Michael Baldwin has lived in South West France, and published a volume of poetry about the region, a collection that earned him the Cholmondeley Award. He has also won the Rediffusion Prize for his work in documentary television. Formerly chairman of the Arvon foundation at Lumb Bank, he now lives in Kent and is a Fellow of the Royal Society of Literature.

MICHAEL BALDWIN

The Rape of OC

WARNER BOOKS

A *Warner* Book

First published in Great Britain in 1993
by Little, Brown and Company

This edition published by Warner Books in 1994

Copyright © Michael Baldwin 1993

The moral right of the author has been asserted.

A CIP catalogue record for this book
is available from the British Library.

ISBN 0 7515 0624 9

Printed in England by Clays Ltd, St Ives plc

Warner Books
A Division of
Little, Brown and Company (UK) Limited
Brettenham House
Lancaster Place
London WC2E 7EN

Off all fairheid scho bur the flour,
And eik hir faderis air,
Off lusty laitis and he honour,
Meik bot and debonair.
Scho wynnit in a bigly bour;
On fold wes none so fair;
princis luvit hir paramour,
In cuntreis our all quhair.

Robert Henryson
from THE BLUDY SERK

The blood-crossed Knight, the Holy Warrior, hooded with
iron, the seraph of the bleak edge.
Gallops along the world's ridge in moonlight.

Through slits of iron his eyes search for the softness of the
throat, the navel, the armpit, the groin,
Bring him clear of the flung web and the coil that vaults
from the dust . . .

The rider of iron, on the horse shod with vaginas of iron,
Gallops over the womb that makes no claim, that is of stone.
His weapons glitter under the lights of heaven.

Ted Hughes
from GOG

. . . a sacred bow;
A woman, and an arrow on a string;
A pierced boy, image of a star laid low.
That woman, the Great Mother imagining,
Cut out his heart.

W. B. Yeats
from PARNELL'S FUNERAL

For Christine
and
Tony Weeks-Pearson

TABLE OF MATTERS

the Virgin recalls that women may be naughty
together with no harm to God or man.

CAPUT ONE

In which a young woman sees her
parents cruelly pricked and most
vilely ravished, sundry serving
wenches and the Demoiselle of
Coulobres besides.

*T*he mischief started and the best blood was spilt two days before the feast of La Madeleine, our own Saint Mary of Magdala.

It was the eleventh year of Pope Innocent's reign on earth, and the twelve hundred and ninth of Our Lord's in Heaven. One God or the Other saw to it that the day was hot.

As always in the middle months of summer, our little river Hérault flowed slack, though hard enough to pass with a laden donkey. For those who wore armour there were just three ways to cross it, all within a bowshot of our front door. There was the stone bridge, the underwater bridge, and the ford; then nothing else but high banks or bog. When the Pope proclaimed his Crusade we knew it would come our way.

We paid to send out messengers to warn of its approach. The town sent the messengers, but it was Daddy who bought their horses.

Three nights before La Madeleine one of them returned. The foreigners were already at Montpellier or Montagnac or Montmèze. Their army had brought so many wonders that the sight of them struck him in a mumble. They had pavilions and cooking-pots and stallions in skirts. His mount wasn't as tired as his tongue, so we were certain they would be with us soon, say in a week or two, before the next moon was up.

The townsmen held a meeting to discuss how much we should charge them for the use of our bridge. It was decided to grant them free passage as a mark of goodwill, in case they heard tell of the ford and crossed for nothing anyway. Daddy agreed with this logic. He didn't want horsemen thigh-deep in the family's drinking water, horses even less.

Daddy didn't go to the meeting. Mummy needed him to help with me. She said it was time I put up my hair and

3

learned to keep both legs on one side of our gelding instead of riding like a tinker woman. She knew how stubborn I could be, even with her, and promised more trouble for us than anything Pope Innocent could bring. Daddy didn't argue with her. He said he had no time to waste at meetings with blabbermouths. As for this Crusade, it was made up of Christians almost as honest as he was, so he wouldn't hide his women or take us up the mountain to stay with Mummy's relatives.

Don't think my father wasn't a careful man. He had to think of business. He wanted to sell the crusaders some flour, or even raw corn. He was delighted to hear they'd brought cooking-pots. That was why he didn't suggest Mummy ask the maids to fetch in their washing from the bushes, even their personal washing. Spread women's underthings on your bushes and you'll certainly bring soldiers to your door. It seems obvious in hindsight, but I do believe Daddy was the only one of us who understood it at the time.

The bridge the town left open was next to the ford, and almost above it. It was built by the Romans or some other long dead race of giants and sorcerers who could shift rocks. If it belonged to anyone, it belonged to the fairies. It certainly wasn't ours to open or close, any more than was the ford, so we weren't being generous.

All rivers have fords and towns spring up because of them, even without a bridge. So it was with our little St Thibéry, if you can call it a town.

The underwater bridge was our own, and quite a different matter. Daddy made it by chucking in stones. He was nearly a giant himself, but hardly a sorcerer. He constructed it because he was a miller, and needed the waters to believe in him. What he got was a pool full of naked boys, and the weight of them jostling and shouting helped turn his wheel, at least until sunset. Mummy disapproved of naked boys, especially in a place where they were easy to look at and difficult not to hear. I didn't mind them. Nor did the maids.

4

The Mill wasn't next to the river, but stood a tiny meadow away. Our wheel was kept turning by the flood down a race-cut or snye. This last could be slabbed on or off. Daddy said he needed the splashing of boys to shift the water across the ledge, and save him pulling planks.

He wanted to build a new mill at the end of the pool, and drive a bigger wheel; but Mummy refused to live among the gnats, and have eels and frogs for neighbours.

Daddy was the richest man in St Thibéry, and would have been in all of Hérault if he'd lived longer. We didn't boast about it, in case Mummy's relatives took back our milling rights. 'Never brag about success,' Daddy said. 'It only leads others to ask the wrong questions. They've got their castles and their armies and their fancy clothes. I've got twelve bags of gold that are almost thirteen. So who's to tell either of us what's what?'

Mummy rarely mentioned such matters. She had so much importance in her blood that all kinds of great ones hereabouts would stop their horse for her, even when she was in an apron, and call me 'niece', 'god-daughter', or 'cousin', without noticing Daddy till he'd filled their second cup for them. Stupid to go on about her blood, Daddy used to say, especially now it's sleeping with a miller.

She was her parents' eighth child and seventh daughter, so it was that or become a nun. Two of her sisters were forced to be nuns in earnest. Two more were almost as unlucky, being dead of the sickness that comes from sitting idle. Of my remaining aunts, old Alazaïs was mad, so also unmarried, even to God. Not even the keeper of the Count of Toulouse's madhouse would take her.

My uncle, Mummy's brother Crépin, was another idiot in his fashion. He followed my grandfather to the grave a week after inheriting the title. Grief at his good fortune led him to drink too much and die of snake bite. People don't often die of snake bite unless wine assists the poison. They merely rot like bad apples till the swelling drops off. But Uncle Crépin was not only drunk, he was bitten more

5

than once. The stupid man squatted over a pair of mating serpents while relieving himself in the herb-garden, and they both obliged him. They were found underneath his body fastened together like belts at the buckle, their teeth still in his bottom. Grandfather's estates, Mummy's birthright, followed the only daughter nobly married and went back to the Trencavels, which was more or less where they had come from in the first place. 'Land follows blood,' Mummy fretted, 'and blood is where blood itself goes to.'

Mummy's relatives had granted Daddy his milling rights, as I've mentioned, so he was inclined to treat the topic gently. 'A commoner can't own land,' he would say. 'Whereas a nobleman can gather it on his sword or his prick. His prick, as in my sister-in-law Esmengarde's case, is doubtless more comfortable, providing he doesn't have to dig his fields with it after.' Here he would squeeze my mother, who hated squeezing. 'A woman, alas, isn't allowed a sword. And I've only heard of one who wore the other thing, and she was a pope.' With these words he forgave Mummy entirely for her lack of possessions.

He didn't squeeze her this morning. There was a horse between them, smelling of sunshine. More of that in a minute.

'Talking of swords,' Mummy said, 'and perhaps even talking of *things*,' – she was determined I shouldn't use language like Daddy's, especially in broad daylight and the heat of July – 'you'd better not forget there's an army of crusaders strolling this way. Bury our gold in a nice deep hole. Then plant your silver pieces at whichever end of the vegetable patch you're not doing your dirties in this month.'

Daddy's gold was well hidden, so it was unlikely to become a military issue. 'Armies are all the same,' he said. 'They need corn. They eat flour. Since this army is coming here to impress all of us in Oc with the civilized intentions of the King of Paris, it will undoubtedly be willing to pay for it. Unfortunately, Pope Innocent sent it as well, so it won't

6

pay much.' He patted Mummy by proxy and lifted me back on to Nano, our gelding. I was being taught to ride like a lady, and Nano didn't like it. 'They'll bring fine manners, and expect fine manners. Remember they are Northerners, Perronnelle, so keep them at a distance. Fine manners are best at a distance, especially from foreigners.'

Mummy agreed. She approved of distance. She wanted nothing else. It was only two hours before noon, and the day was too warm for her, even by the river. She nagged me to keep my smock and my underskirts tight between my ankles, but I didn't wear them long enough, because of the goose-droppings. She made me sit on that gelding with my legs hanging daft down one side. I had sat on half a dozen horses in my time, not to mention mules and asses, and ridden them till their feet wore out, but always astride. Mummy said I was becoming too old for astride. She said a lady opens her legs for nothing, especially on a horse. 'Our seat on a horse is what shows the world we are women, and what sort of women we are,' she said. 'We keep our right leg against our left, and our eyes above the window-shutters or anyone else on horseback. Our right leg with our left, and not vice versa down the other flank.'

Mummy was quite wrong. If you think how men are made, and I did often, then they are the ones who ought to ride side-saddle. I've never seen one prepared to be so stupid, and I said so.

That was why Daddy was there, and why she hadn't let him go to the meeting last night. He had to get ready to put me on a horse. He was patient about it. Patience was his way with horses and women, if with nothing else. Nano didn't like what was happening, and nor did I. Daddy just lifted me up and waited for the gelding to shrug us apart. Then he put us back together again.

Our struggle interested the little boys in Daddy's pool. It interested the bigger ones as well. The little ones didn't watch me all the time – they had other things to shout about, like the colour of their toes and the size of the fishes – but the bigger ones did. Big and little, they all shrieked and hooted for one reason or another. Nano had a lot to put up with, and so did I. Daddy tried to calm us down, but Mummy was too hot for calm. She shouted at him, then at me. Being a Great Lady's daughter, I was supposed to be quiet as a puddle in summertime. Being a Great Lady, Mummy was allowed to shout. The boys joined in.

There was another sound, to add to my embarrassment. The domestics up at the Mill House had asked permission to follow us into the meadow and see me ride. Mummy had been so firm against this that now they had nothing better to do than peep from the doors and enjoy the spectacle at a distance. I could hear Thistle the scullery girl jeering away; our cook Marie-Bise telling her off but giggling in spite of it; One Eye the scrubber all in a chirp; and a note I hadn't heard before, Mummy's personal woman gasping out a laugh she hadn't been given enough time to practise, because of her years with Mummy. If Constance de Coulobres could laugh with the rest of them, albeit hidden away in a corner, then the sight of me falling off a horse must have been an entertainment that transcended every barrier of class and custom. Our Lord Jesus had to make do with a donkey, as did his Mother; and I thank them both that there were no men to scoff at me. Daddy wouldn't have men in the Mill. He said the place was idle enough without them; and, when it came to the house, a Lady was best at running women. Mummy had only a few menials, but such women as she had were as noisy as a convent when it's time to harvest the grapes.

This hubbub went on for some time. When it ceased, the silence near-to seemed unnatural, especially with Thistle and One Eye still giggling in the background; but they were a pair of lack-brains with no sense of what was proper.

First the big boys stilled in a bunch, then the tinies one by one. It takes a thunderclap to interrupt boys when they're bathing. They stopped this time, though. A great tremble of hoof-iron stopped them. They began, all naked as they were, to run towards the stone bridge, where the sound

8

threatened. The little ones didn't even pick up their clothes. The hoof-iron grew louder. It stirred the soft turf by the river's edge and made Nano fidget.

It didn't deter Mummy, but by now she had very little left to say. Mounted men rode across the bridge. Their hoof-beats lightened on the stonework, like trotting at a fair, but the great disturbance still rumbled after. Six or seven dozen crossed over, two with pennons on their lances, most without lances. One carried a flag that wouldn't stay upright or unwrap itself from its pole, such was the weight of heat. I couldn't see what these people were wearing, not from down on the water-meadow, not even standing on the back of a horse. The parapet was in the way.

The geese didn't hoot at them, though geese always hoot – they had wandered off. Perhaps it was an omen.

'A horse isn't a table,' Mummy scolded. 'So please don't stand on it. Remember you're a lady and use it as a chair.' She meant a fixed table, not one with trestles; Mummy owned several fixed tables. No one else owned as many.

More riders crossed over, and went on crossing until there were perhaps a hundred score of them on our side of the water. I had never seen so many, not at Béziers at the feast for Mummy's cousins, not even at Pézenas for the Madeleine. I couldn't be certain of their number, because counting heads is harder than counting sheep. Unfortunately they didn't turn our way, so Daddy couldn't sell them any flour for themselves or oats for their horses. He stayed very calm about this. 'High folks eat meat for their bread,' he said. 'Flesh and then fish is what obliges Christians. It is my own taste in the matter. So I can't say I blame them.'

Mummy sniffed at 'high folk'. 'They're not "high",' she said. 'Or not all of them. There aren't so many high ones came out of the ark.'

High or low, some of the men carried flags embroidered with crosses, embroidered so stiff that they stood out square like a surcoat with leather in the shoulders or a great lady's

9

neck in its struts. One lot carried actual crosses fashioned from sticks or untrimmed lumps of wood.

A few bore lanterns dangling from poles, even though it was daylight. This was a very foreign trick, but what made these men strangest of all was the colour of their faces. They weren't a healthy brown, but plum-coloured or pink, as if unused to sunlight. A few were as stone-white as they would look if their heads had been dipped in Daddy's flour or, whiter than that, plastered in lime.

Their silence was strange, too. Put two of our people together on horseback and they'll shout at one another, shout or at least laugh, not to mention giddy-up their nags. Yet here were thousands of men, and they all rode with only the clatter of their hoof-irons and the noise of falling horseshit to show they were real.

They went on towards Béziers, and since they hadn't turned our way or called 'hello' we did our best to forget them. This may seem strange, but not to us. We lived by a bridge, so we were used to seeing people. As Daddy said often, 'If you don't like people, live somewhere else.' Besides, it was a whole bow-shot away, and we had Mummy to stop us from noticing them.

I don't know whether the boys spoke to the horsemen, or whether the horsemen or any of the people they brought with them spoke back. An army is a passing wonder. Even when it stays, the fascination can't last. Water on the other hand attracts boys for ever, especially when it runs from under a bridge to where it can be dammed up in a pool. They can hardly bring themselves to be out of it, unless you ask them to wash their hands in it or beat their mother's bed linen over a wet stone. In which case they'll run for miles, or at least until they find another pool. So it was this time. The water won. I daresay I hadn't slid off Nano's flanks more than a dozen times more before they were all back and splashing about as if the Crusade hadn't been invented.

One of them came over to us. He tugged his hair at Mummy and stood dancing from leg to leg until he could talk to Daddy. He was naked all the way down, the way tiny boys are, the way

Mummy never likes to see them. 'A viper has fallen in,' he shouted. 'And the trout are eating him up.'

Serpents do crawl along the bottom of the water sometimes, and trout will chew anything, but I'd never heard of this.

'It'll be bad luck for someone,' Daddy grunted. Millers are fond of omens, and their families learn not to believe them.

'Eating serpents, are they?' Mummy said to the urchin. 'Make sure they don't eat that thing of yours.' She didn't like men, big or little. As she told me often, it takes ages for a girl to develop into a woman, but no time at all for a lad to get frisky and ruin God's good work with one of those objects they all have hanging down the front of them to tell the weather by. 'The Almighty One should have stuck to bees and seaweed,' she said to me at bedtimes, 'which is how most people tell the weather. Instead he invented that thing. It can't think, and half the time it stops its owner thinking as well. Women are lucky to be different,' she used to go on, 'and praise be they are, or the world would never have thought its way out of the Garden of Eden. The Snake would have eaten us up before anyone found the key.'

My mother frightened the lad into covering himself with his hand. But his thing was in no mood to be covered, so he shielded his eyes instead. He was saved by a great beating of drums and rattling of sticks from the bridge. This led to the boys running off for a second time. A whole army of footmen passed by, and went on passing for what seemed hours, or certainly long enough to bore the lads back to us again. This procession gave our bridge more walking and stomping over than it would otherwise get in a hundred years, and would have shaken it down if it hadn't been built by giants and held up by people's prayers and the milk they leave for the fairies. 'If I had a quarter of a groat for each pair of feet gone over today, I'd be rich enough to buy the sea from God,' Daddy said.

'The sea belongs to the Devil,' Mummy answered. That's the sort of nonsense members of her family do utter, and it was very shortly to get them into trouble, as all the balladmongers testify.

11

'I'd buy it from its owner,' Daddy insisted. His mind was like mine, better at facts in well-stitched boots than ideas in a bubble, and there were plenty of facts stomping over our bridge just now, threatening to blow it down on top of Jericho with their horns and shouting through their hands and tuneless trumpets.

'I preferred the first lot,' Mummy said. 'They were all church-quiet like crusaders should be.'

'That first lot were frightened,' Daddy said. 'I thought it was their Northern manners, but now I think they were frightened. They came along timid in case anyone said boo to them. This second parade is not so scared. It thinks it's a marvellous army, and I daresay it is to those who know about such things. Besides, it's got the first lot tucked away in front of it, and that must make it feel more comfortable.'

For a time there were no more soldiers to see, and scarcely a horseman. There were only pilgrims and quarantine men. Daddy said they weren't here for the fighting, merely to spend their forty days with the Crusade, pick a few purses and locks, and so gain the Pope's blessing.

'They're a rabble,' Mummy said.

'I can't see their cooking-pots,' Daddy agreed. 'Nor their pavilions.'

'There are certainly no stallions in skirts,' I put in. 'Let alone anyone riding side-saddle.'

This chat should have got us back to the kitchen for some soup – Nano had already wandered off to find his own lunch – but the excitement of so much bustle we weren't allowed to look at kept us in place.

We would have been safer with Mummy's relatives in a castle up a mountain, at least for a year or two, then I might have grown up innocent and gentle, and not become famous for deeds that needed doing but were best left undone.

Everything took us an extra long time that morning. I want to get it down exactly, though, because terrible events don't happen often. What I am trying to remember is whether any one of us felt uneasy at the coming past of all these men-at-arms with their light skins and foreign faces. I don't believe we did. All that seemed strange was these crusaders' reluctance to call anyone a greeting. Not a shout as they went through town, not a hallo or a hullaballoo, in spite of all their blowing of notes and blasts. Not a blessing from a pilgrim or palmer. Nor did anyone come asking to meet Daddy, who was famous for miles about, both as a wrestler and for the size of him, especially his waist. The length of his belt was one of the wonders of the world. People in Béziers talked of nothing else, especially each time he grew to need a new one. Soon they wouldn't be able to stretch a cow far enough to make the leather. You would think the leaders of any foreign party would want to see such a thing and meet such a man, not to mention listen to Mummy, who was marvellous too in her way, at least for those who thought she might stop talking.

'Are you sure they're coming merely to impress us with their good manners?' she asked. 'And not for some other reason you'll have to be careful not to offend them about?'

'It's a Crusade,' I offered. 'They've come to bring us Christianity.'

'We've got plenty of that already!'

'They *were* coming so the King of Paris could settle his quarrel with the Count of Toulouse,' Daddy said. 'And so the Pope could pay him back for the death of that messenger of his. But, since it's a Crusade, the Count has had to join it. So they're going to fight the Trencavels instead.'

'Toulouse can't fight us Trencavels. We're related to Toulouse.'

'Only by marriage. Besides, you're a miller's wife, so you're not related to anybody.' Daddy spoke sometimes as if we were a family of torturers and executioners.

'Closely related.'

'Perhaps they're coming to gather land on their pricks,' I suggested to Daddy. I received a slap for my pains, so I'd hardly got the word out before it died on the air like a spent whistle. I treasure the memory of that slap. It's almost the last thing Mummy gave me.

Mounted crusaders were still trotting – perhaps I should say pattering – across our bridge, so many of them that it became filled parapet to parapet with dung, and the air above it shimmered with steam. I could see it dribbling round the cornices like gravy from a saucer – straight into our river of course, though mercifully it couldn't seep below the ford, or not until the rains came. I pitied the footmen among them.

Last night's counsel had been very wise. We would have needed a bold bridge-keeper to ask the pilgrims and quarantine men for a penny a horseshoe. He might have been paid in different coin than he bargained for.

This fouling of our water made me feel thirsty. I sensed a great need to fill my stomach with liquid before the next storm ruined the wells with horseshit and I was forced to follow Daddy's example and drink only wine. I stooped to cup my hands in the stream. It tasted as sweet as olives.

'Don't take it from there,' Mummy called. 'Those little boys do their naughties in it there.'

'So does everyone else,' Daddy said. 'It's what turns the mill.'

'Drink from the stone higher up.'

'That's where they do it from.'

We'd forgotten the boys. One moment they were here again, the next they'd rushed away to find food or catch another glimpse of a soldier – or that is what I thought if I thought of it at all, and I didn't much, nor of the silly stuff my parents were chiding me with. Our pool was so clean, and what boys do is so insignificant compared with what God does from heaven on a windy afternoon that I drank quite happily at the freshness of it.

I crouched there for some time, looking for fish, but really it was my face that took my gaze. I'd sip from its reflection, scoop it all up into bubbles and wrinkles, then watch it grow clean again. I was fond of my face, and thought it beautiful, perhaps because I could only watch it at times like this.

14

Mummy didn't believe in mirrors, not for greensick girls. She said I could plait my hair by feel, and Daddy didn't need one, since his hair was black and curly except where it was bald from butting bulls at the fair.

So that's how it was. I drank water from our stream and our pool, and saw a fair-haired young woman with the stones shining through her, and the fish swimming in and out of her head, and I must say the sight of her unsettled me. I looked into myself until I saw nothing. The water muddied over with what I thought was a bad cloud.

At back of me was an armoured man on horseback. He'd stolen over the lush turf of the water meadow, and now there were others not fifty paces behind him, the settle of their hooves muffled by the sound from the bridge.

Other riders approached from the far side of the river, having ranged round the town searching for foodstuff, or hungry for amusement. They'd glimpsed a host of naked boys. Then they'd noticed us. They'd seen a house surrounded by women's laundry and heard shrieking from urchins small enough to sound like girls. No wonder the boys had run away and the riders surged forward. Now they came across the Hérault, treading as if on nothing, picking their way gingerly in line across Daddy's underwater bridge.

Before I could go to Mummy, the first man dropped down from his horse, caught hold of me by the arm, and began to talk a nonsense I was too frightened to listen to. He was, I thought, their leader. He had what I call a French voice, which is more or less an English voice, in other words a foreign voice; and his face was covered in wet, most of it made by his skin. I had soon come to recognize Frankish Frenchmen, or their English friends, or the Norman Irish (which are all the same people) by their moist red faces and the way they spoil in the sun. I had also found that I could tell them by the speed with which they tried to slip their hand inside my clothes. Most men had the same inclination, but not usually when my parents were there and before they'd had several cups of wine.

15

'You're a young woman of appetizing appearance,' Mummy often said. 'There's no point in overlooking the fact. Should a man seize hold of you in that way I'll not describe, there's only one thing to do. You must kick and shout. Never squeal, screech or scream. Do not panic or do anything in a fluster. Remember whose daughter you are, and kick and shout with dignity.'

I daresay I shouted, and I daresay it was with dignity, because no sound came, he was holding me so hard. I didn't kick. I shrugged myself free, which was easier for the wet of him, and tried to find Mummy. She was already surrounded by men and horses, but determined not to be, since she couldn't stand either sort of animal. So was Daddy. I must say I was proud of her.

'I am Mélisende Trencavel,' she said firmly. 'Mélisende of the Trencavels. This is my daughter. That is my husband.'

My mother kept her own surname for occasions like this, whether from stubbornness or because my grandfather insisted I am not sure. I was allowed to choose. To choose Mummy's name would be unfair to Daddy. To choose Daddy's would be stupid. As Mummy said, 'Traders and peasants do not have families. They have children, and only an urchin could be one of those.' So, in deference to Daddy's Mill, I chose the name St Thibéry, but written out full, Perronnelle de Saint Thibéry. My grandfather was delighted. Some said it was his delight that killed him and caused Uncle Crépin to sit on the serpents. There was another family called Saint Thibéry, but what Grandfather said was, 'If they want to argue about it, let them talk to the Trencavels.' They never had to, for it was not in my own person, or even as a Trencavel, that I was to become famous.

Whether it was Mummy's choice of name, and mine, that killed Grandpapa is an academic matter. They were to prove deadly for the rest of us.

Mummy was by now growing impatient. It was nearly lunch time, and people such as crusaders could not be invited in, no matter how far they had travelled. She was used to the merest breath of her family connections wafting lesser folks out of the meadow. Instead these strangers were behaving rather like the boys in the pool, quite beyond control, there was so much jostling and leering and laughing.

Mummy had to try again. 'My name is Mélisende Trencavel,' she said. 'You know the worth of such a title. You know my station. This is my daughter Perronnelle and my husband.'

The fellow who had surprised me was clearly these persons' leader, though not the sort to stand backwards or forwards or set himself apart. He found it unnecessary to introduce himself, something which annoyed Mummy intensely. 'The Trencavels are forfeit,' he said. 'That's a fact that bears King Philip's seal upon it.'

Mummy took one of her breaths at this, but before she could spend it, the stranger said, 'As for your fancy forenames, my ladies, I have an aunt called Mélisende and a sister called Perronnelle, and I've fathered a child on both of them!'

His men laughed at this, and repeated it, the way men will.

Daddy kept his temper. You don't buy corn by quarrelling, still less sell flour. 'I owe my leat to the Count of Toulouse,' he explained. 'He owns this water, if not its banks. I'm the Count's man, as he'll be pleased to explain to anyone.'

'Toulouse is in full agreement,' the lout said, without benefit of title. 'You're forfeit. It's got Pope Innocent's blessing as well.'

Daddy was a man who could crack skulls in his hands, or wrestle with bears and horses as was well known. 'Moreover,' he said mildly, 'my name's not Trencavel.'

'Nor's mine,' I put in.

'You're living in concubinage with another man's wife? Very well, my good miller, just stand on one side and leave us with the women. We'll do what has to be done.'

'And what's that?' I asked. Females do ask questions down here, though they're not always answered.

'I'm supposed to burn you. But this is a moist place, and I

17

don't like burning women even where it's dry. It makes them smell a lot less sweet.'

The men-at-arms thought this was another great joke. They began eyeing me the way Daddy looked at Mummy when he'd had a drink.

Their leader took hold of me again, but as of right, not necessarily to start a quarrel with Daddy. 'My name is De Montfort,' he said.

His smile was engaging, his breath hot. He still had his teeth, and only a few of them were turning brown. 'I'm Lord Simon's brother – and young Amaury's too, come to that – but I'll not ask my page to show your ladyship my shield. The bend is sinister, like most of them in your own family. I am christened Meudon, after my mother's house. Men don't call me bastard, just the same. They know me as Merdun. The title is honest.' Another jibe at Mummy. 'Merdun means Shit Face in my part of the world.' His hands crawled all over and under me, struggle as I would. 'If I ever do better than worst you can call me saint, but I don't expect to be canonized yet. I'd rather have a pretty woman on my forepiece than any number of candles burning for me in heaven.'

It was taking him a certain amount of time to establish me there, as we wrap up well in these parts to keep the sun out, but his hands were in advance of the rest of him and becoming insolent. 'If a man touches you beneath,' Mummy had said, 'he'll soon be fingering your mind and controlling your thoughts for you. So tell him to get himself out of it!' I did.

My protests went unheard. His fellows were laughing so hard at 'bastard' and 'shit face', and Trencavel most of all, that my moans did nothing above the hubbub.

Daddy wasn't the man for moaning, as they all should have known. He threw back his arms to clear a space for himself to be violent in, and this made Mummy angry, to see me not free and Daddy about to brawl and be vulgar. She began to say something to this effect. Anger catches on person to person very quickly, as is well known, but it surprised us all when one of Merdun de Montfort's men stuck his sword right through her and nearly knocked her off her feet with the thrust of it.

This caused a moment's silence, during which Merdun muttered, 'That's a bit quick, even for one of mine.' Then the Bastard added loudly, 'Don't waste her just because you've pricked her. Use whatever you can.' He handled me encouragingly. 'Always use what you can.'

Daddy's cry came out of him at last. It was terrifying for the sorrow in it. He went into the crowd of them – how many were they? a score? half a hundred? – and threw them aside till he found the fool who'd just hurt Mummy.

This was a lean, draggle-arsed fellow in a jerkin topped with ringmail as rusty-grey as a water rat's winter coat. He snarled at Daddy and squared up to him with the same bloodied half-sword. It was a miserable affair in the context, though awful with Mummy's hurt on it, no longer than a tall man's arm, and crimped at the end. You see knackers use such things on bullocks at the fair. The man waved it in Daddy's face and made as if to slice his throat. He'd just as well have offered to cut his own.

Daddy brushed the blade aside, caught hold of him in a wrestler's squeeze, and shook his back so loose and into so many parts that the fellow immediately died of it. Whereupon three more of them set upon Daddy without even a round of applause. They didn't know he was a champion. All I can remember about that lot is that they wore cleaner mail.

Daddy took the sword away from the nearest of them, upended him by the ankles and clubbed the other two with his head till his brains broke. This caused the rest of the Bastard's men to hesitate, at least for a moment or two, and secured some more silence in which I could help poor Mummy. Merdun de Montfort was so distracted by the fight that he only held me by the elbow and a yard of my hair. I took what distance from him I could and used my wooden sandal on him. Kicking a hauberk is like kicking an iron skirt, bad for the toenails. It did me no good. He held my hair shorter, and shifted his hand to my nape. 'Dear child,' he said. He swept my leg upwards and tried to refit my sandal for me, but he didn't have hands enough or the necessary length of arm. My naked foot distracted him. It excited him so much he held me folded towards him and began to chew on the ends of it. An obscene trick, quite as perverse as· any that the goats get up to when mating. I refused to let him go on with it. I thrashed about so much he was forced to give me my legs back and rummage my chest instead.

Never mind his bussing and fidging. My worries were with Daddy. Mummy's husband was beginning to upset our guests, and some of them were keen to punish him for it.

Fortunately, the great majority of military men find it difficult to overcome people who aren't soldiers. If Daddy had been an army they could have had a battle with him and perhaps won a substantial victory here at St Thibéry, but he was much more unpredictable than an army, and wouldn't keep still long enough to impersonate one.

Soldiers are schooled to act in unison. They achieve remarkable feats of co-ordination, but only through rehearsal. These poor fellows had their minds on other matters, as their shouted obscenities made only too clear to me. They were hoping to work themselves up to an atrocity; but they showed no confidence in their training for such a manoeuvre, still less in their depth of practice. Killing Daddy would divide their forces, they yelled at one another, and no-one was eager to be divided, especially from himself.

If the Bastard had given them an order, they might have laid siege to my father properly, and had done with him. But Merdun was no soldier, or not with me struggling against his thigh, he wasn't. As Daddy often said, 'If a man puts women before his work, he'll prove no good at either.' This great lout of a De Montfort was no exception to the rule. He left his ruffians leaderless, and Daddy still unbloodied, except where a few of the more insolent ones had burst themselves open against his forehead and stomach.

One of them tired of all this shouting to and fro. He pulled an enormous two-handed sword from a scabbard on the rump of his horse (it was too big for a man to wear) and went to mow my father off at the knees with it while he wasn't looking. Daddy was always looking. He hopped over the sword and used the top of his head to butt the fellow in the teeth, so that was an end of him, or of his teeth anyhow.

Daddy didn't need a sword, not even with a mill full of gold to protect. I'd seen him pick a pony off its feet, and carry a donkey a furlong. So had most of the robbers between Pézenas and Béziers. Such men claimed he could lift a brace of oxen, swing a carthorse round his neck, and throw a suckling pig beyond the moon, but I'd never witnessed such things.

It's a pity Merdun's men hadn't heard these stories. If only they'd been fearful enough to leave Mummy alone, Daddy might have remained sufficiently calm to reason with them. If only they'd left her alone.

They wouldn't or they couldn't. She was a comely woman, I'll grant them that, especially now that she was silent because of the sword hole in her, and couldn't keep her legs together because of how it was placed.

What was happening to Mummy and nearly happening to me caused Daddy to lose his concentration. He howled and went pushing towards her, so violently that several of them tried to stop him. One of them was stirring her chest with that famous old foot-soldier's weapon the Roman spikes, perhaps to help her catch her breath. Now he turned them on Daddy and sent them pricking around his underparts like a brace of swordfish under a cockle-boat's belly. (To anyone who has never been visited by Pope Innocent's men or otherwise had the good fortune to view such objects, I'll simply explain them as a pair of iron-on-leather gauntlets with a nine-inch blade on each fist, and a great favourite among the crusaders, whether for fighting or eating hot dough from a stew.)

Anywhere save in bed Daddy was nimble, Mummy said. He wore his coat long because of his standing in the community and station in life. This meant no-one could see what his feet were doing in the grass. Although he was grand, he was practical. He might be shod in felt for the Mill, but out in the meadow he wore overclogs like the rest of us. These made his feet almost as hard as his head. He gathered himself for a wrestler's leap, or his toes did, and caught the man in the gut with a thump like a barrel bursting. Something nasty came out of the fellow's mouth, his lung or his tongue or yesterday's breakfast, and the rest of him splashed down his leggings. His gauntlets fell to the ground for people to be careful not to step on. Goodness knows who was going to clean up our meadow. All that blood in the sunshine began to smell worse than goose-droppings after rain. It drove Nano quite mad, and caused even the military horses to behave strangely.

Without any order being given there now seemed to be a need to move us into the Mill House. This was partly because it contained our other women, more because this was where Merdun hoped to be. He had grabbed me for himself and was coy enough to want to be wicked in privacy, or at least inside four walls. Such a hullaballoo of shrieking and pleading issued from the building, and women calling 'no!' (as if that ever made any difference anywhere in the world!) that he had no difficulty in persuading his rascals to follow him, those who weren't already there ahead of him and squeezing a range of notes from our serving girls so strident that partridge began to rise on the noonday air, and our geese at last became excited. (To deal impartially with the situation, there wasn't enough of Mummy to go around, not even with her lower limbs stripped from ankle to waist; and the sight of Merdun with his hands under my stitching and his knuckles jumping about like spiders in the fireplace must have set them on just a little as well, though I didn't make these allowances for them at the time.)

If ever a family was about to be punished for its extravagance with water it was us. Daddy always said the stuff should be used for turning millstones and nothing else. But what had we done with it? We had allowed naked urchins to swim in it and their screams of delight were bringing evil to our door. Worse, we had wasted it on godliness and personal adornment. Show a brigand a garden strewn with under-linen and other such clouts and comforts, and he will know it serves a house full of women. Show him a house full of women and he will try to convert it into his bordello and bloodbath.

Beside the Mill there were bushes, each of them handy for drying folderols, being so much more airy than rocks. It was Daddy's inspiration this morning that they were smothered in the family's laundry, not just Mummy's grand petticoats and saussures and clouting clothes, but all of mine, which were plenty. Then, as I have already hinted, there were the underthings of Marie-Bise our cook, Thistle the scullery girl, One Eye our young sweeper, together with the pruderies of Constance de Coulobres, Mummy's personal woman and a fine lady in her own right and opinion. Between us and the blackberries (still six weeks from fruit) we were displaying such a litter of woman-cloth that day's eye itself hazed over, and the sun grew misty with blushing. What a sight for Christian warriors it must have been!

Christian they undoubtedly were. Daddy was not to be blamed for thinking so. His mistake was in supposing they would treat us like Christians too.

They treated us as Christians *do*, a philosophical distinction the Bastard's own lips were soon to teach me. As we dragged towards the bushes, in a shuffle midway between a carol and a clap-dance, Shit Face put his tooth in my ear (I thought he'd chewed away the lobe at the time) and called me his juicy little heretic. I recognized Daddy's error as old Badmouth bit me. These Christian soldiers – and, believe me, I saw several of them cross themselves even with their chests bone-naked and the rest of them nothing short of disgusting – didn't come on a Crusade in order to hurt people at large. They were here to rebuke the Trencavels, in other words Mummy and me, and to reform all heretics, in this instance myself and Mummy.

Nor were we and our serving women about to die because of our sex. We were merely going to be raped on that

23

account. We were about to die because Pope Innocent said so.

But the plain fact of the matter is that no-one need have discovered we were women or Trencavels, without being attracted to us in the first place by the virgin fruits on our blackberry bushes.

The Bastard's rogues had by now laid their hands on some of these knick-knacks, and were wearing them and whooping in them, those of the villains that weren't already whooping in their owners. It was very disturbing to see men dressed in petticoats so early in the day, and even worse to see the same men strip naked to scramble their legs into them. They played some unusual games, these strangers, and were using our underthings to polish more than their swords.

The house was all a-scream by now, just like a hen-coop when the fox is in. Mummy hadn't spoken to Marie-Bise as she had to me on the subject, nor to One Eye and Thistle, so the noise of their pain was very unsettling. I was further shocked to be frothed at by a red-headed lout who came romping outside in a dress and pelisse belonging to Constance de Coulobres, one I had glimpsed her wearing not an hour before. He was otherwise stark naked. Impossible to get into anything of Constance de Coulobres with chain-mail on. Even his chest hair was too much for it, the lady of Coulobres being flat above the binder. Below, the cloth was cut full, after the fashion. Not full enough, as I saw when the villain flicked her skirts at me and couldn't drop them down again. My protector was annoyed at this, and squeezed me into his chest as we struggled towards the Mill.

He had a practical reason for hurrying me there. Useless to pretend I'd protected myself from the Bastard's worst simply by struggling so hard against it. As for shouting in a dignified manner, he'd sucked all the breath out of me. What kept him off was the fact that he was hung about with mail, a coat of chain to his knees, and rings of the stuff counterbound round his legs from ankle to I daresay the very top. It is said that a man enjoys a good rape anywhere. In peacetime, perhaps,

24

and in summer clothing. But during a Crusade or suchlike period of strife, only a fool removes his armour in a field. Lesser men have less armour, as Mummy had discovered to her cost. They wear their coats shorter, and little of anything else. Some of these lads wore their hauberks so brief they were dressed in not much more than jerkins, with their legs lagged about in leather straps. A man can get quite a lot of himself out between a couple of rags and a frayed leather strap, whatever his purpose, especially when the sun is warm and the crows have sheep to peck at.

Not Merdun de Montfort. He wore a decent harness of banded mail and was sensible enough to know it ought to be removed in a quiet place and in an orderly manner. He gave a signal – I suppose by tugging my hair – and they carried me, dragged Mummy and drove Daddy into the Mill House. Daddy and I were relatively unharmed. I'm not sure whether Mummy could be called alive at this point. I'm not writing a history of the Crusade, simply giving you the facts.

Our house consisted of four great spaces and a hundred nooks and crannies. There was the grinding room, which was full of turning stones, trunks of oak which Daddy called axletrees, and a tangle of wooden rings with teeth on them. These were Daddy's cogs, and Mummy hadn't been able to take them away from him, nor anything else in the room.

She had contented herself with improving the rest of the house. There was the granary or corn room, the flour store, and a bergerie for cows, goats and geese. Mummy had seized all these spaces, and had them scrubbed clean and polished bright, since they were the nearest to a castle she was ever going to find herself lady of again. 'Cattle live outdoors,' she told Daddy. 'And a shed is quite good enough for corn.' It was a pity about the cows and goats. We missed the warmth of them in winter. And having the place to themselves made the chickens cheeky. You can't keep hens out of anywhere with holes and rafters, and scrambling about on high makes them skinny to eat, as well as encouraging them to hide their eggs in silly places.

We were lugged and driven into the biggest of these three rooms, the old bergerie with its split door and its fireplace. Mummy called it her solar, because it went right up to the roof, and sunlight could force its way in round the end of the beams and under the tiles. It was the hen's favourite roost as well. There was a fire kept lit against the wall, winter and summer, and an iron tub full of broth for Daddy's breakfast or whenever the mood took him. Today there was also a casserole in an earthenware pot. It smelled delicious with all the scents from Mummy's herb garden. She had made it for us herself, with only Marie-Bise and Thistle to help her. Whenever I look back on being ravished, what I most remember is the squawking of hens and the smell of Mummy's casserole. It was into this atmosphere of domestic peace that the brutes dragged me, and set about making the rest of us their meal.

According to the Rules of War, high-born families are not supposed to be treated like this, not even their women. They are worth more with their legs together and their throats uncut. What we didn't know – Daddy certainly didn't – is that a Crusade is not a war, so it doesn't have any rules. So here was poor Mummy with a sword inside her before she could even refuse to offer our visitors a bowl of stew; and the domestic women having their clothes plucked off and their tender parts felt as if they were poultry being cleaned for the spit.

Once we were inside, the Bastard de Montfort let go of me and shook his fingers, which were numb from my hair. I couldn't run back through the door. There were too many men, including mounted men, between myself and the light. Besides, I could no more leave poor Mummy and Daddy than fly up to a crossbeam and roost with the hens. I felt a certain loyalty to the other women too. One of them – I think Thistle – was weeping and pleading in the grinding room, where some of Merdun's louts had chased her or carried her in.

Having my hair free of Merdun's fingers vastly improved my hearing. I heard the sound of stalks being broken, or a clay pot, then a gurgle like the broaching of a flask of aqua-vitae or a firkin of vinegar. Some fool had caught his head in a cog or his foot in a revolving stone, such was the cunning of Daddy's machinery where it changed the uprightness of the turning paddle to the flatness of the grinders. We used to lose a host of chickens and rats that way, and sometimes a cat. No-one, not even Daddy, could stop it or save them, because he was powerless to turn back the waters. Even God only managed it once, and that was for Moses who was a very persuasive man.

This snapping went on for some time, so it must have been a head and then a neck and then a well-made coat of ring-mail being drawn up slowly into an overhead cog, with goodness knows what cost to the teeth of it – Daddy shaped them from heart-of-oak and filed them by hand – because if you slip between a grinder and a tubstone you disappear immediately, or some of you does.

A smelly mess trickled out of the grinding-room door, staining Mummy's woven rushes, which were already splashed by the horses. These rushes weren't bought in, or bartered for flour, but ones Mummy and Constance de Coulobres had picked along the river and plaited with Constance's own fingers to Mummy's direction. Now here they were spotted in blood and belly squeezings.

To my relief, poor Thistle continued to sob and groan. Clearly the mess wasn't her, though very upsetting to me just the same.

Our brains cannot deal with horror straight away, only with the reversal of order. What appalled me most was to see that these mannerless men had brought their horses inside the house, instead of tying them outside. I have spoken of Mummy's rushes. The idea of anyone bringing a horse or even a pony into any room of hers was unthinkable. Yet this was exactly what Merdun's men had done, and not dismounted some of them, either. As I said earlier, horses had once lived in here, but that was before Mummy's time when the house was made comfortable. The room had begun as a barn, and there was space enough for them, and a large enough door for them to enter by. In the winter, the house had been warm with their dung and sweet with their breath, but their droppings had lain on bracken, dry nettles and straw, not upon Mummy's rushes.

A man with his head in a cog causes a distraction, even when there are ladies to be fondled and young women to be stripped and ravished, and wine to be spat in their hair. Daddy seized the moment to make a dash for the grinding room. I do believe he could have rescued me, if only he had got there, he knew so much about the power of the place.

His way was blocked by horses. Whether the horses had riders, I could not tell, what with the stirring of the corn dust, the smoky shafts of sunlight, and the barging and banging. Daddy at once began to head-butt stirrup against rib, and kick against pastern and fetlock, but he could not reach the door (he'd been too fat to creep beneath the belly of a horse since he was ten). He threw one rider towards the hens in the roof, and his nag against the wall behind the fire (or, if there were no riders, he threw two horses). This broke both their necks, and the horse by the fire began to cook its feet. This was no help to Daddy, shuffle horses as he would. The door was still beyond him. His way was dizzied by horses rearing up, and riders or dismounted men beating on his head with their swords. I daresay a stallion or two hoofed him as well. Males are always spiteful when it comes to kicking. Worse, Mummy's floor was becoming sticky with spatter, and no-one's feet are clever when it comes to that, especially with their outdoor clogs on.

The foreigners at last had Daddy penned. There were women shrilling and mewling round the Mill, making music to their ears and breeding impatience. To such men, a young woman shrieking is like a drum to a small boy. They hear her, they have to play on her.

First they had to settle with the drum's owner. If they'd brought any bowmen along, or even one of those Italian foot-soldiers with a wire and spring, they'd have shot him

28

dead and been done with it. He was reducing their capacity for rape. The next best thing to an arrow is a lance or a poleaxe. While a cavalier on a rouncy was levelling up the one, a dismounted groom – bare-legged and bad-tempered from holding other men's horses while they took their turn with one of our women – let go an armful of bridles and mashed Daddy over the pate with the other.

Daddy staggered but remained upright. The blade missed most of his head, except for a tuft or so of scalp which now stuck to it; but the pole fetched him a mighty blow, hurried on by the weight of the axe. Meanwhile, another one of these draggle-arses rushed a sword between his legs – a knacker's man if ever I saw one – and sent blood squirting everywhere. I don't know how much blood a man has in him – they say it depends on his vineyard – but you can catch all of a pig's in a bucket, and Daddy lost much more than that. Then the lance arrived on the spur and trot, with a horse pushed up behind it.

Daddy was standing on the knacker by now, and had the poleaxer between his thumbs and was unpeeling him from his mail, much as he would a crayfish from its shell, when the spike hit him. The horrible weapon passed clean through him sideways on, pinning one elbow to his ribs, and setting up a twitch in the rest of him which was distressing to behold.

Even then I don't think Daddy would have given up if it weren't for my mother's cooking. He was still on his feet, not bellowing any more, but grunting from pain and determination, twisting and revolving about and about like one of his own millstones, and still contriving to knock men over and loosen teeth with the great spoke that transfixed him elbow and rib, when one of the rascals came at him with a ladle full of boiling stew, and another with the whole pot.

'Don't waste the soup!' I heard Merdun exclaim. By then, Daddy was already drenched from topknot to belt-buckle with the scalding fluid, and drooping with the shock of it. He couldn't fall decently, but lay propped up on the lance that impaled him. For a moment or two, it went easing through with the weight of him. Then it snapped.

'Never baste a bull while it's still on the hoof,' Merdun admonished. 'If you've struck it fair, let it stagger off and die in its own time.' He didn't like the look of Daddy once the lance was broken, and gestured a couple of his fellows to slit his neck for him, in case he rose up and did a further mischief to someone.

'Don't cut his throat – his blood'll spoil the women,' someone called, as if these louts were concerned about spoiling anything. He ran forward himself and began to beat Daddy's head in. I've never liked seeing this done to a lamb or a pig when the butcher boy is too drunk to find the artery, but I watched without feeling while they savaged Daddy. There's no time for tears when your own turn is next.

Daddy grunted, swore and tried to get up again, even in death, so they cut him as Merdun ordered. He wouldn't bleed, brave soul. They hacked him, right enough; but he'd shed all his blood from lower down. I've often seen men die since then. No-one did it better than Daddy, though I daresay he disappointed Mummy, joining her like that without a prayer, grunting and perhaps swearing.

Some kind of order was restored to the disorder once Daddy was still. I could not accept he was dead even with the facts of his death before me. Left alone with them, I could perhaps have revived Mummy with a drink of water, then she would have restored Daddy with wine – we all have these silly thoughts, especially when we cannot hold our loved ones and know they have reached the limits of their mortality. Besides, a man does not die as a beast dies, absolutely, and a woman even less so – or certainly in Mummy's case.

So far we had concentrated on murder, which is an untidy business. Now we could have an hour or so of rape. Women would doubtless die from time to time, but women do die all the time: it is part of the wit of Creation that women perish more often than men. Wars were invented to redress the balance but wars kill women too.

I don't know about Daddy's blood 'spoiling' us. It certainly improved everyone else. It is well known that the sight of it makes some fellows frisky. Butchers have a bad name among young females, except the ones that marry them, and they always look over-smug. So it was with this De Montfort brute, who was a lad for the shambles if I ever smelled one.

His eye fell upon Mummy, then upon me. His ear listened to Thistle and One Eye in other parts of the house. His brain inspected the silence, or the thumping laid on silence that was Constance de Coulobres and Marie-Bise. Then he slapped my face to summon attention. 'You can have the Great Lady, my brave lads, or what's left of her. And the lady's ladies as well. Let no one say I am not even-handed in such matters.'

A cheer rose at this, but ours was the only room where men still waited for something to cheer about. Half a dozen louts began to drag my unconscious mother apart by her extremities, principally her legs, while the rest cocked their ears towards the other rooms, but not before they'd heard the Bastard say, 'I'll have first shove at the little virgin on your behalf. It's a thankless task, sweating over a maidenhead, especially while the sun's still up. I wish no man to say I don't lead from in front.' He whispered in my ear, 'It's in a pretty enough box, I must say, this virginity of yours, and there'll be as much pleasure in opening it as in digging for truffles, if only we can find somewhere private.'

A man had never spoken to me like that before – I suppose they call it love-talk – and in other circumstances I might have listened to it differently.

His fellows, or some of them, were hoping for a freak-show, the way they'll watch dwarves and asses at the feast. 'I'm going to give this little one such a roasting,' he promised. He'd already rummaged me so thoroughly that he'd loosened my under-smocks from shoulders to hem, or one of them, without shifting my top-wear, and bits of me were hanging out underneath, those parts a little girl doesn't have and shouldn't show to the world once she acquires them.

'*Oui*,' one of his men shouted. 'Turn her nice and slow on the spit!'

'On my Lord de Montfort's spit, if I know anything about cooking.'

I liked this renewed talk of the flames even less than the rest of the Bastard's suggestions, though that 'I'll give her such a roasting' was a term well used down here, if only out of steamy doorways by men who guzzled wine.

Meanwhile his men were roaring approval and urging him on. '*Oui*,' they said, '*oui*,' as if such a word could be full of wisdom. It's strange, this '*oui*'. I know it, but I don't like it. They pronounce it 'oïl' or 'oï', instead of saying 'oc' as we do; and to hear them chatter you'd think they were spitting out olive pips. Still, I'm writing about the Crusade, not about the Tower of Babel. Ravish me or roast me, it was clear that Merdun intended to have me stark naked first. Thank goodness Mummy had seen to it I was stitched very firmly into stout cloth. When Constance de Coulobres plied a needle she planted the thread close.

Write me down at that moment as a young woman who saw everything and understood nothing. This is in part because nobody acted in any way I had ever witnessed before. This was my first and, I suppose, last Crusade; and its men were behaving like infidels. Or, much worse, they were treating us, who were Christians, to barbarities that Christians are supposed to reserve only for heathens who expect no better. These were men, and yet they were disporting themselves like children, pulling their garments off, getting ready to eat the scrapings of Mummy's casserole half naked, and guzzle all of Daddy's soup in various ways unfastened. At least, that is what I supposed they were doing, because they kept on dashing about, then stopping to do things to Mummy, or admire that brute Merdun manhandling me, or rushing off to where our sweeper and duster could be heard screaming, and our tight-lipped cook and the ladylike Constance de

Coulobres couldn't. It was horrible to hear poor Thistle. If she was only having her throat cut then someone had clearly mislaid her neck. Whatever happened to me, I resolved to be as reserved about it as Mummy had been, or her companion from Coulobres.

I didn't know much about men and their behaviour. I only knew Daddy, and he was a miracle who had been schooled by Mummy; but I always thought that men were little boys who had been taught to keep their clothes on. That's what Mummy said they were. Women, by and large, don't take their clothes off at all, and yet here were naked men giggling about while the Bastard of Montfort tried to undress me.

Daddy had broken that horse he threw into the fireplace, as I think I've mentioned. Certainly it stayed there, with its feet more and more ablaze. Nothing smells worse than hoof glue being cooked on a hot day unless it is a Crusader in his armour. Men from these parts are aware of the ways garlic afflicts them in sunshine. If they're not, their women soon remind them. People from Paris, and foreign countries like that, have no such idea. I daresay Merdun was cleaner than most people – great men souse their bodies in water once a quarter, or certainly every year when winter is past – but he was giving off another odour by now, and so were the rest of them. Men wouldn't know it. Most women do. It's the fume of a bunch of lads growing lusty, and it's worse than billy goats heating themselves for rut. The scent of it in our great room became so strong that it made me giddy, so much so that I nearly swooned from it, in spite of the peril I was in. I strove to keep awake and struggle. As Constance de Coulobres used to say while instructing me in embroidery, 'When a woman goes to thread her needle, she must learn to hold still. If a man tries to thread it, she must keep it moving.' I'd already received one slap across the face – she didn't mention a man might knock your teeth out by way of encouragement – and I daresay she'd received more, enough to make her keep her needle still, anyway.

Forgetting Mummy, who was dead, and myself, who was

33

spoken for, the beasts had as many women at their mercy as a Spanish Arab has wives. Keeping us in separate rooms caused friction. They began to feel the mathematics unfair, the division less than equal. There was the arithmetic to consider – a dozen men with Marie-Bise, a score with little One Eye and, far more difficult, even for an Arab, which a Christian never is, the geometry: woman in bed, woman on cushions, woman on a blanket box or woollen rug, woman on a quern, woman on trestles. Such an argument, and I heard it, contemplated more women than there were; but they had wine to confuse them, and not enough fingers to count us by.

There was also the fact of it being a mill, when they were used to counting women in cottages or castles. So there was revolving woman to contend with, woman turning flat, woman spinning upright, just as earlier there had been woman secured to an axle-tree and her hideously headless man, she suspended in time like one of the fixed stars, he rising above her then having his brains minced in her hair before slipping between the tenses like whatever cut of the moon seems most appropriate. How could they take proper account of a headless man, several asked, especially now his body corporate was no more than a puddle on the floor? Send another one in as a makeweight, or let poor Thistle content herself with the luck the occasion lent her?

This led to debate, and debate to friction, followed by leapings from room to room, men tiring of one queue and changing to another, like idiots foolish enough to buy wine at a fair, this time with more than their tongues hanging out, but their eyes and shirt-tails as well, or whatever serves as a comfort between a warrior and the weight of his armour, mainly a whiff of sweat.

This Crusade didn't like quarrels. A manly absence of rancour was one of its undoubted Christian virtues. It began to reason like this. If having four women in four separate corners leads to hard feelings and a superabundance of exercise, why not have all these women, all together, all in one place, all out in the open, fair and square and plain for everyone to see? So here in Mummy's solar, normally as quiet as a cave of anchorites – by which I mean anchoresses – the last rape was played out.

Thistle and One Eye came first, whether carried, thrown or prodded hardly matters. Thistle came out fighting, and One Eye having fought. Eyes blackened, cheeks bruised, lips cut, teeth missing, blood and the signs of ill-use all about them, they came out to a raucous cheer, as a bull does into the circle. The cheer wasn't for them. It was for all the good that had been done to them.

They didn't handle themselves with dignity, die prettily, look at all elegant or withheld, while those brutes butted and bucked and billy-goated above them, but the fact of them was my inspiration. It's a Latin word Mummy taught me, that *fact*. I wished I'd studied her embroideries of prayers and her slates more often, but she taught me *fact* means being as well as doing, especially for women, and that – since it's all there in a single word – being must mean the same as doing. She held after some strange beliefs, my mother, and since she was dead because of them I decided to look to them while I lived. These women weren't dying because of Mummy's fact, but because they were Mummy's and women. So that was *their* fact.

It was Constance de Coulobres' fact as well. They brought her out in a bundle. The bundle was herself, her arms, her legs, her untied hair – a terrible insult to untie a lady's hair, or unplait the tresses of any grown woman, but just as with One Eye, Thistle and myself, her hair had become their drag rope; and if it was a profanation to unfasten hair, then how great a desecration was it to loose the sash-knot of a woman's girdle, whether stitched or bound; but none of the Mill's women had been allowed to keep cape or cotte or underskirt.

Constance de Coulobres' clothes had been torn off, every cloth of them, or perhaps hacked to pieces with swords, for good stout fabric does not rend easily. Some of it was being used to tug her wide open, chiefly by her legs, but also her

35

arms. Of the rest, what they couldn't bind about her neck
was stuffed into her mouth to rebuke her unwillingness to
speak to them. To the last, she was Mummy's woman,
a Great Lady's lady, and easily the haughtiest person in
the Mill. She never wasted her words, especially on the
lower classes, among whom she numbered all men; and if
there's one thing above all that males cannot stand it's not
being spoken to. They need to be approved of while they
are performing their silly antics. So it was against a total
silence that these smelly fellows kept going in and out of her,
sometimes two by two and by any route; but if ever a woman
was too well brought up to notice, it was the Demoiselle de
Coulobres.

I had never seen a woman so undressed before, not even
myself; and if I ever thought of such a subject it was piece by
piece and back to front as glimpsed in Mummy's mirror, or
studied through the neck of one's undercotte or nightgown.
A woman who plied her needle diligently (she told me) was
anyway too near-sighted to be able to see much of herself.

Thistle came as a complete shock to me. She wasn't
wearing any of her clothes, not even in her mouth. She
was as naked as any urchin in the pool, but without the
river to hide in. I must say that without water on her, and
lacking the benefit of water drops, she looked very different
from a boy. There was both more of her and less of her
in all the parts common sense would have expected. The
sight of females being naked was so unusual that it filled
me with awe. Men may be boys who have learned to keep
their clothes on (not this lot). Women are descended from
creatures who never take their clothes off, except some, I
am told, to sleep – but not in Mummy's house.

Thistle was to get no sleep, unless it was the world's
sleep (and even that would be kinder than the flames they
promised us). If you've ever seen billy goats trying to share
a single female, like frogs on a lily pad, you'll appreciate the
cruelty of her case. The young males don't lounge around
chewing thistles, the way nannies do while they wait for the

buck. They scramble over one another, butting their rivals, meaning no harm to the female, though she is the one who suffers it, and – if she's weak boned – breaks. Thistle wasn't weak boned, but she broke, several times.

I don't know why I compare these foreigners to beasts in the field. Watch any kind of herded cattle and you see good manners, even in pigs, especially in their use of females. The females insist on it. Even the bucks' abuse of one another is only temporary. A matter of mathematics rather than mores.

We had a few domestic sheep, the way some people keep cats (sheep being clean with their droppings, especially if you have a One Eye to sweep up after them). Once the brutes had cut poor Thistle and Marie-Bise out of their undercoats (and Marie-Bise wore extra layers to pad herself from the cooking fire), then broached Daddy's aqua-vitae and other strong waters, they fell to hacking at sweet little Three Legs' neck and Winniemeg's guts before turning the selfsame blades upon One Eye.

One Eye, being coy, had to content herself with most of them. They cut her out of gratitude. As Daddy once explained to Marie-Bise when he thought Mummy and Constance de Coulobres weren't listening, men will always thank a whore with kicks once they have tired of kisses: they cannot bear to have bought so much for so little. One Eye had given them everything for nothing, and totally against her will, so the kindest thing was to kill her. They couldn't burn her without her name being Trencavel, or her being able to furnish them with some other clear proof that she was a heretic, such as claiming that most of human existence belongs to darkness. She did so claim, of course; she tried to spit out this great truth of the Cathars every time she could open her mouth to draw breath or scream; but each time her lips parted they placed themselves between them, so her blasphemies were all in a choke and a mumble, poor sickly profanation of a woman that she was; and rather than listen to such filth, they'd kicked her teeth in long ago, and probably as soon as they met her. Since they couldn't purify her with flame, they were forced to send her to Purgatory unprepared. They opened her belly, as they'd learned from the sheep, then slit her neck as their kindness taught them.

It was at this point that Merdun wormed his hand firmly against my skin, but slowly, enjoying the death of One Eye as he did so.

'I'm too young,' I protested.

'Too young is exactly the right age for a man of my taste,' he agreed. He moved his finger, but I'd managed to wriggle some cloth between myself and it during our conversation.

Since this is an elegy, I had better explain that One Eye had two eyes, but she only opened one at a time, poor thing, because she was always dripping with sweat from the exertions Mummy ordered from her broom. She was comelier than Mummy could bear to see about Daddy, and the only way with prettiness is to keep it busy (Mummy was a true heretic at least in thinking that beauty is the Devil's work). One eye or two, she was about to close both of them for ever. Meanwhile these brutes were certainly giving her plenty to blink about, if not wink.

The Bastard chose this moment to try to ingratiate himself with me. I was so stitched about in chastity cloths – as were the others, at Mummy's insistence, for the protection of Daddy – that this de Montfort monster realized he would either need to summon help with me, such as had been served upon the rest, and which he couldn't bear, or else find some other way to ease me out of a garment or so. He indicated Mummy's corpse, with a peculiar gentleness of expression. A couple of louts were still playing with it, but slowly, like dogs that have fed too often. 'I'd have burned her decently,' he said. 'Alive and properly, without all this. But my fellows killed her before I could give word. She's a great lady, and they did it because they were frightened of her.'

'Tell them to leave her body alone.'

38

'They've not seen the nobility in that kind of detail before. Take it as a mark of their respect.'

Before he could visit such courtesies upon my own person, some of his fellows decided they had a duty to perform. They tossed poor Thistle, or what was left of her, head-first among the burning logs, with Winniemeg's guts thrown on top of her like an amber necklace or a sausage-dressing. Her hair caught fire and flared like a neglected haycock. As it burned, a couple of them quarrelled over her legs, sweating from the heat of the embers.

'That's it,' Merdun roared, leaving off his frontal attack on myself. 'Roast their brains, my brave lads. That's where the heresy lies.' He gave me a kiss that tasted of pepper, and whispered, 'Perhaps I won't need to cook you after all.' His voice was louder as he added, 'A little miss like you is bound to be hot enough already under all that starch!'

This led to another cheer. Apart from the raftered poultry, I was all of ours that was left alive in the place, so quite a weight of anticipation now fell upon me.

'Try to be politic, my dear – even if you won't be polite.' He was back to his whisper again. 'You're only half a Trencavel, and much more than half of a woman. So tell me your thoughts on the matter.'

I resolved to say nothing to this, and indeed nothing further at all. Mummy had instructed me not to talk to strangers unless she was there to present them to me. I might have exchanged a word or two with him while he was hanging from my hair and underthings. I did not intend to be catechized by him. Not in public. Not before foreigners. Mummy had scolded me on such matters often enough, so it was easy to hold my tongue.

Innominata

The caput continues and with it
the débauch until the Virgin is
inducted beyond the Fiery Portal.

My wriggling had caused Merdun to grow red in the face. Whatever I had aroused in him had a fair weight of armour on it, as I have indicated. I have watched stallions being given a chilly reception by mares in the field. They rise up, and then they sink down, often in less than the interval required to burn a short candle; and a stallion does not struggle under ring-mail any more than does the flame on the candle.

I scarcely noticed the men, save those who kept thrusting themselves at me and whose bodies happened to my eye amid trappings so confused that I could see nothing of them. They might have been so many imps with sharp tails and pitchforks. Even the most naked of them kept his helmet on, and those who had taken their hauberks off generally kept the bindings on their legs, even the leather and chains.

Not that I lowered my eyes that far, lest my young woman's gaze should cause their body bits to frisk again, and rise up for the baking like loaves quick with yeast.

With my chin lifted high to spite Merdun, I nonetheless glimpsed so many shifts of flesh that I could not distinguish stomach hair from what grew out of it. They had bushy bodies, most of them, quite different from the women and several of their thigh-pieces were matted in blood, of course not their own. There were some fifty of them to start with. Daddy had reduced their numbers, but more had come in; so there hadn't been enough woman-flesh to go round. The little boys at the pool had been prudent to hide, for once the ruffians found Daddy's wine they fell upon our sheep, as I told you, our goats and even our chickens in ways a Christian respectful of animals and foodstuffs could never imagine beforehand and only recall in a whisper.

These monsters didn't fornicate with a woman in her

entirety, even when she was lifeless and completely at their mercy. They snuffed themselves out among her grouts and orts; they spent their lust in gobbets and entrails. I witnessed the entire anatomy of the Crusade laid bare in Mummy's solar, bone by bone, and feather by feather, and quite a few naked crusaders as well.

It wasn't a pretty sight. Here were men who would quarrel over half a Thistle, almost cooked as she was, enter poor One Eye by twos and threes, even making use of the dead girl's fingers, wrestle to run their hands up Mummy's backbone or cool their palms in the fold of her knees, then squabble into the warmth of Constance de Coulobres' armpit. Didn't they learn anatomy in Paris?

You may think I dwell overlong on this hell, stretch out its entrails sentence by sentence. I pray you have patience, and help me make peace with the horror of it. See the entire rape as a painted pot – would that it were no more – broken in the instant of its falling, but painstakingly and painfully resurrected in these pages by one who would paste the fragments together with the molten hooves of horses or stiff pine gum.

What was in my mind as it happened? I once saw a young hen, followed by some dozen of her day-old chicks, being snuffled after by one of our sows. The sow, great cannibal of the poultry-yard that she was, sipped the chicks up one by one, licking their cheeping into her stomach till they had all disappeared and were digested, still crying out for their unsuspecting mother. The young hen turned as her last chick was taken, just in time to hear its pipe disappear into the sow's grunt and rumble. The hen was too bewildered to be distraught. Her universe had disappeared in a cataclysm. She could only circle and gape. For days after, she was witless. Think of me as that young hen. Then I merely saw it. Now I suffer it alone.

We played our own game of chicks and hens, my parents and I, with the help of our domestics. What a sweet fancy of peace we had, what chirping assurance. We never thought there were pigs to rush in on us – not yard pigs either, but hogs, a rout of wild boar to guzzle our blood and mangle our comfort with the sharpness of their feet.

I'd forgotten our murderers' feet almost in the instant they had demonstrated their use. Horror does those things. It creates such a disturbance of mind that only forgetfulness reigns. Yet hogs and pigs are all snout and hoof, all bite and scrape, as many a peasant child finds to its cost if it tumbles amongst them. So, too, were these crusaders.

They came crowding about Merdun de Montfort, offering to use their feet on me, if that would be of assistance to him, and reminding me of what my mind had so far discarded as being too terrible to dwell upon from among the terrors of these last moments.

Thistle, One Eye, Constance de Coulobres, they had all been savaged and snuffed out after their tormentors' fashion, but none of them with such brutish indifference as had befallen Marie-Bise. The rest had been treated as women can expect in such a circumstance, much as animals in the killing pen, but as living things nonetheless. To stab, to bang on the head, to strangle is to take some account of the life in a captive. It acknowledges the need to subdue it before involving her in her torturers' pleasure.

With Marie-Bise, they discovered a more indolent constraint. Some were shod in pieces of iron, some wore clogs, some riding slippers. None, I think, favoured bands of steel lower than the ankle as was becoming the fashion, and only Merdun had the new sabatoons. They did not remove their footwear for Marie-Bise. Four and four about they did their business with her among the dung and the blood-spattered rushes; and they managed without wrestling. Two would hold her by the legs, one would stand on her head and neck while the fourth had her. Then it was step down, step on and shuffle about. She died quite soon, I think, but they didn't notice.

'Old age!' Merdun scoffed, some time after, to acknowledge she was lifeless, as was Constance de Coulobres, who never could tolerate feet anywhere near her, especially with men at the end of them.

'Old age,' my owner repeated. 'These little women of St Thibéry grow too ancient to live, all save you, my restless one.'

It is true that Marie-Bise was the oldest among us, older than the lady of Coulobres: at thirty-four she was within a year of being as venerable as Mummy. So you could say she died of old age if by claiming so you also admit that having a man stand on your mouth or your turned-aside head does bring antiquity on rather rapidly. Poor Marie-Bise. Cooks need to advance in years, for it is never tomorrow they gather in their pots, but a hundred memories of yesterday: they remember last Christmas' beans, wild garlic still sweet from Eastertide, their grandmother's trick to drip honey into a white herb sauce, a song with a verse and a vinegar for each pickling bit of the pig.

So it was with her. She came to us without a family, but bearing the nickname Crab, out of respect for the louse. Mummy refused to have such a name in her kitchen. So Daddy rechristened her Marie for the Madeleine, and followed it with Kiss. When Mummy was close at hand, Bise meant Chilly Wind, because Daddy said it could, but not near him where no-one was chilly.

Now she was dead. Even the drunkest of her butchers knew she was dead. Everyone was dead, though floppy enough from the heat of the fire. These men-at-arms began to play rag-doll with the corpses, tossing them here and there, propping them together and scoffing at the tumble show. They dressed them in what particles of gown they could find, cloth or else reed and feather. They used Thistle's blackened corpse as the rook-stick to hold up their haycock of dripping meat, like an archer's tally of pheasants, my family women and friends. Thistle, being carbon, snapped, but only my appetite waned at the sight of it, never theirs.

They set Mummy in her place, Mummy who was stiff by nature. They had dressed her again, in finery stolen from

46

her basket, but only to mock her. She was caparisoned agape in a pelisse ripped down the front to keep them on the giggle, a pelisse with its capuchon pulled forward to cover her face and deflect its rebuke. For now her eyes were open, their gaze full upon everyone, and haughty with death, so these men-children had to shield themselves from the scorn in them.

Then the flies came in – unless these villains had the power to change themselves into clegs or wasps. No, these were flies right enough, bubble-green maggot-flies, and fat amber stingers from the shoreline to join them in their dancing like gads or frits. How soon these flies had word of us, but meat is meat, whether woman's or squirrel's. It could have been mine or a mare's at the froth of birth, the flies didn't care. These mannerless fools had left doors open, and the reek carried. This brought the crows as well, arriving timidly on the rafters, then clouding down gently to peck at the eyes of my heart. I'd not seen crows in a house before, not even pies or jackdaws. They're enemies to the living, and bad luck dead.

The drunkards didn't like the flies, which bit and were a nuisance. The crows, though, they found a laughing matter. They sang a song about them, croaking it as the birds croak, and dancing a crow dance as well, flapping their hands, then joining the birds to dig at the corpses, all of them stiff beyond dancing now. Or I think they sang of crows, calling them corbels, which was crow enough for me, crows or black rooks, daws or else ravens all squawking their curse.

You may ask how fifty men could achieve so much evil unchecked. I'll tell you the simple truth of it. Fifty men make a crowd down here, especially when they start sober. Fifty men undrunk enough to sit upright on horseback could conquer even Toulouse on a Feast Day, or any day of the week after the midday meal. Nobody would be awake to stop them. Except for the women, that is; and women soon learn better than to meddle with men who ride in with steel on their heads and carry flame in their hands. This had been made

47

very clear by the noontide's events at St Thibéry. Now my captor had more to teach me, and was impatient to continue the lesson.

Restoring good order to a rape requires cunning as well as character, but the Bastard must have judged that the time was ripe. Lately I'd only heard him whisper against my skull. Now his voice filled the room. 'Well achieved, my brave lads. Well achieved and properly handled.'

No-one answered his cry, or not for the moment. Their brains were gone with crowing, and their throats dissolved in wine.

'I've grown famished from watching you, men of Meudon and the Islands. Now, and by your leave, the De Montforts will feast in private.' He held me from behind, and bent back my shoulders the way you break a chicken for breakfast. 'If any man still needs easing, let him do it at once. Before we cut throats here.' He seemed to like cutting throats, even if they were dead and already cut. 'We'll bring flame to the heresy later, bring it or else spread this fire.' He indicated the burning horse and the charred Thistle. 'For the rest of it, go and water your mounts for a while. Bestow yourselves comfortably.' He encouraged me with his thumbs. 'Meanwhile, tell my brothers nothing, and no man more. I may even lodge here till morning, if the taste sits sweet on my tongue.'

Little comfort for me, yet a morsel of hope even so. If his ruffians would leave us alone together, I might manage to escape. He was stronger than I, but the time must come when his hold on me would slacken. Even the beasts of the field need to change their grip, even the boar with the sow, the buck with the doe.

I couldn't outrun men on horseback, not outside the door in an open field. In the Mill, I knew where to hide from them. Even if they set fire to it, and they would, there was a place by the wheel and under the tumble of the water where I could be safe. I needed them to leave as he asked them.

They were in no hurry to move. Men do not steal away

48

from their lusts with such haste as they rush towards them. These stayed to lick their lips a little, and wonder if there was more to be had, even from the dead. Their tongues might be silent, but their gaze was thoughtful. At what point, if any, would they be bidden to take their turn with me?

I struggled to stay composed. I was on the last rung of purgatory, at the portals of hell itself, here in Mummy's room. There was smoke, the foul smell of hoof, charred flesh both horse and human, offal, blood, and the droppings of crows; and flies rising from the dead in such swarms they might have been clouds of incense, until they whirred closer to splash me with droplets of death.

A tall fellow with flapping sleeves unglued himself from the corpse-dance. He ran his tongue over what he could reach of his face, which was gaunt and hooked as any beak he pranced among, then chuckled his morsel forth. 'You're our leader, Lord Merdun, our owner and only general. There's not a man-at-arms here to dispute your right to the little heathen, be he commoner, aspirant, or gentleman.'

No assenting murmur from the rest of them, just an overall sucking on thought, as men will hark at barkers at a fair, to see how cunning is their pitch.

'And as you are our leader, so shall you lead us. Show us the way with the lass, my lord. Point yourself at her and teach us how you great ones do it.'

They cheered him then. '*Oi!*' they shouted, in that impossible gabble of theirs. '*Oi-oil!* You go first, my lord. We'll follow after.'

'Her head's a bit soft for standing on,' their spokesman said, 'but we'll help any other way that suggests itself to you. She may have a shoulder that cries out for the pressing, or a hand or a limb to be held.'

You should have heard them *oi-ing* and *oiling* and *oui-ing* then. It was like being auctioned in a corsair's slave-market.

'This little one's a lady's daughter,' Merdun proclaimed. 'And not so little either. You lost me money on her mother, you villains. Well, this one is mine. Mine to stir and mine to ransom.'

'Yours until morning, my lord,' one of the chicken-thighs said. 'You have first shove. We'll draw bundles for the rest of her.'

'Sticks or straws, Merdun, short or long. We're going to watch you have her, then we – '

'Then it will be our turn to dance!'

'Then you can ransom what's left.'

'Perhaps you great ones don't know the way with a lady.'

They howled at this.

'Easier than with a boy, my lord. If you know what you're looking for.'

Merdun wasn't the man for this kind of impudence. He let go of me and sent the fellow reeling with a hand-clap to the face that burst him nose to ear.

His cronies weren't stilled so easily. One of them, I think the rook-face who'd begun it, came leaping towards me, forcing Lord Merdun to claim me again. Still staring me down, the fellow removed his clothes to reveal a mass of body hair through which his beastliness poked like a turkey's neck from the steam. It was raw and sticky and all shades of pink, except where the damps had rusted his chain-mail – or perhaps it was freckled? – and every bit as uncomfortable looking as the long-bone when it finally realizes all of its feathers have gone.

This thing came sniffing and spitting against me till Merdun hacked his sword-glove at it, whereupon it dragged its owner in search of the heaped up dead, and made a lunge into Constance de Coulobres who was uppermost. Her dulled eyes opened, then her mouth, through which I thought the bloodied tip of it emerged to crow, or at least the wattle and comb of it, till I realized it was her tongue I saw, which of course was soundless, but I was half out of my wits by now.

'Lads, you shame me,' the Bastard called after him. 'This Crusade moves slowly enough, but you step on fast. You want me to be up with you, and – by Saint Mary! – so I will, stride by stride and saddle by stirrup – I won't say cheek by jowl, because you're an ugly pack of villains. But at least let Merdun take example from that one's buttock and figs, which are currently all I can see of him – '

He had them nodding, then laughing, and now they were cheering as he shoved me towards them to say, 'You want to see my bum wagging over this one? So you shall, so you shall. Clear me a tupping space, and prise her out of her things while someone unhooks my mail.'

The hurrah that followed emptied the barn of livestock. Their shout sent our chickens from the rafters, and frightened away those of their horses that weren't already strung outside to take grass. We lost the crows in that selfsame instant. As for the flies, I didn't notice or care. I had rather be laced head to toe in clegs and pissmires than have the least of those murderers' hands on me, and they already were. They'd ripped the other women naked, so why not me?

What stays with me from then is the silence. They had me to handle at last, and I daresay the thought made some of them breathless. Anyway, it's the woman who makes the noise, and I wouldn't and didn't. I remembered thinking one thought, and it was an entirely stupid one. It was to ask myself why the neighbours didn't rush in to rescue me. They must have known by now. I have seen a deal of this business since, and can answer myself in hindsight. Neighbours never rush in to rescue anyone, not even with women shrieking and animals panicked in the fields. Neighbours will bind your wounds or bury you. They won't join you in Hell.

Hell is where I was. I have spoken of fowls being scattered by my captors' shouts as they fastened on me, even birds of ill-omen. A garment or two of mine must have gone flapping off as well, because I found myself bare-armed, draughty about the back and chilly below the nipples. My belly heaved with struggling, as I strained to be separate and stay silent.

The neighbours still did not rush in.

CHANSON CONTIGUA

Wherein a maidenhead is snatched back from the flames by an apparition on horseback while a mute and a hunchback give grounds for hope.

The Bastard's men stripped me naked at their leisure, except for a shred or two. Whatever rags they left me, I felt completely uncovered. Mummy used to say a woman clads herself in her own entirety or she is nothing.

I was nothing and trying to make something of it, when these louts of Merdun's slipped their hold on me. They stopped tugging at my limbs and last twists of clothing, so I tumbled to the floor.

I clambered upright, and knew that a sound had interrupted them, a note they'd heard once and not recognized. They cowered back and were still; the way rats are beneath a nesting hen if they sense danger approaching, even when the egg is clasped warm on their belly and ready for eating.

Bubbles gurgled down the leat, the wheel creaked over. Outside, the waters ran. Our death was only an interval in summer.

The note came again and drew near. It was chill and became chiller. Someone was playing on a pipe, playing but making no music – unless it was Pan's song or the call of the Devil's shepherd that drives flocks mad. This trill was not made by reeds or anything easy to cut. It was the blast of hollowed wood, midway between bagpipe and trumpet.

Men stood back from me to reach for their swords and gaze at Merdun for guidance. He took hold of me by the wrist as the door burst open.

A figure on a horse swaggered in, with others on foot at its tail.

Merdun's men gaped at his appearance, or those who stood right way of the sunlight did. To me he was a shadow in a shaft of dazzle.

When he moved I saw a man of stone – no, jointed iron.

55

He rode on a caparisoned battle mount, and had no face, just a featureless lump without hair or ears.

Starting up like a tub-stone from the cloth on his shoulders was a helmet that encased his head. Its eye-holes were empty. If there were breath-holes I could not see them. His horse breathed for both of them, with a strange dry rasp, like a serpent moving through straw. His body was draped in a Spanish cross, and his horse's caparison was similarly embroidered. He held his naked sword before him like a crucifix, gripping it by the iron not the handle, but abjectly, as if he rode in to surrender Satan's Kingdom to God.

'Ah,' said Merdun, 'a crusader!'

Nobody relaxed. The Apparition's two retainers stepped forward. One of them was tall but with a hump that pressed him down by the shoulder. He stood leaning on a staff. His companion was short by comparison, slight, smooth-faced and graceful as any badel or hermaphrodite. His fingers fidgeted on a pipe. He was the one who made the Devil's music.

The Bastard's men moved forward, then drew back again, the horseman was so odd.

'That's a fine girl you're holding, and no doubt she's someone's daughter.'

Merdun laughed and rubbed his face in my hair. 'I'm going to cook her. Do you want to eat some?'

'Cook what you've killed. A man shouldn't butcher once the flies are up.'

'The banquet is ready for the spit. My fellows have dressed the meat.'

'I'm proposing to buy it from you.' The iron horseman lifted a bag from his crupper. It was heavy and did not rattle.

'Buy her with what? The Devil's gold?'

'All gold is the Devil's, some men say. Then I say that is a heresy that fools will be burned for.'

'I'm on a Crusade.' The Bastard felt what he could find of my body, as if to illustrate the point. 'I didn't come here to discuss Theology.'

56

'There's a touching confessional,' Ironface said. 'Perhaps you'd care to make it to my sword.'

Merdun's fellows were quick when it came to stabbing Mummy. This time they were as prompt to draw back as to begin. It wasn't a staff the Hunchback leaned on, but a longbow.

The Bastard grimaced his annoyance. He couldn't avoid a challenge, not one offered in front of his men, and he resented their presumption in the matter.

The bag of gold dropped straight to the ground beside Ironface's horse. It was too heavy to toss, or he was too weak to toss it. 'I'll fight you for the woman,' he said. 'I see no need to go as far as death. She's a small matter. If I win, I take her with me. If I lose, then so be it. Either way you have the gold.'

'If Merdun bleed or the devil bleed, she's still ours to keep,' a hidden voice stated.

'And she won't keep long!'

I saw no way this Ironface could win my freedom from such a bunch, unless he did indeed possess devilish powers.

Merdun fondled me lasciviously, then instructed his men to fetch him his horse. 'I am the Bastard de Montfort,' he proclaimed. 'So what is your title?'

'Men also call you Shit Face,' the iron fellow said. 'Content yourself to know me as the One Who Brings Gold.'

'Then tell me your weapon.'

'I'll fight with this Cross.' He reversed his sword and grasped it by the handle.

'Then you'll find it too blunt.' Merdun let go of me and, without bothering to arm himself, mounted the horse they brought him and spurred it into his challenger's mount, almost unseating him with the unexpectedness of his attack. Then he rode roystering back to take up his helmet and sword.

He almost had no need of them. The shock of his charge jolted Ironface's legs and drove the metal into metal higher up, so his whole body flinched. Whatever infernal regions he emerged from, he wasn't impervious to pain.

Merdun gave him no time to recover, but returned to beat him an enormous blow over the casque. Blade and headpiece gonged in unison, with a note so terrible that I doubt whether the Cathedral at Béziers ever rang more loudly for the Madeleine.

'Neither head nor foot,' Ironface chuckled. 'It is in here you'll uncover my heart.' He held out the blazon on his arm. The Bastard struck it, and Ironface chuckled again.

I trembled to hear his voice. It was sinking into his body, and no longer spoke from his face but from the metal of his belly, as if it were an echo caught in an empty suit of armour. Can the Devil bear a cross? He can and does. I've seen it many a time, and heard him called Priest and Cardinal.

This wasn't a proper cross, but a strange Spanish emblem. He handled it disdainfully, and was clumsy with his sword, which was another cross, as if he couldn't bear to touch it. Suppose he won me? Would my soul be any safer in his hands than my body was with Merdun de Montfort?

About and about they went, ill against evil, lust against lack, till my head reeled and I stumbled anew. I was dizzied by the frenzy of their blows and the shrill fear of their horses, as the Bastard pitted the cunning of his forearm against this ghost in cold iron. They fought without rule or favour, and – whatever Ironface proposed – they fought to the death. Save, for him, I believed there could be no death, just a retreat into air, into his chuckle, which grew louder.

The Bastard bore no shield. He didn't need one. He swung round and caught me half-naked against his stirrup, perhaps fearful his ruffians would abuse me. He hoisted me across his saddle, but I clawed off again, dreading the devil's blade. Merdun clung to me as best he could, by wrist, breast, waist, hair. The iron man would not strike near me, nor could Merdun swing his edge. I was half dead when he dropped me.

Mummy's room had begun as a bergerie halfway in size

to any great hall or castle keep. In the old days, bears had been lugged there, cocks and fighting dogs baited in the ring. There was space for horses to circle and others to wait, and for men-at-arms to stand about. There was height for the overhead swinging of blades. Nor was it less terrible when they shook down nests, scattered feathers and eggs.

So we had iron music, curses – which were Merdun's! – the lifting and dropping of hooves, sometimes on stone and rush, sometimes on beloved flesh. And of course horses shit at such times. They respect neither death nor weddings. Surely battles must one day be fought on more respectful engines? No wonder this Ironface chuckled, and not from mockery but sheer enjoyment. Merdun swore at him. He broke oaths too terrible to name in writing. While he did so, Ironface spoke kindly to him, encouraging him to win, laughed a little more, then whispered in his disappeared voice to urge his foe on.

Merdun needed no help, for it was the iron fellow's body that seemed to wilt, if body he had, his edge that flinched at the dint, in spite of his infernal spirit.

Infernal it must be. He signalled with his battered sword, so the smaller of his retainers began to play that devilish pipe again, still out of any known tune, yet at one with the fretting of horses, the crosscut of iron, the discords of death that had been its theme from the beginning. It was never a glee the little badel played, but a requiem.

However Ironface clowned, it was to no avail. Not in the world of men, which was Merdun's and brutish. The Bastard turned his blade aside with increasing ease. 'You're weak, for a devil!'

'I've had less practice in evil than you.'

It was the Bastard's turn to chuckle now. He began to play with Ironface, teasing gaps in his defence as a prelude to striking him a mortal blow, yet still the metal belly chortled on. Ironface held his shield across his body, and parried high cuts from above with his sword. His vital organs, if he had any, were secured by this stratagem, but he could clearly come to incidental harm.

'His legs,' one of Merdun's men advised. 'Trim him by the legs!' They had seen, as I had, that he could feel pain in his legs.

Ironface's men smiled grimly and set their music on.

Their confidence seemed foolish. Their master's strangely protruding lower limbs were an invitation. His shield was unhandy, because borne so high, and his sword arm could not easily be dropped across the body to defend him lower down on the left. He circled and did nothing but chuckle and grow more infirm by the minute. He no longer sat his horse like a man, if he ever had, but wide-limbed as any peg-leg. He rode like a cripple woman rocking on her stool.

Was this the deceitfulness of his devilish art, or was he losing his vital force?

The Bastard asked no questions. He was a man for onset. If Satan opened his mouth at him, he'd pick the lizard from his tongue. He feinted high overhead and crashed his edge down on Ironface's leg, sheering it exactly at the knee.

It hung off in a lump of horror, or rather the armour did, on a single rivet. The flesh inside was severed. It poured blood from the meat and sweat from the bone, more blood than I had seen in the whole of that day.

Merdun's men cheered, then were silent. Ironface was laughing at the mishap, and his laugh lacked pain. The red still gouted from his stump as if his heart had burst above it, but the voice was cheery beneath his hauberk, as if it were the most natural thing in the world to be parted by a sword like this.

The Bastard had seen severed limbs before. He approved of their message. He spurred into the devil's flank and aimed a blow at his neck.

His horse reared unexpectedly and dumped him on the floor before tumbling half on top of him. It was chewing on a dart like a thunderbolt, which lodged in the roof of its brain. The pipe-player rewound the spring on one of those Italian arbalests, which are now called crossbows. God knew where it had come from, unless from the other man's hump.

60

Merdun scrambled to his feet. Dismounted or not, he intended to finish with his foe. He pulled a blade from somebody's belt, a dagger no bigger than a farrier's hoof-pick, and rushed to bury it in Ironface's groin.

I was being ransomed by sorcerers and devils. Ironface twisted the remaining rivet by his knee, caught up his severed leg in its armour, and smashed the Bastard a mighty blow over the helmet with it. He rode into Merdun's gaggle, trampling footmen, corpses, cinders and the remains of the fire, then reared his great shadow round to chase them to oblivion while he hacked them and truncheoned them with his bloodied limb.

The sight of a faceless man attacking them with his own severed leg was too much for them. So was the gore he sprayed them with. It was hotter than Mummy's soup, more caustic than dragon's blood. It stung their faces and scalded their eyes. They fled from the shock of it, but were trapped in a greater terror.

It takes time for several score men to leave a house, even a mill house which is all doors. In that time, the Hunchback wreaked a terrible slaughter among them with his longbow and a quiver full of arrows. It was simply a matter of pull and release for him, pull and release, with no need to aim, let alone rewind an Italian spring. He loosed his arrows without compunction into their backs and buttocks, and so were my parents avenged. If you think chain-mail is good, then see what heart of yew can do to it, aided by the fletcher's craft. Merdun's men squirmed in heaps by the doors, with the Hunchback's goose-quills sticking from their backbones and his barbs eating their bowels.

The Bastard did not lie with them. He had stolen away with those who had fled, despite the blow that had dented his helmet. I was glad not to find him. The iron devil had told me to pick up his dagger and cut him by the cullions and cod. He said I would feel better for it after, even if I was sick in his teeth as I did it. Well, that was Ironface's revenge, not mine; and he was a being without leg or heart, or a human head.

*   *   *

So I was left alone with my saviours from Hell in a charnel house of corpses, my dear ones quite still, my foes in a froth and a murmur. The iron fellow laughed. He examined his stump, while the Hunchback went about Mummy's room with a dirk and cut into backs to pull out his arrows. Sometimes he pushed them through, because of the barbs. This freshness of blood awoke the flies. Flies on an enemy's wound are not jewels, any more than they are on your own.

I might have run mad, begun to scream or at least keen. The little badel crept near, moaned gently in my ear and embraced me. This sweet-favoured monstrosity was mute, but elegant as a cat. The heartbeat along his arm was warm.

Then the Hunchback approached. He too hugged me, but with a bloodied fistful of darts. 'We are your friends,' he grunted in a growl of a voice. 'Believe me, your friends, young lady.' He flourished his dripping arrows. Like the Mute he was hooded, and he wore a beard as well. He did not meet my eyes. His face was all bone and shadow. He apologized for his grisly relics. 'I have to reclaim them,' he said. 'The ordinary goose-quills I could leave. But each of these lovelies flies with the wing-tip of an owl. It is feathered with silence for shooting at night.' He kissed me. His beard was soft as midsummer catkins. It was a human kiss.

I was glad of such a comfort. Ironface was now reunited with his fallen leg-armour and the limb encased in it. He peered into the chasm of its wound and sipped some blood. 'A noble grape,' he chuckled. 'An excellent year. The summer of my birth from a human belly. It is a vintage too sweet to waste.' He fitted his leg back against his stump, or – to be exact – refitted his armour into the hinge at his knee, in spite of the dint in it. 'Well, my brave fellows,' he chuckled, 'I now ride light on the left. Lord Ferblant regrows his tail like a lizard.' His voice was softer and less in his chest, but my heart still beat with terror at his closeness. When other

62

men lose a limb they lie down, at least until the fever has passed.

'Trust us,' he said. His tone was kind, but it came from its depth of iron. 'The proof of your trust will come to you only when you find it has not been misplaced. There is no surer proof than that.'

'These crusaders will come back,' I said.

'Some score of them can never come back, being already here. As for the rest, I think not. They will not boast of evading the Iron Devil and his retinue of demons. To speak of their valour in facing me will be to tell of your parents' rape. I take it the giant is your father, and this noble pillar of nakedness the fleshly cradle he hatched you from?' He indicated Mummy's corpse, having chosen it by the smoothness of its hands.

I should have wept then. I tried to weep. As I did so, the legless iron thing that had rescued me strove to bring me comfort. To be enfolded in his metal arms and clasped to his metal chest was like being cuddled against the anvil by the axe. When he whispered in my ear, it was in a voice without nostril, without breath. He did not even speak sparks. Only the cross on his falding was real. And that, like his accent, was Spanish.

The Mute and the Hunchback meanwhile equipped them-selves with the mattock and spade which Daddy's bowels required to be always close to the rear door. I could not bring myself to join them in their task. Nor did Ironface, the devil man, this self-proclaimed Lord Ferblant. Still, the needs of seven people kept the kitchen garden soft, and there was always the water-meadow.

'Sooner or later someone will come.' The hollow man was changing his tune. 'Not those villains but the cohorts they strayed from. And as an army finds its men slain, so will it search for their slayers. This Crusade is camped all about you. Some of it is eating its midday meal, some of it is preparing its supper, according to when it got up. And some of it is doubtless already asleep, but around you is where it finds itself.'

63

'I must run then.' By run I meant ride. I didn't intend to sit sideways either.

'I suppose you must, now you have made an enemy of it.'

'May I make so bold as to ask you your purpose, Ferblant? Here, I mean.'

'In the land of the living? I have been in Pézenas, rescuing people from witches and sorcerers.'

'There aren't any witches in Hérault.'

'Not now,' he agreed. 'Nor for a good time in the future. Once this Crusade gets itself properly in motion, there won't be many people of any sort.'

The Hunchback and the Mute came back and put their spades up as gently as if they lived in the Mill themselves, and had used them for their own bodily purposes. 'We have buried her parents in the garlic patch,' the Hunchback said. 'And their women here and there among the beans.' His voice was rough, as if something had been stripped from his throat. 'The soil is soft, but it's not deep. The garlic cloves will keep devils off. Dogs will be another matter.'

I needed to cry, but I couldn't. So the Mute touched my face, and I cried. He went on touching me, but I didn't need to be touched. His hands were scented with rose water, in spite of digging in blood.

Ironface gestured for Merdun's men to be dragged out of doors. 'Let them lie naked to the birds,' he said. 'But let us take good care to be gone before the birds tell tales about us.'

A score of corpses takes a deal of time to shift. As his strange henchmen went about the task, the devil fellow regarded me kindly, or at least his eye-holes were inclined towards me in a manner I thought was sympathetic, till he growled, 'Since we talk of bodies, kindly have the modesty to cover your own.'

Tin Legs was prurient, and I had sat before him in my nudity like a little girl.

'Count yourself lucky,' this Ferblant chuckled, 'as in

64

an hour you have been taught every evil that men can do.'

'Not in my own person, praise God.'

'Not yet, perhaps.'

CANTO TWO

In which a maiden has virginal
dreams but awakens in a ditch
to see frogs mating.

shall keep the emotional fruits of my condition to myself, at least for the moment. Their rind is too harsh and their pith too bitter for sharing. If there were any practical consequences of Mummy and Daddy being dead, and of course there were, Ironface and his two companions were at pains to hurry me away from them. 'We must ride to Béziers,' he said.

He was either a devil or some other kind of inferior person, and I did not intend to accept such a being's proposals lightly, so I hesitated before agreeing.

'My master advised against this Crusade,' Ironface said, as if his words would explain everything. 'When his counsel went unheeded, he asked me to report on its progress.'

'So you serve a great one.'

'Without doubt.'

'What great one is that?'

'One who will not be named.'

'Then name yourself, since Ferblant is a nickname and you are clearly no lord!'

'I'm a complicated tale to tell in a hurry!'

I listened no more. The earth's mother, Eve, was beguiled by a stranger's talk, but Mummy had taught me her folly. I dressed quickly and carefully, wrapping myself as for a journey. Then I packed some clothes in a bag, better clothes than those I wore, and followed my new companions across the meadows.

I rode Nano, with my limbs on either side of him. As Daddy had said, 'Horses are forever tupping, so stick to a gelding. Once they start climbing on each other's backs, you'll feel silly on a stallion and sillier still on a mare, especially side-saddle. Choose a male without his figs and be kinder to him in consequence.'

So this should be possible I rode as always with my petticoat and coat tucked short, and no under-surcoat or gown as I would if I were calling on people of importance. To make such a spectacle decent to the foreigners, I wore chausses on my legs much as a peasant might, but more of them and with better cloth in them, bound even beyond my ankles, in fact all the way into my clogs. I say 'decent to the foreigners', meaning 'decent to the enemy' because our own folk are used to such things. If a man hereabouts can afford a second horse – and very few can – he expects his women to share it, without going to the foolery and expense of a skirt saddle. When a man sees a woman's legs in the Hérault, he dilutes his fancy with another swig of wine and forces himself to think of something else. There are legs everywhere on market day, including bare ones, though Mummy never let me wear mine like that. As far as the crusaders went, it might be foolish to suggest I had limbs at all, since women are not ordinarily supposed to possess them; but having been totally humiliated and almost raped had left me with an odd feeling of bravado. Besides, I was riding with an escort of demons, including at least one archer.

I didn't put my hair up, as a grown woman should. I wore it down my back, like the child I no longer was. I was travelling with Ironface, who was possibly made of tin, for Ferblant means tin, and with his Mute and his Hunchback, with only their descriptions to serve as their names. So never mind convention.

Did I truly believe they were demons? I paid very little attention to the problem, once I saw we followed a crooked path towards Béziers rather than the direct route to Hell. The afternoon sunlight was melancholy enough, without the confusion of thought. All I will say is they were not ordinary men. Ordinary men smell, principally of ordinariness. Riding among them, often knee to knee, I could sniff no such matter. My nostrils encountered marsh mallows, dog rose and dock, then juniper leaf and the crushed oils of the garrigue as the gorse and fig bushes crowded our way.

Another human odour was absent. Ironface's wound should have stunk by now. Sour blood would be obnoxious to all but the clegs and meat flies. Yet his leg was scented with grapes rather than gore, as if his body was full of juice.

Someone was wearing spice on his limbs, one of those sickly aromas from Spain, such as the gypsies make for the infidels. I think it was the Mute, who continued to fawn and smile at me, poor little badel that he was. He sucked liquorice, and chewed cloves to keep his teeth from rusting.

I was stupid to leave my hair down, in spite of these distractions.

Our path was moving closer to the old stone road of the Wizards that the Crusade had stuck to, but keeping a less open route. We could hear trumpets above us, and the march of horses heavy with metal, so we chose a more prudent direction.

This new way led to a wood on the edge of a Roman water barrage which was now silted into a desolate salt marsh. We were only a few paces inside the shadow of the trees when we were surrounded by horsemen. Most had been dismounted or asleep in their saddles, but there were some on watch and prompt to challenge us. Several of them snatched at me, and one caught hold of my horse's bridle as if Nano were a row-boat and I were adrift on it.

'I serve the Legate,' Ironface lied. 'I ride with Arnold Almaric, the Pope's man.' He unhooked my reins from the fellow's fingers.

'Then you ride closer to the front of an army than any priest I've ever met.'

They laughed mightily at this. I did not laugh, not with crusaders.

'I'm no priest,' Ironface croaked, and his pelican voice frightened them. 'Though I bear arms in Pope Innocent's name – as do you all, I trust?'

'And who is this malkin?'

I hoped Ironface would show more respect than to call me his daughter.

71

'She's my wife,' his impudence said, with all the ease in the world.

'And rides with her hair down, little Molly-on-my-back? You let her go dishevelled and disgrace you like any tinker woman, or mackerel from the town?'

'She is in mourning for her parents. They died just now of the Plague.' Ironface put his hand to his helm, as if to remove it. 'I am full of the spot myself, else I would show myself to you, fellow.'

This made them draw back in a hurry. 'Well, I'm in no hurry to feel her groin for the buboes,' their leader said. 'Nor yours.'

The Mute cackled his voiceless laugh for them, and this frightened them even more.

'Farewell, Englishman,' Ironface said. 'And may you grow better manners and some teeth to go with them.'

They moved away, and we rode past their encampment without further parley.

'I'm not your wife,' I said to Ironface.

He paid no attention to me. 'This army is scattered everywhere,' he commented. 'And if we continue on horseback into the evening, we shall doubtless blunder into it again. Therefore we must rest and give it time to gather itself into one place.'

'I am not your wife.'

'Nor I the man for wedlock, so don't disturb yourself further in the matter. If I were, I should feel obliged to choose someone much older than fourteen summers.'

He had my age wrong by several years, and I told him so.

'Someone with a more adult intelligence, then.' He pointed ahead to one of the bothies of the Visigoths that besprinkle our landscape. They are round, beehive-shaped structures of stone, each with a little chamber at their heart slightly fuller in diameter than a tall man lying, though such a person could never stand up in one. 'We'll stop here,' he said. 'They are commonly held to be magician's work or fallen from the moon. No crusader will trouble us there, be he ever so strong a Christian. And if anyone passing hears our voices or the Mute's pipe, they'll conclude we are gnomes or ogres.'

'I'll not share a pig-pen with three men,' I said. 'Besides, such monuments only have one door. If anyone chooses to push in a burning log, or sit outside with a sword, we'll be cooked and done.'

'Pert as well as nasty,' Ironface said.

'Nasty as well as pert,' the Hunchback agreed.

The Mute played a derisory tune on his pipe.

'I shall sleep in that ditch,' I said. 'It's dry, and there'll be no rats.' I pointed to the silver grey coils of a Montpellier Serpent, our largest venomous snake. They're aggressive creatures, but content to leave you alone if you don't trifle with them. This one took herself away up the ditch in dignified crusade, but settled at its further end and glinted at us. It was exactly the colour of Ironface's mail. 'Take care it doesn't mistake one of your limbs for its mate,' I advised him, 'or you'll have a wife in earnest.'

Ironface was in a sulk. It was all right for him to speak of wives, but not for me. Still, I owed him a kinder politeness. 'How did you know that horseman was English?' I asked, to start talk up again.

'The English only have two words for whore. Malkin is one. Molly is the other. Whereas I shall call you whore by a dozen if you don't put your hair up, my little nanny-goat.'

We made our encampment. This, in my case, meant no more than planting my bottom in the ditch. I had a cloak to spread, but not one made for this kind of work.

The Hunchback produced bread, and the Mute went foraging for crab-apples. He found crabs instead. These weren't tasteless freshwater crabs from ponds, but sea crabs as big as platters. The sea was a full league off, but there were salt creeks everywhere. We ate them raw and alive, even to the flesh in the pincher, as we did not dare light a fire to make bisque.

Ironface's wound remained fresh, in spite of the heat.

73

There was no chance of cauterizing it, so I offered to find water and bathe it for him. The Mute sighed at my concern, and the Hunchback groaned. I was parading my ignorance again. Devils and the walking dead cannot take hurt – was that to be my conclusion?

Ironface added to my embarrassment by unfastening his injured limb completely. That is he unhooked its armour from the thigh, and shook it. It was empty. No blood, no bone, no flesh, no putrefaction. Such leg as he had, or stump, or tail, was concealed beneath the skirt of his habergeon. Man, monster or mechanism, he had not been recently amputated, if ever. He chuckled. The brains behind that mask of his were as cunning as a mill full of Daddy's cogs.

He removed his other leg at the knee. On the right-hand side he either carried more leg or sought to retain more in the way of deception. 'I like to shed these after a long day in the saddle,' he explained, as if such a riddle offered me anything but surprise. He sipped noisily at the rim of his calf-armour. He was tasting something. He pronounced it good, spoke a brief blessing, and passed the amputation to me. His entire lower limb was a flagon of delicious muscat, not the ferment but the distillation. I felt drunk just to sniff it.

So he was a legless man who rode with firewater for ballast, like a tunny-boat? Or perhaps there was no man in there at all, and his armour held only his voice? I decided not to deliberate further on the matter.

Good wine, fresh crab, bread only a day or two old – their effect on me was instantaneous. Darkness falls quickly at this time of the year when there are no clouds for day to skulk in. The sun sank. I sank.

I had promised myself a midnight or so of quiet weeping, once the others' minds were elsewhere. Instead I heard a cricket chafe his legs together, another cricket answer, and knew I must give myself to sleep.

My companions sat about me, but apart, according my grief both respect and protection. I sobbed an unholy prayer for them. I prayed to treat the three of them, especially Ironface, more politely on the morrow, if I lived to see one. Death did not concern me any more. I had studied it too closely. If it left me alone, so be it. If it came with violence and pain, then it would be over in a minute or an hour. It would pass within the running of a sand or the burning of a candle. Its hurt would be no more than life's last gesture.

My prayer was aimed at no Saint but given to God the Simple One direct. My mind passed very quickly from it into sleep and thence into disturbing visions of what men and women do with one another in the act of love. My dream had nothing to do with the afternoon, because it lacked kicking and stifling. It lacked screams. I heard a sigh as soft as starlight in the midsummer grasses, saw faces come close with kisses, a twining of limbs that were naked and beautiful, as if the angels themselves were mating in Heaven. We rarely spoke of such matters, Mummy and I. I had my first month only recently, and she blessed me and told me it would return in another month. Otherwise I knew only what I was told by Marie-Bise. Wrestling between man and woman she held to be an admirable sport, but said that if Daddy ever wrestled with a woman he would crush her. That is why there is only one of me. Mummy declined to renew the combat, and was jealous of her household of proxies.

So I was left with ill-informed dreams of limbs locking face to face, and of feelings largely unrefined. The limbs did not puzzle me. I had lived by a stream in a meadow. I had sometime or other seen every one of Noah's known beasts at the tup. Everything from tortoises and vipers to Jourdain our stud bull with each of his milchers in turn; I include cocks and hens, and Frédélon the swan whose soulmate the mad Queen Blanche only let him approach for the one purpose.

So I'm not at all baffled by the commerce of lithe limbs. It's how the faces bestow themselves during my most relaxing thoughts that's the puzzle, especially the female ones. Males throughout the entire Kingdom of Animals either grunt and dribble (even vipers leak a horrible stench of almonds) or

75

else they keep their head cocked away in search of a rival or enemy, or even a friendly intruder who might treat them to a three-legged surprise.

What are the female manners in such a case? Goats munch nettles, sows drool swill. I can't imagine Mummy doing either of those things or telling me if she did. Does one look into the distance? Search for a star and watch it turn in the heavens, or hum a troubadour's song under one's breath?

My dream might have been beautiful, but it asked so many questions that it must have represented all manner of anxieties. Only at one moment was it entirely calm, and that was when it included a vision of two frogs mating, both of them with a rapt look on their faces as if God had welcomed them to prayer. The male crouched on the female's back with a far-away gaze as he slowly inflated his bubble. She refused to be distracted by him, or by God, but kept all of her mind on a grasshopper she was sicking up. It was a holy vision, appropriate to the ditch I slept in.

I was woken from it abruptly.

The Mute's face was close to my own and bright with starlight. His two index fingers pressed lightly beneath the lobes of my ears. For a moment I thought he was preparing to throttle me. Then I realized he was waking me without noise.

The other two were already alert, and peering over the lip of the ditch. I crouched up beside them and saw a great pile of naked and half-naked men, some of them in helmets, all mounted on each other's back like a precipice of tortoises. Naked men were no longer a surprise to me, but to see so many of them heaped so high, all pressing earthwards in a convulsive act of integrated concupiscence took me a second or two longer to understand. I am a country girl, so I daresay I was well ahead of my companions in forming an opinion.

How apt was my dream of frogs. Often, when spring is all in a rush and the countryside has not wiped the sleep from her eyes, you may see frogs or even toads make such a mountain. The males are in search of females, their seed is running to waste down their flippers, but the females are still asleep, or at their toilet, or gone into a nunnery beneath the nearest flat stone.

Suddenly the males espy one of their number successfully mounted – whether they see, hear, touch or blunder upon him in the dark, I do not know. Each of them thinks it better to be half a daddy than no daddy at all, and promptly leaps forward to place himself on a heaving tower of rapidly diminishing arithmetic. I have seen them three score to a pile, and the girls of our house claim to have witnessed heaps of several hundred, which is higher than any of them can count.

Let me not take the allegory too far, especially in the presence of so many grunting bottoms. But the plain fact is that when the pyramid is undone – and we women were sometimes spiteful enough to attempt the task: it was a simple way of catching the family's breakfast – there is often no female frog at the heart of it. The whole exercise in geometry has begun from a gigantic piece of misunderstanding, such as a blind male jumping on his companion's back, or a jealous frog rushing to mount a friend who was simply squatting on a pebble. Or perhaps – I've often thought it since – the female was simply appalled at so much bad architecture, and decided her heart was no longer in it, and took herself away from underneath it all.

So it was here.

A shape smaller and more totally unclad than the rest left the pile of glinting bodies and rushed glowing into the ditch to hide. A young woman of Thistle's age (so a year or two older than I) lay panting beside us. She was dressed only in the sweat of a score or so of her nearest oppressors, and was clutching a bottle from which she drank noisily. 'You're making yourself cheap,' she said to it. 'It's like your mother said, "Whoring is steady work, but you need to fix a proper price on your tally-stick".' She became aware of us, as if for the first time, and shared her bottle around with a shrug. '"Easy come, easy go",' she said. 'That's another of the old lady's expressions.'

The bottle contained indifferent Armagnac, and it had obviously been her 'price'. It passed between us only once, before Ironface kept hold of it and urged us further along the ditch, just as some of the crusaders dismounted from one another's backs and fell to squabbling.

Our way was barred by the Montpellier Serpent. It was too cold to move, and on such an occasion capable of being nasty, though its venom is all at the back of its throat. 'Allow me,' the young woman said. She crept ahead of Ironface, who doubtless found crawling difficult, having no knees to creep on, and took the snake – which was as long as she was – in firm hands, gripping it gently behind the head. Serpents have frequently been beguiled by naked women, ever since that First One stole into the Garden. It snuggled itself up to her. 'I've held men's cockles and penny-dum-didos that have been bigger than you,' she murmured. 'But none of them so pretty!' Before it could make itself comfortable she tossed it through the night air towards her former customers, where it bit some, and frightened several, and doubtless confused itself. They dared not bruise its head with their heels, as most of them were naked.

That is how I met Mamelie la Mamelonne. I thought I recognized her nature immediately. She was like One Eye and Thistle, with quite a lot of Marie-Bise's wisdom to season her understanding. It was only later than I came to detect in her certain traits of Constance de Coulobres and even Mummy herself. That was a day or two later, when I was rather more grown up.

We couldn't slip away from these roystering crusaders until daylight had made a mess of things, and moving after the sun was up presented a host of problems. 'Riding with a virgin and a whore,' Ironface explained, 'is bound to slow a warrior down, even an invincible campaigner like myself. He's forever protecting the one and collecting for the other.'

The Hunchback thought this a splendid joke, but we women didn't laugh at it. The Mute simply wound up his crossbow and pulled faces at a little donkey that wandered from a thicket where it had been pretending to be venison. What it lacked in wind it made up for in flatulence, and its socket-bones stood taller than its ears. Mamelie explained it belonged to her.

Finding where we had put our own horses took a little time, and helping La Mamelonne discover her clothes took even longer, so much so that we began to suspect she travelled without them. In the end, I gave her an undercotte and a pelisse from my bag. 'That makes us friends,' she said, dusting the thumbprints from her breasts. 'Gifts from a man are just payment. From a woman, they come different, especially in your case. The cloth of that under-smock sits softer on my belly than anything I've ever known, including an Arab's kiss.'

Mummy and Constance de Coulobres had never spoken like this, and probably would not even have had an opinion on such matters. I tried to understand my new friend a little more closely. 'Why were you lying under all those men?' I asked her.

'It's what I do for a living.'

'Why were they all in such a heap?'

'They were drunk and they were in a hurry.'

'How much did they pay you?'

'They let me stay alive. Your life is often the best thing a soldier can offer you.'

My own recent experiences forced me to agree with her. 'Tell me your name,' I said. 'I mean your *real* name.'

'I've no time to remember it. I can't even think just now.'

As I grew to know her, I found that Mamelie la Mamelonne could rarely discover much time for thinking. She dreamed often, and sometimes she reflected, but think? Not Mamelie. This made her a philosopher, and like most philosophers she was frequently wrong.

Her discourse was always entertaining, though. I had my own thoughts, as could be expected, but they were immediately broken into by her answering some question of the Hunchback's. 'The difference between a whore and a concubine? Some say it's the length of the word. Some say it's the length of the service. Basically, it's money, take it from me. A whore gets a pittance, the other one gets nothing. Unless you count gee-gaws and trinkets. But a clever girl can steal trinkets any day of the week.'

'Suppose I were to require your services,' Ironface asked, 'professionally speaking, that is. How much would you charge me?'

'Nothing,' she said promptly. 'You're a friend, and a friend need do no more than ask.' She gazed at the faceless lump of his head, his all-over metal shine that made him look more like a scum lizard than anything human. 'Of course, once a friend asks me that, he no longer stands so tall in the hierarchy of my affections!'

Mummy would have agreed with her. She had always stressed that there are some things that men, by which she meant Daddy, don't pester a woman for.

I was delighted to see La Mamelonne wore her hair as long as I did. 'In my profession, only bawds put their hair up,' she insisted. 'I'm a woman, not a woman keeper.'

In her innocent wickedness she was a little girl, and in years scarcely older than myself or One Eye, or Thistle, as I've already said, though plumper than all three of us together, perhaps through being stretched so often.

And why was I travelling with such people? At the simplest, because I saw no-one else to be with. Mummy's family, Trencavel, was a perilous connection for me. So where was I to be, save with my new companions? Was I to go to Daddy's lot, and learn to soak peas?

Ironface spoke, as if in answer to my darkest questions. 'You think because I allow men to call me Ferblant that my chest was created by a tinker! Well, look what other knights wear – a fishnet of straps and wires. A hauberk is not built by an armourer – no, nor by a smith. And as for a tinker, he would not cut so ill. It takes but a lorimer, a strap-and-buckle maker, to fashion an ordinary coat of mail. A woman could do the same with her needle.'

'And knit me a Ferblant too, a gentleman who can shed his limbs like a lizard, and perhaps all his other organs as well.' His armour was no concern of mine. It was what, if anything, was inside it that bothered me. 'Lord Ferblant,' I teased. 'Lord Tin? Can there be such a person?'

La Mamelonne came rushing in to soothe us – if anyone can rush anywhere or soothe anyone on a donkey that farts. 'Names!' she said. 'What's in a name?' Her tongue was all of a gallop. 'Married men'll call you anything to get what they want.'

'Married men come to you?' Our whore was an endless source of curiosity.

'Only when their wives send them. When I started selling love for money, which I did as soon as I stopped giving it away for pleasure, which I did as soon as I discovered there was no pleasure in it, I was called "Blatte", which is how they name a cockroach in Paris. Men like to put you down. I'd be called "Blatte" by customers whose fingers had been crawling all over me. Then they'd grow respectful and call me Bubby once their hands had steadied themselves on my body-handles. I won't let them call me by woman's other bit, though, because my ooolooolooo was fashioned for me by God.'

'You mustn't say God made our shameful parts,' I scolded. 'It's a heresy to pretend so!'

'Believe me, no, my little chick. It's only a hundred Hail Marys. What is going to get all the Trencavels burnt, and all you other Perfect Ones, is saying anything is made by the Devil. Anything except bad luck, that is. Of course the Devil made that. But he could never design an oooolooolooo. That's why he's so attracted to them.'

Mummy never said oooolooolooo. She said 'your *self*' in a peculiar tone of voice. Or 'down there' or 'there'. Marie-Bise said it was ooolaaalaaa, but then cooks have different words for everything, even vegetables.

I had no time to weep at such recollections. La Mamelonne was a sovereign antidote to weeping. 'Nowadays,' she said, but lost herself momentarily as her tiny donkey folded beneath her like one of those arrangements of sticks that town people use for drying clothes. 'Nowadays I'm known as Sifflet,' she laughed, picking the beast up by the shoulder bones.

'That means Bellows!'

'It's because I creak a lot. Men like to hear me creaking, though you're young for such talk, Perronnelle. They like to know it's a woman they're at, and not a hedgehog – men hereabouts, anyhow. People from Paris, and especially the English, would rather play fuckyfuck with a hole in the wall.'

The Hunchback laughed and the Mute shuddered aloud. Even Ironface amused himself in his foreign fashion. The little donkey didn't laugh, but it did the next best thing. It kept its head under her pelisse, which was my pelisse, for the rest of the journey, proving, as she said, that even beasts of burden were at home inside her skirts.

It is only a few leagues to Béziers from St Thibéry. You wouldn't make it fifteen if you went by the sea, or thirty by the mountains; so it amazed me we took so long. This was because Ferblant insisted on doubling about. At Cabrials he sent his Hunchback to buy bread. At Bachéléry he told his Mute to perform conjuring tricks for wine – which he did very prettily, making a puncheon disappear and almost causing us to be stoned and have our ears clipped in payment. When we progressed to St Jean de Libron I knew we were going backwards, like ships tacking wide of the wind. An army moves slowly enough – it may waste the forenoon foraging for breakfast – but these crusaders couldn't be far behind. They might even be once more ahead of us.

I watched the city walls deepen from sunlit to shade as noon moved past them, the cathedral change from a golden bug to the blackest of beetles, and I grew afraid. This Ironface Ferblant was himself a crusader, was he not? He had been

afflicted by a moment's pity in my case. He had offended a
mighty one, or the mighty one's brother, for the merest slip
of a girl, and she from a family they had come here on oath
to burn. Surely he regretted such a rash step?

I turned Nano towards him. Before I could speak, he said,
'I hesitate before Béziers, and my hesitation is this. I do not
wish to be known among your great ones.'

'And why not, pray?'

'Because I have a parchment that says they shall be cinders,
and all that are found about them.'

'You talk as if the city will be taken.'

'You know your own people, and you have witnessed these.
Can you believe otherwise?'

Presumptuous fellow. My kinsman Raymond-Roger was a
noted warrior and huntsman. Although young, he had a list
of chivalric feats to his name as long as Daddy's waistband.
I got ready to say so. Instead I heard a pounding, and turned
to see such a tower of dust in the east that it looked as if
night had opened her cloak behind us just an hour into the
afternoon. 'Crusaders!' I called.

There was no way of escaping them, their vanguard came
on so fast.

Ironface seemed to exult at their coming. I was once more
fearful I would be sold back to my enemies, or betrayed in
some other way. But my private liar and devil was doing no
more than prepare himself for a further bout of deception,
such as he practised on all men equally. For the moment,
he hissed, 'It's easy to hide in a crowd, so put your hair up,
Perronnelle.'

It takes me nine minutes to plait my locks, even indoors
with no wind blowing, but La Mamelonne fastened my tresses
in a knot, and I hid the resulting mass in my hood. We rode
to meet the head of the column.

Ironface held out his sword before him like a cross. He
was again giving that silly greeting the crusaders learn from
their songs. It is a foolish gesture, even with a blunt sword,

which most of them are. They nick their fingers and do terrible damage to their horses.

He greeted the outriders in Latin. This marked him as a priest in their eyes, and stopped them asking further. His helmet was a problem for them, and some of them looked as if they would like to throw him into a pond, perhaps because being crusaders they had too many priests among them already. We were saved from damage, at least for the moment, by the arrival of the main body of horsemen.

A great chatter of nobility rode at their head. Among them, I learned later, were the Duke of Burgundy and the Counts of Nevers and St Pol, as well as the Archbishops of Reims, Sen and Rouen, and six bishops; but Mummy used to talk to such people almost daily.

Two men rode apart. One of them, a skinny fellow whose cuffs were trimmed with squirrel, was evidently a priest of some rank – he had the belly to prove it, in spite of being built like a climbing vine. The other was middle sized, quick and sleek. He was about fifty years old. His face reminded me of someone, perhaps a wrestler Daddy had broken.

Squirrel Cuff nodded towards Ironface and said, 'I know this fellow, and once knew his features where he now has none. He was a good man, stout for the Cross, however he rides.'

'Sat a bit too close to the fire, did he? I mistrust a man who travels with whores and strumpets, whatever his quality. And as for the deformed one' – his companion spat towards the Hunchback and crossed himself – 'a hump is the Devil's luggage. It's never fastened on a fellow without good reason.'

There was no answer I could give to whore or strumpet, not without saying Trencavel. I did as La Mamelonne, smiled and said nothing. But great ones love to show their importance, even before whores and strumpets. So it was I heard Squirrel Cuff say, 'Those who killed my friend Peter of Castelnau shall assuredly die.' He gazed towards the dark hulk of Béziers, with the sun still glinting on its towers and crenellations, and its birds shifting and settling, as if it were a sheep's gut full of maggots. 'My friend and God's. And the Pope's legate. This man's comrade in blood.' Once more he indicated Ironface in a way that suggested the devil fellow was mortal.

'I hear what you're saying, Arnold Almaric. You feel that if we kill enough people we'll catch the right ones.'

'No,' Arnaud said. 'I'm not suggesting that, my Lord of Montfort.'

'I need to be clear. You speak for God. I can only talk for the army these faint hearts have no-one to lead.'

So this was Simon de Montfort, the half-brother the Bastard had boasted about. No wonder the face seemed familiar. The likeness was strong.

The 'faint hearts' were presumably his fellow nobles. He gestured towards them where they waited at the head of the column while the dust settled back on them like flies onto dungy oxen.

'Courtiers and quarantine men,' he scoffed. 'In forty days time their wives will have called them home.'

'You'll cook the more heretics, and cook them the better for their absence.'

'When the dukes and archbishops go home, they'll take the army with them. Then Toulouse will change sides again.'

'By then you'll have swallowed young Trencavel and have no need of Toulouse. If you're short of an army, there'll be land within your gift. You'll be able to fee those young barons to stay with you.'

'It depends how far you trust me, Arnold Almaric.'

'I trust you to look after yourself. And how far do you trust me?'

'Till sunset tonight, and perhaps after dawn tomorrow. That's as far as I'll trust anyone.'

Almaric continued to glare towards Béziers as if his gaze alone could set it burning. 'Tomorrow will be long enough,' he said. 'We'll eat them on the Feast of the Madeleine.'

'It may take an hour. It may need a season. Something of how it goes will depend on how good these Bitterois are at resisting a siege. Most, in my experience, will depend on luck.'

'God is our luck!' The cleric wheeled his horse, leaving Simon de Montfort to say, 'A man makes his own luck. And then he thanks God for it.' He spoke to himself.

Ferblant was among great men, where he claimed to belong, but he wasn't listening to them. His horse was almost a dray, like most battle mounts. He let it rub nostrils with Nano, while he plunged his own mask inside my hood and kept it there, like a donkey nosing a sack for oats.

The iron-headed monster! Did he think he was playing kiss-dance at Christmas after his earlier claims that I was his wife?

I heard a familiar voice, and knew why he hid. It was Merdun. The illegitimate one had ridden out of nowhere and was swearing a rumble of oaths into his brother's ear.

Simon disliked being sworn at. 'You grow fat, Merdun!'

'It's the wind, brother.'

'Before a battle, many suffer from it.'

Ironface and I burrowed into each other's hoods like monks at a funeral. Merdun belched to consolidate his argument. 'It won't be a battle, my brother. We shall overcome them without a whisper.'

'So we shall have a massacre. You are good at those, men tell me.'

'Let them fear for their tongues, these men. I do what Christ puts upon me. And what will you do to the burghers of Béziers, my brother?'

Lord Simon laughed, as if it were a rhetorical question merely.

'Tell me,' the Bastard persisted. 'It is a truth my fellows wish to share with me. So what will you do once we carry the attack?'

'I shall put them to the torch and the sword for keeping their wall against me. You know the rules of war.'

'Aye, the prick and the torch. They will hold their wall

against you because you have proclaimed them heretics who shall certainly be burned.'

'I do as Arnold Amalric orders. Were they wise, they would leave their fair city to me and run. But they're not wise, and I praise God for it. Their heads are puncheons of aqua-vitae and their bellies tubs of tripe. They'll burn better for the pickling, but their guts will smell.'

'Not their women, Simon. Their women are delicate.' The Bastard pursed his lips like a man sucking figs.

'You spatter like a nag's tail.'

Arnaud Almaric returned at the gallop, and re-entered the conversation briskly. 'Women, is it? You're in luck, Merdun.' He needed the brothers to be at peace with one another. 'My priests have found out a woman for you.'

There, among the houses at St Jean de Libron, a brace of chaplains were holding a young female captive. She neither struggled nor spoke, and the holy men watched her with fascination. They knew she would soon be dead.

She was a slim girl, with a face like a fish. Her mouth was open and eager, and her body moved in curious ways, even when it was still. Men would not notice the face of a body that moved like that.

'I know thát twitch,' La Mamelonne breathed beside me. 'That's a feast day whore called Violette la Vierge.'

'Can you have a virgin whore?'

'You can have what you like, dear.' Then she was breathless with fear for herself.

'Let the search begin,' Arnaud Almaric ordered.

By this he meant them to undress the girl. They produced an old woman for the task, but she had arthritic fingers, so the priests were happy to assist her.

'We're not going to strip *all* the heretics, are we?' The senior De Montfort was growing fretful at the delay.

'Only the pretty ones,' the Bastard chuckled.

'This one's not one of your Cathari,' Almaric said. 'She's accused of witchcraft. Well, we must cleanse as we go. The girl is a manifest witch-woman.'

'No she's not,' Mamelie muttered. 'She's a kiss-and-run whore.'

Whatever she was, she hadn't been stitched into her cotte and petticotte by Constance de Coulobres, so they had her out of them in no time at all. These priests were deft at undressing women.

Her body was free of blemish, except for a small mole on her left shoulder-blade.

'It's the Devil's teat,' Arnold Almaric proclaimed. 'She's suckled a child on the blood of her back!'

'She's a virgin,' the old crone said. 'She's a virgin, so there's the proof of it. The Devil only takes virgins to wife and to motherhood.'

'Just like the Holy Ghost,' the Bastard agreed.

'Entered unnaturally and delivered unnaturally.' Almaric tested her maidenhead with his finger and agreed that it was good. 'Burn her,' he commanded. 'Burn her on a clean fire, and sweep the embers away afterwards. Then cook me some supper.' He scowled about him, the way the righteous do. I saw his features from close up. Their skin was purple as a raisin, especially on his nose. The blood wriggled slowly round his nostrils, as if there were worms swimming in it. If ever a man's thoughts were made of maggots, it was this one's.

These witch tests and sorcery tests are a fine entertainment, but they are hard on women. Also they do not operate entirely in favour of the accused, even the innocent accused. It is well known, for example, that a witch can pluck a stone from a pot of boiling water and come to no harm. So – rightly – young women who can perform this feat are found guilty of witchcraft. But nobody seems to concern himself with the plight of the young women who are found not guilty. Several such in the Great Assize at Béziers have died from the injuries that established their innocence, and I know one who is so maimed she has to carry her hand in a cloth even after an interval of years.

A fairer test, my father said, is to place a red-hot spoon

on the tongue. A woman's tongue is not such a bad thing to burn, and no family is worse for having its females talk a little stiffly.

When a great one burns a woman, he does so seated on his horse. His horse is what marks out a great one, and the less he dismounts the better.

These crusaders didn't build a fire. They kicked down a cottage on itself, and let its own hearth set flame to the rafters. Then they made ready to throw the young witch into them or under them. She was still naked, and her shoulder-blades twitched, but in the presence of so much nobility no-one dared violate her further.

'Quick with your peppers,' Ironface hissed to the Mute. He went from madness to plain silliness. Was he going to cook her with spices?

'Cover that woman,' Simon said, 'before she bewitches the horses.'

No sooner had he spoken than several of the crusaders' mounts reared up and threw them. Others began to prance or fret; a dozen more ran, with or without their riders, towards every part of the landscape. I am told that one knight's rouncy took him into the sea at Le Cap d'Agde, which is several leagues away, and swam to Africa on the other side, where nag and rider changed themselves into camels for fear of what the Moors might do to their Christian parts. Sorcery may not move mountains, but it builds powerful rumours.

'See what she does, though God knows how she does it,' Arnaud Almaric hissed. 'Let us burn her at once, even though the flame's not yet hot, burn her before she – '

Hereupon his own stallion shook its nostrils and screamed like a jay crop-full of poison. The Mute had been fondling its cullions an instant before, fondling then easing them of flies, but now it reared its hind legs up and went curvetting away, running chiefly on its forelegs and its nose, being much troubled about the rear.

'Necromancy!' Almaric shouted. 'Burn her! Burn her!'

Men do not normally take notice of warriors who can't

control their horses, but Arnaud (or Arnold, as he was more commonly known) Almaric was also a mighty priest and dangerous with it, so the cry was taken up, 'Burn her! Burn her!'

'Burn her at once!' Simon said, patting his own horse to keep the Devil from its bottom.

'I have already put her in the flames,' Ironface said. 'I and my men.'

I had not seen him move, only the Hunchback and the Mute, yet once the fire took a proper hold of the cottage and its roof fell in, the Fish Girl could be plainly heard, coughing and laughing and chattering inside, presumably with her private demons, so many were the voices.

She sputtered incessantly; one of her demons screamed in pain, but she would not die. Meanwhile the crusaders grew hoarse with smoke and their mounts were sneezing. We could hear devils howling everywhere.

'The village is possessed,' Simon de Montfort said. 'It's full of nothing but warlocks and sorcerers. Burn it all!'

So they burnt it all, or set flame to it all, while the Fish Girl's body still sneezed and chattered.

'It's that iron fellow!' Merdun shouted, glimpsing us for the first time. 'I know that one. If you're looking for – ' His horse interrupted him by producing a bright green haemorrhage of froth from its reins which were nowhere near its reins, of course, but I do believe it would have passed those too in a moment, and its bit, if it weren't so desperate to kick its buttocks with such an agitation of hoof that it began to shed its ironwork and shake out its pegs. I had never seen such a frenzy in a nag before. It thrashed its limbs about even more violently than a dog does when it scratches a flea in its ear – but a dog only flourishes one leg at the time, whereas this poor beast used all four, and on parts of its anatomy that none of them were built to reach. Horses are usually provided with tails to refresh their bottoms, but this one's was either so agitated it became invisible or it quite simply dropped off in the first spasm of its confusion.

90

It then galloped sideways towards Béziers, but the Bastard was a thoughtful man, and had already dismounted.

'I ate crabs last night, and now I see them everywhere!' Ironface jested. A number of other horses ran sideways, or backwards, or simply knelt in prayer. He led us quickly away, circling from the main body of horsemen by tree and by stone and even by dried-up ditch. They did not see us go. They listened to the Witch Girl burn and they watched the village burn. Perhaps they cooked sausage in the embers, and perhaps the Witch Girl still chattered to them from their plates.

She certainly chattered to us. She chattered brightly but incoherently from the standing pools and the shadows of the vines, while La Mamelonne seemed to grow fatter and fatter and the little donkey faltered even more than usual. Her borrowed surcotte and pelisse were swollen almost to bursting. Not for the first time I wondered if she were pregnant.

'What miracle overtook their horses?' I gasped, as we scurried onward.

'You'd dance pretty lively yourself, with a pepper in your behind. I'm sorry we've no time for you to try, Perronnelle.'

Mamelie giggled, I think because her tummy was gurgling so much it sounded as if she'd swallowed the Fish Girl.

'Time for you women to dismount,' Ironface said. 'It's your turn to carry the ass for a change.'

I only saw one woman besides myself, and I was on Nano and not astride a donkey. Ironface was forgetting his manners again, and needed telling so.

Mamelie's ass with its high shoulder-bones, low ears and unmilitary tendency to fart resolved the situation by giving way beneath its load and collapsing in a heap of hoof and rib, dumping the pot-bellied La Mamelonne in the dust as a consequence. She swore, and her belly, clearly possessed of a demon, began to cry out in tongues.

Her clothes, which were once my clothes, were excellently

91

stitched. I have made this point before. They needed to be. Not only did Mamelie's own legs fall out of them, bound tight against the gout as they both were, but a second pair followed. These were neater, narrower and entirely naked. It was fortunate for my peace of mind that they did not match the first pair, or I might have thought the little whore had turned quadruped, and strained my intelligence to encompass such a miracle of nature.

As it was, a pale bottom with a navel round the back of it, two breasts and a wart on a shoulder-blade followed shortly afterwards and began to flop their nakedness on the dirt like a newly fished trout, then the rest of the Fish Girl, quieter than usual and ventriloquizing less because gasping for air, stepped out to join them.

Ironface's stratagem was clear to me at last. While the Mute had done his bidding and slipped among the crusaders to stuff their stallion's arses with peppers, La Mamelonne had simply slipped Violette la Vierge up her skirt or down her collar, whichever way was deftest. All Ferblant had contributed afterwards was a lie or two, principally about burning the Fish Girl or witch as Arnold Almaric would insist on calling her. Well, Ironface was deft with lies, so praise him for what he was good at.

The body of Violette la Vierge, Fish Girl, Witch, or kiss-and-run whore, began to dance in the fields for us, for dancing was all it knew. It's a good thing my bag was capacious and could manage another cotte to cover its nakedness, or the Hunchback would have run mad with desire, and he was already carrying the donkey.

'Put some clothes on that wart, then dance yourself off,' Ferblant told her, 'and don't be so free with your Devil's nipple again.' He gave her a coin or two, and she clung to his tin legs in gratitude. 'Dance by yourself,' he insisted, kicking himself free of affection. 'I can't travel with all the whores in Christendom. I shall get my master a bad name.'

So she wept, and she danced and disappeared from sight, this time with clothes on. Clothes but no clogs, so her blisters glowed redder than the sunset, and her cries, always strange, grew stronger and stranger.

Somehow I didn't think this would be my last encounter with Violette la Vierge. She danced towards Béziers, and we made our way there too, however reluctantly Ironface travelled.

'Remember, little Perronnelle, I want no truck with your great ones.'

'You'll be welcome enough,' I taunted him. 'You can make their dogs a present of donkey's meat for the Feast.'

'Aye,' he muttered. 'I'd rather feast with their dogs.'

Talking wasn't easy. The Hunchback carried the sick ass, which still broke wind like a mountain, and La Mamelonne rode his horse.

'Once La Madeleine dawns tomorrow,' he went on, 'I fancy their dogs will be the only ones eating.'

Ironface worried me, whether he was don or devil, or simply a dwarf hidden away in a man-size coat of mail. I was still too young to dissemble. I had to let people know my mind, even my enemies. After an interval I said, 'What side are you on, Ferblant? What is your cause?'

'I serve the truth. That is all my master asks of me,' the iron fellow said.

'This "master" of yours – is he God or man?'

'He is much less than God, by his own admission. And much more than man, by my opinion of him.' He caught at me with his gloved fingers. His hands were real enough. He was wearing armoured mittens, with holes for the fingers. Those fingers had fingernails, and those nails were as dirty as the day was hot. 'My master is my own affair, and I his. Enough that he has me. He is my sun and I his shadow. The rest is a riddle. Guess its answer and I will neither deny nor confirm the truth of it.' He let go of me, and pushed me away. His grip had been strong.

'Your riddle, Ferblant?' I pushed him back again.

'My master came barefoot,' he said, level voiced. 'And I walked barefoot behind him. When I had legs – ' his

93

voice broke on this, ' – when I had legs, I was the tail of his horse.' He cackled with laughter. 'There, you have my riddle, Goldenhair.'

Ironface was his own riddle. He had a steel head, sometimes without eyes, tin legs that were hollow, and intervals of flesh in between. All I knew of him were his fingers, but before the Feast was over I was to see crows fly with the fingers of men and children in their mouths, and dogs and cats with worse.

'That donkey is dead!' Ironface told La Mamelonne, after the Hunchback had worn it round his neck for a further hour or so.

'Nonsense,' she protested. 'I can still hear it dreaming – farting at least.'

'It's dead and it's beginning to smell.'

Someone undoubtedly stank, but I hadn't remarked on the fact, as Mummy had taught me not to sniff at people on a hot day.

Mamelie slid from the Hunchback's horse, then walked behind the wind to lift her donkey's eyelids. It dribbled at her, but otherwise said nothing. 'It's in a very deep sleep,' she admitted.

The Hunchback threw it down with a curse, and kicked it. 'Stone dead,' he growled. 'Dead as a sack of salt, and nowhere so useful. I've had its tail between my legs all afternoon, and its dicker in my ear, not to mention a hindfoot harder than a farrier's anvil. I'm bruised all over, and what have I got to show for it?'

La Mamelonne wasn't listening. She pretended to be elsewhere – she told me a whore often does – and assumed her donkey was doing likewise.

By the time she returned, it was in a ditch with a pile of rocks on top of it, and nothing left but its smell and a dislocated foreleg stiff in the air. She caught hold of this and began to kiss it, as if it were a parent's forgiving hand or Pope Innocent's ring finger, while Ferblant intoned the burial service from the hollow parts of his head. This again made me suspicious of him, as donkeys aren't allowed in Heaven, or not by Christians. La Mamelonne wept.

I couldn't stand tears. 'Anyone would think he was your father,' I scolded.

'Would that he were,' she sobbed. 'Have you ever seen a foreleg so proud or a prick so big?'

'Only on a horse,' I agreed, having little experience of forelegs otherwise.

Canto Three

Wherein the Virgin is beset by priests and magicians then a whore lifts her skirts to uncover the falling tower, all this followed by catastrophes too terrible to presage.

We were allowed to enter Béziers by the ancient Domitienne Gate, which was currently no bigger than a postern and soon to be sealed off against the approaching crusaders. The gate-keeper demanded a password. My mother's name was password enough.

'No-one can batter this down,' I said. 'And look at the height of those walls.'

My cousins' castle filled the evening sky to our left, and the town's other ramparts were almost as lofty.

'That Simon of Montfort is a very determined man,' Ironface countered. 'Like all failures, he can only get better. If the priests and the princes grant him direction of their main battle, he'll soon find a way past your defences. If not, he'll wait till the other idiots have piled themselves into a mountain of dead in front of your best stonework, then climb up and step over the top.'

'He's a coward then.'

'I grant you he's clever,' the Hunchback said.

Meanwhile we strode about. A young woman was allowed to stride in those days, but not with her hair down.

'Don't walk so fast,' Ironface cautioned me. 'You'll damage your virginity.'

'What do you suppose holds it together?' Mamelie asked him. 'A placket stitch?'

He boxed her ears for this, but tenderly, with his mailed glove off. To me he said, 'As you will, Virgin!'

Thus my maidenhead became current. Thanks to Merdun I had almost lost it. Now Ironface gave it back to me as a nickname. I received it anxiously. It conferred a mythical status some females found hard to slough, even those with fifteen grandchildren.

I was a nightwalker. I saw Béziers with peeled eyes. A

young countrywoman visiting town with her parents goes in blinkers. It was painful to be without them, but their absence brought my gaze closer to truth.

The place was full of miracles and apparitions, and stuffed with more wickedness than anywhere in the whole vicomté of Toulouse. Men went in women's costume here, and women in men's, and I lost count of half-men with breasts, damsels with beards, and other such badels. If these excrescences were afflictions I pitied them. Most of them were paint.

There was love going on, celebrated openly between all manner of persons, including these. It was sold on the streets, and sometimes bartered or diced for, or lost at chin-sticks. I was disgusted and intrigued to see how freely men, women and other creatures embraced, going boldly to the lifting of cottes, the parting of pelisses, the lascivious opening of clouting clothes, even among those dressed in rags and cobwebs.

Inside these clouts or cobwebs, their hands all found the same thing, whether they were mauling man, maid, or hermaphrodite – or as far as my eyes could follow them they did, which was as far as Ferblant would let them go. What they found was sweat and shadow, exactly as Constance de Coulobres had told me at the age of fourteen when a troubadour had strummed a dirty song at me, and I had mistakenly thought it funny. Merdun the Bastard had taught me about lust in Mummy's kitchen, and lust had been stark naked and bloody; but this was a higher thing, this love men sang about, this sweat and shadow; and once I could smell the sweat I knew it wasn't funny at all.

I turned towards Mamelie for an explanation, but she had already gone off into the night.

'She has to earn us our soup and our breakfast,' Ferblant said. 'I spent all my gold yesterday.'

'It's shameful to ask a woman to sell her body for your personal advancement, even a whore. You can't do it.'

'I can and must,' old Ironface chuckled. 'Besides, La Mamelonne is no longer a whore. She's what she's always wanted to be – a kept woman. Saint Mamelie's got four bellies to feed, as well as her own, and it makes her very happy.'

'I thought you were her friend, Ferblant.'

'I am, Virgin. I'm also her keeper. And you, although pure as the petals on the tree, have become her bawd. She wears your petticoats among men; and it is your pleats and plunkets they fondle her through. For this she will bring you soup. How you blush, Perronnelle. I can feel the heat of you even on a hot night. Virgin and bawd, it's an agreeable paradox like so much else in life. Let it simmer gently in that pretty head of yours and don't overcook it.'

At this, the sky decided to rain, but not enough to empty the streets. St Mary Magdalen, patron of perfumers, glove makers, tanners and repentant women, wept a whole minute at Ferblant's paradox and my confusion.

Few men there lived more than another day to remember that minute. Those that did, swear she wept blood. Meanwhile they gazed where I gazed, and having no dear ones nor dead ones to distract them, I daresay they enjoyed themselves.

I watched a man who swallowed fire, and a man who swallowed swords and a man who swallowed ropes and serpents, and I don't think any of these men were related. Then a man offered himself to me with pictures all over his body, pictures he said were painted underneath his skin. The rain might have proved him a liar if La Madeleine had wept some more truth on him – but, that being said, he could hardly repaint himself every morning, so there must have been some cunning way of fixing the pattern on the bits of his skin he couldn't reach. The Hunchback said perhaps he had been flayed alive or was an angel stepped down from a great cathedral window. Ironface said people who are flayed alive dance rapidly towards death, and if an angel had come from the glass we would have heard of it, because there aren't above ten lots of patterned glass in the world, and they're all famous.

This man wasn't alone. He had a woman with a flower

101

on her face who claimed the rest of her body was likewise, but Ferblant still lacked coin, and La Mamelonne (briefly returned from trembling her knees in alleys or under stalls selling fruit) said she wasn't going to spend good money to see another woman naked. She said we must wait till tomorrow evening after the Saint had eaten her feast, when everyone would take their clothes off for free, and we wouldn't be able to tell the experts from the idiots except for those with pictures on their bottoms or snakes between their legs.

Then came a man who juggled with knives, and another who balanced three footstools on his nose while a dog dressed like a devil climbed up and down them, and once fell asleep at the top. There was a man stood on a pyramid of women or badels or other beings too immodest to look at, though the Mute seemed very pleased about them, and there was a woman who turned somersaults in the air. She wasn't dressed like a woman, but these tumblers never are, nor dressed like men either: both sexes go without skirts and look nearly the same, except for the obvious differences you can guess at from studying babies or living near a farmyard.

The jongleurs with musical instruments fascinated the Mute, whether they drummed or piped or jangled. Ferblant said they were Satan's work most of them, then corrected himself when he remembered it was heretical to say such things, except in Béziers which was full of heretics anyway. Besides, who was old Ironface to speak of devils?

Most of all, I listened to the mountebanks and those who sold nostrums. I kept on giggling with grief, and said I wanted to purchase a medicine to heal me of having a man's hands go listening under my petty cotte. Ironface told me sharply there was no cure for this, only patience.

Hunchback hated my giggling, but he showed me I could buy cures here, whether powders, prayers or philacteries (which are a kind of delayed spell). I saw a cow's udder being cleared of the wart with a hot stick, and a mare being comforted against piles with a jelly which was said to be equally good for a woman after childbirth, or delicious when eaten on toast.

All sorts of affliction were paraded here, as is common at any fair, certainly on a saint's birthday. There were men with the stoop, men with the stump, and hunchbacks with the cold shoulder. I saw scrofulas, whitlows, mormals, strawberry rash, and all sorts and condition of itch, including the jumping kind and the one that only comes to idiots that take their clothes off.

There was a nun took a nostrum and spat up a tapeworm longer than a stilt, but by the time we could see it, the head was all that was left, as her confessor had come and taken the rest of it away in a pan full of holy water, saying it was God's or created by God. Everything was God's since we had a heresy. If you were a priest, it was quite a challenge.

The tapeworm itself was as nothing, not when there were snakes and snakefish in earthen jars, and unborn babies in an iron pot as well as a saltwater mermaid, a fish with its own head but the lower parts of a woman, which its owner said was the ideal woman anyway, since she could drink and fornicate but not speak.

There were men with patterns pricked in their skins, and women allowed to somersault and cartwheel in the streets with nothing on their legs but stretched cloth and onlookers' eyes. One wore eyes on her legs, painted eyes, and buttons with mirrors, but people still couldn't avert their gazes from the tumble of her limbs, even when they met themselves face to face.

The houses were tall, and some of the ways were so narrow with shade that spit wouldn't dry or run away, but stuck to the stones like slip from a snail's belly. Thank God the Romans built the drains here, so the streets were full of criss-cross cuts that fed the River Orb, or the Fair would have drowned in the stalings of horses and the widdle of men before the Saint shed a single tear or her first rouse was taken. This, I suppose, is the biggest argument against living in towns, that their dwellers use the thoroughfare for functions that countryfolk perform behind a bush or in a barn, whether skinning rabbits or paring cheese.

'This town is fed by a tunnel sewer,' the Hunchback said. 'The Wizards of the past built a tube of brick men say you could ride on horseback through. Did you know that, Perronnelle?'

This wasn't the sort of information I would ever have had from Mummy on visiting a town. Like the angels she acknowledged no bodily function in herself, apart from giving birth to me; though she sometimes perched alone on a box which none of us were allowed to see, because she said it was full of the blinding stones of Heaven. Constance de Coulobres used to push it about the Mill behind her.

'Fed by a tunnel sewer? Is that true, Ferblant?'

'Fed and emptied. I'm familiar with these conduits. They do little good for a town, especially at times of siege.'

This was an undoubted strategic fact, but I lacked the stomach for it, especially when old Ironface chuckled and added, 'Where a town's turds can float so may its enemies' daggers crawl.' I translate this reluctantly, but in his strange idiom he called turds tords, and daggers something completely unpronounceable, whereas we never speak of them.

What was I to think of him? Here was this tin fellow, his armour as dull as a dried-up stream, and not even glinting by torchlight, once again ready with his talk of places underground. He had the brains of a gentleman, and something of a courtier's slippery talk, but he was all deceit and bawdry – and if that wasn't the description of a devil, I didn't know what was.

You may wonder how it was that our party went unnoticed, having a hump, as it did, and a whore and a man with an iron cauldron instead of a head and tubes just like a spider for legs. The fact is we were noticed. We were seen as being one with all the other freaks and mountebanks. People looked at us sometimes as if they expected us to conjure miracles from the air or swallow pins, but there was always plenty to distract them, and Mamelie performed enough tricks for the rest of us anyway.

The animals were the most fascinating sight in Béziers if one wasn't used to marvels. There were horses there with mountains on their back, and these were called camels or drum-drearies according to how many hills they carried, and the camels were as dreary as the other ones, whichever ones they were, because of the colour of their hides. There was also a beast that was grey and as big as a house and had ears like window shutters and a fifth leg hanging from the middle of its face. This had people quarrelling about its name, including Ferblant (who claimed it was an elephant) and priests and other men who should know. It didn't have a mountain on its back, but its droppings were like little hills, and threatened to build an alp in Béziers, or did when it got stuck between the ends of two houses and couldn't move anything except its bowels.

Then there was something I had seen at Béziers before, but prefer not to think about. They had all manner of small hairy children there – I saw at least a dozen being led on chains or strips of leather. These are known as monkeys and when they grow up they have to be kept behind bars and are called apes. Some say they are the natural children of Moors or Blackamoors, but I have seen such people's offspring and know them to be much like ours. Nor are they gypsy children. More convincing is the theory that they are the offspring of badels or hermaphrodites, and I must say the Mute gazed on them very fondly; but Ferblant said they were God's punishment on men who had intercourse with others of their own sex, and that – I suppose – is the most likely explanation of all, the lack of feminine softness bringing them out in hair all over and under their bodies including their hands and ears. I am bound to say I have never seen a pregnant man; but then a life as brief as my own finds scant time to include all the miracles in the world, and it is well known there are faces in church on a Sunday you never see in the week, and saints' days are a kind of Sunday.

These baby apes were a token of all the ills born of man. Once I had seen their faces, Béziers showed me her backside.

I went to the Church of La Madeleine to buy prayers for the repose of Mummy and Daddy's souls, and to pay for more to be said on the morrow before the Mass of her Feast Day. I chose the Church of La Madeleine because hers was the Feast, and both the Cathedral and Saint Aphrodise were beyond the City walls, though doubtless well defended by God.

I gave alms. I bought the best beeswax and lit candles. I spent a thumbnail or two of their burning time on my knees for my loved ones. I also raised a good stout tallow for Constance de Coulobres and found a frail and suitably gentle old spinster to pray for her, at least while I looked. For Marie-Bise, Thistle and One Eye I provided tapers and coin for a fat widow woman to serve them up prayers until breakfast time, with an hourly devotion before my beeswax and tallow. I was unable to afford the eventide of clerics, but Daddy disliked all such people, and my women would understand.

Did I sell another coat from my bag to pay for all this? I did not. La Mamelonne gave me money. She said she'd prefer to spend it on a priest – buying a poor widow's prayers being only slightly better than hiring another woman to dance naked – but she provided money for all, coins from the palms of men who had felt her in lust. I wiped those coins as I took them, and this made me a bawd indeed.

I went from the chapel and passed beyond the church into its precinct, searching as Mamelie had insisted for a suitable priest to sell me his time for a chantery. I wanted one who could promise me good voice for an hour, early in the morning before he was drunk.

I was quickly found by what I was looking for. He had reached the age of fullness, but was tall, bright-eyed and strong, at least what I could see of him. What I couldn't see was hidden in a cope the colour of cattle-stained snow. This made him some kind of Carmelite.

Now, as I write this, we would call him a friar, but even in Mummy's young day there were monks everywhere, except in their monasteries where they were supposed to be. Some of them were sent out to spy on the priests who were heretics (which was most of them), and some to pry among those who were lechers (which was all of them). This meant they were exposed to a great deal of evil; but they were always good for a prayer, if the price was right.

No sooner did he find me, this person I was looking for, than he backed me into a small room, half cave, half cellar, let into the side foundations of the church. I stumbled down a step or two and noticed this was but one perilous cell of many, each with its rush candle and bald-headed cleric. The alley resembled a comb full of honey-bees; I felt as frightened beneath La Madeleine as if I'd fallen into a hive, and its sound was as menacing. The whole wall was abuzz with prayer and protest, as well as those half-noises women make when they are struggling to know better. So he backed me.

I don't back easily, so he prodded me downstairs. The pressure came from his forementioned fullness of body. This was concentrated in an expanding bulge some handspan beneath the jut of his chest. If it was only his belly then it was surprisingly narrow at the tip. Whatever it was, I recoiled from it.

Inside his cell I gasped out what I had come for, and thrust my money against him with a vigour that should have surprised him. His hands took in the money as his eyes did the rest of me. When I had finished speaking, and pushing, and dodging, and stepping over his bulge, I could tell from his expression that he hadn't listened to a word of what I'd asked him. It was my body he was after (or its principal parts, as they term such things in Latin).

Our priests are a very special case. Meet a priest down here and you'll immediately become acquainted with fast hands and a ready underpart, so ready that if you don't recoil on the instant you'll find it blocking the doorway and jamming the latch, as I could now vouch for. Any girl who needs to consult a priest for any reason whatsoever and who hopes to reach womanhood with a flat belly, prefers to stay in the open air – a cloister has too many corners, some of them circular ones where she can be come at both ways at once – and walk fast with a prayer-book or missal held open in front of the gap in her pelisse, not to say cotte-fold or plaquet. If any of his ten fingers, three thumbs (or, in the case of monkish orders, eleven toes) loses its sense of direction she can slam it in a psalm and make an end of it. But I had no such weapon about me.

He kept his hands away. His eyes were so bright he had no need of them. Instead he plucked up the hem of his cope to show me what I had long expected. A friar is nothing but a wine-stained frock (or *froc* as they write in Paris) with a naked man beneath it. He was truly enormous, but monks are supposed to become so. With nothing to support them when their owner is standing up, their particles droop like the breasts of a ten-times mother and cannot be entirely at peace until they touch their noses to the ground to nuzzle out the secrets of the worms. This one was long and dusty at its tip, but no longer limp.

'Praise God for sending you to me,' it said, making no mention of my poor parents at all. 'Praise God and the Holy Mother of Jesus.' Its owner spoke words as well, also at length, 'Thank God and Hail Mary!' One of them was now in Latin.

Priests aren't supposed to fornicate, and the Perfect Ones among the Cathars regard all flesh as unclean, woman's meat being the supreme work of the Devil. Since most of our priests claim to be Perfect Ones, and all but the most exalted of our Perfect Ones are priests, they can each commit their sins on the other side of the heresy, not to say the blanket. Neither finds his essential self involved.

So it was with this one. He was quite content to let his thing do the talking till he found I wouldn't listen to it. Now

108

he had to skip about a bit. 'All a brother such as myself has between his legs is his chastity, and very comforting to the bereaved it can be. If you're frightened of it, there's no need to look at it. I know a jolly little place where we can hide it away from view.'

What Ferblant refused to let me to stretch by striding about was certainly not going to be engorged by such a monstrous abstraction as a holy man's chastity. Unfortunately his needs weren't merely around and beneath me, but beyond and dropping the pin on his door, with perhaps a little left over to use as the latch. How on earth could I protect myself against this fellow who was threatening not to touch me, and was already demonstrating he had no need to use his hands?

They wear a girdle – their devil's bell-rope, Thistle called it – as a symbol of their everlasting purity. Mummy said it was safest to think of it as a slipped halo, and Marie-Bise a high garter; but this one was already off, and the rest of him blocking my view of the light, before I made another of life's discoveries. I was wasting my time defending myself against men. I should fight back. All it needed was a little wit and invention.

His room glowed with candles. I resolved to light another, closer to God.

The wick was dry. It had never been lit. He still sought to dip it in my intended indignity, and the rest of him with it up to his little pink ears. Meanwhile there was wax to hand and in plenty, dripping from the tapers on his *prie-Dieu*. I anointed one with the other, and set them aflame at the same tiny altar.

His cell filled with plain-song, prick-song and notes even higher. He grew a hundred hands, most in a frenzy to extinguish his loins, first by smothering these then by dousing them in weak wine and holy water, but with several fingers left over to pluck the eyes from my head, the gargle from my windpipe, and my heart from the sticky mess of potage he was by now anxious to make of me.

He screamed and shouted fit to bring in a dozen of his

neighbours. Recent experience taught me a dozen was too many, so I caught the tassel of his bell-rope and stuffed it down his throat. I bound his neck and the noisy half of his head in his halo, and knotted it tight so it wouldn't be in such a hurry to slip down again.

Even a Carmelite cannot work miracles for ever. He returned to being a beast with only two hands, one of them scalded with wax. The other was clawing at the cord on his throat, so the way to his portal was relatively uncluttered. I took back my money, and prayed he could untie himself but not too quickly. I left him writhing in a disgusting smell of underbelly, wax and singed hairs, and fled towards the town's decent impurities.

His prodigies continued to haunt me. Not so much his multiplying hands and evaporating pride, as the thousands of eyes that popped from his sockets to wasp about my brain. Stumbling up those stairs was like climbing out of his head.

I wasn't done with enchantment. I should have known that the Feast of La Madeleine was only a moonset away from Midsummer's Eve. I rushed from the alley and there was Mamelie talking with, or listening to, a tall narrow man of singular presence. He was as lofty as Arnold Almaric, and gave off the same black aura in spite of being dressed neck to boot in scarlet, which is a costly cloth and not often seen, especially by church light.

He held Mamelie with his left hand on her right wrist, and seemed to be draining the life out of her the way a spider devours a fly or a wasp sucks a caterpillar by the sphincter. She was numbed by his voice and clearly enjoying the sensation, but men say the fly and the caterpillar feel no pain either, else they would protest more, or band together and end the tyranny.

'This is Dogskin,' she said, as if the name were a normal one, and scarlet dogs a commonplace occurrence.

'It's my midnight title,' he said to me, 'and must be used

only beneath the stars when the candles are out.' He held out his free hand, as if to claw my own blood up as well as hers. 'I am Raymond of Brousses,' he said.

'Perronnelle de Saint Thibéry. I am of the Trencavels. My mother – '

'Ah, the Virgin from the Mill.' He licked the word virgin as if his tongue were between my legs. 'I know you by the light of your hair. And your skin. I have studied you often.'

'I have never seen you before,' I said firmly. 'Nor heard my parents talk of you.'

'Everyone talks of me.' He contradicted me without pride or pretension. 'But few see me, for I often go invisible.'

La Mamelonne crooned and chuckled as if she were a child being sung a funny song.

'As for seeing you, Perronnelle de Saint Thibéry, as I said just now, I have watched you often. I have a water in a pool and a glass in my wallet, and in both of them I see you clear.'

'Stuff,' I said.

'I do not care if you believe me.' He still spoke without emotion. 'I simply tell my maiden acolyte here' – he indicated Mamelie, who was in a trance – 'that you've a mole on your left shoulder-blade exactly like the one I sent Violette la Vierge, which she may feel for to satisfy her trust in me.' He gazed deeply into my eye, which misted, even though I have no mole, birthmark nor even a sunspot about me. 'What other secrets your body has for me I shall tell you when we are alone and your inner self is more truly attentive.'

Hot faced as I was, I choked on the notion of La Mamelonne being anyone's maiden acolyte, though I hoped I was too well-mannered to say so.

'Your thoughts shame you,' he said, gazing at me in a way that made my bowels dissolve. 'Do you not think my Master can make or unmake a maidenhead in an instant, close the loins of this young strumpet as if she were an infant newly born, or invade the thighs of the greatest virgin saint, even Saint Ursula, to leave her defiled and raddled as any whore?'

111

He gazed at me and whispered, 'Scorched by his glory or transported with his ecstasy? Sweet Saint Ursula herself and all ten thousand of her nuns?'

I was glad he mentioned a few other people, because until now he seemed to be talking to me alone, and to parts of my body I preferred not to think about.

'I tell you directly, Perronnelle my little mill-maiden – I shall not touch you with my Master's displeasure by using your other name – I tell you directly that you have been marked for me.'

He paused, and in that pause I heard claws rustle. Then he spoke to La Mamelonne direct. 'When this city falls, you will come within my direction,' he told her.

'Where will that be?' She spoke slowly, like a child being taught politeness and giving her answers by rote.

'At the Chapel of the Bones on Mount Alaric.'

Enough of this hot-bellied witchcraft. I could not stand the silliness any longer. 'And just who says that Béziers will fall?'

He still spoke like a priest, as these pretentious sorcerers do. 'My Master says it will fall, and I have laid a charm to ensure his will prevails. If you do not believe me, Virgin, watch the Gateway of Saint Jacques just after noon tomorrow. Only watch it with your thighs astride a horse, and watch it from outside, for you will see it swing open to admit the courtiers of Hell. They shall devour this place before its silly feast is halfway done.'

'Why are you doing this?' Ironface had come up to reclaim his women. He spoke as if he took such matters seriously. 'Why do you lay so terrible a curse?'

Dogskin of Brousses turned towards me then back again as if to feed the hatred in his glances, which were raw as wolves' eyes in their winter hunger. 'I have cursed Béziers and I will curse Carcassonne, because they are the demesnes of the Trencavels, and my Master loathes them all. He abhors all such who turn from the Light of Jesus but will not seek His Darkness.'

112

'They have long given succour to Cathar priests,' Ironface mused, 'and now it is rumoured the young count wishes to become one of the *Perfecti*.'

'There are two great Rulers of the Universe,' Dogskin whispered. 'The hoops and rings of the All Father's kingdoms are up there,' – his fingers grazed the stars, which were bright on the roof-tops and near – 'but my Master keeps this earth. The Popes know this and fear Him.' I felt his breath in my hair, and my head grow hot if not actually singe. 'That is why they hate these Cathar fools who think they can starve Him out of their lives.' He woke Mamelie by pulling her ear, and then he was indeed invisible. That is he disappeared from among us, an easy enough trick at night.

His voice remained. 'It was my Master did it. My Master prompted Pope Innocent to send his little Crusade and put this heresy away.' His voice went chuckling off. 'An innocent indeed.'

Ironface began to talk, but Dogskin's voice was back at us. 'You have seen Arnold Almaric. Which God would you say he serves – Pope Innocent's or mine?'

'"Maiden"!' I scoffed. '"Virgin acolyte"!'

I hated myself the moment I spoke. Only a second or two earlier I had resolved not to mock La Mamelonne on such a topic. Whore she might be. She was, just the same, my only female friend. But the truth was that Dogskin of Brousses, Scarlet Raymond, had frightened me more in an instant's unveiling of his eyes than the Carmelite Friar had achieved in a whole quarter of an hour with all of his other parts put together and stood end to end.

'I am still a maiden to Dogskin,' the sweet girl said. 'Not just spiritually speaking. He says there are ways into my body that no other man has found, which he will one day uncover for me and dignify.'

'With a knife, no doubt. It will take a sharp blade to reach them, my Mamelie, for they're buried deep.'

'I can see you've just had a terrible experience, or you wouldn't be so cruel to your friend.'

Mercifully Ironface had not been near enough to hear me, nor had the Hunchback and the Mute. Even so, the night seemed so full of menace at its middle hour that I snuggled against her, and began to ask more about this necromantic nobleman. The great family of Brousses was highly born, whatever its pedigree in the black arts.

'I met him last year,' she said. 'He bought me with a gigot of venison – for which degree of recompense I'm any man's – and used me like a donkey. He had so much enjoyment of me in ways I daren't mention to my confessor that he repaid me after with this pack of cards.'

She felt beneath her skirts and found a tiny leather pouch full of numbers and the most amazing pictures, each of them so strange that just to glimpse them through her fingers set my brain madly on fire. As to when he'd passed them to her, she was quite clearly lying; but I contented myself with saying, 'He must have given them to you just now!'

'I have had them a year and studied them throughout eternity.'

'When we found you with all those crusaders on top of you, you were completely naked. And so were most of them. You didn't have a pocket or a placket between you, let alone a purse.'

'A woman's body always has a pocket,' she said. 'And sometimes another one, depending on how she's used. I've learned to keep shifting my valuables around, according to the pressures of circumstance.'

'One of your suggestions is disgusting, the other quite preposterous.'

She stooped towards the cobbles, sighed and spread her cards. 'Do you want to quarrel about anatomy, or are you going to look at my magic pictures?'

I looked at her magic pictures, and I must say they were worth a draughty back. They were unlike anything I had ever seen before, even spread out on a gypsy's drum.

Certainly Marie-Bise, who played such games, had never
drawn anything like these for Constance de Coulobres (who
claimed she didn't). There were men with swords numbered
one to ten, men with coins, men with wands, men with
cups. And as for the ones that were just pretty pictures,
they weren't pretty at all, but wreathed as you imagine the
breath of a dragon, or sometimes see at the fair pricked
out on a juggler's skin. There was a devil and a rabbit
being broken on a wheel, and foxes and wolves howling at
a left-handed moon. There was a man with bandaged legs,
woman's breasts and a halo like a saint; and a naked woman
with a wizard's hat. Her body was as beautiful as Thistle's,
but where her shame should be she was shaven smooth and
a man's thing was hanging from her loins, as long as a snake
or an ox's tail, and looking like a rope with a flower at the
end. I passed on from this through images of war, a man on
a gallows but with his ankle in the noose, not his neck, and
smiling as perhaps he would; bony Death with his sand glass
and scythe; and all kinds of miracles else. Whatever wonders
I had witnessed in Béziers this evening were presaged and
surpassed by Mamelie's painted pictures.

'That's a magic lay,' La Mamelonne whispered, 'a magic
spread and a terrible one.'

I wasn't laying or spreading, just looking. I was particularly
struck by a great tower as bold as any in the walls of the
château behind me, being struck by lightning, till its battlements burst open and its people tumbled out as screaming
cinders of fire.

'We might be lucky,' La Mamelonne muttered, as she
gathered them up and pretended to put them where she
pretended she put them. 'We might just be lucky. You laid
some of them upside down.'

I hadn't laid them or otherwise touched them at all. My
impression was that they had jumped themselves out in a
tumult from beneath her legs as if she had a hutch of devils
up there; but the night was old and I was growing witless
through grief and anxiety.

As we walked through the darkened streets, the cards kept coming back to me, the cards or their pictures which were bigger than the paper they were written on.

'That riven tower,' I said, 'that collapsing masonry with the scenes of misery and ruin – what does it mean?'

'An end of friendship, family and stability,' she intoned, while scratching herself where no lady should, as if to lend credence to an almighty lie. 'Total reversal.'

'That's what happened to me yesterday,' I whispered.

'These cards are powerful figments, and Dogskin a potent sorcerer. He has foreseen where our lives are tending, Perronnelle – from now till the end of the world.'

Dogskin de Brousses and his playing cards weren't the only wonders La Mamelonne provided for us. She also flaunted bread and wine, as well as some new clothes. These last looked outrageous even by the flames of midnight. Heaven knew what the Saint would think of them in the broad light of morning.

These, or the wine, brought the Hunchback and the Mute back into our company. Ironface never strayed far. I realized he couldn't move swiftly on foot. One of his legs clanked as he walked, giving off a sound midway between an anvil and a bucket. I had been aware of the note all evening, but thought it was a flock of belled sheep in the next alley. Now I realized he had been keeping an eye on me.

'Let us walk the streets until morning,' I shouted, striving to stay ahead of Mamelie's wine. 'Walk and enjoy the music of the fair.'

'It might rain,' the Hunchback said gloomily. 'It's already rained once.'

'That was only the ladies of Béziers emptying their chamber pots,' Ironface laughed. 'They won't do it again until breakfast time. Not from upstairs. I agree with Perronnelle. We'll be safer outside.'

'It's all right for a saucepan head dressed in tin to say that,' the Hunchback said. 'The rest of us could catch a fever.'

'Not in the middle of the main square,' Ironface said. 'I want to be there early. Your cousin is going to make a fine speech, Virgin.'

I had quite forgotten the Trencavels without Mummy being near to remind me of them. 'We could all be up at the castle,' I chided, 'safely asleep in a linen bed. If only you weren't so set against it, Ferblant.'

'Your presence would embarrass your cousin,' he said gravely. 'He's just about to run away.'

'Run away? A Trencavel?'

'Even the Trencavels can be sensible, Virgin. And this one is almost as sensible as Simon de Montfort. He knows war only offers a man two choices – to lose or to stay alive.'

'What about his people?'

'Ordinary men and women have only one choice – to stay alive if they can.'

'Stuff!'

'Let's hear what he's got to say for himself. He's an honourable man, your cousin. He won't run away without boasting about it first.'

So we came to the great square outside the Trencavel's castle, and slept in the middle of it from the first cock on. No chamber pots fell on us, and the stars and then the sun were much too bright for the sky to think of emptying her own. (I am well aware that the sky is masculine in all tongues hereabouts. When I've seen a man empty a chamber pot I'll know I've witnessed a miracle indeed.)

Some of us were woken by the stirrings of those who could find no lodging, some of us by being trodden on, and one – my poor Mamelie – by being lain over by a man who said she was a mattress, even though finding a bed on a saint's day is much more costly than having a whore.

Ironface was the last to rise. A great shout brought him upright, if not to his feet. The commotion came from in front of the castle, whose gates swung open to reveal my cousin Raymond-Roger on a very pretty horse. This was all

117

nostrils and teeth, the way such a beast can be when it is handled to get the best out of it. It came prancing into the middle of us, and a mighty crowd we were by now, waiting or waking or just plain curious. Being the mount of a Trencavel this horse had other horses in attendance, but they kept their riders a long way behind it, so their backs wouldn't impede my cousin's mouth once he chose to open it.

I must say I felt proud of him. He was as pretty as his charger, even to the teeth, and that was saying a lot. The citizens of Béziers cheered him again and again, because they loved him. So did the farmers from the outlying hamlets. Mummy always had hopes I might marry him, if she kept me hidden long enough and uncovered me at the right moment. He had a wife already, but this didn't trouble Mummy. 'Being a woman is such a risk,' she used to say. 'That's why life holds so many chances for us all.'

This splendid chance of a man waved us all to silence at last. 'Brave men of Béziers,' he began, 'my fine and courageous lads,' – a good number of us were women, as is common among crowds, but it was early in the day for a nobleman to have his eyes open, so we accepted the compliment in the spirit it was offered us – 'fellow Bitterois, I have invited you here on this holy morning so I may receive your counsel and unveil my great plan of battle.'

I was one of the few people who heard this sentence. If you live in a house of women you become adept at reading lips. When he called the good people of Béziers 'Bitterois' a mighty shout of acclamation went up, scattering doves and seagulls, and drowning out common sense. Bitterois is the citizens of Béziers' own pet name for themselves, and they thought him clever to remember it.

The cheering lasted for some time. I nudged Ironface from excitement and family pride. He withdrew nothing. 'There are lots of Jews about,' he muttered. 'A lot of Jews. Wait for his plan and listen to what the smart people have to say about it.'

If I didn't mind being called a brave lad, I didn't see why a Jew should object to Bitterois.

'Simplicity is the essence of all good campaigns. Simplicity of design and boldness of execution. My plan is simplicity itself. I know I can count on you for boldness, my brave lads, just as you know you can count on me.'

A fair amount of heroic spitting went on at this, but its effect was lost on the ear. You couldn't hear any of it strike the cobblestones, as there were too many feet on them.

My cousin took his next speech at a gallop, and I was surprised how well people kept up with him. 'While these Northerners and other foreigners exhaust themselves in front of our mighty walls, kept at bay by the citizen army of the Bitterois, I shall sally to Carcassonne to fetch a strong reinforcement from among the regulars of their garrison. Then I shall return and grind all the foreigners to pieces against your impregnable battlements. You, my brave men of Béziers, will be the mortar and I and our equally bold friends from Carcassonne the pestle. Such a strategem will lift the siege and put paid to this so-called Crusade at a stroke.'

Most people seemed to agree with him, and he would have got another cheer, if one of the Jews hadn't interrupted matters. 'Carcassonne is fifty leagues away,' he called.

'Not on horseback, my brave fellow. A horse has four legs whereas you have only the two.'

'Aye, it's twice as far on a horse.'

This set the women off. They had started muttering as soon as Raymond-Roger spoke of Carcassonne – my cousin was a pretty fellow, as I keep insisting, and women put their own gloss upon an announcement that someone close to their affections is proposing to gallop off for distant places and other parts. One or two of them began to wail and keen, producing a noise like asses or gypsy women who have lost a roll of lace.

The men were made of sterner stuff. They thought the matter over and decided to drown all this cowardice out with a great cheer. 'Mighty walls' had pleased them no end. It was a pithy expression of the absolute, and with a mouthful of breakfast between ear and ear it must have sounded like poetry and prayer rolled into one, though such things are no more than high-flown nonsense in another language. 'Impregnable battlements' was more of the same, especially if breakfast consisted of wine, and even more exalted because it took longer. What really had them shouting was to be called 'brave lads', especially the old and toothless ones of thirty or more. If you wish to gain a veteran's confidence, there's nothing like calling him a brave lad, Ironface explained. He won't necessarily die for you, but he'll certainly cheer.

'How many people can you bring with you from Carcassonne?' the same Jew asked. He had a thin voice, and it was a pity people felt the need to listen to it. 'Ten score? Even a hundred score men would be swallowed up by the great army that threatens us.' He spoke with a Spanish turn of phrase – I heard the name Solomon of Gerona muttered – and he sounded much too sober to be popular.

'I'm glad you raise the point,' Cousin Raymond-Roger said, 'and feel at home enough here to express your worries so freely, even as a stranger.' He raised his hand as if to deflect wrath from the man. 'In fact, you touch upon the essence of our stratagem.'

'That's it.'

'The essence of his stratagem.' More heroic spitting.

'Time. Time will weaken these crusaders till they are no more than their own shadow. Tell me, what will they eat? Will we invite them to table with our women?' He smiled benignly, the way a great man can, at Solomon of Gerona who had no such plan for them, so declined to answer.

'Here there is good flour in store, and your wells are deep. Out there there is only the flood plain of the Orb. Their water stinks in ditches. They must eat clegs and pissmires or go and catch rabbits from the sea.'

I don't know whether they cheered again. I expect they did. I was deaf to cheering by now. My cousin had a genius for inventing nonsense, and there's nothing like a foolish phrase for making men believe in you. Rabbits from the sea, indeed.

Not everyone was listening to him. Some, like me, were already deafened, some were chewing on bread, some were feeling Mamelie La Mamelonne or looking for others like her (and highly distracting it was for all us other women to be mistaken for her). Wherever she went there would be a queue of unmarried men, or husbands who had got themselves lost in the crowd waiting to touch her, so I knew we should do well for breakfast.

'These crusaders are quarantine men,' Raymond-Roger went on. 'They are here to serve their forty days and so gain the eternal forgiveness Pope Innocent promises them. If only it were so easy.' He spoke as one who had long sought grace himself. 'They sat in their castles in Paris, and they thought' – ('castles in Paris' was a bit like 'rabbits from the sea') – 'that starving outside the walls of Béziers would be an easier forty days than sweating beyond the gates of Jerusalem, and they began to chew their prayers. Let them chew away, because prayer is all they will eat – and forty days is long enough to spend in the wilderness, as our Saviour knew well. Besides, some of this lot think their quarantine began weeks ago, when they first joined their horses to this so-called Crusade.'

The cry was taken up by some, 'What will they eat?' and then taken up again by everyone else who wasn't sleeping, eating or feeling La Mamelonne. 'What will they eat, these quarantine men?'

'Rabbits from the sea!' Mamelie called helpfully from her nest of hands, and a hundred whores shrieked, 'Rabbits from the sea!' as men dived under their skirts to find them.

'They are like to eat your bones,' Solomon of Gerona said. I had positioned myself near, because all such ideas of grand strategy interested me. I don't think anyone else heard him, not with the thinking part of their heads. They closed their ears as soon as he opened his mouth.

All Ironface said was, 'For a heretic, your cousin seems very free with Jesus.'

'Are you a priest or a pedlar?' Solomon asked him. 'Or something in between?' He was one of several Jews in the crowd, as I've said. Like my cousin they had brought their horses, though – as a mark of respect – they didn't sit on them.

Jews aren't supposed to ride horses or wear stones on their knives, but I've never known the law enforced in the whole country of Toulouse or anywhere in Oc, not even the one about wearing black. To wear black in Béziers, especially on a feast day, would only attract attention to yourself, unless you were a very old woman, and Solomon wasn't.

As the meeting broke up, my cousin left the square in a hurry, in case anyone tried to detain him. He galloped out of the city by the Gate of Saint Jacques, which faces south and leads on to the road that runs westward. He took several hundred mounted men with him, the better to persuade several dozen more to return from Carcassonne.

'Never mind,' Ironface said. 'No-one needs horses in a siege. They eat all the oats.'

'Then you can eat them,' Solomon agreed, 'if your religion lets you.' As he swung his shanks over his mare, he said, 'I'm off to Carcassonne with the heroes. There's not a flea left in town, not even on a Christian priest, and that's a bad omen indeed – not a flea, not a louse, not even a greenfly. So I'm going to Carcassonne, where they've still got plenty.'

I caught him by the sleeve and asked him what he meant.

He grinned at me (I was beginning to learn that no man is averse to having his arm felt by a pretty woman). After a moment he said, 'I've studied you Christians. It's a well-known fact that the holy ones among you have rings above your head, your clergy especially. I've stood in the dark at Mass just to be sure of what goes on, and I've seen how those rings get there. They lift their chins from their copes in blessing, give a shuffle and nod as we do – save we keep ourselves clean as our law commands us – and up jump all their body tenants, whether vassal, vavasour or serf, and fly in a glint of candlelight round and round their heads.'

He was already half on the gallop when he turned round

to call, 'There are no fleas at your Mass today. If you travel fast there's still time to catch up with some.'

No fleas in Béziers was unusual indeed. When my cousin's grandfather was murdered by peasant farmers fifty years ago in the church of the Madeleine, again on the Feast of the Madeleine, there wasn't a flea in sight. One of his gentlemen remarked on the fact. 'We're meeting in church with this lot, yet nobody's scratching and I don't itch. It's highly sinister, my lord.' It was. Someone stuck a sword through the viscount's liver as soon as the words were uttered.

I felt sick at heart to hear there were no fleas, especially when La Mamelonne brought us breakfast and confirmed the fact. 'I haven't taken a single flea,' she said, 'not even from sleepers on straw and skin-and-bone itinerants. It's odd.' She yawned and tried to scratch herself, but found no satisfaction. 'I've taken none, and I've not retained my own.' She began calling her pet ones by name beneath her armpits, and begged me to shout for them as well, but my thoughts were already elsewhere and very ill at ease.

'If you can't find a flea on your body,' Daddy used to say to Mummy, 'it not only means you're dead, it means you've been dead for some time.' Mummy never could find one, because Constance de Coulobres used to see to her, so both ladies would sniff at Daddy's innuendo, even though Daddy was quite right, and Mummy certainly wasn't alive in the way other women were, Thistle for example.

Clearly a catastrophe was about to befall Béziers, even though its walls were secure and I couldn't see how. Everyone knew it, except the boastful Bitterois themselves. The fleas knew it. The Jews knew it. My cousin knew it. So did Ferblant and Daddy, who had said the stars were bad, and had already been proved right.

It was in this frame of mind that I resolved to inspect the fortifications. My companions came with me.

There is a ballad says the walls round Béziers are a hundred foot high, taller than a rook-shot, loftier than trees. The words

123

sound well in a ballad, provided a woman doesn't sing them. A woman learns to measure true when she cuts her cloth.

It could be the ballad maker, great mathematician and historian as is claimed, was thinking of a dwarf's foot or a weazle's, or of feet stood on top of one another rather than toe to heel.

There are some, generally Bitterois or other drunks, who speak of yards or bow-pulls, and say the walls, or at least their towers, are a hundred upwards of those. Let fools who are still alive say so if they still dare. A yard is a mighty measure, about the distance Mummy's fist used to be from her shoulder when she smacked One Eye's head for blinking at Daddy, so a hundred skyward of those would be well into the clouds if we had any, and that would be a poem indeed. I am glad that the yard is out of favour in these parts, particularly among archers, of whom we don't have many, there being few among our manhood able to see past their noses by mid-afternoon or capable of stretching a bow more than the length of a thumbnail, or standing upright to do it.

The walls could be a hundred leagues high for all I cared, taller than Babel's tower and fit to tickle the underparts of Heaven. They would be no use to anyone if the enemy could unlock a hole in them, and that was clearly to be the crusaders' stratagem and Arnold Almaric's prayer.

I climbed the narrow tower that stood between the Domitienne Gate and the Fortress of the Trencavels, and watched the Crusading Army approach. I thought of Almaric, then of the De Montforts, both the calm one and the Bastard, and I shuddered. I may have taken a chill from the coolness of the stairway, which smelled like all such places, of drunkards' piss, or I may have caught fear from the numbers approaching us from the East, whose dust already blocked the sun, though our half of the sky was still blue.

The tower was a shallow, one-sided affair – in military parlance, more a curtain than a skirt. Fortunately, none of the fellows who thronged its narrow platform seemed to share my unease at what the day might bring. They chattered a lot, and scoffed beneath the early morning brightness. As with many a brave man, their teeth were black and their spit red. They kept both colours fresh from several puncheons of wine they had the forethought to bring up with them, those and the metal cups they passed about, being delicately mannered. I must say they were full of courage, these self-appointed warriors of the Bitterois. I was particularly struck by the wit with which they would turn aside to refresh the coolness of the stairs.

Once their bladders were empty, these warriors were full of commendable valour. They could see the crusaders coming and count the hordes they were up against, or at least number their dust. Their tower was so tall they didn't blench, but gazed boldly eastward, offering a variety of strategic opinion. Some said they should keep the northerners out and let them starve as my cousin had commanded. Others wanted to have them all in and cut their throats one at the time. Others were so full of wine they contradicted whoever spoke last, calling '*oc*' and '*non*' like a gabble of geese at a mad girl's heels.

Mummy had made a wise observation on the subject, *un mot* she often repeated. 'Show me a brave man, and I'll show you a drunkard or a fool.' She was quoting her brother Crépin, and he was an expert on the subject, being both if not all three.

I pushed my way to the wall amidst weapons of one sort or another – cups and wands, to use the language of the card pieces La Mamelonne had shown me – and viewed the approaching army for myself.

They speak of an army of five hundred thousand men. They say it made a procession seven thousand paces long. It would, wouldn't it? And a bit more besides. If you say that each man needs a footstep to himself, and he needs more, not to mention his horse, then their order of march would be some eighty men wide (and I never saw a warhorse with hindquarters as narrow as a man's, so let us call it a hundred). So fat a procession would fall off the road. Indeed, it would fall off Hérault and perhaps off the edge of the world. Whoever heard of such a number? Whose wombs did they spring from? Are there so many seeded mothers in the cruel part of France, or were they all born of that female Pope in a single miracle of parturition, or struck from the rock by Lord Innocent the Third? Miracle it would be to assemble so many, or even a tenth of so many. A twentieth part would still be a huge army, and much nearer my guess; but then I'm a woman, and can only count with my fingers.

'That's an impressive host of warriors,' one of my companions said gravely, 'though to tell you the truth of it, I can't tell the men from their mirage.'

'I can't even separate them from the pain in my head, to deal with you truly,' another said, just as honestly. 'It's the sunshine.'

'It's the bad wine.'

'It's the wine.'

'Raymond-Roger will need to bring a good few dozen from Carcassonne.'

A long bowshot away from our walls the vanguard of the great army wheeled southwards, and began to open ranks, so for a moment we thought they were spreading themselves to attack us. Their armour glinted brightly in the facing sun, and a very brave sight they were. So were the men of the main party advancing behind them.

The shining ones halted in their wide ranks, and turned themselves into shadows on the instant. One minute they were angels of light, the next they looked as insubstantial as unkept cobwebs. They achieved the transformation by dropping their shields, and tearing off their headpieces and sometimes their hauberks.

'The Count's right,' a voice said. 'They're already dead of starvation or some such ague.'

'Before God and all the Holy Marys, that's the truth of it,' another said.

'Whore of Shit!' another agreed, naming his favourite saint, but he was the one with the headache, and spoke his vileness in the northern tongue, not our own.

He said well. To see our adversaries bareheaded was to gaze upon skeletons and spectres. It seems that the Duke of Burgundy, finicky old Eude the Third, had borrowed extensively from the Jews to helm his front men in casques, and insisted they wore them in consequence. Under our July sun, this had slimmed their heads to the bone, and possibly beyond. On a normal day, it would be like dipping their topknot into a bowl of Marie-Bise's soup. This morning they had just as well plunge it into her stewpot itself, and keep it there till their face floated off.

'There's not so many,' a defender said. 'I can't count more than six and twenty thousand score of them, and I've been over the whole ground twice.'

'Not much at all,' another agreed. 'What's not boys or priests is mostly battle flags, and I'm not scared of either.'

'Flags don't frighten me a bit,' I said, just to be joining in and contributing something. I should have known better than to call attention to myself. When the rats poke their tongues out at the cat, a wise mouse keeps her distance. 'Not a bit,' I repeated boldly, sensing that a siege is no place to be timid.

At St Thibéry I thought I had seen great crosses being borne across the bridge. Now I realized these must have been the gaunt frames and shoulder-pieces of the gonfalons and other penants that streamed from the tops of their poles. I hate such windy regalia even in a saint's procession, and more still when it gloats above the spears of an army. The cloth itself looked crucified, as if these crusaders were turning God into a parade of scarecrows.

I should have paid more attention to what was going on around me.

'Traitor!' someone shouted, interrupting my military reflections. 'Nest of traitors!' he added, dribbling wine in my ear. He wasn't talking to me in particular, but it was me Perronnelle de Saint Thibéry he was referring to.

'Burn them! And that flaxen-haired witch first of all!'

Their hostility took me by surprise.

Ironface had come clanking upstairs, helped by the Hunchback and the Mute, and I must say we made an odd foursome in the drunken light of day what with our lump, our imagined lisp, and our tin head, and myself as a woman not needing to be there. It was something to do with Ironface's appearance that caused our problem, in a way the garrison gave me no time to dwell upon.

'Burn them! Burn them all!' The shout was taken up.

'It's much too warm for a bonfire. Don't waste the wood. Let's sit them on our swords instead.'

I wish they had done. They spared our lives for the moment, because Ferblant told them a pretty story. Instead they dragged us before the acting Seneschal, who recognized me enough to spare us a few minutes more, while he deliberated which way to deal with us. His conclusions were extremely painful. We were sat not upon swords but string, as a prelude to being expelled from Béziers, even myself whose family owned it, and whose mother had intended me to marry it, and thus own it myself.

If only we had been shown through a gate or even kicked through a postern, squeezed through a shot-window or made to crawl out along Ironface's Roman sewer, my pride would have been spared. In the event, as I have indicated, they hung our bottoms in a string and dangled us terrifyingly down from the walls, like so many sheep sent to graze in a snowstorm.

A snowstorm, or even a very low rain cloud, might have afforded our posteriors some protection from the vulgar gaze of the town's enemies. As it was, four timorous sets of buttocks (no longer to be called 'pairs', they were so cross-hatched with cord) hung in their parcels above a vertigo of sunshine and waited for the arrows to come thudding in.

'Never mind,' I consoled the Hunchback. 'The rump, sometimes called the crupper, is a universally deaf little ornament. Our bums won't have to listen to the shots arrive, especially if they're flighted with some of your owl feathers.'

The Mute made a most unmanly sound, snivelling more like a ninny or a hinny, while Ironface rattled his scales. The Hunchback spat against the wall. 'It won't just be arrows,' he said, 'but dirks, quarrels from crossbows, Italianate ballister-shafts, darts from arbalests, javelins, heated harpoons, long-handled shovels, vulgar stones such as the flint, not to mention bladed bolluses with two, three, four and five heads, sling-shots and the occasional flung sword.'

'Man, man, man,' I chided, 'where do you keep your spunk?' the way we country girls will.

At this moment, while our noses were still level with the crenellations of the ramparts, our tormentors ran out of string. We were left suspended in tallest space, and the Hunchback decided to come back at me.

'These crusaders have been on a long march, and deprived of entertainment,' he added. 'Taking a catapult or so to your suspended backside is likely to be a powerful inducement to them.'

My bottom hung lower and looser than the rest. It contented itself with the thought that there were no Pyrrenean eagles about, while at the same time it was perched a mite high for crows and other carrion. Arrows would be a loftier problem, and their beaks peck deep.

I deserved all his mockery, just the same, and much more beside. It was my own inattention to detail that had brought about such a cruel reversal of fortune. I hadn't taken enough care of the way we were dressed.

Woman's clothing is a labyrinth. She lives inside a maze, and has no time to notice the trivial things outside, especially the garments of men. That is my excuse. Grief is its extenuation. Together with the plain fact that, thanks to Ironface, we arrived inside the wall long after dark. Men hardly bother to check their clogs for cattle-dung at such an hour, or their leggings for horse flies.

So the Hunchback's attire went unregarded and scarcely

sniffed at. So too the Mute's. So it should have been for my Lord Ferblant, but he was a devil. When a woman goes riding with a devil, she tries to glimpse his tail.

Instead, I should have noticed him take hold of his gipon, or as some would say his tabard, and turn it inside out. This was to hide his crusader's blazon, lie though this might be. It was a very stupid stratagem, because the backside of a cross is not invisible, especially when the front of it is embroidered. The backside of a cross is simply a cross that is visibly not there.

I did not notice this. Certain townspeople did, the moment he came clanking from the dark of the tower staircase, like a bucket from a well, to slop his sweat in the sunshine. Considering all the circumstances, we were lucky to avoid being butchered outright. The sole indignity these Bitterois had so far inflicted upon us was to run out of string.

'Our cord's too short,' a voice kept on saying.

'If it won't reach the ground we'll have to let them down another way,' said someone else in the chorus.

'Such as cut it.'

'It'll stretch if we cut it.'

'The cleaner we cut it the further it will stretch.'

'Our cord's too short.'

'It's their cord now.'

'We could sell them some more.'

That's townspeople for you, shopkeepers to the last. We had no money for cord or string, nor even a rope of risky hay. Mamelie was our purse, and after buying breakfast and a candle or two for La Madeleine she was empty. We could hear her haggling for more string, a chain, a rope ladder, an assemblage of poles. Her credit was good, she said, but our tormentors couldn't be bought with coin, and certainly not with wine. Their price, and it was a fair one, was a young woman's body. They began to wind me in again.

'You'll be making a terrible mistake,' La Mamelonne admonished them. 'She's a great lady, and much too hoity toity to give real pleasure, especially before lunch. Besides, she's a cousin of the Trencavels. That young Raymond-Roger's bound to come back here sometime, if only to punish you for poking yourselves into his family name. Noblemen are fastidious in such matters, and he may want a gallop with her himself.'

The rascals promised her a sufficiency of string, but only if she undertook to wind all their ropes for them first (or perhaps unwind them: I'm ignorant of such smut). La Mamelonne, in her own person, paid for our freedom by making a small present of herself to each and every member of the tower's garrison, veteran and boy, and even their empty suits of armour. Or that is what I took to be an accurate translation of the ensuing ribaldry. In spite of her largesse, they let us down gracelessly and with a bump.

I was scarcely at large upon Hérault, with the blood not yet returned to my bottom, when I felt a gentle nibbling at my neck such as I now know that lovers use. This was followed by a sweet breath of garlic, clover and wild peppermint kinder than kisses. It was Nano. I had tied him at the Domitienne Gate. No-one had eaten him or otherwise coveted him, so he was mine once more. Ferblant's mount was with him, having kicked her way free of a loosely buckled hobble. Her reappearance didn't surprise me, since nobody would want such an apparition, even if it had cullions, and a decent coat. The Hunchback caught her, and old Iron Lips embraced her. The gesture amazed me, but not the horse.

We hurried south and then west round the wall to avoid the Crusading Army and its cooking-pots, and then south towards the bridge of Saint Jacques in case Béziers decided to drop things on our heads.

'Get on your horse,' Ironface told me, 'but with your capuchon pulled up, and the end of its dangle tucked in. We'll look like a pair of fat abbots with our chaplains trotting at heel.' By 'dangle' he meant 'liripipe'. He had a foreign way with his words.

Nano was so pleased to see me that he left the town's

131

shadow very briskly indeed. The Mute was my chaplain, and his trot had to be more like a gallop, never an easy gait for a beast with only two legs. The Hunchback was our other chaplain, of course, and he galloped at a more comfortable pace, being long in everything below the waist, the shanks especially.

I have explained that the Crusading Army had come by means of the Wizards' Road, the old Voie Domitienne that had been conjured up along with the stone bridge of St Thibéry and the pleasant little arch of St Jacques, where we now found ourselves. Mercifully, the invading hosts did not cross the river Orb to our side of the bridge, or not immediately. So we didn't need another of Ironface's lugubrious bluffs to escape them.

Honour dictated we wait for La Mamelonne during as many hours as it took her to get her thighs out of Béziers, or as much as she had left of them. Imagine my relief when I noticed a series of sunken gardens to the west of the stream. These were rock-rimmed affairs, each like a little castle underground. They had been dug out by the Visigoths, history's second race of Wizards. You will remember that they also fashioned magic bothies of stone, and such like private encirclements a maiden would be foolish to sleep in with men. Their gardens were healthier places where figs could be unwrapped at leisure and cherries plucked. Their great charm was that they were almost invisible, save to eyes that knew the landscape and loved it. So we were able to drop ourselves and our two horses into a shady hold built for us ages ago by these sorcerers who had conquered our land with kindness, being gentle at warfare, gentle at murder and gentler still at rape, as well as considerate to their horses. So you can understand how I snuggled down. They conjured up nothing arrogant or high, the Visigoths, except for Mount Alaric, which their leader built as a sarcophagus for his pet stallion, some say fashioning it from the bones of the animal itself.

Mercifully, the Pope's huge army did not attack at once. It needed to assemble its siege engines, prepare its assault towers, and make ready its ladders and stilts. It had been an eternity on the march, so it also wanted to cut its corns and lance its blisters. That is why its leaders had decided to outflank the city and encamp themselves on a raised piece of ground east of the River Orb, and just south of the hamlet of St Jacques.

Our little nest of figs and stones was across the stream from this hill, which in no way impeded our view of the citadel, several bowshots to the north. We propped our chins upon our forearms in the meadow up above and stood on tiptoe with our bodies well hidden in the garden down below. What a pretty sight the crusaders' encampment made, with its planting of spears, its airy pitching of gonfalons, among which the pavilions of the great ones rose and puffed the air.

The noblemen, the gentry, the gentlemen and the better sort of yeoman had arrived on horseback, so wore their blisters and corns on their backsides. These crouched in their tents or lay face-down across their saddles while they waited for nightfall, not wishing to laugh at one another or make their enemies giggle.

The foot-soldiers and foot-farers at large had their woes in their feet. Swollen ankles, bruised heels, split toenails and all manner of wildlife in their clogs and stockings were calling out to be cooled or fed as appropriate. Fleas are not noted for their patience, nor are those who live with them. These ordinary ones – 'louse-food' as the Hunchback called them – were not allowed the hill, but had to content themselves with the meadow land nearest to the Orb. They came limping across the dried grass, parted the reeds, and began to bathe themselves in the river, some of them naked, all of them unashamed. I do not know what Arnold Almaric and Lord Simon thought of this, if they bothered to notice. But – again as the Hunchback pointed out – they presented the town's defenders with an inviting division of forces.

133

There was time to discuss the matter, because La Mamelonne caught up with us at last. She had no difficulty seeing where we were hidden. Whores always have keen eyes, from resting them so frequently on the sky. 'There's to be a great battle,' she squeaked, still breathless from the briskness of trade, 'a very great battle indeed.'

This was hardly news, save that a siege is not a battle. We scarcely listened to her prating, so keen we were to share what provender she had bought for us with her lewd earnings.

'I had to satisfy every man in the garrison in order to buy you string,' she panted, 'and everyone else in town in order to get you lunch, all except some of the women, that is!'

She bore a skin of wine, a loaf, a fair cheese and a giant onion which proved to be as juicy in the mouth as an apple. We all took a bite or ten from this, playing cherry in the ring, as there is nothing like a blue-skinned onion for sweetening the breath and flavouring the sweat and thus allowing friends to come close to one another on a warm day. It struck me as I chewed and quaffed that a drab's wages were better than I had first thought, because a journeyman has to toil for many a bonded hour before he can afford a cheese, let alone a wineskin – though the wine to fill it comes easy enough. Against this is the fact that whoring is piece-work, and La Mamelonne reckoned to turn over a great number of men in a very brisk time.

She regarded us fondly as we ate, refusing to share with us. 'No thank you,' she explained. 'I ate a second breakfast with a Marshal of Horse not an hour ago, then lunch with a Chevalier du Vicomté – such fellows are ten a groat when warfare's afoot – followed by an early supper with a knife chapman who thought it prudent to dine at noon in case he didn't live until nightfall, there's so much doom in the air. I can always tell when there's to be a disaster – men put their fodder before their poking, though praise be they pick up at the end!'

'How did you manage to leave town?' I asked, mindful of our own difficulties.

134

'A whore may go anywhere,' she explained, 'or she can while a battle's pending. Likewise a bawd or badel. Some man-at-arms simply pushed me from the gate and said, "I've just given you the clap. Go and give it to the crusaders!" The fellow hadn't even touched me, either. Unless it was while my back was turned.'

'You spoke of a battle?' Ironface had filled his legs with her wine, and now was on with the thinking.

'Look for yourself,' she said.

We peeped above the parapet of our tiny Gothic garden, then raised our heads clear. We saw a silly sight indeed.

I've told you that these crusaders, some of them no more than pilgrims or similar horseless people of no account, were doing as the vulgar will always do – lapping up ditch-water and popping their blisters in public.

The sight disgusted me; but then I and my companions were hardly in contact with the world as it was and is. Only our chins were on middle earth. The sensate parts of us, from the toes up, and the necks down, nestled in a place where snails unrolled coolness, and snakes came to mate. We had a blue onion to digest.

The Bitterois were thronging their battlements. They stood closer than us to this picking of corns, and very amusing they found it. I heard quite a few shouted references to the quarantine men's parentage among whores of shit. The phrase does not sound any sweeter in the language of Oc than it does in the louche French of Paris. Then you must understand that the garrison had been standing iron-headed in the sun all morning, and was by now well and truly drunk, the way good troops are once noon has come on.

They began to understand what I had noticed half an hour earlier. The invading army was divided. Its men-at-arms and their mighty leaders were resting on their hammocks. Only the hangers-on were here. An easy opportunity presented itself to reduce their numbers and rebuke their presumption. I sensed a thinning among the defenders' ranks along the ramparts. It is hard to count maggots in cheese, even with

135

eyes like mine, but that is what I sensed. A sortie was being planned. Doubtless it contained elements of social condescension. These presumptuous Northerners were but louts and ragamuffins. The men on the battlements could see as I could that the Duke of Burgundy did not cool his corns among them. Nor did the Counts of Nevers and Saint-Pol. Crépin de Rochefort was not there; nor the resolute Bouchard de Marly; nor were the Poissy brothers, Robert Mauvoisin sieur de Rosny, Geoffroi and Simon de Neauphle, Guy de Levis, or Pierre de Voisins. You do not attack such men as readily as you attack lesser folk. They each stand in stout armour a thousand strong. When one of them coughs, a hundred run to help him. When one of them farts a dozen men excuse themselves. Such names were not here. Even those who did not know what names to expect in the first place could tell that.

What we could see, with the sun high but behind us and the City walls ablaze with brightness, was that the great gate of Saint Jacques, the town's southern portal, stood open.

It should have closed itself immediately. But a track ran down from it and towards the bridge by the Cathedral. The invading riff-raff were treading barefooted on the dust of this track, beneath the very battlements themselves. More, they were leaning on the bridge of the wizards and making free with its masonry. Were they spitting or fishing?

One thing was clear: they were drawing up buckets. They were lowering the level of the stream. They were *stealing Béziers' river*, which to the Bitterois was so precious that they'd spent all this saint's day drinking wine instead of it. The townspeople had worked themselves into a frenzy and stood outside the gate now, puncheons and even sword in hand. A number of peculiar facts struck me. One was that the stream where the pilgrims dabbled was below the town. They did not muddy the water supply, but drank from where it was already dirty – foul from Béziers' washerwomen and the contents of Ironface's great sewer. Another was that to deny travellers – even hostile ones – a drink of murky water was a pretty unchristian parsimony. There were those in town who were allegedly unchristian, no doubt, and according to whose religion water was filth – and the Bitterois certainly made sure the Orb was filthy.

As I loitered there pondering such matters of faith, I was overwhelmed by a spiritual dilemma so acute that I cried aloud for my confessor. It was this. If, according to the Cathars, the Devil made the water these Christians drank from, did he also make the turds that floated in it? The soul, say the Perfect Ones, is God's; Water is the Devil's; but surely they have to admit that the filth of the world is man's? Perhaps they don't. Yet my beautiful Lord Jesus does. 'Thou shalt eat *thine own* shit,' He says. 'And drink *thine own* piss.' What a wondrous exhortation it is, and one that even the most tiny of children remember, having as they do their own bowels pretty constantly in mind. These poor pilgrims were falling a little way short of their Lord's exhortation, as they weren't drinking the fruits of their own bodies but of their enemies', and perhaps this was what made their enemies so unhappy.

Be that as it may, a few hundred Bitterois came out of town by the Gate of Saint Jacques, and arrived in a rush as angry men will. No sooner had these men filled with wine come upon these paupers who were filling themselves with dirty water, than they'd broken one of the pilgrims in half and tossed him into Satan's element. I say 'broken in half' but you must remember I am but a green girl writing, and the truth is probably no more than that some giggling Bitterois pushed him, and his backbone merely happened to spring apart by the time it had come into contact with a sharp rock (did God or the Devil make that stone, Rock Peter Saint Pierre being the name of God's best friend?) which cut him exactly in half like a salmon on a platter.

This enraged the pilgrims. Sober men move fast, and one of them conjured a sword or something sharp from under his palmer's weeds and sheathed it with remarkable adroitness in the guts of the nearest townsman, which upset him no end, and his friends even more, because they lived long enough to make the most of the spectacle.

These good Bitterois from Béziers all had swords and such things in one fist or the other, according to which hand they were drinking from; but it came as such a terrible shock to them to find the enemy also provided with weaponry under their skirts and tucked up their prayer rolls and psalters that they all cried foul and ran back towards town, the tally at that point being exactly one all.

I was immediately to witness the terrors that arise when men who rush to play games of chance leap to conclusions based on over-hasty mathematics.

The grand investment of Béziers began in that selfsame instant. Listen to the ballads, dance with the carol-makers, finger the tapestries and touch the gold illuminations in the margins of monastic incunabula, and you will know it should have lasted five months and been a mirror to hardihood, derring-do and chivalry, even between the sexes. The Bitterois had high wells to drink from, low wells to wash in, and battlements where they could perform everything else at enormous length and from an extravagant height. They boasted fresh wine, live meat and a foison of comely women to gladden their own and their neighbours' beds and keep tidy their streets. Five months? Five brief moons? The investment should have endured five years. It should have outlasted the little adventure at Troy and seen my virginity into old age, or at least until God or Pope Innocent called it off. Unfortunately, Dogskin of Brousses had laid his curse, the Devil Raymond had set his seal upon it, and it was over in five minutes.

I am told it takes a man to understand siege warfare. So let me say what a woman understands, which is exactly what I observed in front of my nose. What I saw was that it is no good having an impregnable wall if some idiot leaves the gate open. At Béziers, some idiot did. He left it open because several hundred fellow idiots were still outside having their throats cut and their heads bashed in, or screaming they were likely to. A woman would never make such a mistake. She learns to lock her doors and keep her idiots, whether geese or children, in order.

The men who stormed the Gate of Saint Jacques weren't soldiers, still less knights-at-arms. The soldiers were sharpening their spears and thrashing the rust from their armour, while the knights-at-arms took their end-of-march siesta. These were poor men, vigorous for God, having nothing else to occupy them. They had been mocked at by drunks, and seen one of their number murdered. They were here to kill heretics for Pope Innocent, and this seemed a good moment to begin.

So the drunks ran away, either up their tower or on through the gate ahead of them. The shell was cracked open. The pilgrims were like ants inside the carapace of a beached crab. They could feast at their leisure, but what should they feast upon? They weren't greedy for wine, for bread, or for women. They hungered for salvation, or, more simply than that, Pope Innocent's irrevocable absolution and remission of their sins. This made them dangerous indeed. Henceforth, even in their atrocities, they could find themselves faultless and know God agreed with them. Meanwhile, there was no blood in their nostril, as they cast about for the simplicities of death.

I am told an ancient woman ran out at them from the gate cottage and began to scold them. She had her soup bubbling on her fire, and bread to consider, so she flapped her black skirts at them and perhaps her white petticoats, as if deflecting cows. A pilgrim or some lesser lout picked up her skirts in a bundle, and I daresay her petticoats, and dropped them in the fire with her old bones in the midst of them. He did this as a prelude to tasting her soup, but the day was too hot for soup. The roof caught fire from her kicking, and ten other roofs besides. It wasn't the Devil's work though Raymond de Brousses had a hand in it.

Women are largely fat, and fat is mainly grease, and their clothes already primed from their cooking. The whole southern quarter with its sun-dried rafters was like a candle, and its dwellers were stone dead before they could scream. The town's hair was on fire, and many of its citizens died at their first gulp of air. One who ran to us later said there was no noxious fume in the streets, just naked flame. Many of the invading rabble perished too, but they had the advantage of being outdoors while the townsfolk were in. Those that survived this first catastrophe on either side were still outside the gate, or had rushed on as far as the square by the Trencavels. Some even drew blades in this place, and for all I know crossed them.

It needed a bold man or a brash woman to lead a counter attack. (I won't speak of throwing water!) There were no bold men that day, not in Béziers. They had all drunk too much and bragged away the best of themselves. Their women were as women are, which is how they have to be once their men have made a nonsense for them. They have to gather their children, hold down their skirts, and pray for the best. Mankind has divided its womenfolk into parcels, whereas in a crisis we are just like men, best in a lump. I had to wait a week or so before I found what women can do when they band together, and that is to work miracles. Here they were martyred one by one, or ten by ten which are similar numbers, rounding up their families or wherever they found themselves. Some had their throats cut, which was kind in its way, and certainly personal, but for the most part the flames came too quickly, so they went into the universal fire, five thousand women or ten thousand women. There's no agreement about numbers, but five thousand is not a lie. And their children, and their livestock if they kept them, and their drunks who were now quite sober and whimpered of headaches the way drunks do.

I don't believe my cousin could have made any difference to them. They had prepared themselves to defend an impregnable wall, but one of their number had done the unthinkable and opened a hole in it. They were ready in armour to repel armoured men moving forward in a phalanx with their ladders and their scaling towers, resolute, firm-footed and slow. They anticipated the interlocking complexities of modern war; their ears were cocked for the whir and rush of missiles from those giant machines that the enemy's engineers had already in part assembled; their brains were alert for trumpets, their hearts awaited drums. Instead they sat on their battlements like pelicans on the rim of a volcano, and watched the streets run with ragamuffins armed with knives and staves cut for walking, and everywhere they surged there was fire, God's old-fashioned miracle and first gift to man. By the time they rallied down from their towers the furnace had already cooked them.

A few of De Montfort's soldiers got in, but too late to extinguish his newly won kingdom. They came in somewhere near the Domitienne Gate where the defences were highest. Whether they scaled the walls, battered them down or vaulted over on their lances or their pricks – and I've heard all those things suggested – is a matter of speculation. It's possible they simply asked for the door to be unlocked.

The flames were too fast for them. I am told that, in places, they were too fast even for the pigeons. An up-draught of burning trimmed them by the tail-feathers. They joined the communal cinder, the all-over stench of singed meat.

We saw none of this from our salad garden. There were no screams, only the occasional shout from our side of the gate. I don't think many hundreds of men rushed into the town, so our first thought was that the citizens would soon make an end of them.

The fire was immediate, but at first we did not notice it. This was because the smoke pall, although huge, formed high up, and made common cause with the crusaders' previous dust of march, which was still rolling over and settling.

No-one will find this easy to believe, no-one who has seen a house burn, or a garth, or a cornstalk, or a stook, or even reeds or withies. They all wear a great wig of smoke, sometimes a steamy silver but mostly heavy and black. And beneath it is the stark eye of the flame, which is yellow turning quickly to red.

The flames stood clear above Béziers' wall, and a bowshot higher at least. But our gaze could not detect them. What we saw was a clarity beyond which there was nothing, as if an endless thunder were ruffling the sky and leaving it midway between a rent and a ripple.

We heard them, no doubt. Our ears found them out in a stormy deafness. I felt the Hunchback nudge me. 'Fore God,' I watched his lips say, 'the whole city is burning!' And this not a minute after the first pilgrim had passed through the walls. 'The whole city is burning.' I could not hear his lips, only spell them out. The air was full of terror, like a great wind too noisy to be heard.

It was this clarity of flame, its unholy suddenness, that made minstrels afterwards write of God's fire, as if it was God who rebuked the evil in Béziers, and not God's evil men, some of whom were more evil than evil itself.

What we could see was the Cathedral precinct, outside the city walls but defended by its own stoutness. We could also view the Evêché with its little house for nuns and another for convertites, all of them vulnerable as are most of Mamelie's friends.

Townswomen ran here first, with their children. They were followed by a scattering of the murderers who were sacking the city. Some were pursued from the Cathedral Gate, but many of the rabble rushed here direct from the bridge or swarmed back from the Gate of Saint Jacques. They knew their victims would come here for sanctuary and that the pickings would be rich. There is no sanctuary from a Crusade. We could hear neither threats nor shrieks, because of the deafness of the fire.

The Bishop's house and the nunnery were soon in flames, as was part of the Cathedral roof. The fleeing townswomen were not engulfed in the furnace, not at first. Their throats were cut. We were too far off to recognize their faces, thank goodness. We could only recognize their throats being cut, from the brilliant transformation of their dress.

Some broke away and rushed towards us. Not the women who had children to drag, but the women who were God's and begged to be lifted up to him. Useless to attempt to aid them by bow or sword; we should have been butchered in our turn, in spite of Ironface's Cross. I was grateful none of these unfortunates ran close enough to put our humanity to the test.

I saw a nun or some other natural victim with half a dozen gaping wounds in her, each of them being enlarged by villains without even the patience to wait for as long as it takes a pot to boil. I call her a nun because she was bald as well as naked; but perhaps she was an ordinary young woman whose hair had simply fallen out at the sight of them. Perhaps she had been scalped or singed.

The nuns of Saint Nazaire had no hair, and the convertites of Saint Jacques shaved their body hair also, according to Mamelie, lest the thought of it offend God. The sight of bald women without body hair inflamed some men's lust, and of bald women with body hair agitated others, and all in different ways, there being so many varieties of desire, most of them ludicrous – especially among men who had knelt before their sword as if it were a cross and kissed the Virgin's feet and vowed to have no desire at all for a whole forty days. Some fell to fornication, never having noticed it before, some to more leisurely slaughter, and this in its turn excited others, especially when they found themselves among women who were bald or otherwise extraordinary through patterns pricked in their skin.

Women with hair in all the usual places had a hard time of it as well, especially once men set fire to them. They did this sometimes to change their appearance, sometimes to get rid of them, sometimes to encourage them to dance. Saint Paul I think says it is better to marry than burn, but the more thoughtful among the crusaders were mindful of the wives they had so recently left in the North and decided

143

it was better to burn than marry down here, even on a hot blanket. Not that they lit many bonfires in Béziers. They lit an individual or two as I say, but in general they were lazy and simply set fire to the town. Béziers was its own bonfire, and its people stopped screaming almost as soon as it was lit. Forgive me if my style is abrupt, but unpleasantness is best taken at a gallop.

So far I speak of the main beastliness being done by louts and hobbinols, but this does the truth scant credit. Among the quarantine men, only the lowborn ravished. It is to be doubted if many of the better sort found their way in. But what of those who came for longer? They were gentlemen at the least, the best blood and cream of a dozen nations, who had taken the Cross as a quick path to women and wine.

No toiling beyond hot seas, or sweating amidst hinnies and camels, not for them. We had both of their wants in Oc, a drunkard's spit from their doorstep. They could enjoy us, and claim the Pope's exemption. Unfortunately the feast of the Madeleine taught them a stranger lust. They discovered it in an hour. They wanted us dead. A woman is just as enjoyable with no breath in her body, just as enjoyable and much less of a scold. Blood is even brighter than wine, and there's much less waste in the spilling of it.

It wasn't their fault that they discovered such matters. It was our devilish Southern climate.

Under their cloudy Northern heaven, Retribution must have seemed close – just above the roof-tops most of the year. Down here, the skies were blue and went upwards for ever. Beneath them, men performed wicked acts with no sense of God on their shoulders.

And, of course, they brought their priests. Those Northern clergy are devout, and dangerous. If the crusaders had simply raped the town, what a party they could have had; but their riff-raff got in first, led by their holy ones. Neither had any sense of humour, just vigorous bad taste. It was the holy ones who set fire to our women in order to protect the lowly ones from their worst natures.

When the whores rushed into Saint Nazaire calling for sanctuary both at porch and high altar, they were followed there by prayerful men who cut their throats. A crusader proper will make decent use of a whore, as La Mamelonne and sometimes the food in our bellies could testify. All these imbeciles could manage was annihilation.

By now the great roof of the Cathedral melted – whether it was copper, lead or pitch dripping down, who is to say? Those holy butchers had acquired a taste for death and its artistry. They prodded nuns and convertites by pole or else spear beneath the several cascades, until they'd changed them to statues, some bald, some dressed, but each of them a monument to wit. They accuse us of acknowledging two Gods down here, one of them the Devil. All I know is that our Devil wouldn't have done that. He wouldn't have thought it funny.

A host of good people were lost with that roof. Acrobats, dancers, breasted men and several oddnesses of woman had climbed there for safety – if they took up their drum-drearies and elephants I never saw them. All of them came splashing down to add colour to the precinct. Those strange hairy babies came last, the ones I mentioned as being born of men's bodies as the result of unnaturalness between men. These children of iniquity were more nimble than ordinary mortals, having hands for feet and fingers on their toes, so they mocked their murderers and the great flame alike by hopping from place to place until there was no more heaven to jump to. Then they too came crashing down. None of these wonders lasted, except one or two nuns encased in stone, because the fire grew too hot for its own invention.

There was a great deal of more ordinary wickedness done in my sight on the near side of the cathedral, but I see no comfort in remembering it. Nor will I record the raping of children or the ravishing of wounds. Such matters are commonplace in any war, especially a Crusade.

They sound more heroic in song, being on the dull side for history.

It was at this moment with Béziers more or less dead – which was within minutes of it being totally alive – that a tree came rushing before us. It had become unfixed at the roots so could hardly be said to run, but here it came flying and dancing. A tree? This was an exaggeration. My wits lacked sleep and went wild with horror. The tree was no more than a sapling or long-legged bush, screaming as it came.

I recognized the Fish Girl at last, but with her skin changed to bark and her clothes cut to ribbons so they flowed like a weeping willow, her hair, her body, her raiment a bright and unnatural green where she had been standing beneath the rushing of water that had cooled an otherwise fatal melt of copper. No wonder they had let her through. She looked like a maenad or a wodwo, or a corpse from last year's pit. The Mute ran and caught her, risking his life. The Hunchback held her down excitedly, while her limbs continued to wriggle beneath his mountainous hump.

She spoke quite clearly for her, but in no speech we could understand.

'She's lost her livelihood,' La Mamelonne translated.

'Nonsense,' Ferblant growled. 'Her life is her livelihood. She's a dancing whore.'

'She's been robbed of her virginity.'

Ferblant was not an original – what devil is? He must have recalled Solomon of Gerona as he said, 'Her virginity? Tell her it is floating above her head. Tell her I can see it shining there.'

The Fish Girl reached up, pulled it down and put it where La Mamelonne told her it belonged. Once it was in place, she spoke her familiar gibberish again, threw off the Hunchback, and began to dance wildly about our sunken garden, knocking down figs.

Arnold Almaric and Simon de Montfort were still in their tents when the bad things happened, but they must have

146

come out in the end. What child can resist a bonfire? Nobody knows for certain what passed between them, though it is reported that Almaric said while he was weeping or picking his nose, 'To defend a heresy with your sword makes you a heretic.' He spoke to comfort Simon, who was scrupulous on the handling of a massacre. It is also reported by some that it was at Saint Nazaire and within a second or two of the Fish Girl's emergence that he fathered the expression attributed to Simon at Minervois an exact year later. Told he was burning Christians as well as heretics, he said, 'Give them all to the flames, and trust God to know his own.'

Was it Arnaud or Simon? For men on the right side, which was always the wrong side, it seemed such a good word to say, this 'Trust God to know his own', that soon everyone was saying it. It made you feel virtuous to kill a man, and – in the case of women and children – positively generous. In fact, I've heard the phrase was invented by the De Montforts' hangman, or by a poet belonging to Bouchard de Marly, but such people are never given credit. If even a dog does something clever in a great one's presence, the great one becomes his master and gains the applause. Dogs, it is true, are rewarded by a bone. But who gets the meat on De Montfort's bone? Clowns and poets get nothing, except a poke at La Mamelonne, which she claims is world enough for any man.

I do believe Ferblant was deeply disturbed by what we witnessed together, but a faceless being cannot show emotion any more than a spider can darn my petticoat. He began to clank his way out of our hole like a stag-beetle rising from its bubble, tugging his mare up behind him. I and Nano followed. This was a silly step to take, but catastrophe induces a certain dullness of mind. We were all aware, too, that since Béziers had been burned rather than taken, its conquerors were unlikely to stay there and gloat. They had no captives to drive before them, and this city was a cauldron too hot for them to cook in. They would need to range about and gather fruit. La Mamelonne was all in a fidget as well. She wasn't the woman to stay on her back for long, even with a pile of men

147

on top of her, and she had no use for the Hunchback, the Mute, and the Fish Girl's ceaseless wittering. She rose up with us. The others collected our belongings in the sunken garden.

The fiery crackle had stilled just enough to let the three of us talk together, but not to hear distant sounds such as the rumble of hooves. I glanced about me quickly, but missed the horsemen's heads in the hollow of the River Orb. So it was that Merdun de Montfort stole upon me a second time, again by water.

It wasn't myself, or not in my own person, who took his attention.

'I see a fat whore,' he shouted, wheeling towards us.

'I'm not a fat whore,' La Mamelonne shrieked. 'I'm a slender whore with a generous belly and huge tits.'

'Haaaaaargh!' the Bastard scoffed, in the way of these Northern bastards, with his aspirates silent and his terminations full of phlegm. 'Haaaaaargh!' and then 'Haaaaaargh!' again, spurring forward, the second of this second set of *Haaaaaarghs* coming not from himself but his horse as it stumbled on to its chest among the cornflowers and mallows of the water margin and began to chew blood.

His men thundered past him in a great charge midway between a hesitation and a gallop. This slowed to a progress midway between a gallop and hesitation, then came to a dead stop as three or four fellows among them stumbled in their turn, themselves rather than their horses chewing blood.

The Mute had shot off one of his darts, and the Hunchback several of his arrows, both from where they crouched with their feet in history and their faces concealed among the ripening fruit. The voiceless one had been unable to bring himself to shorten the life of a nobleman, not when he had a horse to shoot at. The Hunchback, on the other hand, saw no need to kill thoroughbred animals while there were men in abundance.

We had the sun behind us, so there was no way they could tell how many archers we had.

Merdun's men halted, and one of them dismounted to give him a horse and pluck up the fallen animal's caparison. The spare horses came slowly towards us, sensing crab-apple and damp green leaf, and having no living hand to halt them.

The Bastard was baleful. He glared towards Mamelie, drooled, moved forward, then halted again. He wanted her, and would clearly pursue her with a greed as fervent, not to say fervid, as he showed in his hunting of me. Every man in Christendom had had La Mamelonne, and quite a few in Heathenesse, all of the living and many who were now dead. No man had had me. That made us equally precious in his eyes. He had the scent of us both for ever.

I'm not sure his men thought of arrows, in their amazement. Not yet. Here, right before them and wearing the sun, was the devil man they knew, in his face of iron. They thought he had stopped them with firebolts from sources unseen, curses wrapped in air, and whirling spells.

Then the Fish Girl started out of the ground, clearly recognizable as the witch they had burned yesterday, even though she was still a tree. They hesitated further.

'Sorcery,' Merdun shouted, as if he could erase it by saying its name.

Sorcery it was, for the Hunchback reached up and caught her into the shadows, expunging her from the sunshine as she danced against the dazzle.

'That thing with yellow hair,' Merdun bellowed, indicating myself. 'I know that vixen.'

'Then you'll know I bought her from you,' Ironface said, seizing me firmly and in ways I was this time grateful for. 'And reinforced my claim in a fair fight.'

'She should be on top of a bonfire.'

'And you at the end of a rope. You violated her mother.'

These words were less than true, like most sounds uttered by our statue on horseback, but the Bastard turned blue in the face at them just the same and was clearly in no mood for discussion. 'Giddy-hup,' said the Hunchback, and the Mute breathed something to the point. They had already risen from

149

the ground and emptied our new-found saddles of death. So with that pair taking a nag apiece, and mounting Mamelie and Violette la Vierge on the third steed together, we rode round the nearest stack of smoke, and found we were in midnight an hour before sunset.

Ferblant was never a quarantine traveller, a forty-day warrior for Christ. Now he was no longer a crusader, either, but a fugitive from injustice with everyone else in Oc. He hid his blazon in his saddle-bag, and travelled in a jangle of plate armour like the earwig he was.

Once clear of the burning town, we regained the red fires of evening. We rode directly west instead of south and then north. This took us through a scabby high country of worms, wild men and vipers.

Don't think I was happy to leave Merdun unanswered. 'Thing with yellow hair' indeed. What did he think I was – a dandelion?

Caput Contiguum

In which the survivors fall to whoring and the whores to surviving, with much grave matter in addition.

We made good progress for a thousand paces, but it was clear we couldn't go at such a speed for ever. The Fish Girl had shed her leaves, so was once more afflicted with an inclination to dance. Except for one breathless boutade on the rump of their borrowed warhorse, this inevitably meant dismounting from the charger she shared with La Mamelonne. A steed rejected by one whore is unlikely to be good enough for another, so within twenty footsteps Mamelie dismounted too. Shortly afterwards the thing bolted.

Impossible to blame the Hunchback and the Mute for occupying a mount apiece. They were men, and men do such things. Down here, if a gentleman owns a string of prancers he sits himself astride the fleetest, sets his women all together on the fattest, and shares his sword, his spare hats and his cages of falcons between the remaining half a dozen. It is a well-observed custom that a woman is not accorded a whole saddle, lest she gets up to mischief on it. Unless she is such as myself, and related to great ones, in which case she rides sideways and is protected against everything except falling off and bruising her bottom on a rock.

The Fish Girl was no problem. Violette la Vierge could dance her way to Carcassonne faster than we could gallop. But Mamelie was a different matter, being so sore between the legs from buying string that her knees couldn't pass one another. So it was at a hobbled pace, with her astride Nano behind me on a folded coat, that we approached the little village of St Marie la Dragonne just as it caught fire.

Ironface had ridden forward to spy out danger. Now his nag brought him back to us at the best speed his tin legs could squeeze from it. 'The brothers are before us,' he rasped. 'A brace of De Montforts, both the old one and the lusty.'

153

'How can that be?'

Women screamed in the distance, but not for long. He sucked his ankle joint while he listened to them, I suppose drawing wine through its hinge. 'They bring their personal retainers only, and in their own livery, not Christ's. My guess is they've ridden on fast, looking for wages. There's nothing in Béziers save a handful of flame.'

'Now this place is burning.'

'Aye, both saint and dragon. Your land is tinder, Perronnelle, and their smiles are flint.'

'In their personal livery, you say?' The Hunchback stroked the owl in an arrow, then fitted it to the gut-string of his bow.

'Leave it,' Ferblant instructed. 'There are more men in either's blazon than you've got spells in a full quiver.'

'I could quell this Crusade with two pulls of my arm.'

'How you boast. A wise head would be better off counting its fingers. Almaric is not here. Nor the Pope, nor the King. And be certain of something else. While this Merdun is alive, the world needs Simon to keep him in order. Let me give you an instance from Marie la Dragonne.'

We looked between a cork oak and a rock, waiting to see which side we should run, while Ironface told us he had just seen the Bastard with two young sisters, both of them struggling, one beneath each arm, as he bore them off to his pleasure. Simon had stopped him, and had them thrown into the fire. 'Show a woman your favours,' he had said, 'and she'll seize the chance to talk to you. Grant her a moment's prattle and she'll become an object of pity.' Clearly he hadn't studied his brother's views on the matter, but it was a noble thought.

I began to shriek with rage, just the same. Once a girl's mother is dead, and her father is dead, she senses an emptiness where formerly there was light and wisdom. How quickly she rushes to fill this void with pomposities of her own. 'Didn't you try to save them?' I yelled.

He gazed at me as if I were a mad thing.

154

'You protected me. You risked your life to protect me, if tin is alive. They might have been young women of worth and substance.'

'I wouldn't have saved you from burning,' he said. 'Burning is good for the soul, Virgin. It was the other thing I spared you, because no good can come of it, especially just before dying.'

I couldn't think what to say. It was hard enough to say anything. Marie la Dragonne smelled awful, and her people made an even worse stink, perhaps because the flames weren't as hot as at Béziers.

I glanced for the Fish Girl. All of her, including her voice, was missing.

We searched for Violette la Vierge, but we went with caution. The Bastard's men were everywhere, gathering sheep and geese, and up to their old tricks with chickens.

They were teaching Simon's retainers bad habits as well. I found the Fish Girl underneath one of them. He was all in his chinks and chain, and – whatever blazon he wore on his shield – he hadn't thought to take off his Cross before fornicating. He was kissing her throat and bringing it up in a rash. She was biting his eyes.

I don't know what it is people do to one another at such times, so I proceeded with delicacy and caution. 'Do you want this fellow on top of you?' I asked her.

Her giggle was as wild as ever, but her eyes looked sad, and she struggled with him.

The lout swore at me over his shoulder, as if I were interrupting something private. I picked up a large stone and dropped it on his neck. We prised her out from underneath him, and once more she went dancing off.

The Hunchback held out his hand to me, as if I had just done something worthwhile. 'Lady Perronnelle,' he said, his voice thick with all kinds of unsuitable emotion. 'You can call me Gibbu.'

His name, now I had it, was as ugly as his deformity, but

someone had given it to him, and I was grateful to learn it at last.

The Mute had no name, or could not give us one. He held me in his soggy arms for a moment, and I must say I shuddered. I prefer a man with muscle on his bones.

I shuddered even more when he touched the unconscious crusader's head with his boot. The lout's neck was broken. The bone grated and rattled like damaged tiles in a roof.

The Hunchback, Gibbu, picked up the dead man's sword.

'You had better wear it, Perronnelle,' Ironface said. 'It will look as ridiculous as your unmade hair, but it's better than beating in heads.'

The blade was broad but light, and as sharp as need be. If I knew about such things I'd have said it was Spanish.

Violette la Vierge had danced into the distance by now. We decided to follow.

'How can you have a virgin whore?' I asked.

The Hunchback gave a meaningful laugh, but otherwise said nothing.

'I mean how can you be a whore and remain a virgin?'

'That wasn't a fair example you saw just now,' La Mamelonne explained. 'She wasn't working and he was only playing, not paying.'

'Whore's always win,' the Hunchback said. 'You always have to pay them before they'll open their legs for you. Isn't that right, Mamelie?'

La Mamelonne was on her dignity. 'In my case I get paid before they know whether or not I have any legs to open.'

'But if you want to remain a virgin,' I insisted. 'I mean men can be brutal as well as importunate.'

The Hunchback chuckled, but a long way inside his hood and his beard. 'If you want to remain a virgin, Virgin, then you need a friend to drop a rock on your lover's head.'

La Mamelonne couldn't share Nano for ever. Nor could she dance ahead, except on her buttocks, so her progress would be slow even on sandy soil when their load was light. She needed a fresh horse.

There were any number of these tethered, hobbled or simply grazing free in the fields west of Béziers and beyond Marie la Dragonne. We had no difficulty in catching her one. It was a mare, coloured like wine spilled in the street, or over-cooked rhubarb. It was loose, saddled and hungry. It belonged either to a butchering pilgrim or to a cinder, probably the former, so we felt justified in taking it.

'You are a heretic and a Cathar,' Mamelie told it. 'So you'll be wanting a Christian name.' As our one whole man and our two halves helped her into the saddle, she added, 'I shall christen you Pipi.'

The mare grunted at her weight but put up with her prophetic nickname. She had a damaged – or perhaps badly docked – tail which she carried high like a vine stump, and her arse was extremely prim in consequence. Impossible not to notice this little instrument and, in the context of Mamelonne, to study it. The dead donkey had boasted a huge orifice, loose as a scold's mouth, flap-lipped and including the tongue though probably toothless, and – as I have indicated – it spoke often.

This one's bottom was so small it would not even admit the beak of a wren or a child's little finger, and in all the days I was acquainted with it I never saw it void any ordure, in spite of the great capacity of hay, grass, turnip leaf, scum-weed and thistle ingested through Pipi's more noble end.

Imagine my surprise when it farted. It did this the second La Mamelonne was in the saddle, no mealy-mouthed mewly eructation either, but a great polyphonal plainsong of a raspberry louder than four and twenty monks wailing to Saint Mary in Heaven, their only love on earth.

Pipi's hind lips didn't change their expression to utter such an orison, not by so much as the pucker of a kiss.

I rode close behind her. As soon as the first windy chant was over, she started on another. This one was louder, with ninety-nine chapel nuns in chorus and innumerable anchorites chewing bracken in the woods beyond, as they fought to peep in at God's holy altar. Her great, sad, forward eyes were open and alert. Her nether eyelid neither winked nor blinked, but remained solemn enough to be dead.

I began to doubt my senses, not only when it came to Pipi's protracted vespers, but to the whole history of yesterday's farting as well. La Mamelonne was not the culprit. She told me whores never fart: they have the breath pumped out of them too often. Besides, her donkey had broken wind even when she was not mounted on him, even when he had died and was buried.

Here was an indication, if ever there was one, but an indication of what? Pipi sang it again.

We must have a ventriloquist among us. The more I pondered such a miracle, the more I understood it must be Ironface, *he who rode with his mouth covered*, and who could easily have swallowed a trumpet. I already thought he might be some kind of entertainer, a jongleur, a juggler or a speaker of charms. What more likely explanation was there of his entire legless being than that he was a dwarf from the fair, full of all the tricks like conjuring, voice-throwing, curdling milk and scrying generally? He would have caught all these knacks from his own kind. He had legs, and this was my comfort, but sheathed in braggart's armour a tally-stick too long for them. Yes, he must be a dwarf, or something equally cunning – a gnome or even a monkey-child born of unnatural men like those who would have invited his father to the back door of their castle, one of them the nobleman he claimed in kinship. My Uncle Crépin was of their number, and had his bottom bitten in consequence.

He sucked his knee. Pipi couldn't fart while Ferblant sucked his knee. So the tin man was the ventriloquist.

I took no comfort in this. A dwarf may also be a devil, just as the Devil is a dwarf whenever he chooses, in or out of armour.

*   *   *

158

The human jawbone is said to heal fast. Not half so fast as a woman's genitals. La Mamelonne's oooloooloooo needed do no more than rest itself for a brief gallop on a good horse before it was ready for work.

This was to our advantage. We needed to eat, and we were beginning to overhaul those who had deserted Béziers, and other cowards who flew ahead of the Crusade. Solomon of Gerona was here, with a string of packhorses laden with boxes. There were travelling journeymen, stone-cutters, burghers with sense, and a whole rabble who had nothing better to save than their lives, and were energetic enough to think them worth the trouble.

Pipi slowed to a jog-step, and still did not fart. This more than anything convinced me the matter was entirely at Ferblant's discretion, since a windy mare can have a melancholy effect on a recently bereaved man who is seeking solace, and quite put him off the whore who is riding her.

If old Ironface was neither a mountebank nor a warrior, then he was clearly a priest, because he was always haranguing those he was shortly to ask to rob themselves. So he was now with La Mamelonne.

He turned to her as we rode beside the halt, the grieving, the infirm. 'Don't you feel pity,' he asked, 'don't you thrill with awe and shame, to think of all those men who were with you last night, and are now with the living God?'

'No,' she said simply. 'I'm glad they've had their experience of me, since there's none of it in Heaven.'

'Death cut them down amidst the vapours of their lust. Shouldn't they have had a more fitting preparation?'

'They won't get fitted by a priest,' she said, 'not unless they're women. I'll tell you what many of them say to me,' she added, after thought. 'They say that to lie within my arms, by which they mean my legs, is like heaven on earth. I do truly believe that to jig a leg with me is a sinner's best inducement to go among God's angels. If I thought otherwise I would tell you truly.' She began to cry, poor girl, some of the wettest tears I have seen on a woman. The Mute sobbed too, and the Hunchback moaned with desire.

La Mamelonne was never cast down for long, certainly not by Ferblant. She spited his greed by stopping next to the most meagre refuge-seeker in the whole procession. This man was showing a lot of leg, in a tunic rather than a skirt, and the tunic was too short for his bum, so he was not only poor but reach-me-down.

He became king on the instant, for wherever La Mamelonne opened her arms or unfurled her legs so would the world follow.

'Come on, my brave survivors,' she chuckled. 'Come and refresh yourselves in me!'

'Oh, my poor wife!' one sobbed. 'Oh, my poor wife's poor sister!'

'That's where you'll be needing a good whore,' Mamelie explained, 'especially with two women to forget. I don't come cheap, but injured old veterans of five and twenty like yourselves can have me half-price, and any brisk young lad about you can do it free, providing he doesn't get greedy.'

'What's half-price?' some toothless oldster demanded, shifting a sack of silver ornaments from one side of him to the other.

'Half of whatever you've got.'

In the end she did the lot of them for a fistful of wild garlic, a basket of root vegetables and a bucket of wine. 'It may be demeaning,' she said, 'but it's dinner.' It was, too, though as full of wind as someone pretended her mare to be.

Wind is a comfort when you lie under smoking stars on a dewy hill.

Not that we slept very early that evening. We had scarcely looked over our neighbours nor our neighbourhood looked over La Mamelonne, before there came a wailing of women.

These were soon hissed at and told to be quiet. Apparently

someone had died. Townsfolk are unused to the strain of travelling, especially with an army chasing up their behinds. An old man well into his forties found the excitement too much for him. His death left his wife, his mother, his daughters, daughter-in-law and grandchildren feeling as free to indulge the occasion as they would back home.

Ironface put paid to all that. 'The sooner he's a heap of dirt, the sooner they'll realize death is nothing to weep about,' he said to the Hunchback.

'The soil's stony, and I've only a dagger,' Gibbu complained. 'That being said, he'll be easier to hide than a donkey, fat though he is.'

Ironface surprised me but pleased the poor fellow's family by saying a very pretty prayer over the resulting heap, then chanting a ten-minute frost of Latin that cooled their emotions down very nicely. We returned to the embers of our fire, and what was left of our supper.

'Let's hope his grave lasts till morning,' the Hunchback said. 'Or at least until we have all moved on. There's no corpse so snug that the dogs won't uncover it. And as for the wolf and the boar and the bear, they all go deep.'

'It's bad luck to be eaten by a bear,' Ferblant commented. 'Though easier to put up with once you're dead.'

The Mute had news to impart as well. His means of expressing himself were so disgusting I was glad when the matter communicated itself. And this it did. For a second or two I thought our piece of hill was experiencing an earthquake, or the freshly dug soil yielding up its corpse. Then I realized that one of the bereaved family was suffering the pangs of childbirth and struggling to bring forth. We left our food once more.

The dead man's youngest daughter was at work. She was a girl no older than myself and showing all the consternation of a cow calving upside down in a rushing stream. The Mute calmed her at once, possibly because he was the wrong sex to be a midwife and much less chatty, and Ironface's presence always frightened people. I wondered what she thought of her

161

laying-in. She had a dumb-skull, a Hunchback, a woman with untied hair, and Ferblant the faceless one himself, looking like a boggart or something to frighten crows, or a broom dressed in a colander. And all of this by moonlight.

The birth itself was every bit as tedious as watching a snake wriggle out of its skin, and much more noisy. I must say the infant gave off a pleasing note on arrival.

'We have a world here,' Ferblant exulted, 'a whole world. One dies, another is born.' He spoke like a ruler contemplating his kingdom. Not without good reason. A number of young men presented themselves to him during the evening, as if they were bonded militia reporting to a castle for a tour of duty. Old Towerhead accepted this as his due, and enrolled them in his memory. He was the only armed knight among us, even if his titles were no more than a pretence. It looked as if he could approach Carcassonne with a retinue larger than his previous entourage of freaks and whores.

Solomon of Gerona was another natural leader. Men gathered about him because of the importance of his packhorses. As Daddy used to say, 'Let a man hold a string and asses will soon tie themselves to it.'

I liked Solomon of Gerona's talk, so I went to ask him what attracted men to him. 'You're a Jew,' I chided him, 'and a foreigner as well. So why do they gather to you?'

'The Jews because they are Jews. Other men because they want to be the first to hear bad tidings.'

'There's more to you than that,' I protested.

'It seems to me I have already described a great deal. Let me add just this. These lads who lie on the ground about me and their women are like drops of stagnant water. They come to me to learn how to run.'

'I don't follow you.'

'You will. They come to where the stream flows quickest. We Jews have been running for centuries, Lady Perronnelle. We know where the quick waters go, and which are merely eddies.'

'Will Carcassonne be safe for you?'

'It is impregnable, Lady.'

'So was Béziers.'

'Walls are built by men. Sometimes God breaks them with a trumpet.' He smiled kindly, then added, 'Not next time, I think. For my God is not involved, and He was the one who cancelled Jericho.'

I thanked him, and returned to my own end of the hill, where I am bound to report that one or two women gathered themselves to me, as did several of the men who pretended quality. This was because they recognized Mummy in me, or because they saw what I was or recognized who I was connected with.

So our band came to have three leaders, none of us from choice, and fell into three groups. Only one person among us could bind them all together at once, and that was La Mamelonne. She harvested them to her lap like Marie-Bise picking cherries. The men, that is. The women weren't so forward, but sat a long way off with their noses in the air.

I remarked on this to Mamelie, as we finished what was left of her roots. 'Wherever you go,' I said, 'the women fasten their eyelids against you.'

'That's because their eyes have gone missing,' she smiled. 'And their ears too, like as not. They're all under my skirts to find where their husband's bums are hiding,' she laughed. 'I'm not called La Mamelonne for nothing. I'm named Little Tit-Shaped Hill because my tits are hills all men need to climb with their kisses.'

'And who tells you this?'

'Dogface,' she said, serious again. 'Dogface Raymond placed a charm on both my nipples, one for weekdays and one for Sundays.'

'And what about one for the Devil?' Ironface asked. He had left his militia and was all attention to this kind of talk.

'I don't have a Devil's pap,' Mamelie protested. 'Not even Dogface Raymond could give me one of those. I'm a Christian like everyone else down here. That is, I hear Mass every

Sunday while I live, but hope to take the *Consolamentum* on the day I die.'

'That's your religion on Sundays and your death day,' Ironface said. 'What about your weekdays?'

'I'm a witch. I follow the mistletoe serpent and the green girdle.'

'A green girl who practises white magic?'

'Only till the wolf howls midnight.'

'What happens then?'

'My fanny itches and I follow the black path of the moon.'

'Raymond de Brousses?'

'I have seen his stars, sipped black wine in his circle, and let him show me his Horned God.'

'And?'

'I have kissed its parts, yes.'

'No wonder you itch.'

She was like a world, that one, a world in which miracles could be planted.

I belched then, being full of supper and starlight. I belched and said, 'Many men have had you, La Mamelonne.'

'And I've had them.'

'Many men.'

'If you want to think in numbers, yes.' She was being sniffy.

'You've been with six or seven since we started supper.'

'We've all got to eat, haven't we? Besides, one was only a boy, and one his great-grandfather who'd fallen into my lap and wanted to lift himself up by my ears.'

He wasn't lifting himself up when I saw him, more working himself down, but I let that pass. I had important questions to ask. 'How is it, then, that you're never *enceinte*, you know, pregnant?' I used to blush to say the words, but I found I blushed less since meeting Mamelie.

'Pregnant?' she asked. 'What, *me*, with child?' She giggled, delighted at the thought of it. 'I have been, several times, but my Mama taught me how to cough,' she explained. 'I must say I don't like to catch myself with a toad in my hole.'

'How not then?' I felt this was information that every woman should have.

'A girl who doesn't want to find frogs in her pond should keep the tadpoles out of her ditch, that's my first piece of advice to you.' She told me another little trick.

'But that must take lots of time, Mamelie, all that folding and soaking of cloth, and – '

'And time is usually what a girl is clean out of once she's poking with a man, true, Perronelle. Similarly vinegar or a lemon. So what she must do, if she can wriggle her buttocks right and her fellow is amenable, is lie across the moon.'

'Lie across the moon?'

'A whore must always know where the moon is, day or night. Just like a peasant brings his bull to the cow.'

'Horns to the moon?'

'It's a sure way of being pregnant. The sun is even better, of course, but the baby's born with a headache. Well, a whore wants neither moon nor sun, and nor do you. Understand?'

'Perfectly.'

'But I shall be pregnant in a month or two, pregnant but not miscarry. Dogskin says I shall.'

'And who is this Dogskin?' As if I didn't know! 'No man has such power. Who is Dogskin to foretell matters that cannot possibly be known?'

'You may own the skirt on my bottom, Perronnelle. Or you may have done yesterday. *And* the cape on top of that skirt. You do not own my mind's secrets.'

'You have no mind, La Mamelonne, not if you believe in soothsayers.'

'Dogskin of Brousses is no soothsayer. He speaks more sooths than a soothsayer, and some of them are true ones! Ask any cinder in Béziers. He is a great necromancer, and he is my friend and master.' She silenced me as I went to scoff further. 'You were frightened enough when you met him.'

There is no-one so lofty as a whore having a tiff with a

friend, and no whore in the world with as much hoity-toity as La Mamelonne. I felt chilled just the same at her talk of Dogskin Raymond, and chilled even more at my memory of him, as if Evil himself had undressed me.

I shivered, and the Mute stole himself close to comfort me. Gibbu the Hunchback said jokingly, 'Perhaps Perronnelle has seen the devil this sorcerer keeps beneath his cloak.'

No laughter followed. Ironface added gravely, 'He has a devil right enough. I've seen it. A strange little imp of a fellow he keeps in a jar to teach him spells. And if Dogskin frightens no-one else' – this for the Hunchback – 'he frightens me. I used to think that Devil was myself,' he said, 'and so will you, if you ever see his face.'

'We've not seen yours,' I felt bound to say.

'Exactly, my child. You incessantly make us a gift of the obvious. It's a knack of yours.'

My turn to sulk now. To sulk and then shiver about Raymond de Brousses, whose face would not leave my sleep.

I was awake, though, I swear still awake when the evil thing happened. Dogskin Raymond revealed himself as a member of our column. One moment he was a memory, the next he was as I had last known him, a tongue in the air, its voice thick with cinders.

'Fetch her to me,' I heard it whisper to La Mamelonne. 'Bring her,' it boomed closer and more loudly. 'The witch has set me rising like barm in my mother's bun.'

I thought he had gone flying to his chapel on Mount Alaric, on his cloak for all I cared, and his distance from me had let me mock him. Now he was here, or his voice was, and the frankness with which it discussed my effect on him was making even La Mamelonne blush in the firelight.

Thus did Dogskin Raymond proclaim his lust for me, as if my thighs were a fireplace and his body wand no more than a stick of dough with the hot yeast rising. That troubadour had sung as much to me when I was fourteen, and Constance de Coulobres had boxed his ears for him. I had been warned.

Fortunately so. Mamelie had now been plunged into a deep sleep – she was, she said, his acolyte – and now he manifested himself. Still in red, and in a cloak that was more surcotte than pelisse, he brushed her on to her side, then stepped near our embers to proclaim, 'I intend to have you, Perronnelle de Saint Thibéry. Not merely as man to maiden – though be certain I shall thread your itchy little virginity on this which in part shows itself to you – but as my coven bride when I stand forth in the glory of my Lesser Ritual!'

These were awful words, and I giggled at them, so great was their effect on me.

'And on that night, I shall not merely plant your bum on the bracken, my snivelling little apostate, I shall draw off your spirit and hold it naked to me for ever.' He caught me by the chin, before Ironface could clank up to him, or the Hunchback knock his hand aside, though they did. 'What is dross, I shall burn,' he boomed. 'What is pure I shall – '

Gibbu lifted him bodily now, and ran him into the darkness, but his voice stayed constant in sound, as if it were only a thumbnail away from my ear. Then it spoke inside my head. 'I shall ingest you, tripes and chine, even your lungs and your breathing heart. When I have finished with what is flesh about you, only your backbone will be left from the flames.'

He struggled in from the darkness, pushing the Hunchback before him, and rattling Ironface aside. 'I thought so, my Perronnelle, it is your spine that is the serpent in you. Ah! How it tingles! That is all of you that shall wriggle from my fire. It will lie in the frost on Alaric till the moon-wolves lick at it. They will not eat it though, Perronnelle, because they will know it is mine.'

Gibbu threw him back at last, but his voice continued to whisper from the shadows beyond the fire, even though the Mute fanned it awake till it lit everything, and Dogskin was no longer there. 'Your backbone knows me as its Master, Perronnelle. When you dream tonight, you will feel me as the marrow in your spine.'

Foul being. How his voice ate me, as it came from the everlasting darkness beyond our little bonfire.

'Dowse it,' Ironface hissed, and the Mute sprinkled soil on the flame. 'Merdun is a nearer devil than he is, and he kills with more than curses.'

I was speechless for a while after this. It is disturbing to hear a man speak of your innermost parts in the way this Raymond of Brousses did. When beggars called out to me in the street, beggars or woman-hungry palmers, not one of them had thought to mention my lights, my bone-marrow, my tripes or my chine, or spoken of plunging his wand into my spirit.

No sooner was our fire dampened and my mind emptied of visions than a fresh noise disturbed us. A woman was singing a ring song – never a pretty noise at midnight. Then a dozen men joined in and began to cough up a clog dance, or some such drunken counter-measure, and the girl giggled, then shrieked, then howled *no no no* in a silly, high-pitched, knife-on-plate kind of voice like a vixen's when it comes on heat and calls for a mate. None of those things make a pretty noise anytime, unless you are a dog fox; and we had to think of Merdun's men, who were more than conscious of the tails between their legs without listening to a female's shrieks of invitation.

'Stay calm,' Ironface advised. 'Soldier's never move about at night.'

'This may encourage them to an early start,' the Hunchback said. 'It will be dawn in a snore or two – or at least as soon as the sun gets up, and the cock pops out of its bush.'

La Mamelonne woke from her trance, where we had all been content to leave her. 'It's that Violette la Vierge,' she said crossly. 'It's noisy, nasty work is her kind of whoring.'

The Fish Girl skipped towards us then, exhibiting herself in a most shameful fashion, with her legs bare as withies peeled for the plaiting, and her cotte, which was my cotte, and used to no such matter, pulled up round her bottom and plattered out in front like a goose-girl's when she gathers apples.

A dozen men followed her with their mouths hanging open and their skirts agape like hers, those that could afford them. They halted in embarrassment, I thought from glimpsing me but in fact La Mamelonne, then slunk away in the darkness.

'They've all been with me,' Mamelie triumphed. 'When a lad has been with me he has nothing left to give and little more to hope for.'

The Fish Girl let go of her skirt, or its gather of cloth out front, and dropped from it trinkets, coins, fruit, several cob-loaves, a gigot of cured meat, some chap-knives and a wine-skin. She giggled, preened and shook herself until she'd dropped enough to load one of Solomon's pack asses with a saddle or two to spare.

'She's earning more than we can carry,' Ironface complained. 'As for that virginity of hers, someone will have to get rid of it before it becomes the death of us.'

The Hunchback groaned in anticipation, while the Fish Girl continued to giggle and La Mamelonne kept to her sniff. There was nothing here for the Mute.

Ironface went to his mare and found a cloak or some such which he threw over the Fish Girl to cover her for sleep. She didn't lie down all at once, but sank a bit at the time, like a deer when it's struck by an arrow, or a newly born calf. He let her eat some of the bread and fruit she had brought, and she was noisy with it, the way she was with anything else, noisy but beautiful.

'Men pay royally to see a show like that,' Mamelie conceded. 'But that's all she is – a show. Whereas I'm more of a miracle, and they expect their miracles for free.'

'And what would you give for a miracle, Gibbu?' I asked the Hunchback.

'I don't believe in that sort of thing,' he lied. 'In general I believe in nothing.'

The Mute tittered, and that was a new sound. He slipped

his hand between the Hunchback's legs, who surprised me by doing nothing to move it. 'I believe in that,' the Hunchback said after a moment or two.

Ironface thumped his fist on the Fish Girl's blanket. 'Someone will have to get rid of it,' he muttered again.

I was surrounded by freaks and badels and now a macaroon, not to mention the whores. Quite simply I wasn't old enough.

For the third night running, and the third time that night, I tried to compose my soul in silence and shut myself up with my grief. It was not to be. Man is a sparrow among the hailstones, and woman a feather less. How I mourned that feather, for its absence was becoming a torment to me.

Men's thighs prick them often. Even Daddy admitted that, and Mummy proclaimed it all the time. During seasons of pestilence or bloodshed, they supposedly prick harder, and women's loins come to itch and their hearts ache, so the land may be peopled.

I had thought myself to be exempt from all that, but the sight of the blood at St Thibéry then the carnage at Béziers began to work on me in ways I had not foreseen. I did not yet desire commerce with a man, or even long for kisses, but the ordinary weeping of children in our encampment began to take a hold on me, as did their occasional laughter, and I wanted a male for a companion, someone with a brain like Ferblant's, but with a tender voice and a face made of skin not iron. Somebody human.

As I drifted into my sleep, it wasn't Mummy or Daddy that filled my brain, nor poor Marie-Bise and the other domestics, nor the Lady of Coulobres who was so especially good at reproving wicked dreams. It was the throb in me of my own being, which wasn't the least bit sad, but strangely persistent.

There was a being not myself, but mine and mine only, as tall as I was, or as small, but lofty and remote when he began with me as was the darkness between the stars. He had no face, this phantom, only breath and lips, and I felt his hands when he talked to me. He spoke mainly with his lips and fingers. He spoke as a Mass priest would talk, if I could imagine such a one to be pure. I forget what he said, but remember he said it, in a voice that went with holy eyes and a gaze more remote and intent than the frogs in my ditch of dreams when I met La Mamelonne.

The Faceless One breathed on my lips for a long, long time. His mouth tasted of dew and mint and freshness. Then he moved his voice to my ears and began sucking their lobes as if he were a buck rabbit at the tup, only he wasn't tupping me. I felt his weightlessness on my breasts, my belly, and all of my bones; and although there was nothing of him it pressed down heavy and hard.

'Virgin, Virgin,' Ironface's voice was mocking and close to my ears, so was this Ferblant devil no longer inside the armour, but under my cotte and pelisse, licking my spine and the hollow place where it ends, where a beast has its tail and woman her world of expectation?

I pushed the dream away from me and woke to find Ironface still in his mail, or some of it, but wrestling with the Fish Girl, holding Violette la Vierge down hard to a mat of cinders and daisies. He clanked about on top of her, clanked and clattered, just like a crab. I don't know what tubes of iron he had erupted from, or how many joints there were to the pith of him, but they were all of them in a tremble.

As for the Virgin Whore herself, she howled and mowled, first from fright, then in her usual madness, then in joy like a nunnery chanting the *gaudium*.

Bad often comes from good. I have never seen good come from bad. I was shocked to find Ferblant the self-proclaimed Lord taking the Fish Girl by force. The experience was so depressing that I laughed aloud.

'Stop giggling,' Ironface cautioned over his shoulder. 'A woman must learn to laugh like a woman, and chuckle never. Otherwise she'll be mistaken for a chicken and someone will wring her neck.'

171

'I'm giggling because the world is so bad,' I said. 'It was bad yesterday, and tomorrow it will be even worse.' I was angry at being wakened from my dream.

'Each day starts the same as its predecessors,' Ironface rejoined. 'The same and sometimes a little better. That is because God breathes on the glass each dawn and repolishes it.'

He let the Fish Girl climb out of his armour. She didn't run away, still less dance, so he left her and walked to his mare.

They made an odd sight in the rising sun, the soldier crab and the uncivil beast. If Ironface's mare had been a woman, people would have said she had a sagging rump and spiky elbows. I don't see why a horse should be afforded more charity than the rest of us, so let me say at once that she was plain ugly. As he climbed into the saddle – never easy for him – he was mounting an animal that sagged everywhere except for those places where it was sharp. Both ends of it were as pinched as a rat's futtocks, or a worm's arse under water. So even at the charge, against Merdun, say, in the Mill, she looked as if she were retreating, and it was my Lord Ferblant's fate constantly to appear as if he were sitting backwards.

I folded my cloak, mounted my Nano and went up to him. The others were already stirring, except for Mamelie, whose dreams were making her twitch like a fresh ant hill. 'Why do you run from this Crusade, Ferblant? You've taken the Cross?'

'I never took the Cross, little Perronnelle. The Cross took me, a long time ago.'

I hated his 'little Perronnelle'. I was as tall as he, whatever length leg he wore.

He placed an iron hand on my leg, one side or other of the knee. 'Cheer up, Virgin,' he said.

I hated that too, the Virgin, I mean.

The Fish Girl didn't dance any more, nor shriek or sing. She crept up behind Ironface, and sat there shivering on

172

his sloping horse. Someone placed Mamelie, still asleep, on her own.

Only the Jews were up, being prudent. I greeted Solomon as we filed past him. Pipi didn't fart. Ferblant's mind was on other matters.

We rode along the hill, and saw hundreds of families sleeping beside the high track to Carcassonne. The dawn was noisy with their breath, and with hinnies sneezing and horses chomping on air.

CAPUT FOUR

Wherein the wenches of Carcassonne cook crusaders in cognac
and a certain sleepless Virgin
views a youth clad in nothing
but crystal-clear water.

We did not come to Carcassonne. It came to us on the next sunrise, floating upwards in a mauve cloud which burst apart to show us battlements of blocked stone and a triple dozen of pointed towers each as ferocious as a wolf's smile.

We sat up and admired it as the dawn broke behind us. Truly it must be the biggest city in the world, the strongest, the bravest, the most beautiful. Paris by comparison was no more than an island in the mud. The citizens of this place would never become slaves or cinders, I was certain of that. The Crusade would break its nose here, and maybe its tripes and its brains.

We had come down from the high paths, and were now on the old Roman route that led to Carcassonne from the fortified village of Trèbes, having slept against the shadow of Mount Alaric, and almost beneath the cloak of the Magus Dogskin of Brousses. We hurried to break up our camp and ride on.

The enchanted citadel was still a league or two off. Because of the giants' paving slabs and such-like wizard-work, we were able to take this at a pace scarcely short of a gallop. We should have gone faster, our horses were so rested, but the Fish Girl was again stiff from Ferblant's blanket, and once more fastened herself to his saddle; and La Mamelonne held Pipi back from the stride, not liking too much motion beneath her rump unless she was at business or pleasure, and Pipi was neither. The Mute too was uneasy on his horse. He fretted himself over a chafing he pretended to find between the ridge of its backbone and the high part of his legs. Such people do. They have neither manhood nor maidenhead there, nor human finish of any kind, and the absence makes them saddle-sore.

177

A stream ran about and around the Roman road. Twice it ducked under a bridge, and once came over the pavings far enough to wet our skirts. This was the River Aude, and although the land was flat hereabouts, and built largely by flies, its waters showed all the ill-manners of a mountain torrent.

The flood left this side of Carcassonne alone, so lesser men had built their houses between it and the rise of the city. We rode through a maze of little streets and dwellings mean or magnificent, before coming to the outer drop-gate of the citadel.

This drop and drawbridge had its own fort to protect it, and no way of going past it.

There was no-one about, so soon after cock-crow. I decided to address the masonry in a voice as loud as I could muster.

'I am Perronnelle Saint Thibéry,' I said to the wall.

Pipi farted. It was her first time since St Marie la Dragonne.

There was a small shot window beside the gate, and the sound of mare and maiden caused a face to glimmer there.

'I am Perronnelle de Saint Thibéry,' I said, remembering Mummy, 'and consequently I am Lord Raymond-Roger's cousin.'

'So's my arse,' a voice said through the slit, 'and that's got yellow hair as well.'

Pipi farted again.

Clearly the place was better kept than Béziers had ever been. Unfortunately, the fellow did not intend to open it up to us.

Mummy had taught me never to argue with menials, so I was at a loss how to proceed until Ironface stepped forward and pulled off his tabard, which was bloodied on the backside of its cross, whether from the Fish Girl's virginity or fruit he had eaten by the roadside I couldn't tell. 'You see this gippon?' he said. 'I took it from one of those Crusaders, some Norman English Irishman I killed along the way. Receive it for a keepsake and a fee, but let us all in, by

God's holy loins, or they're going to cut our throats in consequence.'

You will need no reminding by now that La Mamelonne's mount did not fart once, nor could it while Ironface was talking.

The fellow dropped his bridge half down, then came out and balanced on the rim of it, scratching his fleas and sundry other parts where the night had left them frisky. 'You've brought your own women, seigneur, and that's in your favour, my lord. Step back from the brink there, or the bridge will chop your toes.' As he went in to finish winding the capstan, we could hear him mutter, 'I never did hear of a crusader bringing women.' And so we stepped above the moat.

'Where is your retinue, my lord?'

Ironface was never the one to embarrass himself at his own self-importance. 'I've some bold lads from Béziers. Send for me when they come, and I'll ride down and vouch for them.'

The moat was a capacious ditch, too high up the hill to hold water, though the River Aude clung close about the walls on the west side.

'What a monstrous chasm,' Gibbu muttered. 'When your cousin's enemies tumble in, there'll be no need for them to drown in their armour, they'll dash their brains out instead.'

I peered down, and at the bottom of this mighty ditch was surprised to see roof tops of thatch, shingle or stone. A whole colony of stalls, sheds and dwellings had sprung up against the foundations of the outer wall, so the morning beneath us was noisy with stitching, hammering, scraping, singing and oath-breaking as craftsmen plied their trade with leather, cloth or bone, or simply chewed what they could find for breakfast.

'It is to be hoped your Trencavel has those hovels stricken down,' Ironface observed. 'They could else serve the Crusade as firewood and cook his foundations till they crack.'

'Pah!' I said, or 'Poh!', or some such word in our dialect, but only because I was giddy.

There was another gate beyond the bridge, this portway's defences so far comprising turret, twin-towered drawbridge, then the bridge on which we now stood – itself stretching too dizzily far to be drawn up – then this further gate which was deeply recessed between two mighty towers of such smoothness and pinkness of stone that Gibbu the Hunchback said they reminded him of nothing so much as La Mamelonne's thighs.

'Fore God, I hope they're kept closer than that!' Ironface said, and the Fish Girl giggled so much she fell off the back of his horse, and almost off the bridge.

'If this place is at all like my wedge,' La Mamelonne said sternly, 'or, as some say, my ooolooolooo, then I do assure you it will be guarded with the absolute of discretion.'

And it was, for this further portal still kept itself shut against us, the only sign of a welcome it could offer being in the level gaze of a stone Virgin that glimmered from its deepest niche, and which Ironface told us was famous.

'If this *is* my fanny, I don't know what *she's* doing,' La Mamelonne added, touching Our Lady by the nose, 'nor what she may be said to represent.'

Now it was the Mute's turn to laugh, and – as I have indicated before – this wasn't a pretty sound. However, it caused the gate to swing open.

Once her nose was inside, Pipi did better than fart. She parted her bum at me without checking her stride, and dropped out the great load of hay, garrigue-grass, mangold and root she had been holding in her sally port for years. Some of this fell in the road, and continued falling, but as her heavens had first opened while her tail was beyond the wall and her hind hooves planted on the wooden slats of the bridge, she dumped her first bushel or so straight onto the hammerers and stitchers beneath it, though mercifully it was too early for anyone to be making soup.

180

Clearly this beautiful City of Carcassonne was highly ben-
eficial to the reins, and sovereign against the least hesitation
in the bowel. No sooner was I inside than I found myself
needing a privy. This is not the sort of matter I have ever
seen fit to discuss with you before, and it need not detain us
because mercifully I was attracted by the smell to a moat-hole
behind the tower.

As I sat in the noisome crevice with my bottom precarious
on a comfort midway between a wishing well and a public
plank, I gazed out upon the innards of the City, and thought
how it could all have been mine if only Mummy had found a
way for me to marry it. Could have been and yet might be.

The castle received us royally, by which I mean well and
according to my station. Gibbu and the Mute were allowed
to wait closely on me, as if they were gentlemen, and La
Mamelonne and Violette la Vierge were persuaded to help
themselves to a little meat and a jug of hot wine in the manner
of ladies rather than women several cobblestones short of
the holy ladder. Ironface comported himself appropriately
enough, with his voice high and his nose tilted. He called
for a fellow to polish his head and another to sharpen my
sword. Both of us were treated with a certain amount of awe in
consequence. It is not true, though the ballads say otherwise,
that once it was honed I used the blade to carve capon and
scrape my back for freckles. The wartiest thing about me was
Daddy's tame toad, and I'd left that at St Thibéry. I did eat a
chicken or two, but broken fairly in my hand. I took no crust
or other crumb, because it is well written that Carcassonne
is built of bread, since that is all its loaves are good for. If
stories gathered around Ironface's name, and they did, then
I do not propose to repeat them for you. I'll give the Devil
his due, but be damned if I sing hymns to him.

My cousin was unable to be civil to us until noon. This
was because he was absent from la Cité, following his hounds
between the Aude and Mount Alaric. Time weighs heavily on
the quality. They are allowed to make war or bring death to

dumb animals, which is why their great halls stink of sour meat. The alternative is to sit among their women and listen to music, but a married man is soon bored with that.

A poor man is lucky. He has stones to trim, and streets to keep free of horse manure, even when there is nowhere to put it except back again. In the afternoon, he can stop holes and hope Satan hasn't beaten him to it. Satan generally has, the young wenches like it so much.

My cousin returned before I had time to ask myself why he wasn't in High Mass mourning the loss of Béziers or galloping his army forth to succour it.

Seemingly, the flood plain was hot, and he had already killed too much for his men to carry. Worse, he had seen horsemen in the distance where the Wizards' Road passes the shadow of Alaric. These had caused him to hurry home, as he had no desire to find the Crusade between himself and a late breakfast.

Normally a huntsman has his men clean his catch in the field. Skinning is best done when the meat is warm, and trimming even sooner, as no male flesh tastes well if the breads are left dangling for more than a second or two after death, which is why we knacker bacon first, smoke it or salt it immediately, and only kill it if we have to.

This skinning, trimming and cleaning is a great festival, especially if you are a crow (waterbirds are always driven away from a kill, as they bring bad luck, gulls especially).

My cousin arrived like a warrior in triumph. He rode into his own hall to a great bracking of bugles and rattling of drums. He took his horse round the circumference of the room while a dozen retainers soused the pair of them with buckets of scented water. His fellow huntsmen meanwhile processed a boar, a bear, a fox and such-like wonders in a straightforward line to the hearth. My cousin waited for the guts to be drawn and placed on the flames, then stepped forward to be draped in their skins and hand out their liver, stomach and hearts to those menials with rank enough to cope with such largesse. Then he waited for a dozen brace of birds to be displayed. He had stooped these with his falcons or even spat at them to bring them down, so modest was he.

I went forward to congratulate him.

'Well, cousin,' he said. We took the wine they had cooked with clove and nutmeg for his breakfast.

'I look for a stag,' Ironface said rudely.

'I have lanced a bear. To kill a bear is a great omen.'

'You cannot eat omens. Your guests must eat pork, and pork is no good to me.'

'Sanglier is not pork. I expect Solomon of Gerona here, and even he will eat sanglier if it is stewed in apple brandy. Are you perchance a Jew, sir?'

'Jews are made of blood and bone, seigneur. I am blood and iron.'

'So long as you are blood. I did not quite catch your name. Nor quality.' Raymond-Roger smiled on me before adding, 'Though any knight or other gentleman who lends his protection to my cousin is of course welcome at my table.' He signalled for some trestles to be pulled and the boards set, meanwhile studying my sword with some amusement. 'There's no need to bring your own cutlery when you visit me, cousin. My fellows will lay out knives, and even some napkins.'

Ferblant spoke to him. He spoke at some length in Castilian Spanish, and not in that damned Catalan men know but cannot speak. I understood him to be tracing his lineage.

My cousin interrupted him to say, 'Well, sir, so we are related, and now we are acquainted. You shall have venison, sir, though I tell you truly I see no hole in your face where you could even force the leg of a chicken, not even the needle bone, nor the whisker of a carp.'

'I shall take it in wine, sir, and breathe it through the nostril.'

Raymond-Roger Trencavel turned away and said to the table at large, 'These Castilians snuff up wine, some of them, till their face drops off. Clearly we are dealing with such a fellow. Well, he comes here with my cousin, and must be used like a gentleman. Also, he speaks of a retinue, and a man who brought me even rats in armour would be welcome.'

'I bring you your own,' Ironface said, 'so no thanks are due. But then your own are in disarray after Béziers.'

Trencavel faced me quickly. 'What is this of Béziers, cousin? The wall is not down?'

'No, but to speak frankly of the rest of it, the whole place is no more than a riddle of cinders, and your militia is ash.'

He went white as I told him how it was. 'Praise God, you did not ride here shouting, though doubtless those who follow will bring their tongues.'

There was nothing to be said to this. The bad news had been with us so long it seemed inconceivable that we should be first with it here.

I had not mentioned my own troubles. Now the chance came unlooked for. My cousin frowned at Gibbu and said, 'What's that fellow?'

'The iron knight's servant and my own warrior,' I answered. I told him about Mummy and the Mill.

'He reminds me of someone.' There was no time for elegies. Raymond-Roger hugged me instead.

After this, the woe unravelled quickly. First Solomon of Gerona arrived. He and his people were well received, as was traditional with the Trencavels and indeed among the whole fiefdom of Toulouse. They distributed gifts of great discretion and largesse in return, and Solomon made it clear that if the South's war needed financing, then he could send messengers to arrange it. The Jews are a reticent tribe, and Solomon more than most, but they treat bad news with respect, and relay it in detail. Solomon's party had gathered on a hillock to see Béziers in flames. Then, as they rode beneath its pall, they had as we know taken the mountain paths followed by the survivors.

There were no tears to be had, that Solomon did not bring, save for those borne by a half dozen horsemen who arrived from Capestang, having followed the Wizard Route of the Romans all the way. These were young men of the seigneury, third and fourth scions of the squirearchy who found themselves without possessions, without hope, and therefore without wives. Having nothing to leave, they left it.

A junior son has little difficulty in betraying his father, so Raymond-Roger was able to discover from them the extent to which their fathers had betrayed him. The country quality had gathered at Capestang from the Trencavel estates around there, and from Montady and Enserune. They had heard of Béziers, and seen its fate in the soot clouds overhead. Perhaps news had reached them of the Mill House at St Thibéry. In any event, they made their submission to the Crusade, reaffirmed the Cross, and bought their families' lives by donating land within the Trencavel gift. I leave aside the fact that this was Spanish land, some of it – my cousin was vavasour to the King of Aragon as well as France. What was interesting was that these gifts were pocketed by Simon de Montfort. He was still so little regarded by the Dukes and other great ones that they let him play tax collector while they kept to dice and cards. At Béziers they had allowed him to gather the cinders. Now he had stag and salmon, and some castles the world would regret.

My cousin embraced the young men, and seated them about his hall. Only then did he give me a glimpse of the religion that burned in him. 'The Cross is made of wood, and thus it has the Devil in it,' he said. 'And yet the fools will kiss it.'

I couldn't answer that. Down here we are all Cathars at heart, yet Christ is in our souls, and the distinctions are too subtle to battle over.

'Like that Etienne de Servian,' my cousin complained. 'He no sooner hears there's to be a Crusade than your wretched Bérenger, Abbot of St Thibéry, has him kissing devils and becoming a Pope's man.'

This was new to me, though Bérenger was known to be persuasive. He even persuaded Mummy to make Daddy grind the Abbey's corn.

185

My cousin again said Gibbu reminded him of something.

'He reminds you of the hill over there,' I said. 'He bears Mount Alaric on his shoulders.'

The Hunchback was a servant, so I need not have noticed him as I spoke. He smiled at me as if I had uttered a kindness about him, instead of a monstrous piece of cruelty and folly.

'Talk to me of that Hunchback. His face is familiar for all his wild hair.'

'The Hunchback is a hunchback.' I might have added he was valiant and a mighty bowman, but I was learning my cousin's ways by now. He hoped to draw me into discussing my family misfortune, and I had no wish to oblige him.

'So young Auntie Vinegar is dead, and that nearly young maiden of Coulobres. These are naughty times, Perronnelle, naughty times. They shall be avenged, I promise you. And that fat champion who dipped his bread in Auntie Vinegar shall be avenged as well.'

'My father died nobly.'

'I've no doubt the miller fell like a wrestler, and doubly a man. As for the rest, he was your mother's husband. Let us not talk of any further propinquity, my Perronnelle.'

'You speak as if I am a bastard.'

'I'm afraid that's the way of it, and how the family has it. The miller was a fine, able man, but we could not consent to his turning quern-stones in our blood. Nor could Auntie Vinegar be married off among the nobility.'

Women are taught not to quarrel, and I loved my cousin too much, yet he had to still me to say, 'It's well known she was carrying the child of one too close to her in blood. Otherwise . . .' – his blush perhaps was real, his words merely diplomatic – 'I saw you when you were seven, Perronnelle, and again when you were thirteen, my lady, and by God I would have had you to wife at either moment, if it were not for this. Alas, by the same swelling that would not let us place your mother among the quality, when that swelling burst forth

186

and was you, because of closeness of blood I dared not find you in my arms – '

'Nor I you perhaps.'

'There – I've offended you!'

'No, not offended,' I whispered, hoping the talk was as quiet as my face was hot. 'Not offended, but surprised just a little.' I took some more meat and thought if this heresy prevailed there would be no fear of the Pope, and should my cousin's wife die, and women do die, then perhaps as Mummy said . . . I chewed, but I could not swallow.

He chose to tell me more. 'Some say it was my Great Uncle, Bernard Aton Trencavel, my grandfather's brother, put yourself in Aunt Vinegar's belly. Others suggest my grandfather, God rest him. Well, we all know a man may not have his niece, any more than tup with his horse.'

The comparison hardly suited Mummy, but these were extravagant times.

'The wickedest whispers hint at Cousin Crépin.'

'Uncle Crépin was her brother.'

'He mayn't even have meant it. He was always blind drunk, and in any case too short-sighted to tell the difference between a boy and a girl, even with their clothes off and the matter pointed out to him.'

'Crépin was an idiot.'

'I see none of it in you, so perhaps it was old Grandad. Well, we shall never know, not now Aunt Vinegar is dead, supposing she ever noticed.'

I had thought my cousin's hall smelled of dead meat. Incest has its scents as well, so perhaps corruption travelled with me. My nose was not to detect the true flavour of the castle, or my brain deduce its source, for several days to come.

This was because our nostrils were full of distraction, and our thoughts even more so. A look-out rushed in to tell us that the Crusade was attacking Trèbes. Then another came shouting that the place was being invested by giants, by bears and bulls on sledges, assisted by ghosts and apparitions. A man would need keen eyes to detect such a distant matter, but monsters come in more sizes than one, so the news was not derided. An elephant may trumpet where an ant farts unnoticed.

The Crusade never did attack Trèbes. Yet Trèbes was attacked, and cruelly abused, and the ghastly odours of its plundering shortly to reach us. If I allow myself to accept what happened, I am bound to confess it was not immediately apparent to me, other than by the nose. It took a dozen messengers with conflicting tales for me to deduce the following:

On this day, the twenty-fifth of July, Raymond de Brousses decided not so much to join the Crusade as to harry the lands of Trencavel on his own account. His hatred of the family's religion went even deeper than his dislike of the Cross.

He had no army for such an enterprise, so had to call upon those infernal legions which were always his to command.

His followers had been preparing long before the feast of the Madeleine, and had scoured Black Mountain, digging up giants and the larger sort of goblins or netting them among the trees. Now they brought forth twenty-five of these monsters, each of them taller than a house, even when folded on sledges. They had been prepared with bungs up their fundament and a nine-day feast of bean-pot in their bellies, together with aqua-vitae, apple brandy, beeswax and fiery gum.

The stench would have been worse than a plague wind, and indeed we began to smell it in the castle a league away in the citadel of Carcassonne, where the afternoon stank viler than pillows stuffed with pig-guts on a hot night, or goose-droppings wrapped around your neck for goitre and the quinsy. As such it was already a mighty stratagem, even before the monsters' stops were pulled and their breeches voided. In Trèbes, men and women became bone-white, and at the first real breath of it their faces hived out in spots. When they filled their lungs a second time, their skins glowed green as copper in a candle-flame. The walls nearest this sulphuric battery freckled with warts and nuggets of yellow plaster.

188

Meanwhile the subterranean winds increased in frenzy. A kind of pother or devil's mustard began to splash across the town's south-eastern quadrant, where roofs tumbled into the street, and buildings crawled about like lizards. Starlings, sparrows and even tiny wrens fell from the bushes with cats in their claws, and when these were not already dead they bit all the town's dogs in a frenzy, or so the rumours ran. I can certainly attest the death of all climbing vines.

As it was at Trèbes, so nearly with Carcassonne.

Mankind has always yearned for the ultimate weapon, the closed tub or tube that will belch flame and fling stones, swords, spears and such-like projectiles including live snakes and dead donkeys over enormous distances, up to the length of an ox furrow or the flight of an arrow. Even Dogskin was not exempt from such a fantasy. He commanded members of his coven to stand close to these expanding giants and ignite their britches.

The noise was impossible to bear. It was as if God had taken all the thunder from a storm, bound it in a cloud and delivered it in a single second. Carcassonne rocked and Trèbes nearly turned over. We saw twenty-five gouts of bright blue flame, followed by a league-long firing forth. The distance could be judged from the fall of trees, the jarring upfling of birds as they were scattered by spigots or wood, brick and such other corkage as the monsters' tails had been stoppered with.

Mercifully a bottom is not so accurate as a bow and arrow. Nothing was propelled towards Carcassonne except a passing gypsy on a camel. Both of these might have fallen in the Aude and been saved, but our walls were in the way and smashed them to bits.

'It's bad luck to kill a camel,' Ironface said.

'And worse to harm a gypsy,' my cousin agreed. 'Cross both their palms with silver, and bury them facing East.'

In spite of this, there was still a mighty stench left over.

This took place on the twenty-fifth, as I say. The first crusaders arrived beyond the out-town walls on the twenty-eighth of

July. The main body of their army, now shrunk to a mere thirty thousand men, was with us on the first of August, by which date the smells became mighty. As a soldier arrives, so he squats, and with not much patience to squat on, nor delicacy of manners either. They have little regard for agriculture, these northerners, and even less for the vine.

Ironface's party had approached Carcassonne through a walled out-town called Le Bourg. This has its own gate into the City, though we had chosen to enter through the more imposing portal of the Narbonnaise. The Aude curls away from the walls of Le Bourg, leaving a marshy interval of grass and gas. The Chanson says the Crusade camped there.

Looking that way, I could see no such matter. Perhaps all its warriors were invisible. Such conditions are commonplace enough, especially after lunch, and the Pope was known to have sent them prayers and ointments, as well as conflicting instructions, and it could be that one or the other took their flesh right away, and let my gaze go through them as if they were walking streams or mad marsh vapour, even their bones. Invisibility would render them exactly so.

My problem with this argument is that there were other warriors camped in the wood and on the hill that lay to the south of the Narbonnaise Gate, and these weren't invisible at all, perhaps through lack of prayers and ointment. It was on this hill and within this wood that the Count of Toulouse set his pavilion by a spring and its ensuing stream. He was clear for us all to recognize, being not a bowshot away. There was no man in all of Carcassonne, my cousin least of all, who would have unleashed an arrow at their noble count – for fear of killing him too quickly. But that was a separate matter, to do with strategy, so clearly not for me.

I saw the Count of Toulouse's pavilions from a tower just west of the Narbonnaise gate. My cousin inspected his defences daily, almost as tirelessly as he rode hunting, and he was pleased to invite me to stand with him. Women are useless on a battlefield, his thinking went; but among the defenders of a siege they have a part of play. No doubt I

190

was a special case, I was a member of the family. I had won my sword from a crusader I clubbed to death with a stone. That is how the stories ran, and they were unusually close to the truth, for stories.

My own presence was easy enough for me to explain. The problem lay in my attendants. My women, if anyone could be said to own either of them, were La Mamelonne and Violette la Vierge. One of these was half a whore, and the other a whore and a half. So what would the citizens think? What could they say, especially their wives?

Very little, and nothing to the detriment of my cousin's cause. He was admired, but the respect was in danger of turning to reverence, and this is too austere an emotion when there is blood to be shed and wounds to bind. Raymond-Roger was a devout man, too devout to go to church or have his wife near him. Some said she was in Albi, some said she sulked in a nunnery, some said she was dead (as, without wishing her harm, I hoped she was). In fact, she was in Spain, which was further than death.

La Mamelonne put the flesh back in people's regard for him. Here was a woman who could lie with thirty crusaders on her belly, and still think of breakfast. She stood above the battlements and made a joke about his uncle, the Count of Toulouse, that set the whole city laughing.

The Count was well known for having the biggest tail in Oc. People spoke of it often, the way women will discuss a pelisse and liripipe, or men a fine horse. The object was not invisible, being as long, as thick and as playful as an elephant's nose, and much more given to spitting, so much so it had fathered half the population of Toulouse.

'There are two sorts of prick,' she explained, to as many of the gentry and the garrison as could cluster about her. 'I've studied the subject at length, and believe me there's only ever been the single exception. There's the limp ones and the limper ones. When the limp ones grow stiff they grow stiff. And when the limper ones grow stiff they grow longer, just like a slug on a leaf.

'Then there's my only exception – I refer, of course, to the lance, quarter-staff and jousting truncheon of my lord of Toulouse, God's viceroy and viscount. If you don't believe me, ask any whore with the clap, because his tool is where she'll have got it.'

'Tell me about Raymond of Toulouse's,' my cousin's friend Roger de Cabaret of Lastours demanded. (He himself had such a big one, men used to speak of his five noble towers – his four stone forts at Cabaret and the fifth piece of masonry he bore beneath his coat.) 'Before God, talk to me about my lord's alp and pinnacle. I need to stop laughing before lunch.'

'It's twice as big as yours,' Mamelie said, whereat Violette la Vierge shrieked in terror. 'Twice as big. As chargers go, it's all of twenty hands high in its stable. But out of stall, it's another matter. I, for one, could never find it.'

Such a roar of laughter arose from our battlements, such a swell of mirth, that it brought the crusaders from their tents, Raymond of Toulouse among them.

'It used to grow so excited to see me,' she went on, 'it would disappear altogether. Raymond of Brousses is so obsessed by the magic of it, he's twice tried to buy it. If the old Count falls on the field of battle, Dogskin is certain to come looking for it. If he's taken in this war, his captors must ransom him separately from his belly-finger.'

'That's why the Pope overruled Arnold Alaric's excommunication of him, and allowed him to join the Crusade,' laughed De Cabaret. 'He knew he would be getting two converts for the price of one.'

'What a man to have as uncle,' my cousin said. 'Not only does he fight on both sides at once, he manages to shake hands with the Devil even when his fingers are fastened in prayer.'

'That's because he's so long beneath the stomach,' chuckled La Mamelonne.

My cousin did not talk like a doomed man, still less walk like one. Soothsayers said he would lose his family's possessions, and pointed to Dogskin Raymond's curse upon him. Raymond had promised him annihilation by Fire, by Earth, by Air and by Water. At Béziers the fire had come magically, as if from Hell or from Heaven, and Dogskin of Brousses had expanded in glory as a consequence. Presumably, his twenty-five farting giants represented his attempt to make good the annihilation by air. If so, they had failed, showing plainly that a necromancer should never seek to implement his own curses. He should send out his verbal squibs and wait for Hell to ignite in sympathy.

Hell was on our side today. As we mocked Raymond of Toulouse, there came a shout from the far side of the City. We heard steel nudge steel, then arrows fly as noisy as partridges shaking their wings above a frosty field.

It took a minute or two to hurry to a vantage tower in the castle itself, and by then the matter was over. The crusaders had ranged around the outer town, dropping off sentinels where the land suggested, then swelling these by reinforced encampments as their people came up from Béziers. So far they had not dared occupy the narrow stretch behind the castle, where our walls were tallest and thrust outwards. This soil was ours to command, for here the River Aude came closest, and was wider by an island.

Simon de Montfort saw the land was empty, so advanced a dozen score knights and mounted men, with as many more on foot, to complete our encirclement. As he passed Le Bourg, the townsmen took their longbows and shot at him. Then he came within threat of our garrison at the Mill Tower and the Tower of the Carpenters. These spent all their arrows and several hundred darts, and hit nothing, but drove him towards the river, where he continued to advance. Again, we shot too early. Crossbows from the castle, sling shot from the barbican, neither achieved a hit, but they pushed him even further to his right, until his flank was in the mud. If he faced us and waited, we might come out and attack him with his back to the water. He turned and began to withdraw.

I recognized him clearly enough, though my eye was distracted by a further waste of arrows, which again hurt no-one but clouded the air like midges. The Bastard did not march with him.

No corpses were strewn before us, and that was a disappointment. Across the town, I had heard not only arrows fly but a sound like blade on blade. As far as I could tell, the dints were caused by the foot-soldiers' knees knocking together as they marched. If a man binds his legs with canvas and iron rings, then it is hard to keep them from touching, especially over rough ground. The lucky ones had nothing on their knees but wore those long English skirts of chain. I was coming to think men shouldn't design armour. It would take me a day or two longer to realize that war is best left to women altogether.

'We stand at such a height here,' my cousin murmured to those about him, 'yet we cannot close off the river.'

Our eyrie was in so tall a place that the Aude with its reedy islands seemed no more than a dribble at our feet. Our own outpost, the Barbican, was a child's castle of pebbles.

'A pity we have no menials here,' De Cabaret observed. 'I'd be interested to see what a longbow could do from such a vantage point.'

'Not enough, believe me,' my cousin said. 'We'd need to post horsemen below the Barbican, or use the River Gate as a sally port.'

Gibbu stepped forward, and men cleared a path for his hump. 'Bowmen win wars,' he said. 'Horsemen only dream them.'

'True enough,' De Cabaret said, as if between equals. 'But can your arrow stretch as far as my dream?'

'He's a long arrow,' La Mamelonne said, but in the background, which is where a whore should be. 'Yet I doubt it's as long as anything of yours.'

Gibbu grounded his bow stock and strung it with a string.

He fitted an arrow – not an owl-feathered slenderness for silence, but a goose-winged shaft which would fly and fly, with a barbless head like a waterbird's beak. This he drew by the length of his arm, and further by the spread of his chest, but it still had the length to let its nib peep over, though we marvelled at his reach and the muscle that would hold his pull steady.

He waited for the wind, angled upward, and loosed.

The arrow flew a long time, so men counted its flight and applauded what they numbered. Then they groaned, though one counted on. Even so mighty an arc sunk this side of the Barbican, planting itself at the very foot of the tower.

'How far from the Barbican to the river?' De Cabaret asked.

'By that far and more again,' my cousin answered. 'Further than the shot you have seen, and that shot would start lower.'

'I do not know a bowman with more reach than me,' Gibbu said, 'nor a shaft with more carry.' He spoke as if it were the most normal thing in the world for a hunchback to boast before great ones.

'So we can't close it off,' De Cabaret mused.

'Not unless you grant me a dozen archers, and set me on that island,' Gibbu persisted. 'Then I could close one half of the ground, the Barbican the other.'

There was a murmur at this, for a lout may win applause without gaining approval.

'I like your spirit,' my cousin said to him, 'but I don't hold with your thinking. It takes a knight to command an outpost, and there's no knight I'll ask to sit on that stink hole in the reeds.'

'Grant me a fletcher with a clean sack of feathers and I'll build enough arrows to sit there by myself.'

'No, fellow.'

'Let me cross to that island before De Montfort sets his flag upon it.'

'No, Hunchback. No.' My cousin turned to Ironface. 'Have

195

your servant hold his tongue.' He swung on Gibbu again, as if even a menial deserved his explanation. 'I want no man outside my walls. A foray, yes. An outpost, no. A captain spends his force by manning outposts – it's one of the first rules of war. Le Bourg and Le Castellare worry me enough. I'll have to take their women inside, and most probably their men.'

'They'll have nothing to drink,' said De Cabaret drily.

'And nowhere to shit,' muttered Ferblant. Being foreign and faceless he could say such things in our councils of war.

'This Crusade has too many leaders,' my cousin said. 'Why don't I bring three or four hundred keen huntsmen to horse, and either chase this De Montfort away from the rest of the army, or attack my Uncle Raymond head on, while he's waiting for his quartermaster to bring up his whores?' He smiled at me for approval.

I smiled back at him. A few dozen men had set fire to Béziers, simply by rubbing their beards together. So a bold charge of several hundred might scatter the invaders' host. Who was I to tell?

Roger de Cabaret was a keen enough huntsman, but I noticed he pulled his chin at this suggestion. However, we hurried down from the castle's Tower of the Chapel, and my cousin gave the order to saddle up.

He was interrupted by a deputation of townsmen. It will always be so, I guess. A leader looks for greatness and sees only distraction.

They were all carrying loaves, and held them towards him. I've mentioned before that their bakers are excellent brickmakers, but I failed to see how this could be laid at my cousin's door.

'Bread,' they said. 'We can't bake bread without water.'

'Eat plenty of meat,' Raymond-Roger advised.

'There's only wild pig, and that sticks in the gut.' Thus did they mock at the feast of kings.

'Nobody in Carcassonne has trouble with his bowels,' my cousin the viscount said. 'Walk outside and sniff.'

They went outside, but they sulked too loudly to sniff.

'Keep back your horsemen till you need them,' Roger de Cabaret advised. 'At some time soon, these northerners will try to cut you off from your river again.'

Ironface's man Gibbu growled at this, as if he had a right to growl in such company.

I settled the debate by fainting. My month was oppressing me – my month and my moon, or the general lack of air.

'Drink some wine, cousin. We're short of water, as they rightly say. We've only two wells in the citadel.'

'Dig some more,' Ironface said. 'And dig them quickly.'

'The level is already dry.'

'Dig deeper.'

My poor cousin was too pained by the message to be incensed by the manner of Ironface's advice. War to such a noble spirit is all hoof and iron. Talk of spades distressed him. He yearned for combat in the open field. I had already seen and smelled enough to know that a siege is different. A siege needs engines. It cries out for cutters of stone. And – on the defending side at least – it needs women.

'You dig your own well, Lord Tin.'

'I have two wells already,' Ferblant laughed. 'One in each leg, and both of them are full.'

When faceless men speak riddles, the wise ones turn away.

Ironface wasn't in the least put out. 'If we're to have no river tomorrow, then I'll go wash in it tonight,' he laughed. 'Aye, and fill my mouth with it, some of it at the least. I've still no space in my legs for water, my limbs are reservoirs for wine, but I'll take by mouth all a mouth may take. Come, Gibbu. Bring the Tongueless One as well. I shall need a squire to unlatch me, and another to rinse the iron from my back.'

He led them towards the Barbican Gate.

La Mamelonne sniffed and the Fish Girl dithered like a starling that's broken its nest. Then they too left me. Washing is not for women, so whores find it hard to confess their need for it. I followed the men towards the river, though naturally with no thought of joining them.

A woman never swims as easily as a man. I have swum, some several dozen times in my life, but it needed such a fire to dry the soggy clothing on my back that the Mill would be full of steam for a whole month after. As for rinsing and scrubbing, I never had a bath, except as an infant when the occasional cleansing of the parts was necessary until one was in control of one's functions. As an adult Mummy and Constance de Coulobres both taught me such grooming was superfluous, save among menfolk, principally the sweaty ones like dykers and first-cut masons, and only for them while they were unmarried or had no woman to cook them clean linen.

Sometimes when I lay unable to sleep at night, I used to dream of taking off my clothes and swimming in our mill pool under the stars as naked as the town boys beneath the midday sun. I would twist inside the coverlet and imagine my white body gliding, not frisking and splashing like the boys, but slipping past the waters like a fish, and with a giant trout's privacy and secret gleaming. But that would have meant taking my clothes off, and even the moon mustn't see me like that.

So I did not seek the shore beneath the Barbican Gate, but walked the closed way towards the Barbican itself. My friends were ahead of me, and below. I heard them laughing beneath the shot windows, yet would catch no sight of them, naked or however else they were.

The first man or person of either sex to cause me to be totally undressed was the Bastard of Montfort. As I had grown so had I split my clothes, and some had tumbled off underneath or assumed new shapes of comfort and cosiness with the aid of patches, panels, and cunning extensions from the needle of Constance de Coulobres, who had devised me a miraculous system of lets and gussets all the way from toddlerhood through my years as a ninnie till I matured to maidenhood and was buxom front and back. 'The way to fit an undergarment is *on the flesh*,' Mummy would say. Naturally enough, I had very few cloths to my limbs that were the same at seventeen as they were when I was three, but an erudite and attentive lover could have been able to read my progress though time patch by ribbon, and stitch by thread, if that fool Merdun hadn't commanded his fellows to deprive me of my history, and a tough time with the Lady of Coulobres' needle they had had of it. I *don't* talk of my overgarments, of course I don't. My cottes, surcottes, bliauts and pelisses were all made of the finest stuffs, brocaded as like as not or otherwise embroidered, furred as appropriate, and each one designed to be dropped on and off – hence the extent of my bounty to La Mamelonne and the Fish Girl. You don't earn top-clothes like mine at the town's end. They come as by right only to people of rank and good taste. 'Men don't give away cloaks in exchange for cuddles,' Daddy used to explain to Marie-Bise when he thought we were otherwise distracted. 'He makes a present of a ribbon, or if she's lucky a scarf or even a folded pin.' Marie-Bise used to have a lot of those, and was quite the talk of St Thibéry, but I never saw her in a pelisse that was better than moderate, nor ever wearing anything quiet and soft.

These were tearful memories, or tearful on the sudden. My month was heavy with me, and my eyes full of dew at haphazard moments. My deeds were in a jumble too. For instance, why was I here – to see three grown men swim naked like boys?

They weren't grown men at all. One was faceless and without his parts; he was legless perhaps or a dwarf or devil encased in tin. Yet he could pin the Fish Girl to his bed, and that was a fancy. One was a hunchback. He was a man I had come to respect as is possible with such people, but he would not want any woman to see his naked deformity. And then there was the Mute, shorn of his sex as well as his tongue, a strange smooth creature such as a Moor might make for his wife's safety and his own pleasure.

I know why I was here, if I was true to myself. My dreams had been troubling me. My sleep had been filled by a Creature who would neither love me nor leave me to peace, a Phantom who commanded my life in words my days could not remember but whose speech was never still. This being was always naked but indistinct, as an angel might be, an angel or the incubus of a terrible temptation. I wondered, when I woke, if one of these three men were invading my sleep. I hoped, if he were, that to glimpse his naked flesh would reveal my dream, and give my longing an identity.

My friends' voices were quiet. There was no footfall below me on the shingle of the river bank. I peeped through a dozen shot windows, and saw only dusk and the early moon.

The Barbican itself was well defended. Its men were garrison militia, serving turn and turn about from their fields in the land of Trencavel, which is half of Oc. They were caught here by the siege, and left to make the best of it. Naturally they were in need of their wives. They treated me respectfully enough, but from the way they eyed me I knew I shouldn't have strayed here alone.

A few short days ago, my life ran clean as a freshly dug spring. Then the Bastard's men had come, and Merdun set his thumb on me. Everywhere I turned since that moment, even in my dreams, I was reminded that man is in ceaseless rut, like a tusker in the thicket. Woman is his sow or his cow, according to her luck.

I had my little herd. Now I'd lost it as I'd nibbled in its footprints. I ran back along the closed way, calling for Ironface, Gibbu, even my Mute. My lack was for a man made of tin, with one of the deformed, for a thing who was sexless – my lack and my love. Yet my longing was for my Phantom, and if I turned aside to weep, my comforter was a whore. Life fits me as appropriate. No sooner do I find myself to be an orphan, than I discover Daddy is not my father and Mummy committed incest to get me.

I ran the length of that corridor several times, that narrow place of shot windows between its two tight walls. I crossed it back and forth. There was no-one in the Aude, neither up nor down, not bather nor drinker, and no-one casking water. Not unless they were hidden from my eye by the swelling of the Barbican itself. Yet I had stood in the Barbican, albeit among the militiamen, and noticed nothing from its ports.

The closed way grew brighter. A moment before, in my terror, I had waded thigh-deep in dusk. Now its floors were paved in light as the fat moon lifted herself above the level of the bow-slots. I stepped back towards her, and once more looked out.

I was facing upstream, to the south. Beneath me, some two hundred footsteps from the Aude, was a pool, a tiny lake of water where the prudent might draw buckets, hard against the foundations of the closed way. It shone like a pouring out of silver. It was secret and unexpected.

So, too, was the youth who stepped from beneath the angle of the wall and plunged his nakedness in the reflected light, which shone too flat for the eye to search among.

He neither swam nor washed, but stood for a while with his back to me, cut at the waist by the water. Then he turned and walked out to one side, his shoulder, his back and what I could glimpse of his chest white with moonlight, his lower limbs dripping with diamonds, his ankles still lost in the water. He turned slightly more, facing direct to the river, then stepped clear of the pool.

His thing shone with diamonds too, but with the moon's fire all beyond it as if it made its own light. Otherwise it was much like the small boys' I was used to watching in Daddy's weir. Like theirs, but there was more of it, though not too much, especially after its owner had immersed it in a flood basin of the River Aude, which is mountain-cold and noted for the greed of its fishes.

It didn't menace me the way the Bastard's men had in their nudity, so I eyed it for a long time, stealing an occasional glance also at the rest of him. It was longer than his wrist and thicker than his finger, in every way as elegant as his very handsome nose, but with a touch more gravitas, though not so sternly fixed. I could have gazed on it for ever, but it saw me and took fright.

He turned towards me fully, noticed my moonlit gaze in the shot window, and showed me in that instant that his was the face of the Phantom. My Phantom was real, was flesh, though this time too far away to touch. Then, when he saw me, he did as my Phantom always did, he disappeared – not from melting away, but by stepping beneath the angle of the wall.

I could hear his breath. I could hear sounds of a person dressing himself, then his footsteps on the stones as he picked his way back towards the castle. I turned and hurried back along the corridor, then down towards the river door, wondering what to say to him, yet knowing he would be the one to begin.

There was nobody there. There was a dampness on the floor inside the gate, but no sign of a footprint. And if I found a footprint, need it be his? Other men had been recently to the river as well.

My Phantom lived. That much was certain. He was real. He was properly alive, an inhabitant of creation. He was neither a love-dream nor a devil sent by Raymond of Brousses. He should have walked this way, yet there were no people here.

Upstairs there were altogether too many, what with Roger de Cabaret, his ladies and his gentlemen, my cousin's knights and scores of retainers preparing the evening's feast.

My friends were back inside. Ironface soon had enough of water, if he ever had water at all. He found a corner nook to spread his weight on the Fish Girl, or her lightness on him. Whoever my Phantom's features belonged to, I hoped they weren't Ferblant's, now masking his lips in steel, his legs in tin, but panting and pasturing away at the writhing Violette la Vierge, that witless creature.

Or the Mute. Could it be him, in spite of his lack? I eyed him between the legs, at the hem of his tunic. He smiled as if knowing my quest, so I turned away.

'Hunchback!' I called, like a lonely child. 'Hunchback! Dear Gibbu!'

'Little Bastard,' he grunted, and pressed me to his beard. I pushed him away, so he growled, 'Yes, Bastard, Perronnelle. I heard what your cousin said. It's a sickness of great ones, never to talk quietly.' He caught at me again, as if I could be used like this. 'From all the Viscount said, I gather your mummy lay very strangely, and in a crooked bed. Is this the woman you sob for in your sleep?'

He got me crying then, though I swore I never would.

'Yes, call me Hunchback, which is how God made me. And I shall call you Bastard, for it's what the Devil wills.'

To Mamelie I said, 'I'm searching for a man.'

'I used to be like that. Poor, poor Perronnelle. Now I'm searching for somewhere without one.' We grew sad together, then she brightened and said, 'Not that there's any such place, not in our whole flat world!'

I won't tell you what a sleep I had with my Phantom the night immediately following. He bothered me from the moment Venus stood above Alaric to long after the first cock, and this merely by talking. Very shortly nearly everyone would die, he said, and I was to take charge of the survivors and lead them to safety, and overthrow the Crusade and Pope Innocent or King Philip or Arnold Almaric. His words confused me because of what his lips were doing while he spoke them, several times causing me to wake during the cool of the night bathed in perspiration. (He did not talk with his mouth, but with his throat and ears, which La Mamelonne assures me is not in the least bit supernatural or unusual, as most lovers do this all the time when they're with a lady.)

Next morning the war started in earnest, and I must say I was glad of it.

The bloodiest, boldest and most effective fighting during the investment of Carcassonne took place in the outlying villages or towns-beyond-the-wall of Le Bourg and Le Castellare. However, the woman Perronnelle must tell you that this part of our campaign, like much else in war, was the result of an accident.

My cousin Raymond-Roger had withdrawn most of the inhabitants of these little towns inside the walls of the City, leaving only idiots, itinerants and a few whores known to be a nuisance. And, for the moment, the men. He had no intention of defending these places, and his decision was wise. You don't bar your front door against a wolf, then open your window and try to strangle it.

He thought that the buildings, and perhaps the whores, would delay the Crusade's advance a little. The house of a famous vintner stood in the suburb of Le Bourg. The vintner himself was a Cathar, and as such a heretic and frightened the crusaders would cook him. He'd fled first to Castelnaudery, then to Montréal, towns where they don't roast meat but eat a lot of beans. He had taken enough wineskins with him to pay for his beans, but had been forced to leave the rest. The men of Carcassonne had all the grape they needed. It would have been a sin against the South and the entire land of Oc to tip out the wine, or otherwise spoil it. My cousin decided it should stay in its barrels and its pits beneath the floor, as an enticement and distraction.

The ruthless Simon de Montfort took no heed of this (I was struggling with my Phantom, but I suppose he took no heed). He left his brother with the whores and the wine, grabbed Raymond of Toulouse by the scruff of the neck and began to move boldly towards the ramparts of the City. He still wasn't in charge of the Crusade. He simply believed in getting up in the morning.

This took my cousin by surprise. He too was up early, but with a proper reason. He was out hunting, certain it would be his last chase before his walls were encircled and invested. Fowlers might creep out, and fishers, but once the enemy dug his lines, it would become difficult to ride forth with a pack of several hundred dogs. Dogs need to be shouted out, and whipped in, and generally have trumpets blown at them. They'll also steal a sleeping man's breakfast, cock their leg against his ear, and otherwise wake an army up.

The walls of Le Bourg were low, especially in the south-east, which was the furthest Simon de Montfort could persuade the Count of Toulouse to march, being nearest to his pavilion. Simon put several hundred of his men across on a short ladder, while Toulouse returned to his bed and the people he had left there.

My cousin was on the river plain north-east of the town. No sooner had he started than he set a fox running. It was smaller than a wild boar but faster than a bear, so not bad for war time. It ran straight through my cousin's hounds only to find its way barred by the river, so it ran through them again – everyone said this was an omen, but an omen of what? – and made for Le Bourg, and some said the vintner's.

The walls of Le Bourg which were low in the south-east were even lower in the north-west. The fox got over them with a hop, skip and scamper. No horseman jumped them clean, though several fools tried. Some rode across by a bank between a tree-stump and a stone, then clattered down the roof-tops. Most, including my cousin and De Cabaret, came in by the gate, which set them two by two like the beasts in the ark, and in very good order for a fight.

They might have taken De Montfort by surprise, or themselves by surprise, but a horse makes a mighty noise on a roof-top, especially when its tiles lack moss in their teeth and they've only the summer dust for their gums; so the crusaders heard them coming and pulled their swords from their saddles.

They also saw the fox, which ran straight at them. They began to cheer the hunt, the way men will. Reynard found himself penned between devil and damnation, as is so often the case in the last few moments. Fortunately for him, he recognized a storm cut, or some other sewer, right behind them, and went between their horses' legs and straight to earth in its banks.

This caused the crusaders to swirl about, some to sniff

Reynard, some to calm their horses, and left half of them with their stirrups hooked together and the other half facing the wrong way, all except a fine knight called Bouchard de Marly, whose war mount embarrassed him by throwing him to the ground and trampling on his beard. My cousin and the best of his hunting party were unable to check their horses or their dogs, and a great confusion followed, which the survivors called a mighty battle, with hound biting horse and horse kicking dog, and the gentry of both parts of France spitting at one another and being rolled on by their steeds.

This was fortunate for my cousin's party, who were embroidered as for hunting, their chests stitched with marigolds, forget-me-nots and lupins, and their heads bound in fur or scarves stolen from women. There wasn't a blade among them, except a couple of flaying knives and the little handsaw my lord De Cabaret carried so he could fashion flutes and whistles while waiting for a scent. The nearest to chain-mail that any of them wore were the rings on their fingers. As for helmets or other such armour-in-chief, I never saw the southern gentry in casques even when they meant to fight. Their retainers sometimes bore helms, but only for cooking eggs.

Confusion never lasts long, particularly when it is to anyone's advantage. Once my cousin's dogs had run home, the hunting party was outnumbered six to one and being driven into the sewer, to the further risk of the fox.

At this moment, at whatever slant of the sun spelled breakfast time, Le Bourg's garrison woke up. Or one of them did. He came wandering outside to kick a few chickens and relieve himself on his neighbour's pig, when he saw the to him unbelievable sight of a hunt tussling with an army and so raised the alarm.

What he actually shouted was 'Rape! Rape!' followed by 'Rape!' again. It is a mighty word in its own right, and full of interest in the early morning. The poor man was neither blind nor a poet. He saw armoured horsemen in a wrestle with gentlefolk dressed in finery and petals. Naturally he thought the citadel had been penetrated, and the best of us dragged from sleep and now brought forth to a steamy conclusion. 'Rape!' he called again. How he explained the presence of our horses, only heaven knows. Most possibly he thought we had them with us in our beds, as menials will believe almost anything of their great ones.

De Montfort was just about to gather himself an armful of the flower of finest chivalry in Oc, and either twist it by the stalk or plant it in a deep vase, when this fellow's fellows rushed from their houses and began shooting arrows at his back.

The carnage caused by these opening volleys was widespread, particularly among the huntsmen, who were only wearing embroidery. But a number of the crusaders' horses were struck in the rump as well, and their squealing made this first passage of arms seem much more equal than it really was. Added to this was the fact that most of these crusaders had come here as a business venture; and there's a well-known governance among military men: *lose a soldier and save yourself his pay. Lose a horse and ride lighter by a shilling.* Nobody wished to lose coins from his purse, so the conflict abated.

I woke now, to find many people in the castle and most in the City already astir, what with the bawling, the baying and the running about of dogs. We had to dash some way through the streets, and then climb the tower of the Le Bourg Gate before we could see what was happening.

I asked for some pack-nags to be saddled, and shields and axes to be piled on their backs. This may seem presumptuous of me, coming from a young woman with wild hair, but I was known to be of the Trencavels and almost everybody else who was empowered to give commands or even offer opinions was outside with the hunting party. Truly, all the men of Carcassonne were ready to issue commands at that moment, but no-one, not even their wives, would listen to them. They shut up and moved briskly enough once my words stung their ear, just as cows go better for a sharp stick in the behind.

Persuading them to go with me was another matter. Still, my lord Ferblant rode along, at least as far as the gate; and wherever he went, the widowers who'd struggled after us from Béziers were sure to follow. Then there were the three young squires from Montady and Enserune, doughty men all, with only their lives to lose. These, to my surprise, were followed closely by six or seven old women, all without teeth and not one of them a day younger than thirty.

I questioned this.

'Whenever men do battle, there's killing,' one said. 'And whenever there's killing there's corpses.' She blew out her gums at me like a frog's bottom, as if the rest of her argument was self-evident. 'Whenever there's corpses, there's pickings,' she triumphed. 'And cleaning up pickings is what women's good at.'

So these fell in, as did Gibbu and the Mute. La Mamelonne was there, and so was Violette la Vierge (though whether the Fish Girl came along for pickings or from sheer empty-headedness I had no time to tell).

The gates bayed open, someone dropped a drawbridge, but with strict instructions to lift it up again afterwards, so out and over we trotted.

I was fifty paces into Le Bourg, and closer to death than that, before I realized that the packhorses the good men of Carcassonne had laden with so little protest belonged in fact to Solomon of Gerona. So he rode too.

'You're a Jew,' I protested. 'And Jews don't fight.'

'Certainly not on a Friday,' he agreed. 'But the sun's hardly up, and there's not a rabbi this side of Spain.'

As we spurred towards the skirmish, he drew an Arab sword of great length and beauty. 'I'll be the first Jew to die for a horse,' he said.

My cousin's hunters were just about to yield, or drown their steeds and kneecaps in a sewer. Only God in Heaven knew what such a choice would do to noblemen with the sensibilities of the Trencavels and the De Cabarets. Their mounts were thoroughbreds too.

The crusaders had their backs to us. We did nothing to encourage them to turn about, but spurred through them, over them, round them, and in all ways past.

It is a perennial topic of military controversy. Set a band of men equipped with chain-mail and swords against a foe furnished in embroidery and battleaxes, and who will prevail? We passed out the battleaxes, and then pressed ourselves into the ground behind them to await the answer to this conundrum.

In my experience, the crusaders were always the victorious ones, providing they kept their horses in a bunch and did not allow themselves to become distracted. There were distractions on this occasion. A haphazard rain of arrows and crossbow quarrels was falling on their horses' rumps. The same rain was dropping through our own party's teeth, so the odds were surprisingly even at the outset.

After a brutish five minutes of blood, mangled men and chargers with their heads parted in the middle, my cousin's people were able to make enough progress forward to allow us to wheel and retreat in good order.

De Montfort did not follow, whether from chivalry and prudence I cannot tell. This was to the good, as it took an age to persuade the townsmen in the City to lower the drawbridge and even longer to unbar the gates.

Once inside we congratulated ourselves. My cousin rewarded me with a kiss, and I clung to Ironface, Violette, Gibbu, the Mute and half of the garrison in turn. Ironface was difficult to kiss, but I kissed him. Old Pot-head's mask was hot on the lips, midway between the skin of a feverish child and Marie-Bise's big tureen just before she dropped in the tripes. But I clung to it till I thought my lips would burn off, such is the ardour of heroic affection.

Several of Count Raymond-Roger's vassals had been driven into the storm drain Le Bourg used as its principal sewer, or tumbled there having been unhorsed during the combat, or had rushed in seeking the fox (according to whose story I listened to). My cousin was decisive in these matters. He told them to burn their clothes, shave their heads and scrub hot wine into as much of the rest of themselves as they had brought home. This was too late to prevent the stink from being brought into the castle, which began to smell worse than the hot end of Reynard's tail.

This brisk morning's work did not earn a place in the Chanson, but then that noble lay fails to honour Simon de Montfort as playing any part in the Crusade until the siege of Carcassonne is well advanced, so you know what credence to lend to it. The Bastard is not sung, not by any name, nor is Solomon of Gerona, whose pack-nags were crucial to the rescue, nor is Bouchard de Marly's beard. So much for History!

If Truth rather than History is to have its say in this account, then I must observe baldly that the nobility of Oc, with my cousin its finest and prettiest flower, had just been rescued from the consequences of its own folly by a motley assortment of orphans, Jews, cripples and women.

I say nothing of the first three categories – you can find examples at any town's end – but once we ladies and lesser women came to play an active role in the conflict there could be no reining us in for the future. This was the first instance since the campaigns of Feminye (which were well before Mummy's time) when those doughty bare-breasted Amazons drew shaft and string across their lopsided chests, that we of the two-legged kind had brought succour and common sense to those of the three-legged variety, for all their prattling and prancing, and the undoubted heroism in their tails.

Nor do I except the endeavours of those half dozen or so toothless crones, who could probably boast all of one hundred and fifty summers between them. They had scurried forth as pillagers – a recognized profession in times of strife – but finding few dead men to strip, at least at the outset, had busily set about making some of their own with their corpse-hooks and snipping sheers.

Their work was not yet done. It transpired a mighty slaughter was afoot all unknown to us, while we of Raymond-Roger's party were refreshing our parched throats with spiced wine and cooling our other parts with scented oils, eaux-de-vie, crushed fruit and anything wet that was not water. The howling of this latest event reached us at last, so again we hurried to the towers overlooking Le Bourg, and sought ways to view it.

The battle from which we had fled had not stopped. Our people retreated, as did De Montfort's men who now rode away entirely. (We heard from our watchmen to the North that he had defeated Reynard – or some other fox – and hurried to make a present of its pelt and tail to Count Raymond of Toulouse, whose tent was full of tail and skin anyway.) Yet, in the absence of these warring bands, the townsmen of Le Bourg battled on, being left to fend for themselves with a much clearer view of things.

While my cousin had been shaking his fist at De Montfort, these doughty townsmen had saved the day by shooting off arrows. During our rescue, they had woken up in strength. Some two thousand of them now stood here and there, loosing their darts into their neighbour's wall, the next street, or – most properly – over the roof-tops towards where they fancied the action to be. 'At the ditch!' one shouted. 'It's at the ditch!' 'Along the ditch!', 'In the ditch!' the cry was taken up. So they loosed their arrows at the battle, those that had them. Those that hadn't, made some, or made some more. Those with crossbows soon ran out of quarrels, but – in the absence of their wives who would have been more cautious in such matters – made do by shooting off knives, skillets, knitting needles and pokers from the fire.

Unfortunately the storm dyke and sewer ran from one end of Le Bourg to the other. Their aim was often good but it was towards an imprecise aiming point. Very few of them shot themselves, but in the course of an hour or so huge numbers of them were stricken by the darts of friends elsewhere in town. Some dozen score were killed outright, particularly those transfixed by basting forks and ox-skewers, and as many more were left maimed and demanding the assistance of barbers, leech-gatherers, apothecaries and such-like healers of hurt. Thus does a war garner in its glorious dead.

'They should be encouraged to shoot all day,' Ironface observed. 'There'll be less mouths to feed.'

'Amen,' Solomon of Gerona said. Thus our two wisest heads were in concurrence.

The most happy outcome of this slaughter was the making of many more widows. The young women of Le Bourg stood with us on the ramparts of the Citadel and watched in amazement while their men killed one another, and then they became angry, and very suitable for deployment as warriors. Recent widows make the most doughty fighters of either sex. I knew this from experience. We already had several among the survivors from Béziers, and a dozen more as a result of drinking accidents in Carcassonne. Now we were gaining hundreds.

It was then that Simon de Montfort came back over the town wall. He wasn't in charge this time, but accompanied, preceded and superceded by Burgundy, Nevers and St Pol, a whole squadron of Bishops, and some thousands of their men.

'To horse,' Raymond-Roger shouted, with no thought of his safety.

'Wisdom should keep us here,' De Cabaret observed.

'My people are all outside.'

'Well, well, then, we must saddle up.'

The Crusade was a splendid sight, with its crosses painted on its cloth, and its mail catching the properly risen sun.

'It's a splendid sight,' I said to Ironface.

'And quite the safest side to be fighting on,' he complained. Just the same, he armed himself quickly enough, for a coward.

*   *   *

Much has been sung about the Battle of Le Bourg, which ought properly to be called the Second Battle of Le Bourg, but I do not propose to detain History further by feeding it with facts.

Once through the gate, our sally-party took a little time to assemble. In the end we drew ourselves up in two main battles – we of the nobility with our knights, gentlemen, and other mounted forces in one, and of course some thousand of yeomen on foot, all in shield and chain; and the generality of women in the other. Most of these bore only domestic armaments – ladles, meat-knives, fire-rakes and logs from the hearth – but their anger stood tall with them, and no-one in Trencavel's party felt safe to restrain them or persuade them to return home.

We rode and strode down. The townsmen were distracted by their shooting games, so did not anywhere bother to defend their wall, which was everywhere indefensible. Allowing for the riddle of the streets, it is my opinion that the opposing armies met halfway.

All the ballads agree that the skirmish lasted for two and three-quarter hours. I did not see it all, or even much of it, because I was fighting some of it. Corpses already littered the streets as we rode down. By the time we rode back, some streets were piled high with them, and for the first time since the Crusade was proclaimed, the north of France also gained widows and orphans.

We were by now well and truly divided among a maze of tiny lanes, walls, gardens, alleys, startled cats and sudden ambush, and it was not long before I found myself among a group of our women, in spite of my instinct to keep myself to the chivalry. In the space of two or three minutes – say the burning of a long straw or a short taper – I was to learn more about warfare than a knight-at-arms ever learns, or lives to speak about. Our widows and other town wenches, angry for their cottages and menfolk, simply fell upon the first organized column of crusaders and tore it apart. The crusaders saw us, hesitated while the married ones among them advised caution, and in their little moment of confusion we killed them. They screamed, of course, but a woman with children is used to a scream or two, and only too glad to pay somebody back for them.

Men-at-arms are at an immediate disadvantage when they fight ordinary citizens and peasants. When they encounter women in hand to hand – not to say hand to claw – combat they are in an even worse case, the knighthood and nobility, the whole priggish chivalry, most of all.

A trained man on horseback expects to meet sword, axe and lance, and nothing more. Whenever javelins and arrows begin to fly, he has foot-men to rush to catch them and send them back again, or at least get in their way. Sword, axe and lance he can absolutely thrive on, especially when used sparingly by gentlemen of similar gentility.

He is less prepared for an attack with pitchforks, log tongs, cattle-prods, branding irons, tree trunks, chains, limbs from the shambles, roof-tiles, hot ladles, stale turds, and clouds of pepper.

He is positively heroic against overhead cuts with a poleaxe, far less happy when someone sneaks beneath the belly of his horse and saws away at his saddle girth or feels for his bollocks with a vegetable knife, and women in general know their way around such things.

Time was what we were fighting for in Le Bourg – time for the townsmen to pick up themselves and their wounded, time for them, and then us, to withdraw in good order through an embattled gate.

I do not think there would have been enough time if it weren't for the women, and the speed with which we understood what was needed of us, principally our unbridled ferocity which kept us from harm if not from hurt.

A woman grows used to a little blood, what with the kitchen, childbirth and that other thing. Beyond these, she is always chopping or pricking her finger. So a battlefield, if anything, reminds her of home, and only makes her cry if she is foolish enough to be homesick. I remember whispering

214

together with an aging widow-dame of five and twenty, while we were straightening our swords. 'I've got ten children,' she said, 'all of them boys. It's good to come to war for some peace and quiet.' We went back to castrating crusaders.

I don't want to make too much of this. To hack a man by the cods is a terrible thing, and even worse by the bold bronze herrings, especially for the poor unfortunate concerned. But I can wholeheartedly recommend the adventure if you wish to disrupt an advancing phalanx of horsemen, as we did several times that day. It is not so much the damage achieved as the damage anticipated that yields such a robust splendour of result.

As an example, Merdun arrived on the scene about now, surrounded by the very louts who had done such damage to my home just a brief week earlier. 'Burn that witch!' he called when he saw me. 'Burn her and be – '

He was rolling his eyes and tossing his head and not exact with his glances, so it was several dozen of us, and not myself alone, who went howling at the Bastard and his men with a glittering assortment of knives, woodsaws, pig-picklers, meat-axes and bared teeth, as well as the two swords I have just mentioned.

No time to chop a thigh or cut a cullion. His retainers' horses rushed through us, past us, and away with them, to Merdun's total embarrassment. I might have had him to myself for a moment or two, but the Fish Girl set fire to his leggings with a ladle full of charcoal and caused him to follow them pell mell down the storm drain and into the River Aude.

How did so little gain so much? Women, as is well known, open their legs to allow a thread to pass through. A man slams his shut, be it against blade, ballister or hot lips. Slams them into one another and locks them together like a leather-cutter's vice with the wormwheel turned tight.

This is safe enough if he has nothing between them but sweat and warm air. If there's a horse in the way, or even a donkey, it jumps forward as if kick-started by a pair of hot

215

spurs. A nag is trained to recognize its master's knees. That's why it prefers to be ridden by a woman.

If they'd dismounted from their horses, some of these Northerners, they'd have made shorter work of us, or at least stayed edge to edge with us longer. Dismounted or set their bums atop some safe ones.

Forget the silly ballad about the palfrey and the destrier. The best battlenag is a carthorse, a rouncy. Otherwise a gelding is the advised mount. Unfortunately, a member of the chivalry is permitted none of these. He must go sensitive on a mare or frisky on a stallion, and it has to be a recognized pedigree of destrier, not a palfrey or a hunter.

I saw the folly of all this when a splendid body of horsemen came up the Road of the Tower as if they would carry the gate by the masculine force of their understanding. They brushed De Cabaret aside, forced their way past Raymond-Roger before the first cloud of rust had settled, then pushed through the retreating townsmen at the walk that leads to a charge, that awesome, stiff-legged gait a Norman Englishman calls *pace*. I believe they belonged to Crépin de Rochefort or even one of the dukes. There was only us left to halt them, and not enough of us by ten.

They should have come on geldings. As it was, La Mamelonne ran down an alley with a shovelful of straw and mare's menstrual blood. She came out between some cottages behind the third row of the crusader's cavalry, and smeared a few of their chargers' rumps with the stuff, irrespective of their sex. No one clubbed her head. They took her for a gypsy, bringing them good luck. Not wishing to trust too long on her own, she tossed the rest of her shovelful high in the air, taking care to run before it settled back again.

The entire cohort fell to whinneying, dribbling, kicking up their heels and mounting one another up and down the town like the bullfrogs in my dream or flies on the dung of harvest. The lucky riders fell off and had their throats cut.

The unlucky ones were pinned between a nag's back and a stallion's belly.

We did cut their throats, I'm afraid, or some of us did when we could stop ourselves laughing. We did in fact stop quite quickly, because those of us who weren't recent orphans were recent widows, and there's no-one so close to tears and generally quick tempered as a recent widow. A man makes most women bad-tempered anyway, as Mummy would testify, but to have a husband killed midway through an argument in which he says he will be perfectly safe fighting and she says he will be far better off hiding among her brooms and cleaning rags increases a wife's anger substantially. Assemble a half hundred or so of such women and it is simple to encourage them to use these same brooms and rags as bludgeons and firebombs. They'll go on boiling soup, no doubt, but with a huge preference for tipping it over heads.

My cousin came up to congratulate us, and I had no further difficulty in persuading him of our usefulness. He had a cool brain in the mornings. Being married himself, he also seized immediately on the dangers inherent in using women as warriors – namely that we need to be pointed carefully in the right direction, as our inclination is to kill all men equally.

Fortunately he had a task to distract us. It may seem unfeeling of this scion of the Trencavels to launch his kinswoman and vassal-widows on an armed sortie, but the fact is that most people killed in close-quarter sword-play die from tripping over their own legs, and this was hardly likely to happen to us. He knew us for the nimble creatures we were and are.

'That house at the end of the street,' Raymond-Roger whispered. 'It belongs to old Xavier Goulue, the vintner. If we can push that far, or any one of us, I want us to set a torch to it.'

No murmurs of disapproval at burning the drink, or not many, not from women experienced in what wine does to men.

217

'I've held back from doing this,' he explained. 'But we've enough grape in the Citadel to keep us full of swagger. There's all manner of barrel ends in there, and two centuries of leas-drippings. Old Xavier swears he's aqua-vitae a-plenty to blow up all of Oc, and we've got trouble enough with the diarrhoea already.' He paused and said, 'Any questions?'

'You talk too much,' a corpse-stripper said.

I thought La Mamelonne would hold back from such a venture, but she said spirits were only useful at childbirth, and she wasn't pregnant yet. Meanwhile we had to charge down a street full of armoured crusaders determined to march up it.

Women are different from men, the poet says. They have one less limb but contain more surprises.

The crusaders had our lack clearly in mind. We had warriors on foot to contend with, ever the dangerous ones. As Mummy used to say, 'There's little harm a man can do while he's sitting on his horse.' This lot were eyeing us and the City walls behind us, and were clearly intent on clambering over one or the other of us as soon as possible, with or without ladders.

The surprise we were full of this time was to charge them just as they thought they were stalking us. 'Remember to cover your noses, ladies!' La Mamelonne called, as she and some several hundred of us ran at them with a shriek. It was timely advice.

When you strike a man's armour, even half-heartedly, you send up a great cloud of rust and dust which you hope will fill his eyes but stay out of your own. Many of the bravest warriors blink as they swing their swords, not from fear of retribution, but to save blearing their gaze and pricking their lids with the consequence of success.

Our shriek infected these fellows with such a confusion that we didn't need to strike them often. A woman is supposed to run away when she screams, or cower in the corner – ask any man – not dash ahead and mow people off at the knees with a half-sword; and the women with proper weapons did tend to

218

strike low, because of their weakness of wrist, and in places a trained man was not taught wards or parries to protect. Those ladies armed with scullery-irons were less predictable, and my own slight Spanish sword and corn-heaving forearms could knock off a head whenever the impulse took me – which was not infrequently since I left the Mill.

The crusaders opened rank before us partly from surprise, more certainly because they knew themselves to be formed up in depth. Some of them – the bachelors, no doubt – mistook our charge for panic even so late in their education, and assumed we were attempting to break out of Le Bourg and run away as fast as our limber white legs would carry us. They gave ground the better to engulf us.

I hadn't been inside a house since leaving St Thibéry, and very comfortable it was until La Mamelonne set fire to it with a ladle full of charcoal such as some of them were carrying, and the Fish Girl torched it accidentally by dancing through the parlour and knocking something over. Flinging oneself about in such a place is as dangerous as introducing a dragon into a pepper mill. 'Get her out of here,' La Mamelonne said. 'One breath of that cordial, and she'll sneeze fit to suck the roof on top of us, and there's enough here to make her fart as well.' Thus do whores pay pretty compliments to one another.

Old Xavier's casks were full of wonderful stuff, whether ullage or spillage or flammable air. The first one broached burned with a clear blue flame like angels' wings. There was no time to enjoy another.

'Come on, ladies,' Mamelie cried, granting title where none was due. 'If we don't leave now we'll fry like woodcocks in the honey ... Pick up a skin and a baling spoon as you go, girls!'

She was carrying a twist of burning tallow, doubtless with some nun's hair at the core of it – this vintner Goulue afforded nothing but the best – and she glittered among us with a wicked look in her eye.

Some of the enemy had followed some of us in, and some of us were keeping some of them out, or others as the case might be, but we had nothing further to fear from the foot-weary legions. They retreated as men always will once the fire reaches cooking heat. Our problem now was a fresh arrival of horses and such eminences as sat upon them – warm wine and hot women being potent bringers-up of the nobility, especially when their swords are sharp and they can feel the sun on their thighs.

They arrived in several dozens that may well have been hundreds – until my hands encountered Nano in the crush, I could see only legs, and a horse has more of these than a man and moves them more quickly. Then I swung myself astride and came face to face with one of those rascals who had given Mummy such a poking and prodding. He was hardly quality, no doubt, but momentarily he was all I saw, both from the pressure of History and because he was already half-unbuckled and showing us women brown legs, brown arms and brown everything, this being the way Merdun's men preferred to fight.

La Mamelonne recognized him for what he was, if not who. She knew him to be in need of forgiveness, so at once dashed him with a baler of holy water.

He screamed. The monster screamed, and that was music. Old Xavier's aqua fortis was too much for his sunburn. All these Northerners have lily skins, whatever colour they go in the South. He shook himself about as it trickled under his mail. He was spread astride a horse so it found all of his ticklish places and he reached accordingly. His fellows laughed, or recoiled at the tang of spirit and hot leg he was giving off, so were enough distracted for La Mamelonne to slip forward and set fire to the brew.

This cured his sunburn, and his horse, if equus can ever be cooked on the full gallop. We caught eight or nine others in this way, knights, squires, or footmen on each other's backs the better to gain a view. Then we retreated from the confusion we had caused.

*   *   *

I haven't concealed the fact that we were losing the Battle for Le Bourg. Indeed, we were almost the only people still fighting it. Its walls were always indefensible, and Raymond-Roger's aim in prolonging the skirmish was simply to allow the townsmen to salvage their pride and arms then retreat in good order to the Citadel.

History hasn't treated him kindly in this. You know what I think of History. It even suggests that by deploying us, his fullness of women, beyond the City gates he was seeking to do no more than reduce the surplus. This is a calumny. Whatever he was as a warrior – and I believe he was a great one – there was nothing underhand about my cousin. He was too spiritual a man ever to pursue an untruth. Indeed, he was soon to take the way of the *Consolamentum* and the *Endura*, and become spirit entire in his quest for the good.

He did not command his women. The women were their own and commanded themselves. Whoever gave orders to a widow in the tower of her grief? Hers is a lonely, high place that no words can reach. Whoever, come to that, heard of commanding a corpse-stripper?

These were not pleased at our setting men on fire. It ruined the value of their corpses, they complained, by melting rings, chapping purses, and scarring knife-handles. A man's small-cloths were never the same after he'd been burned in them, they said, and quite unsaleable, even after washing. The body, too, was often 'spoiled in its intrinsics'. This last was chilly news, so I reduce the woman's phrase verbatim. While some of these ladies pillaged trinkets, others apparently took anatomical parts to sell to witches, apothecaries, and Raymond de Brousses. They also collected skin for the great monasteries, many of whose books were bound in the stuff.

One should never gossip on a field of battle, even while retreating. I had dismounted, and was leading my horse out of kindness to those who had none, when we were surrounded by crusaders in their hundreds, then in their thousands, and lastly by what seemed their whole army. They were reluctant to overwhelm us for fear of crushing one another, but it was clear we could not reach the Le Bourg Gate into the Citadel a short way behind us. Nor could its drawbridge be lowered, for fear of repeating the very error that had led to the demise of Béziers.

Men began to point me out, so I mounted Nano again in order to have a clearer view of them. I'd heard one of the corpse-strippers wondering whether to offer me to them for a ransom, or even for straight profit. Mummy had always insisted to me that a woman is far safer with her bottom planted on a horse than she'll ever be with it settled on a daisy, so aloft I swung and wheeled hither and thither about.

The enemy cheered. They cheered my hair, my sword, and the way I sat Nano, who was my only King and consequently well beneath me. They also cheered because I am a pretty young woman, as I occasionally reminded myself, and because some knew me to be a Trencavel and because I was undoubtedly current. Wherever the Crusade was, there was I, Bastard or no Bastard. So they cheered and, very gently, set about catching me.

I fought. We all fought. We were used to fighting. Our side did very well. Being all circular as we were, they could only come at our circumference, and that limited their advantage over us. So we shouted and chopped at one another. A sword fight is all shouting and chopping. Having a high, feminine voice I prefer to leave my foe to do the shouting, while I get on with the chopping. Such a singularity of purpose gives me the edge.

Did I wear armour? The Chanson speaks of me as if the only armour I wore was a chastity belt. Let me say just this. If I wear armour you shall hear about it. As to whether or not I wore a chastity belt, ask my horse.

After a few moments' blade to blade with me they fell back and howled, none of them deeply hurt, but with chops and chins looking like a bad morning at the barber's. Only one of them came to real harm, and that was when a fellow aimed a mighty blow at me and removed his neighbour's head instead. Even so, we were losing. Our brave little band was melting

222

round the edges. Put a group of women among a horde of men, and the occasional widow will invariably become nibbled off.

Another cheer, more mighty than the one which had greeted my leap to saddle, and again I had breathing space. One moment I was confronting the entire Crusade single-handed with just a few hundred helpers, the next these inconstant Northerners had discovered a fresh attraction, the way louts will at a fair.

A pair, or – as farmers would say – a team, of gigantic breasts were bobbing up and down like oxen on a drag-shaft, only moving with a vigour far beyond anything possible to ox, bull, or stallion as they frisked moist-nosed at the heart of the battle and cleared or rather *cleaved* a space for themselves at the very centre of things, the way breasts will when they present themselves naked among thirsty men, and bring the rest of their woman briskly behind as she strives to retain a grip on their halter and keep the rest of her body up with them.

I was as astonished as any man facing us to see a woman without clothes, alone and cheerful on a battlefield, or rather the breasts of the woman cheerful and unalone, having one another and the rest of her for company. Unlike the enemy, however, I was possessed of an explanation. I had seen those breasts before.

They could only belong to my friend and miracle Mamelie la Mamelonne, one breast Mamelie, one La Mamelonne, with her heart and belly attached to them like tuns on a tumbril, the whole woman running through Le Bourg and drawing the enemy laughing and panting behind her. They galloped in a circle, then ran towards the flood plain of the River Aude with half the Crusade in pursuit.

This was not the end of it. No sooner was she going – they going, she gone – than there came a mad, strained cry. Had Violette la Vierge been banished from Ironface's bed? For here she was, *dancing again*, prancing through the streets equally nude and brazen all below, though naturally whiter-skinned, tighter-bosomed than Mamelie, and slighter round the parts that overhang the legs as she afforded the sunshine an unabashed view of her wishbone and fin.

Poor, mad little Fishtail. If the men had all been Merdun's she might have got away with it, or got away with something. Alas, there were other men there, men like the Bastard's brother, who saw no need for prancing women until well beyond sundown. He, or someone like him, called for archers to shoot her.

Here was a pretty sight, and a most enchanting prospect. It halted the war entirely. To see a hind run before arrows is most lively entertainment. To see a naked woman brought down, and she scarcely more than a girl, is an even more intriguing *divertissement*, whether by volley or at a venture.

Praise God they'd brought no crossbows, or the climax would have been immediate. But their ballisters were all in bed with their arbalests, as was the Count of Toulouse, so they had to make do with the more traditional forms of toxophily, and thus give themselves, and the Fish Girl, a much longer run, allowing her perhaps another half a minute to live (I could hear La Mamelonne's parts returning, but surely not in time to save her?).

Forward stepped the Duc of St Pol's archers, forward then a half-step again. What a bold sight they made, as they spread their shoulders to shoot! These were all longbowmen of the old persuasion, each his own fletcher and arrowsmith, each man a master of cutting and feathering, a magician of wicked flight. They spread, they spread, they spread – yet none pulled so wide as Gibbu. Nor, in the end, could they shoot.

The naked Fish Girl had a most interesting effect on them, they being without women, she being a woman and more, with each little nook and cranny of her, as well as each point of vantage, wobbling and warbling about, themselves already warmed and put in the mood for wobbling by the stampeding parcels and particles of the lovely La Mamelonne.

An unstrung old-fashioned longbow is as high as its man and a whole hand more. Strung, it offers a powerful disincentive to priapism. An archer masks his forearm in a brassard against the fret and chafing of his bowstring. Lower down, he keeps the rest of himself well tucked in, and he learns to protect it with prudence and common sense.

These men could no longer shoot, or not persistently or at range, and nowise in a volley. Just as an Amazon was unable to clear her breast with her string, so had it cauterized by her mother in girlhood, so these fellows dared not pass their tented tunics and orgulous crotches with their bottom six inches of ashplant, or not with certainty, not even when their bows were cobbled from strips of yew instead. They loosed off a dart or two, but uncertain as straws in an adverse wind. The Fish Girl laughed at them and went skipping on.

His pole is only a part of an archer's worry, and so it was here, and this further depressed their aim. When a man stands forth, his problem is to know what stands forth after, so bowmen assure me. A man's prick (as the cattle drovers call it) is only there as a kind of fence peg or prop to save his balls (as our town urchins hold them) from becoming involved in catastrophe. Heart-rending indeed for an archer to find his white-meats and nether breads entangled in a bowstring – almost as complicated an agony as catching them in a harp.

It was against a background of such considerations that the Fish Girl was able to dance away from the feeble droop of their arrows. Several darts transfixed her clothing even so, at great damage to my surcotte, but that was spread out by the City moat to air and herself naked as a skate in mudtime, though not so brown or spotty.

Meanwhile La Mamelonne's heralded and frequently applauded return to us was approaching its grand climacteric, by which I mean the great panting gallop of her breasts sometimes ahead, sometimes above, sometimes below the no-less-plunging frenzy of her knees, with her smiling face in the midst of all and her hair involving everything, including her naughty places, which also smiled. No wonder there came a halt to our fighting. How could men's eyes avoid her, or their brains compete? When she was on the move she presented such a glitter of nostril, nipple and kneecap, each of them with its dimple, that she caused them more excitement than a quintet of racing stallions in a pen. When she stopped, she was as I say all hair and urchin freckles, from the great blonde haycock on her head to the under-branch darkness of the rest of her, as she flaunted her vistas like an endless succession of armpits.

Constance de Coulobres had spoken to me of Chimera, the mythical beast of the ancients with its oddly assorted parts. The lady of Coulobres was as near to being a scholar as a woman may be, having held an abbot's ring in childhood and examined his monastic scrolls. She often narrated the wonders of a being which spoke fire through its nostril, and for the rest was but leg and tail. La Mamelonne was such a miracle, but more beautiful and more splendid. Had Chimera appeared, or the Eagleman, or the Dragon, our fight would have gone on. But we had La Mamelonne, the Fish Girl, and then *mirabile dictu et mirabile visu*, as ecclesiastic lechers say, La Mamelonne again!

Her effect on our own people was terrible, even on our citizen militia, but remember they had drunk no fresh water for a week, nor in their whole lives, some of them. I do believe that it was the sight of her breasts, coupled – if I may use such a word – with the saintly serenity of her eyes, that caused my cousin to turn in his last days to God. If men could have broken rank they would have fallen on their knees and worshipped La Mamelonne then. Light began for them with her nakedness. When she covered the sweat in her navel there was darkness.

I have spoken of the ferocity of we women, which came from sprinkling our anger on our sadness. To see so many of their archers standing forward with their parts more forward again, and thus preventing their first move to shoot, this filled us with a terrible rage.

'Charge!' one of our corpse-cutters shrieked. 'Charge and strike low!'

The first row of bowmen turned into the second, and

collapsed their cod-poles into each other to the owners' considerable detriment. A proud stand of belly lances became a sorry push of pike. The Crusade was briefly undone. The townsmen we women were protecting regained the City Gate, with Violette dancing ahead of them, La Mamelonne still naked, but bearing our gratitude and dressed in her pride.

The portal was, unfortunately, closed before the last of us were quite within.

Only the boldest of the women and the bravest of the men now stood with us. Although this description accounts for most of our female warriors, it does not include many others, so our tally was small as the enemy backed us into the gateway and our garrison leant overhead to drop slops on them. I was learning war slowly, and the clearest lesson I bore from the skirmish by the wall is that stale soup is an abominable weapon, and stones are even less productive than dumplings if they fall on the wrong side.

Our foe were a constant surprise to me, largely because there were so many of them, and all different like chess-pieces. Our current assailants gnatted at us with such an abundance of swords and such-like points that they might have been a walking cheval de frise or one of those iron hedgehogs with which engineers line the tops of towers. The surprise was not their ardour – like us they were hungry for lunch – but their strange dark faces. These weren't Northerners on the quarantine, but trained men from Lombardy or Aragon, or some such distant place. Nor had they come because they enjoyed war. They were here because they knew about it, and I soon began to wish they were somewhere else.

They carried embossed shields, rather like Spanish trays. They didn't hold them out for us to hit, but kept darting from behind them with terrible flourishes of carnage.

If your battle lacks inspiration, then you must look to forethought. As the townspeople of Le Bourg had been stampeding through the portal behind us, Ironface had strewn

227

the whole area with dried nettles which had been kept to fodder goats. There were all manner of such flammables and chewables hereabouts, and our saviour now torched them with a flambeau, I think the cresset cone that burned night and day by the gate.

Our enemies drew back in a stench of singed leggings. One of them grabbed at the torch, as if eager to set fire to himself, and as he executed this gesture Ironface removed him with a sword.

Our horses were pretty hot about the hoof by now. So were the women who clung to their stirrups. Nobody liked running forward again, but even Nano knew he couldn't trot through a wall, or leap over this one, so once more our foe fell away before us, some howling, some coughing, some stepping back from the stink of old soup and other such ordures that our friends had cast down from above and which now cooked with the crusaders among the hot nettles.

Here Simon de Montfort at last achieved a proper mention in the ballads, long after Ironface, myself and La Mamelonne. As we burst through the ring of dark faces to encounter their army proper, one of his gentlemen fell off his horse in front of us, and De Montfort swept him on to his own. This undoubtedly saved the man from losing his finery to our corpse-pickers.

We rode in a circle before the Le Bourg Gate, while they shot arrows at us. Then we shook ourselves into some kind of brisker gallop towards the river, hoping to regain the City by the postern behind the Barbican.

This would have been the coward's stratagem, so I am glad it did not work. Only those with horses could have come that way. Our women urged us to leave them, knowing their town better than we, and thinking to hide there; but no-one can hide in a battle any more than at a wedding, so I am glad we stayed close to them.

This was because our retreat was frustrated by the re-emergence of Merdun de Montfort's party from the Aude, where their recent misfortunes had propelled them. They had taken the opportunity, some of them, to slip from their armour and rinse their smallpieces, obeying the dictum that a warrior must maintain his principal weapons in a thorough state of readiness.

Their advance not only barred our way down the only lane open to us, it brought me tooth to tooth with Shitface himself. As I rode through the flames then wheeled in front of them, the Bastard shouted, 'Not even burning will stay that witch, not though we hang her in gibbets and bonfires. When we catch her, we'll flay her alive, her and the devil she rides with.'

So are great reputations made, by the tongues of reprobates and men who spit in wine. Meanwhile, since there was no riding round Merdun, I resolved to go through him. Now seemed as good a time as any to cut him from his horse and avenge Mummy and the good miller I called Daddy.

I spurred up to him, right knee to right knee, and for a very brisk moment he found my Spanish sword too lively for him, while Nano, perhaps recognizing the smell of his horse, was content to dance a jig with it, much as Ironface's had done a week or so earlier.

The Bastard was not the man to lose a fight, nor to let somebody else win one, especially a woman. He pushed me away with his shield and called in a loud voice for the Crusade to arrest me.

The Crusade was unwilling to do so. As so often when heroic deeds are being done and History written, the commonality of mankind is content to watch.

'Pah!' said Merdun. 'I gain nothing by vanquishing a woman.'

'And lose everything by being vanquished by her.' I stuck my sword in my scabbard and rode on past him right up to one of his fellows. If he thought I was done with jousting he was mistaken. There was an axe there I recognized and had come seeking out. I caught it from his hand and twirled it overhead. Its edge was dull and stained. If Daddy's life blood still disfigured it, so much the better. Pray God his force dried into the blade as well, mightier than querns or millraces. I turned and struck the Bastard such a blow as would cut a dynasty in half.

He neither ducked under it nor lifted his shield. I believe, in truth, he aimed to cut me beneath my uplifted arm, forgetting the axe in his contempt for the sex that wielded it.

I could chop wood. I could flog a donkey. With battleaxes my aim was poor. I missed Merdun's face, I missed shoulder, forearm and knee, perhaps because I aimed at the sneer that floated off from him. Instead, I smote his horse and cleaved it clean in two, parting head from body at the deep end of the neck.

It walked with him a little, then they tumbled both together. As they did so, I heard a terrible cry arise from among the crusaders, the one they were prompt with whenever anyone got the better of them. 'Witchcraft!' they whispered. They did not shout it aloud, but if ten thousand tongues hiss at once, even the breath of lizards sounds like barking.

So what had I achieved, as I stuck my heels into Nano's belly? Immortality, of course, coupled with the further miracle of our women being drawn up the walls in harness two dozen at a time. When a town is prepared for a siege, it has its sheep-cranes all ready. The crusaders were distracted by seeing a man on a headless horse, so the shepherds of Carcassonne were able to put theirs to immediate employment.

Meanwhile, Merdun's men were behind me, and the lane to the Aude lay open. Even as I realized this, I heard horsemen moving through the streets and lateral alleys that cut across it.

My way was barred by some score of tidy men on tidy palfreys who held their swords towards me like so many crucifixes. One took a pace or two forward, but kept a tight hold on his steed's mane, in case he had to salvage its head. 'Tell me your name, Sorceress.'

'My name is Perronnelle,' I announced.

'I have heard men speak of one such, a heretic from among the Trencavels.'

'No heretic, by Saint Mary.'

'Even your own faith says that the Devil made women. By such small light shall we burn you.'

I was about to retreat, but all journeys backward are squalid. 'I have been a victim of the rape of St Thibéry, and a spectator at the massacre at Béziers. At Carcassonne I propose to be active for my family.'

'So what does that mean, Whore of the Night?'

'If any villain or knight-at-arms dare come to me sword in hand – or brandishing his other weapon – he can expect me to mash him in the face with whatever blade I can lay my hands on, including this axe.' I swung it flat, spattering them with horse blood. It was well I did so, for I struck iron behind me at the finish to my swing, having caught the belly chain of one among many who had stolen up on me. There was only an alley to go down, so I did.

I slid poor Nano on his knees round a corner, and then on his belly – a manoeuvre no stallion could tolerate – only to find myself in the midst of another troop. One caught at my bridle, so I cut him across the mouth. Then each of them snatched at part of me, principally my horse, and around we all went as they tugged to unseat me.

It is never easy to be a woman in such a circumstance, because of the disgusting ways in which men behave even while you are trying to kill them. One made as if to test the varnish on my saddle by sliding his hand straight between my legs. 'Push your face under here,' he called to his squire, 'and you'll have a beard in no time.'

This is a common recipe for baldness, too common some would say, but I am not an apothecary, so I sliced through his armour at the elbow, and I suppose his arm as well, because his hand clung to me for some hours afterwards, occasioning comment. The rest of them, not in the least deterred by losing a tooth and a forearm between them, set about dragging me from Nano's back.

Whereupon there came a scream rather than a shout, and Ferblant rode out of nowhere with a couched lance which removed someone's head and carried it for twenty paces before his body caught up with it again. La Mamelonne, Gibbu and the Mute charged behind him.

Ironface was a terrible sight, and already sung about often, so my murderers broke and fled, leaving me a forearm for a saddle and Old Tin Legs himself with a head on his spike, with most of its body attached to it.

He cleaned his lance, and we retreated towards the Citadel in our turn. 'I wanted a new head,' he said regretfully, 'and I'm in need of a body, but these were too dead to be of service to me.'

Not so the severed arm. It kept up an agitation with the fingers which in other circumstances might have been pleasurable. As it was, I was in no mood for such fancies. I had a Phantom to consider, and my memories of his naked body bathing made my nights more than fatiguing. Fighting would be sufficient for my daytimes. You think those thoughts as you rise up a wall in a sheep-basket. My brain only had space for one more. It was this.

The last time I had been roped over space in such company, and against such a city wall, the place had been incinerated within an hour. Was this an omen, or had I lived so long my life would now repeat itself?

Caput Continues

And tells how we were beset back as well as front and front as well as back not only by Count Cunning of Toulouse but also by the Spanish King of Aragon yet wore cushions on our arm and threw widows in their teeth.

very great battle must have its chapter, men say. A caput each time you draw a sword. In wartime, breath itself is a battle, and despair may be found even beneath a woman's skirts.

My first move on passing over the City wall was to dust myself free of sheep oil and embrace my companion Lord Tin, press Gibbu to my bosom and lastly the Mute, all of these having levitated with me, then call loudly for wine.

I daresay men brought me some, or offered what they had, but the cup was interrupted on its way to my lips by such a neighing and a clattering, such a whinneying, a winching and a cursing as ears will ever hear.

My lovely Nano came floating over the wall in his turn, as did the three other horses, all on cords so thin that men on the other side could only admire the sorcery of their flight, and refrain from shooting at them lest they cast their shafts into a miracle.

To hoist a horse atop a wall is one thing – he will perch there as proud as a weather-vane on a roof or a cockbird on the back feathers of his bride – but try to fly Pegasus down again and you'll encounter a dimmer matter. I had to lead Nano around the battlements almost unto the castle before he could acknowledge a stairway gentle enough to step down, and then deign to descend. Similarly with the other steeds. There wasn't a destrier among them. Although valiant as centaurs they weren't built for climbing chimneys, being more like sausages on legs, and they slunk along the parapet like bedbugs above a candle.

What with his fear of flying, and perpetual terror of falling, Nano was a sausage that quickly lost his stuffing, making me once again praise the holy design of nature that causes mankind to lead horses by their noses rather than their tails.

To have strode by Nano's north end at such a moment (if you can picture the City map and plot our aerial peregrination upon it) would have been more stupid than planting your head in a heifer's bottom to cure your hair of dandruff – effective, but foolish. Those who stepped behind me, alas, had mine or some other liquefactive quadruped in front of them, and I prayed God they wore clogs rather than slippers upon their feet. As it was, we all walked fast to avoid becoming statues.

You don't often encounter horse dung above a battlement – men and squirrels being the more usual animals to find themselves without time to run downstairs – so the droppings and stalings of our assorted flyers are given an undue prominence in the ballads, and all subsequent disaster attributed to them.

However that may be, we were all of us downstairs before even the quickest of troubadours had opened himself a quatrain, let alone closed one up. We stood with our feet firmly planted on the flagstones of my cousin's barony, bestowed according to rank and with wine cup in hand, and contemplated the very paradox with which I opened this chapter: the unpleasantnesses that lurk even beneath a woman's skirting.

'You are playing with something in your skirts,' my cousin accused.

'Somebody's got to.' La Mamelonne was sitting like a queen in the eagle-legged, lion-headed chair that belonged to Raymond-Roger's mother in her lifetime and, until now, in death. She rummaged beneath her hems and showed him one of her magic cards, then another and another, some of them on vellum, several on wood or slate, so bright and bold in their colouring that the depictures on them moved.

'What witchcraft or tarot-toc is that?' my cousin asked. His wounds were only scratches, and such cuts make men irritable.

'Visions and curses which I had from Raymond de Brousses.'

My cousin reached for a card.

'Dogskin gave me these,' she said.

'De Brousses is a gentleman,' Raymond-Roger countered.

'How do you tell a gentleman in Oc?' Ironface inquired.

'He lost a horse to me at dice.' My cousin turned his hand. His card was made of stone and showed a riven tower by a dried-up stream. As we watched it, the tower took fire and was hideously burning, scorching my cousin's fingers so he dropped the card from his hand. He kicked it back to La Mamelonne, who muffled it in her skirt. 'You bring me Béziers too late,' he said. 'There it was my brethren ate cinder tarts.'

A great cry followed this. 'Castellare!' men called. 'The enemy has breached Le Castellare.'

The axe was still wet with the Bastard's horse, my sword blade not yet dulling to rust. I went to find Nano, who I prayed was empty.

'Doesn't your arm ache?' La Mamelonne asked as I stumbled to horse.

'I thought I might pad it with a scarf or else a bandage.' Even in war our talk is of apparel.

'Don't bind your arm beneath your shield,' La Mamelonne advised. 'Use a quuushshn.'

'What's a quuushshn?'

'Something that I can't spell,' she said. 'If you can find one in the castle, it will be softer than a cushion and plumper on your arm.'

I couldn't find a quuushshn, or even a quishan which is how the English write it. The cushion I did find served me very well. I didn't use it to stuff a man-sized shield but a small practice-buckler. Let the men be brutal. I could be fast, which is a woman's way, or La Mamelonne's way. ('Fast and always first, if you're to gain any pleasure in life,' she was forever saying. I never understood her advice as offered, but in a fight it made excellent sense, and many was the poor fellow I finished with before he'd even got his weapons unbuckled. I wasn't a murderess. Just a simple gash across the nose was enough to send most of them snivelling back to their wives

237

in the North of France to make sure they still had their sense of smell. If they wore an old-fashioned helmet with a nose-spike I used to cut off their chins, which was crueller because several of them didn't have any, and not so much as a whisker between my sword and their Adam's apple.) Such speech is a prolepsis, however, which of all figures is a cold one, according to Constance de Coulobres. Le Castellare by contrast was hot.

Even we women sweated worse than horses, and our steeds themselves were in a terrible case, as if made of froth, as indeed most of God's creatures are, and far more agreeable than dust on a warm day. But by this time, everyone in Carcassonne was a skeleton or even thinner, what with perspiration and this other matter I and the historians keep on coming towards.

Raymond-Roger had no salt. The crusaders had salt, but not us. While the Trencavels had ridden hunting, the great ones of the North had set Simon de Montfort to collect my cousin's vassals. He had also secured my cousin's salt at Capestang, which is good for nothing but salt. We had more meat to spread it on than the crusaders, but no salt to spread.

This meant that our skins were for ever wet and our bowels unstoppered. A moist forehead does not make for courage, and a man who cannot avoid leaking on his leggings is of little use as a warrior. Once his fundament is ajar, or even half-unlatched, he'll shy from the shadow of his own horse, and who can blame him?

My cousin began to assemble his saltless ones beyond the Gateway of Le Castellare. 'They stink of defeat!' he cried. 'So what use is the charge? I can smell their fear from here.'

'They smell of shit,' I advised him, in my best mill tongue. 'And that is not always the same thing.'

'I shall ride beside your cousin the Lady of Saint Thibéry,' Roger de Cabaret said. 'That way I shall breathe only lavender water and the flowers of the valley.'

'Wait!' La Mamelonne commanded.

'What will you do?' my cousin scoffed. 'Show me a lily flower painted on a card? Or bring me a sniff of Dogskin?'

Whoring is a resourceful trade. Its pursuit, for a woman, is rather like the act of love for a man. It doesn't take much to begin, but a great deal to keep it up. It needs the wizardry of its furnishings, and so it was now. Not every bulge beneath La Mamelonne's cotte was Mamelie herself, not even the best ones. She went beneath her skirts and, in answer to my cousin, brought forth not cards but a wine-skin full of perfumed water, that she used to keep herself and Pipi sweet, and to flavour her customers' beards. She sprinkled this liberally round our lads and their mounts so we no longer stank of fear but rode forth smelling like a courtship bower or the herb store of a great house.

This confused the enemy mightily. They didn't know whether to fight us or fuck us, and not a few of them were strewn about the alleyways in consequence.

There was little derring-do in Le Castellare, and even less chivalry. What I chiefly remember is that we rode at the crusaders just as they rode at us. I found myself going forward into a lane too narrow to hold more than a fragment of the battle, no more revealing than a single ribbon unravelled from a tapestry. Then I was driven back by a big fellow with a mass of chain on his chest.

This was no good for a weak-wristed woman to feel his heart through, so I parted his face with my battleaxe. Then I saw a great, red-headed lout who had a lance halfway through the top of his body. He ran two or three anxious footsteps to the front, completely at odds with himself, just like a chicken with the croup. I don't know what became of him, but I doubt if it was very much more.

'Mama!' one was calling, which is the English for *maman* or, as I say, mummy. How dared he remind me of her! I gave him Daddy's axe to taste. It quieted him on the instant. Then I combed a couple more through the chest.

This chain-mail is in no way so good as a castle wall, even

though it feels twice as heavy. A link sufficiently thick to turn aside a sword is bound to have holes big enough to admit the first inch of a knife, or the painful part of a spear. Arrows simply slip through a soldier's armour like truth through the eye of a needle, and the shafts from a longbow pop out the other side. I've seen men lying dead, or feeling far from well, with half a dozen spikes growing from them. Men who have been shot through like this, and turned into so many short-spined hedgehogs, make a battleground a highly dangerous place to plant your feet. All the chain-mail does for an arrow is to make it impossible to draw out.

These events came scrambled upon me, so that is how I remember them. In truth, the breaching of Le Castellare, and the to-and-fro screaming of its women all about us, took my cousin and even the cool-headed Roger de Cabaret by surprise. The walls were so strong here, the defence accounted to be so determined, that not even the children of the suburb had been taken into the City. As we formed up, then gathered again, these were for ever underfoot with the cats and the chickens. None fell beneath the hoof, and that was a matter of miracle, but each time we charged they were with us, then rushing through our ranks like storm water in a drain or the streams that tumble off Alaric.

Their mothers found them at last, and shepherded them into huddles, their mothers and those old men whose backs were too weak for the main business of life, which today was killing. Then they were guided into the invincible fastness of the City itself, through the Razès Gate.

Meanwhile, the young unmarried women were of use to us, gathering up arrows and stones.

'Bad luck to use your enemy's flights,' I heard Ironface grumble.

'Worse still to find his barb in your own gut,' Gibbu said. He tore his captured arrows by their beaks just the same, and rid them of their points so that they would bounce off stone and take the enemy's oncoming horses in the belly. 'At a hundred paces there's no need for barbs,' he said to me, as if War was to be my trade and I must learn its craft and press my lips to its mystery. 'At such a distance I could shoot a feathered stick through a man.' He did so, and again. 'Even a reed or the dried core of a thistle.' The Mute ran up to kiss him, then wound up his crossbow in its turn. It was a wonderful invention, like all things foreign, but took longer to set than the weights on a clock, and was as unhandy to use as man is with man in the act of love.

'If you tear them by the barb, they'll be drawn and volleyed back again,' Ironface grumbled at him.

'So I shall recognize them when they come, and acknowledge the acquaintance.'

'You've barbs enough in your own gut already.'

'But no iron in my soul.' Gibbu gathered Ironface into his arms and set him back on his horse just as another great charge of crusaders bore down upon us. They came on heavy and slow, like men with no puff for the chase but stomach enough for the killing.

These were Guy de Levis' men, with Bouchard de Marly's alongside, together with those of Guillaume de Poissy, Robert Mauvoisin, Roger des Essarts, Pierre de Cissey and Robert de Picquingny; all friends of De Montfort, and practised in warfare besides. These had come with artillerists and engineers, and all manner of sawyers and their equipment, and so had we been surprised. While their masters were riding over roofs in Le Bourg, their journeymen captains had been working.

First, and most obviously, they had erected a battery of mangonels to catapult rocks against the suburb's battlements or ring of defended house-backs and so broach them. Fragments of hillside, and some say whole hills, had come crunching one a minute into the wall by Fontgrande and St Hilaire with a pain like teeth being pulled, for those still young enough to remember the sound.

Then, in spite of the stony soil, they had dug a mine under the defences and lit a furnace inside the very bowels of Le

241

Castellare's foundations. This had smouldered beneath the crack where the mangonels were at work, till its heat rotted the rocks as well as sending a great stench of marsh clay and excrement across the town. An hour ago this noxious damp had exploded and the wall had come crashing down like a mountain built on sulphur. The enemy had ridden in as soon as beams could be laid across the fiery pit.

Nor was this enough for them. Their sawyers had built them a Cat, a prowling tower on wheels, taller than any roof in town. We could see it now, sitting above the tiles. I think all of us were in awe at the wonder of it. With this they had overlooked the defenders, stolen close enough to hail darts and sling-shot into them, then stepped out over the wall by six and by twelve, and finally a bushel at the time, with men entering the tower by its foot to replenish the hordes that hurried forth overhead.

All this I saw. I lend no credence to the stories of scorpions and slither-tails and eagles trained by these Northerners and now fighting with them. Nor of a fire-breathing worm, a friend of Pope Innocent's, which was burrowing hourly towards the heart of us. Men had as soon talk to me of rabbits with swords in their gums as gossip of Papal Serpents.

What I saw now was their black-headed Cat grinning over us all with the sun in its eyes as their horsemen came on and still on.

'Saw them by their feet,' an old woman cried. 'Lie down boldly and serve them on the hoof!'

Mad old thing, she threw herself down with a knife in her teeth to wait belly-up before their advancing heartbeat.

A squire dipped his lance at her, but Gibbu shot him from his horse. Whereupon a dozen of our women rushed forward and lay down beside her. Then, if I still could count, went a dozen more. 'Safer to lie beneath a horse than wait like this for a man,' one of the corpse-strippers shouted. 'You can see what a horse is doing.' She removed an embroidered riding slipper and its jewelled spur, I think with the foot inside it.

Or perhaps it was the looting of his property made the knight howl down at her.

The effect on the enemy was terrible. Horses hate treading on women or anything slippery, especially when disturbed by an arrow while planting their feet. If they did stamp ahead, some of them were cobbled on the fetlock, while their riders were trimmed by the ankle.

The Mute tried to run forward with his basket of peppers, but Ironface stopped him. 'Don't get behind them,' he said. 'They may run this way.'

'Frightened, Ferblant?'

'Yes,' he said, his voice dry as a lizard's. 'I'm frightened they'll use our women for cobblestones.'

The attack found itself unable to press its own front forward or pass it by, so it broke formation and turned back.

As the vista widened down road and past square, we saw that the crusaders lay dead in their dozens. Hard to tell blood from blood, but it seemed to me our own people had perished by the score. This did not include the townsmen, whose crude leather guard-coats of pigskin and oxhide had let in points enough to slay them in their hundreds.

'We have saved what we can,' my cousin called. 'Let us fall back on the City in good order!'

The women of Castellare had been rescued; their owners or other menfolk who survived were contained within or stood behind our ranks, so his plan was the right one.

These crusaders were in no mind to let us follow it. Unlike ourselves, the men facing us now had not been fighting this morning; nor would one charge be the end of them if they had been. They were here to beat us, and came on again remorseless and slow, this time by our left flank, which was dangerous to us, since it covered the gateway to the City, the Portal of Razès.

Things could have gone badly for us at this moment. We still had to pass a great number of townsmen through this gateway behind our left, then ourselves, then our own rearguard. Had they pushed us boldly in, we might have been turned by the flank and quite cut off.

They were distracted by the group of women who gathered themselves on foot about La Mamelonne. Thinking these were merely refugees from La Castellare, and having no direct news of what our cod-cutters did to discomfort their allies in Le Bourg, they gathered themselves street by street and tried to force their advantage upon us. They should have known better.

When the Wizards overran Oc to breathe fire upon our ancestors and force them to build roads and eat stone, they came here under the leadership of King Caesar. This magician was a famous warrior among the Giants, able to command wolves and eagles into battle as well as horses, and to write on water with a stick. So it was he composed a book full of the Spells of War, which he passed to his hundred sons, some of whom became mortal and made copies of this treatise on parchments which they sold to the monks in return for being shrunk to normal size.

Caesar's book of cobwebs only once explains how to fight with the two-legged half of mankind. This is when it describes the Wizards' wars in Britain, which in those days was peopled only by women, all of whom lived like bees.

Their queens dwelt in chariots drawn by flying oxen, and when they wished to become impregnated they mated with a race of female magicians who had penises but died if they used them. The skins of these magic women were bright blue, so they disguised themselves from head to foot in flax and hid in circles of stone. The wizard defeated the bee-women by tying scythes to his wheels and dividing them into three parts. Since he had a penis of his own, he extirpated the blue women entirely.

Usually he fought on beaches or plains or walking on the sea. He warns armies about standing with their backs to a forest, but fails to advise against fighting in town, even against bee-women.

If the crusaders could have caught us on open ground they

would have overcome us by sheer weight of arms. But they had to come at us down streets and alleyways, whereas we had the advantage of our view along the foot of the City wall. La Mamelonne, on our left flank, stood at the marketplace where all the roads converged at the City Gate. If she advanced her front, if any of us entered the maze of dwellings which was now as full of crusaders in ring-mail as hornet lanterns are of stings, then the advantage of the larger view would be lost. We could see enough not to lose. If we were foolish enough to try to win we should become blind again. We dared not go too far.

Taking a saucy step forward is what whores are about. She tied Pipi to a stump, dismounted, and called to them to run at her. A man with his legs astride a wide horse is never entirely at easte if you compel him to come at you between walls at the gallop, especially with ten of his friends alongside him in an alleyway designed to accommodate no more than a scag with her panier of bread (the Carcassonne loaf has been mentioned before. It is built with these passageways in mind: hard ended and crusted like a beetle). They saw her. They had not seen her before. They ran at her, barging their kneecaps together and crushing their thighs against saddles already painful with the afternoon sun. Man to woman like this, especially those who sat above the salt and were less used to such matters, they were in prime condition to find themselves with their cruppers on fire and their balls cut off.

Our corpse-strippers watched her tip her third measure of spirit over a taper, and decided there was too much costly saddlery going to waste. They rushed forward to help her. This brought the Battle of Le Castellare to a standstill.

One day a wizard – or blacksmith – will invent mightier weapons, and the feminine half of mankind will come to hold the strings of them or remain as nothing. Even without them, the difference between a knight with his sword and lance and two or three angry women with pitchforks was not unimaginably large, especially if he fell from his horse. A middle-sized man weighs much the same as a bundle of wet hay, and we turn such fodder often, and throw it into the loft when it's cooked and dry.

Much remains to be written of the cruelty of war, but I am bound to confess that very few crusaders were killed by us women directly. As La Mamelonne said while she was soothing Pipi, 'It's not being turned on a pitchfork or stilt-pole that kills a man. Nor is it being tossed over the roof that does it. It's falling on the cobbles at the other side of the house.'

So it was our sally-party was able to regain the Portal of Razès, La Mamelonne and the corpse-strippers last of all. They had collected all manner of lewd particles in their buckets, some for the apothecaries, some to joke about later. My cousin pulled a face at having such offal in his castle and about his cooking-pots, but he sensed their usefulness when he heard the jokes of jesters and clowns, and was prudent enough to say nothing.

Simon de Montfort was there at the last. His neighbours and vassals from Paris had fought the actual Battle of Le Castellare, but he was there at the Portal of Razès to witness the corpse-strippers' barbarities.

Did a gentleman mutilate his fellows thus, the retribution would be terrible, especially from one such as himself, who was one of the world's *just men*, and there are none so cruel as these. But when our widows splashed his ears with a load of bollocks and other tripe, he merely asked his squire for a napkin and remarked that women are full of tricks, especially the very young and the extremely old. His wisdom has been corrupted to a *mot* I often hear quoted: *Well, well – girls will be girls*!

Lucky for our sex that he took such a reasonable view of the matter, for he never put out any woman's eyes, however many he placed upon the bonfire, nor caused her bowels to be searched with swords. What he could do to men is a matter of record and regret, though he hadn't taken charge yet, merely come to see the fight.

*   *   *

246

A woman shouldn't wash often, lest she rinse herself away, especially in summer. She should wrap up well against the heat, and hope to dry back into herself. Her flesh is like a candle-flame – its sweat is precious. If man is as tallow, then woman is purest beeswax and should be hoarded drop by drop.

Whores are different. They are always scrubbing something. La Mamelonne used to soak herself several times a day, dunking whole lumps of her anatomy in raw water as if they were piglets being pickled in brine.

Her back was of special concern to her, and coy though she was, she was never too modest to refuse my help with it. Otherwise she would have had to go behind herself with a long-handled broom, and such-like contortions. As it was, once we were arrived in Carcassonne there would always be some little corner of my cousin's castle ringing to our merry laughter as I helped her rinse the grasses from her shoulder-blades or pick pebbles from her bottom.

This is all beside our History, and of no interest to anyone but myself. Not so her hair. She was for ever scrubbing away at that, and knotting it and wringing it, and generally dealing with it the way a capable wife and servant treats linen in a puddle or even unrotted flax. Any girl else would know that combing is better than cleaning, and brushing more healthy than both, since hair needs to be full of its own juice if it is to stay manageable.

Poor Mamelie. Perhaps she had secret guilts, or endured feelings of shame and unchastity – though her mummy and grandmother were whores, and her family suffered from no tradition of anything different. She would scrub and rub-a-dub at tresses with the life quite drowned out of them, complaining all the time of scurf, or bird lime or flaky, when I knew that what she was after being rid of were the oaths trapped in her ear, and the loathsome dribble of kisses.

Her hair started a good deal darker than mine, and the dawn after I met her it was midway between tired auburn and fair (though that was after it had been trodden on and

peered through by that great pile of crusaders). Old wives
say it is impossible to wash colour from hair, unless it has
been put there by bark or berries, but that depends on what
you wash it in.

Once we were well established in the ancient fortress of
Carcassonne, Mamelie used horse urine by the bucketful.
This is reputed to be highly effective against scurf and flaky,
if not so good as the stalings of pig or deer, though the one of
these is hard to find and the other almost impossible to collect.

I was glad to see La Mamelonne rinse her locks thoroughly
in the River Aude from time to time, and do her best to cancel
the horse piss with rose water or aqua fortis and nutmeg.
Meantimes, they grew lighter and lighter. I don't like that
Northern word *blond*, far preferring our own *blant* or *blanc*,
but *blondes* is what they became, even more than mine were. I
at least retained a touch of faded dandelion about the ears and
other hems, like an old man with soup in his moustache, but
Mamelie was all ash on the instant and like to become snow
in a fortnight. If we ever needed to disguise her, we should
have to wrap her head in mud. Meanwhile, her colouring was
like a banner, a gonfalon even. Mine was only a pennant by
comparison. I sincerely hope this did not irritate me.

After the Battle of Le Castellare, which followed close
upon our no less triumphant defeat in Le Bourg, I beguiled
myself an instant with Mamelie's tresses, just the same.

Then I went to look to my resting place where the Phantom
laid his finger on me, and I was fast asleep.

I say the Phantom, but he came later, even if only by a
candle-flame's sputter. What laid me in sleep's arms was my
need for love, which is like any woman's, or like the cuckoo's.
When you stand close to death and risk her kiss, you need a
little reassurance at the end of the day.

He was there the moment I closed my eyes, not a breath
sooner than longed for. He crouched over me, the way a
dream will, and immediately asserted himself. 'France needs
you,' he said, or some such nonsense. 'France is calling you.'
(What was this France, or who and where? It was no place

or person I knew. We call Philip Augustus the King of Paris, and where is that, but an island in the mind?)

I had an island in mind immediately my Phantom spoke to me, and my mind was on my thighs, which were witless enough. He spoke no more words, having breathed his apocalypse in my ear, but sunk his lips immediately to a spot I can only describe as a thumbnail away from my left nipple, and equidistant round it, a thumbnail away then shorter by a thumb as he closed his mouth.

'What should I do if I am ever unfortunate enough to experience such a dream?' I had once asked Constance de Coulobres.

'Take charge of it immediately,' she had answered.

My dream or Dream was already in charge of me, boot and saddle, spur and crop, and was proceeding as always to have his way. What he did first, this divine diabolo, was suck against my breast even as I'm told an infant will, as if trying to have my heart out. Being a man, he had my lungs as well, what with the weight of him and the taste of his hair in my mouth, which was like rain on midsummer bracken or cobwebs when the bats begin flight.

'Need,' he mumbled, not to mention France again, or Toulouse or Trencavel or Oc, because it was his need we were talking of now, as always with men.

I took charge nonetheless. 'What do you mean?' I demanded of my visitant. 'Tell me what – ' As well talk to an Incubus, or try to interrupt a priest, which I suppose he might have been. He had his cotte up by now, if he'd ever had one, his cotte up, and mine, and his leggings away.

I didn't wear clothes to fasten or unfasten, so much as have layers in the manner of snakes or, in a funny sense, caterpillars. Merdun the Bastard had loosened quite a lot of me, and so had his men, without coming down to my final thread which was kindly placed and made so strong it might have had a whole sheep plaited in it and not just the harvest of its back. This I have told you, but dreams spare their breath so my Phantom was faster than Merdun

249

to undress me. He had me naked in an instant, shaking out my body parts and unfurling my wings to reassure both of us there was nothing torn, like a boy with a moth or Archangel Gabriel with the damps of Sunrise.

What he did next so discomforted me at its beginnings and coddled me at the end, while tormenting me with such a seesawing delirious alternation of light and dark, open and close, breath and not breath, gawp and gasp, that I can only describe it as a Revelation, I think with a capital letter, because even to think about it makes me clench my teeth and growl.

How was it that a dream could teach me so much, if dream he only was? There you have the nub of him, as I certainly did. Was he only a dream, that could leave my soul bone-naked? I already knew him to live in the flesh. I had seen him bathing. So did my Phantom lay flesh on me now? Or was my flesh its own Phantom?

A castle is not a mill, and this is its principal disadvantage. It has much space, but few spaces, a heavenly vastness of room yet no rooms. Nothing is private, not even the privvies. If the lord lies down with the ladlemaid then there are five hundred eyes to see and, if necessary, applaud. As great ones consummate their wedding, the trumpets sound. When the Chatelaine groans in her birth pangs, there are kettledrums to muffle her cries, lest they disturb bed-guests at their beverage (as Northerners call their midnight mull) or call-guests with the Treacle (named after the Trinity and consequently a third part spirit), or distress the least of their dogs. Once the child bursts forth from her, the whole town knows the sex of it before she has time to glimpse its head past her own falling belly. If she dies, and women die often enough without being surrounded by such barking drunkenness, then the shire is dewed with weeping before her husband leaves the hunt to fetch the mass priest to her viaticum.

My cousin was a private man, so little of this was for him. He could not bear his mate about him and, as our troubles gathered, he was the only person in Carcassonne I never saw at stool. So I doubt it was he who stooped over me, whatever his protestations of longing that first evening.

What we had for sleeping, and we women for our bathing, was a folding frame of curtains. At night, all the great halls of the castle were divided as one arranges sheep-pens, though not by bavins and hurdles but by hangings laced on lines of string. At such times only the impudent peep. The children whose pastime it was were shut away tight with their nurses. So we all slept sly.

I was better off than most. Though low enough in my cousin's family, I stood high in his esteem. He gave us what men call a bower, which may be no more than a hole in the wall, but at Carcassonne the walls are thick, and so therefore are the outer recesses of its castle keep. A mill house could sit inside them, so our bower was a fine, large room. There Ironface lay also as my only knight. So did Gibbu his man and the Mute his thing, though a little beyond the curtain. The Fish Girl slept as the two men allowed her, and Mamelie at such times was always La Mamelonne. There's a saying in the language of Oc: 'Put a whore in a castle, and she'll soon move the rest of you out.' Mamelie was too sweetly generous for such strictures, but whether she stood or slept, or simply painted gum on her fingernails, she was a woman who needed her leg-room. A palace might hold her awhile, but with little space left for a queen.

So I gasped, thrashed my limbs, and cried out, half waking to find Mamelie stifling my lips as if to reassure sleep. This almost put an end to my Phantom, whose body rolled away from me like mountain mist, leaving my thighs covered with dew. 'Wake up,' La Mamelonne was saying. 'Wake or sleep properly, even if you snore!' Snore is not a pretty word, especially between friends in the early evening, and the Phantom evaporated entirely, all except his voice which though stiff and stern continued to say nothing, and which he left in my hand which was firmly between my legs.

I had less clothes on than I had thought, though more

251

than I'd dreamed, and my mind was unbalanced in consequence.

When sleep is full of such visions, why should a woman
need a man? 'Was it you who helped me to bed by undressing
me?' I asked Mamelie.

'I wish I could claim credit, my pet, but I can't. Nor for the
dream that so clearly possessed you. I was with a gentleman,
and you know what that entails – a lot of my time and all of
his attention.'

'What gentleman was that?'

'One of those about Roger de Cabaret. Not for money,
either. Call it folly – which in my case stops well short of
love. It looks as if some such visited you, and perhaps the
very man himself.'

Was the evening as warm as my cheeks found it, even
among so much stone?

'He's an active little cock-bird,' La Mamelonne chuckled.
'And his thing is of a size with the rest of him. Not an
enormity like old "Towers" de Cabaret himself, but one that
will perch in anyone's nest.' She combed my hair with her
fingers. 'More of a wren than a buzzard or a bustard, and
certainly no-one's idea of a goose.'

'Do men vary so much?'

'They do, my dove, and there's their danger to us. This
one could slip between a matron's legs entirely unnoticed. It
probably wouldn't attract a virgin's attention either – simply
do its business, spread its wings and be gone. But think of
nine months later.'

'I do, often.'

'So do I, pretty. This castle has put such a fulness in
me.'

I spoke no more, but drifted again towards sleep. Great
events occurred in my slumber, but none of them to me.

My cousin kept his spurs on. He, and a few gentlemen
whose bottoms were still glued to their horses, rode back
through the Portal of Razès and into Le Castellare. His

252

party included Roger de Cabaret and some of his own people.

If you consider that spears had been rattling against the Portal of Razès just a brief dream earlier, spears and javelins and arrows, then you may conclude my cousin already had the urge to die. He had glory enough without needing more on his sword-point. In the event, he was divinely inspired.

La Castellare was empty. The crusaders had gone, possibly in error, perhaps thinking some other man's men stood guard, but gone they had. My cousin found a few of them drinking looted wine, and leaning officiously on a single spear that wasn't long enough to accommodate all of their hands.

At the very first charge, those that didn't take fright at the battlecry 'Trencavel', and jump the moon in their drunkenness, became so appalled at the sight of De Cabaret that they drowned themselves in the River Aude. Le Castellare was again in our hands.

My cousin was in no mood to keep it. What he rode for was water. They told me that each of the several dozen men in his party carried two buckets, even the gentlemen, because everyone in Carcassonne was thirsty for a drink other than wine. Le Castellare had a well, and our own two wells were dry.

Unfortunately, the town took fire before we could sip its juices. One moment the coolness beckoned, the next instant Le Castellare was hotly aflame. Some say the crusaders torched it as they ran away, others that my cousin set it burning from policy or pique. The truth is it did it to itself, the way a stack of grass will burst forth, consumed with its own heat before the kine can eat it.

If you doubt that water can burn, be certain of it now. Or say with La Mamelonne that Dogskin of Brousses had cursed us detail by detail, even to the stones that lined this well.

It was the dropping of one of our buckets past these stones that struck sparks enough to light a thatch. Wherever this Crusade went, the elementals of fire were present. A man did not have to follow the Cross, or even the sword, to call them down. There were salamanders in bed with us, as the heat in my own thighs could testify. Whether they expressed the wrath of God or Pope Innocent's displeasure only the Holy Dominic could tell. I heard of lovers burning as soon as their bodies touched, as if he had an imp within his candle and her bush were so much tinder. But there! I was talking in my sleep!

I woke to find the Mute in the room, and La Mamelonne once again shaking me by the shoulder. The eyes of both were full of flame, not for one another and still less for me, but because Le Castellare was by now burning as merrily as a bonfire before you throw the ox onto it. Our shot window did not overlook it direct, but we had its reflection in the Aude, and a torching makes its own sunrise. Meanwhile, my favourite whore shook me. 'Wake up,' she said. 'We have great things afoot, like kings and parchment. Stir your bones, my Perronnelle, and enjoy the terrible events that pass.'

Gibbu groaned in his sleep. He sucked on the memories in his beard, rolling about the floor as if he needed to shift his hump and cuddle it. My lord Ferblant's devil began to babble inside its iron. I swear I saw a tongue or some such moistness flicker behind the bars of his head, just as silver fish run in the hearth when the griddle is lifted.

'My liege,' he groaned, 'my lord and temporal Master, oh my own Sire, my honourable slippery one.'

'Another relative of yours?' I asked him, stirring at his belly lump with my clogs, which I still slept in.

Such a being cannot leap upright. He levitated beside his planted spear, and clattered after us. Leaving Gibbu, we others strode through the midnight castle to see what was afoot, as Mamelie called it.

It must be a matter of moment. She put her hair up for the first and last time, then called me to fasten my girdle, it being the only visible sign of maidenhood about me.

In the main hall we found the curtains drawn back from the bedding, the sleepers kicked up, and the air fresh with pomanders and the burning of pine. Cousin Raymond-Roger,

254

Towers de Cabaret the Lord of Lastours, and several jolly bits of barons grouped themselves about a kingly presence with the biggest and blackest *small* beard I have ever seen. He was a handsome man, exquisitely put together by tailors from the sort of cloth normally used to make women and cushions. It was white about the backside from the sweat of his horse.

The most remarkable thing to look at was not the monarch himself, though he was pretty enough. It was a floor piece his retainers had made by throwing their shields to the ground. Our own shields were rough at the edges, handsome when clean, but now spattered with blood and the consequent attention of carrion, principally their body droppings.

These shields were Spanish bright, looking like gold barred with silver, but without the dullness of precious metals. They lay upon the flagstones like so many mirrors, showing us the hall and its roof-rods in a mighty reflection, just like a pool of that miraculous water we did not have. Their gemstones were splendid too, and sat there as fat as frogs.

'It's the King of Aragon,' La Mamelonne whispered. 'Young Pierre, Pedro or Peter according to what ballad you read.'

'How do you know that?'

'Because I told her so,' Ironface said. 'I galloped with the little sprattling in a dream just now, and you wake me only to turn my eyes into my own head. They see what they already saw, and such visions make me uneasy.'

The great ones were taking a treacle together. It was the wrong time for a treacle, but my cousin and His Royal Highness of Aragon doubtless thirsted for the ghost in it.

The songs tell how this king had lain all summer at Collioure, which is a fish-town beyond Narbonne. Some say it was for lust of a woman, or women – they all smell of seaweed there – some say for love of the mermaids who drive men mad with desire then do nothing to slake them, just like we wise virgins inland. Be that as it may, he had heard of his vassal's plight and he and several hundred knights had dragged themselves away from such tails or scales as they found on the beach and come to Carcassonne without females of any sort, and consequently at a brisk gallop.

'You have ridden far,' my cousin said. 'And in troubled times.'

'I come well protected. I have what you see, and six score of my best horses wait at your gate for water.'

'Our wells are dark. Their water flows only by daylight. They must slake themselves in the Aude, and their riders be contented with wine.' My cousin waved a finger, and listened for the rolling of casks.

'Last night I slept by the sea at Collioure.'

'The sea makes a noisy blanket, my liege.'

'And a beguiling one, if you find a woman's toes in it,' Roger de Cabaret said.

King Peter flushed at this, and men say his shields darkened too, for no-one likes to hear his truths uncovered in a jest.

'You will sleep softly here,' my cousin said quickly. 'This place may be stones, but each one bids you welcome.'

'Your stones stand in walls, and I cannot lie one side of them while the Cross is planted on the other.'

'The Cross goes as men carry it. I have another nailed up in my Cathedral here.'

'A Crusade has been proclaimed. It is unthinkable to me that you, as my vassal from here to the Pyrenees, do not join it.'

'I cannot.'

'Join it or stand aside. But *oppose* it?'

'I have other masters than you. Shall half of me be on one side and half upon the other?'

'Raymond of Toulouse manages well enough. What other master do you have, unless it is the old King of Paris who demanded this Crusade?'

'I was thinking of my people.'

'Heretics mostly. Heretics and harlots.' He noticed La Mamelonne for the first time, and gestured towards us as if plucking us both from his beard.

'They are my people.'

The King laughed at this and quite recovered his temper, as if my cousin had said something witty and pithy and worth a monarch's time to ride and hear, no matter how many toes and their women he left in bed behind him. When he spoke again, it was quietly. 'God gave me this earth to lend you. He told me nothing of lending it to your people. So let me tell you what the Count of Nevers says.' He led my cousin away from De Cabaret, and all I heard was whispers. When the King whispered, it was hard and urgent, like a mother scolding her child.

As he did so, La Mamelonne's fingers separated on my sleeve then dug themselves into my arm. 'I have that man up my skirts,' she said.

'He queues there behind many, and I pray there will be many more to come.'

'I have him on a card, idiot.'

'Painted by Dogskin de Brousses?'

'My Master didn't paint those cards. They were given to him on his mountain by a Dragon.'

'So was my thimble.'

'And I know whose cave you keep it in. That man is called Imperatrix.'

'He is Peter the Second of Aragon.'

'He is called Imperatrix, and upside down he means weakness.'

'Pah!'

'Frailty at the best, and at the worst treachery.'

The King walked beyond his shields, and there he was, inverted in the mirror of their glittering.

'A trap,' Mamelie whispered, 'a most terrible, magical trap.'

Gibbu was awake and at my elbow. 'He's only a king,' he growled. 'I've never put an arrow through a king, no matter which way up.'

The King was still holding his cup. Now he dashed it into the fire, and made as if to walk away. 'Let me hear from you,' he called. 'Till then, this treacle has snakes in it.' He returned to kiss my cousin, even so.

'The viper,' Gibbu said. 'When a king embraces a man like that, it says no more than a priest's kiss to a maiden – he has trouble in mind.'

'My countess must continue in your safe keeping,' my cousin called after him.

'And your young son.'

My cousin's bride had fled to Spain. Alas, she wasn't beneath the King's blanket at Collioure, and since I wasn't Raymond of Brousses I couldn't put her there.

So it was King Peter of Aragon took up his shields and rode back into the night.

After some six or seven minutes blowing on his hands although it wasn't cold, my cousin called to his personal squire and followed after him.

Lord Roger de Cabaret of Lastours had spent the same interval picking his teeth, and otherwise counting that he had some. Now he swore very loudly and strode away too.

'Follow them,' Ironface advised.

'I'm a woman.'

'And as such are allowed nothing, I grant you. But if you choose to do what is not allowed, being a woman no-one will hinder you.'

I went on foot where the others went by horse, and hateful it was once I took my clogs off, as I had to if I wished to remain silent.

My cousin was proposing to leave the Citadel by the Narbonne Gate which led towards the crusaders' principal encampment. The Baron de Cabaret had caught up with him and stopped him, at least for the moment. The two men sat on their horses, arguing furiously. Their squires had dismounted, out of deference, and sat a short way off.

I halted before I was lit by the cresset in the archway. It must have been burning pig grease that night, for it sputtered like an evil thing.

'You make too great a sacrifice,' Baron Roger was pleading. 'Let us put some horsemen together – all of our horsemen on all of our horses – and have ourselves a sally at them. You see how limply they fight.'

'Bad counsel when I advised it myself and you in your wisdom stopped me. Bad counsel now, my dear friend. No, Towers – I must go. I have promise of safe passage from the Count of Nevers out there, guaranteed by the king who brought it.'

'But the terms you propose – '

'I am my own terms, and my body is my ransom. But what am I, and where have my wits all gone?' He caught at De Cabaret by the blazon on his overshirt. 'My five are uncertain and the sixth is a chaos!' He glanced around and growled, 'It's that damned witch! She makes my thigh rise even in the blood of combat. God knows what such a yeast is doing to my mind.'

I felt a pang of jealousy for La Mamelonne. Could a man of my cousin's lineage be so much in love with a whore?

'Then have her, my friend. She's yours for the plucking. Have her and let us get on with the war.'

'Don't you think I haven't thought of it, planned for it, dreamed of it? She's my own blood, Towers. My own blood and begotten on my blood, possibly by my father on his niece the Vinegar Woman of Saint Thibéry.'

A long silence fell, then Lastours said, 'Does she know – '

'She knows something. She knows – '

I never learned what it was I was supposed to know. I was of course shocked to hear of my married cousin's love for me. This delighted me so much that I was unable to cry out and join my protest to Lastours' as the young viscount left town.

Thus Raymond-Roger rode forth on a whim to surrender my mother's ambition for me, together with the world's most impregnable fortress.

CANTO FIVE

In which the invincible City
founders in flux and Cousin
Raymond-Roger is kept more
dead than alive in his own
pickle.

eny a man water and his bowels will invent it for him as surely as if Moses struck him on the bottom with a stick. Once his body loses moisture he must take salt by the mouth and liquid by the bucket, or immediately die. Raymond-Roger's people were beginning to die. He did not ride forth for me, but as a final expression of his own compassion and common sense, which he was frightened would be obscured by desire.

It was dawn when I retraced my footsteps to the castle from the Citadel's great portal of Narbonne. As I did so, corpses from the Plague of Carcassonne were being placed in the streets. There were no edicts to forbid this, and no will to heed them if there were. The gutters ran with excrement, and wall to wall the cobblestones were ankle-deep in flies. King Peter's advice to my cousin came not a day too soon.

As I picked my way home, my mind was like my stomach, full of grave matters. A siege is a noble thing. During Philip Augustus' Crusade, and Simon's Crusade, then King Saint Louis' Crusade, we saw a lot of them, all conducted according to the Rules of War and the no less hallowed Procedures of Warriors. A warrior is like everyone else, the treatises agree: he needs to eat and he needs to drink. What even King Caesar's treatise neglects to mention is that he has a healthy desire to shit as well, and it is when we turn to this problem that we see how so many sieges become unstuck – or stuck, according to which side of the wall you find yourself on.

Those on the outside have very few problems of this sort. When they wish to disgorge themselves they have the wide world to do it in, and the nobility and the gentry as well as their generals to show them how to do it.

Those on the inside are not all of them warriors, and more than a few of them are several degrees less than nobility. 'Lowborn people rarely know how to do it.' This was one of Mummy's everlasting themes, to which Daddy would add, 'Ignorant people can't find where to do it.' Not in Carcassonne they couldn't. They shat everywhere. That was before they were ill. Once they were ill, they still shat everywhere, when they could reach anywhere, but they did it more often. The Crusade didn't need siege engines. It just had to wait until the citizens remembered shitting. Once they did, they couldn't forget it. Nor are they to be blamed for the woe of their own excesses. People accustomed to using the bottom of their kitchen gardens find it hard to go from the top of a castle wall. Although they can't dig a hole in a paving stone, doing it in the street makes them feel closer to home.

Once inside the castle I was quick to tell what had happened, though I said nothing of Raymond-Roger's love for me.

'The poor man is deranged,' was all La Mamelonne would say. 'Clearly, he is besotted with my body.'

'He should have brought our salt from Capestang,' Ironface pronounced in his wisdom, 'and kept his wife with him. The crusaders have no such problems.'

Here he spoke truth. Simon de Montfort had taken our salt, and the rest of the Crusade had borrowed our virgins. They all had our water. Even without resorting to water there is nothing tightens a young man's bottom so much as swallowing salt and poking a pretty woman. Exercise it with several, and it becomes narrower than a gnat's.

So they had all our virgins and they had all our salt. Whereas we, especially the women among us, had neither.

'I think I'll go wash myself in wine and await his return,' La Mamelonne said. 'You coming, Perronnelle?'

I didn't see the need. My body never smells, only my soul when its thoughts are impure. That is why prayer is more cleansing than soap.

I was kneeling in a corner with Ironface, Gibbu and the Mute when my cousin returned. I hurried back to the great hall. Knowing that he loved me put me in a great tingle to see him, in spite of the gravity of our situation. The thought that he also lusted after me set up even more of an agitation, mostly in those parts of me that only my Phantom knew about. When I saw Raymond-Roger standing alone by his fire, alone though surrounded by his squires and courtiers, I realized how fortunate I was he had been too honourable to force his attentions upon me. I lacked the defences of a married woman. Married women wear chastity belts. Their husbands turn the lock, then throw the key in the moat. To be so protected, I needed to have a husband, and he needed to have a moat.

My cousin called Roger de Cabaret to his side, and spoke to him briefly. Then he addressed us all. 'I have been among these crusaders and I have arranged terms. Let me tell you what those terms are, and how I came to them. Then you can go forth and broadcast them among the good folk that throng our City and its citadel. Let them know that the bargain that has been struck is promised by the Count of Nevers, and with other mighty ones signatory. It is guaranteed by Raymond of Toulouse and King Peter of Aragon. There is no help but to trust them.'

There came not a single murmur at this. I believe most men were too dry-mouthed even to cough.

The crusaders' proposal was a sorry enough matter. My cousin's life was to be spared, and he was to have his freedom. He must leave at once and take only twelve people with him, these to be of his own choice. In return, his vicomté was forfeit; Carcassonne was forfeit. All the people in it, including those from Le Bourg and Le Castellare and the broad demesnes about, all were forfeit. Only his witches' dozen could ride away.

Still scarce an outcry. One or two of us with saliva still in our veins managed to raise a spit that stayed wet as far as the floor. We wanted to know what the crusaders intended for the rest of us. Would they burn us, rape us, or set us to grind corn?

'My party would, of course, include Roger de Cabaret of Lastours and my cousin Perronnelle de Saint Thibéry.'

Possibly I blushed as he spoke, and certainly I did so when he allowed himself to glance at me after. Yet my thoughts were with Gibbu the Hunchback and that poor little Mute, as well as with Ironface my devil and La Mamelonne the whore. These, quite certainly, would not ride with the party afforded safe conduct.

'I did not accept such a covenant,' my cousin announced. 'Nor will I. My love is for you all, my people. Nor have you ever done less than deserve it.'

How they cheered, dry-mouthed or not. How we all cheered. So we were to fight on. Bad news enough, but better than the alternative.

'In a week we shall die of thirst,' the Viscount said. 'Those of us who are not already dead with fever.'

These were grave words, and heavier for being true. So we heard them in silence.

'With this in mind, I have agreed to forfeit my City but let its people walk free. My own self is to be your ransom.'

A great wailing arose at this, the louder for having La Mamelonne back again. It was much too noisy to be entirely sincere.

'My own surrender will have bought ten thousand free-doms,' my cousin told them. 'Ten thousand? No, more by another ten.' He turned away, and left others to tell us the worst of it. These greedy Northerners would not allow us to return to our homes in Le Bourg or Le Castellare. We must build anew on the far side of the river. If we had stomach to build at all.

My cousin said nothing more after this. Not to the world, and not to me. It was De Cabaret who gave orders for the gates to be thrown open, and to allow the Crusade to enter our mighty portals.

'Quick!' Ironface said. 'We must hide where we can, and be prompt to leave when we may. Twice they have called you a witch, Perronnelle. And Merdun de Montfort claims you for his own. I too am not exempt from his displeasure. We have the Fish Girl to protect from the cinders as well.'

'What about me?' wailed La Mamelonne.

'Somebody will collect you as a souvenir.'

To live among great ones offers a man little protection. In case we needed reminding of this point, several courtiers were taken ill in the great hall of the castle. They fell to the floor and died in puddles of blood exactly where they had been standing a moment or two earlier.

'Keep a garlic up each nostril and an onion in your mouth,' Ironface advised.

'Why not two grapes and an apple?' La Mamelonne asked.

We all had to relieve ourselves before anyone could answer her. None of us yet suffered from the aquatic flux, still less the gory deluge. We went out of terror and local necessity.

So it was that when my cousin Raymond-Roger Trencavel rode down to welcome his new guests, the bottoms of his vassals from the lowest to the highest were uncovered in salute. So it was too when the Crusade marched in to drumbeat and trumpet, and a great display of flags.

I speak of all manner of dukes and archbishops, as well as Eudes III of Burgundy, Hervé IV of Nevers, the Count of Saint-Pol, the Count of Auxerre, the Count of Genervois, Adhémar of Poitiers, and even Raymond VI of Toulouse, weak-kneed from whoring and frequent changes of side. Not one of these great ones saw a properly covered backside during the whole of their parade through Carcassonne.

Nor did Simon, Amaury and Merdun de Montfort, Bouchard de Marly, Guillaume de Poissy, Robert Mauvoisin, Roger des Essarts, Roger des Andelys, Pierre de Cissey, Robert de Picquigny, Guy de Levis, Guillaume de Contres, Lambert de Thury, Alain de Roucy, Robert de Forceville and Enguerrand de Boves, all of whose gums were chewing on pomanders and noses sniffing at posies and snuffing up petals as they rode past our terrible salute.

Only those two great Irishmen Hughes de Lacy and Reinier de Chaudron rode entirely unprotected. Theirs and their retainers' eyes were full of tears at the stench that pervaded the Citadel because, as they sobbed to all and sundry about them, it reminded them of home.

I have no doubt that it was the vanquished state of our bowels that saved us from wholesale rape. The crusaders themselves, and their historians, put it down to military good order and discipline, as well as their civilized respect for treaties; but we all knew that this was nonsense.

According to the Rules of War, rape is an act of violence *against the person*. It is not a crime, because it is permissible in certain circumstances, which, as I had discovered at St Thibéry, translates into any old circumstances that take a warrior's fancy on a warm afternoon.

Besides, you need to be a person to have a person. We weren't persons, we were heretics, and as such entirely forfeit. It was, I swear, only this windy blazoning of bottoms that protected and afforded us, as they say, safe passage.

Enough of that. We didn't readjust our garments a moment too soon. These crusaders were very brisk in matters of hygiene, as the Romans and Northerners call the unnatural practice of cleanliness. They collected all the corpses on to the square in front of the castle, and set them on fire with oil from the tuns of animal grease and tree wax we kept for our cressets. They cleared our wells of bodies too, and burnt all people else who couldn't cover their bottoms before this operation was completed, calling to each one as they did so that they were to have no regrets as they were clearly at death's door anyway.

Then, with averted nostrils and handkerchiefs stuffed in their mouths, they hurried us out of town. As we left, we heard in the midst of their scoffing that they in their greater military wisdom would only be allowed to squat in two places. The commoners would sit backwards upon the battlements and aim themselves into the moat, like so many pigeons and crows. The nobility were to restrict themselves to a privy funnel in one of the towers of the castle. This necessitated their climbing to an upper room, but they could use this aperture with perfect ease and freedom, secure in the knowledge that its pipe would not disgorge itself until it reached the cellar or, as some would say, the dungeon that was to be Raymond-Roger's lodging for as long as he remained in his own château as his guests' principal guest.

'We can't let them do that to him,' I protested, as we slunk away. 'It's an affront to his blood.'

'And an even greater insult to his other faculties,' Ironface countered.

Since he was a devil, made of Spanish tin, I took no notice of him.

We were forced to cross the stone bridge over the Aude, which was another prehistoric miracle constructed by Wizards, and made to remain in what I can only call an encampment. There is nothing on that side of the river except a large, damp field stretching all the way to the sky-line. The part where we were confined was little better than a marsh with bumps in it. The more prudent among us chose to dwell on the bumps, and so a great number of factions formed.

I insisted that La Mamelonne share my hill with the rest of our party, rather than find one of her own, or there would have been an impossible division of the common people's concentration. The minute the townsfolk identified me as a Trencavel, they came flocking around me, principally so they could spit in my face. They preferred to blame my cousin for their misfortunes, which were great, rather than thank him for their lives, which were insignificant enough.

I reminded them of this very sharply. The men soon agreed with me, the way men will when they are spoken to by a woman, as it saves them listening any further. Then they went back to cursing and scratching themselves, which is what men do. The women tended to congregate in groups, finding it a pleasant change to talk among themselves now they no longer had to scrape carrots for people who never listened to them. They told me they felt safer *en masse*.

Their main fear was rape, as was mine. Their other obsession was the clap, the one being attendant upon the other. It was easy to understand their concern.

We were being guarded here by the Irishmen I have already mentioned. The Barons Hughes de Lacy and Reinier de Chaudron were well enough disposed towards their charges, being civilized gentlemen able to speak French as well as anyone else from the North, which is of course very badly.

Their men were another matter. The Irish are like the English. They allow themselves to own their retainers. Once you own a man, he becomes as snappy as a chained dog. Such a fellow finds it very agreeable to be disagreeable to a woman. Give him a wine-skin to suck and it puts him in mind of all kinds of wickedness.

According to La Chanson, these Irishmen and other Frenchmen from England deflowered seventeen thousand three hundred and forty-nine virgins between Béziers and Carcassonne, and gave the clap to several regiments of nuns, beginning at St Marie la Dragonne and only stopping at Le Pech Mary, where they were ordered to eat salt instead. The Chanson overstates the matter. Its author Guillaume le Tudèle is a poet as well as a historian. If he were merely a historian his facts would be in an even worse pickle.

There aren't enough young women in bud at any one time in all of the Southern Country, never mind bloom and leaf. A nearer guess is that most of the Irish raping was done by Merdun de Montfort working in disguise. Such a man exaggerates. He had difficulty unfastening his link-mail, as I could testify, and anyway could not count. The Crusade itself did not believe in rape or anything else that slowed it down, and Simon de Montfort discovered there were better ways to gather land than on his – (but there! I mustn't forever be quoting Daddy); and Arnold or Arnaud Almaric's stern reproof to the Bastard has frequently been quoted: 'Put away your prick.

I'm after an Archbishopric.' Though this wasn't how he got one.

As for the regiments of nuns, a single story will suffice. According to the Abbess of Trèbes, an entire convent there was raped by the Irish and subsequently came down with the clap. The Mother Superior, the Holy Constance de Puichéric who was herself violated, claimed a miracle *because, even after this, the sisters of Trèbes were undoubtedly virgins, secure in their maidenheads.* The local Bishop was sceptical, having had several of the sisters and their affliction himself, and refused to send the claim any further, and certainly not to Pope Innocent in Rome.

This clap, or as we say *clape*, is a terrible disease, so no wonder we were frightened of our Irish bullies. It is bad for women in the first place, and for all who would seek the solace of matrimony in the second and all subsequent places, since it has a stultifying effect on posterity by affecting the male children's cockleorams. It is said to be worse than aqua-vitae, making the said little fowls (or as these Northerners call them, *oiseaux* or *robinets*, by which they mean their spigots or firkin-plugs) hide their beaks and the rest of their heads for shame when they should be strutting like lances rampant, or at least couched. Alas, we have a lot of clape in the South, and have even named a mountain after it near Narbonne close to Arnold's archbishopric, and a wine also, which like the disease runs a nasty shade of pink.

So we kept ourselves in groups and away from those who guarded us, whether they were Irishmen or the women's own husbands.

Once these last had done with spitting at the fair name of Trencavel, I let my tongue begin to wag. 'Ladies,' I said, 'and women of the town. You must prevail upon your menfolk, who sit here in their thousands, to rise against these foreigners who pretend to guard us but number themselves only in hundreds. Let them overthrow their oppressors and take back our Citadel.'

271

This was convincingly said, but no-one was ready to harken to me. Once women are granted a little freedom, they prefer to talk *about* men rather than talk *to* them, especially the ones they are married to. So it was here. Not one of them moved.

'It's no good, my dove,' La Mamelonne advised me. 'Believe me, pigeon, you'll never win an argument about numbers until your listeners have learned to count.'

She was a sweet girl, and doubtless spoke true, but I was determined to spur our townsfolk to action, and rescue my cousin from his dungeon. For the moment, this was not to be.

'You two whores over there!' an Irishman called. 'Report to me at once. I've got some work for the pair of you.'

Nobody was in a hurry to move. There weren't two whores, and even if there were, I wasn't one of them.

'You two lovelies who are doing all the chatting!' the same fellow roared in that odd speech of theirs. 'The one with the blonde wig and the one with a halo! Get off your bottoms and bring your bums over here!'

This was unlooked for, but there was no help for it, so over we went.

'If that pack of foreigners want to be filthy with us,' Mamelie my sweet girl whispered, 'just you keep wriggling until I find time to interpose myself. They won't be able to tell which from who once we all fall down in a heap!'

'Sluggards,' our bully said, seizing us by the lobes of our ears, but totally without malice. 'They want a couple of malkins to take themselves over the bridge and up to the castle.'

'Who does?' asked Mamelie.

'Why?' was my best query.

'Ask me no questions.' He relinquished our earlobes in favour of our bottoms. 'I daresay one of our great ones craves a glimpse of your tails, to see which of you's the mermaid and which one's the mackerel.'

Such talk is clever, and would have marked the fellow out for Mummy as being above the common mould. So would the deft way he used his sword to prod us towards the bridge.

Once across the water, all was made plain to us. We were met by a knight and set very decently on a spare horse, to save us further walking.

'Lord Simon has bought you,' he said, giving each of us a lump of silver as big as an infant's tooth. 'He does not want you for himself, but to win a little wager with his brother.'

This was chill news to both of us, but the man's squire was behind us, and the street too tight to turn in, so we couldn't run away. Meanwhile our keeper gossiped on.

'It seems that fellow Trencavel, once lord in these parts, has partaken of the Great Flux. He's done it by a brutish act of self-will, to vex those of us that own him.' His hoof-iron struck sparks from the temper of the paving stones, then our own nag followed with tinder and drum, so it was a second or two before we heard any more chatter. 'In short, he now lies dying.'

I was speechless to hear of my poor cousin's plight.

'Death is the one thing I can't save a man from,' La Mamelonne said, with becoming modesty.

'You can help him one way, as Lord Simon wills. You can open your legs for him, and thus save him.'

'Stuff,' said my friend. 'If I so much as lift my undercotte in his presence, he'll think he's already in Heaven and expire on the instant.'

'See it like this, and hence solve the wager of the De Montforts. This Trencavel has undertaken the *Endura*, so he's committed himself to die. If the Flux and its fever don't kill him, the *Endura* will. You understand what I'm talking about, ladies?'

The *Endura* was the fast to death of the heretics of Oc, the pilgrimage into the sphere of the soul, and yes, we understood.

'If you can remind the little monk that kneels between

273

his thighs to prop itself upright for a moment, even on one leg – '

'I know a trick,' La Mamelonne confessed.

'Just long enough for one of you, or both of you, to lift your skirts and hang your haloes round its neck, and perhaps slide them down over its shoulders – '

'There's no need to develop such a line of persuasion,' I told him sternly. 'Especially with me.'

'Especially with her,' La Mamelonne echoed.

It's just as Mummy had said. These lower members of the squirearchy can never hold their tongues. 'Consequently, young Trencavel will break his *Endura* by reason of the aforesaid holy knowledge of a woman's carnal possibilities. Breaking his *Endura* will put him in a better cast of mind to restore himself to health. This will please Baron Simon no end, and also help Merdun the Bastard win his brother's bet.'

So we clattered on, numb with grief and terror, and entered Le Bourg.

Nothing of the battle remained, except for house tiles underfoot, the stench of burnt thatch, and a litter of wasted arrows. The corpses had been cleared, but the reek of blood was everywhere.

'What's the stake?' La Mamelonne asked, just to be saying something.

'A nunnery. Lord Simon wants its vines and the Bastard needs its women.'

'Then both of them will win.'

We were approaching the Citadel, and close to the forbidding masonry of its Gateway, so it was good to find a glimmer of hope.

'You don't know these De Montforts. Whoever takes the prize will spite his vanquished brother by burning whatever he's no use for.'

'Then the Bastard must win,' La Mamelonne said, with a glint in her eye. 'Our liege lord shall besmirch his *Endura*. We can't let De Montfort lay his hands on those vines.'

274

After a moment's thought, I agreed with her.

He'd already burned nuns at Béziers and St Marie la Dragonne, and might acquire a taste for it.

Mamelie was praying secretly, whispering her prayer from our horse's back. 'Praise God I'm only a whore,' she breathed, 'so no-one need look at my face.'

I must play mackerel too. We had to go to my cousin's dungeon, stay there, and bring ourselves out again, all without being recognized. If the Bastard so much as glimpsed me, then never mind nuns or vines, they'd build us a personal bonfire. Many other men knew me as well. I'd ridden in front of an army. I'd seen enough of my face in the water to understand its beauty was unique.

As for the rest of this evil wager, I must save Raymond-Roger, even if La Mamelonne did so in my stead, and left me jealous for ever. It was a cruel choice, this rescuing the Bastard's convent from the flames, or sparing Lord Simon's crop. I saw in it an allegory of my own sweet fever. When it came to my cousin, my love kept to a nunnery, and tended a vineyard too – the one inside the other and both between my legs and hideously burning.

From the City Gate, we were led up to the castle, with Mamelie praying every step of the way. Our knight and his squire helped us to dismount. We did so to the cheers of several hundred men-at-arms, and stole into the great hall with our hoods pulled up and our faces covered. I would have jumped into the courtyard well if only I could have done so, or crept like a mouse into the capuchon and liripipe of my own pelisse.

'Walk this way, gentlewomen. I pray you approach the fire.' Simon de Montfort was summoning us, if I remembered his voice aright. To those who crowded around us, he said, 'Bring that pair over here, and stand them against the roast. The sooner they're searching themselves for vermin, the quicker I'll see what my silver has bought me. The heat'll fetch them out of those hoods – aye, and their clouting clothes.'

We did not scratch, nor uncover ourselves by as much as

275

a forelock. During our days in the castle Mamelie had asked me to make certain she was clean. As for myself, men have come to call me holy. I can't be, for it's well known I never wore a flea in my life.

Simon de Montfort was not the man to humiliate a woman, even a whore, or not by his direct order. He would burn us by the hundred, and do so very willingly, but abusiveness was not in his nature. Still with my head down, I heard him call, 'This is a formal wager, brother. Don't you want to look at what we're going to tempt young Raymond-Roger with, myself praying he'll fast himself to Heaven, yourself believing no man's strong enough to turn his back on sin?'

'That's right,' a drunken voice shouted. 'Make the women uncover!'

Crusaders howled their agreement, then listened for the Bastard's answer. So did we, for our lives trembled on it.

'I'm busy with the dice.' This with a rattle of the bones in their cup. 'Too busy to number the toothmarks on a drab's cheek. So pray don't ask me!'

'Take them to the fool that was Trencavel, then.' If De Montfort was grieved at Merdun's insolence, he wasn't the man to show it. 'Lead them as they are, and conduct them unchecked. Let the former Viscount discover all their treasures by himself.'

Men hurried us across the flagstones towards the tower called Pinte. It rose within the château itself, and stood taller than any. On different levels it was watch platform, guardroom, armoury, bagnio, cesspit and jakes. Beneath it were all the rungs of hell.

As we skidded down the greasy steps to its dungeon, I understood what should have been plain to me long since. Lord Simon now had rule throughout the Citadel. The dukes and other great ones had returned to their scented pavilions. They had finished their quarantine and would march their armies homeward. Meanwhile an adventurer had closed his fist on Carcassonne. He owned my cousin's carcass, and intended to boil his bones.

276

Fists beat the first of several doors above our hoods, and those on the other side drummed answer. Something else was certain. Witnesses would have been appointed to oversee this wager. The curious too would be here.

There would be eyes enough to watch us, so how could we avoid being found out? If we were to do my cousin any good, we should have to uncover something of ourselves, if only our faces.

The Tower called Pinte is square. This is unusual in Oc, but like the bridge at St Thibéry it was built by the ancient wizards who always laid things straight.

Dreadful punishments have been meted out in Pinte, and the Tower of Prisons, as befits the City's importance. Giants have been walled up to starve, and women sentenced for witchcraft or similar feminine skills have been settled among dry plaster. Then the rains or the moisture of their bodies have made it harden. They cry out it squeezes their skeletons and bruises their meat with agonies more severe than *la peine forte et dure*, as they call it in England, where it is sometimes offered to heretics who have ceased to care about their future.

These tricks are commonplace. At Pinte they were performed beneath its tower merely for the amusement of the castle guests.

I trod with care, and noticed very little. There was the nonsense of my hood, and the trouble with my footing, but the truth was that the dungeon was full of memories only a poet would trouble with. Even to breathe in a hole like that was to hear the walls sigh back at me.

In truth, I did not breathe. These crusaders had promised the townsfolk when they banished us they would enclose my cousin in a cesspit, but otherwise do him no harm, and they were good enough to keep their word.

Our keepers no longer followed us. We sniffed out a tiny circle of light, and there was the former viscount Trencavel.

They had provided him with a candle of the best tallow, and

all the food he could eat. I believe they offered him only venison and lean pork once he had started his *Endura*. Till then he
had bread and beans, but the instinct for kindness was there.

'Cousin,' I whispered. 'It's your cousin Perronnelle, and
a whore sent to comfort you.'

He sighed.

The poor man was like a drunkard fallen asleep beneath
the tails of cattle, or underneath a roosting tree; and we would
be the same unless we left here soon, so many were the evils
that slithered down on us.

There was no other way to help him than to tear off some of
our underclothes and set to work. We began with Mamelie's
petticoat.

We thought no more of the guards, or of those that bore
witness to a wager. Great delicacies came to pass, and a
dozen indelicacies too, but their eyes were all away, or if
not remained unconsidered. I have said those fellows hung
back. They had good reason to do so, the pit was so grossly
furnished.

'Cousin,' I whispered again. All must be whispers here,
for a voice travels far through stone.

'Ah, cousin,' he mumbled back, not at me but La
Mamelonne, whose linen we tore up now. And this was
certainly unseen. Men watch wild goats at rut, but not the
pigs in their sty. If mermaids frisked in the sewer, who would
seek out their play?

There was water here, running live from the rock and
dripping through the walls. So we used the Devil's water
to clean off the filth of men.

He tried to say something now, but his speech was mostly
blood. I would have said he was dying, if he were any more
clearly alive, but he wasn't one to have a woman weep
for him.

I cleaned his eyelids and his beard, and washed his teeth
with water. Then I helped La Mamelonne scrub away at the
flux on his lower portions, till his nobility was once more
revealed.

He had nothing to wear on his bumbarts, not so much as a crawling infant. As I still went ignorant of what men wore beneath their coats and cottes round such places, I could provide him with nothing. But I bound his calves and thighs with leggings torn fresh from Mamelie's petticoat, much as I would a colicky horse.

All this time we heard crusaders coughing and laughing up above, and making what I thought were obscene pretences till foul stuff fell about us and I realized this melancholy place of his imprisonment was not merely a cess where men tipped their waste, but was indeed beneath a jakes. It was full of the fever of the ages, the Citadel's Great Flux, and also of these messy examples of the Northerners' good health that now jumped down and slithered about us like rats.

Sickness gives rise to many things. Let me report that, as Mamelie finished sousing away the filth from where he lay, then trimmed the wick of his candle, I tied a knot round my cousin's knee and found his manhood fully restored to him. His body might sprawl like the old rotting giant in the legend, but his Knighthood stood proud above it.

If ever there was confirmation of our heresy's truth, it was now. Man is his own dichotomy. He is flesh. He is soul. And when his great mass of flesh nods a-weary at death's portal, he keeps a separate particle that is every inch spirit.

It was towards Mamelie La Mamelonne that this resurrected warrior turned his gentle eye, to me that he spoke. 'Before the Great God of Purity, cousin,' he said, 'Auntie, your mother, was right. I should have married you to my bed. And I yet may, if only – '

He moaned and mumbled on, the way lovers do, which is not unlike the groans men make dying. 'Is that lovely radiance indeed my cousin?' He gazed from one to the other of us, woman and woman about. 'Are you the maid of my blood? You have been my nightly dream,' he sobbed, 'a dream now palpable as fever.' He sobbed again. We all sobbed. 'I think you're no more than a candle-flame – you'll blow yourself out in an instant.'

279

'No,' we both said.

'I promise you, cousin,' I added. 'I promise you.'

'Angel or *ignis fatuus*?' His features lost themselves in shadow. He whispered, 'I think you're no more than a moth – no, a moth would not live here. I'm already dead.' The giant began to crumble, but the warrior was still firm in his conclusions. 'All I see is a bird of the mist, a bright marsh bird. A wisp-bubble of burning vapours risen from the cess I lie upon.'

'We are here to help you, cousin. The townspeople will – '

La Mamelonne gave his body a squeeze, and the giant died a little more.

The spirit nodded on and spoke its mind. 'Sister,' it cried. 'Oh, my poor unacknowledged sister and my love!' Something of him caught me by the hand and covered it with kisses. 'Oh, sister, sister.'

'He thinks you're a nun,' La Mamelonne said. 'If that's the game a man wants to play, then I'm the one to oblige him, even on his death bed.'

His eye rolled from one to the other of us and back again. 'Oh, my Perronnelle,' he said, 'what a miracle of fair hair. My brain is so weak I'm forever seeing two of you.'

I don't know what we should have done after that. Save the vines and respect his body's ruin? Save the nuns and admire the stiffness of his soul?

La Mamelonne reached her customary conclusion, and was half-up with her cotte and half-down with her bottom when the unthinkable happened.

Merdun the Bastard swaggered in, with a retinue of shadows. He glimpsed the naked stiffness in the candle-flame, or perhaps he saw me fit another candle to its cup. 'I've won!' he triumphed. 'The wager and its stake are clearly mine! I'm now the proud possessor of an aviary of nuns!'

I showed him the candle, and this showed him myself. 'All and everything is an illusion,' I proclaimed. 'Nothing yet is consummate.'

He waved his villains out by flourishing the orange he held against his nose. 'So I've found you,' he said. 'There's not much room for running,' he added. 'We'll use the Viscount as our pillow.'

'You've found yourself a whore,' La Mamelonne said. 'I warn you quite frankly – she's got spots in her water.'

'Brief weeks ago she was pure and proclaiming her virginity.'

'That's the cunning of her,' Mamelie said. 'Sin often seems like that, but it gives you spots in your – '

'Be content with what you've brought me to,' I said.

'So I'll sit you on my sword, if not on my – '

'Let *me* sit on *that*,' La Mamelonne proposed. 'I do the nobility for free.'

Once again the sweet girl was offering to save me.

The retainers weren't the same rogues-at-arms who had pillaged the Mill House at St Thibéry, or Merdun would have been obliged to act against one or the other of us in spite of the invincible smell.

As it was, the invincible smell defeated him. The dungeon of the tower called Pinte held the distillation of every ordure known to man or horse, so the Bastard retreated from it before he had so much as unbuckled his belt. Just to incline his nostril was enough.

We knelt hurriedly at prayer in the little shrine of cleanliness we had prepared for my cousin to lie in. His eyes were closed, but at least his limbs were clean.

I'm no good at talking to God. La Mamelonne approached her orisons with ease and dignity. 'O my Great Lord,' she said. 'I thank You, I thank You, and I thank You again.' She spoke to Him as to any other man who offered her trinkets.

'We bless You for keeping your servants safe thus far,' I put in.

'I Mamelie La Mamelonne in all my names am especially grateful to you for making me pregnant just now.'

'The Bastard didn't lay a finger on you!'

'I speak of the Trencavel.'

'You did not – you scarcely touched him.'

'Life can be quick, my pigeon.' As we rose to take our leave of the place, she added, 'Believe me, I am truly blessed. I was last pregnant as recently as yesterday, and that time felt very different.'

Mamelie was often *enceinte* for a moment or two, and frequently professed as much to excuse herself from working with a man with bad breath or too many teeth. She said she could effect a miscarriage by stepping over a stone or showing her bottom to a puddle.

This obsession that she was carrying a miraculous child was foolish and dangerous. Men would punish her for it even more readily than they would for being a witch with pictures of tomorrow up her skirt and a notorious apostle of Dogskin Raymond.

If she said she bore the seed of the dying Trencavel, she would not only lose the love of her last friend on earth, who I take to be myself, but she would also burn – not as an act of superstition, but as a matter of politics and greed, whose kindling is inexhaustible.

She was in wilful mood when we left my cousin and climbed up a step or two. We were at once in a guardroom full of ribald men (find me a guardroom full of ribald women and I'll show you a far kinder place) who began to paw at us the way soldiers will when they've put aside their cups and spears and have nothing else for their hands to rest on.

'These are the drabs from across the river,' one said. 'They'll not have had a man inside their legs since this evening's sunset.'

'Unless it's the Trencavel.'

'Purer than pure.'

'Better than virgins, and not so shrill.'

They didn't seem to notice the dungeon's smell on us, partly because they had it in their lungs already, more because their noses had their own bodies to contend with, and they were either foul or holy according to your point of view.

I expected La Mamelonne to lie across the stonework on her back, and distract the louts' attention, as was usual. Instead, she struck the first of them across the gums with her mitten, and cried out, 'Leave me alone. I'm an honest woman.'

'All the better,' he said. He fondled her forecloth and tried to unfasten her napkin.

These were actions she normally performed for herself uninvited. Tonight she screamed, 'I'm pregnant. I'm pregnant,' as if a lie could be her excuse. Then she bit him.

'Pregnant!' he howled. 'So was my mother.' He rebuked her with a slap. 'How dare you compare yourself with her!'

This got the evening off to a very brisk start.

All score of us were plunged into a wrestle round the guardroom, and a slippery game of catch-as-catch-can it was between three dozen hands, La Mamelonne's body and my virtue.

I say slippery because we were still covered in scum from downstairs, and a slimy woman is a ticklish thing to hold.

Unfortunately, this rapid exercise in the heat began to dry us off and, as soon as we were metamorphosed from mudpats into good brown bricks, these fellows found we stuck so snugly in the fist they were able to close their fingers on us. They at once began to hold us against them in ways I had only encountered once before and did not wish to feel repeated.

As I have explained before it takes a good long time to unclothe me, let alone unclout me, and La Mamelonne (or Mamelie as her naked self is) can clad herself faster than any man who has not cleaned fish or stuffed sausages can possibly undress her again, so we remained in charge of the battle and would continue so unless they grew savage.

To be fair to them, apart from punching us and kicking us, savagery formed no part of their intention. Instead, they waved coin at us. If La Mamelonne weren't in such a religious mood she could have earned more money in that guardroom than she had in the past month of honest endeavour.

As it was, she stood on her dignity. This nearly ruined things for both of us.

'Come on, my pigeon,' she called out to me. 'Your turn to fly. Stop fluttering about. Show them your tail feathers!' She spoke as one whore might speak to another. As she apologized after, her advancing pregnancy was beginning to derange her mind.

They couldn't all hold us at once. Being orderly people, they didn't try. The warriors, or some of them, began to undress themselves, and a curious sight that was. As I've said before, the ring-mail or link armour is a disturbing thing for a woman to see on a man. It makes him look as if he is wearing a frock made of gypsy earrings, or seem to be wrapped in a shawl of copper fishing net, the sort they use to snare pez or swordfish, save it never works. You need good bait for swordfish, preferably a finger.

Most men wear it on top of a frock, with another on top of it again. Smelly men-at-arms of the sort who held us now put it straight onto their skins, where it settles among their body hair and sometimes never comes up again. I've spoken to women who've touched the naked backs of such men, clutched even, and they tell me they've grown skin above the iron. Even the ones who wash themselves during the warm season bear little rings and diamonds or triangles all over their body like so much scrofula.

One such embraced me now. He held me firmly but tenderly, and at arms' length to let me see how much I had got of him. He was completely naked. His armour had made him toad-coloured, like an everlasting freckle.

His kindness did not notice my reluctance. Instead, he spoke softly to himself, which is how most men talk to women. Although he was a Norman, he was inventive as any troubadour. 'When this little bird I have between my legs grows cocky enough to poke his beak into your nest, what shall I say to him?'

'Tell him to watch out for the weasel,' I said sternly.

He squeezed my shoulders encouragingly. Men never

listen. 'Shall I say he is gathering corn from the bowels of an angel?'

Before Constance de Coulobres could lean down from Heaven and box his ears for him, or I dispute the extent of this heresy, his fingers slipped.

We were all growing very sweaty by now, and this sudden outpouring of fear and perspiration refreshed the mud on mine and La Mamelonne's bodies to such an extent that we again became as elusive as eels and thrice as artful.

A woman cannot run for ever, especially in a small room full of large men. We were saved by the door crashing open, and a voice calling through it, *'Stand to your pikes!'* followed by, *'Guard, port your weapons!'*

These are military terms, common enough among the Normans and other warriors who speak the Parisian tongue, but unknown to myself and La Mamelonne who had only seen service with the Carcassonne militia. Their speaker was commanding the castle guard to stand very still, point its spears into the air, and incline them slightly forward and to the right, in the general direction of the pole star.

He now strode in to see what had become of his voice, and grew extremely angry to find it had lost itself entirely. He was one of those people the great ones from the North keep about them in considerable numbers. Neither serf nor gentleman, he was known as a captain or professional soldier. Such people do not understand much, but what they do understand they grasp very clearly.

What he understood now was that whatever the castle guard was pointing towards the pole star it wasn't its spears.

I have never heard a man sing so rapidly as he began to chant now, not even the troubadour who strummed on Marie-Bise. He had the guard stand to attention, naked though it was, then dress itself instantly in its clothes and its spears without flinching from its eternal *rigor* of immobility.

Some of the warriors pained themselves considerably while pulling on their ring-mail, but he was too mellow hearted to permit himself to laugh.

He ordered us to be flogged instead. Apparently, if a woman of the town meddles with a member of a Northern or Norman guard while the said member is on duty, the standard punishment is forty stripes for her, and no soup for him.

We had meddled not with one but with twenty members of a Northern or Norman guard. This meant our punishment was eight hundred stripes each on the bare back.

This led to a further attempt to strip us, as the need for our backs to be entirely bare beneath the lash was another of those matters that this captain who did not understand much understood very clearly.

While an attempt was again being made to reduce us, or the appropriate portions of us, to nudity, he kindly said we could share the punishment between us and commuted our sentence to four hundred lashes each.

One of the guard tried to speak.

'Silence!' the Captain said. Only Captains may speak when Captains are present.

The guardsman tried to speak again, in spite of the terror in the atmosphere.

'Silence!' the Captain said. This was a word he knew well.

Before he said it, the guardsman pointed out that men commonly die after about two hundred lashes with the whip, and although a woman's flesh is undoubtedly more stubborn in such matters, as witness childbirth and frequent beatings from her husband, no one could be absolutely confident enough about the depth of skin on our backs to be certain that the punishment wouldn't prove to be capital – in which case it should be referred higher.

Something else this Captain knew very clearly was that there is no one higher than a captain.

'Captain,' a voice said. 'They wasn't interfering with us. We was interfering with them.'

This led to what the military call a mutiny, in other words a spontaneous concordat of disagreement, agreement, refusal or outcry. '*Oui!*' they all shouted. '*Oui! Oui! Oui!*' It was the first and last time a Northerner's silly 'wee-wee', which they all pronounced '*oil*' sounded to my ears at least half as sweet as our own rough '*oc*'.

'I am going to let you off your punishment,' the Captain told us sternly, while watching us to make sure we got dressed. 'Not because the evidence convinces me, but because to administer eight hundred lashes will fatigue a warrior's sword arm.'

The guard cheered at this, and lost more soup.

The moment we were dressed he had us thrown from the guardroom, kicked out of Pinte, and rushed from the castle.

We tumbled on to our bottoms and into the courtyard, where we were nearly raped again.

I should say *nearly* raped *nearly* again, lest some slipshod historian conclude from the above that one or more members of the castle guard, by which I mean the member of one or more members of the castle guard, managed to intrude itself at some moment or other into our impossible-to-handle, rapidly-gyrating bodies. It did not.

As we unfastened our bruises from the cobblestones, I was reminded of what all women know and some make tiresome use of, namely that to thrash your arms and legs about in an effort to rise from where you find yourself sitting is to present yourself to the masculine sex in an attractive and provocative manner, principally because it allows glimpses, and sometimes more than glimpses, of those portions of the feminine anatomy that no man would otherwise see.

We were at once surrounded by several hundred crusaders and a great deal of excitement. They continued to crowd us close, though those who were near to us, and those who stood downwind, had to keep a tight hold on their noses.

'We could give them a wash,' said one.

'Souse them at the pump,' said another, 'or pickle them in wine. They'll smell sweeter than gooseberries then.'

We were saved from the indignity of being cleansed by

the arrival of the knight and squire who had conducted us here.

'This meat is Lord Simon's,' our own knight said. 'If any man wishes to dress it any further, go talk to him.'

They swore, but troubled us no more. So our saviour loaded us on our carthorse and said, 'They smell of the sewer pit, as you say. Now my orders are to toss them back on that dunghill across the river where their goodnesses belong.'

CAPUT SIX

In which, having failed to be a whore, our Virgin seeks to play politician, but finds only devils to help her.

The moment we were among the smoke and stench of the encampment, Mamelie went to wash herself, while I rushed towards a crowd of men who smelled much as I did.

They spat when they saw me, as if to acknowledge the fact.

'I have just come from the young Viscount,' I cried. 'He's dying at the hands of these invaders. I've seen him with my own eyes.'

'I saw him once,' said a foxy-nosed lubbock with scabs on his knees. 'He had a cloak embroidered with flowers, and a fine tall horse to make a breeze for it.'

'You've known him since then,' I protested. 'You knew him in Le Bourg and Le Castellare at the head of our main battle. You saw him with harness on his back and with steel in his hand. You saw him save your wife and your babies from fire, and strive to protect the whole rotting sewer you lived in.'

The fellow eyed me strangely at this, and a very good fox he could have been, if only he had the teeth to go with his nose. 'You're a highly persuasive lady,' he said. 'Well you know how to flatter a man. But the truth is I saw no such thing. I saw a pack of mounted fellows with iron on their heads. They might have been noblemen, they might have been scarecrows or even boggarts from the vines for all I saw of their faces.' He fell to scratching his scabs as if he'd caught them in combat. 'I even heard there were women up there, women fighting with swords. If you believe that you'll believe anything.'

'Raymond-Roger's close to death,' I said, sticking to my point.

'I'm not too far away from it myself,' a youngster grunted.

'It will be raining soon. We're not allowed to build walls, and there's nothing here to make into a roof.'

'I wonder what became of his cloak and his horse,' Foxy Nose said. 'I could eat that horse to the last drop of gravy.'

'He'll give cloaks and horses a-plenty to any that rescue him,' I said.

'Not from the Citadel,' the younger man said. 'That Citadel's impregnable. They wouldn't have taken it from us otherwise.'

There was a deal more spitting after these words of wisdom. They carried on regardless of the fact that it was my cousin's suffering that let them have water in their mouths to spit with.

I tried to tell them so. I was saved from becoming foolish by Solomon of Gerona, who had been sitting there dressed in black, as invisible as a rook in an evergreen tree.

'This Crusade isn't easy for any of us to understand,' he confessed. 'And when a person can't understand something, what can he do about it? I speak not only for myself, the one man without a foreskin in all the Land of Oc, but also for you, Perronnelle de Saint Thibéry, the only woman with balls in roughly the same area of country.'

He restored my respect with this measured statement, and I felt better for it as any woman would.

Unfortunately he wasn't finished. 'How can either of us be certain which side we should be on, when Count Raymond of Toulouse is on both sides at once?'

'My cousin knows what side *he* is on,' I reasoned stubbornly. 'He is his own man, and the rest of us belong to him.'

'All of me that belongs to him is my foreskin,' said Solomon gravely, 'and I left that in Gerona.'

'So what about her cousin?' Foxy Nose asked him.

'Part of him belongs to the Count of Toulouse – I forget which part. All of his other parts, including his wife and his offspring, belong to King Peter of Spain. Both of whom have said Simon de Montfort may have him.'

292

'Peter of Spain is a Spaniard,' I stated.

'You have a point there,' Solomon said. 'A very good point indeed. I wonder why no one has made it before.'

'As for Raymond of Toulouse, my cousin has twice as many castles as he does.'

'True,' said Solomon. 'But the Count of Toulouse owns ten times as many brothels, and so far these crusaders haven't captured one of them.'

So the cowards had no stomach for a fight. I went to ask their woman to make them change their minds.

On the way to enlist the aid of all the Amazons and corpse-strippers I could muster, I stumbled across a carcass in plate armour. It was Ironface. Thieves had stolen his sword and his blazon, but otherwise his battle gear was complete.

I was plunged into misery when I realized that these outflung and scattered limbs and head were the mortal remains of the being who called himself Lord Ferblant. Since Ironface had once saved my life, it was only appropriate I named him by his assumed title. But there lay all that was left of my Lord Tin, and perhaps everything there ever was.

I was tempted to think he was asleep, but no one, not even a devil, goes to sleep with his head unfastened and a pair of crows eating it.

The contents of his brain pan were sweet to them, so this brace of messy feeders refused to leave. I beat them out of his iron skull. They flapped away and then returned and entered it again. I used my fist. I clubbed them with a long stone. I had to persist.

I intended to pay a proper respect to my friend. He had not fawned on me as the Mute did, nor treated me to gruff good humour like Gibbu the Hunchback. He had been as attentive to me as the one and as rude as the other, just like a father. Not that he could be father. No woman wants a metal box as her daddy, a devil even less. Yet although he was no sort of man, he had saved my life, and done even more for the Fish Girl, bringing Violette la Vierge to sweeter song than a thrush guarding her nest, such was the briskness of his tail.

She, of course, was nowhere to be seen. She never was when the world wanted her. I wept alone.

His chest cage was empty front and back. There was a scabby mess that might have been rust, coagulated sweat or some other residue of mortal or immortal man, particularly one who dwells in body armour. The birds had eaten all there was of him. Unless, as I suspected, there never was anything of him there in the first place.

His arm tubes were empty, save for a morsel of snake parchment that must have been skin. The only proof I had they had ever been otherwise was a memory of grubby fingernails. Even a crow has those, and talons are the undoubted marks of the Great Beast.

The legs smelled of sour wine. I had once seen blood gush from the stump, blind the Bastard's eyes and sting the faces of his underlings as if it were peppery as dragon juice. Then the blood had turned into wine. I had tasted it in the cup. That was old Ironface's miracle.

Ferblant's headpiece held a nest of human hair. His helm was full of fleas, slugs and all manner of vermin attractive to carrion. No wonder the crows had persisted. Slugs are an evil beast, friendly with gnomes and leeches. They'll rise from the soil at the first sign of death, even drunken sleep, as Daddy more than once could testify. Fleas are another matter, particularly *post mortem*. Only a saint has those in such numbers.

Ferblant was a conundrum to the last. I held his teeming brains to my chest, and wondered what had killed him. Had he been struck by a thunderbolt, fallen among thieves or been torn apart by angry women, of whom he knew a great many? He might, quite simply, have been translated. By this I mean nothing blasphemous. Simply that he had returned to the infernal regions that even a Christian knows to lie beneath the hill.

I thought of Ferblant's women not, I hope, jealously but

with a kind of tingling curiosity of the lower parts. The Fish Girl wasn't the only female to have been with him outside and inside his armour, laying herself open to transubstantial delights. There had been others on the journey, followed by an everlasting concourse of the curious in Carcassonne – burghers' wives mainly from Le Bourg and Le Castellare, pining for their homes and seeking a firm root. A man does not satisfy such a longing in a woman without making her become a little bit possessive. Not if he can offer her a firm root.

Lastly I thought of myself. Was Ferblant my Phantom? Could he so transmute himself? Was he my midnight visitant, my whisperer of prophecies, my murmurer of desires? He had a way with words, and a way into my head as well, since my bed was always accessible to him.

My mind returned to the beautiful youth I had seen bathing. Could he have been the magical product of Ironface's will? Ironface had been absent, but might this indeed have been Ironface's diabolic soul made irresistible flesh for a few precious seconds in the fading light? Did devils have such power? Was my dream to be taken from me now he had been swallowed up?

If he *had* been taken back beneath the hill.

I inspected the soil where his armour lay. There was no other trace of him, except for a little circle of charcoal. It might have been Hell's navel, its orifice clenched tight against human inquisitiveness. It looked like the remains of a cooking fire.

I sat there for an age of sorrow. I sat an eternity.

Perhaps it was no longer Ferblant I wept for – how can one mourn a Spanish voice in an emptiness of iron? – perhaps I at last wept properly for Mummy and the fat wrestler I knew as Daddy.

I wept too for my cousin and the wasted seed of the Trencavels, and even more for the mortal sin called incest which was also a human crime. It had led my uncle Trencavel who was also my unacknowledged father to take to his bed a sister, niece, daughter (I could not ponder the relationship) because of her peerless beauty and, in a few quick thrusts of his loins, make her girlhood pregnant with me and transmute her for the rest of her days into Aunt Vinegar.

As I gazed through the stretch marks of tears and listened to the pulse in my wrists I heard a more distant drumming. I heard a tabor being beaten for the march. Its pace was slow and deliberate, as if it guided the footfall of an army. Whoever plied the pom-pom, whether warrior or idiot boy, the sound came from close at hand.

A parade was being tapped, and tapped out proud, here in our defeated encampment.

The note held a wryer echo. Another, more eerie sound came through it, a music I knew well, but had not heard for days.

It was the trill of the Mute's carved pipe. Gibbu called it the 'highwood', and I daresay he named it correctly, save its sound was as low as a woman's sobbing. It was close to a woman's keening, this hermaphrodite's song. It came from the lungs of a degenerate creature whose soul lacked voice as his body did cullions.

First I saw the Mute, my conjuror without a name. Then there was Gibbu, a gruff bearded fellow with manhood enough in his satchel, but who walked like a camel, with the rest of himself on his back.

Then, to my amazement, in step with the one who beat the drum, and apace with the Mute's mad pipe, strode a hundred stalwart men, followed by a hundred more in two companies. These were in the prime of their manhood, not one of them older than five and twenty years, and most of them less than a score.

Such men would strike, then stand firm. They would strike again. They carried weapons to do so, pikes and poleaxes, side-swords and two-handed blades, and their spirits were good. Most of them smiled to salute me, many of them with teeth that had tips and edges, teeth for the most part white.

296

At their rear, like a king in his pomp, and therefore well behind the main battle, rode a ghost.

I say a ghost, because it came in the features of a ghost and in the guise of a ghost. It wore a ghost's armour. This armour was itself no more than an appearance, as the philosophers say. I held the reality in my hand.

Ironhead's chuckle was always a sepulchral one. Lazarus could not have sounded worse as he stepped from the tomb. Terrible now, when he halted to chuckle at me. His voice in its box of iron rattled harsher than the beaks of those crows when they'd pecked inside his harness.

'You're dead,' I accused, touching his breastplate with my boot.

'I changed my clothes,' he laughed. 'My soul was coming out in a freckle. I needed to feel the late summer damps on my bones.'

My clog stirred his fallen armour along the ground. I was speechless to hear his voice again. Let my foot ask the questions.

'Oh, I have a spare coffin, my Virgin. All in parts and packed flat in the paniers in my baggage.'

'On your horse?'

'On the quarter hump of my noble destrier.'

His mare looked as droop-arsed as ever, but I could not bring myself to laugh. 'As well as the harness you wear?'

'I had a young blacksmith cobble me another one.'

'Or perhaps he was a lorimer?' I scoffed.

'There are smiths in plenty, all over this encampment.'

'Or perhaps you're the Chimera from Aragon,' I questioned, 'that breaks itself apart like a serpent with the ratchets – or bones in the potter's field of skeletons?'

'Perhaps I am.'

'Or the little bits of life you find in ditches, that multiply by breeding with their segments?'

He yawned. A ghost may yawn. It's the easiest sound for a ghost to make, a ghost or a devil in armour.

'Do you suppose I can live in pieces like a worm? Or grow another end like a lizard or a spider?'

He vaulted from his horse with an upward pressure of his hands, the way a spectre can that has no weight in its legs. Even so, he used the strength of his arms to let his leg tubes touch gently to the ground, as if there was a gristle above the knee or a softness in the thigh that still might damage from the thrust of iron.

'Ferblant,' I sobbed. I sounded like Mummy when she pretended to forgive poor Daddy for almost everything. 'Ferblant! . . . Ferblant!'

He put a metal arm on my shoulder, a thing he'd done only once before. 'Virgin,' he murmured.

'Don't call me Virgin,' I snapped. It was like being cuddled by a crab. For the second time in our acquaintance I noticed his fingernails. His talons were grubby with the filth of New Carcassonne – tree-stain and the smut of cooking fires.

Unless it were the soot of Hell.

His claw did not shift from my shoulder. 'Your virginity is mine, my Perronnelle, to blazon it as I will. I won it at tourney, and bought it with the rest of you for a bag of gold.' Feeling me struggle against his hand he hissed, 'I ought to wear it on my lance, or keep it in a snake jar of vinegar. Instead I let you walk it abroad.'

I broke free from him at last. Whatever he was, it had no strength in its legs to stop my wrenching to and fro. I offered him a moment's scorn, then said, 'Are you saying that a mere Lord Tin can own a Trencavel?'

'Not in the least,' he chuckled. 'Only a Trencavel can belong to a Trencavel – even a Trencavel disguised as a Saint Thibéry. All that I own, other than the backside of my horse, is your virginity.'

'And what will you do with it?' I scoffed. A wiser tongue than mine might have left the subject alone.

'I may leave it on the hillside like a ring of stones,' he yawned. 'Or I may give it to the Holy Dominic to use as a library. It must be vast, this virginity of yours, my Virgin. You talk of nothing else.'

All this had been uttered to the music of pipe and drum, the thump up and down of ten score pairs of feet.

The Mute had halted beside the cavalcade – there were horsemen too, each company being headed by its proud chevaliers, since you cannot have a leader of military affairs without he wears four legs as well as his own, and preferably five. So the Mute, frail two-legged thing that he was, stood soft-skinned nearby in the manner of musicians, and blew martial notes while the drum marched forward as befitted its importance.

Then the drum too halted, everybody halted to a most military shuffle of the clog and sandal.

Gibbu, a three-legged man if ever I saw one, left off striding with his company, and came to stand hard by Ironface, as if he were the marshal of a great parade.

I noticed that the remaining companies were led by the three young squires from Capestang. They had been doughty at table, and sterner still at the Battles of Le Bourg and Le Castellare. With such men leading such men we might stage a raid to set my cousin free, especially now that Simon de Montfort had lost all his army of pilgrims, and the quarantine counts had gone home and taken their cohorts with them.

Ironface spoke briefly to Gibbu, and the Hunchback sang out a word of command in that language of commands that no civilized woman will ever understand. He blew the sound out as if Ironface were the brain and the lungs, and himself no more than his master's trumpet.

The parade faced its front and grounded the helves of their axes and butts of their spears. The rest placed their right hands on the hilts of their swords like so many troubadours declaring their heart.

They gazed at us. It is hard to be looked at by a parade, so I turned to Ironface.

'These fellows will follow me everywhere,' he boasted.

'So the gentlemen who own them must follow in their turn.'

'So why should they follow you, Ferblant? What lies have you told them?'

Ironface brought his helm close to whisper, 'They follow me because they've seen how I can fight.'

'They've seen how I can fight. And I've done more of it than you.'

'True.' Again that strange rattle of the tongue, like a cricket singing love songs or a meat fly trapped inside a colander. 'True enough, my Virgin. But in my case I'm a man. Since you're a woman they'll take more convincing.'

'You're a devil.'

'Something of that also.'

'If those fellows will follow you, devil, then lead them against the Citadel and set my cousin free. You can wear my virginity as your fee.'

'Against the Citadel? I might as well ask them to cut their throats with spear-grass. As for the other matter – '

'Against the island, then. We could capture the Crusade's great catapults and siege engines, and turn them against the walls of his prison.'

'In a day or two, my Perronnelle.' His voice became un-usually soft and tender, as if his tongue were back inside a human head and that head inside a proper helmet. 'In a day or two, and only if all else fails.' He walked me to one side, holding me by the sleeve then transferring my hand to the vambrace on his forearm, like a knight whose vow prevents the acceptance of such a gift as the one I had offered, but who wears his lady's scarf nonetheless, and wins with it at the joust.

'What else?' I asked him. I clung hard in my turn, clung rather than clutched, the way a questioner will.

'I have a stratagem,' he said. 'Give me another hour to taste it, and then I'll share it with you, I promise.'

I felt for his wrist, but he'd donned an iron gauntlet. There was no hint of a pulse, even inside his elbow, nor of any stirrings else that connected to a heart.

He moved my fingers aside and went back to playing soldiers.

Men think life leaves them time to roll dice. Women know it to be more urgent. I begrudged Ironface his hour and went to look for my corpse-strippers instead.

I found a dozen of them sitting near an old fellow of fifty, discussing the best way to help him die. Some favoured holding his head beneath a pillow, others beneath a pond, while the cruellest ones suggested tickling his feet.

He rose from the ground at this, and staggered off, as some people will when they're already dead enough to grow stubborn.

'He's going to join the militia,' a woman joked. 'We'll lose all of our corpses that way, if we're not careful.'

I suggested they came with me across the river, and killed some crusaders. The pickings would be better.

They said it was too far to go. 'We've got corpses enough nearer home. 'There's scarcely a live man left in the encampment, or not one with salt in his bag.'

'Look there,' one exclaimed, 'and I'll show you an example. There's a death's head in a polished suit.'

'He's either a coffin or a crab,' called another. 'With sour meat inside him whichever he is.'

I needed their support, so I joined them in laughter without turning round.

A hand tugged my sleeve, with a grip like a lobster's. Ironface stood behind me. It was he who had been the butt of their mirth and he did not find it funny.

He led me aside. 'We'll not carry the Citadel,' he said. 'Not even if we get ten thousand to rise against it. We must wait for the quarantine to weaken the crusaders' numbers even more.' He brushed aside my impatience. 'Similarly with their siege engines on the island. We'll not gain a catapult until the watch becomes less wary and their guards grow used to sleeping.'

He snapped his dirty brown fingers and brought Gibbu

and the Mute to his side. The rest of his proud army had dispersed to its women. Its women were my own proud army, and they were dispersed already. 'In the interval we'll go on an embassage.'

'Talk to De Montfort? He'll cut out our tongues and burn what's left of us.'

'We'll be better without your tongue, Perronnelle. Your silence would be a servant to us all.'

For the first time, I heard the Mute laughing.

There was no time to digest the sound before Ironface said, 'I am proposing an embassage to the Holy Dominic.' He caught at my wrist as if to capture my mind by holding my heartbeat. 'He is less than a day away. Dominic of Calaruega may not command the Crusade, but it is his to command. If Raymond-Roger were to die in that tower, it would misplease him greatly.'

'And how do you know this?' I pulled my blood free of his claw. 'Just what kinship do you claim with the Holy Dominic that you pretend to know his thoughts?'

'Do you want to gossip or ride, Perronnelle?'

I rode, and with strange emotions, my heart knocked so sorely. I closed my eyes and my Phantom told me to ride. I nodded with exhaustion again, and he bade me stay and fight. I had to balance my cousin's need against the pangs of my own predicament. I had killed men and cut them. I had lusted for blood and longed after love. Yet I had not confessed my sins since the death of my family. I had come to cross myself with even less feeling than a beggar spits.

There were priests here a-plenty – Ironface sent one reeling as he pushed his way to horse – but they were of Mummy's kind and under my cousin's protection. They were heretics for all their undoubted holiness and belief in God. They believed the Primal Devil made the world, and that Jesus could never be in flesh, for flesh too was Satan's.

I had known bad priests all my life. I had been taught to watch out for their tricks by Constance de Coulobres. As for the rest of them I thought as Daddy had thought, that a priest may be as bad as he likes if only he proclaims the truth and does the right offices, for God will work through him.

Yet here was Nano leading me to the old Roman road of the Wizards as if he were shod with lodestones of magic, and once our steeds were pacing out and their hoofs sparking upon it, I began to think this heresy was no bad notion, or not as practised by ordinary men and women, especially if I took Mummy and La Mamelonne to be examples of the two extremes of heretical opinion.

Mummy believed flesh to be holy enough, all except that piece she detested halfway down the fronts of men and little boys. She knew Jesus was the Son of God because he himself did not have such an object, saying by way of proof that although there were very few depictures of Christ in the world, and even less of God, such ones as there were always showed both of them with their loins covered and plainly without such a satanic appendix.

As for La Mamelonne, she cared nothing at all for the devil's flesh in her body, save to know that it was fat and beautiful. The particle men desired in her even above those twin miracles she let them name her by was so clearly designed by God that she called it by her own magic name ooolooolooo, a term as mysterious in its way and as difficult to write as her other word quuushshn, which she liked to keep between it and her horse.

'Mamelie la Mamelonne,' Ironface said. 'Has anyone seen the idle young faggot?'

'She's resting,' I answered.

'A whore's work is all rest. It's her men who break the sweat.'

'She says she's carrying a holy child.'

'Blasphemy!' He spoke as always as if he knew such matters. 'Manifest blasphemy.'

'She doesn't claim God is the father. She says it's my cousin, who being a nobleman is considerably more eligible.'

'Another attack of wind,' Ironface said crossly. 'She has

a lot of wind, although she blames her horse.' He waited for the Mute to play an imitation on his pipe. 'Tell me, Perronnelle, is it true?'

'If she did it, she did so in the space of a blink.'

'She does all her lovers in the space of a blink,' Gibbu said. 'She claims to bring them Eternity in the flutter of an eyelid.'

Men talk like this once their brains are spread astride a horse.

For myself, I made no prattle except to answer questions. I thought of the Holy Dominic, and wondered if he were not too holy. Like Ironface, he was another crab from a Spanish pond, and I rode with strange enough fish already.

From the encampment to Pennautier would be a brief, brisk gallop, if only a horse could gallop on a pavement of fitted stones. We had to keep to the Wizards' Road, because the land is wet there in places, and a river coils all about in ways more amazing to the eye than when gypsy men at the fair break open their cask of serpents.

We had no business at Pennautier, and they desired to make none with us. First we heard women shrieking, and not pleasantly either, then twenty men and a whole half hundred of boys came out from its walls and shot arrows at us. These for the most part missed, because we rode with our backs to the sunset, and the air was already as nearly dark as made no difference.

The road led us inescapably towards this gaggle of bowmen. We had to pass them or retreat. We decided to pass them.

Ironface insisted they were aiming to miss us, or they would have hit us long since.

If they missed us, I said, how could they hope to find their arrows again, especially after dark?

'Perronnelle speaks true,' Gibbu said, being our archer. He spurred his horse forward and pushed his face into its neck, leaving his hump as exposed above it as a pack-ass's woolsack.

The Mute did the same, but neatly, tucking away his head and folding up his legs till none of him was any wider than the prow of his nag. If anything struck him it could only come from behind, which makes dying more comfortable, as his guts wouldn't fall out when we drew away the arrow.

I wanted none of this, but rode straight ahead, desiring as Mummy would say to do things with dignity.

Meanwhile the shafts of these frenzied toxophilists from Pennautier continued to whir past our ears like so many meat-maddened birds. Each step we galloped forward brought their beaks that much closer to pecking us.

The archers spread themselves out in a comfortable line as if competing at the butt or bringing down autumn duck. Their eyes were hot yellow from the facing sun, with only the whites of their hands clearly visible. They shot so deliberately and long in the pull that I began to believe Ironface was right after all. They were aiming to miss.

They meant to miss me because I wore woman's hair and was friendly of face, and they meant no harm to Gibbu or the Mute because they wore faces of any sort, or did when they had swank enough to show them.

At thirty paces I was convinced these were merely warning shots, instructing us to ride on and leave Pennautier aside from our itinerary, as indeed was our intention. I felt so certain of this that I allowed myself to wonder about the safety of Ironface Ferblant, an infernal being with no features at all, and unable to crouch behind the high parts of his mare because of the stiffness in his armour. I looked and saw he was unscathed. Not an arrow rattled on his tin, nor damaged his horse.

I nearly drew rein amongst them to toss them a coin, or an old loaf of Carcassonne bread which anyone is welcome to. Then I glimpsed Gibbu's hump.

It was stuck with more shafts than a hedgehog has quills, with more of them crowding in by the instant.

At that precise moment a point passed along Nano's neck and under my armpit, and would have drawn blood from me or worse, except for the excellence of Constance de Coulobres' stitching.

Two arrows pierced Ironface, one in the leg, occasioning no more than an instant haemorrhage of wine, and the other straight through the grill of his helmet. Being built like a colander this let the shaft inside, and so far in that it seemed as if a conjuror had swallowed it, liberating a gut-curdling scream, and causing him to sprawl across his pommel and veer in a circle, mercifully overriding a huge number of archers as he did so.

Some of them fell, some of them ran, the rest continued to shoot. With us in their midst, this was largely at one another. Clearly they had not exchanged gossip with the men of Le Bourg.

While the fools began to kill themselves, we burst onward and out. The Mute seized Ironface's bridle, and we led our stricken friends west from Pennautier.

We halted by a narrow wood, scarcely a bowshot beyond the town's ring of houses.

Ironface still leaned sideways like a tree with a rock in its branches. He was so asprawl that the Mute could scarcely prop him into his saddle.

Gibbu had so many shafts in him that the blood remained stoppered inside his hump like oil in a well-bunged tun, or wine in a spigoted firkin. When we drew forth his pain, so would he gush.

We sat him so he could rest his hands on a lump of stone till death weakened him with its comfort. Then we stretched out poor Ironface with his feet in a bush and his shaft mocking Heaven.

Tears filled my eyes, and night fell.

Poor Ferblant. He either had no head, or an arrow had passed clean through it to lodge in a remoter dimension.

It is never easy to watch friends die, even though – in Ironface's case – I already had some experience in the matter. I began to tug gently on the shaft.

It would not come, so I tugged again.

'Take care!' cried an ogre from deep inside the ground. 'You're like to pull off my ear.' Or perhaps it said 'hair', it bellowed from so far away.

I knew the iron fellow could throw his voice even further than lads shy stones at the fair, but to do so as he trembled at death's very gateway and have his wit proceed him underground showed admirable spunk and spirit.

I tugged again, as being the best way to make a brisk end of him.

Ironface screamed. He did not scream as a dead man screams. He screamed like someone who felt tolerably well, or even better than well, until I gave him cause to complain.

He still howled underground, but I was able to judge the note's distance and direction by now. It came from beneath the patch of dirt that lay immediately below his breastplate, and I took that to be closer than the infernal regions. 'You're scratching the back of my neck,' he groaned, 'and like to draw blood if you don't show some care.'

'He's suffering from a bent arrow,' Gibbu explained, also displaying admirable spunk and spirit, especially for a man who resembled a pincushion, with not a crooked shaft about him. 'Alders are always the same. If you coppice them they'll grow fronds straighter than a reedbed, but they're no good for arrows, their wood lacks pith, as I've said several times before.'

That was a long speech for Gibbu, but a dead man should be given his due, so we heard him gravely to the end, did the Mute and I.

Not so Ferblant. 'You'll lack pith,' he said, 'if you don't pull this arrow from my visor so I can fill the space with my head again.'

The Mute urged me aside and eased the shaft free. Its barb caught on the grill, and eventually broke off, causing Ironface to shriek when it dropped down inside and lodged on his scalp. Still, he was able to lift up an eye inside his helmet, and follow it with his snuff and tongue, so he now spoke like a felon through a grating, rather than sounding like a corpse within its sepulchre.

'It's no good bolting my headpiece to my shoulders,' he said, 'unless I can shift up and down inside it with my head. And so I did, when I saw you all cringe about your horses' necks.'

'Coward,' I said. I had pitied his inability to stoop from the rain of arrows, as if one should pity a devil for anything. Yet here he was hiding away inside himself and tucking his head among his own bowels much as a snake conceals its tongue within its coils. 'Coward!'

I turned my attention to the spikes in Gibbu's back.

Gibbu was halfway to his feet, and reaching towards his horse, for all the ferocious injuries he endured. 'Leave them,' he snapped. 'I'll draw them out later.' He appeared to cast about for an explanation. 'That I carry this wen pains me greatly. The wen itself can give me no pain, neither with point nor blade. It is built like a mountain, and as such lacks feeling.' He found a stirrup with his fingers and pulled himself up. 'To hack the whole lump off would be simplicity itself.'

'Then why don't we do it?' I asked. 'Rather than draw arrows.'

'The difficulty lies in knowing where my peduncle ends and my shoulderbone begins,' he said wearily. 'Besides, it would bleed.' He leant against his horse, unable to mount, so great was the weight of the barbs lodged within him. The shafts were a burden too, entering over the neck as they did, and in such droves. 'Moreover, the physicians and astrologers are uncertain as to just what I keep in my hump. It may hold my heart and chines, or simply be full of my dreams. You wouldn't have me cut myself free of those, Lady Perronnelle.'

Ironface helped himself to his feet, then joined me and the Mute in levering Gibbu on to his horse.

The hunchback was an odd apparition, especially by cloudy moonlight. As his mount moved forward, he looked like a bush that was learning how to trot.

308

From Pennautier the way was less watery, so the heavens grew wet for us instead. A short while ago, bowmen had shot at us under a cloudless sky. Now we had a racing wind bringing vapours from the planets, and within half a league the night was crow black and raining heavily.

Neither Gibbu nor the Mute complained. It wasn't their fashion. Nor did I. My cloak was good.

Ironface had mouth enough for us all. 'My armour is awash,' he said. 'I'm catching rust at the joints, and soon I'll have frogs in my helmet. For Godsake let us find a lodging.'

'For God's own sake,' I agreed. Even a Goth's bothie would have done for us, or a tree with tight branches, but 'For Godsake' is a powerful prayer, so we found the little walled town of Pezens instead.

Like Pennautier it was built on a bump and made in a circle, the rear walls of its outermost houses being thickened to provide a defence. Like Pennautier it displayed not the least hint of welcome, and showed no more lights than an owl when its back is turned.

I began to wonder if some crusaders had passed this way, or even a Merdun de Montfort. Yet there was no smell of burning, neither of limb nor log.

Be that as it may, my name would secure a welcome. The road led us to a gateway, and on this we knocked.

The doors did not open, though the heavens stayed ajar. Rain that had been steady now fell in torrents, to the great dissatisfaction of our horses' ears.

I heard tiles shift above my head. Members of the town's militia were manning the roof-tops, brave souls, in spite of the weather. These were our own sort of folk, the salt seed of Oc, and like us resolute against oppression.

'Good people of Pezens,' I called, 'I pray you open your gate to me. I am Perronnelle de Saint Thibéry.'

'She's a woman,' I heard a man's voice say.

'She's a witch then,' a woman replied. 'Either that or something from the river with scales on its back. She'd be drowned else.'

'I am a Trencavel,' I explained, while the Mute's teeth clattered even more noisily than Ironface's armour. 'Perronnelle de Saint Thibéry of the Trencavels.'

'We place our ordures at the end of town,' the woman's voice said again.

'They've heard how your cousin lodges,' Ironface chuckled, in spite of the raindrops on the roof of his head. 'They know he's in the – '

I stopped him. The word is sweet enough, and ordinary enough and quite certainly friendly enough in our dear tongue of Oc. In a foreign voice it sounds most unpleasant.

I am afraid that is how it appeared to the good villagers of Pezens. None of them said or did anything more except drop a rock on us, which struck the crupper of Ironface's horse with a glancing blow and scattered us all in a brisk gallop. If they fired any arrows they either missed us or were blunter than the raindrops.

We skirted the town, and again had difficulty with the river or a rapidly expanding puddle. Whatever it was, it curled all about us.

'Now where?' I asked.

'There's a chapel,' Ironface said, 'not half a league from here. It belongs to the Madeleine and has been blessed by the Holy Dominic himself.'

We turned ourselves towards it as fast as we could find the ford.

A stranger might be forgiven for thinking we had seen enough of Saint Madeleine. He would be wrong. Saint Madeleine is our own saint, and came to us with the fairies.

Horseback is a noisy place, each horse that strides upon stone being rowdier than a smithy with four anvils.

It was lucky for us all that rain softens rock, not in the alchemic sense, but by rinsing it with mud and padding the way with leaves. Lucky it was too that it was the dry end of the year, midway between summer and autumn, when the foliage clings less vigorously to its parent stock, so we were able to pace forward like cattle in a byre, as gently as if we trod upon straw.

Thus we heard nothing of what lay before us, and what lay before us heard nothing of us.

I heard Nano snort, and then Ironface say, 'I am being diluted. There is water in my wine, and my wine is my blood. This wet makes me weaker by the instant.'

I did not feel weaker. I felt as any woman would feel who had raindrops running down the inside of her legs and fidgeting her horse, and other particles of moisture settling on parts of her body that had scarcely known water or sunlight since infancy. I felt prepared to be philosophical.

'What do we have back home that is better?' I asked. 'New Carcassonne is a field. In it I own a space beneath a bough and my portion of a hillock. The bough will be leaking by now, and the hillock washed away.'

A flash of lightning lit the countryside for leagues about, then left us in darkness again.

'Quiet!' growled Gibbu, either to me or the ensuing thunder.

His back appeared less laden than a moment or two before, and he held a bundle of barbs he had pulled from his hump. He fitted one of them to his bow, and peered anxiously ahead, but the lightning was brief this time, not more than a flicker.

I saw no blood on his hump, but on cloth so soused in raindrops who could tell?

So I rode with a second man of parts, a fellow like Ironface – as well as the spider, lizard and scorpion – who could come unscathed through injury, and be unhurt though harmed.

I had no time to wonder at such a miracle. The Mute, a fellow with no parts at all, flung his arm outwards and across as many as he could find of our faces, and we skidded to a halt.

Nano had a delicate mouth and protested at this, but not with a louder note than the rain made gurgling through the topsoil. The laughter that surged up ahead of us continued unabated and went belching on.

'Crusaders!' Ironface hissed. He could not see in the dark, nor poke his eyes through stonework even less, but the noise these Northerners make is unmistakable. They do not laugh from pleasure or joy, but to remind one another they are there. They chuckle like jays. There is no happiness in their mirth.

I heard the Mute wind up his crossbow.

A chapel stood before me, a building no bigger than a shed, but plain enough to see in the altar light that shone through its open door, and the seep of candle-flame oozing as if by magic along the rib ends of its eaves.

A score of wet horses were tethered hereabouts, all of them unhappy. I sensed there were others near at hand, and in the next flicker of lightning I saw several hundred half a bowshot away. Before the darkness came back again I fancied an army of them, spread across the plain. I saw nothing of their riders, but supposed they must be huddled among them in their blankets.

No wonder Pennautier had shot at us, and Pezens barred its doors. If there were other villages about, they were prudent and stayed dark.

Our mounts sensed the other horses, but with scarcely any excitement. The storm fell direct, with the wind beside us, so the horses were like us and got nothing by the nose.

We were turning them gently backwards, when a challenge rang out behind. 'Who lives there, by Pope Innocent and King Philippe, now tell me who lives!' All this in the language of *Oil*, followed by, 'Be still and be recognized.'

We had overridden an outpost in the storm, an outpost or at least a picket.

As we readied our horses and prepared to spur them back at him, the same voice called, 'I've a company of ballisters here, all wound up on the spring, so be steady, you horseman.'

I could see none of his archers and nothing of him. If he could see only one of us, that made his view of the world scarcely better than ours, so I was all for brushing past him at the gallop.

'Those crossbows are a terrible engine,' Ironface whispered. 'They'll go through my armour like grubs through a coffin, and eat that virginity of yours till there's only its skeleton left. I propose we parley.'

I heard Gibbu's shaft growl forward against his bow. 'Parley?' I said. 'What does this parley mean?'

'It means I talk to them.' He went forward and called, 'Good evening, sirs. I am as you see me to be, a knight of King Peter's who comes out of Aragon to serve Pope Innocent's Crusade.'

I was still for running, but the lightning did its duty again.

'I ride with my daughter,' Ironface explained. 'I bring no squire, but a brace of bowmen.'

'Turn back to the Chapel of Saint Madeleine and show yourself.'

It wasn't the Saint who brought our ill-luck, but that silly word 'daughter'. A word full of softness like that excites a warrior's curiosity and makes his sensibilities quicken, no matter how dampened they are by the rain.

We went towards our fate in the chapel.

My nostrils were full enough now, mostly of man and cooked meat, with a thought left over for charcoal and smoke. The place had been desecrated by a cooking fire.

What I saw, as well as a dozen or more of the Northern nobles sitting in their embroidery with their armour off, was Simon de Montfort with a bone between his teeth, the chewing of which took all of his attention and for the moment distracted his curiosity.

There were others of his family seated about, judging from the features of several, so the sight of them was like a horror in a mirror, or would have been if the Bastard had also been there. He wasn't.

'So,' said De Montfort, cleaning his fingers of grease yet

not quite done with his bone. 'Once more we see Almaric's Knight, or as some say priest. I take you to be a priest, and a garbled one at that. You drew no sword in our fight, I think?'

Ironface laughed. It was never a pleasant sound.

'I remember your woman, priest. Last time she rode as your wife, but that was when you were a knight. Daughter sorts well with priest, and makes a more comfortable lie than wife.'

'Sufficient, my lord, that I own her.'

The laughter was general at this. De Montfort did not recognize me from the castle, or not yet he didn't, and no one seemed to know me from the fray. De Montfort's party were only active at Le Castellare, where I rode bare-headed and fair, not hooded like this, and with my head darkened with rain.

'Bring the wench some wine.'

It is a truth that no man recognizes a woman in a whore, nor a lady in either. To which might be added nor a warrior in any of them.

De Montfort motioned us to sit, but only out of respect for his own curiosity. Gibbu and the Mute waited half out-of-door.

Lord Simon continued to gaze at me, the more so since I did not bare my head in his presence. He laughed and picked up his bone. 'We feast continuously,' he said, indicating the altar of the Madeleine. 'For us, all life is a banquet. In this we differ from the English, with whom it is merely that they never stop eating.'

The laughter suggested there was an English baron present, perhaps Simon de Montfort himself, who claimed to be English when it suited him.

'All men dine at their natural hour,' Ironface stated. 'It's a universal truth.'

'An hour after dark,' a Northern voice agreed.

'Two hours before midnight,' a Catalan said.

The Irish knight I had seen before Béziers was there. He

belched. 'The Englishman gorges himself all the time,' he said. 'Just like you French.'

'Your brother the Bastard will be eating thin gruel tonight, Simon,' someone laughed. 'He drinks at Prouille with that Spanish monk from Calaruega – God knows why!'

'He's hungry for nuns!' the Irishman said. 'It's certain he has no taste for prayer.'

So Merdun was ahead of us with the Holy Dominic.

'Perhaps he seeks God in other ways,' De Montfort said lightly.

'Not unless God is a woman, my lord,' Ironface said.

De Montfort was irritated by this turn in the conversation, and by Ironface's cheek most of all. He also tired of what he saw as my continuing ill-manners and Ironface's unwillingness to rebuke me. He spoke to him sharply. 'Turn your pages out of doors, and leave your woman with your horses.'

I rose as if slapped. As I did so, something of Mummy in me overcame prudence, and I threw back my capuchon from my head, I suppose out of an instinct for what is correct.

De Montfort started up as soon as he saw my hair, but I don't know which woman it was he recognized in me, for Gibbu bounded into the room and picked up Ironface in his arms as if he weighed no more than an archer's dolly. A serving man tried to stop him or simply got in the way, so the Mute who was no good at fighting took his ear off in his teeth and spat it in his face.

We found ourselves where we should have been from the beginning – outside in the darkness and running to horse. Ironface could neither run nor get swiftly to his feet or into a saddle, but Gibbu did it all for him as if an arrow had never spiked his own back, and we rode back toward Carcassonne at a gallop.

We were followed, but not by the darts of our captors' ballisters, whether they existed or not. We heard horsemen close behind us, and coming faster because they spread themselves at large instead of trying to gallop as we did on the road of the Roman Wizards.

'Keep to the road nonetheless,' Gibbu said. He spoke true. Even as our pursuers closed up with us, we heard men cry out, and the sound of nags snapping limbs and armoured riders being unhorsed.

After heavy rain, our topsoil is like one of Marie-Bise's pie-crusts: too frail to stand on, but more than tough enough to break your teeth.

That's what these good knights found. As they grew nearer to the river, their nags were stilled from the gallop and planted fetlock deep. The riders flew over the heads of their steeds, I suppose to the immediate detriment of their faces.

This was fortunate, because the storm blew over, and the moon began to poke itself out again.

We seemed to be abandoning our journey to Dominic de Calaruega and retracing our steps towards Carcassonne.

'If De Montfort is that way,' Ironface said, 'we can risk a gallop at the Citadel after all.'

CANTO SEVEN

Wherein sundry corpse-strippers gallop atop the flood to
catch themselves a catapult and
propel themselves into legend.

hilosophers argue about how many spoonfuls of dew must be added to each speck of stardust to create a mushroom. All I know is it takes a woman to bake it into an omelette, and a female chicken to provide the eggs.

Tonight we had more than dew. We had puddles, though it needs no great magic for a storm to make puddles, nor to fit them together into ponds and lakes.

The wonder for us was to ride beneath the wet-looking moon and see drowned rabbits, drowned hedgehogs, drowned serpents and birds mashed down like leaves from the air.

If these last weren't miracles enough, we came across a stag struck by lightning, as dead as one of Gibbu's arrows could make it. The Hunchback was modest enough to point out to us that a bowshot would merely kill the beast, not cook it.

He dismounted and slung it across his horse.

'Yes, it's an omen,' Ironface said to the Mute, as if agreeing to something already said. 'But I'm a Christian, so no-one will tell me what such a sign might mean.'

I was fearful it might tell that the spirit was washed out of New Carcassonne, its menfolk too damp in the spunk for one last fight or even to stand as the stag stands, at bay.

When we got there I found something far worse. Dawn was breaking, and I saw I should have kept my mind on mushrooms. What we had now were growths of a similar kind. A few drops of rain had left the encampment transformed, the way an overnight dew can change a brown field to green and bring it out in succulent globes and buttons, and great flavoursome toadstools as big as platters.

I stood on a slope above the River Aude and was astonished to see roofs of cloth or plank, tented on upright poles and pilings of rock. Beneath them, men had scraped up the

319

beginnings of walls as dams against the running wet, and some had even fashioned bricks from straw and clay.

My eyes were bruised with tiredness, and confused by the soft twilight, but rub them as I would I could not change what they saw. New Carcassonne had turned overnight into a town, as if each of the burghers of Le Bourg and Le Castellare had scavenged like a dung-beetle to conceal a tiny particle of a house somewhere about his person. Even with the sun rising bright behind the Citadel, I could see no other truth in the matter. The rains had come, and instead of going back sword in hand for what was theirs the cowards had put down roots.

'De Montfort wants none of that,' I said. 'What a pity he's away, or he might have stopped it.'

'I pray for a rousting sun,' Ironface said, 'or a wind full of flying stings such as pissmires or gnats to drive them out of doors. If they stay inside, the women will want to make cushions, and the men do nothing but fornicate.'

'True,' said Gibbu. 'They've gone a whole week without either, and making cushions comes as a great hunger to people, especially now the nights grow longer.'

'The miracle is,' I said, 'that after all this rain the river remains dry.'

And it did. Its little windings of water were browner, but it was still not much more than reeds and stones.

'That's because it's made in the high mountains,' Ironface said, 'and clearly the Pyrenees had no storm, or we should see the snow on them.'

Men talk like this if they come from foreign lands. So, apparently, do demons.

Violette the Virgin was very pleased to see us. She had kept a pan of water cooking because La Mamelonne was threatening to give birth by the minute, even though she was only a day and night pregnant. Now that walls had come mushrooming up, she thought better of motherhood and went back to whoring. 'I work better behind doors,' she always said, 'especially when the room is dark. I can delve into their imaginations, and men are always so much more virile in that dimension.'

This left the Fish Girl with a pan of hot water and nothing to put in it. So Gibbu gave her a haunch of stag, and we prayed that La Mamelonne would be paid in roots and onions.

Ironface stole away the main carcass to feed his militia, and I took the other haunch as an inducement to my corpse-strippers.

The plan was that we should make an attack across the river and carry the island where the crusaders kept their artillery. We needed to make our fellows wild and De Montfort angry with them before they settled for being comfortable.

Ironface had no luck at all, even though he beat the drum himself while the Mute played raucous notes on his pipe and Gibbu made martial sounds in general, barking out those incomprehensible commands that usually make a man more excited than a cockerel in a box of hens.

'If we do take up arms,' one of his militia said to him, 'that De Montfort has promised to hang us up by the bollocks and empty our eye-sockets.'

'That's right,' said another. 'He's going to string us by the eye-sockets and pluck forth our balls as if they're worth no more than a pocket full of beads or sweet-meats.'

'They're not,' Ironface told them. 'They're not worth as much. If you were men you would stick your whitebreads on your saddles, clench your legs around them and plant your tight little bums on top of them, then join me in a dash across the river. Come, my brave lads, what do you say?'

'What we are saying is what we said to that messenger from the Countess Trencavel.'

We had heard nothing of this, so naturally Ironface was agog. 'She sends you her commands?'

'She sends us a thousand mounted knights from Spain and bids us ride with them, as you do.'

'Where is this messenger and what became of his message?'

They nodded gravely and pointed with their chins the way

men do when they're proud of something they're too coy to talk about.

Ironface turned and followed Gibbu's finger. He saw a fine piece of armour and a prettily embroidered leg lying among the corpse-strippers.

'He went and caught a cough,' someone sniggered.

'That's right, General. A lump of iron got stuck in his throat.'

'Cold steel, you villains. So what about the message? Will you join these Spaniards of Trencavel at the charge?'

They gazed at Ironface for a long time without speaking, as if measuring him for the corpse-strippers himself. They eyed him so intently that Gibbu notched an arrow on to his bow, and Ironface felt for his sword.

It was the Mute who put paid to their villainy by conjuring a blade from his pipe. His blade was longer than his pipe and, juggler or not, his feat surprised them all, since no man is prompt to lift his hand against a miracle. Then when the same fiery-spirited little badel drew forth a snake as long as a horse's gut and let it lie at their feet, they were vanquished, I won't say for ever but for the second it took them to realize it was dead.

Into that second ran Mamelie La Mamelonne and Violet the Virgin Fish Girl, each of them a whore and both of them a witch. 'Any man who catches me can have me for the price of a salad,' Mamelie shouted, 'or even just the sprig of a leaf,' and ran cartwheeling off.

The Fish Girl began chirping those peculiar cries of hers, vibrating herself as she did so. The effect of her wobble on a line of men was to turn them into a row of lancers with their pikes at the ready. As for those who kept their eyes closed tight, her warble made them squirm with desire.

She went somersaulting and caterwauling after La Mamelonne, with half the manhood of Oc in stiff-legged pursuit. The other half was ahead of her and chasing Mamelie.

'I thought those brutes were about to kill me,' Ironface said.

a drift of midges, but getting more between the teeth
they had bargained for.
much for defensive fire. A weak woman can lightly
an egg in the time it takes a strong man to rewind an
lest, so I knew my little force could now cross over with
er-spreading time to spare.
raise God and all his saints, archangels, angels, seraphim,
rubim, sprites, dominions and powers, that there were no
inary heart-of-yew or ashpole longbowmen among them.
bu could have shot down a whole army in the interval it
taking these fellows to crank up their springs, and Gibbu
some such noble archer behind me proceeded to do just
at. The crossbowmen toppled one by one, all unaware they
re being shot at, each of them crouched so intently above
s weapon he might have been a pullet straining to lay a
luctant egg, for all the use he was.

It was a long haul, this wade against the water, and longer
till for Nano who all unknown to me was towing so much
ehind him he might have burst his heart. Believe me, a
harge is like that. You may only dash ten paces against the
oe, but each footstep becomes its own hour, with a whole
eternity left over in which to pray, remember your parents and
break all the wind Mummy's good manners have restrained
in you since childhood.

My purpose this day became clear as never before. I would
capture a siege engine and use it to batter the Citadel of
Carcassonne. Its knocking might bring out the foe in a sally,
and let us get back inside. At the least, its music would sound
sweet in my cousin's ears, and at last bring him some hope.

I dashed through damp weeds and on to dry stones, with
my cohort dragging behind me.

I came nose to nose with a crusader's spear that had a
frightened crusader at the back of it. As I went to slice off
his chin, my sword cut the strand that bound my comrades
to me, and the net burst open.

I was no longer in the lead. All twenty of my corpse-
strippers were ahead of me, jostling and screaming. For the

326

La Mamelonne never abused her power over men. She
led her own suitors and those following Violette la Vierge
at a brisk pace about the encampment, then home to their
wives who doubtless had a use for them, if only stitching
cushions. They were of no use to Ironface.

I heard only a part of this, though it needed no great
guessing.

I was with my corpse-strippers and saw how they used
the dead cavalier from Aragon. He was a comely young
man with a slit in his throat as big as a bullock's mouth,
and of course quite dead from it. They were stripping his
body, and preparing to bind up his limbs in a net before
stewing him. This was the Norman way to treat noble bones,
as it left a man in a white and tidy bundle for his family
with no way for them to see if he fell ill from the spear
or the spot.

Nor was he the only person being dealt with in some such
way, many having fallen ill with the diarrhoea in last night's
rain or been held beneath a puddle by their wives and their
friends.

There were so many lengths of net all about me, and so
much discarded cloth and clout, as well as a great furnace
of steam, that I was likely to entangle my horse.

I had less luck with them this time than last. Yesterday
they had corpses enough without crossing the stream to
make more. Today they had more than enough. They had
an abundance, and a highly developed inclination to sit upon
it and gloat.

Their good fortune made them cheeky.

'Join forces with you?' one scoffed, 'What, and ride with
your Spanish lover? Be led by a foreign bellamy who never
doffs his tin?'

'Hardly my lover,' I said angrily. 'And still less my leman.
As you've just said, he's never out of his armour.'

'There's others will tell you different.'

'Yes, I'll tell her different. And what I'll tell you is this, my

323

girl, though you'll not need the telling. Where his shell's at its hardest you'll find the sweetest meat!'

A virgin warrior like myself finds it hard to be laughed at by other women, especially when they are foul-mouthed and her friends. I wheeled Nano around with a great cry of rage, and set off to gallop across the river by myself.

To ride at the crusaders' outposts all alone would doubtless prove to be an act of self-slaughter, but I am a woman of undoubted mettle in the teeth of adversity, and very bad-tempered it makes me.

I had failed in my embassage to the Holy Dominic, and found no other way to succour my cousin before or since. Very well, let me die, and poor Nano become horsemeat in a gypsy's soup.

I had reckoned without all the nets and stewing cloths laid all about, and so had the corpse-strippers.

As Nano wheeled into his heroic turn, a piece of string light as gossamer gusted across his saddle and proved itself as strong as the cord that bound Tantalus.

This pulled poor Nano up short, but only for an instant.

In that moment this adamantine gossamer drew tight the net to which it was attached, and through which it ran like a collar, and gathered the whole knotty stratagem about corpses and corpse-strippers alike, as if they were a trawl of deep-sea tunny.

The dead became all of a-bounce, and the living began an instant stagger to retain their footing on the land beneath the net. Once he had overcome their initial slump and set the whole coil moving, Nano set off at a very brisk gallop. There is no steed so determined as a frightened gelding.

We charged in our original direction, namely towards the island in the river, Gibbu's island, where the Crusade had parked it slings and levers, and all its other engines of war.

I knew nothing of my accompaniment. I sensed poor Nano's straining, as if he drew a wagon with the brake on, but thought he merely laboured beneath the weight of my frustration, already made heavier by my towering rage.

We entered the water, which was ᵥ
stones, which were sharp. Whereupon
began to howl in their battle fury, an
up to join them. So we crossed into the
gallop, for some made the brisker for be

When I heard the yelling behind me, I t
such occasions, namely that I had rushed
life without turning round to see what mar
followed me, but knowing that follow they ᵥ
they did, the more readily because the live ᵤ
were women.

The enemy were present in considerab
Gibbu's island. Some of them merely wande
at us with their chain-mail draped over thei
their faces full of cheese. Most of them had
breakfasts, or at least completed their toilets, aₙ
in excellent order with spears and crossbows le
in the high invitation and axes doffed behind t
a thoroughly military fashion. Like the trained ᵥ
were, they showed not the least inclination to ᵣ
onset. This was partly because they knew the we,
armours wouldn't let them get very far, more becaᵤ
them who could see and compute were able to ca
they outnumbered my brave force three dozen to
took no account of any reinforcements they mig
from the Citadel at their back, if anyone there tho
were likely to need them.

Nano panted, snorted and strained beneath me.
a captain among the crusaders call out, 'Steady, n
bowmen. Aim at this apparition, and aim well. Re
you loose over water, so shoot low. Are you ready?

They fired a great fusillade of darts into the river
front of me. Several of these deadly implements skidd
the surface much as boys will skim stones, pricking ᵤ
and confusion from those who dashed behind me. F
rest, a shoal of basking trout splashed to the surface be
having leapt in the first place to take the deadly volley

first time I glimpsed how our majestic and foolhardy charge had come to pass.

'By God,' one of them shrieked, 'that speechifying cow has just made the Northerners a present of our night's supply of corpses.'

'By the beard of Saint Peter's chin,' cried another, 'you're absolutely right. We must kill ourselves some more, or our children will starve!'

I turned from banging an axeman's head against the crossbar of a trebuchet and saw a number of naked bodies floating downstream, and the Viscountess Trencavel's messenger from Aragon still wearing his finery, but now entirely spoiled by rock and water, grinning among the reeds as if he were a gargoyle in an illuminated manuscript.

The shock almost killed me. Not so much the sight itself as the number of words it took me to express it in. While my fingers were tangling with my adversary's chain-mail and testicles, and his head and teeth knocked bits from the trebuchet, a trio of crusaders with two-handed swords tried to mow me off at the head, knees and waist, which are revolting places to seek to cut a woman.

If there had been only one of them, or thirty-three in an orderly line, I might well have been dead by now or at least chopped into small pieces. As it was they got in each other's way. Two of their swords bounced off each other, as if they were a pair of Italians playing at the fence, while the third cut the crusader I held in my fingers clean in half without disturbing his excellent suit of link-mail in the least, so the bottom of him dropped out of it to the great surprise of us all.

Their swords were excellently sharpened (perhaps at the moment of my charge they were preparing to skin a bear or shave an ox) but it was only a rumour born in the heat of battle which suggested that the trebuchet was felled by the might of their onset and brained a multitude of defenders in its tumble. Nor did I take their swords and reduce a whole gallery of these crusaders' siege engines to copse-wood after.

327

History prefers the rumour that says I did. I say I didn't, and I was there.

All three of my assailants' weapons did lodge in the catapult's frame, however, as I ran whingeing and whining between its legs while the brutes tried to hack me apart. They did it less unsightly damage than did the teeth of the fellow who now lay in half on the ground.

Once their weapons were stuck firm, I leapt out to kill them. This, or the sight of their fallen comrade still squirming about and trying to fit himself together, had a curious effect on their courage. I had scarcely put my sword into one of them when it was violently unsheathed from his giblets by all three of them running off.

Once the three of them ran, a hundred decided to follow. We won the battle at that moment. All that remained was to fight it.

Ironface charged towards us across the river, and a fearsome sight he was, especially emerging from water. It was like meeting a lobster on horseback, or an assemblage of soup tureens on a galloping trestle.

Some score of the very young rallied to him as soon as they saw heroic deeds were afoot. Youths with their balls not yet dropped fear little from the likes of Simon de Montfort.

These were joined by a number of fellows of five and twenty, including Foxy Face, once they realized that the moment Ironface charged they would all be liable to forfeit their testicular particles equally, according to the generous canons of Northern law.

They sprang to horse in a mood of blank despair, which quickly changed to grim exuberance as they understood that they might save themselves much pain and gnawing of blankets if they united in a senseless act of mass suicide by throwing themselves at the crusaders' battle line while they could. A man without his ponderables loses his natural ballast on a horse.

They had their wives to consider also. Far better to die

in a moment of glory than endure the hot iron and the cullion-clippers followed by the ceaseless torments of a scold's tongue. They were led by the three young squires from Montady and Enserune who knew they had to fight daily or run out of subjects to talk about at breakfast.

Ironface's three and forty men would have amounted to nothing beside my harpies if not led by the faceless devil himself in his strange armour. He rode as always on a horse that resembled an overgrown ferret and that engaged people in conversation while its rider slew them, such were his tricks of voice-throwing and other kinds of necromancy too obscene to mention. Not all of these were instigated by Ironface. Some were invented by the horse.

The absolute hero and undoubted originator of that inferior or masculine charge was Gibbu.

Once the Hunchback had emptied his quiver, and otherwise seconded my foolhardy dash, he saw what a pickle I and my women had landed ourselves in, now that the crusaders plucked his arrows from their breasts, did up their armour and regrouped themselves for the fray.

He rounded up as many horses as he could find and brought them across the river for my women to ride back upon, together with as many corpses as they could carry.

This distracted the defence. They saw no need for horses, unless armoured men rode them under the belly or swam at their tails. The crossbowmen were by now wound up and waiting, so they fired all their darts into Gibbu's cavaliers, killing a great number. The poor beasts were only waiting in the settlement to be eaten anyway. I don't know if Ironface's mount discussed the matter with any of the survivors, but I daresay they were philosophical enough. They emerged, foaming at the tooth, to aid my women.

These needed no help at all. They fell upon the crusaders' machinery as if they had invented it themselves, and began operating it the way Daddy had run the Mill, by instinct. In an instant they were juicing the enemy out of their armour by winding them up in the winches of their great mangonels or crushing them beneath the counterweights of their trebuchets.

They invented new ways of waging war, my women, including catapulting men into the Citadel. Two would back a knight into his own machinery with their stripping knives, then a third would cut the cord or jerk the lever that sent him into the high winds over the Pyrenees, where he could flap most engagingly among the kites and eagles.

My ladies had repetitive imaginations and if they served one of the enemy this way, they served a hundred.

A number of these fellows lived – or, rather, died – to regret their belief in the notion learned at their granddaddy's knee that women don't understand engines.

La Mamelonne had already taught me everything there was to know about the trebuchet. It projects its missiles at a fixed angle, called 'the magic wedge'. According to Mamelie, artillerists determine it by consulting the line that runs along her groin between her oooloooloo and her upper hipbone when she lies upon her side with her legs straight. She says this is why she is so much in demand among the exponents of siege warfare. They cannot elevate their weapons without her.

If there was anything more than La Mamelonne's everything-to-be-learned about the trebuchet, I deduced it in a flash by watching the corpse-strippers operate one.

Since these hideous engines of indiscriminate destruction always projected their deadly loads at the same angle, it followed that the weight of the projectiles themselves must have a bearing upon where they subsequently landed.

If my women placed an armoured knight in the throwing cup, he stood an excellent chance of flying all the way to the castle courtyard in the Citadel, ready for immediate disposal in the vaults of the Cathedral.

A crusader without his armour, and with nothing more than his cotte flustering around his thighs and flapping about his ankles, tended to fly higher but less far, and consequently stay up longer.

A very pretty sound these lofty flyers made, rather like baby gulls or the top notes on the Mute's pipe. They landed in a number of different places, and it is said some did not return to earth at all, being stolen by birds or eaten by the clouds.

Not all the crusaders ran away, or were impelled by their own siege engines to join the flocks of migrating birds that circled above us. Two of them on horseback were trying to crush me to death between their shields, because as one said, 'I'll not lift my blade against a woman!'

I could do nothing to counter this stratagem. My sword arm was pinned and useless, and Nano was discomforted by the presence of the battle-stallions on either side of him.

Ironface's horse appeared as if by magic, and began to ask the crusaders' mounts if they believed in the undoubted Trinity. This question scarcely troubled the horses, who were orthodox by instinct, but it unsettled their riders, and the Mute unseated them one by one with a large pole.

Immediately after this amazing *coup de main*, Ironface and I, surrounded by our three-and-a-half score followers, began to be herded towards the slaughter by the sustained pressure of our foes. They had the will. They had the numbers. If they could push us to one end of the island and persuade their ballisters to wind up their crossbows again, then they certainly had the destructive power.

We were saved by a surge of our fellow countrymen crossing the water to succour us. I stress water, because the entire character of the river had been changing as our battle raged on. The Aude began as a late summer trickle, stirring if at all like a discarded snake skin as the serpent slipped out of it. Now the water from last night's storm began to fill it bank to bank, and it started to show its muscle.

Soon it was a steady brown flood, and dangerous to cross. There was a fording place by our island, and fortunate it was we had charge of it, or these fresh reinforcements could not have reached us.

This new army was made up of the men who followed La

Mamelonne, and the women who followed the men. Clearly her original plan had gone wrong.

She diverted men who were threatening to murder Ironface by offering them a view of the denuded labyrinths of her own body. Once they followed her, and that perpetual mermaid Violette la Vierge who danced tail to tail with her, she led them briskly towards their own wives.

Their wives in general screamed at them, instead of laying a firm hold on them and entrapping them among their own cushions. No man enjoys being screamed at, so most of them preferred to follow Mamelie and the Fish Girl and keep on running. Their wives followed, many of them still screaming, but a scream is an effective battlecry and carries much more conviction than a cheer.

A battlecry it became, once La Mamelonne appraised herself of the strategic situation and decided to traverse the deepening Aude. Her charge, when it came, was mightier than mine, Ironface's and Gibbu's added together. One way and another she had the entire population of the New Settlement at her heels.

Her arrival nearly sank the island, and the rush of so many panting bodies deepened the river still further, causing it to lap atop the reeds and infiltrate our ankles.

The first consequence was to divert the ballisters' attention towards her own person and the bodies of the rabble who followed her. They could no more loose at her as she heaved her twin orbs and glistening thighs from the water than they could have harmed Aphrodite emerging from the enchafèd flood. The mob from New Carcassonne provided them with a happier target, and this they fired at, angering several.

Then La Mamelonne was among them with whips and scorpions. Some say she charged naked. Some say she was dressed in a river net. Some say she wore open ring-mail above the freckles on her skin. There are those who speak of robes of hair, plaited air, fishscales, foxes' tails and serpents. Others say, but without conviction, that she wore Violette la Vierge about her neck like a scarf, or that they rode two to a horse, with the Fish Girl in front and the only one naked.

Dangerously for my own reputation, they began to say Mamelie was myself, and that it was I who rode at them with my bosom bare as Black Mountain stone and my tresses growing lighter by the minute. They said this even as I stood there, slaying them with my Spanish sword.

What to do, now so many thousands of feet and so many hundreds of hoofs were planted in one small space? This was the crusaders' problem, much more than ours. For an interval after Mamelie's arrival, they were overwhelmed by us all. A few retreated into the narrower channel of water at their back, and waded towards the Barbican of the Citadel. Most were unable to run.

They were seized upon by women who had come here determined to thrash their husbands, but who found a crusader was the next best thing. If they escaped these, they were thrown to the ground by men panting to join their bodies to La Mamelonne's. These were now so near-sighted with desire that they could not tell the difference between a woman wearing water weed and a warrior in an iron skirt.

Not for the first time when Mamelie was near, I witnessed piles of bodies writhing on the ground, and felt certain that the gentle whore was under none of them.

The crusaders were clearly discomforted, but as we had no battle plan and no leader we could not make progress with them for ever. We undoubtedly killed a number of them. The corpse-strippers visited their wrath upon them, as I have said, and then their cruel wit.

Unfortunately for us, these Northerners were used to cruelty and wit. They had their weather. Any man with a wife is acquainted with fury, especially if she is an English one. So it took them very little time to marshal their forces, bring fresh horses over the river from the Citadel, and push back at us.

Many of our men and the majority of our women were

already leaving. The corpse-strippers had inspired our battle, but these were now swimming beside Gibbu's horses, which were laden with their booty, and a gory mess of hacked meat and dented armour it was. Elsewhere, and along the whole curve of the River Aude, wives were reclaiming their husbands from the shrill heroics of the field and leading them towards the greater carnage of the marriage-bed.

All of this, everything I have recounted, took no more than a moment's confusion; and yet, as so often in war, night fell on it.

I was almost alone on an island swarming with the enemy. I had Nano. I had a back damp with sweat. I had my Spanish sword. Ironface was beside me, cackling among the trumpets, and sitting upon a horse that whistled confusing notes to the opposing stallions. The Mute was there. Mamelie was there, and needing to share my mount. I prepared to retreat in good order, as Mummy would have wished.

Gibbu it was who took Nano by the nose and led him into the stream.

The moon was fat, and I daresay we were followed by arrows. I looked at the blood on my sword, and felt the kind of exhausted joy I suppose a woman feels when she has just given birth. Nano half waded, half swam, and I dabbled my blade in the stream.

'Look there, Virgin!' Ironface was clawing my arm even as we broke from the water.

We were faced by a cohort of horsemen, almost as splendid by moonlight as those who had ridden with King Peter of Aragon.

The enemy were before us on our own shore, ten companies of a hundred of them, on higher ground and fresh mounts. Was this to be the end of me?

Mercifully my hair was dry. I shook my head free of stardust and the stains of battle and rode up to meet them as Mummy would have wished. Mamelie slipped down from in front of me and vanished.

I sat with my three remaining friends facing these horse-men, and felt nothing but sadness. My cousin remained unrescued, as I knew he still would be. Just the same, I had failed to achieve a more reasonable ambition. We had not captured a mangonel or trebuchet, though we had destroyed several, and turned others to improbable use.

Meanwhile, there was fighting to do. 'We can make a little circle,' I suggested. 'They'll take time with us then.' I had watched soldiers kill Daddy, who was only one and alone. We were four, and the enemy had no archers. Yes, they would need a little time. 'Make a circle,' I urged my companions, who did nothing but ride wearily forward.

'A magic circle?' Ironface asked me. 'These are your Spanish reinforcements, Perronnelle – the foreigners sent you by your cousin's wife.'

I had no time to dwell on his words, before one of these Aragonese knights rode up to me and saluted. His salute was welcome enough, and better than a sword-thrust any day. His words were a little beyond me. Proud though he was, he talked all at odds with himself. He spoke Oc the way menials do, with a thick tongue, as if he should be tugging his forelock at me.

I found myself sucking my sword arm, for a reason I could not understand, and through a kind of mist I heard him propose I lead these horsemen across the river in a mighty charge against the island and the Citadel.

'Go by the bridge,' I said. 'You have numbers enough to carry the bridge. Then you can come along beneath the Citadel and carry the island from the rear, where the stream is narrowest and the ford at its most wide.'

Gibbu grunted his approval and Ironface chuckled with surprise.

I went back to sucking my arm. I now knew why I did so. I had suffered a cut in the meat above the wrist. I had rinsed my sword in the Aude as I came over, yet the frets in its blade kept running with blood, as if by an evil magic. The blood was my own.

As soon as he saw my trouble, the Mute rushed to bind it for me. I preferred to suck, but was dissuaded. Daddy always said I licked my wounds like a cat.

'Such an inspiration,' the knight from Aragon said. 'How do you think of such a plan?'

'Women make better generals than men,' Ironface said. He spoke mockingly, but he spoke true. We are more used to managing than men. A man does nothing in his life as complicated as stewing a dish of rhubarb – let alone arranging the cooks to prepare a banquet for a big table. All a man can do is eat it, and even then he drops half of it down his chest (and it's women who have the fronts that stick out).

What I said to the knight was, 'Good luck, and may the *Bon Dieu* guide you. I'll not lead you tonight. I have led all day, and my brains are bloodied.'

Ironface muttered to himself, then spoke sharply. 'You must go, Perronnelle. It's a family matter. They need to ride with a member of the family, and there is no son.'

'Foreigners won't follow a woman.'

'Of course they will. History is full of it. Your hair is like a battle flag. Show them your long fair hair.'

La Mamelonne rode up astride Pipi, who looked more like her dead donkey than ever. 'Raymond of Brousses is protecting you with his magic,' she comforted. 'So you have nothing to fear. He wants you for his own.'

'The Good God will protect me.'

'He did not even protect his own Child, so why you?'

Perhaps Raymond de Brousses made me ride. I do not think so. I found myself spurring towards the bridge, even so, at the head of a thousand knights. I wasn't their leader, though the plan was mine. I was merely their talisman, I knew that well. What more could a woman be? Ironface had spoken of a battle flag. A flag can be discarded.

As we rode along the edge of the encampment, to the strange jingle of foreign harness, and the discomfort of alien voices, I heard someone cry in Oc, 'The Maid!' It was taken up. 'Our Maid of the Mountain!' It was a silly shout. I came from a Mill, that stood by a slow stream on flat ground.

The shouts had come from Ironface's militia. They were ready to ride, now there was glory to be had beneath a prudent darkness. We had what many would think an army. So it was, but it was opposed by an entire Crusade.

Ironface dropped back to join his own men. I was urged to the van, then sent forward again, so I rode twenty places clear. Mamelie, God bless the sweet fool, rode up to join me.

We approached the bridge, which was guarded by bowmen and ballisters alike, all stiffened by a stout throng of spears. Had these loosed at us front to front, we would have died. Many did die, but that was later with a sword in the gut or an axe in the skull, which for a warrior is the preferred way to perish. A dart in the throat or an arrow through the breakfast are deemed less agreeable to a man for whom warfare is a living, and the way he is forcibly retired from his profession a source of pride.

These archers on the bridge were a resolute bunch, and so were their pikemen and pushers. They watched La Mamelonne and myself advance upon them. They levelled their bows. Then they ran away.

I know of no historian who blames them.

Once La Mamelonne and I had become the same person in the minds of the enemy, we naturally began to be invested with supernatural powers. Not only did I ride a donkey that could change itself into a horse, I had fair hair that grew whiter and therefore brighter in the heat of battle. I could dress or denude myself in the twinkling of a sword cut, and the miracle of my nudity was this. I was ten times as fat without my clothes on as I was fully clad in an emblazoned gipon and a mountain of armour.

The enemy began to speak of my breasts, which in reality made no more than a seemly bulge within my tunic, as if they were a pair of siege-platforms and battering-rams. I heard them speak of them now, and I heard their teeth chatter.

It was among such a breath of frost on the cool night air

that I heard them shout to one another that I could gallop on water.

When we made our first foray across the river it had been empty, and in many places bone-dry, the reeds only glistening here and there with wet. They took their memory of my first gallop and placed it upon the swirling waters they now saw before them. This invested me with powers belonging to Venus and the Christ, only one of whom was real, and He the Creator incarnate. So they lowered their weapons and ran away.

I crossed the bridge as if dreaming. I did not care if my enemies fled or fought. I was too tired for caring, and felt dizzy from the loss of blood from my arm.

This was fortunate, as the next few minutes would have seemed distinctly unpleasant, if I had been in charge of my faculties.

I have seen no heroes in my life, only some six or seven heroines, and these were mostly women. That being said, let me give these swart knights of Aragon their due. They followed me from the bridge to the Barbican at a very brisk gallop, and if only I could have ridden facing backwards I might have been entertained by heroic sights indeed.

The Citadel towered above us. The moon was high and behind it, leaving us clear to view but the walls blind to our eye.

From somewhere under those walls I heard men shout, 'De Montfort!'

This was taken up as a battlecry. Horses drummed to our left, even above the sound of our own. If it weren't for that 'De Montfort!' and the shudder of the land beneath us I might have thought I heard our own hoofs echoing from the Citadel.

Then there came the smack of iron upon iron, the skidding and halting of hoofs when beasts jar together.

We rode in a phalanx. Our formation was almost cut in two by a column of horsemen charging from the flank.

They came either from the Citadel itself, or from its walls' shadow.

'De Montfort!' again, countered by 'Trencavel! Aragon!' Then the squealing of our mounts, and what frightened men are best at, curses.

The ambush was led by Simon de Montfort himself. It was no surprise to me that he had returned from Pezens. The bone he had sucked last night in the Chapel of the Madeleine did not look as if it would last him for ever.

I reined Nano in, and turned back to find him. If I could, I would give him my sword to taste, and his teeth to eat for breakfast. I was riding too giddy for heroics. I could scarcely stay in the saddle.

The Spaniards wheeled and fought bravely to their flank, as proper warriors should, to a sturdy clatter of shields and a messy tangle of lances.

The crusaders' column regrouped itself. So did our phalanx, half-in and half-out of the walls' shadow. The whole dizzy tapestry wove itself again. One moment the opposing forces rode separate, and tipped with points of starlight. The next they were together and knitting moonbeams. What they stitched were shirts of blood.

The two hundred men of Oc fought valiantly, I made no doubt of it, but they had Ironface at their head and scarcely a lance between them, so they did not look so pretty. Quite soon they had an impulse to retreat towards the bridge.

This time it was properly guarded, so they had to open the way across it. They did so, and this was fortunate for us. The Spaniards quickly lost a great number of their men. They did so with vigour and ease, and very little complaint. They were soldiers and practised at getting rid of people. Soon someone was blowing a trumpet. I supposed this said we were to retreat, and I did so.

The Aragonese horsemen fell back in even better order than they had advanced, as they had less numbers to manage, and fewer of their leaders were left alive to muddle those who were left. If I had felt better, I might have gained a deep understanding of warfare at this point.

What I did discover is that a battle is very simple to watch, and that people lie down very readily, often never to get up again.

I also learned that there's a price to pay. As soon as we were over the bridge, my Aragonese knight came up to me. 'You led us very prettily,' he said. 'You going boldly to our front like that, and yelling your battle cry "Trencavel". My men will follow you anywhere.'

'Thank you,' I said. My arm hurt, but no longer dripped.

'Now they want their reward. I hope you won't mind that there are only a few hundred of them to claim it.' He smiled at me, and leant from his horse to embrace me the way comrades should. 'I'll be first, if you don't mind.' He chuckled and began to unfasten himself, as if a man could manage such an act on horseback. 'I know my lads well, and I love them like brothers, but I'd hate to go after them.' He held me so firmly now that I began to wonder just how weak I was.

The notion that men will follow a woman with only the one object in mind was a novel one to me.

To be fair, I had no gold to give them and no will to cook them a cake.

Ironface moved the Aragonese knight's hand from my arm and said, 'Gibbu has stolen us a trebuchet.'

The Aragonese knight took my arm again.

Praise God Ironface was here to protect me. 'He went swimming for it,' he explained. He didn't move the man's hand a second time.

'This man wants his horsemen to share my virginity,' I protested.

'He's got it on a piece of string,' Ironface chuckled.

'He tells me his men are going to fuck me.'

'We're pulling it over now.'

'After he's done so himself.'

'You didn't think they'd rescue your cousin for nothing, did you?'

340

'They haven't rescued him.'

'Viscountess Trencavel must have mentioned some sort of reward when she sent them from Spain.'

'He's her husband,' I sobbed. 'Let her pay the fee.'

'But he's your flesh and blood, my Virgin. Think of the advantages to yourself. If you let these men do this to you, I shan't be able to call you Virgin again.'

I felt light-headed enough to be tempted by this. However, Ironface removed the knight's hand at last and spoke to him very sternly. 'There's to be no libidinous behaviour between comrades,' he said. 'And lechery even less, especially fornication. It will be the Lord's day almost immediately, if not now, then certainly inside a week.'

The Aragonese knight was not in the least put out by this piece of information. He chose not to understand it. '*Kay?*' he said, which is the noise these Spaniards make when they want to bare their teeth at you. I think Kay is the name of a saint, and a very bad-tempered one.

Either the knight's saint or his bared teeth caused his men to gather round us and flourish their lances.

'This maid is a virgin,' Ironface said patiently. 'And one of the few virgins who is. The enemy ran away from her because she has supernatural powers. Those who ride with her enjoy the magical protection of her virginity. Would you seek to sully such a talisman?'

The Spaniards said that they would, or they mentioned Kay again, who was clearly a very positive saint.

'Others have tried. Their flags have drooped, and their lances withered. Their battle harness has rusted over and their mounts caught the scab.'

His own motley militia were about us now, having finished hauling on Gibbu's string and tugging his captured trebuchet across the river. Most of Ironface's men had the scab already, never mind their horses. They also carried bows and arrows, being riff-raff, and this gave them a marked advantage over gentlemen on horseback who weren't allowed to touch such inferior objects.

'It is because you rode behind the Virgin here that you came through a dangerous battle so lightly,' Ironface went on. 'To lose only six hundred and two score men is a miracle in all the circumstances.'

'Seven hundred and three score,' the knight from Aragon said. 'There are only a few more than two hundred of us left.'

'You must ride with her again.'

Seeing so many bows and arrows, they began to waver. Gibbu appeared by my side, and his wetness and his hump were too much for them. So was his fitted arrow.

'I'll bathe their wounds and bind up their lances,' said a familiar voice. La Mamelonne was here, in a fresh change of clothes and with her hair flying. Since many people thought she was me anyway, I was fully rescued, and lucky to be so.

The Aragonese were fortunate too. I am told a virginity is an awkward object to treat with in the dark, and have no reason to suppose mine would be any more amenable than anyone else's.

I don't know how these Spaniards felt about it. For me, the following dawn was a time of great disappointment.

Daddy used to say a mill was a bit like the chamber pot Mummy kept in her embroidered box. It was a marvellous invention but it couldn't do everything for you.

Gibbu's trebuchet was a marvellous invention too, but it couldn't do anything for us at all.

The townspeople had a meeting about it and said that we were welcome to use it as part of our vain endeavours to rescue my cousin and that they hoped we would succeed with it. They enjoined us merely to be mindful of what we used as projectiles.

Rock was best for pounding rock. They wouldn't let us shoot rock, because rock was a building material. Nor could we use horses. Horses were food.

Solomon of Gerona suggested we use old men. We knew

from our earlier experience on the island that they wouldn't weigh enough to carry, not unless wearing armour or seated on a horse.

'We could stuff their leggings with soil,' Ironface said.

'Soil is a building material,' the aldermen of New Carcassonne told us.

As soon as we turned our backs on it the trebuchet disappeared. It was a building material.

CANTO EIGHT

In which the Lady Perronnelle
and her band of wise ones are
cursed by bears and snared in
enchantment.

'If this encampment had a wall, it would also have a gate,' Ironface said.

'True.'

'If it had a gate, it would be wise of us to lock ourselves out of it.'

The citizens of New Carcassonne were naturally fearful of De Montfort on my account. If they could make him a present of my head on a platter or La Mamelonne's breasts in a handcart they undoubtedly would. Or they would soon. The mood grew on them by the minute as the sun rose higher.

'Understand life for the business it is,' Solomon of Gerona advised me. 'The business it is is business. They've already taken your trebuchet. What else of you is left for them?'

The five of us took our horses and led them by the nose. We held a blade in our hands, as if we were about to cut their throats for breakfast. The Fish Girl danced beside us, and that made six, but we insisted that she leave her clothes in a bag on La Mamelonne's Pipi. To be naked was her nature, and naked she would avoid suspicion.

Once we had reached the place where there should have been a gate, we rode swiftly.

We travelled south, as if towards the great mountains. These were already white with snow. The nearer country was full of bears. These ate Gibbu's arrows but repaid us with coats.

We killed the bears, but not the curse of the bears. Ask any witch, consult any priest – to be cursed by a bear is to fall into discord. We skinned our first bear and left her gristle to the crows. Carcassonne was still in plain sight, and we were able to watch what the men of Le Bourg and Le Castellare were reduced to on my account.

They sent De Montfort a deputation of remorse. My sallies

347

with the Spaniards and the corpse-strippers had cost him some three score of his men, so they approached him with double that number of their own.

La Mamelonne had the sharpest eyes among us. They were honed on the birds and the stars while she lay hard at work, and blunted only a little by having old men blow on them.

La Mamelonne refused to look towards Carcassonne, even though she could see everything for us. She was already cursed by a bear, and sat there among the crows, scolding the Fish Girl.

The Fish Girl danced naked to appease the beast's naked carcass, while the Mute dried its pelt with salt.

Gibbu had long strings in his gaze as well. I did not know how youthful his eyesight was inside his hood and beard, and under the hill of his hump. Nor need I care. He was an archer. He lived for the religion of the yew and ash, which allows a man no leman, nor the near-sighted counting of freckles on a woman's chest. He could number the dew blades on a distant crag, or watch crystals form in the clouds; and that was enough genius for anyone. He told us about these schemers in New Carcassonne. He watched their sacrificial procession for us as it hobbled towards the Citadel.

He said that they sent only the aged and the infirm, and pitiful they were to see. They were all men long in the tooth, or lacking a tooth at all, and as such all fit to be pruned, having far less use for themselves than fellows with younger appetites.

'They're fools to bother,' the Hunchback said when he'd finished. 'De Montfort already has seven hundred deaths to his tally. He has Spanish corpses in Spanish armour, and a great booty of Spanish shields.' He laughed, but the sound wasn't friendly. 'You won him a great victory last night, little virgin.'

Was he too chewing the curse of the bears?

Ironface spat. I heard him. He spat rarely, and only from forgetfulness or quarrel, for such a being's spittle stays with him and lives like a snail on the inside of his tin. Then he chuckled. 'De Montfort will not harm the settlement,' he said. 'A man who has just climbed into bed with the beautiful princess does not notice the gnat that stings his bottom.'

This talk was without meaning, and I said so.

'Fifty castles have surrendered themselves without him even lifting a finger, Perronnelle. So why should he worry that you broke a few mangonels, and stole yourself a trebuchet? He holds all of the South in his hand, and the youth among his family and friends clutch it to their loins as well. And most agreeable it is. Soon he will be Lord of Oc, and his lineage its dynasty.'

'Not while my cousin lives,' I shouted. 'Or this body has breath.'

'In this you will need help.' Ironface spoke tiredly.

'That is why we should seek out my master,' La Mamelonne said. 'I know he is looking for me. The sky rustles with his cloak.'

I shuddered, and glanced towards Mount Alaric, close on our right hand. The wind did blow, but not from the Magus Dogskin. It was a Pyreneean wind, cold as the Frost King in his cave of ice.

'Your master is a blasphemy,' Ironface said. 'I had rather break bread with the Devil in Hell. I say we try again for Dominic of Calaruega.'

'The Holy Dominic would have my offering,' I said, 'if Merdun the Bastard weren't rumoured to be there ahead of us.' I gave them time to remember that fact, then I said, 'I declare us for the high mountains to winter with the shepherds there.'

'The shepherds are in Spain with their sheep.'

'Their wives still keep hearth in the winter hills, and find food for their children. So would they for us. The Crusade will not take an army up there in the snow. Besides, half the land is England's, and half belongs to Aragon.'

'Do you have a parchment that says so, Virgin? And another that says this De Montfort cares a jot?'

'The snow belongs to the sky, not England,' Gibbu said. 'And Peter of Aragon is in love with a pair of women who will not have him, so confuses himself with whores.'

'That's it,' Ironface said. 'A man who shuffles women in bed can keep no count of his acres.'

'Not if those women are me,' La Mamelonne sighed.

We spent a day and a night in this maze of the bears, killing five more, and skinning them of their curses which we rubbed with salt and put on. The sky was full of quarrels and Dogskin Raymond, the sorcerer of Brousses, waited much too near me on the peak of Alaric.

I slept that night with my Phantom. He crouched like a mountain on my chest. 'Run,' he whispered, 'Run!' while he fastened my shoulderbones into the ground.

I woke to the clash of iron. It was dawn. The clouds had come down. There was frost on the grass, and ice in the hollows of the ground. A gently treading deer was shattering the crust of the world with footfalls that sounded to the sleeping ear like axes clattering on armour.

Gibbu was already up, with an arrow fitted. It was my dream that woke him, that or my terror.

Our eyes searched the mist. There was nothing there.

I crouched against his cloak, to get back my body warmth.

La Mamelonne, the Mute, and the Fish Girl slept in a pile of limbs and bearskins with their heads hidden in one another, in a trance that would be hard to break.

Ironface lay alone and a small way off. Or his armour lay. Whether he slept inside or outside I could never tell, any more than I knew whether my dreams were made of mist, or Ironface himself cozened me as my Phantom.

Gibbu lay done again and I dozed against his hump.

I heard a cry a long way off, then woke and wondered if I had dreamed it. It was a signal such as shepherds use to their dogs or their cattle, or to frighten wolves, but without the yodel at the beginning. It was a man's cry, I swear, not a spirit's, and there were words in it. The words were lost as I woke.

350

The next noise was certainly no dream. It was a voice made of voices, a howl without speech, eerie but real. It rose as if in answer to the first, and swelled about the hills, though it came from Carcassonne, from within and beyond stone. It was the sound of women keening.

'A great one dies,' Gibbu said.

Their voices hung about the mist like soot stays in smoke.

'He is mourned, and as he deserves, but by people who are only pretending.'

Ironface's armour spoke. 'I hear the cry "Trencavel!",' it said. 'Your cousin is dead, Perronnelle. Believe me, I hear men shout all over the Citadel, and the note taken up in New Carcassonne.'

My cousin was the only great one in these parts likely to be mourned by women. That much was true, for the Crusade brought no women with it. Even so, I did not hear 'Trencavel'. Nor when I asked him did Gibbu. I felt sick at heart to be reminded of the likelihood of Raymond-Roger's death, yet I found no certainty in it. I said so.

The Mute woke and laid his head to Ironface's armour, then stood up whimpering, holding his ears.

Violette la Vierge had already lain with her face there, twitching her legs. Now she turned about herself in a slow, sad dance, like a stag when the arrow is not properly home, but spins on the point of its fate just the same, digesting it slowly.

The mouth within its armour spoke to me. 'Lay your ear to my breastplate, Virgin, if not your lips to my heart. No, lay it as exact as I lie here. I sleep across grooves in the rock, and I daresay my bones draw echoes from the hill. My armour from helm to heel, and top-knot to tasset, is gonging like a bell with what echoes from Carcassonne.' His fingernails rose to beseech me. 'I tell you your young Viscount is dead.'

The sky grew dark again. There was a mauveness in the dawn like you see inside a mountain when the thunder settles back on it.

Through this gloom a beast came flying, bigger than any bird and dragging its shadow underneath its claws as if it clung to its own death and took its soul back to its eyrie.

I heard the beat of its wings, and my cousin groan in passing. I could tell it was meat-laden, hung about with iron like those vanquished knights my army of corpse-strippers sent whirring over the Citadel.

Then the apparition was gone, creaking like a dragon.

'Devil,' I said. I knelt beside Ironface or his shell, and put my ear to his chest as he bid.

I was blessed by the power that flowed into him. Surely it was the earth-magic of the sorcerers of old. I could hear all of Carcassonne in the echoes of his armour. I was listening to footfalls on paving stones half a league away. I heard them through the veins of the rock. I heard the tread of iron. I heard clogs. I heard slippers. I listened as the Mute had listened, and the Fish Girl. I listened to shouts, to little laughs, a great cheerfulness of whispers.

A man cried the news of my cousin's death to the people of the settlement. The voice was full of triumph. The heresy has paid its debt, it said. The heretic is dead.

'A fool,' Ironface grunted. 'A fool has heaped his kingdom piece by golden piece into the lap of De Montfort's apron.' God knew where his head was. He was listening to the voices in his own belly.

The messenger called again. I heard nothing of the response.

The settlement lay across the river. Our magic vein was cut.

'Devil,' I mourned. 'You're a cunning devil, Ferblant, to burden me with such a sadness.'

I still clung to him with my ear, but he cancelled the hubbub of Carcassonne by causing his gut to rumble. Then he threw me away from him and rose clanking to his feet. 'The echo is now strangled,' he said. 'I grow deaf from listening to it.'

'Devil,' I sobbed. I wept for my cousin.

'It is written in the Miracle of St John,' he said, 'that a

devil may do all things but truly love a woman and fart.' He chuckled. 'Now I swear I truly love you, Perronnelle, and I swear you heard me fart.'

'I swear I know that St John,' I said, 'verse and by verse of his Revelation. And I swear he says no such thing.'

La Mamelonne woke up now, and did her best as so often. 'Lord Raymond-Roger is dead,' she howled. 'My lover is no more.'

'Liar,' I hissed, and never a swan more loudly. 'Your lord for sure. But your lover – '

'And the father of my unborn child,' she spat, and never a goose more proud.

'Your pregnancies come and go,' Ironface said.

'Not this one.' She puffed up her belly till it was even further in front of her than the enormous beehives of her tits.

'A woman's term is nine months,' I insisted.

'A mother's time is her child's, and this little one being a lord will choose to come out when he will.'

'We should have left those bears with their skins,' Gibbu growled, 'and avoided this unseemly strife.'

'We needed the furs,' Ironface said. 'I had rather lie warm while scolds quarrel than freeze slowly to death in the quiet.'

We lit a huge bonfire to light my cousin's soul. Then, quarrelling or just plain sulking as they all were, I made the five of them kneel.

Kneeling was a painful business for Ironface, whether he was dwarf, devil or monkey, but his hollow legs folded behind him at last, and he perched on his tubes like a wounded spider while I began my prayer.

As Raymond-Roger's surrogate widow as well as a mother-to-be, La Mamelonne made a great ceremony of praying. She folded her wrists about themselves and locked her hands towards God in a devotion so grotesque that her forearms might have been knitted from wool. If she contorted her limbs for men even half as adroitly as she did for God then no wonder she was in such demand among them.

Le Bon Dieu was the only one among us who knew what day of the week it was, so I could not tell whether she prayed according to Christ or to some obscure Cathar ritual. Her lips pursed themselves as if she were kissing Dogskin Raymond's bottom. The cloud was still dark overhead, in spite of the bonfire, and she might have believed herself in some such act of devotion.

Gibbu and the Mute knelt better than she because they knelt unnoticeably. The Fish Girl for once was still.

I looked away from Gibbu's hump and towards the fire, and noticed a seventh figure crouch against the flames. It was my Phantom, rosy and hard of flesh, albeit in a hood of mourning. I saw him, gave over my lament and prayed instead for battle. As I prayed he disappeared.

It was a bad prayer. We knelt near the carcass of our last bear, and perhaps the old chuckler brought bad luck as well as discord. He lay like a knight skinned of his armour but left unburied. I had seen his like before, on a card between Mamelie's legs.

A wolf appeared across the fire, sniffed once at Chuckle Tooth and began to eat him. Then he stood back and howled. This brought a dozen more of his kind, who looked at us once, then feasted as he did.

Wolves are not always bad, just mostly so. I've heard of shepherds who could dance with wolves and both part unharmed, and their sheep as well. But these were eating our bear, and becoming bold. Ironface was proof against wolves, but I heard him mutter that we saw Lies devouring Discord.

Daddy used to say that if you let a wolf steal your supper it would eat you for breakfast. I daresay Gibbu had this wisdom in mind, for he strung his bow and fitted an arrow.

The first wolf snarled at him across the fire, showing a great flame of teeth. Gibbu shot him through the open mouth, pinning his tongue to his skull, and knocking his lie back into his brain. His next barb transfixed two of them together and left them dancing rib to rib.

This was supposed to be my prayer for my cousin's soul, but God put an end to that. Gibbu notched his third arrow, and we rose to our feet just as the wolf pack jumped on us.

I thought the violence of Gibbu's shafts would be enough for them. Three of them were dead with all the life smacked out of them, but they lived in a pack, and you can't frighten a pack – again I quote Daddy – because it has no brain for numbers. They were like De Montfort's crusaders. Once one of them decides to fight, you must kill them all. Even when they retreat it is straight towards you with their fangs ajar.

Being a pack they picked on one of us. This was La Mamelonne, but I must say she got herself up very briskly for a widow and stepped to one side with her hands still fastened. So they carried straight on to the Fish Girl who danced into the air and stayed there while Gibbu shot two more and Ironface cut the face off one with his sword.

The Mute discharged that spring of his, and missed entirely. No time to rewind an arbalesque while the fiend is gnawing your fingers, so the Voiceless One lashed about him like the rest of us.

When you fight with a wolf you tuck your chin into your chest to protect your adam's apple, and keep your belly clenched on your gut. Very soon you lose both of them.

The piping was loud but thin. Imagine the way a man whistles his dog, then go higher then higher again, and you'll have the note that saved me.

I thought it was the first thrill of death I heard, for the cloth on my shoulder was rent, and the skin beneath too. My hands dripped blood, and the two-day-old wound in my arm had opened. My friends must surely be dead, all except Ferblant who was too nearly immortal to die, and anyway encased in tin.

The wolves could not count. We had miscalculated also. Our pack was but part of a pack. Their howls had summoned the rest, till we'd staved them off in their hundreds. Mightily we had slain, for I stood on a carpet of wolves whose death had put out the fire, for their corpses now smothered it under.

The trill played on. It was probably inside my ear, but wherever it was, death's little pipe still sounded. I felt the blood run on my arm, and knew I had too much pain to be dead. So I lifted my eyes.

I saw nothing but wolves. Behind the wolves who were slain, beyond those who smothered the bonfire and those whose corpses buried the remains of the bear, I saw yet more wolves ranged around me circle by circle. Some sat with their tongues hanging out, some crouched and licked at their wounds, then put back their heads and yawned to show me their teeth.

Gibbu stood by me. The big man was covered in blood. Every part of him bled except for his hump. That, of course, came to no harm from their fangs, any more than before from arrows, for it is written that only a man's wholeness dies. His infirmities live for ever, passed on to son and grandson.

Ironface came limping towards me. He too was an infirmity. Someone had passed him on.

The rest of us lay together, breathing in sobs.

One of the wolves was huge. He stood up as tall as a bear, then stretched up on his hind legs as high as a very tall man. His belly was hairless and pale, his sex naked and hard, though his front was smeared with old blood.

He leapt to a rock by the fire, still balancing. He howled and his wolves howled back. Then he took off his head.

'Mamelie, my Whore of Night,' it exulted. 'Perronnelle, my Queen of Noon. Tonight we shall feast on Alaric. Tomorrow and all her days, the Whore shall reign as my bride. And what shall the Virgin do?' He leapt towards me and snatched my sword. 'We must see what the mountain will teach you.'

Surrendering to wolves – and being eaten alive – was one thing. Being overawed by a piece of conceit like the Magus Dogskin was quite another. Some of us prepared to fight on.

356

I had lost my sword. Gibbu's quiver was empty. Ironface had been bitten through the elbow joints of his armour, and was shedding gobbets of red stuff thicker than I had ever seen drip from him. It was nearer to the trodden grape than it was to wine, and closer to blood than either.

We were in such a state of hesitation that the wolves seized us easily. Or rather we were fastened on to by men in wolf skins and wolf masks, and most unpleasant their fingers were, since they all had claws on them.

A paw is too imprecise to be insolent, whether it is above your dress or under it. But the real wolves and the feigned wolves set up such a howling together that my wits were altogether deafened. The next thing I knew I was being bound about by creeper and dragged towards Mount Alaric, in the midst of a huge throng of fangs and daggers, while Dogskin Raymond pranced upon rock and tree stump, drooling about my being 'conjured by enchantments and bound about by magic chains'.

Magic nonsense. I was bound by nothing more magic than a creeper from a tree, or a plait of twisted withies. Wrap one around yourself and set a dozen pairs of hands at the end of it and see if you march in any direction other than where they are tugging you.

My friends staggered beside and behind me, ears deafened by howling and the beating of gongs, eyes dazed by dancing and the flicker of flambeaux as we ascended firstly by footholds in the rock, then by ladders through the clouds.

CANTO NINE

Wherein she is dangerously
beset and her bones knitted up
into wands and withies, together with much wickedness too
tedious to tell.

Alaric was a tall mountain to climb, especially with my brain in a mist and my body dripping blood. And for sure my companions found it no easier than I did.

At some point during the ascent Dogskin's wolves and his wolf-men put off their skins entirely and showed themselves nude for the warlocks they were. They danced all about us, howling and tugging on our strings, the men with their bodies smeared in oil, and the women, for they changed themselves to women in increasing numbers, having their throats, chests and bellies stained with moss.

And a toss-bellied shameful dance they made of it. The men had their terses bobbing up and down between such a profusion of naked navels and knees as I hadn't seen since the murder of my parents. The young females' breasts were tossing about as well, and a sick sight they were, like storm waves chopping round your cockle boat, and threatening any moment to splash you in the eye. Hard it was otherwise to tell the sexes apart. Their hair was worn long, the faces of Dogskin's lemans and losels alike made eloquent with limewash, charcoal and crocus round the eyelid, their cheeks pricked red or otherwise depicted, especially the males'. These warlocks and similar brujos paint their features as if they are whores, because the Devil needs men but prefers women.

The centre of a mist is a cold, moist place, especially on a mountain where most things are made of cloud. Yet as we dragged upwards to our accompaniment of spectres, I noticed that the Fish Girl pranced naked, even though held by more cruelly fastened cords than a fly in the dew webs of a spider. How our captors loved her dance, as if they had made her madness themselves and owned her witless fidget simply by beating on their tabors and their drums.

361

La Mamelonne too decided it was time to be naked. While the rest of us sweated for our lives, even in the ice-cold chill of early morning, she kept on saying she was coming home to her Master. She got rid of her cords then her cottes and pelisse, then began to paint herself with the juice of wet bracken or dust from the honey flowers of the gorse whenever she could find one with petals not yet withered. Only the Madeleine knows where she kept her cards after that.

Perhaps Raymond of Brousses had already taken them back from her. For here he was suddenly before us seated by a flat slab of stone, and dealing them out one by one and eyeing them closely as if they held life's last truth and a considerable number of the miracles of hell.

He did not show himself naked now, nor prowl beneath the headpiece of a wolf. He wore his old robes of scarlet, and glowed brighter than a cresset of freshly picked flame. 'Death Seven,' he purred, as if to himself. 'Here we have the heavens jammed shut, and each night the great maleficants lodge in a single keyhole. Saturn, Jupiter, Mars with not a thumbnail between them, so close each to each that when the Mage's eye is tired they wear the same whisker. So what can it mean that on such a day as this, I turn Death Seven in the Major Arcana, but I turn it upside down?'

His hand was not upon the card now, nor the rock, but Mamelie's left breast, which he fingered by the nipple as if pinching a limpet from the stone. 'So is this Death reversed? Does it bring me Double Death in a twin sacrifice? For remember, brazen whore of the donkeys, my temple has two altars. I worship both earth and excrement in the sephiroth of Malkuth whose table is twin cubes.' His fingers worked her by the nipple as if unfastening her heart.

She did not flinch. Our little liar smiled upon him and said, 'I bring you not only myself. I bring you a birth, Master. I bring you such a birth as you cannot dream of, unless you saw it in the waters or read it in your stones.'

'I feel it, Little One. I feel it as I find it, and I found it already in the stars. We live beneath a sky made of soot, so

362

dark is this Crusade. Yet heaven's lights are opening, and the fiery ones approach me in their chariots.'

Her nipple slipped his fingers at last. She moaned in a kind of ecstasy and fell swooning at his feet.

His eyes moved to me. 'I shall take her child from her, my little witch-woman of St Thibéry.'

'I am neither small nor a witch.'

'I shall deliver it with a knife and do all as my planets bid me.'

'If you find her with child – which I doubt.'

Mamelie lay on her side. He pushed at her with his foot until she turned on to her back. Then he felt her with his toe, as if he were a forester sampling a log for his fire.

'I should hate you to spend too much time on the cut,' I said.

'So you plead for her. Let me tell you what my foot tells me. It confirms what the bark of that rowan proclaims. She is bearing a child, and a boy by the berries on that bough.'

'I see no tree, no bark, no bough, and no – '

'Berries? That is because you are a woman. Women see nothing and understand less.' He left his seat by the stone and stood close to me. His breath smelled of running blood, the way a dog's mouth is when it sips the kill. 'Until I have taught them, that is.' He touched my throat with his hands. 'You have much to learn, my lady Perronnelle. I shall keep you long enough to teach you, however many moons it takes.' He let go of me and again prodded Mamelie, then pondered her with his foot. 'Whether you need one moon, or eight of her nine.'

He made a signal I did not understand. One of those about him threw water over her, rinsing away the petals and the moss she had plastered herself with. 'This whore needs only her skin,' he said. 'Such a nakedness should glisten.'

La Mamelonne did not glisten. She glowed. She did not wake.

Scarlet Raymond of Brousses gloated at the success of his trick, but such a being finds very little magic in water. He made another sign, and the puddle in which she lay turned to frost and began to burn, while her body hardened in ice amidst the flames. Her flesh did not scorch, though the heat of her burning was so strong it made me draw back from it. Mamelie continued to breathe, but deeply now, as if enjoying the pyre she lay on.

'So, Perronnelle. You know enough not to fear for your friend. Yet you have no confidence in the fire for yourself. Go on, warm your young bones in the furnace. It is freezing out here.'

I stepped neither forwards nor backwards, while snowflakes fell around me at the power of his command, snowflakes from the black sky he bound us in. I call them flakes of snow, or some such frosty particles, but in truth they might have been blossom from next year's spring or the feathers of a mighty bird, so great was his suggestion. Or they might have been nothing but thoughts in his mind, little whimsies he could shake from his skull to drift about the mountain, hiss into the flames, settle on Gibbu's hood and hump or glaze Ferblant's armour till he stood in tubes of ice.

My fingers grew numb, and my toes in their clogs.

Again he gestured me to step into the fire. Again I would not, in part because I did not dare, in part because I knew that to enter the commands of such a being would put my soul in peril.

'Are you a virgin still, Perronnelle?'

I chose not to answer.

'When I watched you from the millstream in the summer, then you were a maiden. So tell me, are you now?'

'I am as I was, and what that may be you have no way of knowing.'

'I have three ways of knowing, as with every woman else. I can look, I can touch, I can taste you in my bed.'

'If you take me to your bed, I promise you shall die in it.'

He glanced at me sharply, but with a different kind of longing. 'Taste you and test you, Perronnelle, as almost in the summer. A swan once had a maiden, Perronnelle. The swan was a God, and the girl was an idiot as you are, but beautiful as you.' He caught at me again, at my shoulders not my throat. 'I was that God. I was that swan. Remember me in the summer when I was not as now. My mood was jet black, even to my feathers, even to my beak.'

I shuddered at a memory I did not know I kept, concerning the swans at the Mill, our white Queen Blanche and Frédélon her husband.

A black male had appeared last summer and presented himself as a suitor to the mad Queen Blanche. She had less use for a lover than even Mummy had for Daddy in this way, and she treated him as she always treated Frédélon when it wasn't nesting time. Then Frédélon drove him off, and he disappeared from our river. But black he had been, black and deep-throated and overbearing, black as candle carbon or the charcoal of the ash tree. If Raymond of Brousses were a swan, he would be black and dark-voiced like that one.

I shrugged myself free of Dogskin's hands but admitted the memory. Of course I said nothing concerning the childish names we gave them.

'What a pity you will not see St Thibéry again, my lady. If you could go there in a dream, you would find your Frédélon slain, and poor mad Blanche a widowed queen indeed, who waits only for me.'

As I say, I had said nothing of the Mill beasts' names, and was horrified to find how far he could see into my mind.

He tried to clasp me to him again. 'Meanwhile I have a great swan between my legs who cannot help but confess himself to you, since he lifts up his beak just to feel your presence – a white one, Perronnelle, who has an instant need to nod at you.'

All men keep some such beast beneath their tunic, though most are content to address it by a lesser title such as 'my cockerel' or 'little bird'. Even those crusaders from the North speak less of the Dove of Peace than some nameless pecker they term their oiseau. A few weeks ago, during the slaughter of the Mill women, I had seen them in all shapes and sizes with never a white one among them. Though Merdun's men, to be entirely fair, had not boasted about them once, but had been content to let them talk for themselves.

In this case, I looked Dogskin in the eye and kept myself well away from the waterbird that strutted towards me. I dealt with him firmly, as Mummy would have done. 'Your talk is unworthy of your description of yourself,' I told him, and for once I do not think Mélisende Trencavel could have put the matter better.

My utterance took him aback, and he gazed at me with a fresh kind of wonder to find his conceit unveiled. 'Perronnelle,' he hissed, and yes, he was swanlike. 'So why do men call you Perronnelle?'

I did not tell him what he should have known because all men know that it was a name of the Trencavels. I watched his conceit urge him to possess me, and it was conceit, whatever his power, because to call yourself Magus and claim to suck your wisdom from the stars and the stones is to set yourself above the living Christ, and the woman who bore him and the angel who brought him hot from the loins of God. 'Why do they call you Dogskin?' I asked him in my turn.

His face darkened. 'No man calls me that.'

'Dogskin Raymond. All men name you so.'

His rage could invent thunder, but he struggled not to waste himself. He called his dark mood back again, though his eye which had been as empty of reflections as a serpent's or a goat's now burned with a flame brighter than those that burned on Mamelie. 'I am no Dogskin,' he said in that black echo of his. 'My title is Cerberus. The Radiances of Heaven and the Fiery Ones of Hell know me as Baron Cerberus when I celebrate the Feast of my Lesser Ritual.' His voice was less than a whisper, but the whole mountain heard it. 'As for when I work as Magus, when I put on my *ipsissimus* . . .' He shuddered at the wonder of himself. 'You will see me in my power and partake of my ritual. You shall be my feast, even to your infinite particle.' He walked a small way off, to

366

give his brain time to ponder me. 'I promised you when I met you at Béziers, which remember I burnt for you, I promised you in the mountains when I made myself your dream, and I promise you now: myself and my fellow celebrants shall devour all there is of you,' again the brain-aching whisper, 'everything save your backbone, which shall mate with this serpent.' He picked up a tiny green viper that crawled to him from a rock and was still while he kissed it and sucked the venom from its tooth.

I shuddered, for my spine felt his fingers touch me, though his hands were nowhere near.

Then he laid spells on me in a language I had not heard before, a tongue it was clear that not even Ironface under-stood. Yet the wolves knew his meaning, and the wolf-men too. So did his witches and warlocks, and the rest of his huge band of owl-eyed brujos in their nakedness and paint, whether they were sexed, sexless or the worst kind of badel the mind could imagine. There was a multitude of these little monsters, hermaphrodites who could impregnate themselves, if they chose to, and they did while he talked, beings with their male sex below and their womanness above, between their tail and their navel, and milk dripping through the hairs round their dugs they were in such a constant fever of parturition, with their bodies forever playing with themselves then springing apart like mismatched lodestones. Even these understood him, and so did the little snake he still held and kissed while he showed it my future.

Basically we have only the two languages. Oc, which we call ours, and Catalan. The shepherds from the high pastures all speak in Catalan, and so do their sheep, but so do many other people, especially women. We have a lot of chatterers passing through, and if a girl sits by the roadside with her legs apart she soon learns Catalan. It has a quick tongue.

Then we have the witch language, though this was the first time I had heard such a dangerous mixture of noises: part fox, part ass, part owl, and a little of my Aunt Alazaïs when she howls at the new moon. It might have been Old Jewish, their chant, the original Romish tongue of the Wizards, or a Lexicon from a whisper wrapped in a scroll inside the Devil's egg.

'You are right, my white lady Perronnelle,' the Magus Raymond said to me, no longer in witch-talk, and I was again frightened at the ease with which he knew my mind. 'When the swan took the woman, she gave the world three eggs. Yet in all the libraries of the monasteries, the monks number only two of them.' His body floated before me, and retreated. 'So how do I speak from a scroll inside the third?' Again his face swooped at me. 'I have the knowledge by holy right. As I said earlier, I was that God and I was that swan. I kept one part of the product of the woman's body, just as I shall keep the whore's child' – Mamelie still lay naked and unharmed inside the flames – 'and just as I shall keep your own vital particles.' His voice was a gnat inside my ear, and it deafened me with its buzz.

I felt my knees melt into a trance, and my eyes pour from my head like dew on a cold stone, but I told myself my legs were strong and my face ran with no more than tears, so once more my brain steadied.

He again gestured me to enter the flame, and lie beside Mamelie.

'No,' I said. 'For that sweet fool believes in you, whereas I shall never bow before the altars of your conceit.'

The mountain howled at me then, for a mountain has mouths, and the sky too. So the mountain howled, and so did these black beings that were on it. They rushed at me, some with their fangs, some with paw and claw, and tried to unfasten me.

I realized that the trick of the flame was done simply to have me naked. If I entered the fire, such petty mortalities as my cloth would burn, whatever fiendish embargo he placed on my flesh and hair. Well, I would not enter it, so these fiends tugged at my clothes, and breathed a mighty wind as if to make them shred from me.

Gibbu leapt between us, and bounced up and down. These lesser devils drew back from him, fearful of his hump, for it danced quite separate from him as if he bore his death on his shoulders and could not be reconciled with it. Such a dance he did to frighten them, till the Fish Girl sprang naked from his cloak and danced as well, howling her mad cries as if his back had stepped out to present itself with all its bumps and bubbles.

Even without her knees round his neck his hill continued to move by itself. A hump is an infernal wen, unpredictable as a volcano, and it lives beyond the grave.

My stitching held. Doubtless Dogskin could magic my garments off. Nothing less than necromancy could rend them otherwise. Their cloth might not be immortal. The needlework of Constance of Coulobres was.

Only Dogskin Raymond dared approach the Hunchback closely. He did not flinch as Gibbu set a string to his bow. Nor need he, for Gibbu had no arrows left, yet he pulled a trick that made even the Magus pause and lay a hand to his belly as if to make sure his invincible shield was in place.

What Gibbu did was to draw on him, draw a whole clothier's yard. He tugged his ash bow forward and levelled it exact at the centre of Dogskin's head.

'Even with an arrow you could not pierce me,' the Magus said, 'even one the fletcher tips with hook iron or flint.'

'Not with this bow,' Gibbu conceded, 'nor yet with the rainbow on the edge of the storm.' His words made the Dogskin hesitate and gave me, not for the first time, to wonder at him. 'This one is ash, and bears only the magic of the ash, which is strong but too pure for such as you. When I kill you, De Brousses,' – 'It will be no more than my flesh you kill' – 'I acknowledge that. When the moon is ripe for me to pierce such a flesh as yours, I shall come back with yew, yew cut from the heart of a hundred-year tree when the sap runs back but the bough keeps its berries on it.'

He still held his bow with its string full drawn. Raymond stood in awe of its emptiness, as if his eye would read the length of Gibbu's spell measured there between finger and fist. 'Now as to this arrow I shall shoot you with – '

The Magus Dogskin shuddered. He felt Death's pimple growing under his skin. 'No bowmaker nor fletcherman can do me that harm,' he said. 'A crouch-backed soldier such as you cannot touch me.'

'I am my fletcher. God taught me my craft. So watch when he sends me for you, De Brousses, for he'll take me to your heart and a handspan beyond it with a mistletoe tip to a hardwood shaft.'

'No man can kill me.'

'I shall and I will. Dogskin is dead. Which leaves us with your great Baron Cerberus, Magus as he is.' Gibbu lowered his bow at last and stepped forward to whisper, 'That one will go to Hades where he belongs. I shall use the same shaft, oh, but such a cunning hook I shall fashion. Ask your Baron Cerberus what he'll feel when I feed him through the navel with a weazle's gallstone . . .'

Raymond's face darkened and Mamelie's flame was extinguished. She rose and tottered towards me in her nudity, hugging herself against the cold, so I held her in my cloak.

The two men ignored her.

'Ask him yourself when he draws you to his ritual.'

'He'll not ask me to his ritual, Dogskin of Brousses. He knows I'll bring an arrow that will pin him to his backbone with a rodent's pip.'

Raymond drew back, but his wolves and his wolf-men growled up behind him, and made as if to take Gibbu limb from limb.

The Hunchback was ready for them. He unfixed his bow then lifted and unfastened his clothes to do as the shepherds do to protect their lambs. He pissed all about himself in a great circle, saying as he did so, 'And as for Baron Cerberus's *ipsissimus*,' – savouring the word for he found it chimed so pithily with the magic in hand – 'when such a one as you aspires to *ipsissimus*,' and laughed, shaking himself freely in the wolves' teeth. They would not cross his wet, and no more

370

would bears. Those that know animals know they scent their places, and I daresay magicians too, for none of Dogskin's brujos came any closer than half a dozen paces, to their master's annoyance.

Dogskin was in a rage he could not cancel back. It made sparks about the crags of the mountain and drained him for a moment of his essence.

While Dogskin was splitting rocks and causing the sky to tumble, or at least the clouds, Gibbu mouthed on as if speaking by rote: 'The Christ as *ipsissimus* needs no disguise, for He reigns in Heaven. Your little *ipsissimus*, once your Cerberus is dead by me, had better pray to be swallowed by a frog inside a stone. Or we'll drown it in a teardrop, perhaps from this lady's face.' He reassured my cheek with those bluff fingers of his. 'Then we'll give it to Lord Ferblant to keep in a bottle.'

These were brave words, full of hope and heart, even that *ipsissimus* which was new to me and clearly man's talk and made a sound like cows pissing in the soft summer grass. But when all was said, they were only words, and words are but air unless Mummy speaks them, and she was nowhere near, nor her icy daggers any more.

I was nearly in tears at her memory, but La Mamelonne trembled naked beneath my cloak and was all ways as cosy as cuddling a cat, and the great sorcerer of Brousses was about to call the Hunchback's bluff.

He crouched down tiny as a rabbit then breathed through his snarl the way a rabbit does when it finds it has a stone in place of a turnip, and breathed and breathed until he was huge as a dragon, or certainly a bear and with something of the same black look.

He sprung at Gibbu with a ten-stride leap, as if man could fly, or beasts swoop in air.

The string of Gibbu's bow was unhooked, and he had no arrows. This left him with a staff. He caught the jumping Raymond a very brisk poke on the nose with the end of it, then held it by the quarters the way stavers do, conjured a little with shifts and feints and followed with a cunning clout round the ear that sent Dogskin's skull ringing, even on the outside.

Raymond did not so much as shake his head. Imagine smacking a bear with your fist. He would offer you nothing but contempt, and such did the sorcerer feel for the Hunchback. His look said so. As for his nose, it bled all about his feet in tiny pink flowers. He stooped and plucked one, offering it to Gibbu as if it were a present.

Gibbu beat backhanded on his other ear, so now the stars chimed twice.

The Dogskin caught the staff and simply bent it from his hand.

Gibbu howled. He snatched at it again. To steal his bow from an archer is more painful than cutting a wolf from his tail. One or the other will surely bite you. And so it was with Gibbu. He seized Raymond by the fingers, then the arm, and he bit.

The taste was clearly horrible. He spat the sorcerer back at him, and grabbed again for his shaft.

Raymond hopped back a pace or two and taunted him from a short way off. Then, while the Hunchback was still and considering what to do, Lord Raymond raised the staff and bit it in his turn.

It took immediate fire from his mouth, as if it were tinder and the sorcerer's teeth flint.

'Pah!' the Hunchback scoffed.

The heat was real enough, for Dogskin dropped the bow to avoid scorching his fingers. The wood was still green, and perhaps because of this burned with a green flame.

'There are matters yet to teach you about the magic of an ashpole,' the sorcerer said sweetly. His nose had stopped bleeding, and he'd retrieved all his blood-drops in his hand, as if in a little posy. The firewood glowed at his feet.

Gibbu stooped to pick it up nonetheless. It spun round and struck at him, then went wriggling off, singeing the upland grass as it went.

Dogskin Raymond, Magus Cerberus at the least, proffered me his posy of blood and said, 'I think you will join me at my Feast after all. This mountain offers nothing but honey wine and berries. Nothing better for the palate,' he told Ironface and Gibbu and the Mute, turning all about himself like a mounteback preacher. 'This fare must content you until I have delivered the whore of her infant, and the virgin of such virtues as I find in her.'

He took me by the hand and I let my hand be taken. I knew my harm was not yet, and was sufficiently overawed by his magicianship to worry that he might turn me into a serpent if I resisted, or set me on fire.

He reached beside him till his hand found a ladder in the cloud or a step in the rock, and he led us all upward. 'I shall show you the Chapel of the Bones of the Monsters,' he said. 'And the other places built of bones where I have my mansion and my minions their dwelling place.'

Nothing makes sense of my time upon Alaric, unless you believe in the ancient sorceries and know the mountain followed us. Wherever we stepped we were circled by wolves, or bears in a ringdance. These bears were not lugged. They wore no kibes upon their claw nor fetters round their ankle, and no sort of muzzle on their wide-open teeth.

Escorted in this fashion, we came to the Place of Bones and the Chapel of the Monsters.

The monsters had crouched down upon the very top of the mountain. Perhaps a dozen had come here, and here at the beginning of time they had died.

What these monsters must have been is some kind of land whale, or else a mighty forerunner of the Béziers elephant. I say a whale, for their ribs were as big as a church. Yet added to these, and their head and their tail, they had legs with claws like a chicken, just like the Serpent before God cursed him.

Dogface led us to a table in a huge hutch of bones, and commanded his wolves and their maidens to serve us. Then he said, 'Some say these monsters were the steeds of the

Goths, or that one of them at least was King Alaric's horse. But I tell you this whole mountain is his horse, for heroes were bigger then. Witness the achievements of the early Wizards, the soldiers from Rome, and their strength to lift rock.'

This subject interested me, so I sipped honey wine and spoke of the bridge by the Mill, and the road that set its weight upon it. I was given no berries for my banquet, but began with ants' eggs and a green grass salad, followed by a dish of juniper, garlic and snails equal to the finest in the land.

'Those dodmen are sweet,' he said. 'I have trained them to be eaten and purged them of their juices. I shall do much the same with yourself.' Before I could answer wildly he added, 'You may wonder why my wolves spared you, before I was there to forbid them your flesh.' He raised a goblet to his lips and said, 'I give you my wolves and my bears.'

I had no wish to drink to that, but the Fish Girl danced in and drained a cup at him, before dancing out, leaving an echo of her nudity behind, very much to his pleasure.

Mamelie had regained her clothes, or had them retrieved along the way by Dogskin's retinue, but she still shivered in her longing to be returned to the sorcerer's fire, so her presence distracted us all, as did the Fish Girl's absence.

'Your saviours were your horses,' Dogskin went on. 'Talking of horses, and we were.' He signalled, and into this place of bones his witch-women carried four skulls and set them before us before filling our cups.

'There's not a wolf or a dog who will eat human flesh in preference to horse,' he aid. 'No, not even the flesh of a comely woman.' He reached and felt Mamelie both above and below her clothes, as if it were a courtesy to do so.

My mind was on sadder matters. Nano was the only real horse among our mounts, in spite of his overall vanity and underall absence of cullions. The rest had been good for nothing except to charge against crusaders or fart. We had come here with five beasts in all, yet there were only four skulls on the table, and not one of them cried to me for recognition.

374

Nano's absence of balls left him almost as wise as a female, and with much less to distract him in mixed company. Had he kept enough wit between his legs to go stealing off?

The Magus Raymond seemed to discover all manner of tricks beneath Mamelie's cotte and petticoats. He pulled his hands from about her to show us birds with tail feathers made of ears of corn, then bade us look outside.

The Chapel of the Monsters itself put on flesh and began to dance. The giant thigh bones grew claws and a skin soft as lizards. The skulls flashed with shallow eyes, like moons in sour water, and the huge spines grew a crest of scales like the tiles on a cathedral.

Then the other hutches became monsters too, and began to burn, including their eyes. We found ourselves back at the table, and I wondered if we had ever left it.

Meanwhile Dogskin's fingers had finished feeling Mamelie and were feeding me sweetmeats instead. I was a little overcome by the fumes of his honey wine, but I recovered enough of my external powers to recognize that he was expounding his philosophy and proposing my fate.

'My Master is everywhere,' he said, while Ironface yawned aloud inside his head. 'He is into many, and at everyone. That Jesus some men call the Christ wears the only flesh he dare not touch. Women' – he held my hand and shuddered – 'are a special meat to him. He inhabits them because of the infamy of their past. He enters some by the apple and some by the serpent, some by greed's little wormhole inside their brain and some, as I you, by the purse of lasciviousness between their legs as assuredly as he once entered Eve.'

'Ah, so Satan is your Master,' I cried. Seeing his glint of triumph I added, 'That makes you a member of the same old heretical breed as the rest of them.'

His face darkened, and his hands left feeding me crumbs and tightened instead around my throat. This made his face even blacker. 'Fool,' he shouted, shaking my brain in his fury. 'Know that I serve the Great One only, whereas you foolish Southern Cathars believe God made the spirit and Satan the flesh.'

'I was half right,' I mumbled, as he struggled to throw me off the mountain.

Maladroit man. When he could have turned me into a snail with his spells, or a horse-leech in a puddle, he tried to wring my neck with his thumbs in a napkin. When he had my body at his mercy, he and his scores of wolves, he chose to hurl curses at me, some of them in languages not even the starlings could understand. I told him so.

'I shall lock you in a fossil,' he screamed, 'just like these bones.' That was novel, too, but before I could unbruise my neck enough to ask what he meant, 'I shall shut your pedigree in a flint,' he howled, and a lot of gibberish besides, while I hawked up phlegm, saliva, bile and a considerable portion of his great feast, the ants' eggs at least, and the salad grass, as an inevitable aftermath of being strangled, albeit by a magician and a titled nobleman.

'I shall hang your maidenhead in a cage and give it time to ripen,' he whispered, calmer now, and only holding me by the solid parts of my anatomy, such as my knee and shoulderbone.

'Mind it doesn't go off,' I croaked, as if I were Marie-Bise, or even little Thistle. 'Mind it doesn't go off.' I was free of my breakfast at last, and glad to be so.

My comrades, especially La Mamelonne, were drunk or in a slumber from the wine he had fed them, though I have to be fair and say they were all of them tired and had sat down to table without rinsing their fingers or even having their wounds attended to. Gibbu hummed in his sleep, and the Fish Girl came in, lay naked along the table and snored, never a pretty sound in a young woman.

The Magus Raymond lifted her eyelid and peered into whatever was under it. He studied her brain for a long time. 'Beautiful,' he said. 'Witless, but entirely beautiful.'

He turned his attention towards myself, and I waited to hear something at least as complimentary. I did not. 'I have you,' Dogskin said to me. 'I do not yet possess you, but have you I do.'

I. was forced to concur with him on both counts. Strong liquors do not agree with me when taken in excess, especially if there is poison in the cup.

After drinking them, I have discovered in myself an ability to vomit a long time without bringing up my heaviness of head and an overwhelming desire to go to sleep.

I did not sleep now. Our host's and captor's thumbs about my neck had been a powerful and immediate emetic, and I have been unladylike enough not to keep the matter from you. So were his knees on my chest and his toenails in my belly, or however it was the magician's limbs arranged themselves beneath his robes and his slippers.

Gibbu, Ironface and the Mute had not enjoyed this advantage. Nor, if I am counting compliments, had Violette la Vierge and La Mamelonne. They would all have to be ill in their own time. Meanwhile the potion in their goblets could continue its evil work upon them.

Its main effect upon all of us was to induce the kind of dreams that men rather than women tend to boast about, but only if they fancy them to be true. The Mage, Magus or Archimage Dogskin the First Baron Cerberus had already plunged us into a deep state of confusion. He boasted as much to me as he stroked my cheek and tied little knots in my hair.

Then he was hovering all about again, and inspecting the slumbers of his other guests. He signalled, and some of his women carried Mamelie and the Fish Girl away into the night. This had fallen very rapidly after breakfast, the way it does when men and women start peering into flagons or leering over cups. And a strange night it was to become, full of the wild sounds of wolves howling, bears grunting, and the creaking of bones as the mountain began to dance.

Dogskin paid no real attention to my male companions. He instructed his guards to leave them where they lay, all bound about in their fetters of sleep.

By now some of his women had come back. Or perhaps it was all of them; I was beyond counting. They did not lift me, quite as they had the others. Or I don't think they did. They simply raised me upon their fingers and floated me out of doors.

Even so mighty a magician as Raymond of Brousses learns to make do with what he has got. He may be able to conjure palaces in the sky, but they will only be good to wonder at. If he wishes to build something he can step inside, then he will need to break rock, just like the rest of us. Dogskin was not the man for that.

That was why he had feasted us in a hall that had ribs for rafters, and nothing to keep out the weather save his powers of persuasion. So his retinue of feys, fairy women and sorceresses were now obliged to toss me into one of those beehive-shaped bothies of the Goths that litter our hills.

It held nothing except a closed door, a sunken floor, a tallow candle and the Wizard Dogskin.

I don't know whether he had flitted ahead of me while I floated, or simply decided to run there and hide. Now here he was with his fingers busy all about me, as he kindly helped me out of my stained garments.

I would not have accepted his assistance if several of his women hadn't been present, and ready with a change of raiment. The stuff they held out to me was as light as gossamer, a kind of Flemish net that had been blanched moon-white with salt and sunshine. Since I would be naked without it, I was in some hurry to put it on.

I was interrupted by a powerful manifestation of the place's magic. The floor spoke to me. Before my brain could digest this fact by itself, I realized it had two voices, one of which consisted of an outrageous scream. The other voice said simply, 'You don those robes at your peril.'

I hesitated and listened towards the floor for further advice. The voices had been female, and a woman's advice is to be heeded in matters of dress.

The floor breathed gently for a moment. Then it snored. Then it screeched again. Then its speaking voice said, 'If you dress yourself in my Master's robes, then for certain his magic will destroy you.'

I knew the scream and the snore, but took a moment or two longer to recognize the voice. This was because it now spoke sense to me, and it had done very little of that lately.

The floor seemed to move, such was the uncertainty of the light thrown by the candle-flame, and then part of it rose uncertainly to its feet. 'Content yourself with me,' it said to Dogskin Raymond.

The sorcerer began to laugh. I was completely naked by now, and I must have been a funny sight. So must the floor. The part that rose to its feet was fully dressed, but uncertain of its legs. It sank wearily down again, reminding me as it did so very strongly of La Mamelonne. Its other half, the portion which screamed, was as naked as I was, which was almost as naked as the Fish Girl. It snored, and it twitched. It chattered, it screeched. I can do none of those things, even when I am awake.

Meanwhile Dogskin was so enjoying the sight of me that his anatomy began to manifest certain magic alterations to its middle region. I say magic, and it is, although universal. It is a miracle of God's that a portion of mankind that normally hangs its head from shame and keeps itself at prayer well below the torso can come puffing up a handspan clear of the thighs as proud as Pope Innocent in his pulpit. Once a woman realizes she can achieve such a mighty feat of illusion (and I'm told it can often be so) simply by taking her clothes off, then she must experience a strong temptation to repeat the trick. But not with Dogskin Raymond.

Indeed, I was so far removed from pride at my undoubted powers that I began to swoon and fade away from my own sight. I saw my nudity as a mist on which my eyebeams could not fasten. My body seemed to hang beneath my neck like

379

a garment from a nail, discarded and available for anyone to slip on.

I fell towards the floor, which had stopped squeaking and talking, perhaps to make room for me. As I struck it, so I slumbered, and as I did so I felt Raymond's fingers all about me, though thankfully not on my neck.

As so often in the instant of slumber, my Phantom spoke to me. Glad I was to hear him, and even more to anticipate his protective handling of me.

'If you let that devil touch you,' he said.

'I can't help it,' I moaned, mad from desire and overcome by the presence of Dogskin and the effects of his philtre.

'If he steps within your bed, I'll never visit you again.'

'I'm not in a bed,' I complained.

'No, you're lying on top of me, the only situation which a man can find beautiful,' said La Mamelonne.

I woke, having slept only for a second. I came fully back to my senses to discover that my libidinous ravisher had chosen to forebear. He now stood trembling by the door, with all of his innocence undone, and not a popish particle brisk about him.

'By the Great Satan, my lady Perronnelle, by the Horned God himself,' he said as if in an ecstasy, 'you have a Protector. I swear I recognized Asteron from the Twenty-Third Degree, but that's of small matter. Whoever he is, the declension was bad. Why didn't you tell me you slept each night with a Fiery One?'

'Mind your own business,' I said.

'We can all talk in our sleep, if that's what you want!' La Mamelonne complained, and went back to being a floor again.

'What a ritual I shall design for you, Virgin, now that I know you are Radiance's bride. What a coupling shall we have. We shall uproot forests. We shall shake down towers. We shall set running stags. You will be my Sheba and I your noon-hard Solomon.'

'I'm the wrong colour,' I protested.

'Only if she washes,' La Mamelonne agreed.

My darling whore spoke truly. What with Béziers burning, Le Bourg burning, and then Le Castellare, my whole skin was sweetened with an appalling soot. I might lack clothes, but I was no more naked than is a witch woman in her feathers and her moss.

Meanwhile there was another burning. Perhaps the crusaders were obliterating my cousin in the Citadel down there. Or doing what was proper, and boiling his bones. Or perhaps De Montfort had lit another town for himself to be warm at its fire. Whatever it was, its smoke filled the hut where formerly there was cloud. And then there was soot.

Soot is more comfortable than cloud. My head was full of spells and the fume of Dogskin's philtre. I was down upon the floor, so I slept.

CAPUT TEN

In which the Virgin languishes long and prepares herself to become a mighty sacrifice.

ome say I slept a night and a day. Some say a month. Some say a year. The truth is that I was shut inside a dream, where time does not matter. The two whores, or their bodily parts, were mured up with me, and their limbs became my floor and sometimes my entire prison.

We slept more than we woke, and I daresay we experienced similar visions, such was the kindness of God and the strength of Dogskin's potions.

La Mamelonne slumbered most. She had sipped the Mage's mead with a greed akin to lasciviousness, and chewed his meat long and gutsily, whatever its bewitching herbs and confusion of spices. Once inside the bothy, she guzzled every potion he offered her, even between snores, and licked sleep crumb by crumb from his fingertips.

Violette la Vierge did not sleep so much as die. She had neither her meals nor her months, but crouched apart from herself in some kind of separate life, like a bat in winter.

This was not to be wondered at. She was a dancing whore and a screeching whore, and on bad days even a squeaking whore. To shut her up in a hollow stone was as cruel as leaving a bird all season with a cloth thrown over its cage. She withered prettily, like a flower in paper.

La Mamelonne grew very large. This was because she stuffed herself with every platter Raymond fed us, whether vole, mountain pig or the rank flesh of fox. His herbs were mixed for fatness, too. Women were his world. He liked them large enough to ramble over.

The Goths had left us little space. La Mamelonne soon filled all of it. She became the room. In our darkness when dreams were dismal, I began to think that the Fish Girl lodged in her, and myself as well, disposed in pieces about her nooks and crevices. On good nights I perched on a ledge, and breathed the sweeter for it.

'I am not fat,' Mamelie said often. 'Many women are, and except for our hats and our hair it's the chief difference between the sexes. But my sex is different enough already, so there is no need for me to grow fat. I am merely pregnant, and there you have the whole truth of it.'

I had heard this lie before, and the Fish Girl was bad at listening, so we would say nothing, awake or asleep.

'I am made pregnant by that young rip Trencavel,' she said, 'not once but many times and mightily, because there's at least four bunnies in my hutch and everyone of them a Viscount.'

On a good day, Violette would giggle at this. Mamelie knew even less about genealogy than she did about the truth, so the mad girl found it funny, even in her sleep.

Raymond de Brousses believed her, though his brain could count what his fingers felt in her belly, and he knew that she carried no more than one. He fondled it every day. If the embryo was a Trencavel he intended to take it for his own, and stamp his own wickedness upon it.

Mamelie was indeed pregnant. Once inside the stones of the mountain she had nothing else to do but be pregnant. Perhaps Dogskin had fathered the child on her himself. Or it could have been a wolf-child, or the result of her coupling with a bear. When we were dragged up Alaric, the night was full of bear skins. Some of them had men inside, and some of them were monsters.

The babe was certainly not my cousin Raymond-Roger's. Nor was it the Phantom's, whoever he was. When he visited my sleep I used to keep watch on him. He spent hours alone with me in that beehive, and never even entered Mamelie's head.

My cousin died in November. We had come here as his soul departed. By the middle of December I was starved enough to be nearly mad. I daresay I should have been mad, but Ironface saved my mind and Gibbu and the Mute did much for my body by stealing in untainted meats and sometimes bread. Raymond let me keep my retainers, and left them free to come and go, as if I were an imprisoned queen.

'If I could leave you to your fate I would,' Ironface told me, 'and the other two whores as well. But this De Brousses has the mountain well guarded by bears, hobgoblins and wolf-men.'

'It's the wolf-*women* who worry me,' Gibbu said. 'They follow me everywhere. Each time I cut a stick to make arrows, they offer to go bundles with me.'

'It's only because they're cold,' Ironface told him. 'You'd be cold if you were naked. And if you were cold, you'd go bundles with anyone, even an ugly fellow like yourself.'

The Mute giggled. This couldn't be right. I'd heard him giggle once before, and that had been a revelation as well.

'Meanwhile I've washed your clothes,' Ironface said to me. 'That is I've had that one wash them.' He indicated the Mute. 'I think it's very wise of you not to let Dogskin dress you. Take a man's clothes and you put on his magic, and you don't want that next to your skin. You're better off as you are, huddled in your hair like a witch in her cobwebs.'

Gibbu growled. He didn't like the tin man eyeing my nudity, even though I guarded it in tresses and leaves.

'That being said, I'm reminded that the last time I saw you undressed, you were surrounded by dead people. I don't want that to happen again, in case I'm one of them.'

So I put my clothes on, and we sat around La Mamelonne planning ways to escape.

'It will be simplest if you let the sorcerer have that virginity of yours,' Ironface said. 'It will only take a moment or two, and then we can all go home.'

'Why should he want hers when he can have mine?' Mamelie asked.

'He's a member of the lesser nobility,' Ironface went on. 'He'll treat you very gently, and you won't even know he's doing it.'

'That's right,' La Mamelonne said, patting her stomach. 'Noblemen are no good at icky-fuck. They only know about giving people babies.'

'We'll be here even longer if he thinks I'm with child.'

'True,' Ironface agreed. 'For several centuries now, rape by the highly born has been regarded as a pre-contract. If the woman is silly enough to get herself with child, it's taken as a sign that her family have agreed the conditions.'

I opened the bothy door and came face to face with a bear. It wasn't a large one, but its teeth were fully grown, and this fact gave its smile unusual prominence.

'You can't stay sober all the time,' Ironface said, and walked boldly outside. A bear could do nothing to him, except squash his tin.

He tumbled back again. 'Something bit my arm,' he cried. 'And I've just had my head in a wolf's mouth.'

This time I saw nothing but the frost. 'Icicles,' I said. 'You've stuck your neck into a dangle of icicles, that's all.'

'It's the magic of the place.' Gibbu explained. 'Dogskin's water is full of potions.'

'His more than most men's,' La Mamelonne agreed.

We had many such discussions, and in one of them I proposed we postpone our escape until the night of the Magus Dogskin's ritual, whenever that should be. All of his acolytes would be bound to watch, if not actually participate, so his guards would be in one place, and his ambushes called in.

'What do you say to all that?' I asked them.

La Mamelonne saw no need to escape. She said she was where her belly belonged.

The Mute by definition never spoke, and the Fish Girl talked a language only hares understood, so it was to Ironface and Gibbu that I turned for an opinion I could trust.

'Yes,' the Hunchback said. He said nothing more.

'Gibbu thinks with his bottom,' Ironface said. 'That's why he's so full of ideas.'

So now my plans were laid. Gibbu and the Mute would help

me, Ironface not impede me. God knew what La Mamelonne and the Fish Girl would do.

I pretended the plan was my own, but in truth it was the Phantom's. He planted it each night in my ear, and a good thing it was I spent so long naked or I doubt if he would have talked to me. Once I had my clothes on he was forever inside them, perhaps to keep warm, and he scarcely opened his mouth except to disturb me with mumblings which were very hard to listen to, his lips being so close to my body.

What he said, while I was playing the spider witch and he could speak to my ear, was that I must hide myself away for a while. He told me my imprisonment by Dogskin was to be seen as a blessing, save for the death and dishonour at the end of it. Seemingly I was becoming a legend among the crusaders and the commoners of Oc alike, and it is always prudent for a legend to be sparing of itself.

Like any confessor he set about diminishing my own good opinion of myself by reminding me that some of my heroic deeds had been performed by Gibbu, Ironface and the Mute, and even more of them by the corpse-women and La Mamelonne.

La Mamelonne and I should really be considered as the same person, he argued, she plump, me willowy; me younger than she by a full half year, she older by most of eternity; myself with a dangerously tight-bottomed approach to life, herself with her virginity constantly ajar, if not banging open, but, as she insisted, a virginity nonetheless because 'a woman is what she thinks she is, not what men tell her to be, and the same goes for whores'. She rode a donkey and I rode a horse, if Nano were still alive and you could call him a horse; and even when she rode a horse she made it look like a donkey, or did before the bears ate it; but otherwise we were the same, and since we both had fair hair and she wore my clothes, I sometimes wondered if I wasn't the horse she rode on, especially in the bothy with her child's legs dancing all over me.

Then, still like a confessor, my Phantom put himself inside my clothes, and that was the end of concentration and the beginning of comfort. I couldn't have survived so many months in that beehive without him.

CAPUT ELEVEN

In which the whore outgrows sorcery yet the Virgin is set upon by spells.

It is better to be preserved in vinegar than rot in honey. This was Ironface's advice to me, and his comfort against my imprisonment. The trouble was that I was rotting in honey. Each time I sipped at Dogskin's wine or drank a cup of his water, my limbs would melt away and my head become full of bees. I would wake and moan out in thirst, and Gibbu and the Mute would rush to tend me. If they were successful, well and good. Often one of the Mage's bears or wolf-men reached me before them and would I seize the wrong pitcher in my torment. They assured me the water was purest dewfall, and it always tasted sweet. Yet somewhere about it there was a haze of sorcery that sent me into another month's sleep.

So I drowsed my life away by moons and then seasons, and my limbs became as useless as damp straw.

Sometime in May the following year, Dogskin came to look at us. He'd gloated over us daily. Now he inspected us properly, and was at once in a rage.

Mamelie was his main concern. He could scarcely get his eye beyond the door. He'd fed her so fat she was larger than a great tun, not counting her breasts which weighed several barrels more and showed a tidal inclination to sag towards whatever side the moon was on. She'd filled the whole bothy six months earlier, so it was a matter of considerable discretion how we packed ourselves about her, even in sleep. He loved his women large, but not when their immensity threatened to spoil Violette la Vierge and myself, who were also articles in his carnal calendar.

'What have you done to them?' he screamed. 'You pot-bellied whore. You've muffled them out. Look at the Fish Girl – there's none of her left, except legbones and hair.' He tried to push his nose round the doorframe. 'My midsummer ritual demands a total conundrum of feminine meat, not something

so starved it looks like a bird's nest in the reeds. When I come
to impale her on my Wizard's sword it will be like stabbing a
bulrush, or disembowelling bracken. I want a woman on the
end of my – '

Violette began to fidget at this nonsense. His noise was
frightening her out of her long hibernation. Having something
hopping at her back made La Mamelonne itch, then scratch
what disturbed her, so the whole beehive trembled.

'What of the magic child?' thundered Dogskin Raymond.
He reached in to prod her belly with his wand, making her
squeak like an inflated pig's bladder. 'How many fathoms
deep have you drowned him?'

'The Viscounts are lustful,' she retorted. 'All four noblemen are playful and kicking. It's as if I've got a pebble
inside me, and each of my little ones is taking turns at it
with his boot.'

'Silence.' He turned his eye on me, and baleful it was,
baneful too. 'As for this one, I daresay she'll do, if we
can straighten her back and get her legs stretched out.'
He inspected me further. 'All except her bosoms, which
are extremely meagre. Each breast needs to be fuller by a
quarter jug.' He spoke briefly to one of his wolf-women or
something female beyond the door and ordered it to feed
me honey.

'You can't see me properly,' I stated. And he couldn't. I
objected to my body being slighted, when all that was wrong
with it was being mildly crushed by La Mamelonne's shadow.

'Insolence! I shall skin your tongue, miss.'

Nobody calls me that, but I didn't answer further. I had
made my point.

Magus Dogskin of Brousses was in a fresh rage now, a
mathematical fury that exceeded his earlier wrath like a
tempest outblasting a soft spring breeze. This was because
his mind at last got itself sufficiently beyond the porch to
grapple with the geometry of our situation. If La Mamelonne
filled the bothy, she couldn't be brought out through its door.
Nor could we be dragged past or round her.

'Unpick the bothy,' I suggested to him.

'With my sorcerer's hands?' he scorned. 'I keep them unsullied, so I may skein the entrails of gnats or enter the dreams of the dragonfly.'

'Have your wolf-men do it. Or your warriors the bears.' It was the first time either of us had confessed there were such beings. 'Or crack it open with a spell.'

He could have done so easily. He didn't. I could only conclude he dared not shatter this monument of the Visigoths lest by breaking its ring of stones he destroy the magic hold he had on us.

Still in a temper, the Mage withdrew to contemplate his next move. Sorcery may move in circles, but it gets there swiftly and its conclusions are simple. He was back in an instant to reach round the doorframe with a leathern bucket. 'Drink this,' he commanded La Mamelonne. He smiled at her for once. Or the magic rings on his fingers did. 'Drink this on the instant.' The bucket bubbled.

'What is it?' she asked, suspicious of her master at last, and sulking because of his recent rage.

'Only a simple posset.'

'My belly's sore from your prodding. Tell me what's in your posset.'

'Nothing but milk of elderberry, asarabacca, purple splurge, hog's fennel, caraway, sundew, buckthorn, ladies' fingers, dogswood, cascara sagrada, fish oils and dried barbary.'

'Is that all?'

'I forgot to mention agrimony. Drink.' The ruby ring on his index finger sipped at it and invited her to follow.

She put her lips to the bucket. She drank. And what a powerful wizard he was to cure the ailments of three women by administering a simple potion to one. Its effect on us was immediate. She vomited. She vomited for fifteen days and fifteen nights. When she wasn't vomiting, and she did all the time, she voided, also all the time, as if the total flux of Carcassonne were enfolded within her tripes, which now contained nothing but continued to disgorge.

Dogskin fed her his spell, and the Wizards came from the ruins of Béziers and relaid its ancient sewer stone by stone between her tonsils and her bottom while the river waters ran.

And what of Violette the Fish Virgin and myself? I won't tell you how we coped, because our sufferings were too detailed for history. So what then of the child within her in its own womb of water, whether it was one or forty-seven viscounts? What then of the child? Cows chew such slippery leaves to bring their children on, and young wives try tricks with the dried roots of liquorice, either to come to calf or to flush the sin away. So what, amid the downpour, became of Mamelie's child?

So little was it disturbed by its mother's outpourings that I had best write nothing. Nothing or even less was what befell it, even though La Mamelonne was melting into slimness all around it, and long since so skinny we could kick her out of doors.

Something in Dogskin's potion – perhaps the asarabacca, or perhaps he boiled the leaf and the bark of the buckthorn as well as milking its berries – held the little one in place while the rest of the posset turned its mother inside out. So here was poor Mamelie both opened and closed, with her bottom hanging wider than the Portal of Saint Jacques and her birthway tighter than a linnet's (which needs to keep itself fast, for the bird feeds on flax seed which is another name for flux if ever I heard one).

At about the beginning of the third week of her great catarrh, La Mamelonne came on to bleed. This made the wolf-women anxious and the bears grow excited, and brought Raymond de Brousses to us in a rush as if borne by a whirlwind. 'Drink this,' he commanded her. 'Or ingest it and insufflate your cavities how you can.' He could stoop inside the bothy now. La Mamelonne was small and his acolytes had cleaned it. The rings on his fingers were holding an earthen ewer.

396

'What's in it?' I demanded. The poor girl was a fortnight beyond speaking for herself.

'Nothing but a simple infusion of willow-weed, snakeroot, waterpepper, dog's mercury, coriander, mezereon – '

'Mezereon's poisonous,' she croaked.

'So are your reins. Swallow.'

'Drink it,' I told her, and tipped it into her head.

She dried and became pink on the instant, and a frenzy of Dogskin's women busied up to wash her. She looked beautiful.

'The whore is now a perfect size.'

La Mamelonne simpered, and the Fish Girl performed a cartwheel of congratulation, all on one spot in the cavern of the bothy.

'Her bottom is compact as the eye of a bodkin. For two weeks and three days of Saturn, she spattered like a heifer in the field. Now she is a woman again, and can sit upon cushions on a clean carpet.'

We saw neither cushion nor carpet.

'I agree with heifer,' La Mamelonne said. 'A heifer is a virgin cow.'

Cow was right.

Dogskin gazed upon her contentedly, glanced lustfully at me, and then towards the Fish Girl.

Still clad in nothing, she was hanging from the shadows by her ankles.

'Tomorrow I shall prepare you for the Great Ritual.' His hands brushed against us as if he were parting saplings. 'There, at the climax of my arcanum, you will meet Baron Cerberus himself, then myself as my mage, then my image as *ipsissimus*. In one of my personifications, once for each one of you, I shall come to test you all. Test you, then taste you, then scorch you away.' He stood himself close to me, and set his eyes against my eye. 'I shall marry you to fire, my lady Perronnelle. Fire shall be your bridegroom. And as for your virginity . . .'

'Virginity?' I asked him.

397

Constance de Coulobres used to tell me if I was ever unfortunate enough to have to talk to a man other than Daddy, either to say nothing or to repeat what he said.

'Virginity,' I repeated.

The word engulfed him totally. He shuddered at the wonder of it. 'Midsummer is almost upon me,' he said, once his frenzy was done. 'Alas, you will not be able to share it with me, Perronnelle de Saint Thibéry. At midnight on its Eve your own meagre contribution to my pomps will have reached its end!' He regarded La Mamelonne once more, and then Violette la Vierge. 'As for this clutch of whores you stroll about with – '

'I'm not a whore,' La Mamelonne told him. 'Or even if I am, I'm a lady with a horse.'

My Phantom came to see me as soon as Raymond had left. The planets stood still, he said, and the stars were all unfixed. Yet such things though miraculous were entirely without importance, because no man could see them, so great was the pall of burning that hung about the land. 'In part it is God's anger at these butchers from the North,' he told me. 'In part it is Christ's impatience at the heresies of the Cathars, and some say Pope Innocent's as well, for when villainies get up his nose he'll not lift a single prayer to clear away the soot from the darkness of Heaven. Or such do many men say.'

'And what is your own opinion?' I spoke to my angel pertly, since here he was clouding my dreams with words instead of bringing my sleep to its proper satisfaction.

'Superstition,' he said, creeping himself through my cloak. 'Superstition and rumour, and a vile kind of ecclesiastical gossip. Whereas the truth of it lies in alchemy and old-fashioned metaphysics. Consider the nature of smoke.'

We considered the nature of smoke, while the two whores slumbered about me and the evening became very misty.

'Now why does this smoke hang about, so these Northmen can do nothing beneath it? It's because they've been burning women and children too young for Heaven. Their toxins encumber the firmament. What happens when priests burn a witch?' His breath grew warm in my cloak. 'The smoke never lasts nor the smell, for her fume belongs in the abyss, and sinks to its natural home. Set torch to a town or a city, and the fog won't last you a month.'

My cloak was white-hot by now, though it stopped short of actual conflagration.

'Women are inferior matter, their metals baser than base. Their goodness may keep them from Hell, but few of them set foot in Heaven. Burn them, their smoke can't rise. That's why these crusaders do it, to keep their own necks from the sunshine.'

My limbs were in a blister of delight, just to hear his voice, first hot then cold. I was in such a wonder at him, I felt a rush of flame break my skin and all of me come out in a damp freckle.

He wasn't quite done with me, so the holy moment was slow to pass. What he said was, 'Midsummer Eve will not be a day too early for you to escape this mountain, and it may be a wonder too late. This De Montfort has not done a thing of note since the Magus Dogskin walled you up. Not a thing save make all of Oc his own.' He held me very tightly, in a way no angel should. Angels should stand at your bed-foot and whisper lightnings, but this one gripped me close and his breath was sweet as liquorice. 'Yet though he sits on Oc, he does so warily, like a man who finds his bottom full of pimples.' Soft and very certain his embrace. 'Oc is full of pimples, Perronnelle, so now De Montfort seeks to squeeze them.' My Phantom squeezed me for himself and said with measured breath, 'He's moving all his siege train towards Minerve.'

'Minerve is invincible,' I gasped. 'Invincible.'

'So was Jericho. But Joshua had a trumpet. This Simon de Montfort has one also, and soon he'll come to blow upon it. Your people will need you.'

Minerva was a goddess. Perhaps my Phantom was a God,

or even God himself. Whenever soldiers and their women ask me about God, I say he is the World Spirit who holds me very close.

My dream was interrupted by pipe and tabor, as if courtiers were in procession throughout our whole hill of bones. Then came a drumming of fingers on the door.

It was Raymond de Brousses in a new red coat. His rout were outside, wearing scales and claws, like a coven of dragons. Some carried flags and some carried fires.

He scarcely glanced at Mamelie and Violette, but called in his women to strip me and wash me. Before they could begin, and I bark a shin or two, he handed me a liquid in a crystal. There wasn't much of it – about the weight of a young widow's tears in her first winter. Only a thimbleful yet infinitely threatening.

I took it but did not sip. The potion was clear, but scented when I sniffed it. 'Cowbane,' I said. Marie-Bise used cowbane to poison cats. 'You might as well feed me deathcap.'

'Cowbane,' he agreed. 'But diluted and redivided according to the magic principle of four, then again squared and quartered as in all ways befitting the sempiternal quadrant.' His voice was very firm, and I wanted to obey it. 'It will not so much kill you as freeze your senses in a pickle.'

'And leave me as addled as an everlasting drunk.'

'Render your young body numb against the knife.'

'My body prefers to suffer.'

'Then suffer it shall.' He spilled a little liquid on the floor, then splashed some more after. 'There, I've increased your pain by a half, and there's a half again. You must swallow the rest of it. There's a tincture of wild celery and the dust of Spanish beetle. These to promote venereal fancy and fructify the parts.'

'My digestion cannot stomach aphrodisiacs.' Nor did I intend to be lewdly promiscuous with a coven of dragons. 'My confessor has forbidden them.'

'You shall taste as I command, or I'll have my women rub

it all about you in a salve. My witches use such an ointment to set their bodies flying, so I know your skin will drink it.'

This made me so frightened that I resolved to be stern with him. 'In Christ's name in Heaven, I forbid you my soul and I forbid you my maidenhead.'

This did not sound well on the evening air, and I wished I had tried it in Catalan or knew how to speak Arabic.

'Your soul is a fog. And as for the rest of you . . .' He smothered my face in a nest of fingers. 'I'll take it when I will, and leave it when I want to. It's your essence I need, and the string of your spine.' He squeezed as if to peel my skull. 'That and to suck your marrow for its juice and drain your little witch spring.'

Then the Magus Dogskin let go of my brains and added, 'I've no use for virginities as such, except perhaps as pots in which to dry mushrooms.'

He gestured abruptly, and his women cut my clothes off with shears, so my family's sturdy needlework was at last brought down. First they sought to bathe me, then to soothe my limbs with honey, then anoint my personal parts with their sorcerer's ointment, as being the shortest path into a female's thinking.

Raymond couldn't stay for this, in case the sight of my young body drove him mad before dewfall.

His women were foolish, even those who wore the masks of foxes. They left me my clogs and let my feet regain them, so I trod on many claws and quite as many fingers. I kicked the scales off some knees as well, and I daresay the kneebones beneath them. This bathing naked is an obscene practice such as only whores use. Though I am no Cathar there's enough of my Mummy about the hair-roots of my thinking to make me consider water a perilous thing that only boys should dabble in, and Christians never.

They had instructions not to damage me, and before they could be firm our struggle woke Mamelie, and afterwards the Fish Girl. The one fell to screaming, the other to dancing, and all in a space with no room for either.

Then Ironface clattered in and saved me with a blanket.

The women went away. I daresay they told Dogskin they had followed his bidding, when all they had done was wet a little half of me then clutter me up in such a mess of honey I should shortly be attractive to wasps. It's a wonder a queen bee didn't mistake me for home and come and lay eggs in me, or a bumble at least. If one did I was too agitated to notice. I advanced in fear as the night approached.

'You were wise not to step inside his water, Perronnelle. Or any man's else. Worse than all the other elements it's brimful of sorcery. It should only be used sparingly, and never to wash women. Its chief work is to cleanse the smell from a horse.'

These were wise words from Ironface. La Mamelonne and the Fish Girl clearly agreed with him, though I'd sometimes seen the mad one dance naked through the rain. Its drops may be empty of spells, seeds and fishscales, but it's full of sad doubts and all the heartbreak in Heaven. As for Mamelie, I'd scrubbed her back often, and often thought to see her bones melt away in the bath. Whores are like eagles. They have black bones, and that's another fact you won't read in history books.

Both women sank back into sleep as my mind wandered this way and that striving to lock Dogskin away from my thoughts. I wished I could forget him. I could not. I had too much to forget and not enough to remember.

I needed God's comfort but saw no way to find it, for where can it be? We live on this middle world, with the sunshine around us, then the moon, and its tiny stars above the night. Somewhere beyond them is Heaven. How far beyond? Too far for any but the saints or my cousin with his Perfect Ones. I had not seen its golden chain hanging down to fasten us in place, though I knew it was there. I had not found the crystal stairs where the blessed may ascend. Nor was I likely to if I perished in any ritual not consecrated to Christ.

Gibbu came in, then the Mute, both bringing a faggot of

sticks. I watched them anxiously, as they crouched down by Ironface and said nothing.

Dogskin's great midnight was rushing upon me, yet not one of them lifted a finger to comfort me. Were they drugged? Or held in place by the common enchantment? Or did I see matters wrong? Perhaps the women's honey had been full of the magic ointment and my brain was touched after all. I searched their faces.

Dead eyes, gaze averted, no eyes at all but a sieve of iron. Were these the beings I had always suspected them to be? Ferblant the Empty One, his Hunchback, and his Badel without voice or sex were fiends sent to escort me to the portals of Hell where Dogskin of Brousses stood gate-keeper.

Perhaps I had died in my mother's kitchen after all, been slaughtered with my parents, Marie-Bise and the rest of them. Everything from Béziers to Alaric was my soul's last journey, its imaginings forced to follow each twining pathway on the map of the dead.

I knelt along with these and the two sleeping whores, who might be demons also, for what was paint but a devil's face? What was this hole, this tiny stone circle of the Visigoths, but hope's last dungeon?

So I waited for my death on the Eve of the Solstice, or Midsummer's Eve, the Feast of St John. It might be my first death. It might be my second. Whichever death it was, it would be my last.

I glanced from friend to friend, or from devil to devil. Then Ironface leant forward and touched me with his dirty hand.

'I cannot advise you of much, my Virgin – '

'There you go again, with this silly talk of virginity.' I indicated my nakedness.

'Cling to it while you may.' He clung to me while he could. 'What you have is a potent force in white magic. The Christ was born of a virgin, and ones such as Dogskin Raymond hate every facet of her.'

Old Saucepan Head was chill to kiss, cool against lips

that were dry with fear, but as sweet of breath as cloves in a colander.

'You will see terrors, believe me. But terrors that can do you no harm, for believe me again when I say that they will not be real. You will witness mutilation, strangulations, torturings, sacrifices – perhaps of these two whores who are also your friends, perhaps of others – but they will be no more than the tablets of a dream.' He held me again. 'They will be illusion, merely the beginnings of his ritual's conceit. I have studied the Black Circle of this villain of Brousses. I have gone to his stone and sniffed his powders and his alchemies. He will start with coloured smoke and a conjuring trick.'

I shivered, not trusting to believe him. Again my lips felt as cool on the latticework of his head as if I licked a freshly made pomander. My Phantom smelled like this. Was this old liar my dream after all, an angelic wraith in a lobster's shell?

His next words stung. 'His knife is real. I have seen the Magus Dogskin's dagger of sacrifice, and trust me when I say that of all about him its blade is most real.'

He stood away, so I would not miss his point. 'Forget the horrors, as I say. It is when you feel drowsy you must fear. When the drums bemuse you, or the witless lights.'

He went to the door and beckoned the Mute and Gibbu to rise. 'They are coming for you, Perronnelle. Your torment is nigh. Remember not to drink of any cup, whether brought by his maidens, by Dogskin himself, or baby-faced child.'

'I thirst already.'

'It's the fear and his enchantment. Take care most of all not to take any cup I seem to proffer you. Or Gibbu, or the Mute. For it will not be myself or these, but a changeling in the face of confusion. Ourselves shall bring you nothing till the ritual is done.'

He went out of doors into a night full of crickets. There were too many crickets, as if even they were sent to spy on me. I heard the stones tick.

Gibbu and the Mute picked up their faggots.

'What things are they?' I asked. I knew they had no weapons on this hill.

'He told me to collect bavins,' Gibbu said. 'Sticks, straw and brushwood all the better to burn you on. I do as my master bids me.'

'What master is that?'

'No matter who. There is only one bonfire.'

I heard no crickets now, only the sound a snake makes breathing as it moves through straw.

The Mute could not smile, and both men left me on this further note of chill.

Dogskin's women were back. Or perhaps, to speak truly, other women came. The first were dressed as serpents, and it was these I heard breathing, some with painted skins, some entirely naked except for aspic heads and the fangs of vipers. Others came as toads with warts full of venom, others as salamanders, yet more as flies. So here we had earth and water, fire and foul air. Yet most came as serpents, for the snake twines his tail round all other elements and claims himself Quintessence, though philosophers know him truly as the Great One Who Fell. Lucifer was a snake, or some say an eagle, whom men that study birds call a serpent with wings.

So many came to seize me that I dizzied to count them. No time to wonder how they thronged so small a space, perhaps one by one in an endless chain of dancing. It could be, God knows, that I was already drawn outside.

What I remember clearly was they clad me in robes: white for my virginity, with a small band of blue to mock Mother Mary. My head was hooded in red, pleated in a wimple, but reeking with fresh blood, the colour of martyrdom and sacrifice.

Six of the tallest serpents plucked Mamelie from the bothy, and six hopping frogs dragged the Fish Girl after. These handed them in turn to a dozen snakes more. All hissing twelve were painted as colubrines, and kept my

405

friends encircled in bright coils of green. Neither whore was tranced, though both were drugged as always.

A female snake reared up and hopped close on stilts. This venomous apparition put her face down to Mamelie and bit her slowly by the neck. She was a huge Montpellier Serpent, the grey Goddess Malpolon, so her fangs could not be seen, being far back in her throat.

She hissed and bit slowly as Malpolon does. She sucked and bit more, till La Mamelonne grew heavy with the pleasure of her poison. Then she let her weight drop.

The Fish Girl was lifted head down, and bitten by the ankle to cure her foot of dancing. Once her body became still she was lowered gently through the wreathing of serpents, drooping among scales and slipping noose from noose.

Then we three were taken up and pelted by feathers, sometimes merely tickled, sometimes scratched with their quills. Then draped in cobwebs and whipped with grass and nettles, or perhaps stuck with venom, because nowhere did I bleed and in no wise did I itch.

The great din upbore me, and I felt sleepy in spite of it. Was the venom milked from snakes, or did they simply flick me with the drowse of their ointments?

All I know is that I disobeyed Ferblant's injunction. Long before I reached the place of sacrifice, I fell fast asleep.

It may have been a dream, and if a dream my last one. I saw a painted circle on a high lawn on Alaric, and round about this circle stood the Temple of the Monsters. This Temple was roofless. In truth it was nothing but a palisade of bones.

Normally in a dream there's a shift to escape it. You stoop to pick a flower, or lift the magic latch and awaken from sleep. But this dream was a dream of the dream's own situation. Even as I dreamed it the dew fell heavily. I felt the dew fall, and I knew I should wake from dreaming to find the dream was true.

In the dream nonetheless Violette the Fish Girl hung by one ankle from a cross-piece of wood that was nailed but grew branches. She hung there stark naked, twisting slowly and smiling. I knew her for what she was. I had seen her on Mamelie's cards.

Mamelie herself lay outflung on a rock. There were no bands upon her, save some cottons on her fingers. These fixed her hands. Two hawks perched on her toes. She could not move her limbs for their eyes' weight upon her. I knew who she was. She had brought herself forth to show me from between her own legs.

I knew myself also, tied upright to a stake of newly shaven wood. The stake was still growing for its tree was yet planted. It was wet without its bark, and I felt its pulse throb like the old Gothic Life-Tree. It was warm and stood for ever from the loins of the Giant that some men call their earth. I was robed, yet exactly as I'd seen myself fall from Mamelie's skirts.

The Fish Girl was the Fool in the Noose, and Mamelie was Sacrifice. I was Queen Empress Imperatrix who treads down the serpents and holds aloft the stars. Yet her Master is Imperator who shall rape her with his sword to engender plague and miracles the instant he frees her backbone from the safety of her blood.

I was to be Queen of Goodness, the greatest sacrifice of all. I knew this, for all about us we were watched by a thousand eyes.

Still inside the trance of my dream, I heard the voice of Dogskin Raymond, and I heard the Magus say: 'LAMECK CADAT PANCIA *Sorcery is the first reality* VELOUS MERROÉ LAMIDEK *because it begins in illusion.* CALDURECH ANERTON MITRATON *Reality is only transient* MELCIDEAL BARESHCES *for it plants itself in pain.* ZAZEL, FIRIEL.'

He clapped his two hands, which were wet from peeling bark from my tree, so his serpents and his toads, his flies and salamanders gathered all about him. They made their way to Mamelie and entered her body swiftly like beasts into the Ark. He needed the woman's body to draw forth his power, so now all power returned to her. He'd used her magic to enchain me by fashioning this army of demons from the coals of her heart.

Now they disappeared, except for Malpolon the grey Goddess who was also a snake.

I opened my eyes and saw my dream become true, as if my sleep had watched it through my skin. I was bound to a newly peeled tree and clad in robes of sacrifice. My two friends were naked and fastened as I have described, save that Mamelie's feet were no longer held by birds of prey but by forks of wood.

Dogskin appeared as both magician and emperor, exactly as painted on the cards he had lent Mamelie.

He stood by an altar of stone on which a small log was smouldering. Also on the stone there was a naked sword, a hazelwood stick, a dagger with its blade in a green cloth, a copper dish and a large earthenware jar.

He wore scarlet robes with a backcloth of gold, and on his head a tall pointed hat. There were words written on this hat, but I could not read them. There were strange signs too, but I did not know them.

He took up his sword and described a circle on the ground in front of and touching the altar.

Beyond the altar but not touching it he drew a shape that looked like a bent-sided triangle. He didn't use his sword for this, but the hazel stick, which he pointed like a wand.

Then he put down his sword and his stick and took up the earthenware jar. He poured salt in an endless line round the edge of the triangle, going round it three times, always from the outside. Then he dampened the centre of the triangle with liquid from a cup.

He took up the jar again, and marked out his circle with salt, again in a continuous line, this time walking nine times round and pouring from the inside. He did not leave the circle again, reaching out to replace the jar on the altar, and to pick up his hazel wand and his sword.

As he took them in his hands and raised them aloft there came a sigh of affirmation, as if the mountain spoke to him.

408

We were not alone, though we seemed alone. At least a hundred onlookers stood in the shadows beyond the light given off by the burning log.

He threw salt on the ember, salt or salt of peter, and it flared. The onlookers were naked, both women and men. They wore masks depicting the beasts of the mountain: the fox, the eagle, the wolf, the bear and the pig, masks or else these were their living heads. Not all of Dogskin's rout were kennelled in Mamelie, then. There were enough eyes to guard us from flight.

Gibbu stood here, and the Mute also, scarcely further from Dogskin than I was. They neither moved nor spoke. At the feet of each one of them was their bundle of faggots, brought here on the sorcerer's commands to feed the sacrificial fire.

Malpolon hovered about us, transgressing both the circle and the triangle. She was a snake, so she knew no limits.

She came closer, hissing as if to bite me, but I knew she would not bite. Malpolon is our only serpent whose mouth brings dreaming on, so why should the Goddess's poison be different? Dogskin did not want me to sleep, not yet. The huge snake kissed me instead, leaning down from her stilts and oppressing my neck with the weight of her coiling arms.

She kissed me long, licking hard and gloatingly, the way a dog cleans its meat. I spat her kiss back at her, but still she kept on.

So here I was, betrayed by the inactivity of my friends. I felt as the Christ must have felt on his cross, unutterably alone.

I glanced towards Gibbu. He stood hooded and still, so still his cloak might have been hung upon a stick, and his hump also.

The Mute was also frozen as if in a trance, his face shaded by the bent man's shadow. I realized, in horror, that both of them were transfixed by the power of Dogskin's will, perhaps for ever.

Of Ironface himself there was no sign. At the hour of my greatest need, Tin Legs had forsaken me.

It was then that Mamelie groaned a loud sigh, and her limbs pushed and trembled. She was coming into labour.

Mamelie groaned once again, whereat Malpolon disappeared and the night became full of invisible forces. A dagger, not Dogskin's, hovered in the air then stabbed a vertical slit into Mamelie's belly. Dark hands that I could see because they were covered in blood snatched a tiny infant from within her, and the sky howled. I saw the child and the bloodstained hands that held it. I saw nothing else of the phantoms themselves.

Mamelie was awake now and smiling at the hole in her.

Dogskin spoke to the invisible ones, and they gave him an obscene answer, as devils do.

'Give the babe its first suck.'

'She's got teats like a horse's prick.'

The infant lay against Mamelie's breast, but she couldn't take it in her arms.

'Now strangle her quickly.'

The whore's legs thrashed. She lay broken-eyed and still.

'Was that quick enough?'

'Bring the child over here.'

The infant howled through the air, cradled in its arms of blood.

Dogskin snatched it and placed it on the burning log, and the onlookers stepped closer to sigh their approval.

I remembered Ironface's words. 'You will see horrors,' he had said, 'but they will not be real.' He himself had deserted me so why should his advice be true?

Mamelie bled no more. If she were strangled how was it her breast moved as if in sleep?

Again the sorcerer threw salt upon the flames, and in the instant of their burning he became clad in purest white. The Magus was transformed. He was now Baron Cerberus. He touched his sword-point to the tip of his hazel wand and cried in a booming voice, 'PAUMACHIE! APOLOPESEDES!

Our illusions are all ended! Let the sacrifice commence! GENIO!
LIACHIDE! GENIO!'

I heard a rushing through the darkness as if the sky above
Alaric was splitting.

I looked for horrors, but the first being to appear was the
snake-headed Malpolon. Dogskin achieved her return with
a puff of red smoke, and I remembered Ironface saying that
he knew him to be a charlatan, having inspected his powders.
A charlatan with cups full of illusion and a bitter blade to
his knife.

There she swayed, the stilted Goddess of Scales who had
shown herself three times before but who now stood taller
than ever within the magic triangle.

'This is folly,' someone whispered. 'Dangerous folly to
encourage a mere syzygy to step inside the salt.' Was it
Ironface, or Gibbu, he spoke so low? Or did the Mute have
a voice?

Next to Malpolon a woman-shape manifested itself, but
slowly, as if it were made of cloud and forming from its own
mist. This female form was dressed in veils each as fragile
as fog, and these she took off in turn, her body becoming
more corporeal and distinct the further she disrobed.

These veils and swirling vapours revealed a phantom with
mouths and vaginas all over her head and belly and limbs,
even to the backs of her hands. Then she compressed her
will into the semblance of a woman's more normal beauty
with only one of each organ, one vulva, one mouth, that kept
changing places till her flesh grew hideous scales, which she
shed like leaves from a tree.

At last she stood there naked beneath the Goddess
Malpolon. She simpered towards Baron Cerberus, and
then, as if in a dream, I saw that she wore my face.

The heavens were silent now, and the throngs of acolytes
still. The Magus Raymond, name him as I will, pointed with
his sword towards the smoking stars and with his hazel wand
into the abyss beneath the mountain and began a thunderous
invocation.

411

'*In the names of the Great Deus Omnivert, Ruler of Signs, and he who listens from his palace of serpents, Lucifer Lightborne who is King of the Shadows.*'

'I forbid that prayer.' The voice was Ironface's. It came from the darkness beyond the darkness. I could see him nowhere.

Dogskin Baron Cerberus wheeled once about himself, searching for the being who dared interrupt him, then clenched his face again into its ecstasy and said, '*Them I dare not bind. Yet, Greatest Ones, I obdure you according to the Ceremony of Cups and by the power of the life within this woman, whose blood I shall cut for you, and the goodness of this babe, whose gasp I shall extinguish and both their entrails burn, I pray you make apparent within the angles of this quadrant the Guardians of the Universe, all the daemons they bind, themselves and their elements whether of four or fifth, and each and every majesty from within the Triple Azimuth, up to and including Dukes of the Seventeenth Degree.*'

'Quadruple Azimuth,' Ironface's voice corrected him, close behind me now, and placing me in the pathway of the magician's wrath. 'Quadruple as representing in each of its circumferences a sacred letter of Tetragrammaton the Unnameable.'

'Silence!'

'And the fourth but imagined Limb of the Triple Tree.'

'There is no such Limb.' Dogskin's words blistered me now, and I heard Ironface tremble as he sought to shield himself behind my body and the giant's great stake. 'Nor any imagination fiercer than mine. I can perceive no radiance of Kether, still less in Aziluth. And without Aziluth, you timorous one, how can your quadrilateral quadrilingual Azimuth be?'

Ironface's joints rattled. 'Never ask how, but where. For it is there, behind its every maze and sanctuary and on all its paths, that my Master bids me do battle with you.'

My turn to tremble now.

'What the inducement and what the prize?'

412

'Your mastery is the inducement, your ritual the only prize. You are bound to answer me, or abandon them both.' Still sheltering behind me, Ironface whispered, 'Fear not, for he must meet my challenge, even as Merdun de Montfort did, for as soon as he wields his magician's sword and the Dukes are out from their darkness, they will demand to see which one of us has the power.'

'Fool!'

'You are the foolish one, Dogskin of Brousses. Vain and empty. You have no powers save those you pluck from the void – '

'Fool, you interrupt a most mighty Duke – '

'And shall shortly spit in its eye – '

'If you damage this ritual now, then the Dark Ones below the abyss shall run wild, those and the unfixed Daemons of earth, water and sky will loosen the box of the winds.'

'My Master will chain them up, as he chained up the Wolf of Hell.'

'What master is that?'

'I challenge you, Dogskin. I challenge you in that name by His name, for Dogskin is your degree.'

Baron Cerberus roared, and his white robes blackened like salted gold. He no longer guarded himself with his magician's sword or held the female form in check with his wand, or protected his creature Malpolon.

The fog female changed as a dragon will change, breathing the starlight into her, and building up force with the fires of frost.

Ironface, still crouching behind me, laughed.

She shrieked, the woman who wore my face and, for all I could tell, my flesh. She howled neither in pain nor mirth, but as one whose shriek is her essence. She howled to bring on power, the way a wild beast will howl at the moment it takes its kill.

This beauty took hold of the Goddess Malpolon, who was three times taller than she, snapped her stilts in half then in

413

half again, bit off her writing tail, and clawed all her back
to blood.

Malpolon did not hiss; she shrank to an ordinary woman
and screamed like an ordinary woman, for she was a woman
indeed, one of Dogface's inner coven, and masked for his
great illusion.

There was no illusion now, but a terrible reality. The
woman who wore my face neither clawed her nor strangled
more. She had snapped her stilts and her tail, she had scraped
off her skein of scales, and broken the mask from her head;
and now that she was no longer a snake, this duke of a
devil-woman ate her. She chewed flesh from her screaming
flesh, and folded her bones into her mouth as deft as a cat with
a minnow. She ate her till nothing was left but the Goddess's
bloodstained hair, and her blood on the chest and chin of her
destroyer. Then the fiend howled once more.

This howl was of purest joy. It was so stark, so horrifying
in its ecstasy, that it turned the midnight chill. I saw a frost
had formed around us, then heard the dew blades squeak
beneath her as the devil-woman left the triangle that should
have contained her.

She no longer had feet and wore my face no more. She
had claws like the monstrous bones that enclosed us, and
the legs and belly of a bear. Her head was a dog's but not
a dog of this world. It had no nose or nostril; its muzzle
was all mouth and its mouth row upon row of teeth, with
bloodshot eyes at the edge of it. She had eaten Malpolon
except for the Goddess's stilts, and now stood higher than
Malpolon ever stood, as tall as a tree or the Chapel of the
Monster's loftiest bones.

Then she was woman again, still huge and with the
hell-dog's face, and she sidled round the edge of the circle
in which the Magus Raymond strove to protect himself, while
he searched desperately through a parchment of spells.

'You insult me, Baron de Brousses,' she whispered. 'Did
you think you could place a conjuration within my quadrant
yet ignore the necessary obeisances?'

414

'Great One, reveal your name. I am urgent to know you.'

'What – have you name me and so banish me? Go back to your studies till you find my title. Know simply I am a Duke of the Ultimate Degree.'

'My pardon, Great One.'

'Or step from your circle and partake of my power.' She was woman-size again, and wore a woman's face, not my own, but so beautiful that even a woman could fall in love with it.

She spoke to him again, soft and low. It was not her mouth that uttered, but the lips of her loins, their voice more beguiling than Lucifer's to Eve, herself more potent than ever our first mother was or knew how to be.

The Magus trembled both from lust and fear, but he did not move. 'I will give you the flesh of that woman,' he said, pointing to Mamelie, 'if you enter the triangle and yield me your name.'

'I have tasted woman's flesh before. Did you think to place a serpent in my nesting place?'

Ironface chuckled behind me, 'We're free of you, Dogskin of Brousses. You dare not leave your circle now the Dukes are out. Only one is here yet, but think how many you have summoned.'

Still Dogskin implored the wild spirit to do his bidding. 'You have eaten,' he said slyly. 'Yet, have you no other uses for flesh, O Mighty One?'

'I have all female appetites,' the Apparition growled. 'Do you offer your body to slake them?'

'You are a Duke, and may change your form at will. Show yourself as a male. There are women here.'

The devil's breasts grew larger, her voice stayed shrill, but a monstrous spike stood forth from her lovely loins as if all Merdun's rascals had lent her their manhoods end to end. She went swaggering towards where the Fish Girl hung by the foot, and made as if to enter her with this enormous figment of hers, huger and harder than the armour on a wild bull's forehead or the tusk of the Béziers elephant. I shuddered for Violette la Vierge.

415

The Fish Girl screamed and the Apparition chuckled, while the Magus Dogskin studied his parchments for ways to bind her within his power or else banish her beyond the abyss.

Still howling, the Fish Girl began to dance upside down in the air, whirling her arms and legs through the shape my dreams had first hung her in. She danced herself into a blur, but within it one shape was constant, the shape of the bent-ended rolling Cross, which some name the Hammer of the Universe, and some call the Sigil of Luck.

Luck it was for Violette la Vierge, for the Apparition recoiled and faltered, and it was Ironface's turn to chuckle now.

The Apparition snarled, grew plates of armour on its chest and a beard, and went strutting to poor outstretched Mamelie.

The whore's teeth chattered in fright, but she still did honour to her calling. 'What a splendid thing you've got there,' she stammered, 'almost the best one I've seen, give or take a miller's thumb or two. Why don't you rest it down close to me, and I'll show you a trick to get rid of it?'

The Nameless One made a run at her, emitting an ear-cracking roar, but when it came to her body front to front, the hermaphroditic brute saw something in the posture to frighten it. The thing shied away and came charging directly at me.

'I forbid you that virgin,' Dogskin shouted, which of course made the beast more eager. It came trundling up on me like a siege tower behind its battering ram.

'La Mamelonne is bound legs apart, elbows up,' Ironface said, still behind me, 'in exact replica of the Eastern Cross or sigil of Christ Triumphant. Clearly this monster has no stomach for it, no belly-sticker at least. You must make a Cross in your mind, little Virgin, and picture it shining bright to your front, to your side, to your behind and all above you. That way no harm can come to you from man's middle earth or the great pit beneath.'

Words words words. I was slow with this Cross in my

head, or tardy in thinking it forward, and unable to paint it white or illuminate it with due radiance. The Beast was one bound from on to me, and its foretip already gone past my hip in its eagerness, so brisk are these monsters from Hell. I was nearly raped all ends up, and ripped from kneebone to nostril, when Ironface went swaggering forth and made some kind of creaking sign at it, full of far too much base metal for holiness.

The Infernal One tore him apart.

I had seen him slain several times before, but never so swiftly as this. This was the Apparition who, even in its gentleness as a woman, had dragged the Goddess Malpolon limb from limb and eaten all of her except her hair which sprouted this instant on Alaric like a daisy clump. Now she was a man and had a white-hot rod between her legs more uncomfortable to her than a pine pole blistering in a furnace. She needed to cool it in a young woman's blood, with a young woman all around it to ensure it kept flowing. Mine was the blood. I was that young woman. Ironface was in the way.

The Apparition gripped his head in her claws and shook his body off. No trouble, I thought, except for the fury of it. Ironface had hidden in his chest before, but not with his vambrace off, then his cuirass, his greave and his tassets, then his arms and legs in pieces, and his plastron pushed in and pothered out too quick for the gore to run.

The Monster was so anxious to find a man, or a woman, inside the resulting pile of tin that she was distracted for an instant, and made a howling run towards Mamelie's babe where it lay on the altar table. It shattered in her fingertips, being no more than a model made of clay, as I had suspected, with the real birth to come.

The space between La Mamelonne's legs had already concealed many wonders from me and revealed many more, and for the male portion of mankind a plurality of surprises I could only guess at. Its interest for the Apparition, though at a respectful distance from the split Cross she was bound in, was even more evident.

417

I don't believe Mamelie came into labour at that moment
– indeed if I force my mind to return towards fact rather
than content itself with recounting the mere history of a
miracle, I am bound to say she didn't. Nonetheless, from
between her thighs a dwarf was born, who now came charging
out towards the Apparition, calling out Spanish spells and
Christian metaphor in Ironface's best voice.

The fancy that of all Ferblant's organs the speechbox had
survived his recent demolition was a powerful one. So was
the notion that it might be ventriloquizing from Hades or
beyond. The supposition that the trickster was alive was
even stronger. He had stood forth from his armour before
and, now that he had this stunted one to serve his will, he
might well be throwing his voice from a nearer place than
the Hereafter.

The dwarf's bearing was noble, but his face was even
more hideous than the Apparition's it confronted. It looked
as if it had been boiled in a cauldron, or trodden on by a
well-shod horse.

Below the face he wore a tabard, and this was covered with
all manner of crosses, overlaid by an embroidered crusader's
blazon with Spanish bars, much as Ironface had boasted about
his own heart's bone when he first saved me.

The Apparition was fearful of the Cross, or the crosses, or
the face, and backed away. This dwarf was indeed too stupid
to think for himself, so Ironface continued to ventriloquize for
him, mouthing such matters as 'Five wounds, Christ's blood,
Five Joys and Rejoicings of Mother Mary, Five Sorrows of
the Same, Five Senses of the Corporeal Christ and ditto
evermore after,' while causing him to make an endless line
in the air with his fingertip, a line that was neither a circle
nor a cross but moved in a seamless knot of interlocking
triangles not to say pentangles and pentagrams which held
the Apparition transfixed, then compelled her slowly towards
and into the salt.

The Magus Raymond chirped a few defensive spells in
his turn, principally *Tetragrammaton*, which is what these

Wizards say when they will not name the God all men should praise. The force of that word sent the sky splitting and the Apparition howling off into the four winds, all except the forepart of her penis, which being a feminine power she had no need for, so it lay upon the hillside like an enormous log, setting the grasses on fire and growing mauve berries.

Dogface screamed, but to his band of acolytes, 'Smother that dwarf, and strangle the woman on the altar of sacrifice, and use your blades on the whore in the tree. Then bring me the Virgin unharmed. I am exhausted with conjuration. I intend to make spells of another salt, and with a truer wand.'

'Yet still you evade my challenge,' cried Ironface's voice. 'Well, I shall show you miracles now.' The dwarf seized embers and brands from Dogskin's altar, and threw them to illuminate Dogskin's acolytes, who came on none too briskly.

I heard a sound I had not encountered since Le Castellare. A ballister discharged an arbalesque. Then a bow was released, a fresh arrow withdrawn from its quiver even as the first arrow flew, and the string chafed back and released before the flight struck home. So a great bowman hangs his deaths in the air.

I do not know if Gibbu let fly, for the Hunchback stood brooding and still, perhaps till stringing his bow. My Phantom stood beside him, pulling quick and easy, killing Dogskin's scoundrels as fast as they rushed up at him.

The faggot that lay at Gibbu's feet, and at the Mute's also, was nothing but a hoard of arrows and quarrels, a whole year's harvest of shafts cut lovingly from suitable trees as each day progressed, and now shared with my Phantom, who if not real was at least as palpable as midnight, and laughed through white teeth while he killed live men by shooting real arrows.

The dwarf meanwhile fitted Ironface's armour together for him. I saw that he was not a proper dwarf, but was merely an ugly fellow with a full-grown body made short by walking on

419

the stumps of his thighs instead of feet. Someone had cut his hind legs off, but not his prick, which was enormous and which he leant upon. He hid the horrors of his face by putting Ironface's helmet on his head.

I did not see what otherwise became of him, for when I turned round, my Phantom had disappeared, but Gibbu shot now, and the Mute wound his arbalesque all alone.

No sooner was Ironface back, or his voice at least, to roost like a pigeon inside its own armour, than my friends made haste to cut the Fish Girl down without breaking her neck, and to unfasten La Mamelonne from her slab.

When this was done, and as if two naked women weren't enough for them, they set me free from the foul spindle I was fastened against, then ripped the robes from my own back as well, which inevitably led to a baring of my front and a great intrusion of chilliness and early morning starlight.

'You must not stay clad in the cloth of sacrifice,' Ironface said.

'Where's that dwarf?' I asked him. 'And who else saw my lovely Phantom?'

'More to the point, what's become of Dogskin Raymond?' Gibbu said. 'I've got a yew-tipped arrow for that rascal De Brousses.' He hurried off to find him, and the Mute followed after.

'We'll be getting off the mountain,' Ironface called after them. 'You'll not kill that one with an arrow. Or not without dipping it in a treacle I've no time to concoct for you.'

So, with his three naked women supporting him (he said he was still faint from being torn to pieces by a devil), Ironface hurriedly clattered downwards.

Not a wolf, bear or other rascal followed us. A bellyful of iron, flint and fire-hardened wood had proved a powerful disincentive to all of Raymond's minions, so we were left alone to make our way off Alaric.

I was still drunk on ointment, of course, and my brain was nine months' addled by spells and the foul air of that bothy, so I cannot give you an accurate account of the next few hours.

History says that I and my doughty band of warriors made our way off the mountain, and for once I find myself in agreement with it. It makes little mention of what was for me one of life's major miracles, but why should it?

At about full dawn, all four of us were sleeping in a bush, myself and the other two women wrapped up in one another's arms like a parcel of goosepimples.

Here Gibbu found us. He was ever a lad with a nose for a bush, but this was not the principal wonder of him. He was leading a horse.

'Nano!' I cried, waking up half the mountain. My faithful gelding had survived the bears, and looked so entirely beautiful that I would have ridden him side-saddle if Mummy had been there to command me. My saddle-bags had long since been worried off, or stolen by foxes or thieves on stilts, but he still wore a blanket which the Fish Girl was instantly grateful to receive off him.

'I missed the sorcerer, as you say,' Gibbu growled. 'I loosed several times at him, but he bent my shafts in the air, or otherwise baffled them.'

The Mute shivered and showed his arbalesque which the Magus Dogskin had caused to be struck by lightning, just to remind us that Satan still knew a trick or two.

The pair of them had entered the bothy and the magician's palace to retrieve some of La Mamelonne's garments. 'It's best we look after her,' Gibbu explained, 'for a whore must never work naked.'

For me they had brought only the magician's cloak, saying he had flung it down at them from the air.

I refused to put it on. 'I'll be healthier as I am,' I protested.

'Put it on, Perronnelle. Put the heat of his fantasies on. They will serve till we can buy good linen and wool. Think of them not as his cloak, but accept them as the spoils of war. As such, they can never really harm you.'

421

They harmed me. They hurt me to the edge of my wits. Each day I wore that cloak I saw flames in the sky, spinning suns, the air dark with sheeps' skulls flying. Each night I lay down upon it, basilisks possessed me with their serpent thighs, I was raped by Dogskin in the body of a corpse and a skin of dry nettles that pricked me and stung, invaded by straw men with bullrush and thistle.

I wore Raymond's curse while I carried his cloak. I could only pray that, once I had clothes of my own, I should be able to lay madness aside.

Caput Twelve

Wherein the Virgin raises a siege and vanquishes a thousand horses.

had seen my Phantom plain as a cockerel's wishbone, but again he had slipped from my plate. So had the dwarf who had done so much to save me. It would be a lie to pretend I had no theories in the latter case, especially now that Ironface's armour was on the move with his voice inside it, and possibly the dwarf as well.

As for this Phantom, he had never shared my blanket, even in the bothy's coldest and cruellest hours, merely invaded my dreams with his bodily parts, principally his tongue. Now I was without him again, I recalled his last words in my latest dream. He had spoken of Minerve. The De Montfort clan had invaded the Minervois and were investing Minerve. The Season of Bonfires was once more upon us. My war against the Crusade had been dormant for far too long.

Once off the mountain I learned there was a price on my head, so I dared not use my name for currency. It would be hard to purchase clothes and horses. La Mamelonne was too *enceinte* to go whoring for horseflesh. As for the Fish Girl, country folk are proof against her kind of trick. You can't take a peasant's money and run. He needs to see a calf pass heifer and be well into milk before he'll hand over the fourth part of an ear of corn. There was no help for it but have Gibbu win the archery at Lézignan fair, and the Mute play tricks with townsmen's coins.

I sent La Mamelonne up to the high pastures of the Pyrenees. It would be a long walk for her lying-in. 'At least she'll get plenty of grass,' Ironface said, or his voice in its armour did. Violette went with her. The men would be away with their sheep, so the pair could practise purity.

This left me with the three friends who had been with me since the Mill. I say friends, for I know no other word.

425

I say three, even though I had no way of counting how many Ironface was.

My parents had been dead almost a year.

Minerve was like Béziers and Carcassonne, totally impregnable, so I had an idea it would fall quickly. We arrived there, or within hearing of it, on the day before the Madeleine, just as at Béziers. Anyone who studies the history of Oc need only remember the one Saint's date, the twenty-second of July. She isn't called the Weeper for nothing.

I say 'arrived within hearing' because we saw very little of Minerve from our route to it.

It wasn't its altitude that made it impregnable, so much as the way it has been cunningly set about by ravines. From some approaches you can come within a bowshot before you notice anything of it at all. Then you'll glimpse its battlements just as you discover the chasm that separates you from them.

We halted our horses at a more prudent distance, alerted by the sounds of siege.

A properly conducted siege makes a peculiar noise. I don't mean its drums and trumpets, or the messy knife-on-plate clatter of an assault. I refer to the music of its engines.

A trebuchet gives off a note instantly recognizable to anyone who has an ageing relative. You hear the agonizing creak as he swings back in his chair, the abrupt but satisfying crack as he bangs his head on the wall. A mangonel puts one in mind of another geriatric concert. Imagine a gaggle of grandmothers strapping themselves into something tight enough to be worn by their fourteen-year-old serving maids – and they all do – then being startled into sudden movement so their binding breaks. This was the very straining and snap we heard as we crept towards Minerve.

Praise God I have a nose as well as an ear. I knew we were close to the besieging forces as soon as I smelled fresh bread.

426

'Gascons!' Ironface exclaimed. 'I'd recognize their fart anywhere.'

We were in a wood already, but we turned off the road and sent Gibbu ahead to find out what was what.

I burrowed my way into a very tight thicket and discovered that it was already occupied by a pack donkey. 'I thought you'd been burned at the stake long since,' this donkey said to me. 'You are Perronnelle de Saint Thibéry, aren't you? I must say, you're looking rather pallid.'

I recognized its voice, but couldn't make its face fit my memory. 'Solomon,' I said to it at last. 'Solomon of Gerona.'

Ironface and the Mute weren't accustomed to hearing me talk to myself, so joined me in some alarm, and the Mute it was who discovered the Jew's legs up a tree and presumably the rest of him above them.

'What are you doing here?' I asked. I felt certain the town would fall now.

'Chastity belts,' he told me.

'Chastity – you mean you've come to Minerve with a donkey-load of chastity belts?'

'Six donkey-loads.' I heard other beasts munching about the shadows. 'There's a great need for them during times of strife. So many husbands feel the need to be absent from trouble.'

'Men don't buy such objects ready-made?' Ironface said. 'Surely they don't?'

'They do from me,' Solomon said. 'If this war weren't so terrible I should be forced to be thankful for it. As it is, I praise God for allowing me to educate so many of its marriages, Christian and heretic alike.'

'But a man arranges such things for his wife's privities *in private*.'

'Exactly. And this is what puts me ahead of my time. Privacy is what I offer publicly in the marketplace. If a man wants to encompass his lady's *chose* in a lockable unmentionable he has to call his workmen in to fit her.

427

Think of the indignity of displaying your own secrets and her shame, which I take *pudenda* to mean, just *think* of placing such priceless objects on view to your armourer, your locksmith and your farrier. Then suppose you wish to line the machine to prevent unnecessary discomfort to those sweets you treasure so much, you'll need your lorimer, your furrier and a bevy of female silk-snippers to invade the umbrage of her petty cotte as well. Far better test her bottom's girth with your fingers and purchase one of my little engines from round the back of my stall.'

'Can I view one of them?' I asked.

'Only in Minerve. I've sold my entire stock.'

'Why aren't you still inside?'

'The fleas have left,' he said. 'Just as at Béziers. I can't think of a worse omen.'

'Then why are you resting here?'

'I'm waiting for a fresh supply of belts to come up from my smiths in Spain. There are crusaders all about me, and I don't often see the chance to sell to an entire army. The Gascons, in particular, are close to home, and have jealous imaginations.'

Gibbu came back to us. 'Minerve lacks water,' he said flatly. 'Just as Carcassonne.'

'No fleas. No water. That's another reason I'm not there.'

Gibbu had fallen in with a contingent of these selfsame Gascons. They caught him by the balls and the scruff and asked him was he a heretic. He said only his hump was, a joke being as good as a password among such fellows. They were winding up a huge mangonel whose spring was too heavy for its winch, so told him to lend a hand or be off. They gave him a deal of information besides.

The town's wells were shallow, they said, and dry in the summer months. However, there was a fine deep source beyond the battlements, and this could be reached along a covered way.

Simon de Montfort and their own Guy de Lucy saw no hope of overcoming Minerve's defences by direct assault, or even of reaching them with a unified force, their men were so parcelled up by the terrain with trees here, rocks there, little hills and gullies all over the place, and the great chasm of the ravine in front of all.

So they'd ranged their rock-throwing mangonels and trebuchets against the covered way, and were burying it, and its watering-point, beneath a terrible bombardment of stones. They had plenty of ammunition close at hand. All they had to do was dig up one part of Hérault and shoot it at another a little further on.

The bold men and bolder women of Minerve could not venture along the covered way to draw themselves even a cupful of sustenance, for fear of being crushed, decapitated, buried alive or carried into the hereafter by a torrent of rocks and vine-stumps. Reaching the source with a wheeled barrel or even a waterskin on a donkey was out of the question.

So Minerve, just like Carcassonne, was dying of thirst. Not of the flux, or only indirectly.

The principal architect of the town's misfortune was a monstrous trebuchet Simon de Montfort called Malvoisine, and his brother the Bastard (who was here for the pickings) entitled Ugly Girl Next Door. Ugly Girl had dumped a whole hillside on the covered way, and was threatening a mountain, so the men of Minerve had resolved to break her or burn her. Last night they had dashed out to do so.

Unfortunately for them, a gentleman of Gascony had been suffering all evening with the nether drip, and was at that moment sitting on Ugly Girl's crossbeam and using her as a colander. His presence surprised them in more ways than one, and his cries of alarm at being caught with his skirts up and his hauberk asleep in its tent brought his fellow warriors out in force.

The raiding party was driven off, and Guillaume de Minerve sued for terms at first light. Seeing the Gascon at work had proved too much for starving men dying of thirst, sensing him to be so prolific and themselves totally unable.

Simon de Montfort proposed a lenient peace. Guillaume agreed. Then Arnold Almaric forbade it, saying the Pope's treaties needed wax on them, so they would need to light bonfires.

So the fight was continuing, but with very little heart in it, except for those who could expect to be melted to seal Pope Innocent's parchment.

Meanwhile, Minerve was ringed with steel.

'How then shall we get in?' Ironface demanded.

'We shall wait till the place falls, then do what little good we can.'

'There'll be plenty needed,' Gibbu said. 'The town is full of heretics, and Almaric the Papal Legate intends to see bone fires lighted beneath them.'

'What I propose further is that we borrow your asses,' I told Solomon of Gerona, 'together with their panniers and packboxes. We'll leave you our own mounts as surety.'

Solomon did a sum on some Arab beads before saying, 'The surety is adequate. I shall, of course require an inducement.'

'How about a sorcerer's cloak?' I proposed.

'Raymond of Brousses'? That's worth a string of donkeys outright.'

I fetched it from my saddle-bag, bundle of bad dreams that it was. It was a beautiful object, and not even Constance de Coulobres could have stitched it finer. So the deal was struck.

'You still haven't told me how you propose to get in to Minerve,' Gibbu complained to me.

'Perronnelle is going to disguise herself as a chastity belt.'

Was that Ironface's voice, or the dwarf's, or a donkey's?

*　　*　　*

We spent all night in that wood, sharing its innermost thicket with six asses, four horses and Solomon of Gerona.

I passed most of the time trying to stay awake enough to disentangle the Gascons' voices from their intentions, but these men we could smell all around us were part of an army, and armies don't deal in words as such. They speak in trumpets and drums. Trumpets say *Go to bed at night, get up in the morning, range your horses into line*. Drums say *Burn the women and children*. It sounds more comfortable to have a drum say *Burn the women and children* than have a man say it. Drums don't cough at the smoke.

So my dreams were full of military clamour, but completely unmuddled by Dogskin's cloak. Solomon tossed and turned on it, but he was a devout man, and doubtless it would soon lose its potency to rearrange his sleep.

Dawn never breaks in a thicket, so we all slept late. We were wakened by a shout. It began a fair way off, was taken up by the Gascons to our front, then went running onwards, as if ten thousand crusaders had cleared their throats in a ring.

'Minerve has surrendered,' Solomon said. 'I have listened to these fellows for a fortnight, and they have never shouted before.'

'We were told the Pope's Legate won't accept a surrender.'

'Not on terms, perhaps. But unconditionally, wouldn't you think? Unconditionally he can burn everyone he's got firewood for.'

So it was I set about preparing our tiny force. This was simple enough. Three of us had to conceal ourselves inside the panniers of Solomon's donkeys, the fourth had to lead the beasts along.

Gibbu was the obvious choice for this dangerous undertaking. I had first thought of employing the Mute as pack-leader, since his dumbness might prove an advantage. Then I reasoned that he might bode ill for us, since no one likes a hermaphrodite so soon after breakfast.

431

I bade good-bye to Solomon through a crack in his leading pannier, and he paid me an extraordinary compliment. He said, 'Good luck, Perronnelle. If you were a Jewess and beautiful I might think seriously of marrying you. If I weren't wed already and you weren't so stupid.'

I was glad to be out of that thicket. It was darker than the bothy and even more crowded.

Gibbu led us briskly downwards, I guessed into the depths of the ravine. Then our road climbed up again. The panniers were comfortable enough, being cleanly kept to accommodate the female body-fastenings already spoken of. That being said, our bottoms were acutely folded, and we kept slipping round the bums of the mules.

'It must be difficult for Ironface,' I whispered to Gibbu.

'He's lying straight enough. He's stretched out in the only packbox. Or his armour is.'

'Does he have air?'

'Keep quiet, Perronnelle. We're entering Minerve now, and coming up with a column of crusaders.'

Sure enough, our pack-string was halted. I heard a voice say, 'Holla, Crouchback! Tell us your business, and what's in those saddles.'

'My bags are empty. I come to carry corpses into the ravine. If you heed my advice, my friend, you'll be wise enough to leave them alone. I've carried one parcel of corpses already today and none of them died healthy.'

'A witty bent fellow. And a heretic for burning, I've no doubt. Come, rascal. Reveal yourself. Don't you believe the Devil made you?'

'On the contrary, I'm a Christian and believe that God does all his own dirty work.'

'Well, march with us. I see no need of a ravine when we're having a bonfire.'

We went down a street made of ochre stone, or perhaps built of mud, I couldn't tell through the wickerwork. Behind me I heard the Mute's teeth chattering, and a tinny tremble of the joints, presumably Ironface's.

432

Two knights or other gentlemen in saddles rode either side of me. They were pleasant enough with their talk, considering they were on the way to a burning. I suppose victory does this for a man.

'I don't want the place,' one said. 'I don't want it and I don't like it. It's all rocks and heat here. If you go to chase a fox you break your horse in a gully. And as for the women – '

'You break your horse in a gully. There's clearly no pleasure in them. Their skins are baked brown and they stink of foxes too.'

'That Maid of the Mountains is another matter.'

How I thrilled to hear myself spoken of.

'Any maiden from these hills is bound to have sinews like a bear. She'd crush a man with her thighs, and strangle his friend with her ankles. A maid she's likely to remain.'

'Till we get her on the bonfire.'

'Is she truly a virgin?'

'So men say. And born of a virgin mother.'

'She was suckled by a wolf and cut her teeth on a stone.'

The smell of burning became shockingly apparent. I smelled no flesh yet, nor heard cries. My senses were assailed with the smoke of resinous woods and the chuckle of the flames. Then there was a silence, a different smell and a darkness. Our donkeys' hooves still grated on stone, but I felt sure we were inside a building. This conviction became a certainty once I heard a bolt drawn and thrown, a lock turned.

There was a strange odour to the place. Faint enough yet more flavoursome than our hot wickerwork. It was the scent of prayer and tears.

'Gibbu,' I whispered.

'Be quiet.' It was Ironface's voice. 'Do you want our nags thrown on the fire for having devils in their belly?'

I was silent, if a beating heart in a slipping pannier may ever achieve silence.

433

Bars were drawn back again, a key turned. I heard footsteps.

Gibbu's voice growled softly, 'We are too late to save a hundred from the flames. We may yet save a thousand. This place was a convent house, or a house of anchorites. Its women, and some seventy other women from among the Perfect Ones and other heretics have been taken from here and burned. The men were held across the road. They've gone two by two. The fire is hot, and it has been quick.'

'That monster De Montfort,' I shouted, leaping from my basket like a conger from a lobster pot.

Gibbu held me more easily than a man holds an eel and with less damage to my skin. He tugged my donkey's girth down a notch and dropped me back again. 'De Montfort has spared everyone in Minerve except the heretics,' he said. 'All who renounced the heresy and embraced Christ Jesus have been spared also.'

'How many was that?'

'None. Well, to be honest with you, Bouchard de Marly's mother claimed to have seen three women crying on the way to their deaths. These, at her intercession, he spared.'

'What is happening now?' Ironface asked.

'Guy de Levis was unhappy that the first hundred martyrs were offered such an easy choice. Arnold Almaric is enraged that there weren't more martyrs. Merdun de Montfort believes that warfare exists so that women may be enjoyed and their menfolk ransomed.'

'What follows?' Old Tin Tongue continued to wag in his box. 'So what do these dissenters propose?'

'They're rounding all the burghers up, and giving them over to their priests for examination.'

'To test their faith?'

'Their wealth.'

I leapt from my basket again. 'Place these donkeys among the crusaders' horses,' I commanded. Then I ducked down

434

once more, as the door was flung open and Merdun de Montfort stood blinking in.

He wasn't alone, and my hope was that he hadn't seen me, coming from sunshine to dark as he did. I saw he pushed a woman in front of him, even as I hid myself, with others to follow, and this was no surprise.

After a moment or two in my basket I heard chuckles, screams of protest, and the general noises you might expect a group of ladies to make when one of their number is being abused. Then some heads were cuffed, and the protest was stilled.

Then I heard someone, I suppose Merdun himself, trying to take his pleasure with the woman he had caught. 'Ah!' she was moaning, 'No, oh! Oh!' while he was breathing away like a horse with catarrh.

'Poins!' he called. 'Poins!'

'My lord?'

Not for the first time he had a servant to help him in his villainy.

'Poins, here you observe a naked lady. You also observe a chastity belt.'

'It suits her, my lord.'

'So what can I do with her?'

'You can lick her all over, my lord, except for where your tongue is prevented by the chastity belt.'

'I've already done that. So what now?'

'I can fetch levers and break the belt.'

'No levers, Poins. I want you to pick the lock. Her husband's a friend of mine, heretic though she is as most women are. When we come to burn her, I wish him to find his great seal intact, and not be offended.'

Goodness knew where Gibbu was during this exchange. I later realized from the groaning and creaking that I first took to be bodily pleasure bought at the expense of bodily pain that he too was hidden away in a pannier. I nearly rose a third time from my basket to strangle the Bastard where he stood all unfastened, and his Poins creature as well. I am certain there would have been a woman or so there to help me, within or without Solomon's chastity belts.

As it was, some more ladies were pushed through the door by the crusaders, and half of the Crusade's leadership followed to inspect them.

After a few moments of breathing and prodding about, there came a deal of protest, for these weren't women, but ladies, as I have said, and they weren't at all used to prodding.

The Bastard told them to shut up. He was a persuasive fellow however he was dressed, so they did so.

Someone, not Simon de Montfort though he was there, addressed the company at large. 'In the whole land of Oc,' he said, 'there are only three classes of female. Heretics, the women of the enemy, and gentlewomen.' It was Guy de Levis, who believed the Crusade was treating us too leniently. 'The first are to be burned, the second enjoyed as we may, the third sold back to their original owners wherever a price can be agreed and the owners consent to repurchase.' He listened to the agreement of everyone save for this present sample of females concerned. 'If not, such women are to be relocated into one of the other two categories. I except whores, naturally, and people with dark faces. These serve a useful function, and should be spared and at least fed.'

'You want to fix a fair ransom, light a bonfire,' the Bastard said.

'What if they're Christians?' a small voice asked, I swear from a basket.

'Light a fire. Christians are the ones who can afford to stay out of it, even if they're Jews. If you burn the poor, you're certain to burn heretics.'

Simon de Montfort still said nothing, possibly because he regarded the matter with disdain.

When it came to women, Simon wasn't like his brother the Bastard. Merdun lived only to fornicate, or to see his men rape and burn. Simon, on the other hand, is rumoured to have embraced only one woman during his entire stay here, and she was a fairy taken from the sea at Narbonne with a fishtail for legs and scales on her belly; so it is hard to know whether he had her to his bed or cooked her for supper, or stewed what he could and chewed what he couldn't.

Perhaps I began to suffocate in my basket, what with the heat of the day and the donkey, and the enflamed sobbing of women and the hot breath of the crusaders who counted them, but as I thought of Simon and his fishtailed bride I began to wonder why Pope Innocent didn't proclaim his Crusade against our Southern Sea rather than the Oc it dribbled against. It's killed more Christians in its time than all the Pope's wars put together, men of rank and substance some of them, including priests far more elevated in worth than Peter of Castlenau. Also it teems with all manner of monsters, fish with swords on their nose and lobsters that sing – and if these weren't the Devil's work, I didn't know what was.

I was saved from true madness by the door crashing open to let more sunlight in. A voice shouted, 'My lords, the bonfire is refreshed. It is time to bring another batch forth to the burning!'

The leaders of the Crusade went out to enjoy the spectacle, leaving their squires and ordinary men-at-arms to bring forth the ladies they intended to be cinders. Our six donkeys left behind them, with Gibbu once more holding the pack-string.

Ironface's box sat alone on its donkey, but the remaining five beasts were double hung. This left seven empty panniers, and we persuaded seven of the doomed ladies into them, and urged three more to walk near and be ready to fill our own as soon as we chose to vacate them. It was a dangerous stratagem, but the best I could devise.

The convent room had been hung about with cowls, copes, hoods and cloaks of one sort or another, and we carried these in hand. To be a Southern nun was in all likelihood to proclaim oneself a heretic; but unless the ladies were absolutely determined to burn, I knew we could coax them towards a disclaimer.

For the moment we had to keep courage and faith, and allow Gibbu to lead us towards the fire.

'What are you, fellow?' I heard him challenged.

'A corpse carrier.'

'We burn our corpses here.'

'And pollute the sacred embers of their punishment? Six have already died along the path, whether from old age or fright who can tell? I have tossed their bodies into the ravine, and thus kept your bone fire pure. As a good Christian, brother, you should only burn the living. To incinerate the dead is in direct contradiction to the laws of Holy Church.'

'Pass, good friend.'

It was lucky there were no townsfolk here to call the Hunchback 'stranger', but those of the Minervois that weren't assembled to be burned had gone off to the source for a drink of water.

'Steel yourself, my Perronnelle,' I heard Gibbu whisper. 'The known Parfaits are the first to burn, and they're mounting up boldly to stand into the fire.'

I was distressed to witness so much death, even through wickerwork with eyes that were used to the sight. The smell, too, was less than pleasant. However, Ironface stayed me from leaping out by whispering from his box, 'They *chose* this, Perronnelle. They die by their own choice.'

They died by the choice of the man who lit the fire, but there was a farthing of truth in his words so I let them pass without argument. At least I was spared any screams, even such as lobsters make, for the flame was so hot it scorched the voice out of them on the instant of their entering it, but whether it flayed the pain away is another matter.

Enter it they did. It was not in a pit, this fire, but on an elevation, like an altar. The Parfaits, the Perfecti, the

438

Cathars, call them what you will, simply held hands as Gibbu said they had done earlier, and walked boldly up a log pile and upon it.

At this moment, I sent the Mute forth from his pannier to creep us towards a miracle. Ironface came from his box, with Gibbu to lift him down, and a strange sight he must have been for those who do not believe firmly in Resurrection. The men of the Minervois afterwards spoke of corpses coming from the grave in protest, and this must have been the cause of it. Old Tin Legs wore his white crusader's blazon, so once clear of his coffin he presented very little problem.

Gibbu set two children in his place, and two more in the Mute's basket. I stayed in my own pannier, since it seemed early to start waving my locks about.

There were crusaders all about us in abundance, forcing the condemned steadfastly forward, but their eyes were on the burning, especially of the women. One said to Gibbu, right in my ear, 'Long hair catches the flame very prettily.'

Gibbu spat. Hunchbacks are allowed to spit, even when talking to warriors. Once the crusader had stepped out of earshot, he remarked into my cage, 'These beasts will soon burn more than the Parfaits unless we put a stop to it.'

'How is the Mute faring?' I asked Ironface. 'I cannot watch this devil's work much longer.'

He would have been better off in his box. 'The difference between God and Devil is a matter of which side of the flame you stand.'

'Nonsense.'

'Heretics are people who burn,' he insisted. 'Christians are the ones who watch them do it. It's a simple rule of thumb.'

And hear them and smell them after. Smell someone burn and you won't easily forget it. Hear a child among the faggots and the stream will never chuckle again, nor will you listen readily while men talk of God.

'Hush,' Gibbu murmured. 'Old Silent Tongue is about his business, and Simon de Montfort and that Legate Almaric are close behind your donkey.'

I strained to hear what was passing.

I suppose it is possible to lie in a donkey's basket and hear only the beast's ribs creaking. However, burning heretics is a serious matter, and I hoped to eavesdrop on few frankly spoken affairs of state, death being, like drink, a great loosener of tongues.

As it was, Simon de Montfort and the blue-nosed Almaric were in a mumble, the Papal Legate's tongue making no more noise than bats' wings above the general hubbub of the flames.

As far as I could judge, the elder De Montfort said nothing. That was the sort of man he was. He preferred to say nothing when there was nothing to be said.

The most important piece of history I had heard all day was Merdun coming nose to nose with one of Solomon of Gerona's chastity belts and being forced to give it best.

By now there was a sizeable line of women being prodded towards the bonfire. This was the work of Merdun's ruffians, who bore all the women and children they could find this way, I suppose looking for ransom or some other advantage.

There were scores of ordinary folk in Minerve, people in addition to Perfecti, as well as plenty of both sorts who had spent all season fleeing ahead of this vile Crusade. The people were easy to tell. They pleaded and screamed, and begged for their lives in general.

As the Bastard himself drew near I judged the time ripe to stand forth. So I stood up full on my donkey, seizing some crusader's sword as I did so. This was no Spanish blade, and much too heavy for my weakened wrist, but as I lifted it so must it come down, missing Merdun and cutting him off from one of his fellows, who began to spurt blood in a most refreshing fashion.

Gibbu strung his bow and cleared a space by the fire,

while I made the most of my altitude on the donkey. Once I had been seen, I gave the basket over to a brace of children, and prayed God the Mute act on time.

Men who have just won a great victory are vulnerable to surprise, especially when they have done nothing more valiant than deny their enemies a drink. So it was now that these crusaders seemed slow, or bemused when it came to pushing aside the victims lined up for slaughter and making a rush at their slayers.

Or perhaps they thought we were mountebanks about to demonstrate some kind of illusion in the flames, the Hunchback with his arrows, the woman with her too heavy sword. For sure Merdun saw me and said my name, and it was taken up. 'I'm not inside a chastity belt, villain.' Again I tried to slice off any part of him that was nearest. Again he was too dumbfounded to rise to my challenge whether of dint or debate.

The greatest of the crusaders – De Montfort, Bourgogne, Guy de Levis, Bouchard de Marly and the haughtiest of the Gascons – were all astride their horses lest someone mistook them for a heretic and burned them, or for something less than what they were and treated them as such. Only men with work to do, or fellows like the Bastard keen to look a woman in the eye, were on their own two feet.

That being said there were hundreds of riderless horses, hundreds or even thousands tethered all about with no-one on their backs. Some were inside the town, having delivered crusaders within the walls. Many were outside, without saddles, arsons, saddle-bags or caparison, with not even, as Ironface said, the dignity of a bum cloth.

These last were the lucky ones. They had nothing to do with themselves once the Mute had passed by but turn mad and gallop back to Paris.

Those inside the town of Minerve, great Goddess that she was of the old Roman Wizards, suffered a much more complex fate. These in their caparisons, with their shields hanging and banging upon them, began to scream

and snort, then gallop the town in circles, frothing their
way down streets and alleys and sometimes on top of the
roofs amid a great whirl of crows, doves and sparrows, and
stirring all before them, like pig lumps inside a pudding
bowl. Their screams were terrible to contemplate, as were
those of the crusaders who were mangled in their passing,
and quite fit to match the noises uttered by the innocents
on the bonfire, which the moment the horses were loose
ceased its grisly work.

As we herded the women and children into a great chain,
Christian and heretic alike, I rejoiced in the Mute's cunning.
What was so resourceful about him was that he hadn't played
the same trick twice. He no longer sought to unseat the great
ones, as he had during Ironface's rescue of the Fish Girl.
Instead he placed hundreds upon hundreds of fuses inside
the bottoms of untended horses. A pepper is an instant
pain inside the bottom, or any other part, so he delayed
each one's effect by coating it in mud. In this way he had
infiltrated some eight or ten score orifices and impaled each
last one upon its pepper before the first was affected by the
merest blister. Thus the stampede was total and involved
all available horses.

The Parfaits were no longer guarded. The town was no
longer occupied. We were no longer watched, not even by
Merdun de Montfort. Indeed, by the Bastard least of all.
Deprive a knight of his horse and you depose him from
his *raison d'être*, as the philosophers call it. He'll no more
seek to detain you than a naked man herd bullocks.

They didn't run after us, nor send their foot-soldiers to
run. They went after their horses. With a hundred doughty
men, or half that number of my Carcassonne women, I
could have snuffed out the Crusade in an instant.

As it was, I led some three hundred souls all the way back
to Solomon's thicket, while thousands of bemused Northern
Christians sought to hobble and unpepper their horses.

Strange that the Goddess Minerva was born from no
orifice at all, nor had any wisdom concerning the soreness

of women. If she had, she might well have stopped us, and forbidden the Mute his foul tricks. But the warrior deity, patron of root and vine, fell forth from her Daddy's forehead already wearing a breastplate.

CHANSON THIRTEEN

In which Perronnelle travels on high and a maiden is found with child and much grave matter also.

On regaining our horses, I led my band of women due west and into that hideous terrain of gorge and garrigue known as Black Mountain, where only bears and buzzards dwell, and a peculiar breed of dragon which though small is extremely ferocious, especially in the hot season or during the females' *chaleur*.

On our first night under the stars, Gibbu shot a brace of wild pigs, and on the second morning a full dozen crusading horsemen. These men belonged to Bouchard de Marly, as one of them told us, but whether they were sent to seek after us or simply journeying back to Bouchard's château at Saissac there was no time to discover. Gibbu was unhappy not to have slain the fellow outright, especially with a full yard of shaft through the weasand, and was getting ready to kill him with his poignard when he passed away peacefully and naturally through having three of our women sit on him.

Meanwhile we gained swords, horses, and armour – or, as English men say, steeds, gear and tackle, lumpy words for discomforting objects.

I then journeyed south for a week, hoping to leave the lands of the Trencavels and Toulouse, and pass into the territories disputed between the English and King Peter of Aragon, making towards the High Pyrenees but not intending quite that far.

This was a long walk, for all but the children. These skipped most of the way, and hopped the rest, generally to the music of the Mute's pipe.

Our path was made the slower by some score of the women being locked inside Solomon of Gerona's chastity belts. These were not meant for walking in, nor very much else, and reduced their victims to a parlous state of discomfort, chafing and cutting into their upper legs and those other places that by reason of her dress a woman of quality does not usually have to think about. Some of these women had thrown away their husbands, and some of their husbands had simply gone elsewhere once the Crusade came to Minerve, but not before locking up their wives in an Arab bracelet.

I believe I would have left the matter as being beyond any solution, to their continuing discomfort in walking and other bodily functions, but one of them, Matthilde de Azinellet et Olonzac, told me she was *enceinte* and although not imminent felt constrained by these Toledo bumsmiths close to bursting. It was, she explained to me, like having a cork in her wind and a wire round her water.

'It's no good talking to me about the pains of being locked up in a piece of metal,' Ironface said tartly. 'Even when I'm not inside here I feel the discomfort of it.'

'What I suggest – ' Gibbu said.

'Take no notice of him. He's a man and a menial. You should listen to the Mute more often.'

I gazed at the smooth-faced little monster in some amazement, and saw that he had laid aside his pipe and left the dancing children and was now covering his eyes, and hammering on something between his legs.

'Knackering?' I guessed. 'Mushroom gathering? Mending a pair of clogs?' I am no good at such Christmas riddles, and I said so in very blunt terms.

Gibbu interpreted for him far enough to tell me there was a blind blacksmith at Chalabre. Principally a farrier, he was renowned for discretion, whether rescuing children from rat-traps or cutting women out of shrinking jakes or collapsed commodes (as Mummy's box was called), because he couldn't see anything he touched, though he did have a corresponding need to touch it more often.

No sooner had I resolved to approach the Blind Fellow of Chalabre than I knew I must divide my forces. I couldn't walk into a community like Chalabre with several hundred women at my back without promoting a war. I left the unbelted ones in a grove of needle trees, under the guard of Gibbu, while Ironface, the Mute and I took the constrained ones into town.

I had a few coins about my person, and since Mamelie had told me that most men need little inducement to tousle a woman's lower declivities, and will often pay good money just to get their hands there, I had no doubt the smith could at least be persuaded to approach the problem; though success would be another matter.

Smithies are fine hot places, too hot for summer, but have the advantages of being dark, so my ladies and other women would not be able to see what was being done to them.

The smithy was near the edge of town, as was proper, and at the centre of a great lake of horse-spatter, as was usual. The farrier was outside in the street, changing the shoes on a mare. He had her hind hoof between his thighs, and gazed at it, and all about him, with a pair of blue eyes that seemed entirely open and quite used to being looked at.

'What is your name?' I asked him.

'Pierre le Borgne,' he answered, squinting at the hoof, and hammering at it very accurately, considering the danger to the horse and himself.

'Are you blind?'

'If you like.'

'Le Borgne means One Eye.'

He was speaking with a mouthful of nails, you understand, but seemed to give the explanation that Le Borgne was a family name, his father having been unsighted sometimes in one eye, sometimes in the other; but he promised he would be as blind as I wanted. 'I'm a blacksmith,' he explained. 'Not a doctor.'

I wondered whether a doctor, or the town laying-in women, or even a layer-out wouldn't be better, but in the end I took him Matthilde de Azinellet et Olonzac, and he found his way up her skirts with no trouble at all.

She objected to being felt in the street, right where the

449

mare had been standing, but he said the light was better, which a bystander said was the local expression for having more room.

'Are you a married man?' I asked the smith sternly.

'This in no ways feels like the shoe of any beast I've ever touched,' he said with his hand up the poor woman's bliaut and cotte, and his head on one side as if he were listening to his fingertips.

The lady of Azinellet and Olonzac gasped, then screamed, then gasped again, all of this being accompanied by a further inclination of Le Borgne's head and a stiffening of his neck, then a loud straining and snapping.

A monstrous twin hoop of iron, about the same size as – and with all the malice of – a man-trap dropped to the floor between her ankles. 'Do I get to keep the filly or her shoe?' he asked, obviously a joke he'd made often, because he repeated it several times, both for her and the next nineteen women as well.

This was all very well while he was content to work out in the open, though the road was far too open a place for some of my ladies. But for the last dozen or so he felt more comfortable with his head inside their cottes and petticoats and whatever else they wore under that, which if they were like most women on most days was nothing.

They all protested at this, and the town became increasingly raucous at the sight of a man and woman playing horsy-in-her-sack so openly, since all of Chalabre was here by now, all who were living and at least one of the dead, since an old packman died laughing quite early on.

This became quite difficult for us all to bear, though the Mute managed a small collection as well as a tune on his pipe, but our forbearance had a mighty reward at the end, and a huge recompense in goodness, as patience often does. With his head still up the last woman's thereunders, his head, his shoulders, and two scorched hands, Pierre le Borgne cried out, 'St Peter, praise be! It's a miracle! I've recovered the sight of one eye!' Then he brought his blue gaze out into the open, and showed us her chastity belt still clutched in his grimy fingertips.

'Which eye is that?' Ironface asked him.

'The one I couldn't see from before,' Le Borgne answered.

I could do nothing but beat the Mute for providing me with false information, and I couldn't do that because I loved the creature.

We were howled out of town, of course, and through several hamlets after, going with what dignity we could, Ironface and I on horseback, the women on a continuing soreness.

Our rage was increased by meeting Solomon of Gerona on the road. There he was, the architect of these poor female's discomforts, striding along without a care in the world, albeit with neither horse nor donkey to his backside.

'The Crusade has packed up and gone from Minerve,' he shouted, while still a great way off, the way travellers will. 'It's gone principally in search of horses, for which it has a great need, thanks to you, so I saw no point in awaiting a further stock of belts. A man who is anxious for his steed has no time to worry about his wife.' He drew breath, and came close on a chuckle. 'The crusaders' anxiety was so acute, I even managed to sell those six asses of mine to knights in straitened circumstances. They are hardly battle mounts, but nor can a gentleman walk.'

I held out our shattered chastity belts, which were all we had to show for a considerable piece of folly.

'A shame to treat them thus,' he complained. 'I've a spare bunch of keys I might have sold you.'

'Would you consign your own good wife to one of those infernal engines?' I demanded hotly.

'Rebecca? Certainly not.'

'Do you trust her,' Ironface asked him, 'alone all these years in Gerona?'

'I trust her not to let me make a fool of her.'

He wasn't done with the matter yet. Turning back with us quite serenely along the way, he said, 'My belts are

451

remarkable objects, notwithstanding. Toledo steel, Arab craftsmanship, Catalan locks, all the cunning and skill of Fez and Damascus. When the burghers of Minerve raked through De Montfort's bonfire searching for trinkets – '

'Good God!' I cried.

'Why ever should they not?' he asked. 'These people were for the most part strangers to them. When they raked through De Montfort's bonfire, all they found unconsumed were dozen upon dozen of my belts. Blackened and unusable, of course, save as doorknockers and tethering rings, but quite undestroyed by the furnace. There's a remarkable tribute to their smithing. I shall sell thousands more on that story, believe me.'

Back at the grove of needle trees, we found Gibbu teaching archery to some of my younger women. He had cut them shorter bows, but only by reason of their height, not their strength. 'A woman who can draw a pudding round a basin can pull anything else in the world,' he assured me, 'whether it's a bowstring or a cockerel's neck.' They were already outshooting Gibbu's three or four men, and of the female's alleged problems between nipple and string I saw no sign. So at least one book of the Wizards tells a lie.

'Bowmaking is a great sorcery,' Gibbu growled at me, again only treating me to a half welcome, 'but I've no need to part with that. I can fashion all the bows we need. The fletcher's art is merely a mystery. I believe your women could learn it from me well enough, so let them shape our arrows, all except the silent fliers and the magic tips.'

'A fletcher and a bowmaker, all in one body,' Ironface mused.

'Aye, they have need of one another. Yet they are separate masteries, and archery is a third.' He laughed bitterly. 'So why do I have so many skills? I have them because a hunchback must marry with himself.' He regarded our women and children, then myself sadly. 'So now must your women,

Perronnelle. They'll live safer for knowing the little I can teach them.'

I gazed at the Mute's saddle. 'Could you not fashion them an arbalesque?' I asked him. 'Surely a woman's weapon.'

'Arbalesque! Ballister! No, not a woman's weapon, but an Italian trick. Death is a simple trade, Perronnelle, and best taught by those who deal simply.'

Our route now took us past Rivel, where Mummy's second oldest sister, my mad Aunt Alazaïs, has her asylum and castle.

The idea of sleeping all night in a bed, after nearly a year beneath bothy and stars, was highly seductive, though I doubted it would be a clean one, for although my aunt kept servants she also had a famous collection of cats and lizards, and such out-of-arse itinerants as could bear to stay with her in a dwelling Mummy said was no more than a draughty basket of serpents.

It was sunset as we approached it. My women must sleep outside and my few men even more so, but at least within high walls and with a well nearby for water. Once more I gave them into Gibbu's keeping, for I knew that their bodies were safe from him, and his from theirs.

Leaving my charges and their children to the warmth of the horses, I led Ironface and the Mute indoors, to find a pot bubbling in the main hall and a hog dripping into the flames, with its back scorching and crackling in the happiest manner possible, in spite of the stench of its tusks.

Madness burns crooked candles, they say, but its hearth is always warm. A woman servant brought us a posset and then a mull, and carried soup out into the yard, presumably on higher instruction, though it was a full hour before we saw my aunt.

She was in her nightdress, or what I took to be her nightdress, with her hair down her neck and one old breast hanging out. I say old, but it looked better than most I have seen, through being never used.

453

She greeted Ironface warmly. 'I recognize you from earlier,' she said. 'You're my husband, aren't you? I'm good at remembering people like that.' She indicated her breast, which seemed chewed around the nipple, though I have little experience in such matters, since my Phantom brings no teeth. 'I must say,' she said to him, 'you're returning rather late for me, in all my new-found blessed circumstance.'

It was then I heard the baby crying.

'I have just been delivered of an heir,' old Alazaïs said. She was by a long way Mummy's senior sister, fifty-five if a day. 'No man has ever been between my legs, I can promise you that, husband. So I am pleased to name God as its father.'

'God moves in a mysterious manner, Lady Trencavel,' my Old Tin Charmer said, 'I can truly affirm so.' He was gazing at something I couldn't see beyond the fire, the slots in his head giving him a sharper vision than mine.

'Nurse,' Aunt Alazaïs called. 'Now where's my infant's nurturer and nourisher? Be good enough to show forth my child and her.'

God is inscrutable indeed. Forward into the firelight stepped the fairest breasts in Christendom, with a boy child plugged onto the nearest and La Mamelonne stepping close behind them.

'That child is mine,' Ironface whispered to me. 'Most children are in Oc, and that one certainly is. So to that extent I am the old maid's husband.' He growled towards Mamelie. 'Well, nurse, what can you say to me?'

'I always said he was to be a Viscount,' Mamelie said. 'If he can't have a Trencavel for his daddy, then at least let him have one for a Mummy. It will make the old sow happy.'

The Fish Girl came tumbling into the firelight as well, as those of us with rank and station ate a supper of roast pig and went alone to our beds.

Perhaps I should keep from beds, for no sooner was I inside this one in Aunt Alazaïs' castle than my Phantom fell upon me, not with word or advice, and especially no counselling of war, but with an all-over kissing and mumbling, an all-round fondling and fumbling, and a ran-tantintivvy of flashing fires all beneath me through a night damp with mist and dark as liquorice. He brought no war, as I say, and if I heard drums it was only my own blood beating in my sleep.

No, he brought me no war, my Phantom, and no peace either. A man should have his *oiseau* as a woman her *chose*, his little bird between the legs to peck inside the nest, his loin all hard and striving within the softness of my groin; yet neither *oiseau*, pecking bird, no, not loin, shaft, spear nor spindle, he brought me none of these, not even in a dream.

What sort of man was my Phantom? What kind of dream my dream?

CANTO FOURTEEN

In which our heroine learns that her Phantom bears two legs only where a better man carries three, yet he teaches most excellent mysteries and slays a beast in her head.

La Mamelonne was content to abandon her 'young Viscount' to my Aunt Alazaïs. As she said, 'He'll have a lunatic for a mother, but a castle to lose her in.'

She and the Fish Girl continued with us towards Belcaire, which was where I had always intended they should be. There they could learn carding, spinning, knitting and weaving with the rest of my women, and archery too. If La Mamelonne wished to spend any time on her back up there, then there were only some five or six fellows to do it with, which would seem to her like monogamy and undoubtedly lead to an overall improvement.

It was mid August when we reached a settlement of shepherds' families midway between Montaillou and Belcaire. The shepherds were away on transhumance in Spain. Their women were unhappy to see us even so, but I said we were for the most part Parfaits or Perfecti, would build our own dwellings, help them with their work and pay them money. There were several lies among this list of inducements, so I pray they were only influenced by the truthful ones.

Gibbu built me a shelter inside a day, and a hut within a week. After that, I could only sit in it and feel frustrated. My Phantom visited me often during my moments of meditation, but when I spoke to him about his unwillingness to come to the push, he withdrew from my bed, even when I made way for him by unfastening my clothes, and contented himself with talking matters of high politics, as if I were the second female pope, or at very least a queen.

I felt frustrated by the last eleven months. Was my only contribution to this war to confront evil in a bothy then conduct three hundred women and children away from a bonfire?

The ice crept down from the High Pyrenees and laid

459

its fingers across my heart and between my legs. Snow began to fall.

My women grumbled. They were free of their chastity belts but there were no men to thank them for the fact. They could get nothing from the five or six remaining shepherds and the few townsmen who had marched with us, because La Mamelonne spoiled all these for general use, keeping them drained like the dugs of an old ewe, or two ewes for those with a mathematical bent and a knowledge of husbandry.

Seeing the Mute surrounded by so many dissatisfied women and being unable to lift as much as a finger to help them, I knew once and for all that he was a badel. I once thought he might be the Reality behind the Illusion of my Phantom, but he loved no-one unless it was Gibbu, and I found such a passion strange indeed. The Hunchback loved only himself.

As for Ironface, he made himself free. I often heard giggles coming from his hut, and peered inside to glimpse his armour hanging from a nail or lying in pieces along a shelf. Exactly what it was that crept out of it, what manner of man or shape and size of devilment, only a few privy ladies could tell. And they didn't.

I knew it was only a few in spite of his boasting. I knew this because more and more women begged Gibbu to teach them archery, no matter how tired their fingers were from carding and weaving. As they shot their bows with increasing violence and accuracy, I became convinced that it was my own person their imaginations were loosing at, until my face and bottom were stuck full of imaginary arrows. In their own way they were angry enough to become a substantial military force, which I must educate and harness before they skinned me alive or baked me in a pie.

I learned something from them that placed my Phantom in error as a source of information. He had told me, while cosseting my mind in Dogskin's bothy and keeping my body warm, that De Montfort had seized some fifty castles and seigneuries during the autumn months.

So he had. Yet it seems that once his quarantine cavaliers and great army of pilgrims withdrew to their wives, the majority of his castles restored themselves quietly to their rightful owners. Only a few of his closest friends and lieutenants, such as Bouchard de Marly at Saissac, managed to garrison his gifts to them. Some had left them to stand idle until such time as they could fetch their women and their tapestries, with the result that the rats and the pigeons and the peasantry had crept back into them, and invited their squirarchy to return them to their former order. Others, the doughty ones, barred themselves up inside, only to be strangled in their lonely beds or have their balls cut off in their courtyards. De Montfort spent all winter and most of the spring riding over Oc and poking out men's eyes and removing their tongues so they could neither see nor speak of the humiliations being visited upon him. It wasn't until the summer that his wife Alice de Montmorency recruited him an army sizeable enough to do something of military consequence, such as burning women and children at Minerve. Once more it included quarantine men and prick-in-hand pilgrims.

When I meet simple people who don't understand crusades they often ask me how such a war that led to so much death and suffering could happen. I tell them the truth. I say it happened because the Count of Toulouse was foolish and the Northern barons greedy. Once you understand that daft old Raymond of Toulouse owned half of France and Simon de Montfort had nothing but his horse and an English title he couldn't claim, the whole matter becomes plain, even to simple people. Intelligent men compose ballads and complex histories, so don't seem able to follow simple explanations. They put the war down to sorcery instead. What I say to them is that anyone who's watched a rat steal corn has seen all the sorcery he needs to understand this Crusade of ours, and probably every other Crusade as well.

Meanwhile, I make no secret of it, I was developing itchy

thighs. These, and the itchy thighs of my women, were to have a considerable bearing on the conduct of the war, even though I neither hear nor read any subsequent account of them.

This is because men are such liars. Women, in general, tell the truth. Or rather we tell lots of little truths that men find it convenient not to understand, truths such as most drunkards snore, or giving birth is occasionally harder work than running under your falcon or riding behind your dogs. War is wasteful: there's another of our little truths. It is regarded as little only because spoken by women.

We heard, in our huts above Belcaire, of what happened in Pézenas to the girl child who mentioned this truth aloud while skipping among her brothers. It was on the big side as little truths go, and certainly a mad thing for any one female to say. It frightened them all so much that they told Roger de Servian who told Simon de Montfort who told the Executioner of Limoux to go all the way there and cut her limbs off, including her head. Yet war *is* wasteful. My women sat around in their huts and said it often, but there were no men to ignore them while they said it; so they stitched jerkins, cut arrows or fitted slates into waddings of cloth to make themselves hauberks to keep out the cold, whether of spearpoint or icicle.

The question is how did we know of these ideas and events from Pézenas, Limoux and all over Oc, save by such messengers as my Phantom and the occasional returning shepherd?

It was because, and I must state the matter baldly, one woman's thighs did not itch, and this in spite of my best intentions for them. All autumn, and well into a terrible winter, men made pilgrimage to the sacred *parvise*, portal and orifice of Mamelie la Mamelonne. Her beautiful breasts, her tapering thighs, the various apertures of her intelligence and the occasional treasures of her tongue had been unavailable to them while she had been *enceinte* and held as dough in the sacrilegious hands of Dogskin of Brousses.

When such pilgrims came, they brought us blistered feet,

anticipating loins, and such welcome gifts of bacon or wheat flour as penitents generally bestow upon a hungry whore. And, of course, they brought us news.

Unfortunately they carried our news, by which I mean news of us, back with them again. Not only did they state that the mammary miracles of the fabled La Mamelonne were starkly aglow in the Southern mountains which they themselves outshone, while the great cathedral of her thighs likewise stood almost empty, they spoke of her riding a white horse, bow in hand, and calling for wholehearted and total war.

Mamelie never called for war, merely for more, but her unuttered challenge was bruited abroad, and mine also. Even as these amorous pilgrims had soothing commerce with the world's only renewable woman, they also glimpsed the Maid of the Mountains, Perronnelle the Pure, my sulking and fiery self with long hair streaming longer and fairer, naked on an even whiter horse and calling disaster to the Crusade.

How did we know such matters? Because La Mamelonne's further pilgrims brought news of our news back with them in turn. It was all lies, every bit of it, except for my calling disaster to the Crusade. I never rode naked, nor was Nano white, and if ever I braved the icicles I clad myself in cloaks and my gelding in blankets. It was merely that men who walk a long way uphill in pursuit of venery develop eyes that can make light of any woman's clothing, at least until they've found their way to a satisfactory conclusion beneath it.

No sooner did I receive this news than I clapped my hands and called all my women together. I spoke to them of woman in time of war, I spoke to them of spirited woman, I spoke to them of spiritual woman. There are two sorts of spiritual, I told them. One can be a woman who follows the ways of the spirit, or a woman who turns her back on the ways of the flesh. Mummy had seen herself as one of the former, at least on Sundays. In fact, she was one of the latter, and haughty with it. A hairy fist between the legs would distress her greatly, especially if Daddy's arm were attached to it.

She loved him mightily, I told them, just the same. She loved him with the doglike devotion any woman can afford to show a man of temper who does exactly as she tells him. When it came to Mummy, Daddy was frisky but obedient, just like a hunting dog. He spoke of a married man's life as being just like a dog's in the field. Allowed to bark at the game, to fetch it and carry it, but never to close his teeth. Mummy would sniff when he said things like that. She was, as I explained to them, an intensely spiritual woman. She needed no-one to place a chastity belt between her legs. She needed it between her teeth, like some of this lot. Daddy said his things, nonetheless, especially on Sundays. He said them to remind himself he was a man of spirit, just as I spoke now to reaffirm that I was a woman of pith and phlegm.

Their eyes glazed as I spoke, their chins sank, some of them nodded off into a winter sleep. I realized what a stark hold both my reminiscences and my oratory had upon their imaginations.

I would have developed the moment further, but our meeting was interrupted by another trickle of Mamelie's devotees, each of them with glittering eyes, bulging sacks and thighs like pine-trees. They were in a hurry to couple with the paragon of their dreams, they said, because Mamelie's fame and my challenge had angered one of the De Montforts.

They couldn't remember which one, so great was their hurry to find their hackles unfastened, merely that he was threatening the upper valleys of the Aude with five hundred horsemen.

Solomon of Gerona had been dormant since his arrival among us, possibly out of respect to his absent wife. Now he hurried to make suggestions. He could arrange to fetch us ten score Arab shields from Toledo, and undertake to have them available to us within three months of dispatching his messenger. Or would we prefer a hundred strong sledges and three score climbing ropes, so we could make good our escape into Spain to take refuge with King Peter of Aragon, a man who adored pretty faces, and the yard or so of flesh he found beneath them?

Warfare always makes a chafferman think of trade. I had to put Solomon firmly in place, and assert myself boldly. I called my women once more together, bidding them dress in their sheepskin cottes and where possible their slates and wadding. 'We do not know which of his cursed tribe this De Montfort is,' I said, 'whether Great Simon, Amaury his son, or his brother Shitface of Meudon-next-Paris, known among us simply as Merdun the Bastard. Nor do we know whether he brings his men up here to burn us or bung us, or both.' Seeing I had the full attention of what wits they had, I added, 'All we can be certain of is that he will not succeed. We are acquainted with these mountains, their passes, their defiles, their treacherous places. We have the archers,' I told them, 'we have the will, we sit among this heaven-high pile of rocks.' Seeing that some of them still gazed timorously about themselves, for none of them was used to fighting or had seen my Spanish sword dealing slaughter at Le Bourg or Le Castellare, I added gently, 'A woman can run faster up a mountain than an armoured horseman can ride, or follow on foot.'

'Suppose you grow short of breath,' Solomon asked, 'or twist an ankle. Won't you have need of chastity belts?'

Two of my Minervoises picked him up and threw him outside into the snow, but I truly believe the question was part of his cunning, just the same, as there was no thought of defeat thereafter. Send one man flying and you can treat another hundred likewise.

'We march at first light tomorrow,' I told them. 'Bring your arrows, pack some bread and wear firm clogs. I need take no girls, no old women, no women with children, and no woman with child.' This last ruled out the half dozen or so who had been unbuckling the legs of friend Ironface to find which way his lizard would scamper. It left me with some hundred able-bodied young women who would shoot straight and strike hard.

We left at dawn, as I intended. It was a bleak day, thigh-deep in winter. Ironface, Gibbu and the Mute rode with me, but no longer the Fish Girl or La Mamelonne. I had a more urgent task for them than wasting them as warriors.

La Mamelonne had to keep all of our visitors on top of her, not all at once but in continual contiguous rotation. It was the Fish Girl's duty to follow any man who cried off and beguile him back again. We couldn't have any flap-mouthed chasers after women running down from the high pastures and blabbing our intentions to our enemy.

The Defile of Pierre-Lys is an awesome place. Yet our enemies needed to pass here or ride over inhospitable peaks, where black whirlwinds dwelt and some say dragons, and which were anyway tiled with ice and piled beneath clouds that set solid all the way up to the underside of Heaven.

We reached it at noon on the second day, having gone by the Gorges of Rebenty. No sooner had we arrived than we heard horsemen moving up below us. They were a long way down the pass, stepping with what urgency they could. The Wizard Caesar warns in his Book of War of the dangers that beset generals who concentrate forward. I recalled his words, and realized he was right. I could only rejoice that God had spared us by an hour and found time for us to be ahead of them.

'The light's thinning,' Ironface complained.

'"Retreat by darkness, never advance",' I quoted, I think from the same source. 'The sun is already behind us, the cloud heavy. They'll not see us as they enter the defile, but the whites of their faces will be clear to us as they come on. If they're foolish enough to be Crossed we'll have them white-bellied as well from their gipons and tabards.'

Even those of us in coats of sheepskin wore fleeces dark with oil. Most of us dressed even blacker.

'No need to spread ourselves out,' I cautioned. 'We give ourselves shooting room only. We stand on one side of the

466

defile, with the slope favouring us at our backs. Gibbu will take the right flank, the Mute and Ironface Lord Ferblant the left. I shall be at the centre.'

Gibbu nodded his approval, and the women looked happy not to be divided, as I now knew not to divide them.

'Loose at their faces when they come close,' I cautioned, 'at their chests if you loose long. If they do not see us early, expect them to come close.'

Again Gibbu nodded.

'Spend no arrows on their horses,' I said. 'Once we bring down horses, we'll lose their riders in the dark.' A leader chatters on in such a fashion to still the timid hearts. I learned these matters quickly, once the sense of them was not denied to me by men. They are dull enough tricks, but easier to take in than tatting in linen or steaming a pie.

Women may hate to share a kitchen, but put ten of us together in a neighbour's yard with an agreement to cook a pig, and one of us will cut its throat, one scrub its guts, one offer to pick juniper, one to find garlic. Nor will we object to there being a leader if there's a need for one, especially if the leader offers to scrub its guts or go up its nostrils for its brain.

'When this De Montfort comes,' I said, 'I shall scrub his guts and go up his nostril for his brain.'

The horsemen were talking beneath us, but quiet and low. It wasn't the chatter of men afraid of ambush but of riders who are wary of the ground. Now they were near enough for us to hear them word by word, and it was mostly oaths they spoke, being like most men and lacking anything original to say.

We took our bows forward from our faces, with our flight fingers still, as Gibbu had taught us.

'Twenty paces will do very nicely,' I said. '*Now!*' I loosed and stepped forward, uncovering my hair to the light.

We emptied twenty saddles in a damp crash of iron, flesh tumbling sickly on to water and rock. Some horses came on, others shied back, one with its rider's head dangling under its hoofs, which caused a mad consternation in the steeds all about it.

We had loosed either badly or foolishly, spending an arrow from each of a hundred of us with so little result. I should have thought to share our aim down the enemy's line of march, but what was done was done. We loosed once more together, but at horsemen spinning about. If we killed a dozen this time, it was better than I could count.

'Shoot as you will,' I said.

Gibbu began his usual slaughter, and my other women pulled slow and long.

'The light's gone,' Ironface muttered. 'We'll be better rolling down rocks.'

I don't think any of us lifted as much as a pebble. Nothing came past us, or up to us, save a riderless horse then another. We were shooting into darkness, seeing neither crosses nor faces, when the miracle happened. We heard shouts, gravel shifting, hoofs sliding on stone, groans, dripping water and a softness being mushed by horseshoes, whether flesh or snow, then sounds like a mountain slipping, first a loosening of popplestones, then tree stumps, rock, a rolled down disappearing avalanche of crushing. Horses squealed as if they had forgotten their voices until now. We listened to bones break, stones snap and men cry aloud, then the throating of a single crow that was now the only live thing near us. It went grunting on and on.

Gibbu either laughed or wept. I thought he laughed, but when I stepped near to him I saw he was weeping. 'Their forward men tumbled,' he said, 'then their horses rolled back. This brought down more of them. Then the mountain fell.'

After a mountain falls, or a piece of it, and the echoes die down, there is only the silence to listen to.

We couldn't go anywhere, not after dark in the frozen hills. We lit a fire with year-old scatterings we found beyond a waterfall. It took us an hour's chafing and rubbing to draw a flame, but we kindled some logs at last, then fed their red-hot embers to a second pile of branches lower down.

We did this to find warmth and heat dough, but the flames showed out enemies to us also. Not all of these had tumbled into the ravine. Some lay close about us, these being the ones brought down by our first loose of arrows. A few of my women studied them, I think from compassion more than curiosity, in case there were any yet living.

'This one was their leader,' one said. 'He was among the first, and his voice was loudest.'

I went down to look.

He lay marked by his shield, though the bent of its blazon wasn't sinister. Why should it be? I saw no need for us bastards to be decorated as a separate breed. There my affinities with this one ended. I touched him with my clog, and found his bones already frosting. Merdun de Montfort was dead.

The Bastard lay with more shafts in his head than his helmet had room for. He was recognizable to commonsense just the same, from his escutcheon and the overall look of him. The strangeness was that disfiguring death had not unfeatured him. What the shafts forced apart his cheek-mail held together, so he looked like a face in a tapestry, stuck with needles, spoiled but thoroughly recognizable for what it was. I looked at him, and the rascals about him. I remembered Mummy, Constance de Coloubres, Marie-Bise, One Eye and Thistle. It had taken many months more than a year, but now they were answered. They might lie in a garlic patch, but they were answered.

I could not sleep that night. It might have been that the air was too cold for breathing. It might have been that my mind was stitching pictures. It had needles enough. It had my frozen tears.

My Phantom did not come to me, and Gibbu could not bring himself to speak. He seemed awed by a vision of death too vast for his encompassing, a sliding hill that had taken off five hundred men. Merdun's death, the little death, offered him no comfort, though his own shaft as well as one of mine grew from the Bastard's head. Ironface gave himself over to the sympathy of his women. Perhaps they lined his freezing armour with their hands. The Mute's pipe was still.

Dawn came late because of the thickness in the air, which was presently snowing. Save that the night almost froze us to death, it broke too soon for me.

We had several people with frostbite among us, and one woman with frozen feet. She pulled her clogs off to rub some life into herself, and found her toes still inside them. She felt no pain, and said that she would not miss them.

'Toes are an ugly thing in a woman,' Ironface said. He suffered from no such ugliness himself.

I have been to the Defile of Pierre-Lys in the summer-time and it does not look steep. Its walls are sheer enough in places, but not the rake of its gorge end to end.

True I chose to fight from a hump, down which waters trickled, and in winter there was a spill of ice. I still do not see why five hundred men fell, or from how to where. I truly believe God must have tipped the defile on end, the way a clown tilts a ladder.

It could only be God. The place was too heavy for a man, even a man like Daddy.

I looked at our enemies' faces, their eyes glazing over like so many rimy cobbles. Their limbs lay in an endless tumble, sprawling a long way down. The snow was falling steadily, and the crows were feeding. The mountain was already dissolving them.

'Go and cut forth your arrows,' Gibbu instructed. 'It's bad luck to leave your enemy your mark.'

He slid down to recover his own. We did not follow. We were women. We knew how to make arrows. We left them in their holes.

CHANSON FIFTEEN

Wherein rumour furnishes the Maid with a lover she has no need of and several sillinesses consequent.

One thing about a fight, it leaves you in no hurry to have another. When we had stripped those of our enemies who were not yet fastened to the ground by frost, we climbed back up from the defile and hurried towards home. The return journey was quicker, and that's another truth about war. You always leave a battle more briskly than you arrive for it. We were asleep in our huts by sunset and in no mood to come out of them for a season.

When the weather let men into the mountains once more, La Mamelonne's visitors spoke of us winning a mighty battle. Seemingly some six or seven crusaders had survived at the back of the column. They had seen me reveal myself, so the price on my head was now doubled. I was worth a village's supply of mutton for a twelvemonth, though not yet famous enough to be valued in pork.

Meanwhile, my women constituted quite a fighting force, if only I could guide it towards our enemies. Some of them pined for their homes, and even for the husbands who had locked them in Solomon's belts, but since these lay roughly in the direction I needed to point them, I saw no harm in that. I intended to move back into the usurped lands of the Trencavels.

As far as the shepherd women were concerned, we could not depart too soon. Their men had returned from their transhumance in Spain, and they wished to claim their husbands for their own. It's well known there's nothing like a new face to make a man become restless, especially if it's rumoured to have a belly underneath it.

Then Mamelie's messengers brought us disquieting news. Gossip had it that Simon de Montfort intended to attack Pierre-Roger de Cabaret of Lastours, my cousin's friend 'Towers'.

475

I thought this likely enough. When Carcassonne had fallen, very few Cathars had risked staying in the settlement. Some came to the mountains, some went to Minerve, and some followed De Cabaret back to his own pastures.

Lastours was reputed to be the strongest fortification in Oc. So was Béziers. So was Carcassonne. So was Minerve. So I paid no attention to that. Once Pierre-Roger de Cabaret had retreated behind his walls, he would lose. The crusaders loved siege-warfare. The warriors of Oc did not. All of them, all of us, ate too well and drank too freely to be entirely confident of our drains, even when our castles had them. A siege is no more than an examination of the defenders' drains and water.

I decided to offer Pierre-Roger my advice and support.

My women were delighted to be on the move. They attracted one or two unattached mountain men to our party because it was spring; and some three dozen married shepherds found it appropriate to join us in arms because they were Cathars and natural enemies of the Crusade, as were all people in these high places, and while it wasn't winter they had nothing else to do, except listen to their wives.

I was happy also to have a young woman called Mitten by my side. She had been the La Mamelonne of Belcaire before La Mamelonne herself arrived to dispossess her of the task. She wasn't sorry to retire. A female of about my own age, say some seventeen or eighteen summers, her attitude to whoring was similar to the Fish Girl's, albeit more clearly expressed. She saw it as a reasonable enough employment for any woman able to take the money and run. Unfortunately, you can't steal from a mountain shepherd's side and hope to run ahead of him for long, not up a mountain.

'Why do men call you Mitten?' I asked her, as we stood putting our weapons together.

'Mitten is what women call me,' she said. 'They think anyone can use me to keep his fingers warm. And I must say the men agree.'

'I'm told the Cathar men have a poor opinion of females,' I said.

'Spiritually inferior to the horse,' she agreed. 'That one's the only person here to show me affection and respect.' She indicated Ironface, who was having difficulty climbing into his saddle.

'So you've been with Lord Ferblant?'

'All night long,' she proclaimed. 'On many many occasions when the weather has been cold and I've had nowhere else to go.'

'So what does he do for a woman?' I asked her, feeling unworthy as I spoke the words. 'What *can* he do for her?'

'He prays for me,' she said simply. 'Until dawn, sometimes. I've met no-one else who cares enough to talk to God on my behalf. No-one.'

Strange tidings indeed.

The march from Belcaire to Lastours was a long one. I tried to move secretly, but slowly enough to let rumour run ahead of me.

On the way I lost some half of my women to homes, husbands and men they met along the way. That being said, woman is a sticky creature. Like a freshly made loaf on a messy table she gathers as much as she sheds. As I lost more and more women, so I marched with more and more men. The exchange was not always a fair one, but there were almost as many gentlemen of Oc angry with Simon de Montfort and anxious for war as there were those who were pining for love. I had to hope we attracted some of the former.

La Mamelonne was still a potent recruiting officer. I advised her to keep her wares in check a little, with the result that we gathered two or three bachelors from every village we passed. Nor did they march with glum faces. One evening, after Gibbu had tutored them in the correct drawing of a longbow and the loosing of its arrow, I heard our great whore say, 'Lads, you must cross yourselves, pray and be patient. I am under instruction, and from the Blessed

477

Virgin herself, to give myself to none of you till he's shot all his arrows into Simon de Montfort. So guard your shafts to yourself and keep a full quiver. When that day comes I shall be yours.'

'And what a day that will be,' Gibbu promised, 'when even the promise of it makes your limbs tremble and puts you off your aim.'

'What a day!' they chorused.

'What a day and what a night,' La Mamelonne agreed.

On the ninth day of marching we saw ahead of us that dreadful wilderness known as Black Mountain. Many of my women were lame, because they had walked this far in clogs, whereas Nano wore iron shoes. However, another of those matters I had learned about war is that a leader, whatever else he may be, including a woman, is a man who rides a horse. If you are not a man who rides a horse you can never be a leader.

There was a garrigue all about us, and little hills like eyebrows, but I saw no dragons, only worms that stung. We followed a road by a stream called the Orbiel and at last came to Lastours.

This is a place of four keeps rather than four towers, with sweet lawns about them and flowering chestnuts. My band marched up openly. Our ragged dress and the dirge of the Mute's pipe made us look like a procession of troubadours or strolling entertainers rather than warriors.

Imagine our surprise to find the bridge drawn against us, the portals barred, and the battlements brimming with defenders. They thought we were crusaders! I sent Ironface forward to parley, but he had no page and no trumpet, and received an arrow against his shield and no other sort of answer.

He was in a foul temper at this, so I saw no help but to let my hair down and ride ahead with Mitten and the Mute and announce myself.

I was immediately recognized, either as myself or as La Mamelonne. This led to a deal of shouting between tower and tower, till eventually the door into the fattest one was opened to us, and I was welcomed by Pierre-Roger de Cabaret, my cousin's friend 'Towers', the Lord of Lastours.

'You are waiting for a siege, my lord.'

'I am waiting for Bouchard de Marly whom de Montfort promises will be ahead of him.'

'I have seen three sieges,' I said. 'You know how they ended.' His four towers looked ridiculous, a multiplication of error, and I said so. 'We cannot build castles in Oc.'

'We build them too well. That is why people die in them. A man builds himself a hearth and fortifies it.' He smiled around his quadruple keeps. 'What does he think it's for? Himself, his family, a few dozen retainers at most and his women's women. He wants to be safe against robbers, lepers, the marauding mad. He needs to protect his children from wolves and bears and stories of dragons.' He did not bid me welcome, in case I was one of these. 'Then a war comes, or a crusade, and his vassals claim his protection. People at large claim his protection, Cathars, runaway concubines, Jews. He takes them in. He runs out of food. He has no water and he drowns in shit.' He called someone to dampen his fire against the heat, then said, 'At least Béziers was saved all that.'

'I saw Béziers burn.'

'I saw Raymond-Roger drown in shit. So what do you suggest to me?'

'Let us deal with your enemies outside.'

'In the field? Yes, chivalry prefers the field.'

'We could sally south and attack Pennautier. I heard on the way that De Montfort shuns Carcassonne, and dwells at Pennautier. Pennautier is a tiny place. We could kill this monster at Pennautier and stifle the Crusade.'

'Chivalry could not countenance this.'

'He puts out men's eyes.'

'Men's, yes. Never knights' or cavaliers'. We cannot kill him at Pennautier, Perronnelle.'

'So let us speak of Bouchard de Marly.'

'A doughty warrior, and a formidable tactician. We saw him, you and I, at Le Castellare.'

'When he comes to invest you, march out to meet him. I shall surprise him from the rear.'

Pierre-Roger became uncomfortable at this turn in our talk. Talking to a woman was always difficult for him, speech never being the first activity that suggested itself. 'I don't like this taking behind,' he said. 'To take anyone from behind is dishonourable.'

'I agree it's unmanly,' I said, 'and unchivalric,' learning his language, 'and not at all in accord with the rules of war.'

He motioned for some wine to be brought at this point.

'So why don't you share with me where you'll face this Bouchard de Marly when he comes at you all nose to nose and manly according to the chivalric rules of war? Meanwhile, and without your knowing, I'll have my little force hidden nearby in a bush and be ready to spring out and help you.'

He laughed at this, and we drank a deal of wine together. Thenceforward he began to treat me much more kindly. We had a great feast, and invited the Mute in to play his pipe, the Fish Girl to tumble, and Ironhead to lie.

Many rumours circulate about Pierre-Roger de Cabaret, seigneur of Lastours. Most of them concern myself. He is variously supposed to be my husband, father, paramour, brother or fellow celebrant of the black art, sometimes all of these at once. (I don't mention the ballad that has him my son: mathematics as well as the intricacies of his own lineage are against it.) Suffice to say I was a virgin when I met Lord Pierre-Roger and a virgin when I parted from him, though he always fondled me by the sleeve after the second cup, and did on this occasion. By that date, the summer of 1211, no man had succeeded in getting across me with arm, leg, bridle or blanket, and I took pride in the fact. All the male ever does to a female – and I don't speak of our own kind merely, but goats, cattle and horses, and even rabbits and I daresay snakes – all a man does is leave her worse than she was.

At some such point, and while I still remained the better

for it, a messenger arrived to announce that Bouchard was on the road.

All of us, in our separate ways, went forth to meet him.

The Black Mountain is only a little hill compared with a Pyrenee, and Lastours is scarcely upon the worst of it, so the opportunities for ambush were not great, especially since my host was unwilling to mention the word.

However, there is a place where the road comes close above the River Orbiel, and at a point where it may be kicked down, suggesting that the route lies in the defile of the stream itself. This last is built of more stones than water in summertime, so the detour would not seem sinister, or not to a chivalric man used to fighting fair and square, and in all ways face to face.

Now, as to what bush I hid myself in, let me mention that there was a wood where pines pushed their way above the garrigue not fifty paces beyond where the road was broken. This seemed an admirable place as woods go, and by this point in my military career I had been in several.

The Battle, or more properly, the Skirmish of Lastours happened like this. Bouchard de Marly advanced boldly into the defile our cunning had entrapped him in. His intention was to make a demonstration in force, as my men friends say, before Lastours, then by means of a great blowing of trumpets and shouting of *huzzahs* and *olés* and such-like affronts to the coupling of pigs, the mating of birds, domestic peace and rural order, to compel Pierre-Roger de Cabaret's surrender.

Instead, he met Pierre-Roger and some two dozen score of men at the narrowest point of the river bed. These were well drawn up and skilfully positioned. Pierre-Roger himself led a phalanx of mounted men, knights, their squires and other gentlemen able to afford four legs, on the floor of the ravine. In case these men's horses became over enthusiastic, they were restrained and supported by foot-soldiers, armed largely with poleaxes and pikes.

Lifting his eyes a little, perhaps for inspiration, Bouchard saw the ledge above him and to his front lined with ballisters and sling shooters of various degree.

Bouchard saw no room for trumpets. He put his spurs into his destrier and pointed it at Pierre-Roger, towards whom it charged.

My little band meanwhile, numbering perhaps two hundred archers, had already crept down to the floor of the ravine behind the crusaders. As they made themselves ready to chase after their leader, we shot a storm of arrows into their backsides.

This brought some hundred of them to a dead stop. The light was good, and anyway we crept close enough to loose off our arrows right against their bottoms. Those at the front of the charge felt the momentum behind them slacken, so turned about to exhort their comrades forward. Whereupon we shot a number of those as well.

Bouchard meanwhile rode up to Pierre-Roger with his lance couched, and the confident conviction that he had a squadron of horse treading on his horse's heels.

One of Pierre-Roger's yokels with a poleaxe thought he saw a use for it, and brought it down on to the very top of Bouchard's helmet, hoping to split him from forehead to buttock like a kindling log, and drop him in two pieces, each with its leg on either side of his horse.

This wasn't chivalric, and he wouldn't have been thanked for it. Fortunately Bouchard's speed was such that the blade missed him and his topknot only collided with the haft of the axe, and he dropped before Pierre-Roger's horse in a deep sleep. This left Bouchard as the guest of Pierre-Roger's chivalry, which was enormous, while the remainder of the crusaders retreated boldly towards us.

They started by outnumbering us, and we had scant time for a further flight of arrows. 'Let them through!' I called, sensing they had little inclination to stay with us until Pierre-Roger's men caught up with them again. I confess that my hope was that we might gather ourselves after their passing and direct another flight of arrows under their horses' tails. I was only a female, you understand, and thought that was what war was about.

Unfortunately I was brought face to face with a giant in ornamental armour, who seemed to have tumbled from his horse, and who now rushed upon me with uneven, blundering footsteps, all in spurts and starts, much as a spider runs. I say giant advisedly. He was twice as high as Goliath and almost as tall as the Goddess Malpolon before the devil woman ate her, and with something of that same strange gait, as if built of stilts or ladders, save his movement was quicker.

I screamed. I should like to say shouted, but I screamed, and caught him a mighty whack on the hipbone with my sword, this being as far as I could reach and almost too high for me to lift. With my Spanish blade I might have done something delicate, and circumcized or castrated him. But my vile Northern brute of a broadsword had ironwork as wide as a shovel and was altogether too much for the strength of my hand.

Instead of swinging blow for blow at me, or raising his foot and planting it down with myself beneath it, he howled and turned away.

I couldn't believe my eyes. A dwarf or whingeing squire not yet come to manhood might find it natural to flee from a woman like myself who is all truth, tooth and flowing hair. I have after all frightened off bears, boars, wolves and Norman ladies' husbands in my very short time. But to encounter this tergiversating bumbology in a hard-thewed giant was a terrible surprise.

When he revised his reversal, retraced his retreat and bounced off the side of the ravine to barge back at me with a two-handed sword I could only do what came quickest, which was to kick him in the knackers, and a mighty leap it was.

'Don't,' he wailed, 'don't,' in three different voices all at once, answering me from windpipe, kneecap and thigh, so at last I saw what he wasn't.

He wasn't a giant. Each of his legs was an acrobat in

padded wrappings, and his trunk a third, only this time female, mounted on her own thighs' shoulders as it were. The knackers I had kicked were made up of their laundry and their supper sausage, so no wonder they had howled. It was like kicking a bullock in his dinner, which any farmer will tell you is an epigastric impossibility as well as foul on the nostril.

Enough of such boasting. While I was vanquishing the giant, Bouchard was tumbling off his horse. My ladies rushed up to cut his throat, but, as I have told you, Pierre-Roger had already made him his prisoner.

What a feast we had, Pierre-Roger's people, my women and the shepherds, with Bouchard in our midst with a bandage round his forehead and a jugful of spiced wine. If he didn't have a headache when we took him, he would certainly have on the morrow.

The gentility make war the way they play chess or chequerstones. They like to put the pieces they win into their pockets, then sell them back to their enemies at the start of the next game. They call this chivalry. There's another word for it. It's called ransom. They play this game so strictly that one wonders how so much rapine and slaughter occur. The answer becomes clear enough once you understand that to fall victim to these you have to own something that everyone wants. You have to be a Trencavel or a woman.

At the end of the third day, Pierre-Roger sent for me and said, 'In a week or so, Lord Simon will be here himself to batter my wall down.'

'So what next?'

'What is next is that I have already surrendered to him. I sent my good friend Bouchard to him with terms, and they have been accepted.'

'I have just seen your prisoner drunk against the fire in the great hall.'

'That is because he is back again. The terms are that I am to have my estates and live in peace with Simon as my ally.'

'And the price?'

'Bouchard, of course. But principally yourself. De Montfort wants to burn you, and the whore and the Iron man. All else are pardoned. I'm to surrender you tomorrow. It accords with my honour.'

'Why are you telling me this?'

'So you can escape tonight. It accords with my honour.'

CANTO SIXTEEN

In which the Virgin brings
Count Cunning of Toulouse a
famous victory but fortune takes
it back again.

We rode away as quickly as our lame women could walk. What I understood now was that the rules that govern war were quite separate from those that govern life. If a war killed you or tore your eyeballs out, you could blame neither man nor God, nor even yourself for being there.

We limped all too slowly across the landscape called Cabardès. I was aware of the crusaders in Carcassonne to the south – I could see the Citadel by day, and its cressets by night – as well as De Montfort's garrison in Pennautier, and Bouchard's men in Saissac. When these Northerners sit all around you in castles, your route is never safe from them, particularly on foot and with blisters.

Ironface urged those of us with horses to ride ahead. I asked ride to where, and he had no answer. He wanted me to leave my women and shepherds to their own devices.

In the end, I took refuge in the little walled village of Fraisse-Cabardès. The villagers did not want us, because the Crusade had so far passed them by. On the other hand, I had money, and that made us desirable. Win a battle, and you own the dead.

In Fraisse our people healed their feet, and I turned my mind to the war. The situation, as men brought me news of it, was this. The crusaders held all the most formidable strongholds in Oc. Or, not to be holy on their account, Simon de Montfort's family, friends and vassals did. We, by which I mean the people, held the land all about them. It was an interesting military problem, and teased the brain for solution.

Gibbu was a changed man of late. For a start, he seemed beguiled by the young whore Mitten. She was not his leman, still less his love, but he appeared to find her preferable to the chattering Mamelie and the twittering Fish Girl. The Mute, I noticed, was not a little jealous.

Instead of speaking in growls and grunts, Gibbu essayed long sentences, showing an interesting turn of phrase and most pleasing rhetoric. He seemed to have acquired this faculty since instructing the women in bowmanship a long year since. Talking to women can evidently be an education even for such a rough one as he was; though he continued to be gruff with myself.

Ironface tried to keep him in his place, for he thought all men have their place, and I must not overlook the fact that the Hunchback and the Mute were Lord Ferblant's people, not my own.

Fraisse-Cabardès grew an excellent vine. We were there in late summer, too early for the *vendange*, but the last year's wine was a noble nectar, and inspired me to all manner of strategies for the defeat of the De Montforts and the return of the Trencavels from Aragon. I was sipping it, I think from a store that Ironface kept in his left leg, when Gibbu burst out against him in resentment of his high-handed manner. 'Do not call me your good man,' he shouted. 'You are no man yourself, or not to pay compliments to others.'

'I am a man, and a good one,' Ironface retorted, 'and this village is full of women who will endorse it.'

'Then if you're a man and not a wraith in armour,' Gibbu said, causing me to prick up my ears at his eloquence, 'how is it you never shit, and not once need to piss, or anything scriptural, you're so sewn up in iron?'

The question had been on my own mind for some two and a quarter years, so I must say I waited for the answer.

'I do my one thing inside my left leg and my other inside my right.' He refilled our cups. 'Now ask me why my tubes never smell. It's because I wash the insides of my legs with wine.' He clanked in circles about us and chuckled again. 'And the proof of that, my friends, is that I let you drink it daily. Did ever wine taste so sweet?'

490

Mitten screamed at this, and La Mamelonne looked wise. I thought it best to go and inspect my women's feet. The Roman Wizards inspected one another's feet, I am told, or their leaders did. That's how they walked all over Oc before the Visigoths invented horses.

I did not see any feet, not that day, nor even have time for my own. I was interrupted and led off by a gang of priests, professional soldiers and poets who had also taken up their lodgings in Fraisse in the hopes of being close to me. The priests and the poets were here because I was a notorious virgin, the professional soldiers because I was a noted virgin warrior. The professional soldiers were content to leave my virginity alone for the sake of the warrior in me: the priests and the poets weren't. Priests and poets never can leave a virginity alone.

There is a need among poets to be at the centre, for only there can they see things as they are and turn them into tidings. The fact that so many poets, troubadours and other historians thought Fraisse was the centre meant that I was now extremely famous. Such thoughts can turn a virgin's head, but sitting in Dogskin's bothy for a year had left me proof against almost everything.

My principal concern at the moment, much more pressing than deciding whether Ironface was a supernatural being or had, like Béziers, a Roman sewer under his foundations, was why, if these people could seek me out from all over Oc and in some cases the world, Simon and Bouchard couldn't find me from the end of the road. The truth must be that there were other matters more pressing to them.

The professional soldiers' rumours had it this way. The current state of the war was political. That meant that people like Simon de Montfort could do nothing but prepare cunning strategies, take his swords to the knife-grinder and wait.

What was he waiting for? He was waiting for the Count of Toulouse. Dear old Raymond VI of Toulouse had just been excommunicated again, this time for not doing enough to please the King of Paris and Pope Innocent since the last time he was excommunicated.

Being excommunicated meant that Count Raymond was on our side again. Not because he wanted to fight – he was an artistic man who would rather strum on a pretty woman and listen to his courtiers drink wine – but because Simon might try to annexe his lands on behalf of the King of Paris if he didn't. To annexe lands on behalf of a King apparently always makes him so grateful that he allows a man and his descendants to look after them for the crown for as long as either party can remember the arrangement. Simon already held a quarter of France, my family's quarter, on behalf of dukes and barons the King of Paris was beholden to in consequence. If Simon expelled the Count of Toulouse, or preferably fed him and watered him long enough to allow him to drown himself in his own disease in a dungeon somewhere, then the King of Paris would be beholden to him direct. He could then claim the piece of England he was owed, and the King of Paris and himself would be the two happiest men in the world. Save that Simon de Montfort would be happier than the King of Paris, because his reward would be in castles while the King of Paris could only find satisfaction in a map kept in Heaven.

'This kind of talk is extremely interesting to me,' I would tell the professional fighting men. And truly I did prefer it to the gossip of the poets and the priests as they tried to honour me in a prayer or a ballad in return for being allowed to unpick my stitching or otherwise handle the best of me. 'I have only one question for you. What is Simon de Montfort waiting for?'

Poets and priests can never answer questions like that.

'He is waiting for Raymond of Toulouse to attack him,' the professional fighting men told me.

'Why should he wait for that to happen?'

'Because Raymond of Toulouse is stronger than he is?'

'I am a woman,' I said, 'though the present company has been kind enough not to notice the fact. I mention it simply because the strategies you speak of, allied to the larger political issues you have so kindly outlined to me during the course of several days, are becoming increasingly difficult to reconcile within my limited female intelligence.'

'Ah!' one said. 'Ah! Hah! Hah! Didn't I say she was a tactician?'

'We all said that.'

'And we were right. She's a strategist. Now the reason you cannot make the two sides of the matter fit – '

'Is that you are, at the moment, as bemused as we are.'

'I can gaze upon one end of the loaf,' I agreed, 'and then upon the other, but to tell you the truth I see no bread.'

'It is,' they proclaimed, 'a very crusty problem.'

'Made the more difficult because Simon de Montfort is acting, or pretending to act, or alleged to be acting or pretending to act, according to a strategy proposed by an Irishman.'

This was true, or seemed to be true, or was reported to be true. My head was aching by now, so my body took it away to give my brain time to consider its position. I was told by Ironface, who knew from sleeping with village women who heard it from the gossip of crows, that an Irish baron called Hughes de Lacy had counselled Simon de Montfort to advance 'so nigh to Raymond's idleness that it will regard itself cowardly if it does not advance in its turn.'

What Gibbu knew, from following a curious arrow, and finding one of the Count of Foix's men stuck on the end of it, was that Simon was now walled up inside the castle at Castelnaudery, and that Toulouse was in the town of Castelnaudery itself, together with the Count of Foix and two hundred thousand men.

I have dismissed numbers like this before. Assemble so many men and they will either not fit the world or fall through it like a stone through pie-crust. How could they be expected to find space for themselves in Castelnaudery, even

493

standing ten deep on top of one another, without sinking the town itself?

The fighting men were all about me now, though not my women, who had more sense than to seek out a battle before it sent for them itself.

A leader must be bold and decisive. The Wizard Caesar is adamant about it. 'Well well well,' I said. 'We must consider this Simon in his castle and answer to ourselves is he the rat or is he the cheese.'

'By God,' some said. 'We'll follow her anywhere!'

Others put the matter differently. 'By God,' they said. 'We'll follow her till we see where she goes.'

I thanked the good people of Fraisse-Cabardès, bade my fellows sharpen their weapons and break them free of rust by plunging them once into the dirt, then summoned them to clog and horse.

Ironface rode up beside me. 'Castelnaudery,' he said. 'We must answer to ourselves is Raymond of Toulouse the cat or is he the mouse.'

'I've already made the point.'

'My text is clearer.'

'A great leader is careful never to be understood.'

So, allowing for shepherd, poet and priest, I rode at the head of a mighty army, at least a thousand people, and quite probably as mighty as any in the field that day. As Nano bore me proudly at the head of this throng, it struck me that, in common with other armies, only a very few of us had come to fight. The poets and the priests could watch from a cloister or an orchard; possibly the professional warriors themselves would do no more than make notes on strategy behind a hedge. I was better when I stood with fifty women who could draw a bow, better off by far with my corpse-strippers who knew how to make corpses to strip, and of course with Gibbu, and the Mute and the chattering Lord Tin. None of us were brave, but not one of us would turn away if God whistled for us.

494

La Mamelonne rode with me, and the Fish Girl and Mitten. I didn't think this tournament would find a place for whores. I was mistaken.

Castelnaudery was a day's march off. It took us two, because although we struck boldly towards it on the track through Montolieu and then went up the hill overlooking Alzonne, we soon became aware of a great manoeuvring and countermarching of pack trains and even supplies on wheels here and there along the old paved Road of the Wizards in front of us.

These columns were guarded by horsemen, and these horsemen were spied on by distant horsemen, and these in turn by others, as the whirring of crows and similar angelic shiftings in the sky brought to my notice.

'See those birds,' Ironface said. 'There's not one that doesn't take grain from De Montfort's fingers and exchange intelligence with him in return for a dish of eyeballs.'

'Providing they're not from our sockets,' Gibbu growled, 'I'll let him feed God as he will!'

I saw those birds and the horsemen beneath them, so I went by a sad route across rocky hills and steep valleys full of rivers. I crossed the River Rougeanne, the River Vernassonne, the rivers Lampy, Aizeau, Riplou, Tréboul and Fresquel. The rocky hills were rough and the rivers were wet, especially the Tréboul and Fresquel. I have never known small rivers wetter.

Ride a horse through a stream and you refresh its hoof. March a woman behind it and you rot her foot. Coax a professional warrior across the same finny flood and pearly floor and you settle a similar mildew between his toes as well, but he's always too indolent and negligent to tell you. Look after your army's feet, the Wizard Caesar says. I sometimes wonder if he had an army of women. Most men in Oc will not even acknowledge they have feet, or any extremity at all, especially the poets, not as far as pomandering them or keeping them dry.

It was in this mouldy state of mind that we came to

495

Castelnaudery to find two great armies preparing for battle. The squadrons belonging to the Count of Toulouse practised their swordstick, quarterstaff, linking with the buckler, changing direction on the march whether to trumpet, drum or messages from pigeons, and a whole catalogue of feints and parries from *prime* to *septime* and *octave*, though not in that order, for few of them could count.

I wondered, as I watched them, how I had survived so many struggles without these shifts, but was chastened to remember I had suffered two cuts upon the arm and untold hurt to my women's feet. I had also lost horses to bears. I must not give in to conceit.

I sought the Count of Toulouse in a tavern. I found him snug inside a nest of women and pipers, just as before Carcassonne, and all of them people he paid for a tune.

'Niece,' he smiled, without shifting from his cushion. 'I think I may call you niece, my little Trencavel from St Thibéry. I am glad to hear your tidings.'

'What I must state boldly, sire – '

'What we must advise you is that it is our perception that our friend the Count of Foix has imminent need of you.'

The Count of Foix's army improved itself at tourney, swing-post and spike-the-dolly, changing from poleaxe to lance with both or either hand, drawing sword in the saddle, then tourney and tourney again. I am bound to say that this force looked much more military, warlike and martial than the Count of Toulouse's squadrons, being particularly resolute at tourney, which it practised so hard that it incapacitated and in some cases killed over a dozen score of its finest horsemen. With its own share of two hundred thousand mouths to feed, it probably found it convenient to be without some of them, and a lance in the gut is undoubtedly a potent disincentive to fodder.

I went boldly towards the Count of Foix, who was sitting on a horse – whenever do we leaders not? – and pondering a sketch his courtier had drawn in the gravel at his feet. I assumed he was ordering his battle, straightforward nobleman that he was. Instead I saw it was an unmistakable likeness of my uncle-in-law Toulouse tumbling a mermaid he was trying to transfix with a stallion-like prick that leapt out from his undercotte but otherwise lost its way. I had no notion of the verisimilitude of this last object, and many of us were already dead who were fortunate enough to hear La Mamelonne on the subject from the battlements of Carcassonne, so I came straightway to my own point, which was this.

'Sire,' I said.

He glanced up only briefly and did not even adjust his dress. 'Your place is over there,' he said. 'Take your women with you. My brother Toulouse has done my battle some service, and I thank you all for it. Remember, keep your clothes down to the last, and only uncover yourself entire if ill-fortune renders it necessary.'

I took my women to one side, and found that my uncle-in-law Toulouse had stolen an illumination from the scroll wherein my own fame is written. He had formed up a battle of women and was donating them to the causes of freedom and Oc.

The whores of Toulouse do not, as a rule, ply their trade in brothels. It smacks of organization, and there's little of that in the Count's Kingdom. Still, whenever a man uncorks a bottle of wine or unfastens his clothing to piss, two or three of these ladies will generally hurry forward in case his present occupation should put him in mind of anything further. And, of course, if money is changing hands, as in the buying of horses or a cheese, then women assemble in droves.

Still, the Count was able to gather together some two thousand of them on the left flank of Foix's main battle, and have them secrete themselves in a vineyard.

The Count of Foix had been anxious to dismiss me from his mermaid because he was indeed facing a line of Norman foot-soldiers, and these showed signs of coming on. They were neither supported by nor giving support to horsemen.

This was unusual, but here were stratagems afoot I knew nothing of.

As the crusaders advanced, and they did so only slowly with their horsemen watchful behind them, one of Toulouse's heralds blew a tucket on a trumpet. This was contrary to the Count of Foix's wishes, but then I don't suppose my uncle-in-law had enjoyed his failure with the mermaid in the dirt.

Upon this signal being respected, the whores filed in front of the advancing foe and turned to face them stark naked. I had never seen anything like it, or not in such numbers, not even from behind.

Nor had the crusaders, who had to endure it from the front. Nor had their following horses, which frisked and shied. The effect of a naked woman on an armoured man can be very sudden, as I had seen at Carcassonne; and I have no doubt that if these ladies had bows in their hands, or slings, or anything except their fannies (or *fanons fanions* as the *louches* prefer to term them) a great victory would have followed then and there.

If my uncle Toulouse thought these crusaders could be afflicted by anything other than momentary surprise, he was mistaken. Rape did not occur to them. Their foot-soldiers were Northerners, and wouldn't recognize a naked woman if they saw one, as they now certainly did, let alone two thousand of them.

The nuns of Saint Aphrodise made a demonstration on the opposite flank, and with much more success. There were less of them, by almost two thousand, and they had the advantage of being fully dressed and thus looking like women, even the boys among them, so the usual nonsense followed.

There were only a few dozen pilgrims and quarantine men with this force of crusaders. Wherever people of such extreme religious views see a woman and her clothing all in one place they have a desire to separate the pair of them. Sometimes they throw the woman on a bonfire, sometimes

498

her clothes, but whatever they do they are extremely brisk about it.

They did not have time to burn nuns any more than their more disciplined colleagues permitted themselves to impale whores. A recall sounded. So, before battle was joined, or any response threatened save by our women, the crusading force withdrew in good order.

Modestly I say we outnumbered these Northerners ten to one, without counting our nuns and our whores. If the great figure of two hundred thousand is even remotely credible, then we outnumbered them ten score to one. Yet they had come resolutely on. This should have given us pause.

Instead, our commanders in the field made play with their recall. 'Hah,' scoffed one of Foix's courtiers, 'they come not closer than a bowshot and remember they've forgotten to water their horses!'

'Toulouse showed them his little – !' another laughed. I won't repeat the word. It's never pretty to consider such an object protruding from a relative, particularly when draped in a diminutive. Besides, I've seen not a few of the things myself, and will ride a long way not to look upon another.

No account of this feint is given elsewhere, though its purpose soon became apparent.

The retreating force, or at least the mounted squadron behind it, was commanded by one of the De Marlys, or possibly by Guy de Levis. These men knew of the pack trains moving towards Castelnaudery along the old paved Way of the Wizards. They knew because they had dispatched them to succour De Montfort. They had also sent another longways about by Revel.

What they had failed to set in motion were the forces intended to squeeze Foix and Toulouse against De Montfort's defences. Again, a large number of quarantine men had gone home rather than stay for a proper fight. Southern barons, such as Guillaume Cat, whom the crusaders were compacted with, had defected again rather than confront a force of such overwhelming numbers as Toulouse and Foix were rumoured to have under arms. So the two hundred thousand lie was a successful one.

These pack trains were already arriving. A feint had been necessary to distract us from them. They now needed only to be protected as far as the château.

To attack them this moment would be a waste of our effort. You only get one cavalry charge in a day – it takes until sundown to recover your horsemen. There was a better time than now, and a better place than here. I hurried towards the Count of Foix.

This time he had something drawn in the gravel that was better than a mermaid. He had a map of sunken lanes, the position of squadrons, clumps of trees. It was a picture of the land in front of our nose.

I rode up and this time told him clearly who I was, a Saint Thibéry Trencavel and not a bawd in charge of a parcel of whores.

He seemed pleased to see me.

'Let us not take them here,' I said when our courtesies were done. 'Let them draw near the castle. We can squeeze them there. Better still, crush them as they go through the gate. If we time matters right, with not too many of us, we'll find their defences open and make an end of this De Montfort and his Crusade, all at one go.'

'Indeed you are welcome,' De Foix said.

'I pray you look carefully at the ground, and consider my plan deeply.'

'Is this your best advice in the matter?' The Count of Foix linked his fingers through my bridle as if he were leading Nano to a carol dance. 'Then *charge*!'

He dragged me briskly and thoughtlessly to the attack. So was the great Battle of St Martin Lalande or Saint Misery in the Meadow properly commenced.

The two supply trains had by now united. As soon as they saw us come on, the screen of horsemen put themselves in front of their wagons and pack beasts in good close order, spur beside spur, and awaited our onset with lances levelled and such other weapons as they could muster. There's a saying among gentlemen who fight on horseback that if you have to crack a kneecap it's better to do it on a friend than a foe. These Northerners subscribed to that excellent tenet, and snugged themselves together till their defences interlocked tighter than the scales on a peabug's back.

They broke our first charge, the way a stone breaks a wave, but our wave was too much for the stone so sucked it on. Man for man we had to give them best, and group against group grant them better. Yet so many of us came on with our second wave galloping blind, then a third, and perhaps ranks up to thirty behind, that we made good every boast of the bold Count of Foix and forced our foe from the field of battle. So children chase a spider with water from a bucket. The spider has to scuttle or drown. I never thought a spider a coward for avoiding the weight of water in the bucket. Nor did I think so of them.

The men of the pack train were doughty too. They stood up on their wagons with bows and then swords, or knelt upon the panniers of their mules and hinneys with slings or whatever else they could find. I saw men defending themselves by throwing onions and even apples. One of them unseated one of the Count of Foix's knights by clubbing him with a ham, clearly a fellow with no respect for pork.

Many a packman's sling served him better than David's in the teeth of Goliath, or did if he'd seized the time to fill his shirt with stones. When the horsemen retreated, the Count of Foix's knights were Goliaths indeed. They all took their lances and spears and rode around in circles, desperate to prick themselves a packman. It was a sordid piece of butchery, and not much the better for being perpetrated by men of my own side. I was glad to see several gallop to the kill as easily as they would to stick a pig, only to find themselves chewing on a flint from their intended victim's sling.

They saw my fair hair, these doomed ones with their slings and their arrows, and thought my head a pretty mark to aim at, and worth more than the straw butt at the fair. So the Count again caught my bridle, and led me away as if I were a hostage or a flag. I was no longer a warrior, but a standard dragged to battle. I'd rather be the eagle of an old Wizard legion. It was always planted fairly in the van of the advance, and made to stand upright where the fighting was thickest.

Idle men suppose everyone else to be cast in their own base metal. They do not fret that they themselves are less than gold, for they do not recognize what gold is. So it was with Count Cunning of Toulouse. He tried to distract the crusaders with whores, and paid for those whores to be naked. The crusaders did not take them. They had other targets in mind, and other weapons to hand.

Yet Toulouse wasn't stupid. He judged life as he found it. The crusaders might not be affected by a barrage of strumpets. His own men were glad to be, and it was such men he knew. Or if not his own, then those of the Count of Foix, who were scarcely better.

These, or the foot soldiers and base men among them, left off slaying crusaders, finding them man by man hard to kill, and at once saw a thousand whores reclothing themselves.

I wept to remember St Thibéry, but there's only one object more attractive than a woman's underthings on a bush and that's the woman herself underneath it.

'If the Crusade gets wind of this,' Ironface said, 'our horsemen will have no support in a counter attack.'

Men only do as their betters do. While their villains were foining at whores, the quality gave up sticking carters and began to pillage the wagons and pack beasts. What a triumph it would have been, to have led the train into Castelnaudery as a proper foison of booty, and for each man to share it all, whether his portion was beef or apples.

These knights and these lords, these gentry and gentlemen on horseback, pillaged it there, preferring to loot it in the field pack by pack. They had no use for its beef, and even less for its apples. What they did have a thirst for was the wine of Minerve, and the little casks of aqua-vitae that were clearly made in Heaven.

They were reeling in their cups, this great army of Foix, or quarrelling in the bushes over whores, when Simon de Montfort realized a battle had occurred. He rode boldly from his castle with the few dozen men he had with him, rallied those who had retreated in good order, and charged at the drunken multitudes of his foe.

There are men who will stop to pick their nose even in the teeth of the enemy. To tell true I've never noticed much prevarication among these Northerners. They disliked war enough to know the best way through it was to get on with it.

So it was here. Their horsemen came on, so did their pikemen. De Montfort led them from the centre and showed them how to kill.

My own little band loosed a flight of arrows, then escaped through an orchard. Of the rest, some perished by the sword, others were trampled to death in the retreat. It seemed that the more men we had, the more men De Montfort butchered for us, but always with assistance from ourselves.

CHANSON SEVENTEEN

In which her homecoming en-
rages a swan and stifles all
sensual enterprises.

*T*oulouse was one of those fortunate men who do not feel defeated when they are beaten. It wasn't that he took the longer view, simply that he thought there were more important things in life than trying.

He allowed himself to be beaten westward, his great army to be dissipated and his honour humiliated in a number of skirmishes. An army does not skirmish. His did. Raymond thought all men were like himself, 'readier for a fumble than a fight', as Gibbu said of him. I've heard the matter put more brackishly.

Whatever we could do with arrows we did. Principally we killed crusaders or injured their horses. I soon realized that this part of the war was not for us.

The shepherds left me as soon as Foix was defeated at St Martin Lalande. The transhumance required their attention. Their women had to be left pregnant. Rural people keep a calendar in their loins and their bellies.

I discharged my women soon after. Our war was a people's war. It was just that my women were people and most people weren't. The nobility certainly weren't. They were boys in armour.

Quite a few of my women had nowhere to go. When you've brought down a knight with an arrow, you're unwilling to be yoked to a churl with only a handspan to his lance. Most of them decided to return to the high pastures, where the men were absent and the air smelled clean.

I decided to follow them, and Mamelie and the Fish Girl had a similar longing. Mitten wasn't so sure. Belcaire was where she came from, and where more men than she needed had a use for her.

The priests stopped me going with them, and La Mamelonne too. 'Those people are heretics,' they said, 'and the cause of

507

all our troubles. They say there's evil in the world that God did not make. They say that flesh is filthy and that Christ could not break bread or shit. Also they've a low opinion of women, even their women. We have a low opinion of women too, but we are confident that none of these matters worry Pope Innocent, even though he is not on our side.'

'Where were you during the fight?' I asked them.

'Praying for your safety and retrieving naked females from the field of battle. We cannot let you go, Virgin, or the plump whore. You both have fair hair, and one of you is the Maid of the Mountains and shall be Raymond VI of Toulouse's fourth wife.'

'Never,' we shrieked. 'We shall go on a pilgrimage to the Holy Dominic of Calaruega instead.' Mamelie had stopped speaking by now, probably because she was working, so I added, 'He lives hard by at Prouille.'

'Treachery!' they responded. 'He is the cause of this terrible Crusade; he writes to the Pope; he scolds Simon de Montfort daily; he believes that nuns are as important to God as monks are, even though nuns in general are women.'

'You are nothing more than heretics yourselves,' I said. 'Corrupt in all ways spiritual, and only true to your faith insofar as you would rather fornicate than fast.'

'I cannot lie,' their Bishop said. 'There are some of us who would rather open a comely girl than unfasten the Good Book, and others who prefer to fondle a pretty boy than number the beads in our rosaries. That being said, we are priests, and expect people to do as they are told, especially young women.'

Just then the poets came out from the byre with whoever they had been hiding among. 'Is the battle over?' they asked. 'Did we win?'

I told them I was going home to see my confessor, and called to Nano who was better than any of them, being almost a horse.

*　　*　　*

508

Ironface needed to be with priests and poets, he had the tongue for it. Ultimately he longed to talk to great ones. I arranged to meet him at Prouille; lying creature that he was he claimed to know the Holy Dominic well.

I left La Mamelonne, Mitten and the Fish Girl to work or play as they would. They undertook to send word to me at Prouille in a month or two, but not to go there themselves in case someone made nuns of them.

'I'm not staying near priests,' Mamelie said. 'They never pay.' She was last seen progressing towards Castelnaudery a buttock's length at the time.

Gibbu and the Mute offered to accompany me to St Thibéry. I was touched by this. We decided to treat our horses gently. It was a long way to go, even by the old road of the Wizards, which would be kinder to their wind if not their feet.

In the end it proved to be a four-day ride, starting late, stopping early, sleeping beneath the damp stars of autumn, all three of us as silent as the Mute, who in many ways was the noisy one. Whenever he saw a viper numbed upon the frosty path, or glimpsed a sanglier shepherding her young into a bush, it was as if he wanted to be chattering.

He smiled often. He made mellow music on his pipe. I guessed this was his way home as well as mine.

Gibbu gave us no more of his new-found speechmaking now. He was surly and grew more sullen as we progressed, as if even his hump weighed more heavily each step we took. God knew where the bent one came from, or what manner of man he really was, save that he was valiant and his arrows never missed, whether we ate rabbit, wild duck or fish.

Terrible nightmares continued to haunt me, especially now that we again slept out of doors. The garrigue, one would think, is a private place, as inaccessible as a castle keep, more secure than the huge *donjon* on Quéribus when it drips storm high in the clouds. I was wrong. Nothing is proof against apparitions.

I do not speak of starlight's apparent spectres. The way the gorse just at dawn is on fire with its own holy light, and scrawled all over in the love juice of snails. Little rats are about at such an hour, stag-heads and gauntlets and the beetle that rolls rabbit dung. They all make their noises in the dust. Spiders are the worst villains. They produce a curious scuffle on the dry side of leaves, and worse, much worse in those tufts of grass the dew hasn't softened. A spider shifting all her legs on a pile of loose dryness a handspan from your ear can sound like Goliath beating on his shield – no, not that, I exaggerate, like a band of hunters searching the woodlands for your hiding place. Frogs have stopped belching by then, frogs and the midwife toad. It has grown too cold for the bloodless ones, and for snakes most of all. Though vipers will come and lie upon one's legs for comfort, and a warm snake is always to be feared.

Ironface had told me that he once lay dozing on a pile of leaves while a coluber came and laid her eggs in it, sticky at first, then as hard as bone. Fancy something as wise as a snake leaving its brood for Old Tin Legs to hatch.

I thought of Ironface, because it became gossiped abroad that I saw these visions, heard voices, had a mad sleep. Only he could have spread such stories. The Mute could not. Gibbu would not. Nor would La Mamelonne because, although whores gossip, she liked the talk to be only of herself.

Thinking of Ironface I included him in my dream as soon as I slipped into sleeping. I dreamt of him making love. Unlike my Phantom, he loved without limitations, having a handle as big as a truncheon, by which I mean the jousting pole those hot-headed horsemen use at the tilt. Ironface's member was as long as that, and unlike his legs it wasn't made of tin. It was the only flesh of his I'd seen, except sometimes his fingers, though only in a dream, of course. It was only a dream, to fill the space between waking and the moment when my Phantom came to me and all other dreams were forgotten.

This dream became a nightmare, for in it Ironface seized not Mamelie or the Fish Girl, but the Mute as he lay beside me. And they loved face to face, as if the Mute was some kind of woman shape, such as the Goddess monster I had seen on Alaric, and he wasn't using his fundament in the beastly way that Daddy said the Roman Wizards and the Giants and the English use little boys. I rubbed my eyes, still asleep, for the Mute began to moan and groan like any woman, while Ironface clanked and rattled above him like a tortoise mating, or two of those great counts' horses in link-mail.

My Phantom would not follow such a nightmare, and I woke in the thin dawn light to find Gibbu had already caught a rabbit and was gutting it gently. I had no use for such dreams now, nor for my Phantom. We had slept in the low-lying scrubland that surrounded the estates of Servian, and they reached almost to St Thibéry. I was home.

I didn't come in from the town, and along the water meadow from the bridge. I led us over the home pastures and straight to the vegetable patch that nine seasons ago I had left without a look.

Nano gave little snorts of joy as he felt the water-bedded turf beneath his feet. He was puzzled that no women ran out to meet us, that the geese were gone, and the wheel didn't creak over.

I knelt by my family.

Their graves were uncouth enough, little burrows beneath which the skeletons were almost visible, one on its side, one with legs parted under the banked earth, and all of them rank with nettles and the kind of scab weed that grows where the ground is dank. My family women lay in death as life had tossed them.

Daddy's mound was different. Daddy's mound was a mountain, an Alaric in little, and on the large side for any kind of diminutive. His was the remembered face that choked me with emotion, the giant who had not sired me yet had most truly been my father. I had seen many men die since Daddy died. None of them did it so well. Nor would his life be equalled.

Gibbu hung surly about the burial place, and the Mute moped by his side. I hated the Hunchback for his grump, and disliked him the more because he had played sexton to six of my best people. Yet this was no more than the madness of grief.

'Can I do better for them, Perronnelle? Can I perhaps lift them and bear them to Holy Church?'

Poor Gibbu. I answered him the way a beast answers, by turning back my lips from my teeth.

Rebuffed by my ill-manners he turned away.

To return to one's grief is like re-entering a dream. No sooner had I served him thus, and found myself alone, than a huge hog charged me, a bone-white tusker that had been rooting in a wilderness of bean sticks, bindweed and wattles, and must shortly have snuffled up my parents if we'd left him to truffle undisturbed. He came at me tall as a half-grown horse, as fat and ferocious as a breeding stallion, bristling with horn.

A sanglier only rarely has tusks, though if one bites you by the thigh its teeth will hole you big enough for your heart to drop through.

This one had spikes as I say, curved and wrong tangled like an elephant's, and a loin tusk as well, as polished and hard as anything I had seen when knights were feigning at the joust.

He came at me with his nostrils blubbed open and that strange pink look the paler ones give you when they're snorting for blood. I swear as we tangled eye to eye I saw Raymond de Brousses at the back of him. Then, being a maiden and cautious of any such male, I skipped aside before he tore flesh from me.

He turned, not as a bull turns, but more like a cat when it rolls with a rat. He flopped back on himself fast as if to trap me with the weight of him. Of course, I skipped again, but his teeth cut a bolter from my cotte and left me with a

512

gap like a Valentine, while one of his three tusks tore me by the thigh.

I lay there bruised rather than bleeding and waited for the monster to eat me. No one plays carpet to a pig and lives to speak of it.

As he put his head into my side I felt a shadow step over me. It was Gibbu.

The Hunchback had a sword, but made as if to give him his hand to eat. When the monster snapped at it he found his throat swallowing not fingers but a blade almost to the length of Gibbu's other arm. I was reminded of Daddy's 'When a bear gets its teeth on your wrist don't pull away. Force on ... Force in unto your elbow and seize it by the roots of its tongue!' Gibbu was a man like Daddy. He could strike and stay calm. Yet he carried a bossu on his shoulder. I'd rather play kiss with a parrot.

He picked me up and held me just the same, the front of him covered with blood. Then he showed me the monster's tongue, and such other parts of him he'd stirred through its mouth with his sword.

The beast itself lay against Daddy, and I don't know who had the best of it for size.

'That's a noble head for roasting,' my saviour said. 'Noble head, tooth and tusk. But we'll have him in a stew. He's too old to cook green upon a faggot.'

Gibbu was trembling just the same. He was hurt. We hurried to bind ourselves up. I say ourselves, for I was bloodied where no man could tend me, and although women bathe a man's battle wounds often, the Hunchback refused to let me touch his further.

So we went into the house.

'I had no time to string my bow,' he said.

The Mute followed him gently, as if walking after a God.

I took possession of my kingdom, for a night, for a moon, for a season. We ate that boar, and several pigs otherwise.

513

We ate better than in my cousin's palace, or the castle of Cabaret at Lastours, for we had two bowmen to feed us, and Gibbu was a fisherman too. Here, as never at Carcassonne, we had water. Nor need it be purified with wine, but both of them drunk in their own right as God intended.

As my thigh healed, I came to stroll about. I did so cautiously. We did not advertise our presence. Our neighbours knew we were there, and the town also. But we didn't announce ourselves with a trumpet, or herald myself in a ballad. Servian had declared himself for the Crusade, and was loyal to De Montfort, and there were less honourable enemies equally near.

The leat still flowed, but the slab was open. Neighbours had needed to grind corn and I couldn't expect them to be as frugal with the water as Daddy had been. I was glad to find the Mill smelled worked in.

I found no bone-dust in the cogwheels. The floor of the solar was scrubbed, I suppose by friends, but of course not burnished nor rushed. I heard no chickens in the rafters, and assumed last winter had eaten them.

One matter oppressed me, and reminded me that I had more to fear than flame or lance. As I walked by Daddy's pond, enjoying the Hérault proper, Blanche the White Queen jumped at me, hissing as always like a serpent.

She was mad, that one, madder than a swan has any right to be, but maidens can turn into swans, and swans are sometimes God. Then I saw that she was less than mad. She had been resting there in the reeds, resting and moreover sitting on a clutch. All females are prickly at times like these, and those that know wild things acknowledge their right to be.

She did not return to her eggs, but stood threatening me with her wings, and thrusting her great neck at me. Behind her I saw the first egg break and hatch, and a second beak break through a shell before the first chick was dry.

It was black. Both chicks were blacker than sea coal, or purest jet. So was a third. I remembered those words of

514

Raymond de Brousses. I rushed off to search for Frédélon, who should be guarding his mate on the clutch. I recalled Dogskin's brag as I did so.

His boast, his promise and his prophecy. Frédélon was dead, a whole year dead. I found him just the same, for a death of glued feathers does not disperse easily, and the breastbone and beak outlast a king's catafalque, since in death as in life he is noble, the swan.

Frédélon lay outspread, as Icarus must have been when beached from the sea. His body was grown through and transfixed by bulrushes like so many tusks and lances. He had been slain by the ebony swan who had fathered Queen Blanche's clutch. I looked at his hull of ribs and thought of the Chapel of the Bones. Dogskin's brag was true. Even the bulrushes were black.

The dreams I had in my parents' bed. My Phantom visited me nightly, but he offered no comforts there. Nor dared he in a place so holy to Mummy, where Daddy must draw only gentle breath, and try nothing half-human else.

He spoke to me of defeating the Crusade, by which name he called De Montfort, by starvation, ambush, and poisoning his wells. When I reminded him that men like De Cabaret and the Count of Foix would reject such stratagems as unchivalrous and knavish, he said I must persuade the peasants to it. 'Such a message will take you time, Perronnelle. You must hurry to your task. Hurry! Hurry!'

I startled from this latest dream at midnight, or so I guessed later from the candle and the stars. As I stirred, the great hall doors burst open, side and side about. The solar blazed red with torchlight, as if to make a gift of the sun. Then I was properly awake, and armed men strode in, with swords in their hands and arrows through their faces.

I think Gibbu slew no more than three. 'Back ways out, Perronnelle,' he hissed to me, while other men stumbled on the bodies at the door.

I rolled down from my parents' couch, and found the door

to the patch was already open. As I went, my eye caught to my memory a nobleman on horseback outside the solar door, his face half familiar, and a half dozen other mounted men besides.

The Mute held Nano and our other mounts at the back of the patch, whistling to me softly from beyond the clump of canes that had hidden the boar. Clearly he had been sent out by Gibbu at the first hint of trouble in the meadow.

I had no time to ask myself such questions as 'Can a Mute whistle?' for men rushed at us out of the darkness with swords.

Gibbu took one with his unstrung bow, then breasted another with his horse. I had Nano do likewise, thrashing him about in a mad circle as a gelding will, even among sticks, being unfearful of his balls.

The Mute was unlucky. He screamed aloud – I record it: *screamed* – as an attacker sliced at him before he could swing to horse. He couldn't mount afterwards, his arm kept slipping on its own blood, so he was struck at again. Then Gibbu rode our assailants down and snatched him across his own saddle. So, bruised and breathless, and in one case bloodied, we made off.

I had no time to ponder the Mute's whistle, or consider such philosophies as to what extent the voiceless are truly dumb. Gibbu growled, 'This one is going to bleed to death, if it hasn't already. We'll have to stop.'

Our gallop had taken us naturally enough on to the Wizards' Road. We turned off it to the south and found ourselves in the wood where two years before we had met the crusading horsemen.

'Force further in,' Gibbu swore. 'Further in.' We pushed into a wilderness of unkempt underwood, with the branches bruising us and the leaf stems whipping. The place was wild. If it had ever been coppiced it had remained uncut for centuries. Here he let down the Mute. As he did so, a sky that was clear when I last saw it began to rain.

516

'It wants two hours to dawn,' Gibbu said, 'and it'll take me that long to make a fire.'

I felt for the Mute's wound. It was across the upper right arm and deep into the meat of the shoulder. It bled, but not I thought from a major vessel, unless our friend had already bled dry, and such things happen.

I had no need to touch further around the cut for, hell born that he was, Gibbu rubbed a flame from nothing and we had light before the kindling grew damp.

By the glow of early firelight, my hand found and my eye saw what my brain guessed at from holding the Mute so close. The smooth skin, the hairless cheek I already knew about. The small but undoubtedly female breast meant that if it was a badel I nursed then the Mute was a hermaphrodite indeed. I had known many dreams about the Mute, and now they were answered. A woman's breast can never be a nightmare, even on a man. Then the Mute wasn't a man, as I could have found by uncovering further, only such curiosity would have been prurient.

Gibbu held his sword-point glowing red inside his fire. Now he turned with it to burn cleanness into the Mute's shoulder. Or some burn to cleanse, some to stop blood.

The Mute screamed, sobbed, struggled as if to find words forgotten since the cradle. 'No . . . don't burn me,' he said. 'Don't burn,' in a woman's voice long laid aside, and now taken up slowly. 'Please don't touch me with that,' she said.

Gibbu swore. 'I call on Christ,' he said. 'I call twice. First for this.' He indicated his glowing sword. 'We have no water nor container for water, and I'll not let it spoil.' He hitched up his clothes and piddled on his blade as if neither of us women were there. 'Some say blood does away with water,' he said. 'But I say if it's blood you need it in a bucket to achieve a proper temper.' He gushed liberally enough to cool an armoury forge – show me an Occish male who can't. Then he put both his weapons away and said, 'My second prayer was for this.' He forced through the undergrowth to

517

his horse and came back with his saddle puncheon. 'I thank God my harness stays laden with aqua-vitae,' he said, 'if not with cooking-pots.'

The Mute screamed properly this time, for he poured spirit into the hole in her shoulder and arm and over her young breast. She fainted and stayed so while he splashed more of the stuff into her mouth, and he and I drank the rest of it.

'You could have stopped all this,' I said.

'I didn't know it was a woman,' he growled. 'I'd have married her else, for being so good at holding her tongue.'

'I don't mean that,' I protested, glad he hadn't been a party to deceiving me just the same. 'I mean back at the Mill. You could have loosed at those others as they filled the door.'

'I noticed the Abbot Bérenger, and I hesitated. Then I saw Etienne de Servian, and unstrung my bow.'

'The one gave the other the Cross and urged him to join the Crusade. They're De Montfort's friends. Why spare them?'

'Some men I do not loose at.' he stood up with the puncheon. 'That one will need water,' he said, indicating the Mute. 'I'll bring some.'

That was his only answer. What was I to feel? Not only did Servian bring his crusaders after me. Bérenger, my local abbot, had wanted to seize me as well. To burn me as a witch? My father used to grind his corn.

CAPUT EIGHTEEN

Wherein a sword interrupts a prayer then the Virgin recalls that women may be naughty together with no harm to God or man.

'We shall need a horse,' Gibbu said. 'Two years ago, when Béziers died, you could find horses in the field with no men on them.'

'We did so thrice, and they had the wind.'

'Today there are no such horses.'

We stood in our secret place with the wet turning to dawn, and the dust on the leaves dripping mud where the rain seeped in. There was mud enough already, for the soil was still baked and the waters ran on the top of it, giving us an inch of mire in which the Mute, poor unconscious thing, looked like to freeze or drown, if the blood that had seeped from her didn't make an end of her first.

Gibbu strung his bow, felt for arrows. He had three. 'To separate a man from his horse and a horse from his man is a simple matter,' he sighed. 'The problem is to know which man, which horse. I am not a God, nor even a justice, and certainly less upright than any Executioner I know.' He took off his cloak and wrapped our voiceless unconscious one inside it. 'It may take me a quarter of a candle. I may spend a day. If it costs us a day, this thing will be dead.'

He was gone from the dripping thicket, with no word of comfort for me. I crouched inside our hutch of rain and shivered above the fire, which I fed with dry pieces we had piled from the wet. I handled my shoulders against the cold. I had no cloak, no pelisse, and no sort of cotte to wear out of doors, but such a lightweight thing as summertime sleeps in. Yet I looked at the dying Mute and knew I would have covered her with everything I wore, if only I wore more than anything.

I built up the fire, and beside it laid a raft of those same wet windfall sticks that were no good for burning. I placed more athwart them, then a stuffing of leaves, whether dry or

521

damp, today's or yesteryear's, then lifted her on top of this cradle. Then I held her close in my arms, my body crying for her warmth as she died for lack of mine. We cuddled as I have seen shepherds embrace in a storm, as being our best chance.

Sometimes she muttered and sighed. Each time she stirred, or otherwise tasted her mouth, I took Gibbu's puncheon and poured water in, whether it was rivulet, dewpond or brack. A wound will kill a man unless you water it, I'd heard warriors say. Let me water my new-found woman as well.

Call my body's covering a bliaut, petticoat, shirt, what you will. The fact is my sleeping tabard hung loose at the neck, as well as being short for any crouch of circumstance. To my surprise, the Mute in one of her larger stirrings placed her lips to my right-hand nipple, and began to suck.

She did so without waking, and feeling my dying one so plugged upon me, I thought, 'This is death indeed. She is dying now, and like a baby child is mumbling for her mother.' I nursed her, drawing warmth from her, as she drew a kind of spirit from me, for a maid has no milk, and why it is young men cry out to suck on her I have never fathomed.

I heard horsemen entering our wood. Myself scarcely dressed, and herself only scantily alive, lay cuddling together as I heard their hoofs fretting about.

She opened her eye, and smiled at me, but as hurt ones do, a long way off.

'Tell me your name,' I whispered. We could not bury a nothing, and *Mute* would now never do, whether chalked on a board or cut into stone.

'Guillemette,' she breathed.

'Guillemette what?'

'Mitouche,' she said.

'"Mitouche"?' Again gently, still fearing the horsemen. 'That's a joke.'

'"Nitouche" would be an even bigger one.' She fell once more asleep in my arms.

I was glad my nipple wasn't in her mouth when the horses found us.

'My mare loathes that lumpless thing of yours,' I heard Gibbu say behind me. 'I have two more, both of them stallions. We'll put her on my mare, as these others are ill-used and testy.'

He stooped beneath the dripping branches, comforting Nano and his mare against the male arrivals, then tying the newest pair by the nose. Then he crouched roughly over my baby and took back his cloak. 'I'm frozen,' he said 'Death is chilly work when it's raining.'

Again he went away, leaving me comfortless, and my burden hard-eyed and awake. Back he came with two bundles of everything, *gardes-corps*, chain-mail, leg-wrappings, shirts. 'A brace of louts wearing the cross,' he said. 'Their horses caparisoned in red with lions romping in gold.'

'De Montfort's men.'

'Him or his son's.' He stirred the gear with his foot. 'Roast their seams for fleas. We must hurry that one to shelter, and I don't want to lodge with women who itch.'

The dead men's gipons bore both the warrior Cross and De Montfort's emblem, so we fed the fire further and burnt them to skeins and ashes, good flax that they were. 'Where are the fellows who wore these?' I asked.

'Where only God will find them, and that not until the Last Trump. And looking as only the Good Lord will recognize them, being naked as they came.'

I thought of Guillemette comforted by my breast, and tears for the dead men came into my eye.

'Praise Him for this rain,' he said. 'I had only sword for spade, but they are buried deep.'

Buried without arrows, I noticed. For his quiver again held three, and smelled hot.

We found no lodging before Capestang, but Guillemette was already brightening, what with frequent water and the warmth of her horse. De Montfort's men had been well provided for, so we managed to feed all three of us with a soup of uncooked gruel. Better for Gibbu and me, they carried bread. It was stale and not baked by women, but tasted sweet enough with water.

'The water is good,' Guillemette said. She made her words slowly, and had eyes only for him, especially now she was revealed as a woman.

'That's because it came from a ditch with frogs in it,' he said. 'And the brains of a dead horse.'

She tried to fit no more words together, not while bound upon horseback.

At Capestang there is a shed, just before the wilderness and the marsh, and at the far end of life from the château. Gibbu was cautious with this place, and before going in tugged at his beard, as if fearing to be known in another guise.

The rain had stopped, but Capestang makes its own fog. Guillemette and I crouched on our horses beneath low-spreading trees that looked as if they had salt on their branches. Nano sniffed once at the white grass then gazed longingly towards the horizon, which was distant.

When Gibbu came back it was from another door. 'I ransomed him a stallion and sold him a sword,' he said, 'with promise of a knife to follow. We have a loft with a port, share his soup but give keep to our own horses. It is better this way.' He gazed upon Guillemette without interest or emotion. 'If her blood does not heal, we've a spare mount to offer. Give the Jackdaw a horse and he'll think we've touched his shoulder with a knighthood.'

'I'd expect a year's lodging for a horse,' I grumbled. 'And raiment too. And scarcely less for a sword. Who is this Jackdaw, and what is his degree?'

'Carrion.' Gibbu was spending too many words on me of late. He said nothing more but led us inside.

A pretty enough sight we must have been, two women in short-arsed tunics, both of them spotted with chain-mail, and the one of us holding the other up the way a child leads its baby of rags.

If the Jackdaw – Choucas of Capestang – thought there was anything strange about us he said nothing. He served us soup in a common bowl, soup too thick for spoons. This was good for he offered none. He broke bread for us, and to be fair to him he broke it in abundance with hands frosty from scrabbling in the salt marsh for clams. The soup was full of salt, the wine blue and salty. There are several reasons why wine tastes salty. The reason this tasted so was salt.

Guillemette could eat nothing, though she drank water gratefully enough. Poems have been sung about the water of Capestang, many poems by many minstrels who have tasted it and hurried on. But she drank it, and I was glad for her.

Choucas watched us anxiously the while. There was firelight in the place, but he hovered above us with a candle, smelling of goose-fat and dripping too readily. He was a tall, gaunt man of perhaps thirty-five years, who had no teeth standing to keep his nose from his chin, so Choucas of Capestang looked like a jackdaw indeed. It was to be hoped he didn't try to steal from us.

His own dwelling was the table we ate from, two benches and a sleeping place, or some other kind of mess, in the corner. The fire was against one wall, and didn't look pleased with itself.

'Many people in?' Gibbu was finished with his soup.

Choucas didn't answer him. I felt from the tiredness of his gesture as he turned to lead us towards the loft that he was telling us that people didn't exist any more, that here he was, a man who sold his shed for harbour and soup to go with it, a man who lived solely for people, yet knew not where they were gone and why.

'That's good,' Gibbu said to him. 'I don't like people. Well, you're richer by a sword, and if you treat us with discretion you can keep the stallion.'

'Only when you want a change of soup,' Choucas said. 'Only when you want something else in your soup.'

This was a difficult conversation to hold on a ladder.

The loft was clean enough. There were no chickens, and no four-legged beasts because there was no hill nor height against the house to admit them through the port.

The port was open, so were other breezy spyholes in the roof. The place would be comfortable in the heat, miserable in the cold and wet, and safe for all seasons. Gibbu knew what he was looking for.

There were two benched beds, one large enough for several people, and a truckle scarcely fit for one.

Choucas held his candle this way and that to see how we would dispose ourselves, but Gibbu suggested he climb down his ladder and plant his feet once again on Capestang. Sometimes I wondered at the Hunchback's wit, sometimes at his lack of, but a man with a boss upon the shoulder can never be an ordinary mortal.

I put Guillemette in the bed and crept in beside her. Gibbu took the bow stick that never left his hand and jumped out through the port. His feet splashed through the earth when he landed. Such was Capestang. You always needed a clog on it, and sometimes a boat. The warriors whose clothes I wore had been clad in horsemen's slippers.

I didn't trust Capestang, though its choice seemed safe enough. The château that had surrendered to De Montfort was at the far end of the marsh. It was no more sinister to our safety than any other castle that had defaulted to the Crusade, and that was all of them. Besides, having defaulted it had defected again, declared and redeclared, like the homes of all of our squirarchy and nobility, some through lack of courage, most through lack of conviction, for God sides with a Crusade.

I'll say one thing for Choucas' soups and the cleansing salt in the air. It healed Guillemette quickly, or it did once she took some.

Salt makes for sauciness, too, salty bodies and salty tongues. So it was one night that Gibbu, who scarcely stayed with us, but now sat on our bed wittling sticks to make arrows, said some most curious things.

'Gibbu,' I asked him, 'once this Crusade is over – '

'It will last half a hundred years – '

'Yes, but when it is over, what will you become?'

'I shall be as Raymond de Brousses,' he said, 'and enjoy a whole coven of women.'

'So show us how you'll do that,' Guillemette said, and silly it was to say, while he sat on our bed. 'It's very hard for one man to serve thirteen women, especially on a frosty night.'

'I won't be a man. I'll be personating the Devil. So let the Devil help me, I say. Let him help me do the Devil's work.'

'It's work he wants to keep for himself,' the little flirt said.

He held her by the ankle and replied, 'You can drug them, you can give them short shrift, by which I mean in, out, and on to the next one, saving your seed for your horse, or you can make yourself a crutch, prop or splint,' still toying with her ankle, 'or even a device that will do the whole job for you while your niblins – '

'Yes?' she prompted.

'While your niblins dangles safe inside your hump,' he said with a howl, and leapt through the port into the night.

'Guillemette Mitouche,' I said, 'that was very forward of you,' though she had said no more than Marie-Bise would say to Daddy, or Thistle and the rest when Mummy wasn't there.

'I'm forward,' she admitted. 'I had many lovers when I dwelt in Pézenas.'

'How come you left such a paradise of desire?'

'The women had me burned as a witch,' she said. 'They said no-one could catch as many men as I did and not be a witch. And when I told the bishop it was only a question of knowing when to open my legs and when to hold my tongue, he said it wasn't witchcraft but sorcery, himself having had me often. He set the flame himself.'

'But you're here. I can hold you.' Was there no end to illusion?

'Ironface has a trick to fetch people from bonfires, and well you know it.'

'Then you became a Mute and a badel?'

'He said it was a small price to pay. He said they would look for a woman and find a hermaphrodite invisible. He said no-one would believe a woman could hold her tongue.'

'Tell me about Gibbu.'

'The Hunchback came after. One moment he wasn't. The next he was there. He never lets me love him, even when I cook for him or coax his thigh. You saw him just now, fleeing into the starlight.'

She taught me many tricks as between men and women. She wasn't full of moons and magic like La Mamelonne, but knew how to lie under and when to be over. She told me good lotions and potions, and which leg was up and which should be down.

If only Daddy had met such a genuine instructrix. I might have had brothers and ten sisters more. People used to wonder how a lusty man like my father, married to a handsome woman like my mother who came from a big family, could only give her the one child. They said she had him only once because he was too fat for her and would squash her through the bedspread, and so did I think till I found out what I didn't know then, that she didn't even have him that time. People used to cite the Big Bull of Muret. For a while every peasant around Castelnaudery wanted to breed from it; but when they took their cows along the Big Bull would mount them and break them by the back. He used to make them pregnant, but they couldn't deliver their calves because their bottoms had fallen off. No-one could break Mummy's back, believe me. But if only she'd known Guillemette to teach her to be on top, or permitted herself a proper talk with Daddy's friend Marie-Bise.

Without meeting Guillemette I'm sure I should never have thought of such subtlety. I knew only the beasts of the field.

528

I don't know if you've ever observed them, but the male is always on top from goats right through to cows and including such things as chickens.

All this talk, or the salt and the late arrival of my Phantom would give me most troubled dreams. On one such evening, when Gibbu was hunting rabbits or perhaps outside to guard us, I groaned aloud, waking myself from sleep and finding myself hard up against my bed fellow, whose speech was now fluent and free. 'I don't much care for women,' she said, 'but since you're my friend, Perronnelle, and I see no hope of the long fellow, I'll help you out if you like.' Her kisses were as soft as they had always been when she'd comforted me as the Mute, and all the better for knowing she wasn't a beardless man. She had clever lips and fingers too, so clever I was glad it was a cool night, but in truth she taught me no more than I already knew from Constance de Coulobres: that ladies can be naughty together, unless like Marie-Bise they have bigger things on their mind.

We were naughty together many times at Capestang, as formerly I had begun my education at Constance's hands. Such excesses as we dosed through before sleep could not prevent my Phantom's visits after midnight, and now I more truly knew my Mute I knew this could not be my Phantom, who increased his exhortations to me as his foiled ardour accumulated. Most dreams lie along the surface of our minds, but these cried out in my depths.

'There's a price on your head so huge that even a baron would betray you for it,' he said to me.

'But I've done no more than when last there was a price.'

'You idle but yours is the glory. Two crusaders are missing along the way. They always blame you, Perronnelle. Or a Northerner falls among thieves, they are always thieves with your face. De Montfort's horse casts a shoe, you were seen in the stables or the fodder stalls under the wall.'

Thus did my Phantom and my Guillemette keep me busy.

*   *   *

We stayed inside, myself to hide, Guillemette so her shoulder might stitch itself together.

It was towards evening on one of these days as we lay on our bed neither sleeping nor talking that I saw a sword lift itself through the hatch above the ladder – first the sword, then the sword arm, then the head, ghost white. It was Choucas, more beak on chin than ever. 'I'll claim my stallion,' he said. 'You'll need the sword, or some of you will. There's a De Montfort pennon coming down the road, and two score of horsemen under it.'

Gibbu came into the loft, pulling up through the port. He peered through a roof hole and said, 'Too many to stop with arrows.'

'There's nowhere for them to go but here,' Choucas the Jackdaw said.

Guillemette and I dressed quickly, and made certain other preparations. 'Best if I give myself up,' I said. 'If not they'll burn the Jackdaw's palace. He's to have a horse, Gibbu. Keep our swords till later.' I embraced Choucas. He was a hard man to kiss, having no mouth. At least the space between nose and chin was honest.

He was right. There was nowhere else along the road for horsemen to ride. They halted in front of the shed.

'I shall bring you your chance very soon,' Gibbu said. 'Ride hard.'

I was used to crusaders being cleanly caparisoned. These were the neatest I had yet seen. I stood on Choucas of Capestang's dirt floor and gazed out at some forty horsemen, with a young nobleman sitting swordless and helmetless in front of them.

'Perronnelle de Saint Thibéry,' he called, 'bastard and degenerate of the Trencavels?'

'Who seeks her hand in marriage?' I asked, stepping from the Jackdaw's shed as best I might.

'I am Amaury de Montfort. I have a warrant says I may burn you as a witch, and another says I may flay you alive for sorceries too numerous to delineate.'

530

'Burn me first,' I advised. 'Flay me after.'

'I have moreover the authority of my own opinion – '

'So have men all.'

'– which says I may quarter you as a noblewoman who encompasses treason, or hang you as a whore who dares the same.'

'Oh hang me as a whore,' I said. 'It sounds more comfortable to be hanged as a whore.' I had fashioned myself a cotte from a blanket and a string, and the Mute had done likewise, as I had no desire to be laughed at in a tunic, nor to tell them I wore mail underneath my makeshift *garde-corps*. They laughed nonetheless. Such was the state of Choucas' bedlinen. We stood in sackcloth indeed, and seemed unlikely to wait long for the ashes.

'Did you come here on a horse or a broomstick?'

'I came here on a gelding.' I waited for Choucas to lead me my Nano and hoped Gibbu had an arrow slotted. 'My woman has her mount as well.'

'Put both those whores astride the one horse. Then escort them to the village. We'll hang them together from a single tree.'

'You insult me with astride. I don't know this astride.'

'We will hang you with your legs together, never fear.'

Better than being burned, I thought, pretending to mount Nano with difficulty and having Guillemette come up after me.

Amaury de Montfort placed himself ahead, followed by a quartet of horsemen, then a fellow on either side of me holding strings to Nano's nose.

Nano was restless as they threaded him, and I thought now would be a good time, save for the density of riders at our back. These made the Hunchback's task difficult and our progress uncertain.

'Now!' Gibbu called.

I don't know which dances the most curious jig – a man with an arrow through the neckbone or a mare with a shaft up her fundament. The mounted man on one side of Nano received these blisters; the one not yet mounted on the other received them in the neck.

I stuck my heels into Nano's flanks and set his nose midway between the two rumps ahead of him, and drove him forward with my knees.

Simon de Montfort's son was doubtless a fine fellow at the joust, but quite unhandy when his horse was barged on the bottom. Someone, possibly himself, caught me a most mighty blow on the neck as we pushed past, opening my back with wet and I heard a man yell, presumably himself. Guillemette had cut him with a blade beneath the knee.

You can't gallop two to a horse. Nor could the rest of them come on fast beneath the weight of their shields, whereas we had no such nonsense. Also they were in a mêlée and not all mounted.

I heard cries, curses. I daresay Gibbu had shot some more down, or betrayed his sensibilities by damaging horses. He could send such a storm of arrows that brave men could feel they were being shot at by an army.

Then the Hunchback was past us, this time riding his mare and towing the better stallion. Guillemette shifted to it, and Nano strode lighter.

We rode towards the village with blood running freely down my back.

I don't know how far we rode. I could hardly sit saddle and felt numb beyond the shoulderbone. We left the flat places and climbed high into the garrigue. There, by a sunken garden, there was an ancient Gothic beehive, better than Dogskin Raymond's because entirely without enchantment.

The place stank of fox stalings and was littered with all manner of droppings. Gibbu swept it out with a branch, then built me a nest of leaves.

That night we ate a venison that tasted of pig or a pig that tasted of venison. Sanglier is always rich, so I assume it was the latter. My neck and back were sore, my head dizzy with blood loss. I was unable to keep my meat down, and soon lay in a fever.

532

CHANSON NINETEEN

In which the Virgin craves a war but meets a Saint instead, and rather than listen to evasions learns too many truths to follow.

The truth was that I had been cut through Choucas of Capestang's blanket as well as the tunic of a nameless crusader. God knows what filth was conveyed to my blood by the malignancies in the cloth. He knows this just as surely as He can explain how I came to be sliced across the backbone while Guillemette clung to my neck – save she stooped aside once or twice to hamstring our foe or snick the balls of their horses.

My fever was a ridiculous sickness, full of visions and shivers, but they breed such agues at Capestang and I had swallowed its damps for a month. According to Daddy a woman only catches a fever every seven years, and a man not at all unless a wife cooks him a pie with the mumps. My third seven years was a twelvemonth off and like not to come to me at all unless my knees and teeth fell silent and my shoulder-blades ceased their clattering.

Otherwise that Gothic beehive was a fine enough place in which to be ill. I lived in a fume of dog fox and vixen alike, as well as the stench of my bed which was lined with still-alive gorse and such other leaf as the Hunchback could find, till I stank as if Nano had swallowed a whole rack of nettle and done me the kindness to piddle on me.

Gibbu guarded the bothy, my Phantom found me food, Guillemette gave me water to drink and cooled my brow as she could. Sometimes I knew wakefulness, and at others was less than asleep. I had a vision of Simon de Montfort in a castle, of Amaury de Montfort in a castle, of all the De Montforts in a castle, and of all of us denying them food and then water. They would not die of the flux. These Northerners were too careful for the flux. They would wither very slowly with rheum and dry out like last year's sticks. Then we should cut their throats and treat with them.

535

It was dawn or a little after daylight through the bothy door. Guillemette said to me, 'Wake up, Perronnelle. You are better now. Your cheeks are quite fallen in and you have no breasts, but your back is healed and your bones are no longer chattering.'

I opened my eyes and closed them again but still looked at her.

'Moreover you stink and the shadows on top of your cheeks are blue, but you still have teeth and hair, and your nails when I squeeze them are pink, so we won't be laying you out yet, or not with cloves in your mouth and flax in your other orifices.'

'Where are both of my men?' I asked her.

'Two is it now – when one is too many for most women? Gibbu has gone to get succour, and I've only seen foxes else and a most winsome bear. Do you want to cuddle a bear? I am sure he'll oblige you in a minute.'

She showed me a bow and said Gibbu wished me to pull it till the muscles reformed in my back. He'd left us one each, and had been giving her instruction how to shoot with it, for she'd left her arbalesque at St Thibéry.

Sure enough there was a grunting and snouting at the beehive's opening, and then a crunching of bones as the prowler snuffled up what had been left him there. Guillemette sat with her bow advanced and arrow fitted, but old grouchy didn't try to come in, and at last went muttering away.

'I don't like shooting these men of yours,' she said, or I think she said. I closed my eyes properly then, and when I opened them Gibbu was back.

He had been gone three weeks. Ironface was with him. Not for the first time, I fell against Ironface and clung to him. 'I must leave this place,' I said. 'There are bears all about it, and it reminds me too much of Dogskin's prison on Alaric.'

He lowered me to my couch. 'You must stay here till you are recovered, Perronnelle. There is nowhere else that is safe. Were we on a pilgrim path, I am told there are places a person may buy food and harbour, and attract no attention. Here is no pilgrim path. Now, as I love you, Perronnelle – '

'"Love" me?' My Phantom had come to me when Ironface was not within a hundred leagues, so this could not be he.

'Aye, love you. Shall I say "*sic*" to it, or "*oc*"? Do you find that strange? I would not serve you else. You're a Southerner. You were brought up by a fool, and your mother played the harlot with a male of her own blood and was a heretic. Do you not think I love you, therefore?'

'Justify me that love.'

'I saw a naked girl abused by brutes in the midst of a shambles. So I fell in love. Do you find it strange? It was one of love's oldest dances. It is called Death and the Maiden.'

'I find nothing strange.' Nor did I. I had been impassioned with a dream and pleasured by women. I found nothing strange.

'In my armour there is a dwarf,' said he. 'What my shell piece holds is a half-man only.'

'I do not love that armour or its dwarf,' I said. 'Though I have seen them both and do respect them mightily. And yet I love, but do not know who I love.'

Ironface had taken off his head, like a mantis coupling with his mate. Without his casque or mask he wore a kind of inner breathing piece with larger eyeholes and mouthslot, and pierced all over with dots. He inclined this inner head gravely, and listened to me. Or pretended to. To talk to him was like consulting one of those silver pomanders that showy folk have when they're too lazy to stuff an orange with cloves. It was a beautiful experience, but extraordinarily futile. 'I make no answer to unknown love,' he said.

'Well, make one.'

'I offer none because I have none.'

'Well, construct me one.'

'Try prayer,' he offered. 'Do you pray?'

'Yes. But to which God? The Pope's God does not allow such feelings to exist in women. The Southern God – '

'Ssh – '

'The God of the Perfect Ones acknowledges these feelings exist, but says that flesh is the Devil's creation, and woman is more wicked than a horse.'

'God is the All Father and Only Creator.'

'You seem quite sure about it.'

'It is Christ's teaching.'

'How do you know?'

'Because any other opinion causes men to fry. You must talk to the Holy Dominic as we always intended. I'll arrange it.'

Another Ironface lie? He spoke as if he knew everyone.

'Dominic is the Pope's man.'

'He's not even his own man. He's God's man. He understands the teachings of the Perfect Ones and came here especially to show them their error. But I'll give you another reason for Dominic, greater far than your pewling love. There is to be a mighty battle. The armies are afoot and you together with Dominic could stop it.'

'This time Simon de Montfort will lose.'

'Someone will lose. I have yet to see these Northerners lose, haven't you, Perronnelle? Someone will lose, as you say.'

So I came to Prouille, as I had tried to come two years ago. When I attempted it then I had no price on my head, nor did I think of Dominic as an enemy. I had listened to Ironface and believed that the holy rogue could save my cousin. The Bastard had been with him, and that fact had stopped me, that and meeting the Crusade encamped across our road beyond the Madeleine.

Now the Bastard was dead and no one could deflect me. On the other hand Dominic was a Pope's man. Innocent had called his Crusade and Dominic had blessed it.

We met in the monastery garden. He did a very strange thing, which though I had heard it spoken of I had not seen before. He left his slippers on the path, then walked barefoot across the dirt and knelt before me.

'What does this mean?' I asked. I have never met a priest who was not full of tricks, and I told him so.

538

'It means that as I kneel to you, so I hope you will kneel with me, then both of us to God.'

I knelt and he stayed kneeling. 'So we pray together,' he said.

I made as if to seek the chapel.

'Kneel on God's pebbles,' he said. 'Not upon flagstones cut by men. Cutting those stones was some man's prayer. Kneeling on God's pebble is mine.'

'Do you bless this worm?' I asked him crossly.

'I bless it because God made it. His worm already kneels to Him. So does His wasp and His fruit weevil. His fly on His dung.'

'You are trapping me in a blasphemy,' I said, getting to my feet.

No, Perronnelle. It is contrary talk that blasphemes. To point to one of the atomies in Heaven or on Earth and claim God did not make it is to stand in error. To say the Devil made it, that is the heresy. I came here barefoot from Spain to argue that heresy away.' He had a voice much like Ironface's, harsh and foreign, yet full of music.

'Yet you blessed this Crusade,' I cried out. 'And the Crusade is full of evil.'

'What Christ calls I must bless,' he said. 'And when bad men call on Christ I must bless what they do, not for them but for the sake of the Christ they call on. I tried to stop this Crusade being called.' He climed slowly to his feet, as if kneeling gave him cramp. 'Once it was called, then I blessed it as I could.' He held me by the arm, not as priests had held me before, but as one needing my help. 'I'll ask you a question, Perronnelle de Saint Thibéry and Trencavel. If when the Crusade was called, and before it was called, this Raymond of Toulouse had been true to it, what excuse would greediness have used to take away his land?'

'Greediness is its own excuse,' I snorted.

'Only among lesser men. A great one needs his legality. Consider your poor cousin Trencavel. Had he taken the Cross as Peter of Aragon said he should, what harm could have come to his towns, and in whose name would it have come?'

'You truly believe that?'

'What I know now is that the same Peter of Aragon is here with a hundred thousand men, anxious to attack the very Cross he proclaimed just three years ago. You could deflect him, Perronnelle. You are the cousin of his dispossessed vassal. I hear you have influence with the men he attracts to him – Raymond of Toulouse, Raymond Roger of Foix, Pierre Roger de Cabaret and many more.'

I saw no way to give such a promise, and no way to protect my life here without it.

'I must go,' I said.

'You will be safe here, my lady Perronnelle. It's for certain I could build another monastery by selling you to your enemies, but your enemies are not my friends, and you are my only hope. Believe me when I say that.'

'We did not pray,' I said to him, hoping to get him on God's ground.

'We prayed. We do not need words to pray,' he said. 'Words are only good for argument. When I came among you Cathars, I came out of Spain. I came barefoot and I walked many paths on my knees. My kneecaps made my prayer, and their blisters were my penance. My words unmade the heresy. I needed no sword.'

I stayed at Prouille while Guillemette fretted and my neck healed. I met with the Holy Dominic often, never for long for he had his duties and his holy offices. I met him in the chapel, the library and many times in the grounds and gardens of the monastery.

Sometimes I thought he was trying to beguile me, others that he needed to convert me to views about the need for this Crusade. Certainly he fed my pride.

One day, as I was sitting with him, he said, 'You are lucky, Perronnelle. You do not need to make anything of yourself. All you need to do is believe in yourself as men believe in you.'

'So you desire friendship with my reputation, and not my person.'

'I want to be your friend when you are friends with yourself.'

'I cannot,' I said. 'I have a voice that sits in my head and a face that lies in my dreams.'

'So have we all,' he said. 'We call it our soul.'

'The voice preaches me war. It speaks prophecies. The face kisses my sleep and arouses my flesh.'

'All people have dreams. All people are flesh. Even when there is no other flesh near, we know we are flesh. So let us talk first of your dreams.' He rose as if he could do so quickly and dismissively, but he was always being called by some prayer or other, as such people are. 'The voice has offered you fire, the face shows itself in water. Both are God's elements. You must choose, Perronnelle de Saint Thibéry, between Fire and Water, striving and love. They are different beasts. They are like the bear and the horse. They cannot drink at the same spring.'

'My love feels like air.' In truth, I remembered Thistle's flesh burning in Mummy's fire, and the Bastard's face covering my own in the water.

'That is a nun's love, Perronnelle. Not the world's love. God loves in air.'

'If my love is in the world, why can't I match his face?'

'No one can tell love's face until they are at peace with themselves. It would be simpler to find that peace if any of your companions were truly as they seem.'

'One,' I said, 'is a woman disguised as a man.'

'Is that all?' he said, urgent to leave. 'Is that all, Perronnelle de Saint Thibéry? That is an easy shift. You have one near you who hides his love in the earth and one who dresses his face in fire. Woman to man is an easy shift.'

He interested me, but only as jesters do. They doff their hats and speak riddles, clap their hands and are gone.

Gibbu didn't like it at Prouille, didn't want me to be there. He took Guillemette to the river each day, teaching her to shoot reeds as they rippled in the stream. She couldn't shoot reeds, and he couldn't teach her. Neither could shoot at Prouille. 'A bow pulls only in calm,' he said. 'When the bowman is angry, he makes crooked flight.'

When I asked him what he meant he banged bread on the table. The monks didn't bake proper loaves, but rolled dough into balls no bigger than horses' turds with crust all the way to the middle. They were better for banging than eating, and Gibbu had already thrown one to knock a single magpie dead inside a tree. 'They have broken my teeth,' he said. 'So I use them to kill bad luck.'

'Why don't you like it here?' I persisted.

'You are wrong in the head, Perronnelle. Such places keep you wrong. When you talk to a priest who is pure – and this one is rarer than that, he is holy – he talks of nothing but dreams and voices. You already have nonsense enough of your own. I've lain near you at night and heard you mumble.'

'Gibbu,' I chided, 'where have you found so many words of late? I preferred you when you had none.'

'I've travelled three years among women,' he said. 'And I've lain near you at night.'

'Tell him why we stay here, Ferblant.'

Ironface had been sitting quietly. Now he chuckled and said, 'We stay because I'm hungry for prayer.'

'Dwarves and tinkers don't pray.' Gibbu spoke crossly and took Guillemette outside, perhaps to spear fishes, perhaps to throw bread at the moon.

'Not in your faith, perhaps,' Ironface called after him. 'They do in mine,' he muttered.

'And what faith is that?' I asked him. I had disputed with him before, but never received proper answers.

Nor did I get one now. 'You're unquiet with yourself, Lady Perronnelle, unquiet, ill-tempered, *lumpish*. I've an instinct what will quieten you, but I still believe prayer is a kinder answer. As to myself ... ?' He fidgeted on the battered, metallic stalks of legs. 'Well, if I tell you ...'

542

'You told me too many things, all different.'

'Exactly. So you have my permission to ask the Holy Dominic about me.'

I had used up my time with Dominic, and well he knew it.

'Dominic will see you once more if you say Ironface sent you.'

Was this another lie? He was at his pretence of prayer again.

Dominic was sad when I called to him, sad then amused. 'So,' he said, 'you are not interested in saving Oc for me. You prefer to save a little piece of yourself.'

'Your priests will save Oc. Your priests will save it in your way. They will not save it in blood, but there will be blood. Then they will save it.'

'Do you think so? Look at the bishops hereabouts. One is a great theologian but keeps concubines. Another, undoubtedly devout, is tolerant of heretics among his clergy. Then there is that Arnold Almaric, now Archbishop of Narbonne, who burns people to please Simon de Montfort's greed and his own vengeful pride but disobeys Pope Innocent's instructions. If only your counts and your kings – and I think of Aragon as being half your king – if only your great ones would be friends with Innocent they could clear such people out.'

'And clear out the heresy as well?'

'The heresy is evil. You think it is innocent. I tell you it is evil. What good can it do to a woman to feel that her flesh and the products of her flesh are as the Devil made them?'

'It says the same to a man.'

'Men have ways of finding themselves exempt – haven't you noticed that, Perronnelle?'

'They find themselves exempt in more faiths than that one, which I know best as the faith of the shepherds. I never saw a shepherd place a woman on his fire.'

'In you, my lady of Saint Thibéry, I see the whole problem of Oc. You are not a heretic, and yet you defend the heresy.'

'You said I preferred to save a little piece of myself. What was that piece?'

'Your curiosity. Well, I will tell you about this man you know as Ironface and sometimes Ferblant. I will not say his name, for a long time ago he asked me to bury it.

'Ironface was once a monk, a foundling taken in by a monastery and adopted as its jester. Although remaining a wit, he grew up to rise rapidly. Rather than serve his own interests, he joined my mission to save your heretics, and came with me barefooted from Spain.'

'Barefooted in armour?'

'Then he needed no such shell. Then he was a man. Six years ago a group of plotters, some say heretics, some say Count Raymond's servants – well, you know the story, they stabbed to death the Papal Legate to Toulouse. The man we speak of tried to prevent the assault. He was a bellicose man, saw himself as a monk militant, and before coming to me always wore a sword. That day he had no sword. He was ridden down by the plotters' horses and suffered terrible wounds to his face and limbs. His legs had to be sawn off at the thigh and knee.'

We paused, as if there could be no more to say, but the Holy Dominic had horrors he needed to expel. 'When a man's face is on top of his head, the temptation is to leave it there. A bold friend can push it back again. He had such a friend.' He spread his hands modestly. 'He is, if you like, not ugly, but different.' Again we waited, as if the pause was itself a prayer. 'So the accident deprived him of his features, his legs, and some say his private matters as well. There was no possibility that a man who had lost so much should live. I began to pray for him, because I saw nothing else to do.'

'It was a miracle?'

'A miracle? What is that? Sometimes I think the morning is a miracle.' The Holy Dominic sighed and said, 'The injured man didn't thank God for his life, and certainly not me. The leeches refused to cut him, so did the nearest butcher. The barber wouldn't even draw forth his blood. We remade him with the help of a blacksmith and a slaughterer from the fair.'

After hearing this account of Ferblant's injuries, and still being no nearer to his name, I felt a great desire to hug, squeeze and kiss him – kiss him, I think, most of all. But you can't plant love on a tinker's plate, and the thought of the disfigurement and pain behind his mask brought tears to my eyes, especially since I remembered him as he was on Alaric, having boldly pushed his armour at the Goddess Malpolon, the fiendish female Duke, and sent his own dwarf-like body scuttling forth to combat from between La Mamelonne's legs, from which place had no man ever run willingly before.

So Ironface had let blacksmiths and tinkers make him. He had put aside love and dressed himself in fire. Then this new creature, armed with all the militancy he had felt before meeting Dominic, had cured his own pain by righting wrongs, rescuing Guillemette, saving the Fish Girl, challenging for myself and lending his protection to Gibbu in ways I could not explain, because sometimes it seemed it was the Hunchback who protected us all.

If Ironface had put on fire, by burning the product of fire, how was it that Gibbu put on earth?

And where should Perronnelle unmask love, or see his face in a pure water?

Caput Twenty

Wherein the flower of Southern
chivalry aided by forty thousand Tranters from Aragon sets
a spike in De Montfort's balls
but suffers from slippery hands.

We left on horseback, and Dominic of Calaruega led us on foot towards the gate. I am used to parting from priests and such-like holy men. They always smile at me brightly, but with a sad mist of expectancy in their eye as if I am a lover who has just made them pregnant with a child we must work hard to nurture in the days to come.

Dominic did not look in the least bit *enceint*. He bore no expectations of me whatsoever, certainly not one of hope. He simply had his monks hand us up bread and wine for our journey, patted Ironface's knee, or rather the joint of his armour where it folded against his saddle, then said, 'Water or Fire, Perronnelle? Water is always welcome in a land as parched as this.'

'And fire has already done too much damage,' I agreed.

That was a mistake. He saw advantage in my concurring with him, bade me dismount, then led me back to that piece of dirt in which he was able to perceive God so clearly.

'I do not take up arms against the Cross,' I said. 'I make war only against Simon de Montfort.'

'It is a distinction that many men try to make,' he said, 'but it cannot be made. Still, I bless you, Perronnelle.'

We knelt on the holy dirt we had knelt on before, and I gazed at the selfsame pebble, but it told me nothing new.

When I returned to them at the gate, my friends regarded me sadly, as if I had loitered behind for a kiss. We rode away in a sulk, but determined to be in time for King Peter's battle.

It is easy to track down an army. A great pathway of horse dung leads you unerringly to an enormous concourse of whores. You sniff out the horse dung. You listen for the whores.

What you hear at first are the flies. But among the common buzz as we rode along the way, we were able to pick up some revealing gossip.

Apparently there were three armies in the field. King Peter had ridden over from Spain, as the Holy Dominic had told me, accompanied by several thousand of his most hardy knights and a whole cavalcade of horsemen inferior in rank but of dazzling ability with the lance and the sword. He had also brought some *pietones*, as he agreeably called those base fellows who work with their feet planted on the soil. Some of our wayside buzzers mentioned the number forty, others said forty thousand, no doubt remembering the number of days Christ spent in the wilderness. I offer both figures to you. I saw no live foot-soldiers from Spain before Muret, but a deal of dead ones afterwards, many of them undoubtedly King Peter's Aragonese.

Count Raymond Roger of Foix had also brought an army of horsemen into the field, and his son Roger Bernard again rode with him, and for all I know Aimery and Wolf did as well, though I never saw them. Nor is it clear to me whether or not he brought any foot thrusters, who in my opinion are the proper stuff of battle. You need men to stand firm with bow, crossbow and pike, and a few people with vision, such as myself, on horseback to lead them. I speak of the ideal battle, of course, and as I remember that I have seen men stand near the Count of Foix, rather than ride about him, I am reminded that there are several reasons why a knight should from time to time dismount from his horse.

The man who undoubtedly brought pedestrian warriors by the thousand into the field was my own leader and relative by marriage, Count Raymond of Toulouse. Some of them had come in order to share in a marvellous victory, others with the avowed intention of joining Simon de Montfort, and achieving a marvellous victory the other way. But this is masculine politics, and as such forms no part of my thinking.

The only strategic question of interest is why these three

mighty armies should have chosen to station themselves about Muret. There were enough of them to have gone to Paris or even Rome and brought the whole wretched Crusade to a satisfactory conclusion. Instead, a concourse of some fifty thousand men, or two hundred thousand according to the balladeers, decided to besiege a town of so little value to either side that it was garrisoned only by three dozen of Simon de Montfort's least well-armed veterans. Here he had left his wounded, his old men with stiff joints, and his diseased, all of them without horses. I can only conclude that to my uncle-in-law Count Raymond, the odds must have appeared exactly right, and accept what is now the common view that he did improve as a strategist throughout the entire campaign.

Or perhaps a beleaguered garrison was, again, as at St Martin Lalande, to be the cheese, and this chivalrous ring of steel the mousetrap. For, the buzzers said (or perhaps the flies themselves were talking to us by now, the day was so hot and Nano in such a slimy sweat), one thing was certain: Simon de Montfort was riding here with his most trustworthy ally, his brother-in-law Bouchard de Marly and the few hundred horsemen they could muster between them at this time of the year. Simon de Montfort was not a leader to leave one of his garrisons unsupported. Unlike my uncle of Toulouse, Simon was a man of honour who knew clearly what side he was on. His side was unquestionably his own.

The flies also said that De Montfort and Bouchard de Marly would already have reached Muret, were it not for Simon's need to stop frequently and pray. As always when he sensed numbers were against him he summoned God's own legions to his aid, or that's how the rumour went, and the rumour gave a meaningful laugh and pointed out that we on our side had more warriors in this one field of battle than God could muster angels in all his nine orders throughout the Kingdom of Heaven.

During his frequent halts for prayer, Simon de Montfort managed to wage a very damaging war of words. Firstly he

551

sent messages to the citizens of Toulouse offering to be their count if they would only be so kind as to knock Raymond on the head for him. We who dwelled more widely throughout the county would not have been beguiled by such a nonsense, as we knew what wickednesses Simon himself was capable of. The Toulousains on the other hand had quite enough of Raymond, and being like most townsfolk over nimble of fancy were always on the lookout for a change. Simon's messages were eagerly received in some quarters.

He also wrote a very clear letter to Pope Innocent. King Peter had been Pope Innocent's personal favourite among all the Christian kings. Suddenly, upon the receipt of Simon's letter, he decided that he didn't like Peter at all and ordered him back to Spain. As King Peter himself said, the Pope's missive was cruel enough to have decided him to become a heretic, if only he could make head from tail of what our heresy was about.

Then, quite by chance, Simon stopped for a final bout of prayer at the great abbey of Boulbonne. There the abbot allowed him to intercept a letter from Peter of Spain to a mistress of his who lived at one of the local châteaux, informing her of his wish to call on her. Simon had the abbot make copies of King Peter's supposed *billet doux* and sent it widely abroad, with a commentary upon it stating that the philandering King had not ridden here on matters of state or to succour his vassals, but to wriggle his loins around the cushions with other men's wives.

In fact, Peter the Second of Aragon wasn't the man to write letters to ladies merely to announce his intentions towards them. If he arrived to find someone had been taken off by her husband or was firmly locked away in one of Solomon of Gerona's belts, he would beguile himself instead with the women he kept in his luggage.

Not everybody knew this so, all in all, Simon de Montfort halted for some highly productive prayers as he rode to succour his garrison at Muret. He might be hurrying more slowly than he would if he had less on his mind, but he was still moving much too quickly for the three armies waiting for him.

Muret is a pretty town with walls as inconsequential as those of Le Bourg outside Carcassonne, but with a most imposing fortress beside it. The ramparts of this place are themselves no taller than a reasonably lofty scaling ladder, but a well-conducted garrison would see to it that ladders were difficult to position. This is because its *donjon* stands at the apex of the confluence of the River Louge with the Garonne, so even a modest amount of activity from ballisters or longbowmen would make the fortress impossible to reach, and the town only accessible from the further end where the angle of land is broader. Thus a thoughtful concentration of resources would render the town impregnable. Fortunately for us, its commander had no resources to concentrate. Simon's arrival, when he got here, would strengthen his defences considerably, but do nothing for his ability to counter attack, as Muret was a tight little hole to get out of.

In order to reach it, or rather to reach our armies in the fields and orchards round about, we had to cross the Garonne which is a noble flood at this point, infinitely wider than our own pretty little Hérault at St Thibéry, which is much of a muchness with the Louge, though the Louge is deeper.

Our crossing was facilitated by the great flotilla of boats that had come down from Toulouse to participate in the entertainment or simply to witness the fun. Muret was invested by water as well as land. In addition, the great bulk of the Count's militia had voyaged downstream in a huge armada of barges from Toulouse in order to arrive in the field of Mars with rested feet. So the land warriors arrived on the finny flood, in much the same way as the doughty *pietones* sometimes make shift to position themselves adjacent to their foes by riding up in carts or on the backs of donkeys. *The enemy may kill or cripple you if he will. Don't do it for him with corns or fatigue.* So writes the Great Wizard,

553

and I was glad to find myself at last among warriors who had a grasp of the rudiments of their calling.

Sailors themselves are peculiar people, as I knew from talking to those who voyaged up to St Thibéry in order to listen to my mother. It took us some time to find one of them who would let me float across the Garonne in his boat while sitting upon Nano. Gibbu dismounted, Guillemette dismounted. Even Ironface cried aloud for Gibbu to lift him from his saddle. Although a person of substance, Ironface was not a great leader of men. I, on the other hand, was Perronnelle de Saint Thibéry, the Maid of the Mountains, and people expected to see me on my horse.

Once we reached the further bank, the horse dung no longer lay in cobbles, but in tiny mountains, little alps. Clearly we were close to the field of glory. We followed this chivalric harvest until we reached a fording place in the Louge, well south of the town. Then the brown trail began to circle about, rather like a snake that had snoozed in a winy vat.

Strangely enough, both the Aragonese and the Toulousain encampments were some distance to the north-west of Muret itself, in pleasing meadowland beyond a third river, La Saudrune. Closer to Muret itself there were orchards, some of them walled, and vineyards. It was a beautiful landscape in which poets might dream of fair women and lovers twang on the harp, but I saw little chance of the Aragonese cavalry being able to move briskly through it in their formidable close order, or for Raymond Roger of Foix to lead one of his breakneck charges. Raymond of Toulouse's cavalry concerned me less, as I doubted whether my uncle-in-law would even get himself on the move until long after the battle was won.

Soon we came to some pretty pavilions in red and gold. As we rode upon them I was challenged by a guard in that guttural Spanish speech that all guards have, even the English ones, and very nearly placed under confinement.

'This is Perronnelle de Saint Thibéry of the Trencavels,'

Ironface said loftily, with the Aragonese tongue which is very like our own.

'*El virgen das montes*,' Gibbu translated in his best Catalan.

Once again someone had assumed that since I was a woman I must be a whore.

In what one might generally term the Toulousain lines, the whores had been enclosed within an enormous pavilion to prevent the army's backs and more especially its bottoms from becoming afflicted with sunburn. Sunburn gives a nobleman a very sickly seat upon a horse, and a great commander of battles has already written his opinions that to ride upon the enemy with a lance is far less perilous to a warrior's well-being than spurring into a pretty woman beneath a hedge.

The Spaniards took a different view of the matter, and lucky I was to escape them. A great number of ladies of pleasure placed themselves on offer to King Peter's Aragonese, attracted firstly by the splendours of their armour, and more especially by another consideration I shall mention later. The Spaniards gathered all of these, whether they were bawds, scrub-girls, old-time dickory dollies, masseuses, bagneuses, bagnio testers, lice-pickers, hedgerow whores, handcart hoydens, pack-saddle strumpets, palfrey-by-moonlight dalliers, lick-prickers or local peasant girls looking for fun, and shut them within an open enclosure which they walled rapidly with an impenetrable buckthorn barricade two fathoms tall and a fodder deep. This was to prevent the wenches from infecting their horses or blurring the magnificent bosses in King Peter's shields by breathing on them the better to adjust their faces. The Spaniards had to line up naked to be attended by these women, so as not to damage their armour, and once their first excitement had abated this embarrassing fact reduced the flow of men to a steady trickle.

After the first thunderstorm the whores soon set up a clamour to be released from this enclosure, and sued to be allowed to work in the Toulousain marquee, even if they had to share cushions.

The Aragonese refused to release them, again presenting as a reason the fact that the way to their allies' lines led past the main paddocks. So the ladies stayed there without work or wine for a month or so, many of them being released only when the Holy Dominic recruited them as nuns, or when peasants whose farms had lain in the path of what had by now been several armies wandered disconsolately forth to restock themselves with wives. It is not, as I say, a history I give you, but the straitened circumstances of those that History largely forgets, by which I mean poor men and all classes of women.

There is talk of armadas of corsairs that may soon leave the sea and sail across the sky to empty their chamber pots on us and rain down pestilence and burning darts. And, of course, man had and then lost the flying horse. Once a season after market I used to hear Daddy, and not him alone, talk of going into the mountains to saddle himself a dragon. When men can sail above us with devices such as these, who will take thought of women then? A crusade above the treetops bears no thinking of, still less above the clouds. Who will build their bonfires so high?

I was thinking these thoughts, and dreaming these dreams, when I nearly walked into the backside of a horse, and then stepped among a wreathing of legs more closely intertwined than grass snakes attempting to swallow the same toad. I saw a pair of brown hands walk like diminutive spiders upon a breast of truly pyrenean splendour, and attempt to lay siege to a nipple as noble as the airy Château de Quéribus or Raymond de Pereilhe's *donjon* on Mount Ségur itself.

'Mamelie!' I cried. 'My Mamelie!' ignoring her friend entirely.

It is impossible to express the delight I felt at my reunion with La Mamelonne. She had an Aragonese knight between her legs at the time as I have indicated, but dismounted side-saddle and left him in a swoon kissing daisies in the grass while she stole away from him to embrace me. Another knight, and both of their horses, waited patiently in line behind him, gazing at his friend's undulating bottom and her imagined shape in the grass.

'I often say that making love to me is a religious experience,' she sighed, embracing me fondly all the while. 'And here you may see an example. That poor warrior, many leagues and days on horseback away from his wife in her lonely chastity belt in Spain, can take me in his arms and fall immediately in love with the Universe. Look at him licking daisies as if they be God's own eye, and writhing upon a dock leaf as if floating upon a constellation of angels.'

She stooped, and picked a golden piece from his belt, as indeed she was able to, since there was no embargo about dress in her field, as she had set herself up well away from the thorn-hedged compound. 'I had thought to take only silver,' she explained. 'But when I step aside from my work and see what pleasure I give them . . .' She blew upon the coin, then indicated the labours of her companion, the once reluctant Mitten, the shepherdess whore from the high pastures. 'Look at Mitten,' she said generously. 'They line up to avail themselves of her, especially the near-sighted, and she offers it to them with a will, but she only gives them the one thing and they've had it before.

'Praise God you have called me once more to fight on your side,' she enthused. 'Fighting is so much more simple than whoring, because when it comes to battles I have no reputation to consider. I have done mighty things,' she added modestly, 'and much I hear myself spoken of where men drink wine, but all those deeds have been taken as your own, Perronnelle, and used to augment your notoriety.'

'Before God!' I cried.

'Aye, before God. The Almighty has his scrolls in the sky, and when I lift my eyes to Heaven I see the deeds I have done in battle written in flame upon the eternal parchment as your own.'

557

'Before God,' I cried again, 'and his Son, before Mary his blessèd mother, and before Mary who is Oc's own Saint, the Everlasting Weeper, I stood before you and beside you whatever you did.'

'You're a virgin, Perronnelle. And that is why I love you and will follow you and freely lend you my deeds. A virgin among the flowers of Venus and a virgin on the field of Mars.'

I could not bear to argue with my friend, so was relieved to see Mitten and the Fish Girl finish work in the distance, tidy their pieces of field, and rush to join us.

We all kissed for a long time, and so did Guillemette. The Fish Girl turned somersaults of glee, and then danced cartwheeling about us.

Mitten was enjoying her whoring now it was no longer with shepherds who had such a mean expectancy of her. These Spaniards, in particular, had some beguiling tricks for a woman. One was a fetch they had caught from the Arabs, who were of course everywhere about them. This was to wash their bodies all over and all under at least once a month with water, instead of letting their own sweat cleanse them as intended by God. Such a device is unnecessary in a husband, but makes a stranger easier to know.

The Fish Girl had found a coherent tongue. None of her friends could understand her, but the Spaniards thought she was delightful. She had clearly been bred in Spanish. Then many fish are, such as the swordfish and the octopus and a multitude of tumbling monsters like them.

These demoiselles spoke only one word between them to trouble our reunion. 'That Raymond de Brousses,' La Mamelonne said, 'Dogskin Raymond, my former master – '

I felt my veins curdle at mention of his name, much as if I had been bitten by a viper. I also experienced such a numbness in my secret parts I might almost have sat upon a toad, the one with venom in the warts on its back. 'Urrgh!' I said, it being the sort of noise Mummy told me I mustn't make simply because the milk had caught the thunder. 'Urrgh!'

'Exactly, my Perronnelle. He came whining, wheedling

and wanting me back. Of course I told him no! He even offered me some new cards, and those I kept.' She was still stark naked (or should I rather say noble and nude?) but she took a small key from a chain round her neck, and reached into herself to unlock a little casket. Then she brought forth her magical cards, all of them anointed with depictions from the Mage's prophetic Arcanum. 'I'm afraid you'll not like what you see here, Perronnelle . . .'

Nor did I. Each of these newly painted pieces she produced from the Pandora's Box of her thighs gazed up at me with my own face. Not only was I Temperance, Strength, and the Supplicant and High Priestess, I was the Devil and Death as well. The World turned round my features and, when the Wheel of Fortune spun, I was both the executioner and the condemned, for both the breaker and the broken were my own self. Once again the Hanged Man was a woman, and that woman was as me. I was the twins who tumbled from the Riven Tower, and nowhere did anyone but Perronnelle appear, save in the Lovers, which was a most lascivious card, and showed a naked Dogskin fondling me by the breast. I gazed long at this, and I swear his fingers moved.

I handed this horror back to her. 'What happened next?'

'I spat in his eye. I was chewing a garlic at the time to clear my throat for business, with a little leaf of wormwood and wild peppermint. His eye enflamed with an instant sty, closed itself in a mauve swelling, and presently came up in a monstrous carbuncle that would have lasted an ordinary mortal a fortnight. But being a sorcerer, he summoned some duke or other from the twilight and caused her to gnaw it away. He was angry with me, Perronnelle. What I would call enraged. He threatened to dissolve any bones and bring out my brain in a pimple, so I had to buy him off.'

'How did you manage that?'

'He lusts for me, Perronnelle. He lusts after both of us. But, for me, he – well – *lusts*. He demanded me like a dog. And then used me like a donkey. And then he changed us both into swans and he took me flying to some tumbledown old Mill he said was yours, and had me all goosy-gander under the wheel and inside the race. Then he started pecking my wing feathers out, and laughed, and said he would leave me there. As a pregnant swan, Perronnelle. This other mad bird swam up to me then – '

'Queen Blanche.'

'And said she was his wife and what was I doing with him? Then, after he and this offensive old bird had frightened me almost to death, he let me fly back again.' She reached about her still naked person and found a puncheon of honey wine which she shared with us all.

'Anyway he has made a plot to keep your virginity in a jar and sell your body to Simon de Montfort, who has already contracted him in the matter. Lord Ferblant here is a part of it, as he hates him equally, but of course does not lust after him.'

'There's plenty that do,' Ironface said, but otherwise seemed as chastened by Mamelie's words as I was.

Meanwhile, I had a battle to arrange.

I rode straight to the Pavilion of the Commanders, as it was called. This was the biggest tent in the Toulousain lines, and even grander than the spread of canvas beneath which they kept the two armies' strumpets.

I was received with great honour by my uncle-in-law, and by Raymond Roger of Foix. This time I wasn't mistaken for a whore, even though I was accompanied by whores, because the whores were all shut up in enclosures, and that fact enabled these great ones to concentrate their minds on me, now that I enjoyed a reputation that rode everywhere before my horse. (I had, on this occasion, left Nano outside.)

'What we must do is dig a ditch around the town,' I proposed, 'and deny these crusaders food and water.'

'What we must do is kill this De Montfort with my sword,' Count Raymond Roger of Foix countered. 'After all, he's coming here to kill Count Raymond, King Peter

and myself with his own sword. And he brings friends eager
to assist him!'

This was a distressing news. It added a most unpleasant
ingredient to a conflict that had been in the main friendly
until now.

Seemingly my uncle-in-law was to blame. I was so surprised
to hear that old Raymond the Sixth had actually acted on a
scale large enough to compel Simon de Montfort's attention
that I almost missed the rest of the tale.

Apparently, before coming to Muret he had laid siege to
the castle at Pujol, one of Lord Simon's other forts. This
was as surprising to me as hearing he had got out of his bed
this morning and not turned round to find some five or six
women still tucked up inside it. Yet here was the old fellow
blinking and smiling at us and assuring me it was true.

'So what followed?' I asked him.

The Count of Toulouse, idiot that he was, had taken the
opportunity to butcher the garrison. De Montfort did not
take kindly to such matters. When such a wanton atrocity had
been visited upon his people by one of our local commanders
in the village of Bram, and some of his retainers been hanged
and some blinded, he had ridden there in his wrath and
plucked forth eyes from a hundred heads in return, and
tongues as well, leaving one man one eye to lead the rest
to their masters, and allowing that man his tongue also to
make known great Simon's displeasure.

Raymond of Toulouse had this time taken the matter
further. He had executed three of De Montfort's staunchest
friends at Pujol: Pierre de Cissey, Simon le Saxon and
Roger des Essarts, barons who had been with him since
the beginning. So now the whole crusading chivalry
was incensed at the slaughter of three noble comrades
in arms.

Factors such as these, together with the inescapable
circumstance that battles are still fought largely by men,
threatened to cause the coming conflict in Muret to degenerate into a brawl, but such matters were beyond my control,

561

and even the best of us can only make do with what we have on such occasions.

This sorry tale was just being completed, for my benefit, when a trumpet sounded outside, or without as we say, and some three dozen knights in spurs filed in. They all bore the red and gold mirrors that served them as shields, and which I had last seen at Carcassonne when I led a thousand of these Aragonese to their glorious deaths before the walls of the Citadel there. Before that, of course, I had admired a dazzling display of their ironmongery in the great hall of my cousin's castle.

I was wondering what this latest tableau of glittering manhood and polished metal might mean when the trumpet again sounded without. Then, to a long finger roll on the tabor, building to a thunder of drums proper, in strode King Peter of Aragon. Oh, the splendid informality of the man.

He scarcely noticed the two great counts, but such was my reputation or King Peter's eye for anything dressed in the flesh of a woman that he made straightway towards myself. Constance de Coulobres had taught me how to stoop before a great one, and Mummy had told me never to do so. His Majesty was highly taken by the resulting compromise. He seized my hand warmly and at the same time began to caress my arm near the elbow in a most pleasurable fashion.

'It's a good job that cousin of yours died before he could take the advice I gave him,' he said. 'Or the whole sorry business of this Crusade would be even more complicated than it is already.'

'He did take it,' I said. 'And he's dead because of it. Also he gave away his lands to the Northern counts who gave it to Simon de Montfort.'

'*My* lands, my dear Maid of the Mountains, *my* lands. That is why I am here. I have no quarrel with the Pope, nor with the French King provided he keeps to his little island. My war is against De Montfort.'

'Many people have tried to make that distinction,' I quoted, 'but it cannot be made.'

He did not congratulate me for such an observation. I don't believe he was listening to me, judging from the excitement he was finding in whatever he could feel above my elbow.

The King was just beginning to grow warm faced and breathe rather more loudly when a messenger came in. 'Simon de Montfort and forty score of his horsemen are within the garrison at Muret,' he announced.

King Peter released my arm with an oath. 'Did you count the forty or did you count the score?' he asked the messenger. And with this pleasing jest, and with no further discussion of strategy, he strode out again.

'Now he is walled up,' I told Foix and Toulouse, 'we can starve him into a shadow.'

'I don't want him starved into a shadow,' Raymond of Foix shouted. 'I need to cut him in two with my sword. If he's a shadow, how can I do that?'

'My son-in-law's relative has got a point,' Count Raymond of Toulouse said. 'I think we should allow her to develop it.'

'We can dig a trench,' I said. 'Meanwhile the engineers can fire rocks at him with their trebuchets. They always enjoy doing that.'

'Trenches are all very well for engineers,' the Count of Foix fretted. 'But they are no entertainment for noblemen sitting on horseback.'

'We can't starve him,' Count Raymond of Toulouse said. 'I've just remembered. My brother Baldwin is on his side again this week, so he'll be in there with him.'

'Baldwin is very fat,' I told him. 'Starving would do him good. All his women complain that Baldwin is too fat.'

'Well,' Count Raymond pondered.

None of us could guess that Simon had ridden into Muret only to rinse his teeth, say another prayer, and ride boldly out again. Nor that, while he was rinsing his teeth, Alain de Roucy and Florent de Ville had stolen to church ahead of him to state on oath that they would kill Peter of Aragon.

*   *   *

563

It was clear to me I should gain nothing more for the moment. But as Mummy used to say of Daddy, 'A little and often. A woman gets little by going on at a man, for he has no stamina for listening. Wait till he thinks you have had time enough to forget an idea, then remind him gently that you haven't. He'll soon give up.' With Uncle Raymond, I knew this would always be true, because he could never make up his mind. With the Count of Foix I wasn't so sure. I might have time. I might not. What a pity I didn't consider Simon de Montfort in relation to this question of time.

I took my leave of the two Counts. Since they and the King had all three corps of horsemen each under personal command, I thought I could best beguile the intervening time among the foot-soldiers and engineers. They would certainly profit from some experienced advice.

Ironface had other plans. He decided he would ride with Peter of Aragon. 'Now we have Spaniards in the field,' he said, 'I know where my place is.' In truth, he was after no more than carrying one of those gold embossed shields, with their four crimson bars or gules, but I let it pass.

'I thought you were a Castilian,' I said with a certain petulance nonetheless.

'To attempt to unravel the political geography of the great Iberian Peninsula,' he countered, 'is as futile as explaining the female anatomy by scratching lewd pictures in the dirt.'

I had seen these mysteries scratched in the dirt many times, including once by a courtier to amuse the Count of Foix and his son Roger Bernard. But Ironface was right. Such scribbles explain nothing, especially through the scales of a mermaid, and I daresay Spain is similar.

Meanwhile, I hurried to the banks of the Louge to seek out my militia men.

These militias of Toulouse had arrived by boat, as I already knew, and were very fresh in consequence. I began to see it might be best to ensure one's troops were kept tired if one wished to restrain them within the bounds of military good order and discipline.

'Never mind the Counts and the King,' one said. 'I think we should get some ladders and go up the wall.'

'Dig a trench and starve De Montfort out,' I advised.

'Put some knives in our teeth and go up the wall.'

'Dig a trench.'

'I think we should kick that cow on the head and her uncle of Toulouse with her. Baldwin's got the best idea, fat silly bastard though he is. I think we should let De Montfort be Count of Toulouse.'

'We've got enough of a trench here as it is,' the first one said, indicating the little stream of the Louge which flowed against Muret's walls before making confluence with the Garonne. 'And it's already flooded. Perhaps we should throw in that windbag Perronnelle and use her to float ourselves across.'

I thought it best to let them fetch some ladders.

Just across the stream from us, and only a short spit away, stood the Church of St Sirnan. Outside it, a Northern squire was holding his master's horse. It had been there during the whole of our frank discussion about tactics, an enemy we could gaze upon but not touch, as it required ladders to reach up to it from water level, and there was no certainty that there would be enough of a margin to plant them on.

Simon de Montfort strode out of the church. I had gazed upon him three times already, and I knew the face well. God knows why he needed his horse. He wasn't going anywhere. Save that a great one always rides a horse.

He placed his left leg in the stirrup and the chain-mail on his calf came undone. He brushed away his squire's hands and tugged on a broken strap to tighten the length remaining.

How we jeered. Or, to be fair to Mummy's training of me, how the lewd fellows about me jeered.

He shot us an angry glance, and removed his foot from the stirrup. Whereupon his horse turned and banged at him with its head, almost knocking him off his feet.

He turned towards us, calmly enough, and said, 'Chuckle

on, stall-keepers of Toulouse. I shall be among you in a moment to chase you all home.'

How we loved him for it. He had only his squire with him, and no more than eight hundred horses in the whole town, and here we stood in our thousands.

'As for you, woman of St Thibéry, I hold warrants for your arrest, and a seal against your execution. There are those about you who will parcel your body over to me, and make my parchments good.'

Then he put himself back into his saddle, like a man who meets sadly with fate.

What he did next he did decisively, and clearly with some saint's magic upon him. He rode quickly back behind the church where, unknown to us, his knights and other mounted men were already drawn up in three squadrons. Guillaume des Barres led the first, Bouchard the second, Simon took the third. We heard them command their march, and understood their trumpets. We did not see them leave Muret by the Southern Gate, nor notice them cross the Louge by the little bridge at Salles.

Peter of Aragon was already in the field, probably intending to storm up to the town and frighten it into throwing open its gates. It is hard to know what else he intended, unless it was to startle a fox.

Raymond Roger of Foix decided to ride along with him, perhaps sensing that his horsemen were growing stale and in need of a gallop. They tried to put themselves into better order when they heard Simon's trumpets, and to tighten their cavalcade through the orchards when they realized he had been imbecilic enough to cross the Louge and meet mounted odds of four to one.

My uncle-in-law had gone back to bed the moment I and Raymond Roger left him. Now he got up again, and began to put his horsemen into the field. Our order of battle was changed in consequence. The Count of Foix's men were in the van, the Aragonese came second, and the Toulousain advance moved prudently up from behind.

King Peter need not have entered the fray, but he lived for chivalry, and today he wished the poets to remember him for a gesture that would recall the mythical heroes. He had to change weapons with a comrade, surrender his own superior armoury and take on the other man's luck.

Save for the royal bars, all about him carried his own blazon. Yet, near at hand, rode Ironface, with the simple Spanish cross on his shield and the extravagant but stained holy embroidery on his tabard. Peter was a devout man. What finer exchange could there be? The two had scarcely exchanged sword, shield and cloth, when the crusading cavalry surprised them by bursting from the apple orchard on their right flank.

This gave them no time to concentrate their numbers, according to the Great Wizard's best advice. Turned on the flank, although by inferior forces, they could not offer one another support.

The allies were moving steadily ahead, but trying to wheel, when the crusaders smashed into them at a tremendous gallop.

There are warriors with a good eye for ground, and warriors with a bad eye for ground. Raymond Roger of Foix and Peter the Second of Aragon had no eye for ground at all. They had the best plain in Oc to gallop about on, so they chose to squeeze two thousand men on huge horses into an orchard no bigger than a maiden's pinafore, and push another two thousand up behind them.

The rumours that the King had only come here because he was besotted with a pretty woman were resurrected from this moment. Men said he chose the lush vegetation of the orchard to die in because it reminded him of the glade between her legs. It is a pretty jest, but not one that translates in all languages.

The crusaders' strategy was simple. They did not have one, because the urgency of Simon's destiny gave them no time to discuss the matter. Guillaume des Barres simply forced his way into the end of Raymond Roger's line, slashed a swath through and rolled it up.

Bouchard's men drove even more deeply into the Aragonese, again striking at an angle that converted a battle formation into a column of impotent confusion. As Bouchard's men put their opponents to the sword, Alain de Roucy and Florent de Ville were making good their oath to kill the King. They saw his blazon and pushed their horses up against Ironface's mount.

Ironface's bottom was not firmly planted, nor could his steed be termed a destrier of destruction. Rider and horse shied away, though one of them caught Florent de Ville a passable blow with King Peter's sword.

Alain de Roucy at once shouted out, 'This fellow isn't the King. The King is a better horseman.'

Whereupon King Peter himself, with borrowed blade lifted high, called in a clear voice. 'The King. Here is the King. Who wants him?'

De Roucy, De Ville and their men rode him down.

No sooner did they have King Peter surrounded than they cut him and his horse into collops, much as if making a beef stew, a process which the pair of them resisted valiantly. One of these lumps of meat went on waving its sword long after the King was dismembered, but as a monarch is commonly held to require a head upon which to set his crown, King Peter lost his attraction as a rallying point to his own chivalry, not long after he was perceived to be in gobbets on the grass.

The Aragonese fought nobly to protect themselves, but were quickly reduced. A horse is unhandy at retreating unless you turn it around and ride it wholeheartedly away. It is not a cart to be pushed to and fro. It does not handle well in reverse. These Spaniards were too proud to show their backs to their enemies, and in many cases too well mannered also, so were driven into drainage ditches, against trees and into orchard walls by the fury of the Northerners' attack, where they began to be crushed underfoot like a drift of ripe apples.

568

Their cause was not helped by the dispersal of King Peter. The King died many deaths on that battlefield. This was partly because De Roucy galloped his head in one direction while De Ville took his crown in another, and where a King lies, there did he fall, and wherever he fell so does his story start. It was also because there were three King Peter's in the first place, since he was known also as Pedro and Pierre in all manner of dialects, and spoken of as dying among men he did not even know to exist. He encouraged his knights to dress as well as he did, and then accoutered himself better again, so no wonder he lay all over the place, and ballads began to sprout up about him from under every stone.

What is certain is that some hundred score of those beautiful shields lay about the field, each bearing the King's own blazon of gold barred with gules. Many a local peasant came to hang one on his wall, kept a second for mixing mortar or daub, and gave his wife another for mirroring her hair or serving the family's fish.

Ironface rode hard by this multiply dying King, as was always his intention. He was mistaken for Peter, and then swept aside as we saw, but came riding back again to aid whatever particle of him presented itself for succour.

Unfortunately, such was his lack of legs that Ironface perched as insecurely on a horse as a gnome above an ant hill or a doll on an overstuffed cushion, and was quickly laid low by a collision of lances. He was appalled at the moment of his dissolution to find himself confronted by the three young squires from Montardy, Capestang and Enserune who had served my cousin's cause so nobly in and around Carcassonne, but were now tabarded with the Cross and porting De Montfort's blazon. 'By Saint James of Compestella,' he thundered, 'and the Virgin Florimella of Fontarabia,' but by then he was down under hoof and foot, and being kicked to pieces by horseshoes as well as hammered by halberd and sword.

The Count of Foix was in no better case than the King of Aragon. He kept himself in one piece in the teeth of

569

Guillaume des Barres' onslaught, and plied his sword so valiantly that he soon felt hot blood splashing him beneath his armpit, not all of it his own. But as with the Spanish King his horsemen died around him in droves, and many of them fell behind him, for the crusaders' charge had broken his line. He came into the field with two thousand of his finest, yet when the day was over he could not collect enough people of quality together to make up four boards at chequers, and when he saw this, and counted the lack of hands again, he knew how cruelly he had been defeated.

What of Raymond of Toulouse? It has to be said of him that Count Cunning retained a much firmer strategic grasp of the conflict than either of his more impetuous allies. When Simon de Montfort's squadron rode at him, he perceived that this was indeed very bad ground to be fighting upon. At that moment, he grasped a most important military precept: a battle is always better off being fought in some other place. He also saw what his less mathematically minded comrades-in-arms had disdained to notice, namely that the forces under his immediate command only outnumbered the enemy facing him by some three or four to one, instead of being that eighty thousand to just a few hundred that had made his tartine taste so agreeable at breakfast time.

Putting all of these facts together with remarkable alacrity, he led what he could of himself from the field. Although he gave clear commands for all his cavaliers to retire equally, not all of them were as perceptive as he was, and anyway De Montfort brought his squadron on and through them so briskly that very few of them had the chance.

So far, the whole battle had been admirably conducted by our three commanders of horse. Two formations had died facing forward. No-one had dishonoured himself by dismounting to loot wine or fornicate as at St Martin Lalande. Many knights were most cruelly cut down, with no quarter asked for nor given, but most of them bore this cheerfully enough as being no more than a natural extension of the chivalry each had

570

pursued so wholeheartedly in the hunting field, the jousting alley and the bed. As the Chanson so nobly puts it, 'When Duty calls the Warrior/The Lover must dismount/And allow a younger Rider/To bare his backbone to God.' Death made many widows in those few moments, but all of them could be proud, and doubtless some of them found a younger rider by a diligent application to prayer.

All this bloodshed takes no account of another and far more serious struggle taking place about Muret's own defence works. There, Raymond of Toulouse's pedestrians, if I may so term his infantry, and his assault engineers were making ready to storm the ramparts after a barrage of rocks propelled by the Count's own siege-train of trebuchets, mangonels, and old-fashioned catapults, with some ten thousand militiamen in reserve. A grizzled engineer was briefly in charge of this operation, but his sense of urgency was so diminished by age – he was thirty-seven – that I soon saw the need for me to direct operations myself.

This was to be, for a time, my last battle, and I was glad to observe that, while still only twenty years old, I had in these four years of campaigning learned many martial skills I was fortunate enough to be able to put into practice on this occasion.

For example, by this point in the battle, we were able to place some half a dozen scaling ladders against the wall of the old town and two more up to the ramparts of the fortress itself. *I did not go up any of them.* Not for me the impetuosity and foolhardy derring-do that was bringing so many of the nobility of several nations, unbeknown to myself, into such disarray behind me. I did not go up a single ladder sword in hand, or with some other blade between my teeth, because *I did not get off my horse. A leader of men never dismounts from his horse.* I clung to that fact, and urged Gibbu and Guillemette, who were not leaders but whom I needed about me, to do likewise.

La Mamelonne also stayed mounted, as did Mitten and the Fish Girl, though that last one could easily outrun a horse, even when she was dancing. Whores always like to be on horseback. Indeed, La Mamelonne used to say she hated earwigs so much she would even ply her trade on horseback if she could, since she had never seen an earwig on a horse. It is surprising what trifles could come into my mind during the heat of battle.

I did not even leave my saddle when the garrison commander walked along the battlements of the fortress and punched the leader of our scaling party boldly in the teeth with a mailed gauntlet. No, not even when he used the same arrogant hand to send our ladders clattering down upon our heads. 'Pick those ladders up again,' I told the Toulousain militia, 'and mount up like men. Don't let that dotard rebuke you as if you were babies.'

Stout hearts that they were, they returned to the escalade with scarcely a curse in my direction.

One ladder was a little sluggish, but I reached up from my saddle and pricked some bottoms with my sword. Thus does a leader inculcate urgency and inspire confidence, though I took no pleasure in having blood drop in my eye from a Toulousain buttock.

So we fight our personal wars, yet no matter how hawk-like our gaze nor lofty our perch, Mars and the other monarch deities of conflict are sometimes afforded a larger view.

While I was capturing Muret, Simon de Montfort had wheeled his third meagre squadron of horsemen and was now chasing the survivors of three great mounted armies in my direction.

Most of these had no will to be chased, and had either died bravely along the way or simply disappeared over walls or into treetops as accomplished warriors will when they feel Death's tooth fretting their horses' buttocks and his nostrils sniffing their own.

So De Montfort was now free to gallop among the thousands of Toulousain militia who had been imprudent enough to scoff at him for losing his left trouser leg outside the church of St Sirnan. It would have been better for us all if this chilly Anglo-Norman lord had possessed a better sense of humour.

Only a few of my uncle's own cavalry were bold enough and foolish enough to try to hold him off from slaughtering the thousands of terrified pedestrians and engineers who milled about me trying to benefit from my inspiration and instruction.

This all came as a hideous surprise. However, I saw straight-way what must be done. The crusaders were bloodied from their great charge, and their ranks gapped from attempting to wheel in close order, something else I had learned and knew to be impossible until we can breed a war-horse that runs on casters. I knew I must ride boldly into their gapped ranks, plunge my sword down Simon de Montfort's throat and cut the tripes from his breastbone by means of a single, consummate *coup-de-main*. This would take the heart out of his great charge, and victory would surely follow.

Unfortunately for history, Gibbu did not read the tactical situation as swiftly or as clearsightedly as I did. He took hold of Nano's reins and began to lead me firmly in the opposite direction. Guillemette, La Mamelonne and Mitten all followed us at an extremely brisk gallop. I tried in vain to shift his grip, but that ignorant Hunchback had a grasp like a badger's bite, and there was no way I could unfasten it short of cutting off his hand, and I was loath to do that.

Most of the militia had to retreat on foot, and many were trampled by the crusaders' horses, or cut down by their riders, in both cases contrary to the clear Rules of War I have studied over the years. These heartless Northerners not only butchered archers, pike-men and other men-at-arms who had done them no harm save for recently outnumbering them thirty or forty to one, they also massacred the town's bourgeoisie who had come here on rouncy, coracle or punt for the entirely innocent pastime of wanting to watch their enemy die. Although some of these last had arrived upon horseback, they were not leaders of men so had seen no reason to stay in their saddles and were suffering accordingly.

My own enforced retreat, accompanied by thousands of jostling Toulousains, did in fact reunite me with the main stream of history, in this case the River Garonne. My fellow cowards had come down it by barge and were in a mighty hurry to go back up it again.

I selected the largest vessel I could find and placed my personal entourage firmly aboard it, accepted only a limited number of footmen else, and told the waterman firmly to cast off, as some of us had a price on our heads.

He objected to this, but my sword was long and sharp and Gibbu's arrows could reach further and probe deeper, so he gave orders to fore and aft, as such men call the two ends of a boat, and we were quanted off by a group of muscular rivermen.

I began to direct the way upstream. There was a fair chance we could land above the town, and return to give the crusaders a nasty surprise when their destriers had run out of gallop and themselves had run out of spit. As De Montfort came past me I had seen he'd lost a stirrup and broken a spur, and was reduced to using his fist, so all was not necessarily lost.

Unfortunately I had reckoned without the obduracy of men who live by water. (I had lived by water for seventeen years myself, but that is a different use of the preposition. As Daddy used to say, 'We live by water but we function on wine.') However, the obduracy of men who live by water is well documented.

'We'll not put anyone ashore till we're safe inside Toulouse basin,' the waterman said.

'Make for the bank,' I insisted, 'and set us down.'

'Get off that — horse,' he said, using the kind of nautical language sailors have at their command, even river sailors. 'Get off that — horse and throw the — overboard. It's shitting on my decking.'

'A leader never gets off his horse,' I said firmly, before reminding him he was changing the subject.

'You'll sink the — boat.' (I wish I could reproduce the words more accurately, but so many of them blew away in the wind which came up the River Garonne.) 'You'll — sink the — boat.'

This was a lie, for I perceived very clearly at this point that we were aground on a shingle bank opposite the little hamlet of Le Grand Joffréry.

It was a good thing we had retained our seats, because everyone else was in a terrible panic, especially when the crusaders' infantry, which up till now had nothing to do, followed us down the river and began to rain darts upon us from their crossbows.

'Swim!' I shouted, and spurred Nano boldly into the water. My companions followed. Most of the Toulousains could not swim – there is no reason why any of them should – but drowning in your own town's sewage is a calmer death than writhing in agony with a barbed quarrel in your larger gut, as I tried to explain to as many of them as tried to save themselves by clinging to Nano's stirrups and saddle.

My intimates were fortunate in having horses, as a horse never sinks, not even when filled with breakfast and river water, not even when dead, and our mounts were neither.

This water is a curious element and a highly wayward dimension in which to find yourself during times of stress, such as while you are running away from a battle. I wish I had studied it more closely while at St Thibéry, and had I been a boy I suppose I would have done.

For example, rivers flow. Our own barge had been bearing us upstream towards a haven in Toulouse. The vessels of the entire flotilla were bound in this direction also, helped along by oar, quant and paddle, as well as sails filled by the famous Garonne wind which always blows along the river from the south-west. But rivers flow, as I say, and with or without my stressing the fact or even mentioning it again, its stream was now forcing us irresistibly in the reverse direction, into the teeth of the wind and towards the outstretched hands of our enemies in Muret.

Since the complete Toulousain armada was either grounded opposite Le Grand or Le Petit Jofréry, or its vessels of shallower draught prevented from progressing further by the deeper keels already fastened into the shingle, it has been estimated that some ten thousand warriors and interested bystanders were floating with me.

Many of these were washed ashore at the confluence with the Louge, right by the fortress walls. Others fetched up in the orchards below the town. These the crusaders pulled very eagerly ashore, beat upon the heads, let their bellies feast on swords, or simply nailed to trees. In Muret they had found a great barrel filled with nails, and the orchards below the town and the woods beyond them contained trees without number.

It is defeat that makes most men spiteful. These crusaders enjoy victory too. But in reality they were nailing up my uncle-in-law for butchering their comrades.

Fortunately for him, Uncle Toulouse was nowhere to be found, or he might have had a very curious time of it.

If only they had listened to me, these Kings and these burghers alike, none of this disaster would have happened. Oc would not now be controlled from Paris, which is a foggy, foreign place, but from Zaragossa, which is beautiful on the tongue, even if impossible to say after a glass of wine.

They should have dug a trench all round Muret and laid siege to it properly. It afterwards transpired that there was only food and water within the old town for a day and a night, and only water for a day within the Citadel. But even if the siege had lasted for a season, our men could have had a comfortable time of it. There is plenty to entertain a warrior in a trench. Their wives could have strolled out from Toulouse and taught them knitting, for example, and soon it would have been autumn and the rains would have come and turned their excavations into a moat, so there would have been the fishing as well.

These are strategic considerations. The plain tactical fact is that if we had camped properly about, instead of massing for an unnecessary assault, Simon de Montfort could not have got into Muret, or once in could not then have got out.

I was right, and I took considerable pleasure in saying so to the few people I encountered who were alive enough for me to mention the matter to. This was not a great number, I agree, as we left our dead in carpets, fifteen thousand according to any count I have seen, and of these some four thousand of our chivalry. That is an awful lot of people for a few hundred horsemen to kill in five minutes, so several of our heroes must have died as a result of tripping over their spurs or being brought down by their friends.

I cannot find record of how many people drowned in the Garonne, or floated all those leagues downstream and into the mighty ocean, and perhaps fell off the edge of the world beyond. Ten thousand is the number most frequently mentioned, but I can fix no truth to it one way or the other. All I can say is that the Garonne used to be a meagre river for fish, but nowadays it teams with trout and salmon, and you can draw eels out by the basket, freshwater shrimps as well. Also, there are many mermaids. You never hear tell of those unless there are drowned men's bodies to play with, nor wicked sport to be had with their souls.

I received no gratitude for my good advice. Rather was it misrepresented.

'Ha!' they said. 'We listened to you, and look what happened to us.'

'You listened,' I rejoined, 'but you would not learn.'

'Ha!' they said again.

Thus I fell out of favour as a strategic advisor.

CAPUT TWENTY-ONE

Wherein Ironface becomes an anatomie and is like to become an atomie also and float off like a gnat.

There is nothing like a comprehensive defeat to reaffirm a nation's faith in itself and its leadership, especially when the catastrophe is so total that it precludes argument, excuse or constipation. The survivors huddle together and prop their chins up with barrels and wine-skins, and very soon the future begins to appear in a better light; the past is so terrible, the present so dreary, that tomorrow can only bring hope. When, on a truly happy day, can we ever feel so confident about the future?

Raymond of Toulouse began to be regarded very favourably by his people as a result of his defeat at Muret. He had kept his head when all about him were losing theirs, and often other more valuable limbs besides. Whether hovering on the edge of combat or running decisively away, he had shown himself for what he was, a man who would take no further nonsense from the Crusade without making a great deal of noise in the process, joining it whenever it would let him, and meanwhile forming vigorous alliances with powerful friends.

As for the fatal conduct of the attack, he himself never willingly attacked anyone, as was well known. He had been led astray by that fool from Foix and a whole lot of foreigners from beyond the Pyrenees where the bad weather comes from. That Perronnelle de Saint Thibéry and the whore whose back she rides on were a great deal to blame also. They are both women, of course, or the whore certainly is, and their tongues run away with them. Mercifully, Raymond did not listen to them, does not listen to them, and will not listen to them. Raymond never listens to women. He is always too busy doing the other thing to them. Raymond is a good fellow. Kindly pass the wine-skin.

We thought it best to leave this kind of talk, in case we began to detect a victory in the Battle of Muret after all.

True we lost fifteen thousand men by exchange of arms, and most of another ten thousand drowned, crucified, or captured by mermaids, but several of those Northerners had taken some bad cuts as well, and with any luck some of them would fester.

We hurried back towards the field of battle to look for what remained of Ironface.

The crusaders held the town, but seemed reluctant to sit about the orchards – which some historians hold to be a gesture of defeat: possession of the field itself being a clear indication of victory to writers such as the Great Wizard Caesar.

The field at Muret was undoubtedly in the possession of our glorious dead, and the thousands of crows, and the millions of flies who came to pay cloudy homage to them. It was one of the few occasions on which I have ever seen 'odour made visible' as the troubadours call it, a miasma so thick you could ride across it on a horse. We all had to wrap our nose in a water, and do as much for our mounts as well. Nano, in particular, was very sensitive about the smell of humans.

Most of my old corpse-strippers from Carcassonne were here, but this management of a man's corporeal body after his soul has shuffled off its bloodstained garment was an honourable profession to them, a kindly mystery and an excellent livelihood. Less welcome were the pillagers who came to battlefields not to lay corpses out and tidy away their loose ends, pocketing what they could find along the way as their own just and necessary recompense, but who simply robbed the glorious fallen of their valuables, often chopping off ring fingers, ripping out earrings, then tossing the corpses in a smelly heap, which left visiting relatives with an unfortunate impression, especially if they were not entirely dead.

Such people were as the Saints in Heaven compared with those we saw next. There were the apothecaries' anatomists, corpse-clippers who would despoil a warrior of his parts for the benefit of their employers, those loathsome leeches who sell to maidens love potions made of powdered testicle or lucky purses prettily adorned with noblemen's teeth. Nor are such nostrums of any value to the purchaser. The toothy purses do no more for a woman than cause her to be snapped at by passing dogs, and if she takes a good strong dram of powdered testicle, far from placing men within her power, she is likely to find herself becoming available to every pedlar she meets, unless she is lucky enough to succumb, as happens often in a warm climate, to a sense-restoring diarrhoea or a sobering dose of the pimple.

Such men do not operate openly, but snip away quickly in the shady places, or work at night by lanthorn or candle, often in the company of priests and witches to clear away the ghosts. Muret's field was perfect for them, with its orchards and ditches, and the great city of Toulouse hard by as a market place.

It is possible, just, to regard such quacks as physicians of the heart – I have myself sometimes chewed upon a testicle to call my Phantom into a hardier presence, but always a bullock's and never a man's. Whitebreads we call them, and very sweet they are when fried in a little egg and breadcrumbs.

Yet what can you say to those who enter a corpse to extract its bladderstones, gallstones, kidney stones and similar frips to polish them and sell as jewellery, such like human pearls being in demand among rich city wives, especially when they can be furnished with their previous owner's pedigree? What indeed? These vultures were here in abundance, and curious knives they used for their tricks, similar to those that executioners use when told to withhold a man until he reaches the ultimate prettiness, a sight I have been fortunate not to see often.

Gibbu sent several of these away with a blunt arrow, firing at them as they stooped and aiming at the exact point where the backside makes junction with the intelligence. This would send them screeching into the distance, fingering their knees and flapping their coats. Muret quickly earned a name as a haunted field, full of awful moans and shriekings, and Gibbu's padded shaft up the bottom was responsible for a great deal of this.

So too was the corpses' normal inclination to growl at you if left to expand in the warm sunlight. I have only once heard the discharge of that dreadful weapon the bagpipe, but I can assure you that a noontide corpse in tight armour after a Spanish breakfast can render a very fair imitation of it.

As we sought Ironface's corpse among the elegant ranks of the odorous dead (and reminded ourselves by way of a pomander that they did not, in fairness, smell much worse than the odorous living) Mamelie began to sob. Seeing this had no effect on us brought her properly to weep and soak her chest, if not the battlefield, with piteous tears. 'These brave lads,' she sobbed, 'poor Spanish horsemen in their clean shirts and rusting armour – '

Here we murmured our concern. It is a sad fact about chain-mail, pretty invention though it is, that if you do not treat it like a carpet and bang it daily against the nearest wall it will be as scabby as an autumn tree after a day or so.

This was not what La Mamelonne spoke about. 'When I look at so many marquises, if that is how they call themselves, such a multitude of dons and grandees from every corner of Aragon, when I gaze upon them lying there dead and think there may be some of them unlucky enough to have passed on before they had time to taste the ecstasies of my embrace.'

'Never,' Gibbu said consolingly. 'There may be an unlucky horse or two, but I swear you've had all the able-bodied men.'

A chill swept through the field at this moment, as if a hail cloud was forming overhead. I was distracted enough to suppose it was no more than the effect of riding so close to La Mamelonne, for as a great whore blows hot in her pleasure so she may also be expected to blow cold if offended, and the Hunchback's words seemed unnecessarily cruel to me, when I considered how much Mamelie loved animals.

I was mistaken, and shuddered when I saw the true cause of it. A bright scarlet cloak could be seen leaping across a drainage ditch, the way a bat swoops aside at a fly. Raymond de Brousses always frightened me, whether he arrived in the flesh or as a manifestation. Today he was here in the flesh, for he had brought his shadow. Strange that he should flit here and there in scarlet, yet remind one only of the darkest creatures, such as bats and rooks, and the black-bellied kite. When he had his shadow, it was his shadow you saw and were enfolded by, that and the rings that glittered out from his eyes. When he had no shadow, you shuddered the more to think you might already lie wrapped in it and sunk within his head.

He was here with members of his inner coven, people I had last seen as bears or wolves, or wild things masquerading as men, but clearly recognizable to me after a nine-month study and a night of hideous frenzy.

These unmannerly mannequins and unfeminine females were also plundering corpses, tearing out hearts, eyeballs, and spleens for use in hermetic rituals, and cutting off thumbs, noses, ears and the sexual second finger for use in even blacker arts.

He did not see me. I did not think he saw me. We were masked in our perfumed scarves, as I have already told you, and we turned our horses quickly away from him, though continued to spy over our shoulders. He was ordering his minions to load limbs and lesser collops on to a horse-drawn cart. They also tossed in the occasional nobly featured or well-toothed head, doubtless to feed to one of his lesser dukes or even the dragons he kept upon Alaric. The Magus himself was busy wrapping those private particles I spoke of inside his cloak. These soon constituted a mighty load, but from time to time he would shake out his cloak and there would be nothing there, so great were its powers of transubstantiation.

I say he did not see us, but he had a magic ring on his finger that watched everything for him, and there were birds and beetles to fetch him tales. He was well versed in their speech, and knew the voice of all animals, including the snake which talks to no-one, even when it mates.

Thus it was that one of his coven broke away and came walking crooked towards us. First she was stepping, then striding, then running, until at last she flew over the corpses at the speed of an arrow, but still crooked, like a shaft with a folded tail. I swear she was the twin sister of the Goddess Malpolon, or the Goddess herself reconstituted. Like the Goddess she had filed teeth, and a divided tongue that would not be still.

She held out a paper with a picture drawn thereupon. Bravely La Mamelonne tried to take it, but as she touched it the picture fell off and the paper was blank.

The Goddess offered the paper to me.

'Careful,' Gibbu whispered. 'It will be painted with an invisible poison or a mighty spell.'

I carry my own faith, and with it my convictions. I took the paper. As I touched it and turned it, Dogskin Raymond spoke to me from the very centre of if. *'I have your Lord Ferblant,'* his voice said. *'I hold him between life and death on Alaric, in which place I have bound him in a freeze.'*

The paper chuckled, then shuddered so much from its own delight that it tumbled apart. Dogskin now spoke to me from the palm of the Goddess's hand. *'I set a spell upon Ferblant's armour, upon his blazon and his uplifted sword, but that fool King Peter bore them, so could not defend himself against those that sought his death. No-one seeks Ferblant's death except me.'*

The sky grew darker now, darker while remaining blue, for it still scorched with a fierce sun.

'Yet such is the lust I feel for you, Perronnelle de Saint Thibéry and Trencavel, such is my need for you in pleasure and pain ...'

The Goddess had disappeared and the fragments of her paper. As I glanced about beneath the darkening still brilliant sky, I saw that Raymond had gone also, and his coven and their laden cart.

Only my comrades and the corpses remained, and a crow that was full of Magus Raymond's voice: '*Lord Ferblant and I will await you on Alaric. Myself and the Mighty Ones of Earth, Fire and Air.*'

'He didn't mention Water,' I said.

'No, he didn't mention Water,' Gibbu muttered. 'Nor a thousand things beside.'

CANTO TWO AND TWENTY

In which the Virgin seeks to
repair her dented Lord Tin.

I rode swiftly. I took only Gibbu and Guillemette, my Hunchback and my once Mute, and I made no plan. I was learning from Simon de Montfort, much as I detested him. In battle it was better to be quick, and best of all to be resolute.

From Muret to Alaric was a long, bitter ride. We had to detour to the bridges at Toulouse, because the barges were aground, and the crusaders held the Garonne's only crossing points. Then, no sooner did we clap our knees into our horses, than September decided it was summer no longer. The heavens opened. We could go by the hills and be drier underfoot. We could go by the ancient stones and be nearer. We went the nearer way, the rain continued falling, and the ancient stones flooded along the rivers Hers, Rebenty and Fresquel and all that marshy quagmire where the Aude flows eastward.

Dogskin had brought the weather down by spreading his cloak. He only spread his cloak in order to fly off in it. He might reach Alaric in the draining of a sand or the burning of a candle. Or he might mouth a spell and be there the previous instant. All he had to do was wait for us. It took us three days to reach him.

As we woke on each of these days Gibbu said, 'This is the plot he spoke of to Simon de Montfort. This is what La Mamelonne warned you about. Suppose De Montfort's men are waiting for us.'

'Four years ago Ironface saved my life.'

We would be in the saddle by this time, with our horses splashing through wet.

'Talk to a woman,' the Hunchback grumbled. As if he were some great baron, or even a whole man.

'What do you say, Guillemette?' I asked her.

'I'm a mute,' she said. 'I was better off saying nothing.'

A salmon swam across the road, in one of the many places that the road became a puddle and the puddle made friends with the river. Guillemette shot it. She was now as proficient with a longbow as formerly with her winder and spring. 'Ask the fish,' she suggested.

At the foot of Alaric we met one of Dogskin's bears. It put its teeth round a tree and growled at us.

Gibbu leant from his saddle and clapped it on the ear, sending it sprawling.

'That's a bear,' I gasped. 'Not a man dressed as a bear.'

'You think of everything too late.' He strung his bow.

The wolves were already following us. He turned back and shot the first of them through the belly, then dismounted to slit its ankles together with his knife, hanging it from a stick. 'If this one's a man,' he muttered, 'he'd have been safer disguised as a tortoise.'

He was man right enough. With fur glued on his back and a painted stomach.

The other wolves fled. Gibbu didn't retrieve his arrow.

'You've left the enemy your mark,' I admonished.

'I've left my mark.'

Raymond de Brousses was waiting on the rock where he had first appeared to us as a wolf.

'Don't shoot him,' I cautioned. 'We need him to unlock Ironface from his spell.'

'I want him all in one place before I shoot him.'

I looked where he pointed. Another Dogskin stood across the path from us, and a third, who wore robes as hot as sunrise, stood beyond a bush. The second Dogskin was so pale he seemed made of water. I could see the leaves through him, and the blades of grass. Small creatures swam in his bones, though it was late in the year for spawn.

'Well, my pretty Perronnelle.' All three of him spoke. 'So you accept my conditions.'

I wasn't the only pretty one here, but Guillemette still wore a tunic, as I did, and he took no notice of her womanhood, thinking her a man. Surely a sorcerer should be able to tell such things?

I rode towards Raymond's rock and leapt upon it, but Nano didn't like it under hoof, and skidded. The Mage disappeared. I felt a dampness engulf me. It was water from his other self.

Without looking for Dogskin further, or any particle or trick of him, I left his rock and continued up the mountain. The others rode after me.

Alaric is not an alp. It is a God King's horse and the home of monsters. I climbed to the backbone of the horse and looked for the Chapel of Bones, which was all that was left of the monsters.

'Will you eat?' the Magus Raymond asked when we got there.

He was nowhere to be seen. When he finally appeared to us by his altar he was no longer dressed in red but in a *garde-corps* of black with a hood. He might have been a notary or physician, or the church's least important clerk.

'Where is Ironface?'

'First you must drink from my cup.'

'Show me Ironface and I will take your cup.'

He placed his hands together palm to palm, parted them a little by the thumb, then stooped to scoop water from a puddle, lifting it in the keel formed by his fists. He bade me look in it, and I gazed very cautiously, knowing water to be a dangerous and dazzling element.

I saw Ironface in the shadow of the Mage's palm. He lay white of face with his eyes clenched tightly. He wore no iron, so all I could see was his ugliness, and the lopsided stumps of his legs. He lay as if in death, locked inside a stone or a slab of ice.

'Bring him to me,' I said.

'First you must drink.'

'Bring him and prove he is not dead. Then we shall make our terms.'

'You will drink?'

'I will drink to buy Lord Ferblant's freedom from the mountain. That is my word to you. Be it peril or poison in the cup, or Satan's own darkest spell, I will drink. But only on those terms.'

'And these others will drink?'

'That is for them to say. I see no need of it.'

'If I give the little dwarf his limbs? And for you, foul Hunchback, I could take away the mountain on your back.'

'I'll take the cup.'

'And what does the badel say? Does it still, being mute, say nothing?'

Guillemette said nothing.

'The badel will moisten its lips,' I promised, 'if you do as you say.'

'I make you this further compact,' Gibbu said to him, reaching behind his back to take a bone-white arrow with a slippery shaft. 'Do you know what this is?'

'Blackthorn,' Dogskin muttered. 'I know what it means.'

'A blackthorn point on a buckthorn shaft. Not the best of arrows. It won't kill a deer nor catch a bird on the wing. But it's sovereign for liars. You know the old saw, I daresay. *Spike a liar's tongue and you'll split his heart.* Well, it's blackthorn that riddle is written on, Dogskin, with buckthorn for a pricker. If you tell me a lie and I catch you at a furlong, the thorns can't miss.'

The Magus licked his tongue and said nothing. Perhaps he could already taste the spike.

It had not escaped my attention that Dogskin was not attended by wolf-man or bear or acolyte. His creatures were not here, but of course they were near, and his will was omnipresent, as if his cloak wrapped about the mountain like a mist.

'Bring Ironface,' I urged.

The Magus Raymond of Brousses, dressed only in black, being no more than Dogskin in his Lesser Ritual, approached

594

the rock of his altar and sprinkled it with water from a jar. Then he added salt and the rock split open.

Ferblant lay in its centre, like a grape in the press.

'Fore God,' he groaned, 'I am dead. I can see my naked angel in a dream. She has put on dull armour for me, to show me all Heaven is in mourning.' He put his hands to his battered face, and sobbed. 'And my Hunchback is dead already, and my Mute here before me. See them among the blessèd angels. Could death be more beautiful than this, or its beings more ugly?' He shed tears for a long time.

'Heal his legs,' I commanded.

'When you take my cup. Drink it and you can give him your own. I have no use for your legs, Virgin, only your spine and such fancies as I shall keep about me.'

'Take no mead from his cup,' Ferblant whispered, 'nor any sherbet, sulphur or blood. I have seen this man in Purgatory where the fires grow hotter, tossing down souls from Great Satan's fork.'

'I shall drink nonetheless,' I said. I watched Ferblant's ruin crawl from the riven rock, and Raymond mend his altar with a spell.

Little Stump clung about my knees and sobbed, while the Mage boiled a water and mixed it with flame from his altar's log.

'Lord Ferblant must leave the mountain before I drink,' I warned. 'Or before my comrades have anything to do with your potion.'

'There are pieces of armour in the bothy,' Dogskin said. 'Legwork of his own, the helm is his own, the belly and the breast belonged to King Peter. Let him wrap his body in my trophies, if he will, and let him ride your horse.' He laughed, as if to be mutilated were a kindly conceit. 'A steed without bollocks for a thing without legs.' He watched Ferblant creep away on his crushed and hatcheted ends.

'You promised him legs of his own.'

'So did you, Perronnelle. Legs of your own. We must live in trust a few moments longer.'

'And you'll bring back Frédélon my swan?'

'That swan was my rival, lady. Life has gone too far for the swan.'

Ferblant reappeared in iron. The iron limped, though half of him was a king. He went up to Nano, my horse, and my darling whinnied in fear though poor Nano knew him well.

He lifted one leg into the stirrup with his hands, and Nano stood still while he did so. Then the cripple propped himself on to Nano's back, though he had no more strength than a whisper.

He did not bid me farewell. He could not speak, scarcely ride. Poor Nano was hale enough, being made of grunts and breath, as he paced disconsolately away. But his rider's armour seemed more than half empty, as indeed it was. It still glowed with a sickly spell.

I watched them go down the mountain, as one gazes at a sinking star.

Now Dogskin turned from the flame. His preparations were complete. He mouthed no incantation, no chant, no conjuration of the Secret Ones. But then he was a mighty apothecary as well as a sorcerer, and had already shown me in my days in the bothy that he knew witch-tricks with herbs and powdered stones. I guessed what he mixed us was no more than a common poison, or some such subtle bane as lechers use to quell maidens for their sport.

He divided this filth into three metal cups, each on its stalk, whether goblet or chalice.

'There's no need to drink,' I warned Gibbu and Guillemette.

'We'll stand firm and take it,' the Hunchback growled.

Guillemette played mute, as if they still concocted some foolish strategem.

All I had was my prayer, certainly not my Phantom. I felt him near me in the twilight, but he needed a deeper darkness, though my soul was never darker.

De Brousses knew what bound me to him. It was my own oath, and my love for Ironface.

So before he offered me the cup which would bring me to ruin, he decided to tent my fear. 'When you drink this,' he smiled, 'you will lose the use of your limbs, of your will, of your every sense. Only your pain will remain, and that will be exquisite.' He held it closer, and said, 'At the first gulp – and I know you will deal boldly with me – at the first gulp you will see me in my most loathsome manifestation. I will become Baron Cerberus, and in the form of the Faceless Dog in my Lesser Ritual take your virginity. I shall take it in pain, and I shall sacrifice you in pain, I and my acolytes, till your pain is your only memorial.'

He tipped the cup by my mouth, and I felt its wet on my lips. 'I have already sold your body to the Crusade, who will burn it. Your soul is my own. Only your tongue will be left for Christian burial. Let it prophesy then, if it will.'

While he held me the cup, he was all I saw. Then I took the cup, and the cup became everything. I drank boldly, as he had predicted. I did not sip. As I drank, its rim became a crater of fire, and its contents a lake that tilted slowly towards me, like a mirror lifting from the ground. In that mirror, the Magus no longer wore black, but robes of red, which were fire. I saw his people behind him, not merely his coven, his wolf-men, his bears, but the hierarchies of magical beings his mystery caused to wait on him. I saw the wild ones from between the stars, and the black ones from Hell.

Now that I was dying, he brought all my dead ones back to wait on me. There were men from Le Bourg and Le Castellare, from St Martin Lalande and Muret. There were men with missing eyes, and men without limbs, men with their tongues bitten out and obscene wounds where the anatomists had emptied them of the organs of life. Men I had slain stood there, and men Great Simon had blinded. Men nailed by the Crusade to a tree stood about me, still bearing the branches that fastened them.

Merdun was there, with his head stuck with arrows and his loins naked. Mummy and One Eye were pierced by him in turn, and as they screamed in protest so did he laugh. 'Too young is the right age for me,' he chuckled, and waved a mailed arm to show me the citizens of Béziers in their bright robes of flame, some of them cinders, some of them spectres.

Dogskin Baron Cerberus pushed the Bastard aside, and thrust his own body at me, indolently nude, with his penis erect and his skin painted over with hieroglyphs and sigils. 'I have given you the Elixir,' he exulted, 'and now I give you this,' lounging his body against me, for I found I could not move, but stood as if chained to darkness. 'Now I give you this.' He pushed his teeth close to my ear, and said, 'Have you not heard the agony a cat feels mating, for without the female's pain, no life could ever be?'

I felt his hands lifting my clothes. I still wore my tunic of mail, so he had to return to his altar for a knife to cut the straps.

It was then I realized that he loved me as a man, or lusted as a man, and that tonight the languid potion was his only ritual. Whatever his boast, he would take me as a man, and as a murderer kill me.

He cut my shoulder buckles and thrust his naked loins at me. He was as grotesque as any unloved man, but potent and huge, and with some unfrosted corner of my mind I thought of St Ursula and her maidens, and prayed that God would punish him.

He was interrupted by a cry, then by a sound I had not heard for a year. It was deadly, and chill, yet beautiful as if the wood nymphs called to me.

The wood nymphs were not calling to me. Or not to me only. Dogskin turned and saw a naked woman stand within his triangle of salt. She played a wooden pipe, and she hissed at him slowly.

'I conjure you,' he said to her, but he conjured her too slowly. She stepped beyond the salt.

'You do not know my name,' she said.

He knew her as the Mute, and as a man. He did not

598

recognize the naked Guillemette. 'I know you are no devil, no demon, and no duke. It is commonplace that such beings have no body hair.'

'A Goddess has everything she wants,' she said. 'Do you not remember me as the duke who ate your silly Malpolon?'

He shuddered at this, but it was not a great shudder. He knew she was lying. 'Your turn will come,' he said.

He swung back towards me, straining to invade me and invest me. It was then that the Goddess Guillemette, not liking what she saw, stooped quickly and bit him.

Forgive my witless brain. It can only perceive things as they are and, after Dogskin's potion, it could scarcely see things at all. What I saw was the naked Guillemette stoop her mouth at the one thing I saw clearly, and that one thing grow larger and longer and shift itself entirely.

It left his smoking loins, from which it disappeared entirely, and sprouted like a unicorn's from the middle of his head. It was white now, and slippery, as slender as a bulrush and about that length. And to tell you the truth of the Mage's last spell, it had a pair of silly feathers spliced into its end.

'Blackthorn shafted with buckthorn,' I heard Gibbu say. 'And with owl's flights to guide it. I'm afraid the villain lied, Perronnelle. Ferblant is not walking on your legs, wherever else you've put them.'

He caught me as I fainted. Or if I was long-time fainted, he caught me as I fell.

'I put three more arrows through his brain,' Gibbu said, holding me against him on his horse, 'but I'm afraid his belly cursed me before he died. It said De Montfort would have me, and the pair of you as well.'

We dismounted in a little meadow below Alaric. The grass was chill, but the night was clear. 'No-one will find us,' Gibbu said. 'Nor even bother to seek.'

We tried to make ourselves comfortable, myself still numb from a potion that might yet kill me.

'Your bedding is on your horse,' the Hunchback chuckled.

599

'And I've got you an old cloak of Dogskin's – unless you'll share beds with me.'

I kissed the rough spots of his beard, and I hugged Guillemette. 'Thank you both for my life,' I said. 'There's plenty will thank you for ridding our Oc of Raymond de Brousses.'

I wrapped myself in the sorcerer's blanket. 'Well, he's dead,' I thought, as I fell asleep.

CANTO TWENTY-THREE

Wherein a maidenhead ransomed to the Devil is redeemed by one who would keep it from rusting.

did not escape from Baron Raymond so easily, though I had no fears about sleeping in the dead man's cloak. I am a Christian woman, I say my prayers often, and wash no more of me than is modest. His cloak smelled very sweet as I gathered it about me. These sorcerers chew herbs. They burn tapers full of spices. The spirits bring them perfumes not known upon earth. I had no fears, as I say.

I put everything down to his libidinous potion. The Baron of Brousses desired me as a woman, though the desires of such a one have no decent end. Therefore he filled me with a languid bane, intended to keep my wits ajar and my limbs lubricious, which is how all men desire their females to be, though they are seldom possessed of the means.

It was foolish to think I could sleep on such a dram. True there was no-one near me to desire, not even by as much as a mountain goat. The Dogskin himself had shown me all his talent and most of his intentions, but such things commonly put a young maid off. Then I had been privileged to see my tormentor's face transformed into a Unicorn with a quiver full of arrows. Such sights as these tend to cool one entirely, and leave a sensitive person calm enough for sleep.

No sooner did I drowse than the dram crept upon me. Nothing pleasant happened, save Merdun tried to have me, and after him Dogskin, though each of them confessed that the other one was dead.

These brutes came to have a very dangerous effect on me. My enemies were by now both of them so well known to me that, aided by the dram, they slowly began to assume the comfortableness of friends. As Merdun put it while he was unbuttoning me, 'This isn't the first time I've tried to rape you, Perronnelle.' The Dogskin said the same, though his tongue was more honeyed and he used the words of sorcery.

603

Not a moment too soon my Phantom arrived, and his strong manly presence drove these brutes away. I asked him very sharply where he had been since the Battle of Muret and a night or two before, and he blushed before answering slowly, 'I've been trying to buy a key.'

I told him I was bewildered. I was drugged, and in consequence bewildered. I was very often bewildered. My dreams made me so.

'I've been trying to buy a key from Solomon of Gerona for that thing between your legs.'

I told him, again very sharply, that there was nothing between my legs.

But there was. There was an iron-hard chastity belt, encrusted with knuckles of diamond, and my Phantom couldn't unfasten it, wrestle with it how he would.

I tell you it was the dram, but it was halfway to almost pleasant to lie there dressed in a chastity belt while my true love panted to free me.

This two way up-and-down tugging in my dream began to wake me. As I woke, I began to discern a hardness between my legs, which being warm was also a softness, and feeling to find this chastity belt, I found no belt but a hand.

This hand was undoubtedly real and fastened upon a wrist which joined pretty closely to an arm, which was attached very closely to my Phantom. My Phantom was here in the flesh, but lying outside my dream. Oh the power of Dogskin's dram.

Then I had a shock, but the potion stopped it shocking me. This phantom arm, which was joined to my Phantom's flesh, belonged to the Hunchback's hideous person which was not hideous at all, or not while it busied itself between my legs it wasn't, though it had been for four year's past.

I was certain at that moment that Gibbu was my man, and if not my man then at least my dream. If that was the effect of the sorcerer's potion, well, wine does a similar thing. And if loving this beautiful brute was great Raymond's curse on me, then this brute had taught me my life and saved it often.

I threw aside Dogskin's cloak, and crawled into Gibbu's

bed, which was bitter with the arrows of death. He kissed me, and I smelled no beard. I held him by the shoulders, not the hump, and he touched me as he would, which was much as he had done in my sleep, and as Merdun had done on the noontide before my three friends had rescued me, but this was done in love.

Surprising how much you can see by starlight and how little you need to notice. There's the fumble and feel of it, and quite a lot is done by breathing.

Gibbu's voice altered during all this, no longer so harsh, but most agreeably tender. I put this down to my own changed perception of things, or even the dew, which was settling all over.

As Mummy had said, 'men's are not like little boys' and a great deal of harm can come out of them. So after a few ins and outs, and twining round his cloak, I told him to point it elsewhere. He'd been most obedient till now. I had to speak extremely sternly then.

He did as he was told and I could only see the nose of him, which was as limp as a ghost. His eyes were all stars.

The dew fell, almost in a spattering and its mist became a fog. Night settled closer. There was no holding him back then, or me I dare say; love has to happen sometime, and it comes to one as often in a haycock as a feather bed.

Have you ever lain and looked up at the stars on a clear night? They are a fair way away, too far for bowshots and certainly for spitting. Outside them is the Crystalline or Frozen Sphere, said Constance de Coulobres, and beyond that to keep everything turning are the mighty cogs of the Primum Mobile, Daddy would lecture her in turn. He was quite clear about it, being of a mechanical persuasion. There is no water power to turn the shafts up there, even though the moon is probably weightier than a stone. There is only the Creator's will, which he sends down to it on a golden chain from Heaven. This put God at a considerable distance, and with my lover's hands beneath my clothing I was glad of it.

I was handling what he had, as women sometimes do, and not tasting his beard again either, when my arm fell across his hump.

His hump had vanished. His bossu wasn't there. The discovery almost sank me into a trance again, till I saw how it was, the lump that wouldn't damage with wounds, the face buried deep in the beard, the beard in the hood, the miraculous youth my grief had seen bathing, the Phantom who appeared in the dawn, and once in the night while the Hunchback hung on a stick to shoot off Gibbu's arrows. The gruff voice that was sometimes a growl.

'Tell me your name,' I said.

'I am Bertrand de Servian. I am the brother of that Servian who came to arrest you at the Mill. When I saw Ferblant doing as he did, I knew I must join him in hiding. That is the end of me.'

A Servian is not quite as much as a Trencavel. Very little is. And yet I think Mummy would have approved.

'What else could I do? My brother who came to arrest you was that Étienne de Servian who went to the great Abbé Bérenger of Saint Thibéry and knelt side by side with him to declare for the Cross. Nor has he deserted it since.

'My father, true to his code, declared in all honour to his liege lord the Count of Toulouse. Nor has he deserted his oath. My family seemed grievously split . . .' His voice had been light, now it was gruff again. 'Now the Servians are no more than clowns in the comedy of war, because the Crusade is doomed for both King and Pope; Raymond of Toulouse is true to nothing, unless it's his prick, and that drags him here and there, like a bullock on the drag rope or a comet by its tail.'

I didn't know what to answer to this, for his own tail had behaved, was behaving, like the most wondrous thing.

The one-time Hunchback, young Bertrand of Servian, was not finished with talking any more than he was through with loving. He kept on coming at me and coming until . . . I have heard Marie-Bise and Thistle speak of shuddering all over with joy. This I did not quite experience. But the stars sharpened to such a tingle, even in the high mist of dawn, that even if my limbs did not shudder of themselves they felt Mount Alaric tremble beside and above them as if my bottom was back in Béziers and mounted on an elephant.

I sobbed at this, but stopped when I caught my lover looking at me with so much pride and conceit you might have thought he'd just cooped a field full of geese and lent them a gander.

'The elephant,' I said to explain my tears. 'When those villains did that butchering at Béziers, did the elephant perish too?'

He couldn't answer me, but Alaric juddered above us again, without my feeling anything at all except contentment.

In the morning I couldn't move. I put my stiffness down to the dram.

Caput Four and Twenty

In which they seek an errant executioner but find more headsmen than they need.

'I've waited four and a half years for that Hunchback,' Guillemette said. 'And the first time he takes off his hump, guess who gets it.'

She didn't sulk. We had to ride till we found Ferblant, and that was the end of it. I knew we would have to ride far. We had seen him in his ruin, and his pride would not take kindly to that, not from all we knew of him, nor from what Dominic had told me.

At Trèbes we asked after a knight in unusual armour, a knight mounted on a gelding.

People laughed at us. 'That was no knight,' they said. 'He was Chief Executioner to the Spanish King. You should see his gear. He wears tubes on his legs, which nobody ever saw, and chest-mail too fine to mention. His sword is a miracle, with acid-work all over, basketed in and out with a pattern of twigs and feathers.'

'Which way is he going?'

'Who knows with a man like that? He is seeking work now his King is dead. There is always employment for such a one. We wonder he rides alone, just the same. They usually go in pairs for their protection. They have no friends. Who are you?'

'His friends.'

'Excuse us if we spit.'

At Montolieu he lodged for a second night. A widow found him a corner of her bed, and offered food. He wanted only wine, then was too weak to drink much of it. After a while he fell down drunk.

When she went to help him to the bed, he tried to embrace her in his armour. She'd had quite enough of men, her husband being recently dead and his brother too, but she lifted him to bed after she'd given him a good talking to.

He was only as light as two sticks, she said. She concluded some of him was missing. It turned out she was right.

We asked her what she meant, but she grew surly on the subject and would not mention it again. When we asked about the following morning, this morning, she was sullen and bashful by turns.

'Praise God, he was stronger by daylight,' Bertrand laughed, as we rode away.

'She found he was missing less than she thought,' Guillemette observed. Like Bertrand, she sounded relieved.

I thought Ferblant would put aside this boast of being an executioner, but he'd made it again to the widow, even in his cups, and was like to go on with it longer than was safe. What she had said that had given us first to think was, 'He told me he was Lord High Axeman to the kings of Spain, yet when he came to my coverlet it seemed he was the one whose limbs had been upon the block.' That's no doubt what comes of being married. She had grown more curious in a night than I had allowed myself in four whole years. She had discovered nearly all of his secret, that he had been quartered but not quite drawn. And as to the horrors of his face, no one sees such things in the dark.

We went through the woods above Saissac. Bouchard was inside the château, and I had no wish to bring such a doughty warrior out.

Nor did we want the wildness and the wolves of Black Mountain, so hurried to find lodgings in Revel. There we put up with the farrier, for such men eat good food and have sleeping space for horses.

Here we heard a pretty story, that tasted well between roast pig and wine. The Spanish Executioner was not five minutes ahead of us. Our host had joined a break in his spur, then beaten a tiny dent out from his foot. Five minutes when we halted. We had been feasting five hours, myself with my lover, himself with two women.

Our feasting was lucky, like all things in love. Ironface no longer journeyed alone. Men of his calling always travel in pairs, they told us at Trèbes. So now Ironface rode with such a pair. Paris's Headsman, or the King's Personal Headsman – no-one was sure about his exact title – had been riding to Albi with Simon de Montfort's own executioner. Our friendly liar had ingratiated himself in his usual fashion, and was doubtless now drinking with them to the tricks of their mystery, if I may call such a brutal calling a mystery or even a craft.

'What next?' I demanded. I now had a man, so no mind of my own.

'A problem to sleep on,' Bertrand said. 'We can't go running after a pair like that. One of us will be arrested, and not necessarily Ferblant.'

'Yes,' sighed Guillemette. 'It's a problem to sleep on.'

Of course she was sighing. There was only the one bed. Although Bertrand still rode with his hump – how else to fill his cloak out? – now we knew there wasn't a surly, ill-formed lump beneath it, there was nothing to keep him from the communal blanket.

I placed Guillemette on one edge and himself on the other with myself in between. I had admitted Bertrand de Servian to my suit as was right and proper. So was this sharing of beds, since men do sleep with women, even women they do not know, but separated by ribbons of garlic, or preferably naked swords.

I was recovered from Dogskin's potion by now, and though the dram had enabled me to loosen the Hunchback's tongue and reveal him as my Phantom and my Phantom as a man, I was sure that all else that happened two night's ago, from the loosening of my imaginary love-belt to certain occurrences in the Primum Mobile, were only a dream and should be treated as such.

My lover did not think so. First we had his hands to contend with, then his lips, then his item I had seen himself adoring at Carcassonne and had handled below Alaric in my still-bewitched fantasy, matching memory with desire; all this followed by such a whispering of his 'yes' followed by my 'no', 'yes' – 'no', 'yes' – 'no', that Guillemette muttered crossly, 'If you two must argue with one another, do it with your mouths closed.'

This was excellent advice, save like all good things it placed the woman at an immediate disadvantage.

Taking my silence for assent, Bertrand or Gibbu or my humpless Hunchback – and I called him all three – began to rock me along and drive his points home. My joy was as intense as I remember to have dreamt it, only this time in the heat and embarrassment of our shared bed I was aware of certain matters that are lost in a chilly dewfall or the darkness of a dream. Guillemette sighed and turned her back on me while my body ingested love's infusion of curds and an immediate aroma of dockleaves. I had been granted what the bull gives and the cow gets, so was clearly a virgin no longer if I ever was yesterday.

This left me with a problem it seems churlish to mention. How to leave my lover for even a moment in this closely shared bed, if my body's needs forced me to stoop into the corner. Worse, because so easy to omit with Guillemette my girl friend only pretending slumber while lying in a lather beyond me, how to stay wakeful enough to prevent my rider dismounting on the inappropriate side.

If only all life's problems were so trivial. I was only half alert when I heard the rumble of horsemen.

Horses come and go from a farrier's forecourt, but these are lonely tracks below Black Mountain, and few folk cast a shoe on the dark side of midnight, nor does custom ever come galloping into a smithy by the score.

I tried to leap from bed. I was prevented by the weight of a lover who preferred me to his pillow. As Mummy always said, 'No good can ever come of it.' Nor did it. The air was loud with hoof-iron, then of blades unsheathed.

Guillemette was already up, and trying to string a longbow in the dark. Bertrand reacted slowly – another man spoiled by love. Instead of pinning them two by two, shoulderblade against breastbone, as they came at us up the stair, he let the newcomers catch him struggling with his galligaskins, which those Northerners call garguesques, whenever they bear to mention what they keep down there.

Guillemette shot down two of the fellows who burst in on us, not yolking them both together, but with two good single pulls, each of them through the windpipe.

They made a great bubble and froth at this, and didn't want to die quickly. This annoyed their comrades greatly. Bertrand had latched up his legs by now, and looped a string to his bow. Thinking he was the culprit, they rushed to kick his head in and club him to bits with their feet.

I laid my hands on my sword, though Guillemette, being undressed, was not wearing more than a dagger. We did with these what we could for Bertrand's protection, struggling for a whole minute or more, till the walls were splashed very prettily with blood, and the bedding also. There were several cut lips and black eyes. I counted two of each on Guillemette, and could only gaze sideways myself.

By this time we were properly subdued, and dragged half naked downstairs.

We had slept above the main smithy in what used to be the harness gallery, and before that a loft for sheep. We found the farrier was waiting for us there with Amaury de Montfort and Guy de Sorèze, a local baron whose castle was close to Revel. The farrier had left us to ride to Sorèze. Sorèze had taken his men first to Saissac, presumably to claim the reward, and Amaury de Montfort had come on with some of his uncle Bouchard de Marly's men to make good their numbers. They had the local Bishop with them too.

'I carry warrants for your arrest,' Amaury de Montfort reminded us, 'with a clear seal of death upon them. I could hang you now. I could burn you tomorrow. However, such is not to be your fortune, as being widely considered too good for you.'

615

'These caitiffs are ours,' Guy de Sorèze said, 'and must bear the displeasure of a Bishop's Court.'

'As you see, Christianity is not yet dead in the South, praise be. All over Oc we have discovered such noblemen – '

'Greedier for gold than for God,' I said. 'I am a Christian also, and not one to betray my friends for a bag of the De Montforts' silver.'

'I, too, am often so,' Guillemette professed. 'I always hear Mass on a saints day or Sunday.'

Bertrand was unconscious at our feet, and so said nothing.

'There's a reward for that Hunchback,' said Guy de Sorèze, 'be he dead or merely witless. Shackle him up. Shackle them all up.'

The farrier went to the wall for some logging chains.

'I should prefer to examine the women alone,' the Bishop said, gazing at Guillemette who wore little more than her girdle and dagger.

'I know you, Jacques Peyrolles,' she said. 'You used to examine me enough when you had the care at Montagnac. You examined the best of me then. There is nothing new to find.'

De Montfort's men all laughed at this, but by then the farrier had fastened her about with a four-ended chain.

'I am a daughter of the Trencavels,' I stated. 'Whether you like it or not, De Sorèze, it will take more than you and more than a Bishop's Court to determine my end.'

'It is true, Perronnelle of the Mountains, that I have but little influence,' said Jacques Peyrolles, gathering Guillemette towards him in the meantime, arms and legs by her chain, 'but you'll find I carry weight enough to prosecute any family's bastard, not to mention a bedling degenerate, and such a one as yourself.'

'I am my mother's daughter,' I said. 'And my mother was a Trencavel.'

'Yes, and your mother was a woman. And a woman, what is she?'

By this time the smith had made four bands of metal for my wrists and ankles, and four bands for Bertrand my Belami's also. Sweating from the heat at the end of his bellows, he began to clip on our chains. 'I'll take your swords in payment for these amulets,' he scoffed, 'and your horses as a deposit against your bed and board.' He closed a moist eye and added, 'Only in case you don't come back.' It was a jolly sentence. He said it again. 'Only in case you don't come back!'

As he finished fastening us, and he had to lug and tug at Bertrand on the floor, he said for Guy de Sorèze's benefit: 'These three are potent witches and sorcerers. Whenever did you see a hunchback who is not?'

'That, too, is my father's opinion,' young Amaury agreed. 'They spoke of executioners, and the purchase of corpses. These people work for anatomists and necromancers, and are themselves creatures of darkness.'

'Be careful I don't change you to a snail,' I said. 'You're sweating like a snail – or a battlefield slug.'

Such talk was pointless. Soon one of them would beat me or close my other eye.

All this time I heard Guillemette protesting and screaming from the room next door, which was I believe the farrier's kitchen. Was the Crusade to end for me exactly as it began, echoing to the cries of a woman in torment?

'You're a De Montfort,' I said to young Amaury.

He nodded at me, defensive but bright.

'And you're a something also,' I said to Guy de Sorèze. 'Are you going to stand idly by, and have your men stand by, while yet another priest plays confessor to a defenceless female? Who are the heretics now?'

The Baron Guy said nothing, but his men avoided my gaze. Amaury de Montfort went over to the kitchen door. 'Come away, Jacques,' he called. 'There's a good wine mulling at Saissac, and I daresay a treacle. Leave the Devil's work to his own, I say.'

*　　*　　*

617

We spent a wretched night, all three of us being chained to the horse-rings in the wall. Yet all things are better than they seem. Guillemette wasn't hurt, or not by her Bishop. 'I was protesting at his frotting, and his foutering, and fiche,' she said. 'I was used to giving that one all the effs while he was our curate and I was still on my father's knee. But he used to pay me for them in those days. He used to give me Absolution,' she said. 'And I need Absolution. Tonight he offered nothing in return.'

Bertrand woke in the morning. 'I thought it prudent to give them best,' he said, and fell asleep again. By the time the smithy was stirring and our captors afoot, he opened one eye and said, 'I wish to die as Gibbu the Hunchback. Or as Gibbu at the least. I've no desire to bring further misery on the name of Servian.'

The thought that he was already resigning himself to death quite cast me down again.

Then the farrier's wife came in from the kitchen, bringing us bread and soup. She looked shamefaced at the beginning, but when she saw what a state we were in, and being as women are, she rushed to get our clothes and a needle and thread to stitch us into them, though we could drop a cotte or cloak down over our chains.

I think she was shocked at her husband's betrayal of us, whatever their gain in coin. And like most other women, I suppose she saw naked men not often, and naked women not at all.

The farrier came in and said to us, 'They're waiting for you at horse. I've told them none of you has a mount so they're bringing you a cart or so.' He came to pincer us down from the horse-rings. 'Those chains'll be very comfortable,' he said, 'and better than you deserve. You'll be able to feed yourself and scratch, and all things bodily else.'

Guy de Sorèze came to tell us we were bound for the Ecclesiastical Court at Albi. These Courts find all men guilty, and their best punishment is the bonfire.

No cart could go to Albi, not by Castres and after rain.

But they had a good pair of rouncies and dragged us there on a sled.

'We could walk there quicker,' I said to my companions.

'It's only to make us look foolish,' Guillemette said.

'They won't keep us chained for our arraignment,' Gibbu observed. 'They'll take off our chains for that.'

I saw no escape from a Bishop's Court, not among so many people. At least my love sounded hopeful, and I found some comfort in that.

Our ride, or rather our dredge, to Albi progressed from discomfort to a pain scarcely short of agony. I daresay the route was no more stony, rutted or holed at its end than at its beginning, but whereas one bump can seem no more than a reminder of childhood joys such as being horsed on Daddy's knee, the thousandth comes to agitate a slowly evolving bruise. At the end of the first day on the sled, I began to wish Raymond de Brousses had indeed removed my backbone. It was very little use to me by evening, and excruciating throughout the night.

They shackled us to our sled in a sitting position, and at night we were commonly hung against a wall standing up, generally by horse-bolts, so we had neither rest on our journey nor sleep at its end.

In places where men keep animals there is generally an abundance of gnats and midges, attracted by the damp of their stale. There is also the flea together with his good friend the louse, and their country cousin the hay-tick. If the animals are absent, these brutes need a substitute. They begin about your neck and your earlobes, and by the time a few of them leave to tell their neighbours about you these pastures are either full or used up, so the latecomers graze in all manner of other places Mummy and Constance de Coulobres would never allow me to name.

Nor do they really enjoy you. They would prefer the underparts of a badly ostled horse, so bite ungraciously in ways that express their discontentment.

It would take Guy de Sorèze and his drag horses at least three days to sled us to Albi. We passed through a number of hamlets too mean to mention. The people who lived there would run from their houses – or be turned out by De Sorèze's men – and watch sullenly as our procession of horsemen, carthorses and dredge scraped by them. Once they were told we were going to be burned in Albi they would buck up enough to throw their ordures at us – rotting vegetables, vine stumps and the like. There were only stones at one place – Cahuzac I think – but the village was mainly children and the drunk, silly men who had sired them. The young have no sense of what is appropriate, the male child especially, up to the age of about five and twenty. A stone is a dangerous projectile, and when a whole village throws one simultaneously, the result is difficult to duck, especially close to.

Guy de Sorèze intervened violently to protect us, even though his own men had provoked the trouble, and on his own orders. Whether it was because he realized that over-boisterous villagers were likely to render Court and Executioner unnecessary, or whether it was because several of his destriers were hit by flints on the rump, who can tell?

'I thought they were going to knock your face off before I had a chance to kiss it again,' Bertrand said to me, his mouth bleeding.

'What about kissing me?' Guillemette asked him. We were a pretty trio anyway, after the beating Guy de Sorèze's men had given us a night or two before, with our cut lips thickening and our swollen eyes turning blue round the edges the way they do before the bumps go down and they look mean and black and take a month to grow better. 'What about kissing me, someone?' she asked, being a brave, pithy young woman, and all of us chained shoulder to back on that dredge so that no-one could possibly kiss anyone, not even twisty-headed.

'Kissing in public is a very lewd gesture,' I reminded them. 'Especially between man and woman.'

'I don't mind being lewd so long as I'm alive,' Guillemette

retorted. 'I want to go on being lewd a hundred years longer.'

'I preferred her when she was Mute,' Bertrand said.

We were coming into Castres, a place of importance which I do mention, with no way of tidying our hair, or making ourselves presentable.

At Castres people began to say my name. They had already got wind of our approach and knew my reputation.

This led to our being surrounded by an angry crowd. They didn't want to spit on us or stone us. They wanted to hang us all up by the neck then and there, hang us still fastened to the dredge. In fact, as I began to listen to them more clearly above the hubbub, it was only myself they wanted to hang up by the neck, while I was fastened upon the dredge and my two friends still sat upon it.

I must say I was relieved to hear they meant less harm to Bertrand and Guillemette, but I experienced a tightening of the throat just the same, to think how much weight they proposed to suspend from it.

It also exercised me to discover why I should attract so much obloquy to my own person. Had I not done doughty deeds on their behalf, and attempted to inspire Oc and Raymond of Toulouse to yet more meaningful endeavours?

Apparently this was the main cause of their outcry against me. I had attempted, as a mere woman, to meddle with History. I had stirred things up, as if politics were as easy as mixing a cake.

I have never mixed a cake in my life, and I told them so, but this only infuriated them the more, especially the women.

Eventually Guy de Sorèze had his men-at-arms hold them back from me, while allowing them to make their opinions known round the backsides of the horses, so to speak.

They saw things like this. When the local barons of Oc were in their castles, life was good. They knew where they were. When Simon de Montfort's barons threw them out of

621

their castles and placed themselves inside them, life wasn't bad. They knew where they were. What they didn't want was any more chopping and changing. Bad luck comes in cycles as surely as the stars turn to circles. People who want to chop and change disturb one's peace of mind and are bad for business. And people who want to change things back again are even worse. Nothing in life stays the same. Look at the butterfly. The chicken can't step back into the egg and only a fool would try to make it do so. Meanwhile, since they couldn't have me to themselves, they wished me green sticks, damp kindling, and a slow bonfire.

The crowd blocked our way no more, and our sled was allowed to proceed into the centre of Castres. The rabble did not follow us. Something else took their attention. Something that was greeted with a cheer.

We were taken into an ostler's for our evening's lodgings, not a smithy, so we lacked the benefit of a decent fire. Again we were hooked up by attaching our chains to the horse-rings, and again we had a bad time of it.

Guy de Sorèze's men liked the feeling of security this arrangement gave them. It meant the ostler and his assistants could look after us, and no guard would be needed.

Nor had Guy de Sorèze's men deceived themselves. To be hung up by logging chains from a horse-bolt and its rings is to be harnessed as tight as may be. One is not comfortable. One cannot sleep. One aches almost to death. One is secure.

Before going off duty and watching their master drink a cup of aqua-vitae a guard came to share some of his satisfaction with us. 'We'd have put you up in the town prison, but it's full of whores.'

'We wouldn't mind,' Bertrand said. He was showing a degree of coarseness never easy to accept in an intimate.

'Three to be exact. But that's full. They're taking them to Albi, and putting them on trial for sorcery. Much like yourselves.'

'We're the only whores who're going on trial for sorcery,'

Bertrand insisted. 'You've been listening to the wrong gossips!' A man who wears a hump is allowed to say such things. I wished he weren't.

'There's one of them down there offering to open her legs for anyone who'll bring them a loaf of bread and a jug of wine,' our custodian said. 'Either or both of you ladies feel like treating me likewise?'

A silence followed, even though Bertrand was inside it.

'No comfort, no soup,' was the man's only comment as he left us to hang in our irons.

We passed a most melancholy night at Castres. All nights must be so that hang one in chains like sails on a harbour wall until one comes to resemble a string of ancient garlic, even as far as the smell. Our bodily functions were beginning to afflict us mightily, in that matters we could only discharge in the morning when they released us to be fastened to the dredge or in the evening when they liberated us to the wider freedom of the horse-bolts began to trouble us before midnight was cried and were in an excruciating urgency of need by the time Belami, who has imaginative ears, claimed he could detect the first cock.

This was the second night we spent perpendicular. The trouble with storing felons in the pendulous mode is that everything runs downwards – I speak of nothing unsavoury: we were still in control of our wit – till it fetches up against the snaffle and such-like to cause a stoppage in the blood, rather as storms pile logs under bridges. The wrists and ankles swell. The rest of one sags into a most dropsical ache and the joints feel as if they are locked inside a thickening pickle of fluid.

This renders one even more attractive to mouths that fly in the dark than one normally is when one lives in a horse shed. At Castres I swear I was eaten by grasshoppers and dwelt in by wasps and all manner of insects that normally content themselves with fresh leaves or rotting fruit. My hair became a hive and my ears the kind of caverns into which children shout then listen to hear if the Devil will answer them back, and of course he does. He had a lengthy altercation, question and answer, buzz and echo, with a gnat that entered me by the left ear at about three in the morning and didn't emerge until my guards permitted me to crouch and scratch myself two hours after dawn. Their insolent attentions – the guards, not the insects – were an irritation, but I refused to be hindered by their closeness. No woman who has been forced to sit on Merdun the Bastard's hand for half an hour is likely to be disturbed by louts who merely gawp at her. They jeered as I relieved myself and I gazed back at them and pictured them as I had last seen the sinister son of the De Montforts, each with a dozen arrows through his face.

As I adjusted my clothing I thought: thirst, starvation, dropsy, insect bites, and now this need for the pot – is it any wonder we criminals give such poor account of ourselves and frequently appear grateful to be condemned? I have seen men and women walk quite boldly to their place of execution – if they are still able to walk, that is – because they look forward to dying as a blessed relief from their present condition (I speak only of those who face lenient sentences such as the gallows, the block, stoning, death by the hammer and wedge – though that takes a merry hour or two, unless one has very short legs – and *peines fortes et dures*, which some find cruel, but which at least leaves one with time to collect oneself).

Bertrand my Belami finished with himself without attracting the kind of attention afforded Guillemette and me. But as we were shackled up to our post on the dredge he grumbled, 'What goes on in Castres? Why was last night so noisy?'

He spoke true. It had been noisy. I felt proud of my love for noticing it in the midst of our other discomforts. Who on earth would want to make a noise in Castres, and what about? There are no games of put-the-ball, jump-in-the-ring or fiddlesticks there, and it grows dark early because of the hill to the west and the thickness of people's breath. Men have nothing to do by night-time except go to bed with their

624

wives, and all that women can do is turn over quickly and pretend to be asleep.

'It was the whore,' said the guard who'd spoken to me last night. He patted my braceleted wrists into place by my ears and said, 'I told you that she said she'd let any man do it who brought the three of them bread and wine. Presently every man in the town was there, with clothes unfastened, bringing wine by the tun and bucket, and loaves in a miraculous pile, not to mention sides of beef. She had all of the town, some men going round twice.'

'Why all the noise?' Belami asked.

'That was when their own women's backs grew cold and they began to ask themselves questions. Out they all came in their bedclothes and bonnets, and that's when the fight started and they all got shrill. Then they were given wine and told to cheer up. But their men were still seeing the whore. So they got drunk again, and that's when the fight started and they all got shrill. Some women were shrill all night long.'

'What was the whore's name?' Belami asked.

'She's called the Maid of the Mountains. I had her three times and I'll never forget her.'

'I'm the Maid of the Mountains,' I said.

'I won't forget you either, if you'll give me a chance.'

'It can only be La Mamelonne,' Belami said wistfully.

'Can it?' I believe I spoke crossly.

There was so much bread and wine left down at the jail that our guards decided to give us some.

So we set off for Albi on our last drag. The road was rough, with uncertain edges. In consequence the tow was shortened to keep us closer to the horses. To be behind and below a pair of tails is never pleasant, particularly since neither of these was long enough to remove the resulting flies from our noses.

No sooner were we shackled up than we heard a great cheer from near the town jail, and the sun was briefly darkened by the tossing up of caps.

'The whores are moving,' our guard said.

'Oh to be with the whores,' Belami muttered.

Before I could reprove him, one of our horses did it for me. Immediately afterwards we started away from the ostler's yard at a very brisk drag.

This brought us into the crowd that had been seeing off La Mamelonne. One is never at one's best with flies on one's nose and horse-spatter in one's tresses. Belami it was who faced forward, but Guillemette and I were nape to neck with him and also had our hair roots quickened by the same refreshing shower.

The crowd enjoyed us. That is it jeered at our looks and kicked the rest of us. Like all such crowds it was made up of faces we seemed already to know or got to learn very rapidly. There is nothing like a generous donation of dribble to impress a mouth on one's memory. Then when it hawks a second time it seems like a friend of some standing. You count its teeth to reassure yourself they are still missing, and watch for how far its gums have receded, with considerable anxiety in case this time you receive a gobful of bone.

Thus it was I came to be spat upon by a face I had already studied many times before, a face I could never forget even though my memory of it had long since pronounced it to be no face at all. I can best term it the face of the Triple Executioner. For there was the non-face, the principle face, the masked face, holding its two other heads towards us, so the executioner from Paris and Simon de Montfort's neck-cutter and skin-stripper could spit upon us at will.

Itself could not spit, though I heard something bounce inside its grill like a bird's beak behind bars.

'Ferblant!' Guillemette said (or I think that is what she said) as an accurately delivered twin-ended spatter of Paris mouthwater removed the horse dung from her left upper eyelid. 'Ferblant!'

'Pig of Hell!' De Montfort's man told her back.

'Heretic and Harlot!' the Parisian said to me, the words sounding much more resourceful in a foreign tongue. They found so much favour with the crowd that people began to flap their clogs at us once more, rather than their mouths.

'Great whore of shit!' Ironface hissed at me personally, and I loved him for it. It's a favoured form of greeting throughout Oc, and you often hear men call their wives so, and children their mothers, with real affection. '*Grande putaine de merde!*' repeating it in Frankish (or perhaps that's Spanish?)

He dragged the other two heads away with him, but being unable to spit upon us direct, or at least deliver more than a finely shredded rain, he threw something instead, a stinging, but not bruising, object that bounced off my cheek and rolled upon Belami's lap.

My love retrieved it and unrolled it (our chains at least left our hands free to be of some use to us during the hours of daylight). The crumpled paper or, more exactly, parchment, was covered with neat lettering and a picture in red, blue and gold.

Ironface had tossed us a sheet torn from a missal, and it must have jerked his heart to rip it out almost as much as it had to spit upon us, his old friends and loves.

'So Ironface is still for us,' I said. 'But what, even in his full strength, could he do for us?'

Bertrand began to laugh. 'He could execute us,' he said. Since his knock on the head I had begun to wonder if he was quite right there. He was showing a dangerous yearning for the Hereafter, almost as if he were becoming infected with religion. He said it again. 'Old Ironface would execute us,' he chuckled. 'That would be a help.' He laughed and invited Guillemette to join in.

She didn't. She thought it no more amusing than I did.

CHANSON TWENTY-FIVE

In which all manner of whores and virgins are arraigned for heresies, witchcraft and treasons and so condemned, sundry common folk besides.

Bishop's Court can sit anywhere. All it needs are one or two bishops, a couple of lesser clergy and a goodly supply of wine. This is mixed with iron filings, soot or stinkhorn in order to provide the copious amounts of ink that will be needed to record the examination in brief and the Court's conclusions in extenso. Five minutes of question and answer, even when no answer is given, often give rise to conclusions that require several volumes of the best vellum to encapsulate. Such matters as should women wear plain scarves or fancy hats to cover their hair and shade their faces in church, or did Jean-Jacques Clarges, being a shepherd, indeed fornicate with Widow Loudun's pullets and thus delay their coming on to lay, are properly deliberated and the conclusions recorded in wine mixed with iron filings, soot or stinkhorn and sent to the Vatican. By the time the Vatican has had time to digest an answer, the shepherd Clarges will long since have been hanged for unnaturalness, malice and bestiality, and the village women will have grown too old to go to church anyway. The bishops and lesser clerics will have left themselves a little wine unmixed with stinkhorn to fortify their patience.

That is not how Albi does it. That is how the world does it. Albi takes longer. For a start, being a noted centre of heresy, its Bishop's Courts are called Ecclesiastical Courts, and although they too consist of bishops, Albi requires more of them. In our case it was to be twelve, the number of Christ's apostles, with a thirteenth to act as prosecutor. There were also to be representatives from among the barony, because the Court was only held to be competent to try me for unnaturalness, contempt for Jesus Christ and Pope Innocent, witchcraft, apostasy and heresy. Simon de Montfort had sent from Pennautier to

631

suggest that it would be much simpler to try me for treason also.

It would take a considerable time to collect the barons from the hunting field and the bishops from the nunnery. Meanwhile we were housed in the cellars of a mansion next to the Archbishop's residence in the Cathedral Square, and therefore adjacent to our house of trial and likely place of execution. Our cellar was damp, because of the nearness of the river.

The junior clergy often came to look at us. The local friars in particular would come downstairs daily to poke themselves through the doors at the women. But in general we were well kept and not abused. We were in the overall charge of Guy de Sorèze's men, as we had been from the beginning. We were allowed to wash our faces and buy in changes of linen. Nor were we shackled, save by the feet.

There were twelve of us in our cellar, eleven women and my Belami, who still insisted on being Gibbu. It was part of our prosecutor's intention to present us as a coven, even though we came from different places, and thus easily ensure bonfires for all.

Six of the women I did not know. They were ordinary peasant girls from around Albi who had offended either a neighbour in some way or their own parents by refusing to be married to the local maniac, or a scrofulous half-cousin with warts and carbuncles, as well as the local disease of brown mouth. Easy to denounce such waywardness as witchcraft, and hold the maid's supposed blastings and spell-mumblings to have caused old fellows to go dribbling mad and young louts to break out in pimples and festers. The brown mouth would not be given in evidence, as half of the local bishops suffered from it anyway.

The other three women were, of course, the same parcel of friends and whores who had preceded us through cheering crowds behind cleaner horses and on a smoother dredge.

My beloved Mamelie was one of them, and at last with us, though much more hoity-toity as a result of her public following. The Fish Girl had been sledded alongside her, but found scant room for dancing in our cellar, and was consequently in a decline. When we tried to gain her a little more space for five minutes a day, say the length of a corridor, Guy de Sorèze refused us, and my chatty guard said she would dance soon enough once they'd skinned her and lit a flame around her ankles.

Mitten was there too, and philosophical about her likely fate. She said so many men had scalded her bottom and in other ways abused her in her brief span of years that she didn't mind what further heat she was sat upon. She also told us something I certainly did not know, namely that it was the practice to burn witches on a nest of green sticks, which begin with steam and smoke, and once this fume comes on to rise and obscure matters from the vulgar gaze, the executioner commonly creeps close and strangles them from behind. Thus did we live in hope.

The only question to answer was why Mamelie, the Fish Girl and Mitten had been arrested in the first place, save that La Mamelonne had been a sorceress and still kept magic pictures in her body for any priest to find, while Mitten was a high pasture heretic, and Violette quite mad. Yet most people are one or the other, or something very much like, and expect to live out their natural term – seventy years for a man and twenty-three for a woman – without being flayed or burned. Childbirth and runaway horses threaten enough trouble.

The plain fact of the matter is that they were arrested on the direct orders of my uncle-in-law the Count of Toulouse. He had all of the whores in Oc rounded up either for his own entertainment or to enclose as nuns to appease the Pope. He recognized my friends as being immoral particles from among my own entourage and saw a chance to ingratiate himself with Simon de Montfort by handing them over while he fashioned yet another sword to stab him in the back. So do great ones conduct themselves in relation to affairs of state.

I take no account of the rumour that my uncle had it in

for La Mamelonne because of the truths she had circulated concerning the febrile state of his pricker. One never likes to think ill of one's relations, and I had no way of testing either end of that story. As I say, we lived in hope.

We lived well. Although Violette la Vierge and Mitten made it known in their various ways that they considered themselves retired, and wished to deny men any further use of their bodies as carnal receptacles, and thus ease their twin souls' passage to Heaven, La Mamelonne stated boldly that she intended to honour her many admirers by working up to the very last moment, and if possible beyond it.

The ecclesiastical authorities allowed her an upstairs room for the purpose. Indeed, all of Albi and the Tarn, if not the whole of Oc, would have been in a riot if they hadn't. She was to have a plentiful supply of cloths and clean riverwater also, for it is well known that whores like to scrub their bodies many times a day for the delight of the foul fellows they lie among.

She was then free to entertain the burghers, the local peasantry, and an increasing band of pilgrims and devotees, many of the latter being those same men who had followed her as her own palmers south into the Pyrenees, but who now found their needles pointing in the reverse direction and leading them unerringly north towards Albi.

She was permitted to charge what she would for allowing men to worship at her holy places, but principally their own means and our keep. Her body, she continued to stress, was a shrine not a collection of sacred relics, and a cathedral more than either. In private moments with me she said she preferred to think of it as one of those inspirational pastures into which the saints were wont to stray, and there amid blossom, bud and bough see suns spin in the sky, and listen to the All Father make known His most excellent mysteries. In short La Mamelonne was a divine landscape, a place of miracles. With such a piece of holy coin in our possession, the resting eleven of us ate well. Mamelie, poor girl, scarcely had time to open her mouth.

Did she have to pay a price for being allowed to donate herself to charity? I am afraid she did. She was required to pleasure Guy de Sorèze and his men gratis, and the hundreds of local clergy as well. With the latter, even what she gave them freely cost her twice over, because a priest not only begs things from you, he scolds you while he takes it.

'How do you put up with it?' I asked her.

'I keep them short of breath,' she explained. Omniscient lovely, she thought of everything, but even she could not put a term upon our imprisonment, or guess with any optimism at our fate.

Our friendly guard was more helpful. 'You'll either be flayed or burned,' he said, 'or you may be lucky and find yourself being drawn, which I agree is painful, then hanged and quartered. I don't think there's much chance of the prong, or death by the hot iron, do you? And as for being broken on a wheel, Albi doesn't have one, and I haven't heard any carpenters being busy. The place is full of dry rot anyway. Apparently, felons used to break the wheel here in the old days, and that was painful for everyone.'

'How soon can they entice their bishops and barons together?' I asked him.

'By the Madeleine, anyway. The City has a really splendid fair for La Madeleine, as you know, and it goes on for days, even beyond the Saint's day herself. There'll be twelve of you to dispose of, even if we can't find any more young women to arrest in the meantime. They'll save you and the great whore and the Hunchback till last, of course.'

Our guard guessed correctly. The Grand Consistorie, the Consitorium of Bishops or Ecclesiastic Court of Albi was convened in early July two clear Mondays before the Feast of the Madeleine. It was the sixteenth year of Pope Innocent's reign, and the fifth summer of his humiliation of the Land of Oc.

The Court sat in the great hall of the Archbishop's Palace, with the Archbishop himself presiding. His throne was

flanked by enough bishops, canons and such-like dignitaries
of the church to lend weight to the occasion, their bottoms
being squeezed on to two benches, one on either side of him.
Amaury de Montfort and Guy de Sorèze were here to furnish
the necessary secular gravitas, and to ensure we were at the
least hanged, boiled, fried or gridded for something – or
for nothing if it was deemed suitable, provided we were
hanged, boiled, fried or gridded at the end of it. These two
noblemen sat upon padded stools to the left of the court.
All other people stood.

We were to be examined on the Court's behalf by
Guillemette's old persecutor, Jacques Peyrolles, Bishop of
Revel, who was the only person permitted to move about.

Bertrand was wrong in one particular. We were shackled
for our arraignment, fettered singly but secured hand and
foot. There was to be no escape from this place, and not
much hope afterwards. The only person among us who had
any chance of freedom at any time had been Mamelie from
her upstairs room, but she had been too busy whoring to
consider the matter.

The twelve of us stood in a line facing the bishops while
Peyrolles proposed to his Grace the Archbishop exactly how
the twelve of us were to be proceeded with.

I was the principal accused. All the others were merely
implicated witnesses as to the fact of my guilt, a collection of
heretics and witches whom the Court might find it convenient
to sentence as it finished its business with them. If I were
found guilty, then they would be found guilty with me. If
I were not found guilty, or before I was pronounced to be
guilty, they could themselves be judged culpable of capital
error, in which case I should become guilty by attraction.

Jacques Peyrolles explained that it was sometimes convenient to limit or select the charges against an individual in
accordance with the punishments locally available. However,
the Archbishop would be pleased to learn that an almost
infinite number of refinements were possible, as Belibaste
the King of Paris's Chief High Executioner was passing

through Albi, and his services had been retained. He was a man infinitely experienced in the art. Added to that, Ferblant, Headsman and Torturer Extraordinary to the late King Peter of Aragon was travelling with him, as was Jourdain, Viscount Simon de Montfort's own headsman and torturer. All three of these initiates had been required to interrupt their journey till the business of the Madeleine was concluded.

'Are these fellows accomplished skinners?'

'They are, my lord.'

'Can they remove eyes without rending the lids?'

'They can, my lord.'

'Do they draw and can they peel back fingers?'

'They can draw both male and female, my lord. And have their implements ready and sharp about them.'

'There the whole matter may rest,' the Archbishop pronounced. 'The Court will rise and consider its verdict.'

This took us aback, and Jacques Peyrolles as well. 'With respect, my lord Archbishop, the Vatican will need to know what the accused are being charged with, and something of the weight of testimony against them.'

'The female – who is she? Perronnelle de Saint Thibéry – is manifestly and notoriously a woman. She has turned simple wives' minds away from their duty to their husbands, and in other ways offended His Holiness the Pope. Need any more be said?'

'A great deal, my lord. She is guilty of a great deal besides. I venture to suggest your grace would find it hard to go beyond a scourging and a burning for being a notorious woman and corrupter of other women.'

'True. Very true. Pray proceed.'

In the end I was charged with being a whore, a heretic, a most notorious horse-thief and murderess, a suborner of marriages, a witch, a traitor to King Philippe, and a traducer of the vassalage of the Count of Toulouse. I was accused of being a Trencavel, as well as the Church's most constant detractor and an enemy of Pope Innocent the Second. I had eaten children alive and dead, raw and cooked, had lascivious commerce with asses and goats, and been seen riding about fields of battle in the company of naked women, a diabolical familiar and a ritual doll fashioned from tin. I had also mixed potions and laid spells against Simon de Montfort, the Viscount of Carcassonne, causing his wife's teeth to drop out in an attempt to starve the said Alice de Montmorency to death.

This was a standard accusation, and nobody seemed in the least surprised by it. It would have been a waste of bishops to charge me with less.

First to be examined were the six peasant girls. Jacques Peyrolles placed them in a line and told them to speak up. They said nothing, not knowing what they were accused of, and not having seen so many pairs of eyes watching them in their lives, not even sheep's, or goats' or geese's.

After five minutes of silence, Peyrolles said triumphantly, 'You see, my lord Archbishops, she strikes them all dumb.'

'Vuisande,' I called to one of them, 'tell them your name and where you come from.'

'I am Vuisande Strawberry Face, and I live with my parents at Dourgn,' the girl said. She began to weep.

'They speak only at her command,' Jacques Peyrolles observed. 'Is it not true you were in an esbat with this woman's coven at Belcaire, where she taught you to dance with sticks between your legs, to swallow fire and talk to devils?'

Since none of them had been further than two leagues from Albi in their lives, nor clapped eyes on me until I was imprisoned with them, they hung their heads at this question also.

'Enough,' the Archbishop instructed, 'these are manifest women and should not be proceeded against further. I sentence this Vuisande to be delivered from evil by being burned alive and her soul thus returned to her Maker.'

'Amen,' said Jacques Peyrolles.

'The other five women are more stubborn cases.'

638

'Put to the torment, then burned, my lord Archbishop?'

'That would be excessive, I feel. These are only women, as I have remarked before, and susceptible in consequence. Nor are they the principals in this case. Let us deal leniently and instruct they be flayed alive in the public square and their skins exhibited. That should be sufficient for them.'

'Does your Consistorie conclude the woman Saint Thibéry to be guilty by attraction, my lord?'

The bishops put their heads together on their benches, and the Archbishop snapped, 'She is so. Indeed she is.'

'And will you pronounce sentence at this time?'

'Only on these lesser charges. I must proceed equitably. She will be sentenced as I have already indicated.'

'Skinned or incinerated, my lord?'

'Both.'

'And are all others among the accused to be deemed guilty by attraction?'

'That must be the inescapable conclusion. On the lesser counts only.'

'And their punishment?'

'Skin them, of course. Skin them with the rest. My bishops may wish to add things later, according to canon law when they have scrutinized the appropriate decretals.'

The Consistorie rose for its midday meal, and made it plain that it saw no need to reconvene until the morrow.

The next day we began later. The great hall was stuffy and hot, and everyone in a temper.

'Stand forth, Gibbu the Hunchback.'

Bertrand my Belami stood forth, his shoulders and back lump drooping in a most uncomely manner after being so long in the chains.

'Now, Hunchback, you are accused of being a most notorious Hunchback. What do you say to that?'

'I have attracted some attention to myself, yes.'

'Because of the hump the Devil fastened on to you?'

'Because of my bow and arrow.'

'What of this unspeakably loathsome hump you carry on your back? Is it not noteworthy in its own right?'

'I must confess it is. It has had darts shot at it, and abuse flung at it from the lips of fools, even as recently as now.'

'So you curse the Devil for it?' Jacques Peyrolles winked largely at his bench of bishops and barons, then spun upon Belami.

'What are you leering at me for, if you find my hump so ugly?'

'You curse the Devil? Answer.'

'I never think of him. God has already cursed him.'

'You curse him for causing you to have a hump.'

'God makes humps. The Devil can make nothing, except mischief.'

'So God made your hump?' Bishop Peyrolles was extremely disappointed to elicit a conclusion bristling with Christian orthodoxy.

'To the extent that he made the man who made it.'

'A marvellously precise fellow. He means his father, my lord Archbishop. What next, my lord?'

'Flay him. He is manifestly innocent of heresy but guilty of all else by attraction. Let him be skinned, and his tongue first, along with the silly women!'

Guillemette was in a rather more difficult position than we were. Apparently the farrier at Revel had abused her in his kitchen at much the same time as Jacques Peyrolles had been feeling her grossly about. Like many a louche fellow who tangles his fingers in a young woman's fastenings, the farrier found it convenient to say she'd bewitched him. And, of course, there were rewards in Guillemette's case, being my own.

The farrier was a witty enough fellow while he was chaining us up and mouthing slanders, but in a court of ecclesiastics he was likely to make a fool of himself. Jacques Peyrolles must almost have knitted thumbs with him up Guillemette's skirts, so found it more than convenient to oblige him. After all, Guillemette had already been sentenced by attraction.

'You say the woman Guillemette is a witch who snared you by means of libidinous chantings and posturings?'

'I do, my lord Bishop. I know she is a witch. My dillypin rose as stiff as a pintle just to look at her across the room, and it's very near-sighted usually.'

Guillemette tossed her head at this, and Peyrolles quickly motioned the farrier to continue.

'Then when I unbuttoned her top piece and fell to sucking her boobies I was immediately in a deep swoon. That's when you came in, my lord.'

There was a degree of consternation at this, on Peyrolle's part at least.

'What is moreover they tasted bitter. One like a kernel inside a plum, the other of salt.'

'I was sweating, you old fool.' Guillemette called out. 'So were you. And the holy one too.'

This outburst was followed by laughter and some jeering, all from behind us, where members of the town's assembly were standing with their wives. These worthies had not cried aloud, of course, but where the mighty walk, so will the rabble follow.

'She had obviously coated them with poison,' Peyrolles observed.

The Archbishop was annoyed at the way things were going, and incensed at his prosecutor most of all. 'If she poisoned you, she could hardly have bewitched you.' He snapped at the farrier. 'Now which was it? Make your mind up.'

'She bewitched me, sir. Her sorcery was apparent in her being able to bring me back to life having poisoned me.'

'Enough of this rubbish,' the Archbishop insisted. 'A man's lustful organ that can see across the room! Mammaries under clean linen that taste of sweat! What will men and women think of next? Bring me some boiling oil.'

It took half an hour to prepare the brazier, and almost as long to heat the cauldron, but once the oil was bubbling and squeaking with a delicious aroma of freshly peeled olives we knew it was time to begin.

'Trial by ordeal is a known method of procedure in these magical cases,' the Archbishop observed.

All those present, except for the farrier and ourselves, murmured their agreement.

'So the executioner will souse firstly the man's member and secondly the woman's nipple, and we'll soon see who squeaks the loudest.'

The Great Executioner Belibaste, Jourdain and our own Ferblant must have been waiting at the back of the hall, but it was a surprise to us all when Ironface creaked forward, removed the farrier's short-cotte and left him naked except for his leggings. Then, taking the man's virile member firmly in hand, but with its short-sighted eye uncovered, Ironface advanced the poor fool towards the cauldron.

The farrier began to howl before he was within a thought's length of the bubbling juice, then with his member firmly planted inside it he wailed like a cat in a red-hot bucket and fainted clean away.

Guillemette held her tongue, although Ironface advanced her nipple, or what there was of it in the warm weather, as boldly towards the torment as he had lugged the lout's tersis. Perhaps she was aided by the kindly ironwork of his mitten, and by the haze that hovered about the cauldron, who can tell? The fact is a nipple is shorter than the other thing, by a good few thumbnails, even when the latter is badly frightened.

'Not a scream,' Ironface stated, shocking them with his Spanish voice, 'and not a mark on her, my lord.' In his mask and his tabard borrowed from the dead king, he was highly convincing.

'Take the lying fellow outside, and have one of you scourge him soundly,' the Archbishop ordered. 'His wife may apply a poultice of cold clay or somesuch – or she may if she wants any more out of it – but see to it the villain is scourged.'

Ironface dragged the poor fool away, I think by his elbow.

It was good to see our friend recovering his strength during our months in prison.

'You've done it wrong,' some of the townspeople protested. 'If she doesn't howl or mark it means she's a witch.'

'Not in Albi, it doesn't.'

'Burn her. Burn her at once.'

I began to fear Ironface had overstepped himself by leaving Guillemette unblistered, but the Archbishop said firmly, 'There's no wind, good people. No wind at all. If you burn a young and well-covered woman such as she, her scent will stay around for half a week, and the whole centre of town smell most unpleasant.'

There was a moment's distraction while the menials of the archbishopric threw strips of meat into the boiling oil, and followed them with garlic pips and some roots, interrupting proceedings the way such scullions will.

The Archbishop ordered the Consistorie to rise, and Guillemette almost had the chance to slip away. Indeed, Peyrolles was looking at her as if in return for a suck of her other nipple he would willingly give her a ride to safety on the back of his horse.

The Archbishop had a tidier mind, however. 'Skin her,' he commanded. 'Guilty by attraction and association. So let her be flayed like the rest of them.'

'Thank you, my lord Archbishop,' Guillemette said. 'May I make a request? Will you take my skin into your own bed, for I don't want that Jacques Peyrolles laying his hands on me again, not by so much as a finger.'

The Archbishop took just a short time for his midday meal, and loitered only briefly afterwards. Seven people were already to be flayed on or before the Feast of the Madeleine, and one burned, with Mitten, La Mamelonne, the Fish Girl and myself certain to add to their numbers. People needed to get away and send invitations to their friends, not listen to formalities in a room that stank of fried garlic and singed foreskin.

643

Violette la Vierge presented his grace the Archbishop with no problems whatsoever. She tried to dance towards Jacques Peyrolles, tripped over her chains, then began to sing the story of her life before she was asked to give any account of herself. Her words made no sense, so I had clearly caused her to be possessed of devils.

Consistorie was almost minded to exonerate her. Almost but not quite. She was already guilty by attraction, and even if she weren't it seemed safer to sentence her to the bonfire. At least she would escape flaying.

I, on the other hand, had been demonstrated to be totally evil. Here was a woman possessed by many devils, all of them mine. I was sentenced to be burnt a second time after my flaying, and my charred pelvis and all other bones remaining to be broken with an iron and scattered about town. All this before the Court had dealt with me!

Now it was La Mamelonne's turn. Her march forward, naturally gappy-legged, was greeted by a cheer from the back of the hall. She was the one people had come to see.

'What is your name, woman? Tell his Grace your name.'

'Mamelie La Mamelonne.'

'Your true name.'

'By that name I am universally known – that and Maid of the Mountains.'

'The name you were born with.'

'His Grace wasn't born with Archbishop, was he?'

'Very well. You refuse to give your name. Let us now turn to your relationship with the notorious witch and traitor, Perronnelle de Saint Thibéry.'

'She's innocent,' La Mamelonne said.

There was an outcry at this. Mamelie was known as the truthful whore. She had promised to have every man in Oc before she died, and she had kept her word, unless they were dead before her, in which case she intended to oblige them later.

'Innocent,' the prosecutor wondered. 'How innocent?

'She has the reputation,' La Mamelonne said. 'But it was I who did all of her deeds.'

'You are wasting our time with preposterous lies.'

'None of my lies are preposterous,' Mamelie assured him. 'They are carefully chosen so as not to be.' She gave them no time to digest this. 'Consider the ungainsayable fact that she's a virgin – '

'Pray God they don't attempt to gainsay it!' I heard Bertrand groan.

'How can such a one spread herself wide enough to get her thighs down a horse, especially with a warrior's leggings on and link-mail all the way to the top of them?'

The bishops fell to murmuring at this, and the barons too, La Mamelonne having touched on so many lascivious matters, most of them my own.

'Legs are a very lewd thing in a woman,' one of them muttered. 'Wearing legs makes her lower than a herma-phrodite or a stag-beetle.'

Poor sweet Mamelie. Was she attempting to save my life or salvage her own reputation?

'Legs,' the bishops murmured. 'A virgin with legs. Who-ever heard of such a thing?'

Jacques Peyrolle returned to the attack. 'The virginity of this Saint Thibéry woman is something the Reverend Bishops will want to look into,' he said, causing Bertrand my Belami to groan again. 'What we require to know for the minute is how you, a self-confessed whore – '

'*Professed*,' Mamelie corrected him, 'a self-*professed* whore. The greatest whore there is or ever likely to be, even in the whole Kingdom of Heaven. You have a Cathedral here in Albi that men will ride a dozen miles to see. They'll cross continents for what I've got between my legs, continents. If the Church weren't so well thought of,' she said, with an ingrati-ating smile I disliked her for, 'and Pope Innocent the Second so popular in the whole land of Oc, my body would become an entire religion. As it is, it's got converts world wide as well as others who gaze down upon it from the Hereafter.'

'Heresy,' the bishops were saying, and aloud. 'This is heresy indeed. She's comparing her — ' (and here they all used a Latin, Romish or Wizard's word beginning with a capital cough I would never otherwise have heard of), 'what in lay parlance we call her cruncher to a church door.'

'A Cathedral door,' La Mamelonne insisted.

No one interrupts a prosecutor for long. Having passed over the golden opportunity she had presented him with to burn her for blasphemy, Peyrolles wanted to have her skinned alive for treason instead. This was reasonable enough, as the populace enjoys a good skinning, and no one more than an archbishop, but it began to indicate that our tormentor wasn't quite as quick-witted as he might have been, because he had her by attraction anyway.

'You leave my friend Perronnelle alone,' she told him in the meantime. 'I am the Maid of the Mountains. I am related to the Trencavels, having been with child by the poor late Viscount, my little boy as such being rightfully heir apparent to half the Land of Oc, and not that monster De Montfort, whose half-brother I recently slew in hand-to-hand combat.'

'Skin her,' the Archbishop instructed. 'Start with her tongue, and let us not forget her cough.' He said cough, then fell to coughing himself at the thought of it, then pronounced the unspeakable Romish word of the Wizards again. What a race they were, these long-dead sorcerers and giants. They knew how to lift great stones, and thread them into a magic arch, but had nothing elegant to say about my poor doomed Mamelie's parvise, which later men wrote ballads about and honoured in songs, and I daresay angels in Heaven did also.

However, it was growing late. The Archbishop of Albi took a cup of wine, and agreed to Jacques Peyrolles' request for water. We languished as ever in our daylong thirst, but our wait was nearly over. They were ready for me.

I scarcely remember the farce of it. They were already going to burn me and flay me, or flay me and burn me, and perhaps scourge me, all as a result of my guilt by attraction. I saw no point in being guilty after retraction. I confessed all. 'I am Perronnelle,' I said. 'I am a daughter of the Trencavels. I am the Maid of the Mountains. But I am no heretic. I believe in Jesus Christ. I believe he is God Incarnate. I believe – '

'A manifest liar who presumes upon the Faith. Flay her.'

'And what is this flaying good for, my lord Archbishop?'

'It will cure you of corns,' he said. 'And of warts and freckles.' He was a witty fellow, but they keep a good vineyard at Albi, and he had drunk several cups.

Thus it was we were handed over to our executioners. Poor Ferblant. What must he be going through at this moment? What terrible feelings of inadequacy and fright at his impending exposure? 'He couldn't even skin a rabbit cleanly,' my Belami observed. 'Nor carve a roast porker without dropping the knife.'

When I say handed over to our executioners, I mean returned to our cellar but placed within their overall charge. They now possessed our clothes and the rest of us, but they weren't allowed to have their way with us women, save by way of payment for a neater finish. Strangely, with death so near, most women needed to hoard all their moments to themselves. Even La Mamelonne refused them. 'I've never had a headsman,' she told Belibaste, 'or not unless he left his chopper outside unnoticed. I'll take gypsies. I don't mind tinkers. But I never go with hoof-cooks or skinners. I make it a rule. So you're debarred from me on both counts.'

The executioners were bound to honour such a wish. It was their duty not to inflict themselves upon us in our last days, for a punishment was a punishment and must not be added to, and if anything served up as a little less. Thus it was that a felon among the Giants and Wizards of King Caesar's Court, sentenced to forty lashes with the scourge, would only receive thirty-nine, lest his tormentors missed a count. So we women could not be abused in our persons, nor otherwise mishandled. Such behaviour would violate the awful mystery of our sentence, and awful it was to be.

'I wonder how they'll lighten our punishment,' I asked Belami. 'So as not to exceed the prescription, I mean.'

'Perhaps they'll not skin your left ear,' he suggested. He began to laugh. 'In my case I'm sure they'll not lift the hide from my hump.'

How we chuckled together. That would be a brave moment, wouldn't it, when they stripped us for the torment and my lover's hump fell off?

We two were to be last, of course, and saved over till the last day of the Feast, the Virgin and the Hunchback. What an entertainment we were supposed to be, yet here we were neither. I almost couldn't wait to see the rabble's disappointment. Not that they could find out in my case unless I told them.

So it was the Fair grew near, and with it the Feast of the Madeleine, with its quoits, its tumblers, its griddle cakes and its fun. There would be prayers and fastings and weepings, but principally the Madeleine would be fun.

Its chief fun would be with us.

To flay a woman alive is truly regarded as a most remarkable and noteworthy spectacle, an entertainment that folk will travel many leagues to witness and discuss for years afterwards if they are lucky enough to glimpse any part of such an event. There are the drums, the trumpets, the soldiers in their uniforms, the braziers, the splendid racks of knives, the great folk sitting close about determined to give their full attention to some woman who is often of absolutely no account otherwise but is now to be afforded hours of the minutest scrutiny from thousands. It confers the kind of fame upon a person that all but the nobility aim at and every young female dreams of but is rarely fortunate enough to achieve. For one's life to become the object of so many men's attentions, and for so many details of it to linger

648

on in their memories, and to die moreover knowing that one will also give pleasure posthumously! Even when one has stopped writhing and screaming to the muffling accompaniment of pipe and drum there are the innumerable tricks that the executioner and his assistants in one of their more pleasing guises as clowns can play in public with your skin. *And to know all this in advance!* A bullock, for example, cannot take the same kind of joy from becoming a pair of gloves.

There is, too, the added feature that in order to be flayed a person has first to be undressed. Most men, even married men, would not otherwise be afforded such an instructive spectacle. Women in general do not as a rule allow themselves to be naked even for an instant, lest they provoke or embarrass themselves or, by baring too much of their appearance, affect a larger disturbance in the balance of nature. Even when a woman seeks to change her clothing she is for ever drawing one thing on as she slips the other thing off so that draughts and the sunshine may not come at her. Yet here is a flaying, which both requires a woman to be entirely naked and renders her insensitive to any possible interplay between her own nudity and the weather.

I know we hear reports of women bathing themselves, women not whores, and – worse – undressing before they enter the bath, but these gadfly buzzes come mainly from Italy and among the Arabs in Spain. Let these habits stay there, I say. A woman is like a gourd, perfectly happy in her own skin and within her own juice, and can last for ever if not meddled with.

These may seem strange matters to linger upon. But an execution is like that. It takes over from the natural ordering of events and leaves the mind free to wander.

It was Jourdain, De Montfort's own executioner, who arranged to lead the first of us out, mercifully not one of us. Even an hour's life longer is precious, and I couldn't bear to see Mitten or the Fish Girl die so soon, not that flaying is ever soon.

De Montfort's executioner sent for the young woman called

Grazide, and she immediately grew upset at being called, asking why it shouldn't be one of us instead, or couldn't a sheep be skinned in her place, as if the conclusions of an Archbishop's Consistorie could ever be annulled by such a preposterous suggestion. They stripped her and dragged her outside on a choke-rope which, as with a heifer, makes struggling unprofitable.

Here the good folk of Albi showed themselves to be lacking a certain sense of what is fitting and proper. They deprived poor Grazide of her clothes inside the confines of the prison instead of outside in the Cathedral Square. Being the inhabitants of a mean town, they probably intended our clothes to be all of the executioners' wages, and so left them unspoiled indoors, instead of teasing the crowd by having the victim denuded piecemeal for their delight – a ceremony which, properly conducted, can take several minutes or even as long as half an hour if the woman is bashful enough and comely enough, as Grazide certainly was. Even as they undressed her, the poor girl said, 'Now let them hurry to take my skin, for I cannot bear to be recognized in it after this.'

We heard a single scream as the knife touched her, a cry so exquisite that it pierced the stonework. Then we heard the crowd cry out with a great 'Ah!' It wasn't the usual mockery the rabble makes at seeing someone protest too much at having, say, an ear prised off, but it was a sigh of deep disappointment, rage even.

There was no more screaming, but no drumbeat either, nor any shrill of trumpets. Normally, after the condemned has uttered her first howl or so, and the crowd have been given a taste of her voice, the music begins to play, partly to drown out her agony, but more to soothe the executioner so that he and his assistants can get on with their work and proceed with a steady hand. A false move can so easily tear the skin – after all, we women are not bullocks: we are not made of leather – and, worse, do the victim a serious mischief, thus causing her to die sooner than is appropriate

650

if she is to benefit enough from her experience to reach a proper state of repentance.

None of this was to be, however. There were no more screams, no trumpets, no drums, but a continuing clamour came from the crowd, which soon began to dampen enough for us to hear a woman's sobbing, presumably Grazide's, above it.

This sobbing grew more insistent. She did not scream again, but her sobbing became louder. This was most unnatural. Was she able to bear her torments with such composure, and were the crowd and her executioners prepared to let her die so? Or had there been some manifestation of Divine pleasure or disapproval? Were the good people of Albi and the outlying hamlets enjoying the martyrdom of one whom the Almighty's finger rested upon? Did Grazide have the stoicism of the blessèd saints? Her sobbing was loud, and it grew louder still.

This was because it was coming nearer. An instant later the doorway was unbarred and she was thrown among us and allowed to regain her clothes. Her left shoulder bled from a shallow incision, carved upon it with a most libidinous swirl of the knife. As the executioners term it, 'First the kiss and then the caress.' The kiss had very naturally caused her to scream, and she had sobbed thereafter, saving her breath for the caress, which was likely to take longer in the enduring than those attentions men are more normally capable of offering.

We hurried to bind her wound with a rag torn from one of La Mamelonne's cottes.

'It's raining,' she gasped. 'A storm's come on. I've been spared by Almighty God until first thing tomorrow. Never will an evening seem so sweet!'

Presently we heard the executioners come down the corridor, Ironface among them. De Montfort's man and the King's man sounded bad tempered and bitter. It would mean another day's enforced stay here, in addition to the several they had already been contracted for.

Ironface was much more cheerful, a certain sign of increasing good health. 'Never mind, gentlemen,' he chuckled, 'another day's work must mean more pay.'

'I'll leave some bitch half-skinned else,' the King's man threatened.

We heard them go into a room and close the door.

An executioner is a man, and has needs like any other. Christ would be among the first to admit it. His is a hot, smelly, dirty trade, spent with bellows and branding iron among drying blood, sour vomit and people divested of their tripes, and tripes bereaved of their people. If such a fellow ever so much as glimpses Heaven it will be through the frame of a gallows with the heels twitching above him. Yes, an executioner has needs, and the foremost of these is a bucket of wine.

We heard Belibaste moan. We heard Jourdain sneer. Then came Ferblant's voice like a saw jamming in damp wood, like an axe in a knot, a rasp toothing old iron. We heard him and began to curse him. He was making his colleagues drunk, quarrelsome at least. And angry men and men who drink strong waters develop unsteady heads. Grazide required steadiness tomorrow. So did Vuisande. So did the rest of them.

The executioners' door came open and they sent Jourdain for drink.

'He's a fool,' I heard Ironface say. 'A sweet, kind Godfearing fool, but an idiot nonetheless.'

Jourdain came back from the guardroom with a recharged bucket of wine, and the door closed, leaving us with a lungful of sweat, garlic and breathed-up grape which is what such simple souls smell of.

The door came open again and they sent Belibaste for drink.

'He's a fool,' I heard Ironface say. 'Direct, straightforward, honest, but an imbecile notwithstanding.'

'I've seen better things in fishbaskets,' Jourdain agreed. 'And kinder on the nostril.'

Belibaste came back heavy-footed from the nag of the bucket, and Belami asked him to lighten it in our direction, as of course we had no more wine of our own now that Mamelie was resting.

'What, this?' the King's axeman asked, glad to set it down. 'I can't let a prisoner have this.' He took it up again and held it towards our bars. 'This is raw distillation, the essential spirit itself and potent as armagnac. One little sniff of this would shrivel your hump.' He staggered away with it. This time the door stayed open.

If only it had shut again. These twin torturers, the qualified ones, were discussing the tricks of their trade, and how they should proceed with us on the morrow and the days thereafter.

'I shall start at the head, exactly by the left ear,' Belibaste proclaimed.

'And I, as is proper, by the foot, and of the foot the toe.' Jourdain was adamant about it. 'Skin a woman's face and you mar her looks entire at the outset, not to say obscure her expression, and thus spoil things for the crowd.'

They quarrelled a little, but in the good-natured way such fellows show when you know that even when they punch one another it will be in jest.

'Well, Ferblant of the Spanish King, tell us how you would skin these Maids of the Mountain, whether the fat or the thin.'

'Aye, speak up, Ferblant.'

Ferblant was slow to answer, and when he did so he spoke tiredly. 'I shall begin by making a pair of gloves of her hands, and you shall wear them on your fingers.'

'Then what will you make of her —?' (I see no need to write such a word, and it would doubtless pain many people that De Montfort's Torturer even knew it to speak, or that the High Executioner to the King of Paris had in all his life heard it often enough to be able to recognize it.)

Ferblant said nothing to this, being no doubt aware that I was listening to him. So Jourdain it was who persisted and said, 'He is an evasive fellow, this Diego. He's told us what he will make of these women, but not how he will start with them – whether by hand or foot.'

'Aye, speak your mind, Spaniard. Or we shall banish you from our mystery. Where will you begin with the Maids of the Mountains?'

I should have known Ironface would be obscene on my behalf, not to say downright saucy in matters that made me wince. 'When I start with that one,' he said reflectively, 'or the other one according to fortune, I shall start neither by the head nor the toe, most especially because she's a woman.' He had all of our attentions now, never mind theirs, and our guards were staying by to drink and listen too. 'If you think about a woman you might think she's already designed to take the knife, and conclude she's made to be flayed exactly as the Good God intended.' He drank a little aqua-vitae, or such I judged Belibaste's bucket to be. 'I mean – a man is finished entire, and his body comes entire, whereas a woman has her join, and there she's already divided.' We heard him drink some more.

'So you'll start the women there?'

He drank some more, taking it in noisily through his grill.

'So why not the man?'

'Because a man hasn't got the identical sort of there,' said Jourdain with a laugh. 'Just the same, I'd start the fellow there, because you may as well do his frisk while he's fresh enough to feel it. If not, his whole Adam's wasted, and you treat him no better than a woman if you don't give the crowd the benefit of starting him there.'

'Now, brother, you begin to contradict yourself,' Ironface grunted. We heard him come clanking along towards us.

'Where are you going, Ferblant?'

'I'm going to empty my legs.'

'They've drunk enough.'

So had Belibaste and Jourdain, most of the guards and once again Jourdain and Belibaste who were redoubling their intake of leas-distillings by the instant. They were now so befuddled that they had taken on Ironface's lewderies as their own.

'Now, brother. Now, brother,' Belibaste said, 'you do begin to contradict yourself as the Diego said.'

'Contradict myself? I said I'd skin her there and I said I'd skin him there. Where's the contradiction?'

'You said a woman's different from a man, and of course man is the nobler, but you're treating them no different. You're refusing them their difference, and there's your contradiction.'

'Aye, there's your contradiction,' Ironface called. He came clanking back with an extra bucket, which he passed among the guards.

'It's their difference makes them different, you dullard. Not my cunning with the flay.'

Belibaste was speaking very slowly now, or was it Jourdain? Whoever it was spoke to thickening ears and draughty heads, and finished the sentence through his nose. The snore took a long time to leave him, gave up trying and was immediately superseded by another.

The guards slept the way such people do sleep, brutishly.

Ironface unlocked our door, and passed Bertrand a mallet and wedge. 'Knock off their leg irons,' he said. 'We'll do their wrists later, when we're away from here.' As we stepped over the guards, he said, 'I thought those fools would never sleep. They've had pure spirit, belladonna and all the foxglove I could pick.'

Night had fallen, the way it does while drunken men talk.

We took our guards' horses. These were still Guy de Sorèze's men, though not for much longer if Ironface spoke true. Their mounts were kept snaffled in the yard, and Ironface had already saddled them while he was supposed to be emptying his legs. He himself had ridden here on Nano, and I made no effort to regain the old dear for the moment. Tin Legs needed something safe and sturdy.

We have come into the hills. No-one is going to search for us among the garrigue, and we can last here a little longer. Then Bertrand intends to present me to the Servians as his intended bride. He, at least, is anonymous, Gibbu the Hunchback is no more, and as his wife I shall be anonymous also. A woman always is.

Whether we shall live in the Mill, protected by the Seigneurs of Servian, or in some corner of a castle, who can tell? I hope in the Mill, because I intend to keep Mamelie and the others about me, though La Mamelonne is a crowd wherever she lodges.

As for Grazide, Strawberry Face and the rest of them, I hesitate to say for how long Ironface can make good his claim to bring happiness to six young women, or whether Guillemette can content herself with him. For the moment they all seem keen to try. It isn't so much, as Belami observes, that Ferblant used to be a monk and in consequence has juice enough for everyone, as that when people are returned to life as recently as ourselves have been, there is little room in it for jealousy, at least for a day or two.

In the meantime, several of us are *enceintes*, being peasants and foolish. I wait to see if any of the children are born with tails and stag's ears. So, I suspect, do their mothers.